# THE UNITED FEDERATION MARINE CORPS

## THE RYCK LYSANDER TRILOGY

## BOOK 1: RECRUIT
## BOOK 2: SERGEANT
## BOOK 3: LIEUTENANT

Colonel Jonathan P. Brazee
USMCR (Ret)



Semper Fi Press

A Semper Fi Press Book

November 2014



ISBN-13: 978-0692338551 (Semper Fi Press)

ISBN-10: 0692338551

Printed in the United States of America



This is a work of fiction. All of the characters, names, incidents, organizations, and dialogue in this novel are either the products of the author's imagination or are used fictitiously.

Acknowledgements:

I want to thank all those who took the time to pre-read this book, catching my mistakes in both content and typing. I want to thank Tom Rogers, and Anne Gentilucci, my content editors, and John Baker, my copy editor, for catching my many typos and mistakes. I want to thank all those who took the time to pre-read this book, catching my mistakes in both content and typing. A special shout out goes to my comrades at VFW Post 9951 in Bangkok for their help, to the Royal Marines at the Once A Marine website for teaching me about British Royal Marine traditions and slang, and to Dr Alan Whiting, CDR, USN (Ret), my old Naval Academy roommate and physicist and astronomer extraordinaire, for his assistance in astrophysics.. All remaining typos and inaccuracies are solely my fault.

# *BOOK 1: RECRUIT*

# *Atacama*

Sergeant John Nbele barely glanced at his heads-up display as he climbed the huge rise of tailings leading to the open pit mine. Small green triangles being projected onto his visor represented each of the men in the squad, and all were moving in the squad V formation, two fire teams out front, one trailing between them.

This was the sergeant's fifth campaign, but his first as a squad leader. He'd risen up through the ranks quickly, with two meritorious promotions, the last one a battlefield promotion for valor on Case's World.[1] He knew he was on the fast track, and this operation would cement his reputation as not only a fierce fighter, but also as a leader of Marines.

He didn't really expect this campaign to amount to much. Atacama was sparsely populated, and the miners didn't have a military as such, only a small police-slash-guard force (the type of guards Marines and Legionnaires called Jimmylegs) that was formed to protect the mines. They had no heavy weapons. John had bet a bottle of Jack, the real stuff from Earth, not the fake shit that most people drank, with Royal Teristry, a sergeant in B Company, that the Jimmylegs would bolt at the sight of the platoon's Marines in the assault.

His suit subtly shifted to remain vertical as he started up the tailings. Wearing a suit was pretty easy. Most recruits could walk, run, and jump within 30 minutes of being introduced to them. Still, there were a few tricks. Sgt Nbele's body instinctively wanted to lean into the hill as he climbed, and he had to relax and let the suit take over.

The suit was the 980 kg mechanical monster each of his Marines wore, the PICS, or Personal Integrated Combat Units. With its sandwiched Ceramic Array and LTC (Lutetium Tungsten Carbide) armor, it was impervious to all small arms and most larger

---

[1] **Case's World**: A Class 2 planet in Sector 14. Two corporate proxies started a war for control of the entire planet, causing the Federation to send in the Marines to quell the fighting before turning the mission over to the FCDC

weapons. While the Corp's PICS were not the modern Rigaudeau-3s that that Legion and some world militias had, or even the Brotherhood's Saul line of combat armor, it was more than enough proof for the poorly armed miners. Naval intelligence had assured the Marine command of that.

"Bentley, close it up," he sent to the PFC in First Fire Team.

Corporal Kim should have caught his lagging Marine. He, as the squad leader shouldn't have to be getting after individual Marines. He'd have to have a one-on-one with Kim when all this was over. He stared directly at Bentley's triangular avatar, blinking his eyes once long and hard to initiate a full data dump. The Marine's data filled his visor. Heart rate, respiration, suit dynamics, all were within normal range. Bentley's nerves were fine; he had just lost focus.

That was a bad precedent. While this mission should be a cakewalk, losing focus on a more dangerous battlefield was a recipe for disaster. Nbele's battlefield promotion on Case's World was a result of his squad leader on that mission "losing focus." Three Marines had been KIA,[2] and Nbele had had to jump into the breach to save the rest.

He blinked away Bentley, then brought up Kim.

"Cpl Kim, monitor your Marines. I don't need to be keeping Bentley in line," he said on the direct person-to-person comms.

"Aye-aye, Sergeant," was the reply.

Sgt Nbele's Second Squad was the point of main effort. He and his 12 Marines were the heavy squad, the ones with PICS. First Squad had taken a blocking position at a crossroads on the other side of the mine, some 15 kms out. Third was providing security for the platoon headquarters back at the LZ.[3] Normally, 13 Marines, even suited, would be too few to be operating like this, but no one expected much if any resistance. Third Platoon had taken its objective, the mine headquarters at the planetary capital, over an hour ago without a fight.

His leading fire teams crested the tailings, ready to descend into the pit. He switched to monitor Cpl Kim's view, which showed

---

[2] **KIA**: Killed in Action
[3] **LZ**: Landing Zone

up to the right of his visor. There were the same pieces of heavy equipment in the pit as he had seen on the satellite photo, but it was still good to get confirmation. There wasn't any sign of miners.

As always, the projected display was somewhat transparent so he could still see the real world through the image. He wanted a better view, so he picked up his pace from inside the V formation. His suit's servos adjusted. While it didn't take any more effort from him, the motion of the suit swung into a higher tempo as he went up the rest of the incline. Cresting the hill, he could see down into the pit, and he closed Kim's feed.

The pit was huge, maybe 1,500 meters across and 400 meters deep. Unlike the open pit mines he'd seen elsewhere, this one had several smaller sub-mine heads, holes leading deeper into the ground as they followed veins. From the plans they had downloaded, he knew those mine shafts went on for kilometers underground.

He held up the squad as he linked to the eye in the sky. The drone circled somewhere out of sight, but the feed was clear. There was no sign of any movement in the pit. It was possible that the miners had bugged out, but a leader who wanted to live a long and prosperous life didn't assume anything. He checked all his data feeds, but everything was quiet. He considered sending out one of the two dragonflies housed in his sleeve to get a close-up look, but the threat was pretty low, and he wanted to save them in case he might need them later.

"Zipper-six, this is Zipper-two. There is no indication of any enemy activity. We are commencing our descent into the mine, over," he sent to his platoon commander, careful, as always to keep the Houseman slums out of his voice when on the radio.

"Roger than, Two. Keep your heads down. Six, out."

Sgt Nbele gave the command, and the squad started moving down into the mine pit. Their march discipline remained tight with good dispersion and they descended. Unless the mine was abandoned, there had to be eyes on them now, and the more professional the Marines looked the more intimidating and the less likely that any Jimmylegs would want to tangle with them. Loyalty to an employer could only go so far.

He glanced to his left for a visual on Kim's team. The icons projected onto his visor gave him an exact picture of their movement, but human nature sometimes took over, and he wanted to see them with his eyes. He could see three of the four Marines as they made their way through the rocks and dirt of the pit slope.

He blinked at Kim's icon to bring him up on a direct comms when with a flash, his visor's electronics went blank and his suit came to a sudden halt. His PICS had failed, something that had never happened to him before. He thumbed the emergency reset, but nothing changed. He tried it again, but with the same result. Of all the times for this to happen it had to happen now, on his first assault as a squad leader! He cursed CWO2 Slyth, the company ordinance officer, the man in charge of keeping the suits operational.

His Marines were well-trained. They would continue the mission, but he would be out of it. Cpl Castallano would have to take over the assault. It was only then that he looked out at Kim's fire team. While the projections on his visor were gone, he could still see through it. The three Marines in sight had also stopped, one in mid-stride.

Sgt Nbele's heart sank. This wasn't a simple malfunction. Something had taken down all the PICS, not that he could imagine what could possibly do that. But he couldn't ignore the evidence before his eyes. He kept hitting the reset, hoping against hope that it would finally work, but his suit remained a quiet prison. He started calculating. Third Squad was 15 km away, and with the lone company Stork, they could get there in a couple of minutes. But he didn't know where that transport was. It might take 30 minutes or more to get it to Third's position, then another five embark, reach the mine, and debark.

Sgt Nbele felt his frustration threaten to take over. He took five deep breaths to calm himself. They would just have to wait there for however long it took for rescue. It wasn't as if the miners had any heavy weapons with which to attack them. With the power of the suits out, the kickbacks, the tiny jets that went off when a projectile hit the skin of a suit, thereby slowing down the projectile, wouldn't work, but the inherent protection of the sandwiched armor would still be effective.

Something stirred in his peripheral vision. He leaned forward, pushing his face closer to the clear visor, trying to see to the right. At the edge of his field of vision, several men came out of one of the mine shafts, hugging the rock walls. One took out what looked to be nothing more than a folded umbrella. Sgt Nbele had no idea what it was until the miner pointed it at the sky, and with a flash, a rocket-like missile took off. The men ducked back into the shaft. Whatever that rocket was, it was certainly homemade, and if its target was the eye-in-the-sky, that drone had countermeasures.

His cheek was pressed against the visor as he tried to watch. A few moments later, the miners hesitantly came out again. They were searching the sky. They were a long way off, but with his electronics dead and zoom non-functioning, it seemed as if they were arguing on what to do.

More men came out, several pointing to where the Marines were. One man had the controls of an industrial mule which towed a piece of equipment out of one of the mine entrances, and with that in trace, he started guiding the mule up the slope, following the other men as they approached the Marines.

Sergeant Nbele kept hitting his reset, but still nothing changed. His suit was dead. He wasn't sure what the miners could have done. The suits were hardened against EMP[4] attacks, so as long as they were intact, the suits should work. Obviously, though, the miners had managed to disable them somehow.

Halfway up the slope, several miners grouped together. Arms were pointed, then three men split off to move towards Cpl Kim's team. Two, including the guy controlling the mule, came forward towards Sgt Nbele, and another three started to the squad leader's right, most likely heading to Second Fire Team. They were out of his field of view within moments.

As the mule trundled forward, its six tires having no problem purchasing the rough ground, the sergeant's heart sank as he

---

[4] **EMP**: Electromagnetic Pulse. A type of weapon designed to scramble or destroy electronics by emitting a pulse electromagnetic energy.

suddenly recognized what it was towing. It was a powerful industrial drill. As a boy in the Houseman slums, the young John had dreamed of working in the road construction on the planet, where crews were blasting tunnels in the mountain ranges. One of their pieces of equipment was this type of drill. Sgt Nbele wasn't sure if the hardened LTC bit could penetrate the LTC in his suit's armor, but he knew he didn't want to find out.

With all power gone from his suit, the first blast actually rocked him. A cloud of dust rose up from where Cpl Kim's team was frozen. Sgt Nbele stared as explosion after explosion sent more plumes upwards.

"Get some!" he shouted as he realized the explosions were supporting artillery from his unit.

The incoming rounds started walking across the slope towards him. He glanced back to see the two miners who had been approaching him run pell-mell back down the slope to save themselves.

"Fuckin' A, I owe you bastards," he said in awe as round after round landed. "Screw Teristry, that Jack is comin' to you guys!"

Shrapnel pinged as it hit his suit. It didn't do any harm, as the arty Marines firing the shells would have known. But against unarmored miners, it would be devastating. Sgt Nbele looked back over to the left. The three Marines he could see were still standing, but at least one of the miners was down, a bloody mess heaped in the dirt. He couldn't see the other two miners, but they had to be down as well.

It looked like the two men who had been approaching him had made it to safety, but the drill seemed to have taken a direct hit as the rounds were walked from his left to right. He wanted to shout out with joy each time a round landed. Too soon, though, the rounds stopped.

The platoon only had one tube, the old but venerable M229. It fired a 155 mm shell that packed a powerful punch. Some shells were anti-personnel, such as what had just been used, some were anti-armor, some were EMP and other pulse-type rounds. The gun was a great piece of gear, but even with advances in shell-casing technology, the rounds were still heavy and took up space. A mere

Marine squad could only carry so much. They weren't some planet-bound militia that could stockpile huge stores of rounds ready for use. They had to carry in whatever they thought they might need.

Sgt Nbele thought the platoon HQ had most likely expended all their anti-personnel rounds in that fire for effect. The question was if the miners knew that as well. Nbele hoped that the threat of more rounds would keep them in their hidey-holes until the rest of the platoon could come and get the squad out of this mess. Then the miners would find out what it meant to face the Marines.

Motion back at the entrance to the mine shaft caught his eye. The miners had to know that time was limited before reinforcements could arrive. If they were going to do something about his squad, they would have to act fast.

Four men darted out, and by bounding back and forth, hitting the deck before bouncing back up for another burst of 15 meters, they made their way up to the mule in front of Sgt Nbele. Once there, they stood up and stared at it.

*Typical civilians*, he thought as he saw that. *All that dodgin' and bobbin' to get up the slope, then they stand around gawkin'. I wish to God I'd left a sniper up behind us.*

The mule looked worse for wear. He could see that several of the tires were blown. He hoped the drill had been messed up, too. All four men turned as one to look directly at him. They were only about 30 meters away, and Sgt Nbele could see them arguing, several times pointing to the ground between them and him.

One guy got on the control and started the mule up again. It lurched forward, then the drive shaft of one wheel started to spin while pieces of the tire flew off. Two of the men got behind the mule and pushed. It lurched forward again, this time going maybe five meters before getting stuck once more. Once more, the men got behind, and with brute force, got it moving again.

Whatever Sgt Nbele had hoped about the mule and its cargo, it looked like the miners would make it up to him. If they did, he had to rely on his armor to keep him safe until help could arrive. No matter how many scenarios he went over in his mind, nothing he could think of would make any difference. He had no secret powers, no way to fight back. He didn't even have some way to jury-rig a suicide blast that would take them out with him like what happened in the war flicks.

Within a surprisingly short time, the miners were right in front of him. One of them, an older guy with a two-day's stubble covering his face, stood on the mule to stare inside Sgt Nbele's visor. The guy looked like anyone. Dark complected with a narrow face, the only thing notable about him was his icy-grey eyes. Even with the eyes, though, Nbele would never have given the man a second glance if he passed him walking down the street. He seemed so, well *normal.* The man looked to be studying him as well. After a few moments, he shrugged and got back off the mule.

As the men struggled to horse around the drill, Sgt Nbele had a sudden urge to take a piss. With his suit powerless, though, he didn't know if the catchment gel would work, and he would be damned if he was going to piss down his legs with the miners out there. He couldn't see the drill bit anymore, but when it clanked against this armor, he almost let his bladder go.

He heard the muffled whine as the drill was turned on. His suit dampened most of the outside sounds, but as the drill bit started to try and force a way into his suit, the screeching reverberated loudly. Sgt Nbele felt the vibrations, and his suit tilted slightly back before the drill skittered to the side and lost contact.

His armor had held!

They wrestled the drill back, and set the bit directly on his front carapace. Once again, as the bit made contact, the sound filled the inside of the suit. But just as before, the suit deflected the drill, sending it off to the side. This seemed to put a pause to things as the men stopped and started discussing the issue.

"Fuck you too, you freakin' slugs," he said quietly to himself. "Just keep a'tryin', and before you know it, the lieutenant's goin' to get here, and pow, fuck you up but good! So you keep talkin' and jabberin' like that you stupid negats."

The men obviously came to a decision. Two of them got on the mule and put their hands on his chest carapace. Both seemed to be avoiding looking into the visor to see him. They looked back at the mule operator, and the vehicle gave a lurch. He heard it hit him low on the legs as it rocked him. It wasn't enough to tip him over though. But it backed up and lurched forward again, the men pushing as it hit him. The mule couldn't back up much or the two guys on top would fall, but even a foot or so gave it room to gain some momentum. One the third push, Sgt Nbele thought he was going to fall over, but the suit's mass kept it upright. It took four more tries before that magic center of balance was surpassed. He teetered for a moment before falling over backwards.

Without the motion suppressors working, Sgt Nbele had the breath knocked out of him as he fell, something digging heavily into his back. The suits were pretty comfortable to wear normally, but without power, they were only so much junk.

On his back, he could only see the sky. He scanned what he could, waiting to see the Stork come into view with the rest of the platoon onboard. What he did see was the same guy who had looked at him before. The man leaned over to look into the visor. They stared at each other for a moment before the man crossed himself, bringing his fingers his lips as he finished the cross. Then he nodded and stepped back out of view.

When the drilling started again, the noise filled his ears. It kept going, though, not skittering off his armor. They must have gotten him wedged, or maybe the drill itself wedged. They still would have to penetrate his armor, though. It might be over 50 years old, but it was pretty formidable.

The sounds of the drilling changed pitch, getting lower. A sense of panic filled the squad leader. That meant the drill bit had gained purchase. The sound reverberated everywhere, but he tried to locate from where it emanated. With the vibrations that he could now feel, it seemed to be from about his waist, maybe where the chest carapace met the pelvic shield. The newest Legionaire suits were seamless, but the old Marine suits were not. Could the drill bit have gained some sort of purchase there?

The vibration started getting stronger, and the sounds of the bit slowed down even more.

"Break you mother!" he shouted at the unseen LTC bit.

Looking down in the small gap between the skin of his suit and his chest, he had a momentary glimpse of a spinning metallic shaft before it plunged into his groin. He was overcome by an intense flash of agony before his world went dark.

********************

Private Ryck Lysander wiped the sweat from his brow as he caught his breath. He'd just brought up the platoon's entire load of the M887 anti-personal rounds for the M229. He was not a trained artillery Marine, and as the newest of newbies, just reporting in two days prior to embarkation, he hadn't been assigned to a squad and was instead the platoon runner, which meant doing whatever the platoon sergeant wanted him to do. In this case, it was to hump arty shells.

When Second Squad had somehow disappeared from the net, a sense of alarm, if not panic, had swept the platoon headquarters. The eye-in-the-sky had shown the Marines suddenly stopping cold before some miners had appeared in the pit and the drone was knocked offline. Lieutenant Prowse and SSgt England had a heated discussion for a few moments as they reported back up to the company and went over their options. The platoon commander ordered Sgt Dixon, the arty team leader to saturate the open pit with anti-personnel fire. There wasn't any way to know how effective the support had been. The lieutenant had been burning up the comm lines with the company commander, demanding the Navy get eyes on the objective and the Stork pilot to get the transport back.

"Get your gear, boot. We're going in with the lieutenant," Doc Silestre told him.

The platoon corpsman calmly checked the charge on his M99.[5] Ryck hurriedly checked his, too. He hadn't fired his weapon, so it was still at 100%, enough to fire close to 1,000 rounds of the hypervelocity darts.

"What are we going to be doing?" he asked.

---

[5] **M99**: The basic personal weapon of the Marines. It is a lightweight carbine that fires hypervelocity 4 mm darts via a magnetic rings that pull the darts down the barrel.

"Go get our guys, you dumbshit," the doc told him.

Ryck wanted to clarify that he meant what their orders would be and what he was supposed to do, but he bit his tongue. He tried to look alert as the lieutenant and platoon sergeant made last-minute plans. This wasn't going to be some well-planned op but more of an immediate-action drill. The problem was that Ryck hadn't been with the unit long enough to rehearse any of the drills back on the Dirtball, and aboard the *Adelaide*, there hadn't been much room for any sort of physical training.

Within moments, the platoon headquarters and Third Squad were forming up just as the Stork came floating over the LZ, its turbo fans rotating to the vertical so the big transport could land. SSgt England already had the Marines moving before the Stork touched down, jumping up on the ramp while it was still a half a meter in the air. Ryck followed the rest of the Marines up into the belly of the bird.

"Boot, you stick with me like glue. I want you on my ass," SSgt England's voice came over his ear bud, the triple tones preceding the voice message indicating that they were on a direct person-to-person circuit.

Ryck started to acknowledge when the double tone of an open-platoon circuit cut him off. The lieutenant started giving out his order as the Stork rose smoothly into the air. He spoke calmly, but Ryck could sense the underlying tension in his voice, even over the M919 small unit communication modules. They didn't know what had frozen Second Squad or knocked out the drone, so the Stork would come in low and drop them below the lip of the mine before bolting off to pick up Third Squad. Two fire teams of Third, along with SSgt England and the squad leader, Sgt Piccalo-Tensing, designated Element A, would move up and over the western side of the pit and get to the Marines below them. The remaining fire team and the rest of the platoon headquarters, Element B, would provide cover from the eastern side of the pit, then move down once Element A had consolidated its position. This was a very basic plan, nothing like what Ryck had conducted in his almost 10 months at recruit training and then another three months at IUT[6] at Camp

Otrakovskiy. He knew there wasn't much time for anything else, but still, he expected something a little more . . . well, he didn't know what he expected, but it wasn't this.

Ryck still didn't know what he was supposed to do, but the platoon sergeant had told him to stay on his ass, so that was what Ryck was going to follow. He checked his M99 once more out of nervous habit before looking up at the other Marines. No one showed any signs of the butterflies that threatened to take over his own stomach. He wasn't sure if he was scared or excited, and he really didn't make an effort to figure out which it was. This was what he'd been trained to do. This was why he had left Prophesy.

He tried to lean the M99 on his thigh, but it slid off his trousers, his "skins," which were slightly stiffened with the inserted armor protection, or "bones," and he almost dropped it, barely catching it with one gloved hand. Despite the imminent combat he faced, his mind snapped back to boot where dropping a weapon was a cardinal sin. He gave a sigh of relief that he hadn't dropped it as he secured his weapon.

And that was all the time he had. With less than two klicks to the mine, the Stork had them there quickly. It flew in with the gentle approach that still amazed Ryck. Something so big shouldn't fly as smooth as a maglev.

The big bird flared, then the back ramp was lowered and the Marines poured out. Ryck followed the staff sergeant, trying to orient himself. Within moments, the Stork took off, leaving the two elements alone to make their way up to the lip of the mine. Ryck tried to keep aware of his surroundings while still watching the ground in front of him in order to stay on his feet.

As they reached the lip of the mine, SSgt England motioned them down. He edged a small fiber-eye over the lip to see what was visible while they waited for the lieutenant to start the supporting fire.

"We've got three, I repeat three combatants at my 10 o'clock, 550 meters from our present position, standing next to our

---

[6] **IUT**: Infantry Unit Training

friendlies. The friendlies look to be down, over" the staff sergeant sent over the net to the lieutenant.

Two beeps then indicated that he had switched to the element circuit, followed by "Listen up. Do not, I repeat, do not stop to assist any of the downed Marines. We need to get to the mine entrance and inside, so get through the kill zone quickly. The lieutenant and Doc will see to Second Squad. Got it? I want each of you to acknowledge. No stopping, over."

Each Marine responded that he understood. No stopping.

Ryck checked his M99 once more. He hadn't fired yet, so nothing would have changed, but still, he had to check. He couldn't see where the other element was, so he hugged the dirt, listening to his heart pounding. If Second Squad, suited up in their PICS had been taken out, what could they do with only their skins and bones?

Lieutenant Prowse finally had Element B in position, and on order, the element opened fire. Element A immediately pushed over the lip and into the mine. Ryck had a glimpse of a miner off to his front left turning to flee, only to be cut down from the Marines' fire. Ryck hadn't even tried to fire himself. That was Element B's job, and he was having enough trouble following SSgt England as they raced pell-mell down the slope. It wasn't really pell-mell, though. Their jerky movements were reasoned. From an assaulted position's perspective, the rush was intended to make it difficult to bring the Marines under fire with any degree of effectiveness, and the Marines practiced this kind of movement until it was second nature to them. Ryck hadn't had much experience yet, though, so he just focused on keeping up with the staff sergeant.

Trying to watch his element leader, look for the enemy, and observe his step, proved too much for him. He stumbled and fell, rolling over several times before he could get back to his feet. His bones protected him from too much damage to anything other than his pride. He focused a little more on his footing, relying on Element B in back of him to take out any threat.

Ryck felt *extremely* exposed as they rushed to the bottom of the pit and the openings into the mine itself. He felt that he would be hit at any moment. The sight of a downed Marine, his PICS torn open, did not help. They rushed forward to their objective. There were two other doors, both larger to accommodate trucks, but the lieutenant had chosen the smaller of the three entrances, one only about two meters wide.

Just before reaching bottom, a blast erupted in front of Ryck. Smoke billowed up, and a body was thrown in the air. It came back down to land in a heap. Without hesitation, two other Marines closed in on the body, grabbed it, and pulled it forward.

Within moments, all the Marines reached the mined rock wall at the bottom into which the openings were cut. The Marines spread out on either side of their target door. Ryck slammed his back up against the rock, looking over to his right where the injured Marine was on his ass, leaning up against the rock wall as well. It was Cpl Singh. The bones provided excellent ballistic protection, but they did little to provide structural support. Singh's left leg was gruesomely twisted, the front of the foot facing back, the knee twisted at a 90-degree angle to the side. The mine blast had also damaged his skin's nanos. The small sensors and syntho-chromatophores in the fabric of his utilities, his skins, had obviously been knocked out of whack. His blouse had already shifted the color and pattern to match the rock against which he leaned, but the trou had turned to black. His non-stop stream of cursing actually calmed Ryck. If the corporal could keep that up, then he would be OK once the Navy docs got a hold of him.

Ryck subconsciously felt his own skins for the armor in them. It was hard to believe that what looked like stiff, heavy paper, the "bones," could give any support when slid into the pockets of his skins. They were pliable and permitted movement when they were in the skins, but when hit by a projectile, the molecular structure instantly crystallized to provide a casing that was proof against most small arms projectiles. Like all recruits, Ryck had watched a DI back at Camp Charles get shot right in the chest at close range with no injury, but seeing a demonstration of that and trusting his own armor to work as well was a huge jump in confidence.

He tore his eyes off the injured corporal to look back to where LCpl Smith was placing the small breaching charge against the solid metal door of the entrance. Although weighing less than a kilo, it nonetheless packed a huge punch. If anyone was waiting on the other side of the door for the Marines, the blast would either take them out or render them incapable of offering any resistance.

"Fire in the hole!" Smitty yelled out before jumping back to hug the wall.

The breaching charge was very directional and could be dialed to various degrees of dispersion, but even with 10 meters between him and the door, Ryck moved away another step, pushing back up against the rock.

The resultant explosion was huge, much larger than the breaching charge alone would have made. Not only was the door breached, but also some of the rock jamb was blown off, sending rubble out into the mine pit.

"Those fracheads booby-trapped the son-of-a-bitch," Smitty shouted out. "They about got my ass."

By booby-trapping the door, the miners had ensured no one could have survived the resultant explosion on the inside. SSgt England realized that and was already in motion, rushing the blown entrance. Ryck hurried to catch up as they ducked inside the dust-filled room. Ryck cautiously crept forward about five meters and knelt across from the staff sergeant, M99 pointing down the passage leading deeper inside the mine. He couldn't see much, but he had practiced the action enough times in training even if he hadn't practiced it with these specific Marines.

Just inside the door was a holding room of some sort. What once had probably been a desk was now kindling. Ryck was kneeling in a short passage that led out of the room. As the dust settled, he could see the passage led to a T. Ryck knew that miners could be lying in wait right around the corner.

He focused on the edge of the T, barely listening to SSgt England's message to the lieutenant that they had breached the entrance. The element held its position, not moving deeper until the lieutenant could bring Element B down the slope. Ryck's team would have to move then as it would be too crowded for both elements in the room. The lieutenant came into the room, discussed it with the staff sergeant, then decided that Element A would clear the passage to the left, where the mine plans indicated the main spaces lay, while Element B would secure the entrance and clear the passage to the right.

SSgt England relayed the plan to the element. With Singh down, Pallas took over that fire team. The element was down to nine Marines in total, which didn't seem like much, but in a narrow corridor, though, it was crowded. They performed a bounding overwatch, one team rushing forward before kneeling and covering the front, then the other team getting up, moving past the covering team before it, too, kneeled and provided cover. The staff sergeant and Ryck kept attaching themselves to the back of whichever team was moving forward. Several times they had to stop and clear rooms that had been cut into the rock, but there was no sign of any of the miners.

The electricity was still running, so the corridor was well-lit. If the power went out, they would have to rely on their NVDs.[7] Deep inside a mine, though, there would be no ambient light for the NVDs to magnify, though, so they would have to turn on their infrared torches as well, and that never provided as good a field of vision as ambient light provided.

Ryck had been both excited and nervous as they entered the mine. Now, as odd as it seemed to him, he was getting almost bored as they got up, rushed, and got down again. There was no opposition, and Ryck wondered if the miners had fled. The mine was hot, and while his skins were wicking away his sweat, a little air conditioning would have been welcomed.

When the roof of the corridor collapse ahead of him, it took him a moment to realize what had happened. One moment, he was following SSgt England and Pallas' team, the next, the roof fell in front of him, the team, the squad leader, and the staff sergeant disappearing in front of him as rocks fell at his feet. He started to turn around to Cpl Büyük and his team when something impacted on his side above his waist. He looked where he felt the impact. The bone insert there had crystallized and was only now beginning to soften. Then it hit him. He'd been shot!

---

[7] **NVD**: Night vision device

In the corridor, there were only two directions in which he could go: forward or back. With the rubble on the floor, he could crouch and hope it offered some cover. But that would only delay the inevitable choice of what to do next. So that left attack or retreat.

Ryck didn't know how many miners were in front of him. He also forgot that just behind him, Cpl Büyük and three other Marines were only a few meters away. He just reverted to the mindset of over a year of training. He didn't think of danger, he didn't think of much. With a mindless yell, he rushed forward, bounding over the rubble on the deck and the four Marines trapped there.

He was vaguely aware of Büyük's team following him, but he had zeroed in on what was in front of him. About 15 meters ahead, another corridor branched off, and at that intersection, part of a person barely showed, holding an old chemical rifle pointed back at him. The lights had been turned off at the intersection, but the flashes from the muzzle told Ryck he was being taken under fire. Just below his left collarbone, he felt the impact again of another round, the stiffening of the bone insert there absorbing the impact. Another four centimeters higher, and the round would have hit his unprotected neck. Primitive weapon or not, a lead slug would really ruin his day.

Ryck sent a burst of fire back, aiming at the weapon itself. The darts moved at extremely high speeds, and when they hit, they generally created dust as the small needles pulverized metal, wood, or flesh. Ryck could see that he hit the old rifle, at least, and it fell to the deck. He couldn't tell if he had hit the person wielding it.

Ryck never stopped. He rushed forward, reaching the intersection in seconds. Without pausing, he turned into the other corridor. In front of him, he could make out two men. One was on the ground, his left arm bleeding. The other was kneeling, one arm around the other's back, as if to help him up. Ryck's undivided attention was caught by what was in the other miner's hand. From countless flicks, he recognized the Peacemaker in the man's hand. The old handgun looked enormous as he swung it up to point at Ryck.

The Peacemaker was a sonic disrupter. It had that certain historical panache that some weapons seem to capture among the public. That panache was lost on Ryck, though. Even with his body armor, that weapon would be deadly. The bones would stop and reflect the blast, at least where they covered, but with his exposed face, his head would be turned into so much mush. The weapon had a very limited range, and took a lot of energy, but this close to the miner, Ryck wouldn't stand a chance.

Without thinking, Ryck fired his M99 on full auto, stitching from low and left to high and right, exactly as he was taught at recruit training. Multiple rounds hit both men, and they immediately collapsed. Ryck stared at them, his intense adrenaline boost turning to numb amazement. He'd just killed two men—two living, breathing men.

Cpl Büyük rushed up in back of him, staring around at the two men who seemed to collapse like slowly deflating balloons. They were already gone, but their bodies both continued to settle around each other.

The M99 darts did not leave too many visible signs of damage. They were small, only a few millimeters across. What they were, though, was very, very fast, and not much could stop their progress. When they hit soft flesh, the vanes that kept them running true flipped out, becoming four small blades that slice through muscle and blood vessels.

From the front, the two men—boys might be more accurate—looked like they had fallen asleep in each other's arms. Blood was seeping out through a number of entrance wounds, but their miner's overalls were still whole, and in the shadowy light, the dark blood was not extremely noticeable.

"Damn, boot. Nice shooting," the corporal said to him.

Ryck felt both elated and a little nauseous at the same time. He was elated that he was still alive, that he had won this small battle of life and death. He had vindicated all those months of training. But these two men were not just electrons in the latest game. These were two people, and he had killed them. The first one, the one with the bloody arm, looked barely into his teens. He could have been a schoolboy back on Prophesy.

"Jenkins, you and the boot stay here and secure this intersection. Hu and Aesop, back to Pallas' team and let's see to them."

Without a word, LCpl Jenkins flopped down on the deck, pulling one of the dead miners closer to provide a tiny bit of cover and act as a rifle rest. Ryck was a little more hesitant as he mimicked the more experienced Marine, gingerly placing his own M99 on the shoulder of the younger miner. The boy's sightless eyes stared back at him.

More to escape that gaze than anything else, Ryck made a quick glance back to where, much to his surprise, the buried Marines were being helped out from under the rubble. They were covered in dust, and one of them, who Ryck couldn't make out, was limping and had to be helped to the side of the corridor where he could sit, but no one looked seriously hurt.

"Um, boot, what say you look down there, you know, where the targets are?" Jenkins asked with a sarcastic tone.

Ryck wheeled his head around to look back down the corridor. He studiously kept his eyes elevated to escape the accusing gaze of his rifle rest. He was quite relieved when Third Squad arrived on the scene and made a passage of lines to clear further down the mine. He'd done what he'd been trained to do, and he felt no regrets. In all truth, he felt elated. Still, staring at his victims' faces from centimeters away was a little much for a boot like him.

# *Prophesy*
# *Thirteen months earlier . . .*

## *Chapter 1*

Ryck knelt next to the field of GKA Wheat, picking up some of the dirt and letting it tumble through his fingers to the ground. A good portion of it simply blew away as dust. United Ag had GM'd the GKA strain specifically for Prophesy, optimized for the planet's soil mix and lack of water. "Lack of water" did not mean "no" water, though, but since the bankruptcy and closing of the Prophesy Communal Development Corporation, PCDC, the water had ceased to flow in the irrigation canals with not enough rainfall to fill the reservoirs.

Ryck hadn't been born yet when his father had made the investment to become a shareholder in PCDC, moving the family from Ellison to Prophesy for a fresh start. Ryck didn't know anything about Ellison other than the fact that his parents and older brother had made a home there in a small apartment. He couldn't imagine living like that, in a small apartment in a huge building. The open plains of Prophesy were all he had known while growing up. Life had been tough on the newly terraformed world, but for Ryck, life was good. He reveled in the freedom to run around on his own without constant parental supervision. Together with Lysa, his twin, they had the full run of not only their own property, but also that of the entire community, something they never could have had on Ellison. The urban goliath of that planet was not conducive to children running around free and unsupervised. He was vaguely aware of his father's struggles to get crops in, but that didn't affect his early childhood of school and play.

Things changed when Ryck was 10, though, when PCDC went belly up. The planet was not completely terraformed, and without PCDC pulling up the water locked deep within the rocks, the reservoirs dried up, and the little moisture already released in the air was not enough to sustain a normal agricultural cycle.

PCDC had been a subsidiary of the universal giant, Excel Holdings, Ltd. When PCDC folded, not only was Ryck's father's stock worthless, but also through some legal machinations, he owed Excel for the remainder of his initial settlement buy-in. With the then value of the crops being grown at the time, that meant Excel would get 2/3 of the revenue for the wheat for the next 25 Earth years, which corresponded to 27 crop cycles on Prophesy.

That did not take into account that with PCDC gone, the planet's ecosystem itself tried to swing back to its natural equilibrium, and that meant a dry, dusty landscape. Crop yields plummeted, and it became clear that with interest on the debt, the family could never hope to pay it off.

Ryck's father tried, though. He scraped together some cash, and along with Mr. Choo on the next plot, tried to dig their own shared well. Over 200 dry meters later, they had reached the limit of the capabilities of the small drilling company they had hired, and they had no money to bring in a company with a bigger rig.

Ryck watched his father transform from the irreverent, fun-loving man he had known into someone breaking his back and spirit in an attempt to merely survive. Myke, his older brother, dropped out of school to help, but with less and less rain, even the GKA Wheat suffered, providing smaller and smaller yields.

The tipping point was when Ryck's mother caught the Dust. Ryck was fifteen at the time and still in school. He and Lysa had come home from school that fateful day when Myke met them at the door. He took both of them in his arms, saying nothing. Fear had swept through Ryck. He didn't know what was wrong, just that it was something big.

"Mom's got the Dust," he told them.

Ryck had just stared at his older brother, speechless. "The Dust" was the name given to the virus that struck the settlers each year. Not many people contracted it, but for those who did, 80% died within hours, coughing out their lungs. Ryck and Lysa quietly followed Myke to the community clinic.

Their mother lay on the hospital bed, her face sallow. Their father sat by her side, holding her hand. Every few minutes, she would erupt into a coughing fit. The first time she did that after they got there, Ryck jumped up and ran to her, grabbing her other hand. Behind him, he could hear Lysa quietly sobbing.

The virus that caused the Dust had been identified, but without PCDC's funding, the research to figure out an effective treatment had been abandoned. With new worlds opening up, there were so many new diseases that the big pharmaceuticals focused on those diseases where they could help the most people—and make the most profit. On Prophesy, the medical technicians could treat the symptoms and ease the suffering, but that was all. Survival was up to the individual. Some made it, some did not. Ryck's mother was one of those who did not. With her family around her, she had one last coughing attack before she died, gasping for one final breath before letting go.

With Ryck's mother gone, his father sunk even further into depression. He still tried to farm, but it had become obvious that he was never going to be able to dig himself out of debt. Ryck offered to quit school to help out, but his father refused the offer.

A year after his mother's death, almost to the day, Ryck's father was driving the family Deere when it overturned into the gully that lined the western edge of the property. He was ejected from the cab and killed as he tumbled down the rocks.

Myke had erupted when TerraLife refused to pay the insurance policy, claiming "suspicious" circumstances of his father's death and citing their dad's treatment for depression as evidence of suicide. Myke fought the decision, but to no avail. Privately, Ryck thought the insurance company might have been correct. His father had been extremely withdrawn before the accident, and the insurance payout would have given the farm five or six more years of operating expenses. Most importantly, it would erase the debt to Excel. Ryck and Lysa were born on Prophesy, so legally, they could not owe a settlement buy-in. Myke had been a minor at the time, so he could not be assessed the fee, either. While the three of them still owed operating debts for seeds and fuel that came with the property, personal debts could not be assessed on surviving children.

Myke lasted one more year on the family farm. Ryck and Lysa had come home from school, excited about their upcoming high school graduation ceremony, to find Myke gone. A note with the single word "Sorry" was left on the kitchen table. Three weeks later, diploma in hand, Ryck turned from student to farmer.

For two years, he struggled. The first year, despite not knowing what he was doing but with the help from Mr. Choo, he'd managed to barely keep afloat. This year, though, the wheat crop had almost totally failed. Only the monk melons growing in a small patch near the house had come in well, but even if he sold them himself at the market, the revenue would not come close to what he needed for the next crop's planting. With his credit maxed out to get the Deere back up and running, he didn't think the co-op would be lending him anything.

He dropped the remaining dirt from his hand and glanced up at the sun. Its unrelenting rays had burnt out every last drop of moisture from the soil. As a kid, he had loved the bright sunshine. Now, the sun had become his enemy, at least to his mind.

*Well, that's that*, he thought to himself. *It's done.*

He slowly stood up, and without a backwards glance, walked up the gentle slope and to the home compound. It already looked deserted. The old coop in which his mother had tried to raise chickens was leaning precariously to the right, waiting for the next strong wind to knock it over. Ruined parts for the Deere had been discarded near the shed, good only for scrap. Only the house itself looked like it hadn't been abandoned. The bright pink curtains that were visible through the open kitchen window were about the only splash of color in the washed-out scene.

Ryck kicked off his shoes as he came in the front door. It was only late afternoon, earlier than when he usually quit work. Lysa wouldn't be back for quite some time yet. He decided that maybe a good meal was in order. Opening up the cabinet, he took out the last two bottles of Recife Pinot Noir. This was all that was left of the case his father had brought from Ellison. He busied himself in the kitchen, more to take his mind off things than anything else as he cut the onions, carrots, garlic, and Hank's Beef. Hank's Beef was not really good for bourguignon. The texture was too soft, and it didn't hold up well to slow cooking. Ryck would rather be using Sunshine or even Healthy Choice, but all he had was Hank's. As a kid, he thought there really was a person named Hank who raised actual cows. He'd been oddly disappointed to learn that "Hank" was a corporation, and the "ranch" was a soy and peanut-processing factory in the capital.

He browned the beef, taking care not to let it break apart, then put it in the slow cooker. In the same pan, he browned the veggies before adding them to the beef. When his mom had made bourguignon, she had also used lardons, which she had Mr. Compton make for her. Compton was long gone, after having given up his farm, but Ryck liked to think that his own version without the pork was just fine.

He opened one bottle of wine. Lysa would be upset at his lack of manners, but she wasn't there, so he tilted the bottle up and took a long swallow. Ryck wasn't overly fond of most off-world products, but wine was different. They had a synthetic local "wine" available, but to Ryck, it could just as easily have been purple-colored vodka, good for getting drunk, but not much else. The real stuff, though, well, he could get used to having a glass of that with each meal.

With a sigh, he emptied the bottle into the slow cooker, closed the lid, and turned it on low. He'd make noodles later, something that tasted so much better when made by hand. Bourguignon was Lysa's favorite meal, so hopefully, that would ease the blow.

It was almost seven hours later, the aroma of the meal filling the home, when the front door opened. Ryck was sitting in his father's easy chair, back towards the door when his sister entered. He tried to ignore her, but her skintight blue jumpsuit had tiny luminescent micro-LEDs embedded in the fabric that lit in strategic areas as the fabric stretched and pulled. She was a flashing advertisement of her womanly curves. She didn't like to talk when she was in her working clothes, though, so he didn't say a word as she walked past him and into her room.

"Something sure smells good," she remarked as she came back out about five minutes later. "Special occasion?"

"Anytime you come home is a special occasion," he said.

"Ah, no wonder you're still single, with lines like that," she told him as she settled in their mom's chair, her legs drawn up under her.

She had come in the home dressed in high-tech sluttiness. Now she sat in baggy cotton pants and an oversized t-shirt, all trace of make-up on her face gone. She looked younger than their 19 years.

He'd opened the second bottle of wine about two hours before to let it breathe. Getting up, he poured her a glass and took one for himself.

"The Recife? This is a special occasion. And I smell bourguignon. What gives?"

"Eat first, then talk," he said.

Normally, they ate in front of their parents' chairs watching the vid. Today, though, the formal table seemed more appropriate. They ate their meal mostly in silence, only talking to pass the food to each other. Lysa knew something big was up, and Ryck was trying to marshal his thoughts. Finally, though, dinner was over and the table cleared.

"OK, little brother, what's up?" she asked as she pushed his chair around and sat side-saddle on his lap, her arms around his neck.

Lysa had been born first, 12 minutes before Ryck, and she had lorded that over him as children. Now "little brother" had just become part of his name, so to speak.

"The wheat crop's failed," he simply said. "Nothing to harvest."

"I know. I've been watching. Maybe the next crop will come in."

"It's just this. I don't think we can get credit for seeds. We're still maxed out from the Deere repairs from, what, three years ago?" he asked.

"You know I can probably swing the seeds. We won't need that money for another month or so, and I've got several friends who'll be happy to help."

Ryck knew what kind of "friends" she meant. He never pried into what she was doing, but it was obvious. He had kept quiet both because it was her choice, and frankly, they needed the money she brought in.

"It's just that, I mean, uh, I don't know. I mean, I don't know if we should plant again. Who knows if next year'll be better? I mean, ah, grub. I don't want you to be working like you do just to support us."

There, he'd said it. It was out in the open.

Lysa leaned back, then slowly got up and pulled out one of the dining chairs and sat down. She seemed to be considering what to say next.

"You have a problem with what I do? With how I support us?" she quietly asked.

"No, no, you've got me wrong. I am so grateful for you. For what you've done. It's just that I don't think it's worth it. Not your work, but the farm. I don't think we can ever make a living here."

"So, what're you saying?" she asked, her voice sounding only slightly mollified.

"What I'm saying is," he said, pausing to take a deep breath, "is that I don't want to farm anymore. I'm done with it."

Telling her that was a huge weight off of his shoulders. What had been an internal debate was now out there for his sister to hear.

She was quiet for a full minute while Ryck waited to hear her response. If she disagreed, he wasn't quite sure what he'd do.

Finally, she asked, "So what would we do with the farm?"

"Oh, you can have it. I can sign everything over to you."

She gave a chuckle, then asked, "You think I want it? With the debts, the work? Do I look like a farm girl to you?" She raised two hands to frame her face. "Do I want this lovely skin wind and sunburnt? Not on your life, little brother, not on your life. Let's see if Old Man Choo wants it. He might pay enough to cover our debts."

Ryck was shocked. This was their home. They had grown up together in it. And Lysa was ready to toss it, just like that. Of course he was ready to leave, but he hadn't thought Lysa would be willing, too.

"So, what are you going to do? Find work in Williamson?" she asked him.

"I'm going to the capital, yeah, but not to work there. I'm thinking of the Legion."

"The Legion? You sure?"

"Kinda sure. I don't think I can work inside, cooped up in an office or a factory. And what skills do I have? I can't even farm, and that's my job," he told her with a smile on his face.

"Oh wow! My little brother's going to be a soldier-boy? That blows my mind."

"Well, I'm not 100% sure, but I want to go down and learn more. They might not even take me," he told her.

"Not take you? A good, strapping farmboy like you? Of course they'll take you."

"Well, we'll see. But what about you? If we sell to Mr. Choo, what are you going to do?"

She hesitated. Ryck knew his twin, and he knew she was wondering what she could and could not tell him. He leaned forward and took her right hand in both of his.

"If I get into the Legion, I'll be off-world. We'll need to keep in contact. I can't do that if you don't tell me where you are," he said.

"Oh, grub. Well, I've got a friend, and he, well, he says he wants to marry me."

"A friend?" he asked.

He knew what kind of men her "friends" were.

"Oh, don't get too grubbing sanctimonious on me now. Yes, Barret, my 'friend,' asked me over four months ago. He's been keeping food on our table since then, so he's your 'friend,' too, there, big boy. You've seen him. He was the guy who took me home last week when you were trying to fix the power junction."

Ryck tried to think back. A fairly new Lexus had skimmed into the yard in a cloud of dust. He had purposely not watched directly, but in his peripheral vision, an older man had gotten out and come around to open the passenger door. Lysa had gotten out of the car, kissed the man on the cheek, then hurried into the home. Ryck had wanted the man off their property, but the guy had just stood there for a minute or so, watching Lysa, before getting back in the Lexus and driving off.

"That guy? But he's . . ."

"Old? Unattractive? Is that what you were going to say?"

"No, I mean . . ."

"Can it, Ryck. I know you and I know what you were going to say. But let me say this first. Yeah, he's older. And yeah, he isn't the most handsome guy around. But he has a good heart. He treats me like a lady, not like those other grubbing bungmen. He treats me with respect. And yeah, I know you saw his car, so yeah, he's got money. He can give me the life I want. We both watched mom and dad scrabble in the dust of this grubbing farm, we watched it kill them. We watched the dust drive away Myke. I don't want that. I want a nice life, where I can live comfortably, where my kids, your future nieces and nephews, little brother, can live a normal life. I wouldn't marry any grubbing asshole just because he has money, but Barret, he's a good man, and I think I love him."

Ryck was taken aback. He had no idea. He generally tried not to think of Lysa's job. He knew that strangers paid her to have drinks with them, and several gave her more money or gifts. Whether she did more than share drinks with them was something he didn't know, nor did he want to know. Because of the possibility that she offered more than just company, though, he resented all the men whom she encountered through the job. It was a huge 180 for him to try and grasp that the men might not all be the perverted, despicable garbage that he had made them out to be in his mind. But he trusted his twin. If she said this Barret guy was a good man, well, that was that. It was going to take awhile for it to really sink in, but if that was what Lysa wanted, that was what he wanted, too.

"OK, I believe you. But, I don't get it. If he asked you four months ago, why are you still here with me?"

Lysa broke out in laughter before answering, "Oh, little brother, you really are an innocent. How could I leave you here, working the farm alone? You wouldn't have lasted a month without me. But now, if you really are going to enlist . . ."

". . . you are free to go on with your life without having to take care of me," he finished her sentence for her.

He got up, walked over to her, and this time, he sat in her lap. He lay his head down on her shoulder while she reached up to pat it.

"No matter what, we need to keep in touch," he murmured into her shoulder. "I'll be damned if I'm going to let you raise my nieces and nephews without me getting to know them."

"And spoil them, I know," she added.

"We're family, you and me. You might be getting married, but we're still blood. 'Why?' Because there's no . . ."

". . . 'I' in the Lysander family," she completed the family motto, one their father had drilled into their heads. It was a philosophy so ingrained in him that he'd even kept the "i's" out of each of his children's first names.

For the first time in months, maybe years, Ryck felt at peace sitting on his sister's lap. He didn't know what his future would bring, what their futures would bring, but he was anxious to find out.

"Oof, little brother. You're not so little anymore. How about getting your fat butt off of me and pour me another glass of that Recife. No use keeping it around, right?"

Ryck got up, poured them both another glass.

"To our futures," he said in a toast. "Whatever may come, and may it be wonderful, we will always be family."

## Chapter 2

The maglev whispered to a stop at Jacob Station. The maglev was an exception to the planet's infrastructure problems. It still worked perfectly despite the collapse of PCDC.

Ryck had stayed on the farm for another week, helping Lysa set up the auction of it, then selling the bulk of their personal possessions. They'd raised enough to get out of debt for the repairs and supplies to run the farm after Myke had left and even have a bit left over. They hadn't sold everything, though. They'd kept some family heirlooms. Lysa had taken some into Barret's home, and Ryck had rented a small storage locker for his things, paying for a year's rent out of his share of the sales proceedings.

Barret had turned out to be a nice, if too-eager-to-please guy. Ryck was surprised to find out that he actually liked the man. He obviously adored Lysa, and that was good enough for Ryck. Ryck and Lysa had made their goodbyes after handing over the deed to the property to Mr. Choo. Ryck had figured Lysa would take him to the station, but it was Barret who had driven him. During the ride, Barret had haltingly explained that he loved Lysa, that he would take care of her, and asked if Ryck would give them his blessing. It felt strange that a forty-year-old man was asking a 19-year-old one for a blessing, but it made Ryck feel appreciation for the man's heart. They even had an awkward hug at the station as Ryck boarded the maglev.

The maglev ride had been smooth, and Ryck had fallen asleep during the three hours it took to arrive in Williamson. Jacob Station, as the main station for both of the western maglev lines, was packed with people moving to and fro, all locked into their own thoughts and purposes. Five young men, maybe a little older than Ryck, squatted against a wall, simply watching the people walk by. They seemed out of the flow of humanity, and their languid insolence grated on Ryck's nerves. He refused to catch any of their eyes as he hurried past to catch a tram to Corporate Center.

The tram was not as well-kept as the maglev, and it was crammed full. Ryck couldn't get a seat, and his country boy mindset was wary of the dangers of city life. He swung his backpack around to his front and wrapped his arms around it. He knew better than to take much with him, but other than what he'd put in storage, this was the entirety of his worldly possessions. He was sure that given the chance, someone would slit his pack and slide all his belongings out.

The tram finally pulled into Corporate Center. The name of the station had stuck despite PCDC pulling off the planet. The Federation had installed an interim governing body when PCDC folded. "Interim" had lasted eight years (so far) as the Federation tried to find a corporate backer to take over.

Ryck went up the escalator and into the sun-lit square. He'd made an appointment with the Legion recruiter for 2:30, and he had plenty of time before that, but he was anxious to get going, so he went into the Federation Building, passing through the security scan and following the directions he'd received at the information desk for the recruiting stations. The Navy Liaison Office was the first one he passed in the corridor. The Navy held the prestige in the Federation. With no official standing army, the Navy formed the bulk of the armed forces of the Federation. They were deeply involved in politics, and the current Federation chairman, like a number of his predecessors, had been Navy admirals. The main office was all glass and metal, with smartly-dressed sailors rushing about their business. There were about five separate offices lining the corridor with the recruitment station at the end. A number of blue chairs were in the small reception area of the office, each one filled with a young man or woman.

Ryck had considered the Navy, of course. It was a sure way to move up in the world, but the thought of being encased in a ship for his enlistment seemed a little claustrophobic. He realized that most Navy jobs did not entail being in space, but he didn't want some sort of desk job. He wanted to get out and see some action. He'd considered the almost mythical SEALs, but his research revealed that only 3% of those who volunteered made it through the training, and if he washed out, he would have had no say in where the Navy would stick him next or what job he would have.

No, the Legion would be a better choice. The Legion was only semi-official, not a true branch of the Federation government.

It was still technically sponsored by France, one of the last independent nations of old Earth, but everyone realized the Federation still helped support it. While it could be hired out by planetary governments or corporations for missions, the Federation was not above using it for missions that it could not send the Navy or Marines on due to legal issues.

Ryck made his way down to the Legion offices. There were four other guys sitting in the line of chairs in the hallway in front of the recruiting office. Ryck reported into the legionnaire sitting at the reception desk and was told to take a seat. Where he waited. And waited. At 3:00, he went back up to the legionnaire.

"Sorry, but we're running behind," the soldier told him. "You'll just have to take a seat and wait."

"I shoulda told ya," the guy next to him said as Ryck sat back down. "I be waitin' since lunch time. Somtin's goin' on in dere, and we just be coolin' our heels out here."

Ryck had already noted the black trousers and dark blue shirt, the indication that his seat companion was probably a Torritite, but the accent was a dead giveaway.

"Ryck Lysander," he told the guy, holding out his hand. "My appointment was at 2:30."

"Joshua Hope-of-Life," the guy replied, taking Ryck's hand in a surprisingly strong grip.

"So, you're joining the Legion?" Ryck asked, a question evident in his voice.

The Torritites were a fundamentalist religious sect. There weren't any Torritite communities up near Ryck, but he knew there were several to the south of Williamson. They generally kept to themselves in big combined families, running their farms as communal property. It seemed odd to see a Torty there signing up for the military.

"Don' ask. I know what you question. You Gentiles think we Brethren all be peace-lovin' do-gooders. We do believe in what the Good Book says about lovin' your neighbor, but that only goes so far. I be named for Joshua, and he was a soldier most 'standing. He took down Jericho's walls, after all."

Ryck leaned back. He hadn't wanted to piss the guy off. He'd just been curious.

"I didn't mean anything. I just was surprised. I thought you guys kept to yourself and all," he stammered out.

Joshua raised his eyes and mouthed something silently before turning back to Ryck. "Take my pardon, Ryck. No offense takin' or givin'. It's just here, in Williamson, with every soul lookin' and gawkin' at me, like they know me, well, forgive me for assumin' anything about you."

"Don't worry about it," Ryck said. "I was just curious. I thought you couldn't fight or hit people back."

"Well, we turn the other cheek, true, but that's only afore we light the other guy up," he said with a laugh. "Truly, though, we always have men in the military, especially afta Sygylla. Sometimes in the militia, but some of us, we go Navy, Marines, or Legion. We even got an admiral now with the squids."

"No grubbing shit?" Ryck asked. "Oh sorry, I didn't mean to curse like that."

"Yeah, no grubbing mother grubber shit," Joshua said with a laugh. "We be religious and all, but don't worry none about cursin'. We don' take the Lord's name in vain, but everythin' else be fair game."

Ryck realized he liked Joshua. He'd never had contact with a Torty before, and except for his way of speaking and his clothes, he could be anyone else Ryck had ever known. Before too long, even the clothing difference would be gone when they were wearing the Legion kepi and 42's.

They sat together, getting to know about each other as they waited for their interview. Their daily lives were really not that much different beyond their family organization. With Ryck, it had been their small five-member family, then eventually just Lysa and him. Joshua, though, lived in an extended family with nine mothers, 12 fathers, and 36 siblings. Ryck couldn't imagine living like that, but as far as the rest: the farming, the schooling, the sports, the entertainment, the girl-chasing, they were surprisingly the same.

"Ryck Lysander, what the hell are you doing here, aside from the obvious, I mean," a voice called out.

Ryck looked up to see Proctor Miller standing there. Proctor was from the next settlement to the north of his. They attended different schools, but had competed against each other in lineball, b-ball, and they'd even wrestled each other. They couldn't really be called good friends, but they were at least friendly competitors.

Ryck jumped up to shake Proctor's hand.

"Good to see you! I'm here just enlisting. How about you? You here for the Legion, too?"

"Legion? No way. I've already been accepted into the Marines. I'm just here to get my ticket to report in. The Marine's are where it's at, there, Ryck. Not the fancy-ass Legion. Oh, no offense intended," he added, as two of the others waiting overheard him and started to get up.

"Really, Ryck. Why do you want to join the Legion? They're mercenaries," he asked in a subdued voice.

"We all be mercenaries, Marines, Navy, or Legion. Only the militias be true home fighters," Joshua said, standing up beside Ryck.

"Oh, Proctor, this is Joshua Hope-is- . . . Joshua, what's your last name again?"

"Hope-of-Life," Joshua said, holding out his hand to Proctor.

"Good to meet you," Proctor said. "And there's a lot of truth to what you just said. But the militias and the planetary armies never leave their home planet, never go off-world. I want to see our galaxy. I want to go places. I'm not cut out to be a sailor. That leaves the Legion and the Marines, and at least the Marines don't get hired out as mercenaries. The Marines fight for a cause."

"And you don' think the Fed uses the Marines for its own purposes? Things not for altruistic causes?" Joshua asked.

"Of course I know that," Proctor conceded. "But not as much as the Legion is used by whoever has the bigger bank account."

"But I keep hearing about how the Marines have to take second-hand equipment. Even some armies are better armed, and the Legion had all the newest gear," Ryck said.

"True, but those armies don't have the power of the Navy behind them, and when are we ever going to fight the Legion? Besides, any Marine can kick any kepi-wearing froggie if it came to that," he said, then, "Easy does it, fellow. You're not even a legionnaire, yet, and I'm just trash-talking," he said to one of the other waiting guys who had actually stood up upon overhearing Proctor's boast. "We love the Legion, and you guys are all superhuman soldiers," he added.

"Just not as tough as Marines," he whispered to Ryck and Joshua as the guy sat back down.

"Look, I'm going down to get my ticket out of here. Why don't you two come down with me? It won't hurt to just get some information, right? Then you can come back down here if you still want to get in line for your kepi," Proctor said.

"I don't know," Ryck said. "I've got an appointment, and what if they call my name while I'm gone?"

"Hey, what time be your appointment?" Joshua asked the guy who was the one who had started to take offense at Proctor's earlier words.

"Eleven," the guy said, obviously still not completely mollified by Proctor's apologies.

"See, they aren't going to get to you for a long time. Come on down with me," Proctor said.

"I . . . well, I think the Legion gives more opportunities. I can appreciate what you're saying, but . . ." Ryck said before Joshua interrupted.

"I'll do it. Lead on."

Ryck turned to stare at Joshua.

"You're joining the Marines? What about the Legion?" Ryck asked.

He'd only just met Joshua, but the thought of going to Camerone for recruit training with Joshua sounded a whole lot better than going without anyone he knew.

"Not to join. But to get information be the smart thing to do. I considered the Marines, but my brother be a legionnaire, so I chose the Legion. Our good friend here," he said, indicating the guy with the eleven o'clock appointment, "still waits, so we have time. I be tired of sittin' here, so a walk will let me get off my grubbin' ass and stretch my legs."

"Well, just to get more information?" Ryck asked.

"Just info," Proctor assured him.

"I guess it wouldn't hurt. Maybe we can hit the snack bar and get something to eat, too," Ryck told them.

Ryck and Joshua followed Proctor further down the hallway while Proctor told them about his orders, about his departure in three days, about how his girlfriend had come with him and they were shacking up in the Holiday Inn until he left. Proctor hadn't even gotten warmed up when they reached the Marine recruiting station.

Where the Navy office was opulent in a technically-advanced setting and the Legion's office was understated, but classy, the Marine Corps recruiting station was Spartan. There was a plastocrete desk serving for reception, and on a poster on the wall in back of it was an image of a steely-eyed young man in the Marine Dress Blues staring at whomever would be standing in front of the desk. His chest was adorned in ribbons. Unlike at the Navy and Legion recruiting offices, there was no one waiting. In fact, there was no one in the front office at all.

Proctor started to reach over the front reception desk when a door opened and a Marine and a young man walked out. The Marine was in a khaki shirt and blue trousers, a red stripe running down each leg. His left arm was shorter than normal and covered in the blue bio-wrap that indicated his arm was in the process of being regenerated. Ryck couldn't help but wonder what happened to his original arm.

"That is what we can offer you. After that, it would be in your hands. We aren't going to coddle you, but we will give you the opportunity to maximize your capabilities. That we can promise you," the Marine was saying.

"You've got my number. If you have any further questions, I'm here for you," he continued, shaking the young man's hands.

"Mr. Miller. You're here for your ticket," the Marine said as the young guy left the office. "Let me get that."

He pulled out his PA, and hit a few keys. "Open your PA and give it to me," he told Proctor.

Proctor complied, and the Marine tapped his PA on Proctor's.

"OK, you've got it. Be there three hours prior. Take only the items on the list I gave you. Nothing else," he told Proctor before taking his hand and shaking it. "And are these your friends coming to see you off? A couple nights on the town before we own your soul?"

If the Marine thought it odd that a Torritite would be hanging out with "Gentiles," he never let that show.

"No, Staff Sergeant Wassari, these are my friends, Ryck and Joshua. I just rescued them from in front of the Legion recruiting station, and I thought that since they have to wait anyway, they might as well come down and talk to you, you know, only for information, of course."

"The Legion? Good unit. Good men. They're not Marines, of course, but if that's what you want to achieve in your life, then I'm sure you will do well. But as Mr. Miller says, it doesn't hurt to find out about the Corps and how we differ from the rest. Why don't you step back into my lair and have a seat?" he asked.

*Said the spider to the fly*, Ryck thought.

"I'll wait for you here," Proctor said, taking a seat. "Maybe we can get dinner together after you're all done for the day."

Ryck followed Joshua into the Marine's office.

Forty-five minutes later, new Marine Corps recruits Ryck Lysander and Joshua Hope-of-Life walked back out to a smiling Proctor.

# *Tarawa: Recruit Training*

## *Chapter 3*

The ship landed in the middle of the night on Tarawa.[8] The recruits debarked the *Sally Ling* when most of the passengers were either in the casino or in their staterooms asleep. The other passengers probably had no idea that more than 300 recruits had shared the voyage from Vegas. They'd been confined to their billets on F Deck since coming on board. The recruits had been quietly herded out of a cargo hatch, so as not to disturb the paying passengers' night.

It was still hot when they walked down the ramp despite the late hour. Ryck strained to make out anything about where he would be spending the next 42 weeks. It was just a standard spaceport, though, and as it didn't have the glamour and non-stop advertising of Vegas' main spaceport, it was not much different from the one back on Prophesy. There were a few murmurs coming from the recruits, but most of them walked in silence.

That silence lasted until they passed through the door over which hung the innocuous sign with "RECEIVING" printed on it. Several civilians directed them to a processing center with five desks in the front. Each recruit gave his name and was scanned. Told to move in by their handlers, they were led outside where buses waited. Ryck got on board, saving seats for Joshua and Proctor.

"That wasn't too bad," Proctor said as he got on and took the seat.

"Yeah, I thought it would be tougher. I know the training itself will be harder, but I guess it isn't as bad as what we read on the net," Ryck said.

The buses hissed as they lifted off the ground, and the drivers eased the rigs forward. The three recruits were in the second-to-last bus, and as they moved through the streets of

---

[8] **Tarawa**: Originally named Hollison, the planet was renamed when it became the prime training base and headquarters for the Federation Marines.

Gibraltar, they tried to catch a view of the city's infamous nightlife. Either that nightlife was somewhere else in the city, or the extent of it was something else that had been exaggerated on the net.

It was after midnight, but excitement kept most of them awake as the busses picked up speed outside the city. Recruits talked in quiet voices as they discussed what was ahead of them. An hour later, the lights of Camp Charles broke the darkness. Everyone on board shut up as the buses slowed down in front of the gates. Two Marines in their dress blues were manning it, and they motioned the buses to enter. Ryck pushed his face up against the window to be able to see the arch over the gate, *Per Terra et Mare*[9] written in gold-colored metal tubing.

The buses pulled into a courtyard and stopped. Their civilian guide stood up in front of the bus, turning to face them.

"OK, this is it. Welcome to Camp Charles. I need all of you to file off the bus, then cross in front and to the area to our left."

"What do we do then?" a voice asked towards the rear of the bus..

"Oh, someone will tell you what to do. Don't worry about that," the man said with a chuckle. "And good luck," he added as they started to file off.

Ryck, Joshua, and Proctor stuck together as they moved past the bus and into a square with buildings closing in on three sides. Three hundred plus recruits milled about, wondering what was next. Two doors in the one of the buildings opened, sending light out into the square.

"Come on you spineless worms, get your sorry asses on the yellow footprints!" a voice yelled out from the building.

Ryck couldn't see who was yelling, and he couldn't see any yellow footprints, but he pushed ahead in the herd. He'd read about the infamous yellow footprints before leaving Prophesy and expected them, but reading about something and experiencing it were two different things. Despite himself, he could feel his heart rate soar.

---

[9] ***Per Terra et Mare***: "By Land and Sea." The motto of the Spanish *Infantería de Marina,* the oldest extant Marine Corps at the time of the formation of the Federation Marine Corps

"Come on," he told Joshua. "Push. We don't want to be the last ones there."

"Move it, move it!" the voice screamed out. "I can't believe what I'm seeing here! I refuse to see what pieces of shit think they can be Marines!"

Other voices chimed in, coming from the sides. Ryck glanced around, and caught sight of a drill instructor closing in from behind. Like a minnow trying to escape a pike, he darted forward, pushing other recruits aside, not wanting to let the drill instructor get close. He'd lost Joshua and Proctor, but he saw the yellow footprints on the floor and got on top of the first free one he reached.

The DIs continued to scream, their orders only interrupted by their observations on the worth of this batch of recruits; that worth wasn't much. In position on his claimed footprints, he could see the DI in front of him. The man was red in the face and seemed to be in the throes of an epileptic fit. He was screaming out his displeasure, and Ryck was in awe of the man's mastery of expressing his distaste. Ryck let his eyes drift down to the DI's arms. He couldn't remember if the stripes on the sleeves of his uniform meant the DI was a sergeant or corporal.

"You eyeballing me, you piece of slime?" the DI shouted at Ryck.

The shorter DI rushed forward, bending down slightly, then crooking his neck to look right up Ryck's nostrils, it seemed to him.

"You don't rate eyeballing me, farm boy. You keep your eyeballs locked to the front, got it?"

"Yes, sir!" Ryck shouted, looking straight ahead.

"'Sir?' 'Sir?' Do I look like a fucking officer? I work for a living. It's 'Aye-aye sergeant,' or 'aye-aye drill instructor.' Don't ever call me sir."

"Yes, sir, sergeant!" Ryck stammered out.

"'Sir?' What the hell did I just tell you? Can't you follow a simple order?" the DI screamed.

"Uh, aye-aye, sergeant!" he managed to get out.

"Oh my loving Mary! I asked you a question! You answer yes or no. Not 'aye-aye.' If I tell you to do something, then it's 'aye-aye.' My three-year-old niece can manage that!"

Ryck had to think a moment before offering, "Yes, sergeant."

He wasn't sure he was correct, but the DI had moved on to torment someone else. Ryck let out a sigh of relief.

*How did he know I was a farm boy*, he wondered. *Do I look like one?*

The next few hours were a blur. A roll call was made, and Ryck remembered to respond with the "Here, drill instructor" as directed. Quite a few other recruits couldn't manage even that, and they paid the price with pushups. They were broken into groups, then herded to the barber, where their heads were shaved, to the sick bay, as Ryck learned the medical facility was called, for an analysis, and to uniform issue. Ryck had a complete physical two days before leaving Prophesy, so he wondered why another physical was necessary. Did they think they'd gotten some disqualifying condition while en route?

Uniform issue was done within moments. They were lined up and handed a bundle of clothing, then told to march into an adjoining room to change. The uniforms were plain brown trousers and a shirt, a belt, boots, and a helmet. There hadn't seemed to be any rhyme or reason to the issuance, and there didn't look to be any nano-sizing that would adjust the uniforms to each recruit, but the uniforms seemed to fit. The old clothes that they had been wearing were put into plastic bags, sealed, and then taken away.

Dawn was already breaking four hours later when they were marched into a cafeteria. They went through the receiving line to get their breakfast. Ryck caught a glimpse of Joshua, but they'd all been warned to keep their eyes to the front, so he couldn't risk trying to catch his attention. He just sat down and shoveled in the food. It was tasteless, but he didn't care. It was energy, and he'd had a feeling he was going to need as much energy as he could over the course of the day.

Twenty minutes later, they were herded into an auditorium where they sat and waited.

"What do you think is next?" the recruit to his left whispered.

Ryck ignored the question. He wasn't going to give the DIs any reason to target him.

After another 10 minutes or so, a voice rang out with "Attention on deck!"

Ryck jumped to his feet, eyes to the front as everyone stood up. With his peripheral vision, he saw eight Marines making their way down the center aisle and up on the stage. One Marine moved to center stage with another to his left. Another Marine took a position behind him, with a Marine to his left as well. A final four Marines marched to stand at attention in back of them.

"At ease, recruits," the one who had taken center stage said. "Take your seats. I am Captain Petrov, company commander for Delta Company, 1st Recruit Training Battalion," he continued after the auditorium settled down. "To my left is First Sergeant Tyliman, the company chief drill instructor. Behind me is the series commander and series senior drill instructor, and behind them are the four senior drill instructors for the recruit platoons that make up the Follow Series. Each of you has been assigned to a training platoon. The number below the name on your chest is the number of your platoon. Get used to it. That platoon will be your home and family for the next 42 weeks."

Despite himself, Ryck glanced down at the white tag on his chest. Below the "Lysander, R." was the number "1044."

"All of you have volunteered to become a Federation Marine. Many of you will not make it through recruit training. Some will wash out, some will quit. A few of you will probably die during training."

That made Ryck take notice. He knew that Marines faced danger in battle, but in recruit training?

"One thing I need to make absolutely clear," the captain went on, "is that we are not here to make you Marines. We are only here to give you the opportunity to earn the title of Marine. Whether you earn that title or not is up to you. We will not coddle you, we will not lead you by the hand. All we will do is show you the way. It will be up to you to make the journey and grab the prize at the end.

"We have recruits from 53 planets here in the class, coming from 81 separate governing bodies. Some of your governments have been at odds with each other. All that stops here. The only tie you have now is to your squad, to your platoon, to the Corps. When you are sworn in, you are cutting the ties to the past.

"Four other platoons in the Lead Series were formed yesterday. In a few minutes, you will formally join them, and your training will officially begin. I won't wish you good luck. We don't want Marines who were lucky to make it through training. We want Marines who fought for the title, who kicked and clawed past all the bad luck thrown their way to succeed."

The captain paused to scan the auditorium. Ryck couldn't tell if he looked disappointed or please with the gathered recruits.

"First Sergeant, bring the recruits to attention," he told the Marine to his left.

That Marine stepped forward before bellowing out, "Company, atten-hut!" and then "Raise your right hand and repeat after Captain Petrov," once everyone was standing.

"I, state your name," the captain started, to be followed by an uneven chorus from the recruits,

*. . .do solemnly swear, to support and defend Articles of Council of the United Federation, against all enemies, foreign and domestic; that I will bear true faith and allegiance to the same and above all others; and that I will obey the orders of the Chairman of the United Federation and the orders of the officers appointed over me, according to the Uniform Code of Military Justice. So help me God.*

"You are now officially recruits in the United Federation Marine Corps," the company commander said.

He did an about-face and said to the six Marines now in front of him, "Series commander, take charge of your series and carry out the remainder of the training schedule."

He did another about face, and without a word, marched off the stage and down the center aisle, followed by his first sergeant. Ryck risked a glance, then jerked his head back forward as four sets of drill instructors marched down the aisles to the front of the auditorium.

Recruit training had begun.

## *Chapter 4*

No Initial huffed alongside Ryck, his mouth open as he gasped for air. Up ahead, just outside the Liberty gate, Ryck could see Drill Instructor Despri waiting for them.

"Come on, No Initial, another 500 meters and we're done," he got out between his own breathing. "Cold water, aircon; think of it."

Moreau just nodded, too winded to speak. "No Initial" Moreau was a big guy, almost two meters tall, and a solid 120 kg. He looked the part, but he'd struggled during the heavy PT[10] the recruits had been put through the first four days of training, particularly during the runs. This run had "only" been six kilometers, two loops between the gate and The Lost Lady, a rock formation south of the camp wall, but it was with a 35 kg ruck full of sand. The training rucks weren't like the nice commercial rucks available to any civilian. This was basically a synthetic fiber sack with two thin straps that dug into the recruits' shoulders as they ran.

Moreau was from Tai 'pao, and like most of the residents there, he had only one name. That didn't fit the Marine standard, so his name tag read "Moreau, N.I.." The "N.I." quickly turned into "No Initial."

Ryck didn't know if No Initial was going to make it. Platoon 1044 had already lost five recruits: one was whisked away less than an hour after they'd been sworn in for reasons that still fueled the rumor mill four days later. The other four recruits had simply quit. No one knew what had become of them. Technically, most recruits could not just give up their obligations once sworn in, but as the DIs kept drilling into their heads, the Marine Corps did not want anyone less than the best in its ranks. The Navy might snag a few depending on the reasons a recruit quit, his capabilities, and his enlistment contract, but the general consensus was that most who quit during training would just be sent home.

---

[10] **PT**: Physical Training

If No Initial was having so many problems with the PT now, Ryck wondered how he would cope when the tempo was increased. One of the required events during the Crucible just before graduation was a 25 km run with 50 kg on their backs. If you couldn't keep up or quit, it was either get out or get recycled.

The PT was kicking Ryck's ass, too, but he managed to struggle through it. It was kicking everyone's ass except for Clary Won and Born Brilliant. Clary was just a stud, but Born Brilliant seemed to escape to some other plane and breeze through when the going got rough.

"Tighten it up, ladies," Drill Instructor Lorenz said as he ran beside the loose formation. He was carrying the same ruck as the recruits, and it looked like it was loaded with twice as much sand as any of them had. "Look good coming in."

Ryck hated him at the moment. How could he look so good, so at ease, when most of them were dying?

Ryck knew the heavy PT was part of the indoctrination, but still, why the rucks? As Marines, they would be in PICS battle suits, or at least with exoskeleton assists embedded into their uniforms. When would they have to carry loads like this without assistance, with only their God-given bodies? He tried to put that thought out of his mind. His was not to reason why, after all.

Moreau started to fall back.

"Grab my ruck," Ryck told him, hoping against hope that Moreau wouldn't hear the offer or wouldn't take it.

The sudden pull against him threw that hope out the window. He sighed and leaned into the run, pulling No Initial along. It was only 300 meters, then 200, then 100. The platoon started to slow down, over 75 pairs of feet preparing to come to a halt at the gate. Drill Instructor Despiri watch them approach, then motioned his arm around, pointing back out along the trail.

"Not together," he said in his usual clipped manner. "Again."

The moans were not suppressed as Drill Instructor Lorenz swung the platoon around and back on the trail to The Lost Lady.

"Do it right the first time, ladies, and we won't have to go at it again," he told them.

Ryck wasn't sure how 75 men could make the run and stay in formation. There were others besides No Initial who were struggling, some straggling behind. As far as Ryck was concerned, let those guys run another loop. Let the ones who kept up stop and rest. At least No Initial had let go of him as they had approached the gate.

He tried to adjust the ruck on his back to a more comfortable position, but that was hopeless. Three more kilometers, and they'd better all be in formation when they got back or someone might be facing a blanket party.

## *Chapter 5*

Ryck slid into the seat, grateful to be off his feet. This was their first history class, and one of the few training events in which there were no DIs. Drill Instructor Lorenz, looking refreshed and as if he hadn't just been with them on the nine kilometer ruck run, had marched the platoon to the classroom, then left after each rank had filed in.

The platoon already had a number of classes in subjects such as rank structure, military etiquette, Marine Corps organization, and the UCMJ.[11] Some of the other platoons had already started history classes, but with only one instructor, classes had to be juggled. They were scheduled for 20 hours in the classroom before graduation. Ryck wasn't sure just why recruits needed that much time, but any time without the DIs was welcome.

Dr. Berber stood at the front of the classroom, watching each file of recruits march in and take a seat. When the last recruit sat down, he started right in.

"When was the first Marine Corps formed?" he asked without any attempt at an introduction.

Not that an introduction was really needed. Everyone knew about Dr. Berber. He'd been a Marine, but he was a fixture at Camp Charles and had been teaching there for over 40 years. He was a lean, almost skeletal figure, and he spoke with a sharp staccato.

Several hand shot up. Ryck kept his face neutral, hiding the distaste he had for the springbutts. Recruit training was not a place to put yourself in the limelight where you could draw attention to yourself.

"You," Dr. Berber said, pointing a long arm at Doggie Jenkins.

"Doggie" was an appropriate name for a guy who kept seeking approval. Ryck could almost imagine a tail under his trou, wagging in excitement.

---

[11] **UCMJ**: The Uniform Code of Military Justice. These are the rules and regulations governing servicemen and women in the Federation armed forces.

"The *Infantería de Marina,* established on February 27, 1537, by Charles the First, for whom this camp was named," Doggie recited.

"Wrong!" shouted Dr. Berber.

That caught Ryck's attention. Doggie was not any sort of history buff. What he'd just said was right out of our Marine Corps Handbook, the printed book that recruits were required to carry at all times. The book was filled with all sorts of Marine Corps knowledge, not the least being the origins of the Corps.

"The *Infantería de Marina* was the oldest extant Marine Corps when the Federation Marine Corps was formed. But there were many different naval infantry, or marine units formed before that. During the Chinese Warring States of 481-221 BC, soldiers armed with dagger-halberds were put on ships to ward off boarders. The ancient Greeks used hoplites as naval infantry. Mighty Imperial Rome, though, in the year 68 AD, might have been the first government to form specific marine units, the First and Second Adiutrix. The point I am making is two-fold. The first is listen to the question, not just in history, but in life. I asked one thing, and our volunteer there, Mr. Jenkins," he said after peering at Doggie's nametag, "answered what he thought I asked instead of what I asked. Doing that in combat could have drastic consequences. The second point is that from the time of navies, there had to be soldiers to protect them. These soldiers of the seas are your direct forebears. We didn't need Chuck the First to suddenly come up with the idea. All he did was put into a decree what was already a proven need. That need has not changed from the time of war galleys to our newest Prion Class carrier today.

"I hope you will take the advantage of not only listening, but also learning from this class. Yes, I know that you miss your drill instructors," he said to the laughter breaking out in the classroom, "and you need them to tell you how to fart," as even louder laughter broke out. "But this is your heritage. This is what makes you what you are. I'm not going to be ratting out any of you if you fall asleep, but I hope you have the pride and discipline to listen and learn."

The "falling asleep" comment hit home. Ryck had it in the back of his mind to do just that if he could get away with it. But Dr.

Berber's comment and appeal to their own sense of discipline instilled something more in him. He was going to be a Marine, and he should know its history, what would soon be his history.

"Settle back and relax. I will let you know," Dr. Berber said, stomping his foot in an exaggerated manner, "what you will have to know for the test. What you think the Corps doesn't test everything here at Camp Charles?" he said to the groans that had come at the word "test." "The Corps tests everything, so get used to it. Anyway, I'll let you know what will be tested," he said, once again making the exaggerated stomp. "But what I want you to absorb is the makings of the Marines and how our own culture has been developed. We work closely with the Navy, but we are different animals.

"Over our twenty classes together, we will examine the birth of dedicated naval infantry units, of the proliferation and periodic demise of marine units, of the 43 national and three planetary Marine Corps that were combined to form the Federation Marines, and of our own Federation Marine Corps history, our greatest battles and heroes. Much of this will directly affect you, from why we celebrate both February 27 and November 10 as our Marine Corps birthday, why NCOs wear the red stripe on their blues, and why a drummer in the Marine band wears a leopard skin over his uniform.

"Today, we will go over the foundation of how naval infantry was developed."

A vid of some sort of war gallery appeared over his arena.

"I won't be foot-stomping anything during this class. There won't be anything on the test from today, so just listen and let it sink in.

"The first recorded naval battle was the Battle of the Delta, between the Egyptians under Ramses III and a group known as the Sea Peoples. In this battle, which took place around 1175 BC, the ships were used as platforms from which archers could fire towards shore-based troops, so in a way, the naval infantry preceded the use of a navy ship as a weapon in and of itself. Ships continued to be more of floating transports, and it wasn't until the rise of the Greeks and Phoenicians around 1000 BC that the war galley was developed. This is what is called a *triaconter*, or 'thirty-oared ship.' Not only could it transport troops, but also it could attack and destroy other ships, quite often through ramming" he said, pointing to the image above his desk arena. Another image of a galley appeared, and the first one turned to face it before oars started it forward towards the new ship.

Ryck leaned forward in his seat. He had a feeling that the 20 hours he was scheduled to be in class with the good doctor were going to be interesting.

## *Chapter 6*

Recruit Squad Leader Ryck Lysander took a few steps to his left and yelled "Hodges, get your grubbing team up in position!"

This was the first training evolution in his new recruit billet, and he was bound and determined to keep it all the way through graduation. He didn't need Hodges to get him fired before he'd even had a chance to show the DIs what he was capable of.

They were outside the camp walls, in TA103, "Training Area 103," a good-sized expanse of open ground. It wasn't as clear as a parade deck, but it was as close to being clear as any other training area. There were a few gentles rises and one gully, but a DI could pretty much view the entire area. Ryck couldn't afford to focus on any of the other squads in sight, though. He had to watch his four fire teams as they walked through the various formations they'd just learned.

As he'd wondered before, he wasn't sure why they were walking around, their M99s in hand, but nothing else. No comms, no armor, nothing. Ryck knew they'd never be without their comms, and trying to control four fire teams by shouting was not the most efficient way of getting the job done. Why not just give them a club and animal skins, and let them grunt out their commands?

Not that the M99s they carried were anything more than clubs, and not very effective cubs at that. Ryck had been thrilled when he'd been issued his, but that thrill faded when he realized the weapon was a liability to a recruit. Not only did it have the bright pink safety tie that kept the chamber from closing, showing the world that he wasn't trusted yet to have a live weapon, but also even dropping it, much less getting separated from it, resulted in a punishment that was better blocked out of the mind. One recruit DOR'd[12] right in the middle of his pushups he'd been assigned for dropping his. The DIs had been in his face, screaming, and the guy

---

[12] **DOR**: Drop on Request. This is the formal term for a recruit quitting recruit training.

just stopped. Leaving his weapon on the deck, he'd just stood up, then walked back toward the barracks.

"Are you DOR'ing?" the top hat had screamed.

"Yep," had been the reply.

As if a switch had been thrown, the DIs quit their tirade. Drill Instructor Lorenz picked up the recruit's M99 and slung it on his back as the other DIs turned their attention back to the rest of the platoon.

Ryck had already forgotten the recruit's name. He was only one of six recruits who were gone.

"Damn it Hodges, get your team up!" he shouted again, running a few steps toward him until he stumbled over a rock and almost went to his knees.

He risked a glance back to the bleachers where they had been given their lesson. Not only were his DIs there watching, but also the series commander and senior were there as well, all observing the training. Ryck hoped no one had noticed him stumbling.

Recruit Hodges slowly moved his fire team up in position. The DI field instructor had told them that formations like this had been the mainstay of military operations since warfare began, but Ryck thought that had no bearing on modern warfare. Marines were not going to be trudging into battle in nice little squad V's, Wedges, or Echelons. Even the most ill-equipped enemy would be able to hold off a company of Marines if this was all they did. They might just as well line up in three ranks and conduct volley fire at the enemy.

They finally made it to the yellow flag that indicated they had to shift to the next formation. This changing formations was called "Battle Drill." Ryck looked down at his instruction sheet.

"OK, listen up! We're going to a Squad V," he shouted, holding up both arms at an angle above his head.

At least the fire teams didn't have to change formations at the same time, something for which Ryck was grateful. That would be a royal clusterfuck. He shifted to his own position as he watched the fire teams slowly make the change.

"Hodges! Where are you supposed to be in a Squad V? To the right of the formation! No, to your other right! You see Fourth

Fire Team there? You think you both are going to march together?" Ryck shouted as he sprinted towards his wayward team.

Observers be damned, Ryck was going to grab that grubbing idiot by the collar and drag him into position if he had to.

## *Chapter 7*

Ryck strapped on his armor. Not the body armor they would be issued at the end of Phase 2, but plastic armor, gloves, and a helmet that looked like some old-time football gear. This was pugil stick training, what some said was the highlight of Phase 1.

Ryck wouldn't call it the highlight, himself. What was next? Jousting? Sword fighting? He thought in that in today's Marine Corps, the weapons were just slightly more advanced than smacking each other with padded sticks. It didn't matter what Ryck thought, though. For the Drill Instructors, this was life and death. Competition between squads, platoons, and companies was the very lifeblood of the DIs. Each unit had to do better than the rest, and the DIs held their recruits' victories over each other. The pugil stick tournament was the first major competition within the company, and the all the DIs were anxious for an early victory.

They'd been introduced to the sticks in the morning session. There was actually some technique involved, but from what was the undercurrent being discussed, the actual bouts were more like two recruits simply trying to bash out each other's brains.

Now, after chow and after a class on first aid, which Ryck thought was appropriate just prior to the tourney, it was time to have at it. It was First Squad against Second, Third against Fourth. The final platoon winners would go up against the other platoon champ in a death match at the end of Phase 1.

Ryck figured he would be matched against Raj Simperson, the Third Squad leader, but the DIs chose No Initial as his first opponent. Ryck's first reaction was *why me?* No Initial was huge, but then as he thought about it, Ryck figured this would be a way for him to shine. Ryck already knew that No Initial didn't have stamina and that he was slow. All Ryck would have to do would be to dance around, darting in and out, landing what blows he could until the big guy from Craxion 4 tired.

With his gear on and checked by Drill Instructor Lorenz, Ryck joined the rest of the squad around the huge sawdust-filled circle just to the east of the obstacle course. The circle was only used for pugil stick training. A recruit would think this was sacred ground. Woe and behold any recruit who happened to try and walk across it. That had happened to Hodges when he was told to go back to the start of the obstacle course back on T4, or "Training Day 4," and what happened to him was something Ryck never wanted to see again. He thought Hodges was going to DOR right there, but somehow, the guy had stuck through his "motivational training."

First Squad and Second were going at it. Some bouts were quick, some took time. Du Boc, a smaller recruit from Harmony, and Graeme Styles, a heavy-worlder from Rio Tinto, had an epic battle, with all the recruits and drill instructors cheering. Du was quicker than the stockier Graeme, and he kept up a tremendous flurry of blows that the heavy-worlder absorbed as he tracked down his lighter opponent. Heavy-worlder or not, though, Du was getting through, staggering Graeme twice. Finally, as Du darted in for another shot, Graeme connected, almost sending Du down. Somehow, Du stayed up as Graeme waded in. Several blows hit Du from each side, yet he would just not give up. His helmet was knocked askew, blinding him. Graeme lunged forward to take advantage of it, but Du lashed out with a wild roundhouse swing, going yard. Somehow, he connected against Graeme's head, and the Rio Tinto recruit almost went down.

The rest of the recruits, even those in Third and Fourth Squads, were going crazy. Just to his right, the Second Squad "coach," Drill Instructor Mendez, was in full apoplectic fit mode, screaming as it looked that Du might pull it out.

The recruits wore big, bulky gloves while fighting, and these gloves fit through the padding on the sticks to allow a combatant to get a firm grip. It was considered a coward's loss to drop a pugil stick, akin to a Spartan coming home without his shield, so the gloves and handhold made it easier to hang on, almost locking the hand in place. This didn't make the gloves very useful for anything else though, and when Du removed one hand to try and twist his helmet back so he could see again, he couldn't get a good grasp on it.

When Graeme's next blow hit him, it smashed through Du's hand and lifted the taller, but lighter recruit up right off his feet to crash down in the sawdust. Lying flat on his back, Du weakly lifted his left hand, which had somehow still retained its grip on his pugil stick. This was no coward's loss.

Graeme strode forward, and for a moment, Ryck thought the guy was still in attack mode. When the bloodlust was up, anything could happen, and more than once, DIs had to wade in to separate fighters. Graeme was a heavy-worlder, too, and while Ryck had never really known one, he knew their reputation as undisciplined brawlers. He was surprised, then, when Graeme merely bent over to help Du to his feet. Graeme even held up Du's arm in the victor pose. The senior moved into the ring and held up both of their arms. Winning was drilled into each recruit's head, but it seemed that even in losing, Du had gained the DIs' respect.

Despite himself, Ryck could feel his own competitive blood boil. This might be antiquated, it might be useless, but Ryck was getting psyched. He wondered what his chances were to emerge as the platoon champ. He was already a squad leader, but that was assigned to him. Platoon pugil stick champ would be earned.

When First and Second completed the first round, the winners were all taken to the side where they would await the winners between Third and Fourth. Due to drops, the squads were not even, so two recruits from First had joined Third for their first bout. If they won though, it would still be a First Squad win.

Drill Instructor Lorenz gathered them all around before they started their bouts.

"I can give you an 'oorah' speech, but frankly, if it isn't in you, then I'm not going implant it into your heart with a 30-second speech. This, recruits, is up to you. No one else. Yeah, I want you to win, because I'd love to stick it in Drill Instructor Temperance," he said, holding one hand up as if it were in back of the neck of someone, then taking his right and driving it up as if thrusting a knife, then twisting it back and forth. "If you lose, you're going to wish you hadn't, I promise you. But that's not why you want to win. You should need to win because you're the baddest, meanest motherfuckers around, and you want the world to know it."

He looked around at the 18 of the recruits in turn, catching each one of them eye-to eye, before saying, "OK, bring it in. On three. One, two three!"

"Fourth Squad, 1044! We bring it!" they shouted almost in uniform.

Then it was time. Despite himself, Ryck forgot about his previously-held notion that pugil stick bouts were a waste of time. He jumped up and down, shaking out his arms, feeling the aggressor in him surface. He was going to kick some grubbing ass! He didn't lose that when the first two recruits in Fourth Squad fell quick victim to their Third Squad opponents. He was going to break that trend.

"So what are you going to do, Recruit Lysander?" Drill Instructor Lorenz asked him as he gave Ryck's equipment one last check.

"He ain't nothing but a grub, Drill Instructor. He can't even run. He's got no heart, I'm gonna dash in and hit him, then I'm gonna . . ."

"Don't give me all the details, recruit. Just tell me what you're going to do."

"Uh . . . oh, I'm going to destroy him! Oorah!" Ryck shouted.

"OK, go do it."

Ryck stepped into the ring and approached the center. He and No Initial got there at the same time. The TDI running the bouts started going over the rules once more.

*I don't need no grubbing rules*, Ryck thought, tuning out the Green Shirt. *No rules in war!*

He looked at No Initial. Ryck knew the recruit was stronger than he was, but Ryck also knew he owed Ryck. Without Ryck helping him, he would have fallen out of a number of runs. So Ryck knew No Initial wouldn't go after him too hard. And that was his Achilles' Heel.

Ryck has considered putting on his warface, the expression of determination and mayhem that most of the recruits had tried to cultivate. But he thought it better to lull No Initial by not seeming too aggressive. Instead, he smiled and gave a shrug. Just two friends who would do enough to appease the DIs, but not enough to really hurt each other. No Initial smiled back. He was copacetic with it.

The Green Shirt was done and stepped back. He raised the whistle to his lips.

Ryck tried to look relaxed. At the whistle, he was going to spring before No Initial could react and knock the big guy on his ass for a quick win. He almost felt sorry for him. They had just agreed to an unspoken arrangement to take it easy, and Ryck was going to break that to win. But Ryck was tired of carrying No Initial around, both literally and figuratively. Better he learn his lesson here at the Depot then in combat.

The whistle sounded, and Ryck lunged. He had his pugil stick swinging in an uppercut, ready to connect with No Initial's chin. He barely saw No Initial's own stick swinging, then he saw nothing at all.

## *Chapter 8*

"Doggie, check for the DIs," Hamilton Ceres, the recruit squad leader for First said. Hamilton had gathered Doggie and the other three squad leaders, the platoon guide, the whiskey locker recruit, and the scribe for an impromptu meeting. Doggie was the "house mouse," the recruit tasked with cleaning the DIs' office, so if he checked and a DI was still there, it should rouse no suspicion.

The seven of them, the entirety of the recruit leadership in the platoon, waited silently in the head until Doggie came back with news that the DIs were gone. They could get down to business. Ryck already had a good idea on what Hamilton wanted to tell them. Earlier in the day, Seth MacPruit, a recruit in First, had told Hamilton to fuck off, reminding the squad leader that Hamilton was a recruit just like the rest of them, and that he had no real authority over him. Technically, that was true. The recruit squad leaders were only acting squad leaders. All authority was in the hands of the DIs. If Hamilton was having a problem with Seth, then he could go to the DI and report the other recruit, but that would show a lack of leadership capability, and Hamilton could be stripped of his position right then and there.

Seth knew that. Seth also knew that Hamilton couldn't force him to comply with any order. Seth was a Combined Martial Arts phenom, actually having fought in the Ultimate Warrior Tournament, winning his weight class at the planetary level before bowing out. He proclaimed this loudly and often from their first training day, and many of the other recruits, Ryck included, thought he was spewing so much BS. But in the Marine Corps Martial Art class four days before, he'd taken on the instructor, a MCMA black belt, and handily beat him. Seth was the real deal.

Seth was also an asshole. Now that the others knew what he was capable of in a fight, he'd become even more arrogant and unruly. Telling Hamilton to fuck off was the final straw.

"So, I know you all know why I've called you here. The question is what do we do about it," Hamilton told the group, keeping his voice low.

The DIs might not be in their office, but they had a habit of turning up anywhere at any time. This meeting, after lights out, was against the rules, and recruits who broke the rules almost always wished they hadn't after they'd been caught.

"Not much of a choice, as I see it," John McGruder said without much emotion. "We can't let anyone flaunt our authority."

"I hear you, Mac, but we really don't have any authority," Shaymall Cammille, the platoon guide said.

The guide was the top recruit billet, naturally assigned to the recruit who the DIs thought was the strongest. That opinion affected the rest of the recruits, and he was unconsciously considered the first among equals by the others.

"Bullshit, Shay-man. The Senior gave me this position, and that's all the perking authority I fucking need. Ham, you need to call this perking arsehole out. Now," Mac said.

Hamilton visibly blanched before stammering out, "I can do it, I mean I can call him out, but shit on me, you saw him with that DI. He flattened the guy. A MCMA black belt! I'd only last an ant's heartbeat."

Mac rolled his eyes, but Ryck answered for him, "Not just you, Hamilton. You call him out, but all of us take care of him. You bring him in here, and we'll be waiting."

The thought had obviously never occurred to Hamilton, and he seemed to think it over for a moment before asking, "But what does that say about me? That I can't handle my own problems? And is it fair, eight against one?"

"Stick it, Ham," Mac told him. "All's fair in perking love and war. We love that arsehole as a fellow Marine recruit, as a platoon mate, but this is war when he thinks he's too perking special to follow the rules. And when he tells you to fuck off, he's telling all of us to fuck off. So all of us need to give him a little 'extra instruction' on following orders. A beasting he's asking for, and a beasting we'll give him."

"You mean a 'beating?'" Ham asked, obviously confused.

"What? No. Don't you speak Standard? This is a 'beating,'" he said, mimicking the pounding on a drum. "This is a 'beasting'" he added, pounding one fist into the his other open palm.

Hamilton took in Mac's meaning before looking at each of the others in turn.

"Do you all agree with that?"

Each one of them nodded, even if Doggie's nod was late and without enthusiasm.

"And none of you think I'm wimping out?" Hamilton asked.

Each head shook in a "no."

"OK, then. So I guess it's now or never. Let me go get him and bring him back here," he said as he left the showers and made his way into the darkened squadbay.

The seven recruits moved closer to the entrance to the showers so they wouldn't be seen when Hamilton and Seth walked up.

"Shit, shit, shit . . ." Doggie whispered to himself, fear evident in his voice to those who overheard him.

Ryck sympathized, but he was not going to voice that. Even with eight of them, Seth was a grubbing monster, and there could be some serious ass-kicking going on—not all of it on Seth. He swung his arms back and forth, trying to get ready, only stopping when he heard murmuring as the two recruits approached.

"I gotta give you props. I never thought you had the balls to call me out. It ain't gonna make any difference 'cause I'm still gonna to take you apart, but I gotta respect your effort," Seth said as they walked into the showers.

He stopped dead as the seven recruits waiting moved to surround him. Hamilton stepped back to join the circle of recruits.

"Hey, what's this bullshit? It jus' me an' fuckhead here. This is between me an' him," Seth protested.

"Well, you see, Mac-Pisshead, it's like this. When a chav like you goes and disrespects one of us, you disrespect all of us. So we all need to sort of, you know, show you the error of your ways."

Seth stood there looking at them, hands on his hips.

"What a bunch of fucking marigolds. My great-granny's got more balls than you, an' she's been dead for two years," he said with a sneer on his face. "I guess I'll have to show you the fucking error of *your* ways. You don't mess with me! Which one of you pussies is first?" he asked getting up on the balls of his feet, fists raised.

Mac rushed him, head down, arms outstretched. Seth's foot caught him on the chin, folding him in a heap on the tile deck. Seth somehow kept his foot going, bringing it to his right, connecting with the side of Du Boc's neck, sending him to his knees. At that moment, Ryck's fist connected with the back of Seth's neck, right below the skull. Seth staggered forward, clearly stunned, and Shaymall's fist came up in a picture perfect-uppercut, catching Seth on the chin. He went down hard, head bouncing off the tile. Despite Seth being down and out, several more punches and kicks were thrown at his unresponsive body, the last by Du after the recruit squad leader got back up to his feet.

Ryck's heart was pounding. It had all happened so quickly. His fist hurt, but the adrenaline kept most of the pain at bay. He had to concentrate on calming down. Taking care of Seth was only half of the equation. Now they had to get back into their racks before there was a bed check.

Shaymall was checking on Mac, who was just coming to. Ryck joined him as they pulled Mac into a sitting position.

"Mother fuck! What train hit me?" he asked groggily. "What about Mac-Pisshead?" he asked, trying to see around the two other recruits.

"Lesson learned," Shaymall said. "He was too busy with you, so we got him."

"Copacetic! Figured that would work. That perking arsehole knew I was the harry von bad one, right? Knew he had to take me out first, right?" Mac said, his words only slightly slurred.

"You were right, Mac," Shaymall answered. "Think you can get up? We need to get back in our racks."

"Oh, sure, man," Mac responded.

With a little help, the two of them got Mac out of the showers and up into his rack before going back and helping carry the limp body of Seth to his rack, an upper bunk. They had to push him up, stepping on the rack below to get him in. Ryck stepped on Seth's bunkmate in the process, but that recruit never said a word.

The seven of them got Seth up and under his sheets, then scattered for their own racks. Ryck had just gotten in and pulled up his sheets when the front hatch opened. A flashlight pierced the darkness and swept over the sleeping, or at least prone, recruits.

"All quiet, fire watch?" the unseen DI asked the recruit standing at the fire watch podium at the front of the squadbay.

Recruit Dixby Zeller, who had observed everything except for what actually occurred in the showers, said, "All quiet, Drill Instructor!"

"OK, carry on," the voice reached out to them.

The next morning, despite two recruits with very visible bruises, the DIs seemed not to notice that anything had happened during the night.

## *Chapter 9*

"Fucking A, Calderón, get it right! Look at the grubbing diagram, for J's sake!" Ryck said as he looked over Recruit Jorge Calderón's junk-on-the-bunk.

This was the last scheduled function in Phase 1 of recruit training, and Ryck wanted to make sure it was done right. Recruits from the other platoons had started calling 1044 the "booger platoon," and Drill Instructor Phantawisangtong, the platoon "heavy hat," was on the warpath. Du had already lost his billet as squad leader, and his replacement, Scotland Blythe, lasted less than two hours before he was relieved.

Phase 1 had been boring—it had been a bitch, but a boring bitch. It had been PT, close order drill, more PT, basic tactical formations, history classes, more PT, inspections, martial arts training, swimming, pugil stick bouts, more PT, and still more PT. Ryck hated it. He hated doing things he'd never do once he was actually in the Corps. He hated the stupid pink safety tie that rendered his weapon inoperable, and he really hated the "pink baby" catcalls they got from the more advanced recruits. The history classes turned out to be pretty interesting, but Ryck wanted to fire his M99, he wanted to maneuver in a PICS. This inspection was so the DIs could check their gear for their trip to the range in the morning, their first training event of Phase 2. No more pink babies!

Calderón was a gumball. Frankly, Ryck was surprised that he had made it to T24. Twenty-four days of difficult training, and this royal fuck-up couldn't do anything right. Ryck was sure he spent 80% of his squad leader time with the guy, and that was a burden. Ryck might be a recruit squad leader, but the key word was "recruit." He still had to hit every training objective for himself just like everyone else. Sometimes, he resented being held accountable for the others, but still, he liked the ego boost. He was bound and determined to keep his billet all the way to graduation, something almost never achieved.

Calderón placed his Goodell at the top right of his rack. The molecular blade was supposed to go on the top left side, not the right.

"Damn it! Can't you fucking read? I've had about had it with you," Ryck told the other recruit. "I've got to get my own gear laid out, and we've got less than ten minutes to get it done, so you're on your own. King Tong's going to fry your ass if you screw it up."

At the mention of the nickname the platoon had given the heavy hat, Calderón looked up in alarm as if the drill instructor was already there. Ryck just turned away, not willing to waste another precious second on that lost cause.

He hurried to get his own gear laid out and had just finished when the fire watch called the squadbay to attention and the entire DI team marched in. Ryck jumped to the foot of his rack and came to the position of attention, hoping everyone was inspection-ready. He'd checked the others, of course, and they had been making good progress—all except Calderón, that was.

*I hope the sorry sack of shit fucks up*, he thought. *And then Despiri or Tong'll see the guy just can't cut it and recommend him for a retention hearing.*

The DIs started their inspection at the other end of the barracks. Ryck could hear low murmurs as they spoke to the recruits being inspected. Once, there was a huge crash coming from Second Squad's area as gear was thrown on the floor. King Tong was going at it but good, and Ryck pitied whomever was at the receiving end of that tirade.

It took awhile as the sounds of inspections got closer and closer, but finally, Senior Drill Instructor Despiri moved in front of Ryck.

"Recruit Lysander ready for inspection, Senior Drill Instructor Despiri!" he told the DI.

Ryck wasn't sure if he should be relieved or worried that he'd drawn Despri. The drill instructor didn't scream and shout as much as the others, but he was very demanding, and his eyes missed nothing. Ryck made an about-face and stood ready to respond to any questions the DI might ask during the inspection. He slightly broke his position to look out of the corner of his eyes at Despiri, trying to gauge the progress as the DI inspected his gear.

"Serial number?" Despiri asked.

"4795553744, Senior Drill Instructor" he responded immediately.

That was an easy one. He had his M99 memorized five minutes after being issued it.

Despiri picked up Ryck's powerpack from the rack, then turned it around to look at the back.

"Wrong. Again, serial number?"

Ryck was confused. DIs always asked for the weapon's serial number, not anything else. Ryck didn't have a clue as to the powerpack's serial number.

"I . . . uh . . .this recruit does not know his powerpack's serial number, Drill Instructor," he stammered out.

"Find out. And if a question or order is not clear, clarify it. You have five items with serial numbers on your rack. I could have been asking about any one of them," the DI said.

"Aye-aye, Senior Drill Instructor Despiri," Ryck said.

Despiri gave one more glance at the gear on the rack before turning to move on to Hodge's rack. Ryck let out a sigh of relief. Despite getting caught by the blindside, it seemed his gear was passable. He returned to his position of attention at the end of the rack, listening in as the DIs hit the rest of his squad. He caught some corrections, and Lipitski stumbled over the normal combat load of M505 grenades, but it seemed like it was going well—until King Tong, of all DIs, hit Calderón's rack. Ryck heard the recruit report ready for inspection, and not 15 seconds later, the eruption began. King Tong was in rare form, screaming at the top of his lungs. Ryck could hear gear being slammed on the deck.

*Serves the shithead right*, he thought, a small smile creeping onto his face despite him being at attention.

"Who's your squad leader?" King Tong shouted, despite knowing the answer, and Ryck blanched for a moment. He knew he would be questioned, but all he had to do was be straightforward and recite the facts. The prime fact was that Calderón was not suited to be a Marine.

Ryck heard a murmur in response, then "Recruit Lysander, front and center!" from the DI.

Ryck did a right face, then double-timed down the three racks to where King Tong waited.

Ryck didn't even have a chance to report in before King Tong went off, "What kind of sorry-ass preparation is this? Didn't Recruit *Calder-none* know we were having a junk-on-the-bunk? Didn't he think it was important that his gear be squared away before you piss-poor excuses go to the field?"

Drill Instructors were not supposed to alter any recruit's name, but no one ever complained. Suicide by DI was not something anyone wanted to experience.

"Yes, Drill Instructor Phantawisangtong," he said, stumbling over the name slightly.

All of the recruits practiced saying his name, afraid of messing it up, but the stress might have gotten to Ryck.

"Recruit Calderón was aware of the inspection. He was told to get his gear ready. This recruit attempted to assist Recruit Calderón, but it was hopeless. This recruit told him to get it done, and it was up to him to pass or fail."

"You told him to get it done. And he did not do as ordered, is that what you are saying?" King Tong asked.

"Yes, Drill Instructor!"

"Recruit Squad Leader Lysander, in your most expert opinion, does Recruit Calderón have what it takes to be a Marine?" King Tong asked.

This was it. The bottom line. Ryck had to respond truthfully.

"No, Drill Instructor, this recruit does not believe that Recruit Calderón has it in him to be a Marine. He is not Marine material."

There was silence in the squadbay. Ryck could almost feel the attention of 66 recruits and eight DIs on him.

"Recruit Squad Leader Lysander," Senior Drill Instructor Despiri's voice cut through to him. "Are you Recruit Calderón's squad leader?"

"Yes Senior Drill Instructor!"

"Was it your task to get your squad ready for inspection?"

"Yes, Senior Drill Instructor!"

"If you are going into a fight, are you just going to tell your Marines to have their proper battle load, or are you going to check them?"

"Uh . . ." he started, unable to forego the using the "uh" sound, "No Senior Drill Instructor. This recruit would inspect each Marine."

This wasn't going as he expected.

"Yet during this inspection, you decided to let one of your charges sink or swim on his own?"

"Yes, Senior Drill Instructor," he responded, his heart falling.

"In battle, one unprepared Marine can get his unit killed. Here, one unprepared recruit means your squad has failed the inspection. Drill Instructor Phantawisangtong, at the conclusion of this inspection, take Third Squad out on a run to the Lost Lady, full rucks."

Ryck grimaced. The squad might be pissed at him, but they should be pissed at Calderón. He was the idiot who couldn't even prepare for a junk-on-the-bunk.

"Recruit Lysander, hand me your tab," Despiri said.

Ryck's heart fell. The tab was a small red piece of fabric that attached to his left collar. It was the only thing that visually identified him as a recruit squad leader. He slowly reached up and took it off, handing it to the senior when the DI walked up to him. Despiri took it without a word, then turned towards King Tong. It wasn't the heavy hat, though, to whom the senior was facing.

"Recruit Squad Leader Calderón, you will have 10 minutes at the conclusion of this inspection to have your squad, in full kit, mustered on the parade deck. I suggest you make sure everyone is ready to go," he said, handing Calderón the tab.

Ryck's plan on keeping his billet until graduation was over, just like that.

## *Chapter 10*

Ryck was excited. This was their first time in the RCET, the Realistic Combat Environment Trainer. He'd played in the vanilla civilian version of the game before back on Prophesy, but wearing a sim-helmet and "walking" around in his bedroom, fighting others online was a far cry from what he expected in the real deal. He'd watched a Discovery show on military training once, so he had an idea of what the RCET was like, and the show had just enhanced his expectations.

The civilian operator was a young guy, not much older than most of the recruits, but Ryck listened intently to the brief. The first evolution would be fire team formations. Nothing this afternoon would be graded, but that would change the next morning. Scores would be tallied for the fire team, squad, and platoon stages, and those scores would reflect on platoon standings. The highest scoring platoon would not only have a big boost to its total running score, but also it would receive a purple "battle streamer" to attach to the guidon through graduation. The RCET streamer and the red marksmanship streamer were the only two such streamers that could be earned by a platoon, and 1044 hadn't done so well at the range the week before. This was not only the platoon's last chance to earn a recruit streamer, but it should pull it out of being the consensus company booger platoon.

Finally, the operator was done with his brief. It was time to get going. Third and Fourth squads went to Arena B where several more civilians were handing out the armor inserts. Actual personal armor would not be issued until the start of Phase 3, but as RCET was to be conducted in full combat gear, training armor would be used. As they had discovered in Phase 1, the training armor was not only in bad shape, but the "one size fits most" philosophy meant that even if the inserts sort of fit a recruit, they never quite matched up with a recruit's body, especially at the joints. Although the recruits were all assured that their own armor would be tailor-made for each of them, the beat-up training armor inserts were a royal pain in the ass.

The battle helmets were almost as bad. They had been introduced to the helmets during Phase 1, so the recruits knew how to operate them, but these had seen years of use. There was no way to fit nor optimize them for each recruit, so most of the capabilities had simply been disconnected. Each first-person visual would be recorded and would be transmitted in real time to the monitors so the RCET personnel, the DIs, and the other recruits could observe what was happening. Monitors would also show the overall picture as well as what the electronic bad guys would be seeing as the recruits approached them. All of this would be recorded and used to analyze and critique each event.

Ryck had tried on three helmets before finding one that was close to fitting. Despite the antiseptic smell, he could imagine the sweat of hundreds, maybe thousands of recruits who had worn this particular helmet before him. The mere thought made his forehead itch where the brow-pad rested against it.

Geared up, Ryck was ready to go. He checked his weapon out of force of habit. At least, now that the platoon had finished Range Week, the recruits were trusted to handle their weapons and no longer needed the horrid pink safety ties.

When the Arena Chief finally gave the OK, Ryck eagerly stepped forward. As the First Fire Team rifleman, he was the first to get inspected. Pink tie or not, one of the operators gave his weapon a safety check, as professionally as any DI. First, he cleared the weapon. They'd been off the range for four days, and this was probably the 10th time his M99 had been cleared to make sure there were no rounds in the chamber. As the darts were inserted in self-contained magazines, and as none of the recruits had access to any ammo lockers, Ryck wasn't sure when he was supposed to have found a magazine and gotten a round loaded since the last time his weapon had been checked. After clearing the M99, the operator initiated the SFA. The Simulated Firing Attachment would calculate a dart trajectory and transmit that to the RCET computer where it would be inserted into the simulation enabling the RCET brain to be the high judge and jury as to what would be happening if this was an actual combat mission with Ryck firing real rounds at a real enemy.

Ryck received the OK, and he stepped through the hatch into the Arena.

*Copacetic!* was all he could think. *No, this was beyond copacetic, this was, grubbing "fantasmagorical," as the Earth recruits say.*

With his little commercial sim-helmet back at home, the game was pretty awesome. But now, being in the Arena rendered playing at home as the black-and-white version.

He was not observing the game, he was *in* it. Intellectually, he knew he was in a huge room, 700 meters long and 200 meters wide, adjoining another just like it with a wall that could be removed, making a single 400-meter wide space. The room was empty except for the equipment needed to run it.

Ryck knew that from the brief and from what he had seen on the vids, but now, his senses rejected that explanation. At the moment, Ryck was in a partially wooded landscape, standing on dark brown dirt covered with brown leaf-fall. A breeze brushed up against him, and he could smell the dusky aroma of vegetation. He scanned the scene. Small birds flitted from branch to branch. Sunlight filtered through the trees. The detail was amazing.

He was aware of someone joining him. That would be Preston "Wagons" Ho, the team AR man.

"Oh, wow. Fantasmagorical!" Wagons said.

Ryck almost laughed out loud. He called that one right. Ryck didn't use all the slang used by recruits from other planets, but this time, the Earth phrase fit. Some words, such as "copacetic," which was the catch phrase of Captain Titan in the *Swordbinder* series, were more universally popular. Other words, such as "fantasmagorical," or even Ryck's own use of "grubbing," were more regional.

Within a few more minutes, Hodges and Calderón had joined them. Calderón had lasted as squad leader for less than 24 hours before being fired. Hodges, of all people, was now the fire team leader. Hodges still seemed lost at times, but he had raised a few eyebrows on the range. The guy could shoot.

Ryck and Wagons had already discussed their situation. With the two weaker recruits in the team, it would be up to them to pull the team through, even if Hodges was the leader.

The four of them quickly moved into a wedge. Ryck had the point, Hodges was behind him and to his right, Calderón was even with Hodges and to Ryck's left, while Wagons was in trace of Ryck and behind the other two. Their first mission would be a simple movement to contact.

"Fire team, you may begin," a voice told them over their comms.

Ryck didn't wait for Hodges; he simply stepped off, senses on high alert.

He scanned the area in front of him, trying to see any movement, any trip wires, any sign of danger. He knew that this could be a simple movement, just to let them get used to the simulation, but somehow, he doubted it. There would be bad guys out there.

He had been intensely aware that what he was seeing would be on a monitor outside, but he quickly forgot about that. He had immersed himself in the scenario.

*What is that?* he asked himself.

He held up one fist, the ancient hand-and-arm signal to stop, and edged over to look at the ground in front of him. Something had caught his eye. It was a stick, but it looked out of place. Carefully, he pulled back the grass from around it, the front of his mind reveling in the tactile feel of the grass despite the back of his mind knowing there was nothing actually there.

"What is it, Lysander?" Hodges asked.

"Maybe a booby trap, over," Ryck responded.

Ryck examined it from every angle possible, wishing his helmet had full capabilities so he could do one of the several scans an operational helmet could make. Finally, he decided it was just a stick.

He started moving the team forward again. The terrain seemed to rise as if they were walking up a hill. Once again, Ryck knew the room was level, but his senses warred with that knowledge. He wondered at the technology that made all of this possible. This was head and shoulders above what he'd ever experienced in any game before.

*Focus!* he reminded himself. *Think about how amazing this is after the exercise!*

They continued forward, tension building. If they were going to be hit, it would have to be soon. Simple logistics told them that with seven fire teams—four from Fourth Squad and only three now from Third Squad—and the number of runs each team was scheduled for the day, each go-through could only take up so much time.

Ryck just happened to be looking right at a jumble of logs ahead when the enemy rose and fired. Instinctively, Ryck pulled the trigger, lifting his M99 from low and left to high and right, stitching a line across his target. This was a technique taught during the last two days of Range Week, after initial qualification, and Ryck was surprised that it worked just as well in this scenario as on an open rifle range. The enemy disappeared, whether hit or merely taking cover, Ryck would find out during the debrief.

He half-waited for Hodges to shout out an order, and when nothing was forthcoming, he did what Wagons and he had decided earlier. Charge the bastards. They had practiced this during Immediate Action Drills, so Wagons and he thought that would be a good excuse if reacting without orders was considered a no-no.

He saw movement to his front left, so he went right at it, weapon blazing. A line of fire reached back out to him. The helmets didn't have many of the capabilities of an actual combat helmet, but due to the nature of the training, the ballistic indictor was enabled. A trace appeared on the visor showing the trajectory of the incoming rounds. The trace started from Ryck's right, then began to sweep towards him. Ryck dove to the deck untouched. He tried to peer ahead and see who had fired at him. He had a general idea about from where the rounds had come, but he couldn't see anything. An explosion sounded to the front, and dirt and debris fell around him. Ryck could actually feel the clods hit his body.

By now, Hodges was yammering over the comms, asking for an update. He sounded excited, but not in a good way. There was a hint of panic to his voice. At the fire team level, the recruits could communicate directly with each other. The fire team comms circuit was open between the four of them.

"We've got at least three hostiles to my eleven o'clock. I'm gonna shift to the right, so cover me," Ryck transmitted.

"Roger that," Wagons' voice came over the circuit. "Give me a count, then move."

"Roger. I am moving in three . . . two . . . one!"

At "one," Ryck jumped to his feet and darted to his 2 o'clock—and his helmet siren went off.

"Mother grubber!" he shouted as he stopped and dutifully got back down on the ground. He was "dead" and so could not participate in any more action—not that he could even if he wanted to. Getting killed also disabled his SFA, keeping him from firing any more simulated rounds.

He'd been looking forward when he'd been hit, and he'd seen no trace coming at him. Still sitting, he looked back. Hodges was in back of him, looking guilty.

*That fucking idiot shot me!* Ryck thought. *I'm gonna kick his grubbing ass!*

The rest of the engagement didn't take long. Wagons lasted the longest at another two minutes. Once he went down, the simulation faded. They were sitting in an empty space. The trees, dirt, smells, enemy: all were gone.

Ryck had been killed, and by friendly fire, of all things. The fire team had gotten wiped out. But damn it all, it had been a perking blast! He couldn't wait for their next turn in the breach.

"Fire team, return to the front hatch," came over the helmet comms.

Looking back, an innocuous red "EXIT" sign showed them the way.

## *Chapter 11*

Ryck watched the server plop the shit-on-a-shingle on his plate. He actually liked the gloppy mess, but he had to wonder just how many millions of soldiers had been fed it over the centuries. He was pretty sure Roman legionnaires had fueled their marches into Gaul with it. Hadn't Dr. Berber said they'd been fed some sort of gruel? Wasn't gruel kind of like shit-on-a-shingle?

He moved on down the line, grabbing a panderfruit. The Roman's hadn't eaten those, though. The hybrid fruit had only been introduced about ten years before. Their ability to withstand rough handling and their long shelf life had made them an instant hit with industrial food service. They were pretty damn delicious, too. Ryck had never actually tried one before getting to Camp Charles, and now he was hooked on them.

He squirted some ketchup and polly sauce on his breakfast, a combination that some of the other recruits thought was vile, grabbed a cup of coffee, and looked around for a seat. Platoon 1045 had preceded them in the chow line, and he saw Joshua had taken a seat at the far end of his platoon area. He waved Ryck over.

There were no rules about where a recruit sat to eat, but common practice was to eat with the others in the unit. Joshua had seen Ryck and had taken a seat at the edge of 1045's grouping. The empty seats next to him were being taken up by 1044 recruits, so Ryck could sit there and still catch up with Joshua. They'd only known each other for a few days back home before shipping and then while en route, but still, it was good to see someone from home. Without time the opportunity to socialize, even if Joshua was only in the next squadbay, he might as well have been on another planet most of the time.

"Take a load off, brother-boy," Joshua said as Ryck walked over. "Oh, man, what you doin' to that grubbing food, there?" he added, pointing at the ketchup-and-polly-sauce mix.

"What you grubbing doing to that grubbing food?" one of the recruits next to Joshua mimicked.

"You grubbing mother grubber, grub off," another said, drawing a laugh from those around Joshua.

"Not only is he from the booger platoon, but he's one of Josh's homeys," chimed in a third recruit. "Are you another farmer boy? Josh here's a right solid recruit, even if he talks like shit. And he still can't tell us what 'grubbing' means."

"Well, please allow me the opportunity to introduce you to my planetary compatriot, Mr. Ryck Lysander. To respond to your enquiry, affirmative, Mr. Lysander was an agricultural engineer at his former abode. Currently, in the present time continuum, he occupies the position of Marine Corps recruit," Joshua said with an affected accent, one hand raised, little finger extended. "Even if he be from the booger platoon," he added, back to his Tortillite accent.

Ryck extended his middle finger before picking up his fork. "Good to see you, too. And great to meet all of you grubbing freaks," he added to the others.

Recruit culture had a decided aggressive nature with smack-talk rampant. He didn't take the planetary comments seriously. Heck, he had given out worse. The "booger platoon" comment cut though, not that he was going to let anyone know that. More of 1044's recruits took their seats, but this was a chance to talk to Joshua.

"You heard about Proctor, right?" Ryck asked.

"Yeah, DOR'd. That shocked me, I be sayin'. Did you talk to him?" Joshua asked.

"Only for a minute. I was platoon runner for the day and had to take some papers to the company office. He was out on the bench, waiting," Ryck told him.

The "bench" was right outside the company office hatch. Any recruits leaving training, whether being dropped or by DOR, sat on the bench while awaiting their series and company commander interviews. Occasionally, a recruit being dropped could convince the officers to overrule the DIs and give a recruit another chance, but normally, once they had plopped their butt on the bench, it was the start of an inextirpable exit process. The other recruits considered it bad juju to catch the eye of anyone on the bench, so they were usually studiously ignored.

"I asked him what happened, and he said it was just too tough. I didn't have much time to ask anything else, and, you know . . ."

"Yeah, I know. You didn't want any of that bad karma rubbing off. He was on a 556 contract, right? So he's goin' to be a squid now?" Joshua asked.

"Yeah. Remember, he already got his enlistment bonus, so he has to serve for three years in the Navy," Ryck confirmed.

Most of the recruits were on a normal 550 contract. This enlistment contract technically provided only for the opportunity to serve. If a recruit DOR'd or was dropped, then no harm, no foul. The recruit usually just went home. The 556 contract was given only offered to highly-qualified recruits, and it came with certain guarantees along with an enlistment bonus. If a recruit was dropped, he might or might not be required to "pay back" his bonus with service in the Navy. It depended on just why he was being dropped. If a 556 baby DOR'd though, it was usually to be shipped off for three year's service as a sailor.

"He got us to switch to the Corps, but he be DOR'in' himself. That be messed up. That *is* messed up," he said, correcting himself.

On Prophesy, the Tortillites seemed to take pride in their differences, including their manner of speaking, almost keeping those differences as badges of distinction. At Camp Charles, though, there was a significant gravitation to the center, that being Earth Standard. At least Joshua's accent and speech really wasn't that much different. Many of the recruits came from planets where another language was primary, but they also spoke Standard as did 99% of humanity. Some recruits had more difficulty. There was K'Ato Pluz from First Squad, for example. The DIs rode him unmercifully on his almost incomprehensible speech. The rest of the squad had to drill him on cleaning up his Standard.

"So what else is goin' on with you?" Joshua asked. "1044 goin' to stay booger platoon?"

"Oh, man, don't even think it," Ryck said. "King Tong's going batshit crazy. He says he's never had a booger platoon, and we're not going to be the first. I swear, if I have to 'visit' The Lost Lady one more time, I'm just going to lose it."

"You know our heavy hat, Sorensen, right? Even he thinks Phana-whatever-tong be certified looney," Joshua said. "1042's supposed to be messin' up, too. You think you can catch them?"

"I don't know. We've got platoon RCET tomorrow. That's a graded event. I think we're doing OK, but who the hell knows?"

"Well, good luck on that," Joshua said as the first of the recruits in his platoon started standing to get rid of their trays. "What about your sister? She OK?" he asked before shoveling in the last of his eggs.

"Check it out," Ryck said, pulling out his PDA and opening the gallery and selecting a photo.

"She got married? And look at her! If my dear mama wouldn't die of a heart attack, if you had told me she was this hot, I would have come an' grabbed her!"

"In your grubbing dreams," Ryck told him. "She got married Friday night. That's what she said, at least, but maybe it was really in the morning. I think she's trying to adjust date and time since I'm over here on Tarawa. So she either meant Friday night in Williamson, Friday night here at Camp Charles, or Friday night Universal Greenwich."

"1045, get it moving," Joshua's platoon guide shouted out.

"It seems as if my esteemed leader desires our presence post haste in order to stave off the incipient vitriol of our drill instructors, so while I would love to offer discourse on your sibling's matrimony, I must take leave, monsieur," Joshua said as he stood up and offered a sweeping Three Musketeers bow. "Adieu!"

Ryck laughed out loud before responding, "You're still a grubbing land-worm, even if you can manage to sound like a pantywaist."

"You wound me, comrade," Joshua said, still in character, as he walked off.

"What's with him?" Hodges asked from the other side of Ryck. "Why's he talking like that?"

"Oh you know. He's with 1045, and they are all messed in the head there," Ryck said before focusing back on his shit-on-a-shingle.

## *Chapter 12*

Ryck liked RCET, but he absolutely loved Camp Lympstone, where the field training was conducted. During Phases 1 and 2, the platoon DIs were God and Satan combined with full and constant control over the recruits. At Lympstone, the DIs were still ever-present, but the TDIs[13] took over more of the recruits' time. The TDIs were not pushovers, though. They would still explode with the best of the DIs, and they would still assign "motivational training," but the focus was more on teaching recruits the skills they needed to function as combat Marines.

Camp Charles was no Hilton resort, but it was plush when compared to Lympstone. Recruits slept in small two-man tents called "bivvies," bathed in field showers, and ate combat rations twice a day. It was rough, uncomfortable, and Spartan—and Ryck couldn't get enough.

As with the Legion, a Marine's origin was meaningless. What mattered was being a Marine. However, tradition had it that the senior TDI at Lympstone came from the UK back on Earth or from Mollytot, Liverpool, or Barclays, the three UK-settled worlds. Master Sergeant Cletton Smith was no exception to this tradition. He was a short, very dark-skinned SNCO,[14] whose eyes seemed to miss nothing. The officer in charge was Major Simms, who unlike most of the officers at Camp Charles, did not observe from afar but actively got involved with the recruits. Training Drill Instructor Smith scared Ryck, as he scared most recruits, but Ryck knew his place with him. It was disconcerting, though, when running during PT to have Major Simms show up, jogging beside a recruit, casually asking how things were going.

Part of the Lympstone experience was the use of an entirely new vocabulary. Chow was no longer chow, for example, but "scran," and the one hot scran each day was served in a "galley," not a mess hall. The first few days at Charles had been bad enough,

---

[13] **TDI**: Training Drill Instructor
[14] **SNCO**: Staff Non-commissioned Officer

learning to use, for example, "head" instead of toilet, "deck" instead of floor, and "hatch" instead of door. At Lympstone, they took it even further, and messing up was sure to result in push-ups—or "press-ups," that is. The TDI who took it most to heart was not even from a British background. The bull-necked Training Drill Instructor Jorge Jarumba was from Rio Tinto. The Tintoites still spoke Spanish as their primary language, yet the TDI was the most fervent keeper of the tradition.

"You ready?" Recruit Fire Team Leader Lysander asked Wagons.

Ryck had been promoted back to fire team leader two more times—which meant he'd been fired from the position, too. The platoon as a whole was down to 52 recruits. Ben Sutcliff had broken a leg on the obstacle course and been recycled, but the rest had been either drops or DORs. The recruits were now organized into three squads of either three or four fire teams each. Somehow, beyond all of Ryck's expectations, his fire team, with Wagons, Hodges, and Calderón was intact. Hodges was even showing signs of developing into an asset.

"I was born ready," Wagons replied. "Let's kick some ass, OK?"

'That's fine, except we're only facing hulks and targets out there. No incoming," Ryck said.

"Plenty of incoming, there, recruit," Wagons told him.

"You know what I mean. No rounds from an aggressor. The 'incoming' is our supporting arms," Ryck said.

Today's training evolution was to be the first of many combined arms exercises. The recruits had practiced every movement up to a company level. They had done it under simulated fire, with enemy "hits" recorded, assessing simulated casualties. They had moved against each other in mini-war games. What they had not yet done was move in conjunction with Navy and Marine Corps space, air, artillery, and armor assets. The day before, they had sat in the stands at Range 109 while the artillery had lit up the range. It had been an amazing sight, and the concussions could be felt shaking their very bones. It had been both impressive and frightening. For the day's evolution they would have to maneuver in conjunction with not only that level of destruction, but also the presence of a tank.

"Five mikes!" Shaymall shouted out. "Squad leaders, get at them."

Ryck glanced up as the squad's current leader, Harris Thompson, made a quick check of First Fire Team. With the new skins issued on the last day of Phase 2, there wasn't as much to check. There was the omnipresent weapons safety check and a quick check of the required battle gear, but their personal Marine armor had proven to be pretty much as advertised. The body armor consisted of two levels. The first was the "skins." The trousers and blouse looked and felt like normal civvies aside from the cammo patterns. The fabric, though, was interwoven with nano-fibers which offered some ballistic and fire protection, monitored physical readings, and chameleoned to the surroundings. The chameleon function was disabled during boot and was set on a dull yellow for all recruits and then changing to other colors for different training functions, but this was the actual working uniform each recruit would take with him into the fleet.

The second level was the added armor. Each Marine had a custom-fitted set of armor inserts, the "bones." The inserts weren't actually inserted into the skins, though. The bones, which weighed only 5 kg in total, came in 22 pieces, not counting the gloves. Each piece was pushed up against the appropriate body part, and it immediately lampreyed onto the fabric, drawing both power and the appropriate camouflage pattern from it.

During the first week of Phase 1, each recruit had been required to get his bones on within 30 seconds. Ryck's first attempt was over one-and-a-half minutes, and he thought 30 seconds was impossible. It really hadn't taken too many more attempts, though, to reach the required speed. By now, it had already become second nature.

Harris was shouting at them to get in the bleachers, so Ryck and the other three trooped over and filed in to take their seats. One good thing about Lympstone was that they basically took their "squadbay" with them. Their bivvies were lined up 20 meters in back of the bleachers for Range 109, the Combined Firing Range.

Their one hot would be packed out to them, so they had no nice galley at which to sit, but they were not humping back and forth each day while at the range.

Captain Jericho welcomed them to the range and the day's evolution. At Charles, the officers did formal inspections and handled interviews for drops or anything else that came up, and they sometimes observed training, but at Lympstone, they were more involved. Each and every safety brief was conducted by an officer. Captain Jericho had done many of their briefs, so he was a familiar face. He had the frame prosthetic that hid his regen for both legs. Rumor had it that this was his fourth regen: two as an enlisted Marine, two as an officer. Regens were rejected after too many attempts, and Ryck didn't know just how many times that was. If Captain Jericho deployed again and lost another arm or leg, could his body handle one more regen? Would he actually go through life with a prosthetic? That was a sobering thought.

The safety speech was pretty much the same as for every other training evolution: listen to the TDIs, pay attention to everything, keep the weapon on safe until ready to fire, make sure to identify a target before firing, and so on. The platoon had been doing pretty well in this area, at least. Ben-ben had been their only casualty, and he would be back in a follow-on training company. Platoon 1042 had two recruits seriously hurt, and one of them wasn't likely to ever fully recover. The worst case was in 1043, though. A recruit had suddenly dropped dead during a simple training run back on T4. They'd only gone a klick or so when bam, he was gone. He was rushed to sickbay within minutes, but the docs couldn't bring him back.

Captain Jericho finally finished, and Gunny de Gruit took over. The gunny was the TDI in charge of combined arms training, and he went over the first evolution for the umpteenth time.

*We know, we know*, Ryck thought, careful to keep an expression of rapt attention on his face, though. Let's get this thing going!

It really was a simple evolution. Each squad would move on line up the range, firing at targets as they popped up. Supporting fires would precede them, walking them up to the objective, which was a trenchline about a klick away. Once they reached the trenchline, the exercise would cease, and they would march back in a column to the start.

There were two platoons doing the exercise, and 1044 would go second, so Ryck settled in for a long wait for his squad's turn. The first squad to go was lined up, their armor shifting to the red of live-fire training. For this evolution, the recruit squad leader didn't give any orders. A TDI took over that, standing in the center of the squad line, and two other TDIs followed on either flank. Their skins and bones were adjusted to the bright green of their normal identifying colors, making them stand out against the recruits.

Training Drill Instructor de Gruit gave the OK, and the squad hesitantly stepped off. Within moments, the impacts of the 60mm mortars were visible, 100 meters downrange. The mortars' ECR[15] could be adjusted from 10-60 meters. When the recruits had been introduced to the rounds, boxes had been set up on the range, and a TDI casually sauntered to within about 15 meters from the closest of the boxes. He turned to look back at the expectant recruits as the mortars were fired. Three rounds landed spot on in the middle of the assembled boxes, and they were totally destroyed. The TDI was untouched, and he just as casually sauntered back to the bleachers. The recruits were taught that the mortars sent out a blanket of poly-matrix darts with the darts disintegrating to dust at a set range, but it was a relief to see this actually work in a real life demonstration.

Despite knowing this, several of the recruits in 1045's First Squad faltered as the mortars landed. Ryck could sympathize with them—he'd even flinched sitting in the stands another 50 meters back, but he knew they deserved the hell the TDIs dropped on them. One lesson drilled into them over and over was that with combined arms, it was vital to keep in formation. Even when individual infantry positions could be monitored by the arty or mortar sections, a mortar took some time to impact, and moving out of an expected formation could be dangerous.

---

[15] **ECR**: Effective Casualty Radius. This is the radius at which a projected 50% of those within the radius would suffer from the round's impact and detonation.

In combat, things tended to be more fluid, but in training, it was safety, safety, safety. The envelope would be pushed, especially in Phase 5, so the staff worked to minimize casualties in the earlier phases. Too many dead recruits wouldn't make the bigwigs back in the Federation Council happy.

To the side of the range, a big M1 Davis had been sitting idle. It was in defilade, so the recruits could not really see much of the tank, but when it opened up with its 75 mm hypervelocity rail gun, the excitement level perceptibly rose in the bleachers. The firing report was rather subdued, more of a crack as the round exceeded Mach 5, but the explosion as the round impacted on a truck hulk was awe-inspiring. This was the first time any of the recruits had actually witness a tank firing.

"That's what I want to do," Wagons whispered beside him. "Armor is where it's at."

Quite a few of the recruits wanted to go armor, but they would have to prove themselves as infantry first. Those with the aptitude would be siphoned off, just as with other branches. With armor, though, there were size limitations. Larger Marines just need not apply.

The Davis fired only once, then the 81 and 120mm mortars and the 105 and 155 howitzers opened up while Marine air came streaking in, all while the squad moved forward. Several times, targets popped up, and the recruits opened fire. Their reports sounded like little pop guns in the midst of all the bigger explosions.

Finally, the recruits reached their objective. Flashing range lights indicated a cold range, and the squad was marched back. The recruits took their positions in the stands. Ryck could see they were pretty amped, but he couldn't just wander over to them and ask them how it had been.

The range staff and TDIs were going over the monitors, and it took them a good five minutes before the next squad was given the order to get in position. When the squad started moving, it was pretty much a repeat. They got on line, there were lots of explosions, and they reached the objective.

When the third squad made their run, the Davis' impact had faded. It had only been assigned one target, an old truck of some sort, and after hitting it twice, it was pretty much scrap. The hypervelocity round didn't have much to hit, and impacting on the ground was not half as spectacular as when the round hit a vehicle.

Fourth platoon's last squad offered something different in the routine, though, and not in a good way. They were about 500 meters downrange when the range lights flashed, sending the range cold. Ryck couldn't see what had happened. He was too far away for a direct view, and he was not in position to see the monitors, but one of the greenshirts came back escorting a recruit. They reached the stands, and one of Fourth Platoon's DIs, not the Lympstone TDIs, took over, leading the ashen-faced recruit off the range and back to the bivvie. Ryck didn't really know the recruit, but he knew he wouldn't want to be in his shoes, whatever he had done.

The TDI marched back out to the where the squad was still in a line. The whirling red lights changed to a steady green, and the loudspeakers announced a hot range.

Finally, it was 1044's turn. First Squad was ready, with Second on deck. When First stepped off, Third Squad left the bleachers to get its check. Ryck felt the excitement building as the TDI inspected each Marine, even tugging on every piece of bone. They were pretty foolproof, as far as Ryck could see, and he thought the degree of inspection was overkill. But it impressed upon him the fact that this really was a dangerous situation. If the TDIs were that cautious, maybe he should be, too.

Ryck was ready to go, but there was still quite a bit of standing around and waiting. First had to finish, which it eventually did, and Second had to take off. Third Squad moved into position, and they could finally see downrange again. They watched Second maneuver down the range, eventually reaching the objective before coming back. It had been a long day, but it was finally Third Squad's turn in the breach.

The TDIs accompanying the recruit squads had been alternating between two teams. Third Squad had Training Drill Instructor Hyunh as the squad leader and TDIs Papagana and Rose to assist him.

"Pay attention to me at all times," Hyunh told them once more. "You've seen everyone else go through. Now it's your turn, so let's get it done."

The lights turned to green, and Hyunh gave the "Move out" order.

With one step, Ryck was over the white line that was the boundary for the range. It was only half a meter, but it was a different world. One step back, and he was simply at Lympstone. One step forward, and he was in a live impact area, one in which death was falling from the sky.

"Keep it even," Hyunh intoned over the comms. "First team, you're lagging."

Ryck was aware of Training Drill Instructor Papagana moving First Team forward, but he was concentrating on his own movement. He focused on keeping his position, but still looking forward, expecting the impact of the 60's. Even though he was anticipating it, he jumped when the rounds landed. The explosions had to be closer than they were for the other squads! But nothing reached them.

"Keep moving," TDI Hyunh went on, his voice sounding calm and collected.

There was a crack as the tank round went zipping by to their right, but the 60's had grabbed their attention more. With the Davis round, there was a plume of dirt ahead at impact, and that was about it.

"First Team, you are still lagging. Get on line." Training Drill Instructor Hyunh said, his voice sounding a little harsher over the comms.

Ryck risked a quick glance to his left where First Team was moving. They had curved back a bit, and the green shirt with them was physically pushing someone—Tad, it looked like--to get him back in line with the rest. Making a quick glance to the right, he could see that Second Team was even with his own Third Team.

When the first of the 81s and the howitzer rounds impacted, Ryck could feel the concussion hitting his chest. His lungs actually compressed from the pressure waves. Clods of dirt followed the smoke into the air to come raining back down, a few clods reaching their line.

"Last warning, First Team. Get online or I'm going to shut this down," TDI Hyunh said.

Ryck wondered if he was chewing out the other TDI, the one with First. Of course, that would never be on the open circuit.

"Oh fuck! Too far!" Ryck heard, not over the circuit, but through the air as Hyunh started running to the left, coming right behind him. Then, on the open circuit, "Get back, that's too far forward. Cease fire, cease fire! All hands freeze!"

Ryck stopped in his tracks. Training Drill Instructor Hyunh had shut down the range, and he was running to the left to pull back First Team. Ryck expected an explosion of shouting, whether that was to the TDI who was with First or to the recruits, he wasn't sure.

The explosion he did see was not what he expected. Even though a cease fire had been called, there had been rounds in the air, and now they were impacting. The first couple were well ahead of them, as they had been so far. The third, though, was short, and it landed just in front of Mike Yount, who had stopped and was looking back at the TDI. Mike was violently blown forward, something that etched itself in Ryck's mind before the blast reached him as well. Ryck was knocked down, and he felt the impact of the shrapnel or darts from the big round pepper him.

Stunned, Ryck lay on the ground, vaguely aware of shouting through his ringing ears. He was sure he'd been killed. Hands grabbed him, turning him over.

"You OK?" one of the TDIs asked him.

Ryck looked at his left front, where he'd been hit. He didn't see anything major. He flexed his left arm. It worked.

"You're OK," the TDI told him before dashing off to someone else.

Ryck was surprised. Looking closer as his bones, he could see a few faint marks. The armor had saved him. He got to his feet, looking around to see if he could help. The range corpsman had already opened someone's armor and was working on him feverishly. From 20 meters away, the bright red blood stood out like a neon sign. Training Drill Instructor Rose stood over the corpsman, helmet off. It was only then that Ryck took in the bright green armor. It was Hyunh.

Ryck took a faltering step forward when King Tong rushed by, shouting, "Get back to the bleachers, Lysander."

Ryck took one more look around, wanting to help. It looked like there were five prone bodies, all of whom had people around them. Several recruits were slowly moving back. A TDI was rounding up all the rest of the recruits, those who were not injured, and sending them back in a column. Ryck turned to join them. The walk back to the bleachers seemed to take forever. Halfway back, a field ambulance blew past them, bringing more corpsmen to the scene. Finally, Ryck got back and was told to sit. Yet another corpsman checked him out, giving him the OK. Ryck was relieved, but as he looked back downrange, and the Stork that had landed to casevac those hurt, he realized that there, but for the Grace of God, could have been him.

The platoon had lost its first members.

## *Chapter 13*

"Squad leaders, perform your EVA[16] checks" King Tong shouted out.

Ryck locked his weapon in the leg holster, a simple magnetic lock that kept the M99 out of the way while EVA, but readily available. The weapon could actually fire in the vacuum of open space, but there wouldn't be any soft targets at which to fire.

This was Ryck's third time as recruit squad leader. At T288, there were only seven days left until graduation, and Ryck was determined to keep the billet until the end. Of course, two of the remaining days were The Crucible, the final test of a recruit's mettle and worthiness to become a Marine. Ryck could easily lose the billet during that non-stop hell.

He snapped back to the job at hand. This was the final practical app for Phase Four, space training. The first part of the training phase had been conducted back at Camp Charles, in classrooms and mock-ups. For such a modern setting, the mock-ups had been surprisingly basic. There was a hulk of a section of a cargo ship on its side in the dirt, then a simple model of an airlock. The recruits "cycled" through the airlock, then "flew" through the space to the hulk to perform forced entry procedures. It had been a bit surreal, seemingly floating through "space" in the bright sunlight, then "floating weightlessly" through the hulk's corridors to rescue the ship's crew (four hopelessly degraded dummies). All of that has been done in the skins and bones as the EVA suits were too valuable to use on the ground at Camp Charles. Each recruit had practiced getting in and out of an EVA, of course, and operating the suits' systems, but that was with one of the three suits at the space training classroom.

This final exercise was with the real thing, though. Marines would not be issued their own EVA suit unless they were assigned to a ship, so this was once more a bit of trying to make do with what was available. Recruit Dharma, a heavy-worlder in 1043, couldn't even get a suit within the safety parameters, so he wasn't going to

---

[16] **EVA**: Extra-vehicular Activity

participate. The suits would not be perfect fits, of course, but unlike the training events back on Tarawa's surface, a poorly fitting suit had more severe ramifications, and Dharma's shoulders were just too broad and he was too short for any of the standard suits.

Ryck called up his four fire team leaders. When he'd first been a recruit squad leader, he'd had four fire teams then, too, but now, 1044's Fourth Squad had been merged with Third due to drops. Hodges and Wagons, from the old Fourth, were both fire team leaders, but the other two were No Initial and Raj from the old Third. Ryck was rather surprised that both Hodges and No Initial were still in the program, but he had to grudgingly give them their just due. Both had come along quite well, and if Ryck was to get fired again, he thought Hodges might actually get the nod as the new recruit squad leader.

"Have you completed the suit checks?' he asked them. All nodded back, so he continued, "Check each other, then I'll be doing my check in three."

Ryck knew that there would be no sabotage by the DIs on this evolution. The inherent danger was too great. But that made it all the more reason to have a thorough check before they went out. He was nervous, even if one of the DIs did re-inspect each recruit after he did his inspection.

There wasn't much room in the prep hold aboard the *Castor Wong*, the navy corvette assigned to the training. Ryck was forced too close to each recruit as he inspected them, but he just repeated the inspection checklist as a mantra, checking each and every step. The recruits had no live ammo, but he checked the dummies and blanks as if they were live. Each recruit looked good, although he had Carl Kingsman reseat his M99.

Usually, for this type of training evolution, it was only the TDIs who ran the show. This time, though, the platoon DIs, the series senior, and the series commander were there to assist as well. Even Captain Petrov, the company commander, was there to observe. After Ryck conducted his inspection, no less than three others re-inspected the squad. King Tong was one of the inspectors, then one of the TDIs conducted another. Captain Terzey, the series commander, inspected them one final time.

The hold light went from red to amber. It was almost time. TDI Flores went over the procedure yet once more. Each squad would cycle out the lock, make the jump to the target ship, go through the forced entry (simulated, of course: the *Wilma Pritchard* was too valuable to actually blow holes in her), then conduct the movement to the bridge and rescue the hostages. There would be a safety officer at the *Wong's* airlock and another at the airlock on the *Pritchard.* A TDI would handle the debarkation of the *Wong*, another would run the jump, and yet one more would lead each squad during the assault phase.

Once the bridge was secured, the tactical phase would be over, and the squad would move to the forward airlock where they would cycle out, then take one of the EVA sleds back to the *Wong.* There were three types of sleds, and it would be basically first come, first served. Ryck wanted one of the single-man sleds, but with the graded part of the exercise completed, any sled should be a blast.

The *Castor Wong*, as a corvette, was not a huge vessel, so only one platoon was embarked at a time. The cycle for a platoon was about two-and-a-half hours, so while there was time to get everyone through in the course of the day, the schedule had to be kept. 1043 had already completed its training, and the other two platoons were still down at the spaceport awaiting their turn.

Ryck wanted to get it over with. First Squad, though, was, as usual, first to go. At least with them gone, there was more room in the hold. The series senior took that opportunity to inspect the squad again. That made six total inspections.

The hold had ½ gravity, which made preparation and inspections easier than null grav. Even at ½ gravity, though, the suit was somewhat bulky, somewhat heavy, and quite uncomfortable. It would be better when they left the ship, Ryck knew. They had already spent one training day outside the *Wong*, tethered together, but enough to get the feel of weightlessness and maneuvering in it. But in the ship, the suit pulled down on the shoulders, hips, and knees. The fabric of the suit itself wasn't bad, and the helmet was surprisingly light, but the thruster pack and ammunition magazines pulled down and back. The suits could be worn in gravity, either on a planet or aboard a ship, but they were designed for weightlessness. On a planet though, at least the thruster pack could be dropped.

Second Squad, with its three fire teams, was next to go, and the hold became roomier still. He went to each fire team leader and went over the plan once again. This had to go without a hitch.

"You ready, Lysander?" King Tong asked as he came up.

"Yes, Drill Instructor Phantawisangtong, we are ready to kick some ass," Ryck replied.

"Don't worry too much about that. Just make sure no one does anything stupid," the DI told him.

The DIs were still DIs, and incentive training was still on the menu. But either the recruits were getting used to the harassment or the DIs were mellowing a bit. Even King Tong could act like an actual human being—at least at times.

The light finally changed to amber. They were up.

"Lock them up," the TDI told them.

Each recruit closed his face shield and pressurized his suit. Ryck could feel it puff out slightly as the air circulated. This created one more degree of insulation, but it also allowed sweat to be whisked away.

Before each recruit was allowed into the lock, one TDI and the safety officer conducted a final check of the integrity of each suit.

With 15 recruits, a TDI, two DIs, a navy operator, and a safety officer, the airlock was crowded. The inner lock closing had a degree of finality. Each recruit and Marine had to report by name to the Navy airlock operator that he was ready before the air was pumped out. The red airlock light turned to green and the outer lock opened.

Outside the lock, four Marines in their bright green suits waited for them. Ryck recognized SDI Despiri through his face shield, but he couldn't make out the others. Thrusters were not to be initiated within the lock; each recruit stepped to the edge and pushed off with their legs. Still within the ship, gravity pulled them down. Looking out into to vastness of space, but still feeling a "down," Ryck had to steel himself to push off. His mind told him he was about to fall to his death. It wasn't until he cleared the lock and was in the weightlessness of open space that the vertigo disappeared.

"Form it up," a voice intoned over the comms.

The jump would be done with four teams in a column with Ryck behind the first one. Each group of red-suited recruits would be accompanied by a green-suited DI.

Ahead of them, about 300 meters away, was the *Wilma Pritchard*. Every recruit for the last 30 years, at least, had been aboard her. She was an old freighter that the Corps purchased for training. She stayed in a geosynchronous orbit, too fragile to make repeated landing and take offs. Each time she came in for her annual maintenance, people took bets on whether she would be deemed spaceworthy enough to take off again. Rumor had it that the Corps wanted to scrap her, but with anti-piracy as one of the Corps' primary missions, they had to keep her up and running. Aside from a few fast Gulfstreams for the brass to use to get around, she was the only real spaceship in the Marine's fleet. Many of the tactical aircraft could get into space of course, but not to travel across space to other solar systems.

With small jets of the thrusters, the recruits got into position. In front of Ryck, two recruits collided with each other, one spinning off a good 10 meters before he could stop himself and edge back. Without a real working display, Ryck couldn't tell who the two were, but he intended to have words with them when they got back.

Finally in place, the DI with First Fire Team signaled them with a simple arm signal to move out. Ryck followed in trace, careful to keep far enough back not to run into the team. He felt naked without having the tether that had kept them together and around the *Wong* the day before.

The thrusters had enough power to push Marines along at a healthy acceleration. There were rumors of lost Marines corpses travelling between the galaxies at close to the speed of light. Ryck doubted that there was enough fuel to accelerate to those speeds, but he didn't want to test that. Of course, being recruit training, the red training EVA suits had their thrusters modified to keep them slower. Any power, though, in weightlessness, had the mathematical capability to reach a high velocity. It would just take a recruit EVA suit much, much longer to reach such a speed.

Their point of entry on the *Wilma* was facing them. A green-suited DI was clearly visible in the bright, harsh light of Tarawa's sun. He seemed to grow larger as the recruits got closer.

The DI with First made the cutting motion at what was about half-way to the ship. They had been moving under low acceleration, but even with only 300 meters, they had to reverse that to slow down again. Ryck had no sensation, really, of motion, but when he followed suit and began to decelerate, he was "pushed forward" slightly against the front of his suit. It took a moment of two, but he could sense his approach was slowing. He gave the tiny jets on his heels a spurt, bringing him around, but he hoped he would stop just at the lock without having to use his legs to halt on the *Wilma's* skin.

Ryck had just come to a halt a meter or so from the ship when the open circuit blared with "Recruit Thomas, reverse your thrust. You are too hot!"

Grant Thomas was with Second Fire Team, one of the recruits originally with Third Squad. He was from Earth itself. Grant was one of the guys who was always just there. He didn't make waves for good or bad.

Ryck looked "up," or at least away from the *Wilma* and back towards the *Wong*. A growing recruit in red was coming at him. One of the DIs lunged forward, but the distance was too great and he missed the recruit. Ryck reached out to stop Grant, who was coming in way too fast. That wasn't the smartest thing to do in weightlessness. Grant hit Ryck, spinning him aside before the wayward recruit hit the side of the *Wilma*. He bounced off before being slammed back. A moment later, a DI reached him, manually turning off the thrusters at the feed valve.

In reality, Grant had probably been moving at less than a couple of kilometers an hour, certainly nothing extraordinary had he been down on Tarawa's surface. In space, though, that was too fast.

The comms crackled as the DIs and the safety officer asked for updates. After a quick check, the Di who had turned off the thrusters gave the OK, and the training was given the go ahead.

Grant was going to get his ass chewed but good, but open space was not the place for that.

The breaching chamber, or the "can opener," had been previously ferried over by 1042. At first glance, it looked like nothing more than a fat metal tube. What it had, though, was the capability to open up almost any ship that existed. Usually, it was put over the target ship's airlock, but it could force entry into the ship anywhere. Going through the airlock, though, would keep the target ship spaceworthy. Ship line owners, while they wanted pirated vessels recovered, wanted their ships to still be able to ply their routes without extensive time in the yards.

First Fire Team, led by No Initial, maneuvered the can opener over the airlock. The DIs drifted over to observe as it was put into position. Of course, there would be no breach of the *Wilma*. Once in final position, the breaching itself would be simulated with a TDI inside simply cycling through the *Wilma's* lock.

Ryck glanced back at the rest of the squad. The two remaining teams hung in space, ready to move forward and enter the ship. Something caught his eye, though, against the blackness of space. A small puff of vapor suddenly sprouted out from the waist of the recruit nearest to him. The puff started turning the recruit around. It was Grant. There was a breach in his suit. Small breaches from microdust were closed by the suit's internal repair nanos, but as Ryck watched, the breach opened wider, sending out more air.

The recruits were supposed to stay off the comms during the transit, keeping them clear for emergencies. Ryck figured this was an emergency. So did Grant.

"Help!" Grant screamed as he started spinning away.

His thrusters were far more powerful than the force of the escaping air, but he evidently didn't think of that. He was panicking as he was losing his oxygen. He actually still had air being fed into the suit faster than it was being expelled, but if the spreading rip got too big, he would have an catastrophic suit failure.

"Emergency, emergency!" Ryck shouted, not knowing what else to say.

Grant was slowly spinning now, moving away from the others. Ryck was the closest to him, so he turned himself around and blasted forward, colliding with Grant in a classic tackle. He wrapped his arms around Grant's waist, plastering his chest against the rip in Grant's suit. He pulled as tightly as he could. He had to get Grant inside a ship. The *Wilma* was not ready, and looking around Grant's waist, he could see that the *Wong's* forward airlock was not closed as it awaited the arrival of the previous squad on the sleds.

"Recruit Lysander to the captain of the *Wong*, keep your forward airlock open. I am returning with Recruit Thomas!" he shouted into his mic.

He ignored the blast of comms chatter as he tried to align the two of them on the *Wong*, then gave his thruster a blast.

He felt the thrust build up before it cut off. Had his thruster failed?

"Lysander, do not engage your thruster. Do you understand? Keep your hold on Thomas, but do not engage your thruster," King Tong's voice broke through the voices as his speaker switched to a direct circuit.

It was only then that Ryck became aware of three green-suited figures around him. He felt hands on him as the DIs took in the situation, probably discussing things on another circuit. Ryck had been cut off the open circuit. He just sat there, arms clamped around Grant, who had stopped moving. Ryck hoped he was OK.

Finally, King Tong's voice came back to him. "Recruit Lysander, listen carefully. We are going to tow you back to the Wong. No matter what happens, you keep squeezing Recruit Thomas just like you are doing. We've told him to be completely still. You do not let go until we tell you to. You got that?"

"Yes, drill instructor. I've got it."

With his face pressed up against Grant's waist, Ryck couldn't see much, but he felt his suit adjust as hands grabbed him. Within moments, he started to move. He squeezed harder on Grant, not wanting to lose his grip. At one point, Grant started to squirm, but he stopped suddenly. Ryck hoped that was because someone told him to stop and not that he had passed out—or worse.

It seemed like forever to him, but it was probably closer to two minutes before the DIs reversed thrust at the last moment, slamming them headfirst into the Wong's open airlock. The gravity hit them, and they fell to the deck. Ryck almost lost his grip.

The outer door closed behind them, and the air started rushing in. Sound from something outside his suit once again returned to Ryck.

"OK, Lysander, you can let go," a voice, a real voice, not over the comms, said as hands reached down to pull apart his arms.

Ryck let go and sat back, looking to where he had seen the breach in Grant's suit. It was larger than he had thought, a good 30 cms across. The suits were not supposed to fail like that, but these were old, ill-fitting suits. Hitting the side of the *Wilma* as hard as Grant had done must have started the failure, something beyond the old suit's nanos to repair.

It took a few more moments for the air to cycle completely through and the inner door to open. Several Marines and a corpsman rushed in. Grant's helmet had already been popped, and he sat there, eyes wide in contained panic. He was breathing heavily.

Ryck popped his own helmet. He felt relief that Grant was OK. Up until that moment, adrenalin had been coursing through him. Now, it left his body, and he started trembling.

"So, Recruit Lysander, you were all set to order the captain of the *Wong* to keep the airlock open, then take your buddy back to the ship all by your lonesome? With me and the other DIs there at the scene?' King Tong asked, standing over him.

Ryck felt his heart fall. Had he screwed up again? Of course, the DIs were more capable of handling the situation than he was.

"I . . . uh, I guess I wasn't thinking. I just saw him and reacted," he stammered out, getting to his feet.

"That you did. Sometimes, though, reaction is the best action. You saw an emergency, then did something about it. Trying to take him back on your lonesome might have been a little much, but you did manage to limit the breach on Thomas' suit. If it had grown into a catastrophic failure before the rest of us got there, who knows what would have happened?"

"I didn't screw up?"

King Tong laughed, then said, "No, you didn't screw up. Hugging another recruit was an odd way of saving his sorry ass, but it worked. Good job, Ryck. Good fucking job."

Relief swept over him. He was glad that Grant was OK, of course, but he felt a twinge of guilt that he was happier that he was still a recruit squad leader. He hadn't been fired.

## *Chapter 12*

*Ten more steps. That's all. Just ten more steps.*

Ryck had been reciting that mantra for the last hour, trying to fool his tired body that the Crucible was almost over. It wasn't true, and he knew it wasn't true, but it was the only way he knew to keep going.

He'd been pretty excited when DIs had rushed into the squadbay, throwing gas grenades almost 40 hours before. This was the start of the Crucible, where each recruit would finally be forged into a Marine. This was the culmination of over 290 days on Tarawa. Ryck was confident that he could not only survive, but excel. Nothing could stop him.

The first six hours had been brutal, but not one recruit had dropped. They had the pass/fail 25 km ruck run, the obstacle course, and over an hour of "motivational" PT. They had done all of this before during training. The only difference was that this was with the entire company. It had actually felt invigorating being out there on the grinder, doing flutter kicks, push-ups, good morning darlings, and squat thrusts with close to 500 other recruits. The run was not as fun. Being towards the rear of the company for the first half of the run, they had mercilessly accordioned, slowing down almost to stop at times only to have to then sprint to catch up. At least after the half-way point, they had switched the order of march, and the lead series was in the rear. For something that had loomed over their heads, though, since T1, it was a relief to have it over, with not one 1044 recruit dropping out.

Immediately after the run came the "Road to Heaven." During the last week of training, the recruits were run through events taken from all the 46 extant corps that had been combined to form the Federation Marine Corps. The Road to Heaven came courtesy of the Republic of China Marine Corps. The recruits stripped down to their skivvies, then belly-crawled, rolled, and performed maneuvers to get down 50 meters of jumbled lava rock, all the time screaming "I fear no pain!" No one dropped, but the cuts on their bodies stung with sweat, something that would only get worse as the Crucible continued.

After that welcome-to-the-Crucible, they had broken back into platoons to go tactical. Storks had lifted them to the mountain training area on the other side of the valley where they were given a patrol mission. The patrol went up and down the almost impassible terrain. That was bad enough, but the cold was unrelenting. It was here that 1044 had their first drop. Garret Shin had sat down in the snow during a five-minute break and simply didn't get back up. He was whisked away by two of the DIs. No one knew if he DOR'd or was suffering from a cold-related injury. So close to the end, no one wanted to pry into it, the old superstition about knowing too much kicking in. The recruits studiously ignored what had taken place.

By morning, they had reached their objective. But no Storks would be taking them to their final destination. It was a 65 km march down the mountains and across the valley to Camp Prettyjohn and Mount Motherfucker. Camp Prettyjohn, named for a British Royal Marine hero, was a restricted base for special operations training. The recruits had never been taken there, but Mount Motherfucker was in full view of Camp Charles, hanging over them like their own version of hell. It wasn't so much its appearance, but rather its reputation. Rising up almost 2,500 feet above the valley floor, it actually seemed innocuous, almost serene. But each recruit knew that he had to make it to the summit with his weapon and full kit. Ryck had often gazed at the mountain while at Charles, thinking he could run up it. But that was without being up for two days during the Crucible and after a 65 km hump to the base.

The hump itself had been a bitch. They had to move tactically, making two river crossings in the route. Several times, they had been ambushed by other DIs, getting gassed in the process. After the last ambush, three of the recruits had been "killed," forcing the rest to carry not only them, but their gear as well.

Ryck barely noticed as they entered Prettyjohn. He had often wondered what the snake-eaters did there, but as they passed through the gate, he was too tired to care. He knew he should be urging the recruits in the squad on, but with half of Duc's gear in his pack, Duc being one of the "dead" recruits, he had turned inward just to keep going.

At the base of Mount Motherfucker, he might as well have been looking up Mount Ascent back on Prophesy. The treeless mountain would have offered a stunning vista of the valley and Camp Charles 10 kilometers or so to the south, but that would be if they had time to sit and take in the view. The dirt path leading up was fairly even, but the operational word was "up." Ryck managed one "let's keep it tight" before he just leaned forward, trying to keep himself moving.

Tradition had it that there had been a "Mount Motherfucker" since the early Marines on Earth, something the brass liked so much that on the Federated Marines' first base on New Beginnings, they had searched for one there. This was going to be the United States Marines' contribution to the final week. When they had again moved to Tarawa, this current mountain was chosen to carry on the tradition. It had seemed more uplifting when they had first heard of the tradition. Humping up it, Ryck probably joined thousands and thousands of Marine recruits who had wished that this was one tradition that would have died.

At about 500 feet up, Duc quietly slipped out of the makeshift stretcher being carried by No Initial and Petir Borisovitch, letting John Emerson get on. John's feet were mangled with huge blisters, but at the last stop, he'd just jammed his bloody feet back into his boots, refusing the let the corpsman see them. The DIs had to have noticed the switch, but not one took issue with it.

Ryck was vaguely aware of another platoon marching up the mountain on an adjoining trail, but he was focused on his own mission. He had to will one foot being put in front of the other. When he bumped into the recruit in front of him, it took him a moment to realize that he wasn't moving.

Hodges was in front of him, bent over at the waist, hands on his knees. His weapon dangled, the butt in the dirt, but the sling still in his hands.

Ryck straightened up, catching his breath. They were moving up the trail in a column of twos, all pretense at tactical dispersion gone. To his right, Seth MacPruit was doggedly marching. With a hand attached to Seth's ruck was Ham Ceres. Seth was pulling Ham, the very guy who had arranged for Seth's beasting in the showers so long ago. Seth was still an asshole, but he had come around. If he could do that, then so could Ryck.

"Come on, Terry," he told Hodges. "Just a little more. Grab my ruck and let me pull you."

He moved past the recruit, and felt the tug as Hodges grabbed the "dead man's strap" on the side of Ryck's ruck.

*Ten more steps. That's all. Just ten more steps.*

Then suddenly it really was only ten more steps. They crested a ridge, and there, lining the dirt path, were the company's DIs and officers. Behind them were a number of the TDIs. Ryck was confused for a moment, but as he passed Captain Petrov, the officer slapped him on the back with a "Good job, Marine."

It took a moment for that to sink in. "Marine?"

It wasn't a mistake, though. Each Marine on the top of the mountain greeted them, saying the same thing. They had made it. They were Marines!

Several corpsmen were up there as well, and they quickly took those who needed help from the arms of those who had carried them up the hill. 1043 was already there, along with 1039 from the lead platoon. Most of them were on their butts with their rucks off, but they shouted out their greetings. 1044 was not the first to finish, but it wasn't the last, either.

"Keep your heads up!" Ryck told the others as they moved to their staging area.

He wanted nothing more than to flop down on the ground, but he was going to keep it strong until the end. They reached the small 1044 sign that indicated their staging area, and Ryck managed to keep on his feet until each recruit . . . each *Marine*, that was, sat down. He checked them for water before he eased down himself. He didn't think he would ever get up again.

When 1045 marched up, he surprised himself, though. Led by their platoon guide, Joshua Hope-is-Life, he couldn't help himself. He jumped up and ran to embrace his friend.

"Hey, Marine," Ryck said, "you grubbing son-of-a-bitch. We made it!"

## Chapter 14

Ryck held his eyes high as the colonel gave his speech. He'd never even seen the man before. He didn't really give him much thought. Boot camp consisted of his fellow recruits, the DIs, the TDIs, even some of the officers. Out of the corner of his eyes, he could just make out the colonel, up on the podium in his dress blues.

In front of him, though, was the contingent from Eltsworld. Not many family members had come to graduation, but at least fifty Eltsworlders had made the trip in a private ship, and they made quite an impression in the minton-robes and head coverings, the colors changing with each movement or shift of the breeze. They comprised the extended family of Dhakwan Nagi, "Duckman," from 1045. Since their arrival the day before, rumors had started swirling about Duckman, that he was some sort royal prince, out to prove his courage as a warrior before going back to take over the government.

Ryck would have loved for Lysa to come, but with a new baby, and more importantly, with the cost of a ticket, it just didn't make much sense. It didn't matter, though. What mattered was that he had made it. In two more days, he was shipping off to his first duty station, The Third Marine Division at Camp Kolesnikov on Alexander. He would have to attend the 12-week IUT, Initial Unit Training, there before getting to his unit, but it would be as a Marine, not as a recruit.

". . . and so I am proud to be sending you to where your Marine Corps career will take you. I know you will make me proud, you will make the Corps proud, but more importantly, you will make yourself proud. From our forefathers, *Per Terra et Mare*, P*er Mare, Per Terram, Qua Patet Orbis, and Semper Fidelis.* And from the here and now, *Audaces Fortuna Iuvat,* Marines.

"Captain Petrov, you may dismiss your Marines," the colonel told the company commander.

The company commander saluted, did an about-face, then called forward the first sergeant and turned over the company to him. He took a step back, did an about-face, and marched off, the other officers following him as the seniors replaced them.

Ryck could feel the excitement build in him. He waited eagerly for the seniors to get the command. SSgt Despiri received the order, did an about-face, and stared at the new Marines for a moment.

"Platoon 1044, dismissed!" he barked out.

"Aye-aye!" they yelled out in chorus, taking one step back before performing an about-face.

The band kicked in as the platoon erupted into cheers. Ryck pounded the back of Shaymall, who as the platoon guide, sported the single stripe of a Private First Class on his sleeve.

"We did it!" he shouted as he was pulled off Shaymall and bear-hugged by No Initial. The next few minutes were a scrum of hugs, arm punches, and back-pounding. These were his brothers, the men with whom he'd accomplished the toughest challenge of this life. He couldn't have made it without them, and he knew they had needed him. Hodges, No Initial, Duc, Wagons, Ham, Mac, even MacPruit, they were all family. They were all going their separate ways, but this was a watershed moment that none would forget.

The platoons started breaking up, a few Marines going into the stands to greet family, others seeking friends in other platoons. Ryck started to wander over to 1045, but Joshua met him half way. They gripped arms, Roman style, before pulling each other in for another bear hug.

"Congratulations, Marine," they said in unison.

"Well, you glad we went Marines instead of the Legion?" Ryck asked.

"Damn right I am. You?"

"Nothing but the best, and fuck the rest," Ryck responded with a laugh. "When you taking off?"

"Tonight, 2200," Joshua told him.

"Wish I could go," Ryck said.

Joshua's parents had sent a ticket for back home for graduation leave. Joshua would be spending two uncharged weeks back there before reporting to First Marine Division right back here on Tarawa. Ryck could have taken the same leave, but he really didn't have the money to spend on the ticket, and even if he went back to Prophesy, he didn't have a home there. He could stay with

Lysa and her family, but with little Kylee there now, he didn't want to intrude.

"I'll be stopping by and seeing your sis and niece, bro. Tell them all what a bad-ass you are."

"Me a bad-ass? What about you?" Ryck asked, pointing at the PFC stripes Joshua had earned as the 1045 guide.

"Ah, I jus' fooled them but good. Act like you know what you be doing, and they all believe it. 'Sides, we all know what you did up there on the *Wong*."

"Well, yeah, I guess."

They both stood there for a moment, not knowing what to say.

"Hey Ryck! You coming?" Ham shouted out. Most of the platoon was going to go out in town to sample the infamous nightlife and probably get stinking drunk, and the new Marines were drifting back to the squad bay.

"Yeah, give me a sec, OK?"

"Well, I'll be seeing you. Keep in touch, brother," he told Joshua.

"Yeah, you too. Fair winds and following seas and all of that."

They shook hands, then turned to join their platoon mates.

Ryck picked up his pace. He was going to tie one on, and one of those bastards was going to buy him the first round!

# *Third Marine Division Embarked on the FSS Adelaide*

## *Chapter 15*

"Ready to get off this motherfucker?" Sparta asked him.

"Right skippy, there, corporal. Let's diddi ho," Private First Class Ryck Lysander responded.

Ryck was still the platoon boot, but taking out two of the miners had given him a degree of credibility. He'd been tested and blooded. Once the insurrection had been put down (not that they were allowed to use the "I" word), the lieutenant had even put him in for a meritorious promotion to PFC. He would have made it anyway in another month and a half, but this gave him a leg up on most of the rest of his recruit class. More than the stripe, though, when it came time to assign him to a squad, Sgt Piccalo-Tensing had fought for him. He joined Cpl Pallas' fire team, which was down a man with Cpl Singh casevac'd back to the Dirtball. It felt good to Ryck to belong to a unit instead of being just an add-on.

The platoon had taken a heavy hit. Four of the Marines in Second Squad had been opened up like a can of sardines by the miners and killed. Three Marines had been injured enough while clearing the mine to warrant being casevac'd. This was supposed to have been a cakewalk, but that was before someone at UTOM Industries, the company that performed maintenance of the PICS, had both interjected a trojan in the electronics, then sold the information on how to exploit that breach to the miners. A patch had already been installed on the suits, and NIS was supposedly hot on the trail of tracking down the traitor. The scuttlebutt was that the breach was a pretty simple one, but one that could not have been implanted in the Legion's Rigaudeau-3 suits. Underlying the fuck-up was the knowledge that the Marines had gotten off easy. They did not need the PICS to suppress a tax revolt on a piddly-ass mining planet like Atacama. If the suits had been neutralized while in combat with a real opponent, however, it might have been a disaster of epic proportions.

The issue with the suits, though, had kept the Marines on Atacama longer than usual while the vulnerability was investigated. By Federation charter, the Marines were not allowed to remain on a "peaceful" world while in a combat posture. In other words, they were not occupation nor police troops. They had a limited amount of time to consolidate, then leave the planet to the Federation Civil Development Corps.[17] The FCDC was there to "assist in the restoration of civil order and commerce," but they had an awful lot of military gear and men to use it all for a supposed bunch of engineers and economists. With the security breach, though, the Council had extended the timeline of the campaign for an extra 45 days.

With the bulk of the FCDC kept off the planet, the Marines had taken over most of the processing of the civilians. This was something the Marines didn't like to do, and they lacked the manpower to do it well. Certain FCDC teams were assigned to the Marines and even given Marine uniforms, so at least the interrogation of the leaders of the revolt was left to someone else. Ryck had watched four of these fake Marines march into the internment camp while he was on watch and drag off one of the women there. Ryck had no love lost for the miners, but he didn't want to think of what would happen to that woman. It was her own fault, wasn't it? Refusing to pay the taxes to the Federation, the same Federation that paid for the Navy, the Marines, and the FCDC to protect them? The Federation was the strongest power in the known galaxy, but still, there were threats, both from the other non-aligned planets and groups as well as conflicts between planets within the Federation's sphere.

All of that was way above Ryck's pay grade. What he did know was that he hadn't joined the Corps to be a prison guard. The eight weeks he'd spent being just that had been more than enough.

---

[17] **Federation Civil Development Corps**: The FCDC is the federation's answer to a land Army. Heavily armed and outfitted, it is not technically a military which gives the Federation more leeway in its deployment.

At least he wasn't the junior man in the platoon anymore, even if he was still the boot, although the reason for that was not what he would have wished. Two Marines in Third Fire Team, LCpls Verrit and Samuelson had been caught fucking one of the detainees. There was no indication that this was anything other than consensual, so there was no court convened for rape, but contact like that was strictly verboten, and both men had been busted to private and would serve 30 days in the brig after they returned to the Dirtball. Ryck had talked to Sams about it, and the big guy had smiled and said it was totally worth it, even with the brig time and getting busted.

Now, finally, it was time to leave. All their gear had already been embarked, and with the FCDC personnel on deck, they were free to leave for the trip back to the Dirtball. Rumor had it that they were getting a diversion to Vegas for three days liberty, but the brass refused to confirm that. Like most Marines, Ryck had been on Vegas on the way to Tarawa for boot, but he had never gotten out of the spaceport.

Ryck shouldered his ruck and filed after Sparta. He didn't look back as he entered the *Adelaide's* personnel hatch.

## *Chapter 16*

"You are one sick mother," Sams said as he sat down, looking at Ryck's breakfast.

"Eat me," came Ryck's rote reply.

Food aboard the *Adelaide* was pretty damn good, even for a farmboy such as Ryck who was used to a degree of "real" food. Sure, his family had a home fabricator, and sure, they bought manufactured food, but being on a farm and surrounded by other farmers, Ryck had often eaten natural food, even meats. While some of the other Marines, mostly from the big industrialized worlds, blanched at the thought of eating animal flesh, to Ryck, it was special treat. He thought those who said animal flesh was not "normal" were pretty weird, given that some of the bases for the fabricators came from pulverized insects, coal by-products, or other things best not imagined.

The Navy being the Navy, the *Adelaide* had one hellacious commercial fabricator. It shouldn't have made a difference as the bases were all the same and a fabricator followed set formulas, but the senior chief in charge of the mess could whip up some tasty chow, better than a grunt could expect. It was common knowledge that the officers got some natural foods in their mess, but Ryck didn't care. The crew's mess was plenty fine. Even the bacon he was eating tasted natural. Ryck knew that it was made from a mixture of some of the twelve bases that fed the fabricator, but when he ate it, it seemed like the real deal to him. Sams wasn't commenting on that, but with what Ryck had covered it.

As a young boy, bacon had been Ryck's favorite food—real bacon, not the fake bacon made by Sunshine or Healthy Choice. On each birthday, that was what he wanted. That and ice cream. Fab ice cream was pretty indistinguishable from hand-cranked ice-cream made from cow's cream, even if the luxury brands such as Swiss Heaven or Ben and Jerry's tried to convince people otherwise. Their little home fabricator could do a pretty decent job on sweet sauces, too, such as chocolate and strawberry. Ryck, though, loved the raspberry sauce, and he lathered it over his ice cream. On his seventh birthday, he had jokingly said he was going to put the sauce on his bacon. All his family had laughed at that, telling him that was silly. Ryck had meant it as a joke, but their reaction raised a degree of stubbornness in him. They couldn't tell him he was silly. So he insisted on it. His mother had given in, and with ten slices of sizzling bacon on his plate, had hesitantly dribbled the raspberry sauce on it.

"More," he had insisted.

His parents, Myke, and Lysa watched him as he defiantly raised a forkful of raspberry-covered bacon to his mouth and put it in his mouth. He had thought he would have to choke it down, doing it just to show his family that he was not some little kid, but to his surprise, he actually liked it. Now, aboard the Navy ship where fab bacon was offered for each breakfast and he could dial fab raspberry sauce from the dessert line anytime he wanted, this had become his daily ritual.

"Really, man, why do you always do that? That and your ketchup and polly sauce shit you put on stuff?" Sams persisted.

Ryck just raised his middle finger in response.

Life aboard the *Adelaide* was an odd confluence of relaxation, stimulation, and boredom. There really wasn't that much for Marines to do. They had cleaned and re-cleaned all their gear. They had taken care of some admin. The little "gym" on the ship was not much and large enough for only a handful of people at a time. On the plus side, the ship's entertainment system was immense, with what had to be every flick, song, book, and show ever recorded. They couldn't communicate with the outside while in bubble space (unless a message torp was sent to pierce their bubble, and that was done only for extremely high-priority communications), so camming family or friends was out until they dropped back into real space, but still, there was more available to watch than anyone could view in their lifetime. The food was great, and there was plenty of rack time. It should have been a Marine's dream, but in reality, after a day or two, most Marines became antsy. They wanted to do something, not just be cargo.

Sams sat down and dug into his pancakes. He made exaggerated eating sounds, smacking his lips.

"Enjoy it now, Sams, 'cause you ain't getting any of that when your ass is locked up in the brig," T-Rex told him.

T-Rex was LCpl Sylvester Harrington Smith Pulaski. He was an immensely strong Marine, with broad shoulders that had to give the armorers nervous breakdowns when it came to fitting him. He had essentially no neck and seemingly little short arms, hence the "T-Rex" nickname. He was also about the smartest Marine Ryck had met, with a broad knowledge on just about everything. He spoke as if he was barely educated, but that didn't fool anyone.

"Don't need food there. I'll have my memories of the lovely Miss Sorada to fulfill me," Sams said dramatically, his voice pitched higher than normal.

"Hope she was really worth it, when we all are out on the ville, getting some," T-Rex replied.

"Oh, she was, she was. Better than any D-town ho, that's for sure."

That brought a round of laughter. Ryck was glad he wasn't facing the same fate as Sams, but still, there was a degree of envy in him. Getting laid while one a mission had a certain swashbuckling flair, something to tell the other grandpaps as they sat around the retirement home years from now.

Ryck took another bite of his bacon, looking around at the other Marines. He'd been with the unit only a short time, but somehow, it seemed longer. He felt like he fit in, as if this life was made for him. This was a long way from the dusty fields of Prophesy, but sitting in the crews mess, light-years from the farm, it seemed as if it was destined. He felt more at home than in the house where he'd been raised.

Not completely at home, though. Two sailors took their trays to the next table and sat down, their connectors clearly visible on the backs of their shaved heads. Unlike the other sailors, navigators, as these two were, and gunners never wore covers. The interfaces they needed to connect to the cybercomps that kept the ship's bubble whole and the ship on course, or in the case of the gunners, that enabled them to control the ship's weapons systems, were surgically implanted into their brains through the back of their skulls. The "cybos" generally kept to themselves, an elite among the rest of the crew. They gave Ryck the creeps, though. The Marines also used biofaces, of course, but theirs were patches that were placed on the skin, not drilled through the skull.

Ryck tore his gaze off of their heads and speared his last piece of bacon, mushing it around his plate to mop up the last of his sauce. He popped it in his mouth and contemplated going back for another serving. There was nothing to stop him, nor would anyone even care, but he decided against it as a show of inner discipline.

Sgt Piccalo-Tensing entered the mess decks, spied the Marines, and made a beeline to them.

"Shit, what's PT got for us now?" Wan asked, quickly pushing more of his food into his mouth as if afraid he wouldn't get the chance to finish.

"What's up, Sergeant?" Pallas asked.

Cpl Pallas and Sgt Piccalo-Tensing were both NCOs, but Pallas seemed more at home with the non-rates. There seemed to be an underlying tension between the two men that Ryck didn't understand.

"Word just came out, and I thought I would pass it to you. We're dropping out of bubble space at 1400. At 1800, liberty is being called. Vegas."

There was a moment of silence before whoops of joy rang out, not just from the Marines, but from the sailors who had been sitting within earshot. Vegas! Some Marines might go through an entire enlistment without getting to any of the fabled four liberty ports of Vegas, Kukson, Ramp it Up, or Pattaya.

"Liberty brief will be at 1700 in the chapel. And there will be an inspection. No raggedly ass Marines will be allowed off the ship," the squad leader said before turning around and leaving.

"My fucking grandmother! Vegas!" one of the sailors said.

Ryck didn't quite understand the reference of that, but he understood the tone of the sailor's comment.

"Vegas! This is going to be epic!" Sams said.

"What do you mean, there, brig rat?" T-Rex asked.

"No, no, I've got my brig time back on the Dirtball!" Sams protested.

"You sure? Seems to me you're not in the brig now because this ship doesn't have one. I think you're restricted to the ship," Cpl Pallas told him.

"No fucking way! I gotta go see England," Sams said, jumping up, half-eaten breakfast still covering his tray.

He jammed the tray into the galley window and rushed off to see the staff sergeant, almost at the run.

"They really going to keep him on the ship?" Wan asked.

"Nah, they won't, but it's good to yank his chain. He's been bragging about nailing that miner so much, he needed to be taken down a notch," T-Rex told him.

"That said," Cpl Pallas added, "your civvies really need to pass muster for a place like Vegas. I don't know about you all, but I didn't expect this, and I think I might need to hit the ship's store for something better than my ripped t-shirt."

Even on a combat mission, Marines always travelled with at least one set of civvies. Ryck's were brand new, so he thought they would be fine. It wouldn't hurt to check them, though. No way he wanted to be delayed in getting off the ship.

Vegas!

## *Chapter 17*

"You're really trolling for more brig time, aren't you?" Pallas asked Sams as the private showed off the new tattoo on his upper arm, a Star, Globe and Anchor with "Third Marine Division" written below it.

Ryck took another swig of his Bud while he examined Sams' bodywork. Tattoos were against Marine regs. It has something to do with how tattoos could affect both regen and how biosensors monitored the body's readings. There was no such restriction in the Navy, and many Marines got them when they left the service, but active duty Marines were required to keep their bodies clean. No tats, no genmods.

"Ah, that's the beauty of this. Look!" Sams said while flexing his biceps.

He reached across with his left hand and pushed at something. To Ryck's surprise, the tattoo disappeared. That caught his interest.

He leaned closer to look and asked, "How did you do that?"

Wan, Pallas, Hu, T-Rex, and Smitty leaned forward, too, Hu knocking over his Slicer Lite to spill on the peanut covered floor of the bar.

"Alcohol abuse!" was shouted out by the rest of them in unison, as was expected, but their attention was on Sams as he did something else with his left hand that caused the tattoo to re-appear.

"It ain't a tattoo. Me and Aesop here," he started, tilting his head back on the lance corporal who'd come in with him, "saw this place over on Sahara, by the Poseidon Club, and we went in. This is what they call a 'refractive body art,' or some bullshit. It has to do with light waves and such, and when I touch this point here," he said, indicating a small point at the top of the anchor, "it polarizes so it goes stealth-like."

He pushed the spot, and the tattoo disappeared again. Cpl Pallas reached out and grabbed the bigger Marine by the arm and pulled him closer so he could see the arm better. He ran a finger over the spot where the tattoo had been visible only a few seconds before.

"No shit!" Hu said, reaching out to touch Sams' arm as well.

"I don't know," T-Rex said. "It looks like a tattoo, and I bet the first sergeant's going to have your ass over it."

"It's not a tattoo," Aesop said. "They had it all explained. This is brand new techno."

"So where's yours if it ain't a tat?" T-Rex asked him.

"Well, they said it wasn't a tattoo, but like you said, you think the first sergeant's going to buy that? I've got seven more months in this green machine, and I'm getting out with the stripes on my sleeves. I need my VSEB[18] if I'm going to go to school."

"Chicken shit excuse if you ask me. You're out with your liberty buddy, and you let him do that if you think it might be illegal? Sams might be a busted-down private, but all that means is you still outrank him," Pallas reminded him.

Marines and sailors were not allowed to wander alone while on ship's liberty. Vegas was a safe haven—other than losing your money, not much else would happen as the police kept a pretty tight lock on the tourist spots on the planet. Almost "anything goes" in Vegas, but the police kept violent crimes at a minimum. They wanted tourists to come back again and spend more. It was common knowledge that for a place such as Vegas, the liberty buddy concept was more there to protect Vegas from Marines and sailors than the other way around.

The two newcomers grabbed seats as Sams ordered another round for everyone. Hu, Sams, and Wan continued to discuss the regulatory ramifications of Sams' "refractive body art." Hu was debating on getting one himself. Pallas and T-Rex were discussing the NFL and the upcoming season. Smitty, getting deeper into his cups was softly singing to himself. Ryck just leaned back to watch the dancers on the stage. To say they were hot was an understatement, and Ryck had been socially and physically celibate since leaving Prophesy. The tall redhead on the left was particularly

---

[18] **VSEB**: Veterans Service Educational Benefits—payments made to approved schools for veterans who were received Honorable Discharges.

stunning. Like all the rest, she had on bikini bottoms made with the same flashing LED fabric as Lysa used to wear while "working," but while he hated Lysa wearing the fabric, on this undulating goddess, it seemed pretty natural. Of course, he rather liked the rest of her body better where nothing was left to the imagination. What he was able to imagine was what he would like to be doing with her.

"I see you enjoy what a woman can offer," a soft voice said in his ear, startling him out of his reverie.

He looked back to where a blue woman was standing. Blue skin and yellow hair. Very little clothing.

"May I sit down?" she asked.

"Uh, uh, sure," Ryck stammered out, pulling a chair from the next table to beside him.

"Your buddies seem to be interested in other things," she said, pointing a long blue finger at them.

They might have been discussing other things a moment before, but as she sat, she had all of their undivided attention. When she smiled at them, her teeth dazzling white, before putting one hand on Ryck's arm and turning her body to face him, they shrugged and went back to what they had been doing, even if glances kept being shot her way.

"So, what's your name?" she asked Ryck.

"Private First Class Ryck Lysander," he told her.

She leaned her head up and gave a trill of musical laughter. "So your mother named you 'Private First Class'?"

"No, no. My mother and father named me Ryck. I'm a private first class in the Marines."

"OK, Private First Class Ryck Lysander, sorry for teasing you like that. It is just that you are so cute!"

She put her hand back lightly on his arm. It was barely touching him, but he was extremely conscious of it.

Ryck stared at her hand for a moment, then followed the arm up to the rest of her. She was blue, all right. That was her skin color, not some tight-fitting clothing. She was a deep, almost incandescent blue. Her hair was bright yellow, and her eyes seemed to glow with the same shade as her hair. She had on a small v-neck halter and nancishorts, both the same shade of blue as her skin, but with the lights in the bar, it was hard to tell where fabric left off and skin began. Ryck thought back to his Grand Lit class back at school. They had spent a week on comic books, anime, and shorts, and one of the comics had been an old 20th Century volume of X-Men. This woman reminded him of one of the characters in that comic named Mystique. She didn't quite look like what he remembered of the fictional character, but the blue skin color trumped other aspects of their respective appearances. He wanted to ask of her skin was a genmod, or if it was superficial. He knew he shouldn't stare, but she didn't seem to mind his attention.

"Are you enjoying Vegas?" she asked.

"Uh, yeah, sure. It's great. We've only been here a few hours, though. We're on the . . ." he started, then realized that he shouldn't be talking about military details.

"You're on the *Adelaide*, and you are just back from Atacama where they had a tax revolt. Yes, we know all about the comings and goings of ships here in Vegas," she said as her face broke out in a dazzling smile.

That took Ryck by surprise. Was she grilling him on military secrets? He glanced back at the others. Cpl Pallas was sitting on the other side of him, and the NCO seemed to have heard her, because he was looking back at Ryck, smile on his face. He lifted up his bottle of Bud in a mock salute to Ryck, then turned back. The lack of security awareness seemed weird to him, but if Sparta didn't think much about it, it had to be OK.

"By the way, I'm Purety," she said, offering her hand.

"Uh, hi Purety."

There were a few chortles from the others and one sarcastic-sounding "smooth move, there." The other Marines had given him the field of battle, but they still had the two of them under reconnaissance.

"So, you boy's have been deployed for awhile with nothing to do. Saved up all your pay, right?" she asked him.

"Yeah, you've got that right. Nothing we could spend it on there. But Vegas, you know, this place can suck it out of you. I've already contributed to your economy on the blackjack tables," he said, trying to be funny.

He didn't quite get the reaction he'd expected.

"Lost it already? Everything?" she said, pulling back ever-so-slightly.

"Oh no, nothing like that," he said hurriedly. "It wasn't much. I've got most of it here," he added, patting his back pocket and wallet.

Seemingly mollified, she leaned back in to him, took his arm, and said, "Good. There are better things to do with your money. Much better."

As she said the second "better,' she leaned even further forward, pushing her left breast up against his arm.

Ryck wasn't naive. He hadn't needed the liberty brief where the sailors and Marines had been warned that while prostitution was legal on Vegas, as it was throughout the Federation, with a few exceptions, as a matter of civil rights, it tended to be a very costly proposition. There would be no pay advances for anyone who spent all of his money, so making sure it stretched out for the entire four-day liberty was up to each individual.

Still, it had been a long time, and she was a very sexy woman. Her blue skin added to the attraction. It seemed more appropriate, somehow, that if he was going to enjoy the company of a working girl in Vegas, she should be rather unique, and Purety certainly fit that bill. He hadn't planned on doing anything other than drinking and gambling, maybe taking in a show. He hadn't wanted to connect himself in any way to the men who used to buy Lysa drinks. But sitting next to Purety, he felt his resolve begin to falter. This was Vegas, after all, with their hundreds-of-years-old motto of "What Happens in Vegas, Stays in Vegas."

She scooted a little closer, this time pressing her leg up against his. Her leg was bare, but he had on full Dekes. Still, the heavy fabric of the Dekes did nothing to lessen the electricity that flowed into his leg.

"So, you interested in partying?" she asked him in a husky voice.

Ryck was just about to give in when the recall button on his collar sounded. Groans and curses sounded from other sailors and Marines as they realized what the buzzing buttons meant. Their liberty was cut short. Something was up, and they had to get back to the ship.

"You heard it, gents. Let's get going," Cpl Pallas told them as he stood, swiping his card to clear his tab. "Pay up if you haven't already, and we've got 20 mikes to get back to the shuttle. Wan, you and T-Rex make sure Smitty gets back. OK, move it!"

Ryck stood up and looked back down at Purety.

"Uh, sorry, I mean, I wanted to, but I've gotta go."

She shrugged indifferently. "I know. Go ahead."

Her voice had lost some of the sultriness. Despite her still exotic looks, she suddenly sounded like anyone else at a humdrum job; bored and wishing she was someplace else. He wanted to say something more, but as the others started to rush off, he simply turned away and sprinted off to the shuttle port.

## *Chapter 18*

The entire company was crowded into the ship's mess, the only place large enough other than the shuttle bay where everyone could gather. The *Adelaide* was only a destroyer, not one of the larger troop transports. Major Paulan, the detachment commander, stood up to speak, and the room quieted. Something big was up.

"Listen up, Marines," the skinny major said, his voice surprisingly deep for coming out of such a small frame. "We've got a real situation here. The passenger ferry *Robin* was hijacked two hours ago. We are at full throttle now to try and pick up the spoor. If we find it, we will track down the ship and rescue the crew and passengers."

That caught their attention. Anti-piracy was part of the Navy's mission, but that usually meant blasting pirates or their bases into their component atoms. Sometimes, though, that meant a rescue, and that required Marines. The *Adelaide* was probably the closest ship in the immediate vicinity with embarked Marines, so that had to be why the ship was given the mission.

If the pirated vessel was a bubble ship, then time was of an essence. When a ship entered bubble space, there was a warp in the fabric of real space, but one that faded with time. If a Navy ship could find that spoor, they could somehow follow the ship, even through bubble space, and track it down.

Ryck didn't understand how they could do that. In a class back at recruit training, it was explained that it worked the same way as hadron communications. That confused him, though. He understood the concept of hadron comms. The physics of it was that the key components were split-manufactured by twinning. Up to 32 receptors could be made, and they reacted to any outside stimulus in unison, even when separated. Push one up, and the other 31 would instantaneously go up in the exact same manner, even if light years apart. Make communicators out of these receptors, send them across the galaxy, and camming was possible from one to the other. Cross-connect to other comm hubs, and a person could cam with pretty much anyone in the known galaxy, at least within Federation space. That was intrinsically obvious to Ryck and made perfect sense.

He didn't, though understand how a Navy ship could sniff out the bubble spoor, "taste" it (the term used by the class instructor), then lock it in. They weren't twinned, after all. There was no connection between them at the hadron level. It didn't make any sense, and Ryck wondered if there wasn't another explanation, one highly classified. Regardless, he just had to accept that this was within the Navy's capabilities.

"It looks like the pirates are SOG," the major added, eliciting a murmur from the Marines.

Soldiers of God were criminals, their religious-sounding name notwithstanding. They had rained terror on the Reaches, wiping out entire communities, recording their torture and rape and sending those flicks out over the open net. Their leader, who went by the name of All Seeing, narrated each flick, explaining that God told them to kill and pillage. When they entered the inner core, hitting planets, stations, and ships, the leeward edge of both the Federation and the Brotherhood started to panic. No one knew where SOG originated nor where they got their ships.

They were not always successful. Several ships were destroyed by Federation or Brotherhood Navy ships, and DNA regression studies on what human remains could be gathered showed that there was no single ethnic or regional source. It seemed as if SOG came from a wide variety of worlds and people, probably recruited from the flotsam of society.

The Reaches, by definition, were widespread and sparsely populated. Even with modern technology, the SOG's homeworld remained hidden. That was until an SOG pirate mothership was purposefully damaged, but not destroyed, and allowed to "escape." Two Shrike pilots, operating well beyond the range of the little fighters, followed in trace, stealth projectors at max output. One disappeared into bubble space, but the other found the homeworld and torped back the coordinates to the waiting combined fleet. The fleet arrived, and with the main guns of the FS *Russia* and the Brotherhood battleship *Retribution* slaved together, the admiral of the Federation fleet and the archbishop of the Brotherhood fleet jointly pushed the firing button, sending no less than twelve planet busters to destroy the homeworld of the SOG.

Unfortunately, within a year, SOG was back. All Seeing was probably killed when the planet was destroyed, but others rose in his place, and SOG was back in the space lanes. They started taking freighters, disappearing with valuable cargos. They took some planetary militia ships, and even a destroyer from the independent Greenworld. Finally, they had started taking some passenger ships. No ransom was ever requested. The rumors were that the men were made into slaves, the women into wives and breeders.

The major let the rumble die down before continuing, "I don't need to tell you what happened three years ago with the SOG and the *Mount Rainer*."

It had been widely publicized, so pretty much the entire Federation had followed the story. The SOG had gotten aboard the ship as passengers, then taken over the bridge while the rest of the pirates boarded from small shuttles. Over 600 souls were taken captive. The *Ranier* was not a bubble ship, but an old fabric ship. The *FS Wuhan* caught them before they could align for their jump. The Marines assaulted, but when they entered the *Ranier*, they found all of the passengers murdered, most horribly mutilated. The 30 pirates themselves had committed suicide.

"I was part of the boarding team, and I am not ashamed to admit to you that I broke down when I saw what they had done. Rest assured that this is not going to happen during my command."

Several "oorahs" echoed within the mess deck, only to fade in an awkward silence.

"I'm going to turn this over to Lieutenant Silverton for a moment. He's the ship's intel officer, and I think we need to listen to this."

Several Navy officers and crew had arrived with the major and Capt Light Chaser. One of them, obviously a heavy worlder from his physique, stood up to face the Marines.

"As the major said, I'm Lieutenant Silverton," he started. "There has already been a release that the hijacking is the work of the SOG. However, a couple of things stand out. First, this is the furthest into Federation space that the SOG has ever struck.

Second, the announcement that they were the SOG came quite early, sooner than what they normally do. They are still vulnerable, and usually the SOG waits until they are safely away. The Admiralty gives it a very high probability that this is not the SOG, but rather a copy-cat group that is using the *Ranier* incident to forestall pursuit."

That elicited another round of rumbling, and the lieutenant had to hold up his hand to get everyone to quiet down.

"The decision has been made, and this is at the *highest* levels, that SOG or copycat, the *Adelaide*, if at all possible, will track down the *Robin* and take it back, no matter the consequences. The pirates, whether actually SOG or not, will be given the same summary treatment as authorized by Joint Communique 2005."

"Joint Communique 2005" was an official understanding between the Federation, the Brotherhood, and seven independent planets that all civil rights with regards to SOG members were suspended, and summary executions would be conducted on every captured member. The Federation had issued similar rulings before, but those were only in effect in Federation space. This was the first time, to anyone's knowledge outside of it, at least, that the Brotherhood had done away with due process.

The lieutenant sat down, nodding to the major, who stood back up.

"To repeat what the lieutenant said, even if these are copycats, they will be treated like the real deal. You want to play with us, then accept the consequences," he said.

This time, the chorus of "oo-rahs" was louder and sustained.

"According to what I've been told, we should arrive on station in about, uh . . ." he started, then looked down at his watch, ". . . about 45 minutes. Then our Navy brothers need to find the spoor and lock on the trail. Even if successful, the soonest we could possibly launch is in two or three hours. Not much time, so I'm going to turn it over to Capt Light Chaser for the op order. Listen up. We won't have time for a real rehearsal, but we're Marines. We make do, and do it in a most *outstanding* manner! So listen up and get it down, then we've got to get suited up and ready to go. Captain Light Chaser?"

Major Paulan was actually the battalion ops officer, but when the mission to Atacama came up, he'd been given command of the task force of the ground element, the single Stork of the air element, and the small logistics element. Captain Light Chaser was the Fox Company commander, and as such, commanded the company along with the arty and engineer detachment. Navy Captain Webber, the Aidelaide's skipper was the overall commander, and Major Paulan the Marine commander, but Captain Light Chaser would lead the assault.

As the assault force commander, Captain Light Chaser stood up to give the order. He had everyone's undivided attention. Two hours was no time to plan and kick off a ship-to-ship mission. But they would march on and complete the mission. Ryck joined the others, all business, as they received their op order.

## Chapter 19

"Team B, pass through C, but keep it tight," the lieutenant's voice came over the platoon circuit.

"Team B" was the assault element, the bulk of it made up from First and Second Platoons. Third Platoon was the security element, Weapons and the attachments the support element. The support element's job was to make the initial crossing to the *Robin* and secure the breaching chamber. The security element's mission was to breach the ship, then secure the breach. The assault element would immediately follow, pass through Third, and rush to take out any pirates and secure the captives. Speed was of an essence.

"Assault, assault, assault," the Marines of the assault element muttered as they shuffled through the line of security element Marines. The movement was complicated even further by the Stork and the *Aidelaide's* two shuttles filling the hanger deck. The Marines shuffled to the far bulkhead and stopped, still facing outwards.

"This has got to be quicker," the first sergeant broke in on the company circuit. "Much quicker. If we are too slow, those fuckers will smoke check each and every captive."

"You heard him," Capt Light Chaser's unique voice cut in. "Element leaders, get them back and go through this again. Time's getting short, and we could get the go ahead any minute now."

The company had given out the op order in record time, and the Marines had gotten suited up and were ready to go within an hour. Staged in the hanger bay, the company commander had started rehearsals. Walking around in the bay was a far cry from actually flying through space and breaching a hostile ship, but Ryck had to admit that it still helped.

Because of the imminent threat to the captives, a decision had been made to conduct the assault in bubble space. This was highly unusual and extremely risky. Normally, a vessel would be tracked through bubble space, then taken when both ships emerged back into real space. However, once they were in real space, at distances close enough to board, the *Adelaide's* presence would be extremely difficult to mask, and with any warning, the SOG could massacre their prisoners. So it had to be surprise. The SOG would not be expecting it, and their first indication that something was up would be when the breach was made. The fact that a ship takedown could even be accomplished in bubble space was something kept under wraps. Some rumors had leaked out, of course, over the years, but the Naval Civil Information Service had counter-propaganda employed to make those rumors seem ridiculous.

They had been putting on their EVA suits when the word was passed that the *Robin's* spoor had been acquired, and a cheer had echoed throughout the armory. EVA suits were custom made for each Marine, and one of CWO2 Slyth's primary missions in life was to make sure the suits were continually adjusted to keep the fit right. Ryck had just gone through his standard 30-day check two days before they had pulled into Vegas, so his was pretty much right on. But the chief warrant officer, his gunny, and his two sergeants had been pinging back and forth in the crowded armory, taking readings and making last-minute adjustments. Ryck had gotten out of there as soon as he got his OK and made his way to the hanger deck.

Normally, the bay was pressurized, with the Stork and the shuttles passing through a magelectro field. However, with speed as a priority, the only way to get so many Marines and sailors out into flight was through the hanger bay doors. The ship's two airlocks just couldn't cycle the assault force quick enough. And with the shielding of the EVA suits not sturdy enough to fend off the field, it had to be turned off. So the hanger bay was open to bubble space. The Navy deck crew, the assault force, and the Navy prize crew were all suited up, ready to step out the door.

Ryck couldn't help glancing out the huge doors. No stars were visible, of course. There was only a murky, greenish glow. Like every single sailor and Marine there, he knew that no matter what happened, he had to stay within the glow. Drift out, and he would be lost in the emptiness of space, probably lost for good. He didn't have the luck of Derek Housa, a Legionnaire who had gotten thrown out of bubble space, only to be picked up by an ore miner who happened to read his distress beacon, something that had to be a million-to-one shot. Ryck had seen the flick about that when it had come out a few years ago, and the scenes of the Legionnaire floating around all alone in the vastness of space still gave him the heebies.

The *Robin* was not in view yet, either. As soon as it was, the assault would be launched. The Navy bridge crew would be maneuvering the ship closer to the *Robin*, then if they were successful at that, the external projector pods would be extended, effectively spreading the bubble. The pods would move towards the *Robin*, eventually enveloping it, where like two bubbles in a bath, they would merge.

This was the most difficult part of the mission from a technological standpoint. Ryck had heard the process likened to balancing a maglev car on a string of straws, one straw jammed in another until the car was a kilometer in the air. The cybos might weird Ryck out when he saw them out and about the ship, but he wished them well as they tweaked and shifted the pods, more by feel than any hard and set calculations.

Ryck shuffled with the other Marines back to the far side of the bay for another rehearsal. The ship had stopped its rotation in preparation for the assault. Having centripetal force as they exited the hanger was not a good idea. The ship had rotated so the hanger faced the expected direction of where the *Robin* would be, then stopped. With no gravity in the hanger, which unlike the bridge and many of the other spaces had no artificial gravity, the Marines and sailors shuffled their feet to keep in contact. It was considered poor form to have to turn on the EVA's jets to get back into place.

Ryck had just gotten back to his starting point when a voice came over the circuit, "Look, there she is."

Ryck looked out the bay doors, and off in the distance, the *Robin* was appearing as if through a mist. She was nothing out of the ordinary. Like all bubble ships, she was round. A ship did not have to be round to project a bubble, but the shape was far more efficient, and it took far less power to keep the bubble formed around a sphere than any other form. Inside the greenish light of the bubble, she took on a somewhat eerie tone. This appearance was why some people referred to a ship travelling through bubble space as "ghosting."

As expected, the ship was not under rotation. Pirates usually kept captured ships in null G as it kept more passengers uncertain and unwilling to resist.

"Element leaders, get your men in place. Stand by for the go," Capt Light Chaser passed."

"All hands, this is Major Paulen. Do us proud. It's time to earn your big paychecks."

Ryck knew the major had to be chomping at his bit. He would be coming over with the Navy prize team, the sailors necessary to run the *Robin* and affect any required repairs. This would be Captain Light Chaser's assault, and the major had stepped back to allow it, but he had to have been tempted to take the assault himself.

The hanger crew moved into position. They had their own EVA suits, unlike the prize team who were in standard suits. The two officers had their suits shifted to yellow, the enlisted to green. Ryck had though the colors a bit odd at first, but with all the men in the hanger, it really did help to sort things out.

The support element got to the front of the open doors. Two Marines had their hands on each of the four breaching chambers, ready to fly them across to the *Robin*. The other Marines in the team flanked them. Directly behind them, the security element was lined up. They would actually enter the breach and hold it for the assault element to exploit. Ryck took his place behind them, about two meters from the edge of the door. Two meters from open bubble space.

Between the Marines in front of him, Ryck could see the Robin looming larger. It was difficult to tell in space, but it couldn't be more than a couple of hundred meters away. That thought alone was mind-boggling. Both ships were hurtling through bubble space, covering light years in real space, yet they were just meters apart. Real space speed meant nothing.

Ryck felt his excitement rise. This would be his first EVA since the near-disaster during recruit training. He popped his M99 free, checked it, and popped it back into the holster.

Suddenly, the yellow-suited deck officer wheeled and pointed out the doors. For some inexplicable reason, he could not talk on the Marine circuits. The Navy working and Marine tactical circuits were incompatible. The Marines knew the signal, of course, and the first rank stepped off and started flying.

*Thousand one, thousand two, thousand three, thousand four* Ryck counted in his mind. On "four," the next rank stepped off.

Now was the wait. If all went well, the breaching teams could set up and breach the ship within 30 seconds after reaching it. The breaching chambers were adjusted to their shortest length as they were not going to be acting as airlocks. They would be opening the ship up to space.

The security element was given another 30 seconds to secure the breached rooms. The breaching points had been selected compromising between where the air loss would be minimal and where the assaulting Marines could quickly reach where captives were probably be being kept.

At 60 seconds, the assault element would be arriving at each of the four points, ready to dive through the breaches. As the assault element arrived, the breaches would be closed off, extended, then converted to air locks for the follow-on forces.

It was a long, long minute until the deck officer wound up and sent them on their way. Ryck stepped off into space. Ryck was on the left flank of the assault element's line, with only T-Rex outside of him. They would be flying to breach "Tennison." Inside bubble space, it was almost impossible to tell exactly where the bubble "skin" was. It sort of swirled and shimmered, defying comprehension. From what they'd been taught, a person wouldn't know that he had reached the bubble until he was out of it and injected back into real space. Ryck kept glancing towards his left. He figured, though, that if they were drifting too close, Hu would disappear first.

Up ahead of him, the breaching teams had already reached the ship and attached the chambers. With that, the pirates would realize that something was up. This was real, now. Ryck flew on, keeping in formation with the others. What the captain didn't want was to have everyone bunching up at the ship. The four breaches were the bottleneck, and he didn't want confusion to take over.

Ryck was getting closer when the security team around Tennison started to dive into the chamber. They would be reporting back what they found, but that was not on the general assault element circuit. If there was something Ryck needed to know, he would be told.

Ryck glanced over at the other two breaches that were within his view, the fourth being behind the curve of the ship and out of sight. Marines were already inside at "Jakarta," but at "Capetown," there seemed to be a problem, with the security team still outside while the assault element was arriving.

"Team Tennison, get ready to enter. Security has cleared the immediate entry. Stick to the plan and move forward into the passageway. There are two enemy KIA and one rescued hostage," Sgt Piccalo-Tensing passed over the team circuit.

Ryck was running pretty true, and it took only a few minor jets to correct his aim and slow down in order to get into his position in line for entry. He looked down at the telltale on his left gauntlet. Unlike the team leaders who had the positions projected onto their faceshields, just as with the PICS, the riflemen had only repeaters on the flexible patch screen that most wore on their forward shooting arm. It wasn't as detailed as those for the leaders, but it did indicate friendlies. Ryck could see the security team icons as they moved into position within the ship.

Quicker than expected, Ryck approached the ship. He fired two quick jets to slow his approach and took care not to jostle anyone else, sending them tumbling, but he had to keep on the ass of Wan as they dove through the chamber. He crashed into the lance corporal inside the ship as they hit the deck, but Wan was up and moving within seconds. Ryck grabbed his M99 and got his feet under him, pushing forward to the far hatch, just where he'd been briefed it would be. He took in the two dead men, both in various degrees of undress. With their skin exposed to the cold touch of space, it was easy to see where they both had been stitched by the security team's M99s. A naked woman was inside a zip-lock, the clear, flexible emergency pouch that could keep someone alive in the vacuum of space for up to 20 minutes. She was hyperventilating, and a Marine, or probably Doc Stanton, the corpsman with the security element, was with her, trying to calm her down.

Ryck took all that in during the few seconds it took him to cross the compartment, go through the next hatch, down one deck, and turn left to his assigned position. He crouched there, weapon at the ready, waiting for the order to move. The ship's emergency reaction AI had closed off the passages as soon as the breach was made, so no air was rushing out. Gravity was gone, but nothing was trying to push the Marines back out into space. No move would be made to breach the closed hatch 10 meters down the passage until the breaching chamber closed off the initial entry and became a working airlock. Ryck silently counted down the time. The plan was that all the security and assault elements would board the *Robin* within 90 seconds.

Ryck knew his count would be off, given that he'd been diving through and moving during part of it, but the order came to move out when he hit 82 seconds. They were all in the ship and could advance.

Cpl Pallas was up and moving almost before the order was completed. Wan, T-Rex, and Ryck were hot on his tail and they rushed to the hatch in front of them. They were to breach it, then make for a berthing space on the other side while Smitty's team moved on to the ship's passenger galley another 10 meters down. Their sense of urgency was heightened. The necessity for speed had been shoved down their throats while they waited.

T-Rex placed a toad on the edge of the hatch where the locking mechanism hid. The toad was a small, soft, greenish lump that could stick on just about anything. EVA gauntlets or special employment gloves for planetary use were treated to be able to handle them, but as soon as they touched almost anything else, they stuck to it. There was a three-second fuse in each toad, the only solid component to the little explosive, that gave the user a very short time to move back. Toads, or the "E-559 Self-contained Slow Breaching Device," burned more than they actually exploded and could be used in a vacuum or in breathable air. They carried their own supply of oxygen with them, suspended in the combustible material, and could burn through almost any material.

"Fire in the hole!" T-Rex shouted, pushing back.

The toad hissed, then started its burn, the EVA suit visors instantly compensating for the flare. The hatch broke free, and T-Rex gave it a kick, sending it open. Immediately, a burst of fire came back at them, one round, at least, pinging off Ryck's shoulder. As it was not an explosive, the toad only opened and did not clear what was on the other side.

EVA suits could take some punishment, but they were not PICS, nor even bones, although they did give 100% coverage. A high powered weapon would go right through it, and even a lucky shot from small arms could find an opening. All four Marines returned fire en masse, not even fully aware of the target, trusting the very nature of a ship's passageway to focus their rounds.

"Cease fire," Sparta ordered after a good 100 or more rounds were sent down the passage.

Ryck peered ahead. On the other side, a figure writhed suspended above the deck. He had an old M-8 alongside him, but he wasn't paying it any attention. Unlike a typical pirate, he was wearing body armor, or at least a hodgepodge of armor plating, and from the looks of it, the old Proskov carapace he had on had protected him from the Marines' M99s. The only problem was that he had only the torso carapace and a helmet that Ryck didn't even recognize. He had nothing on his arms or legs, and they were torn up pretty bad. One arm was almost gone, and he kept trying to sort of push it back into place with the other.

The four Marines rushed up to him with Wan kicking away his M-8. Ryck automatically started to reach for some ties to secure the man when T-Rex reached forward and pulled up on the man's helmet. He looked like a flick pirate with his unshaven, ratty face. Central casting could not have done better. He looked up at T-Rex and raised his good, or at least not as bad arm, in surrender.

T-Rex calmly put the M99 against the man's forehead and pulled the trigger.

Ryck had almost forgotten. With SOG, there were no prisoners. This went against everything they had been taught since T3 back at recruit training. Ryck didn't like it. They were supposed to be the good guys, the ones upholding law and order. But he understood the orders and would comply if put in that situation. He just hoped he wouldn't have to.

The pirate's body floated back, blood making a string of small globes that were surprisingly beautiful. The little red planets kept going for another two meters before suddenly falling and splattering on the deck to pool there.

With a clear view on where the artificial gravity was working again, the four Marines twisted around so they could land on their feet as they hit that section. Ryck took a moment to glance at his telltale. Smitty's team and already branched off, and Cpl Julio's team was in trace, ready to exploit that mission, which was the point of main effort for this section of the ship as the most logical place for captives to be held. Ryck knew that Sparta would be in pretty constant comms with Sgt PT, SSgt England, and the lieutenant, but too many on the net confused things, so Wan, T-Rex, and he were off the circuit. The comms AI would kick in if Sparta's comms went down for any reason, or if the AIs or the command decided they needed to be brought in. On one hand, Ryck was glad of that. He could focus on his mission, and focus on the other three Marines in his team. On the other hand, he wished he knew what else was going on in the assault. Were the pirates killing the captives? Were they fighting back? Not like the lone pirate T-Rex had blown away, but with any semblance of tactics?

With gravity again, the four Marines rushed forward and were at the berthing hatch within moments. T-Rex reached forward and gently pushed on the entry switch. To all of their surprise, the door rose with a rush. It took all of them a split second to realize that they would not have to breach into the space. Sparta and Wan rushed in first, followed by T-Rex and Ryck. Sparta and Wan split to each side, getting down low while Ryck and T-Rex went in high.

The space was chaos. The bunks were all deployed. This was Berthing 4-19, one of the two male third-class berthing spaces. The bunks folded up and were retracted into the overhead during waking hours. This left space for the passengers to relax, watch flicks, read, or whatever. During sleep hours, all or some of the berths would be lowered, three bunks to a column. With the bunks deployed, there was only a narrow passage between the bunks, a small common area, and a hatch to the heads.

From the main hatch, the passage was twice as wide as those between the bunks, and it lead right to the common area. The first thing Ryck saw was the body of a man, hands tied behind him and a blindfold over his head, lying on his side. The blood pooling under his head did not bode well for his condition.

Ryck jumped when someone, or something, slammed into his legs. He swung his weapon around, ready to blast, barely holding back when the hands tied behind the man's back and the blindfold that had fallen to around his neck registered. The man looked up in resigned despair, a look which slowly shifted as he took Ryck in.

"Help me!" the man shouted, wiggling out from between the bunks and scooting in back of Ryck.

Wan was just in front of Ryck, and when the man appeared, he turned back. He and Ryck caught each other's eyes, then hunkered down in unison, looking for the reason the man was asking for help. In front of them, cursing as he struggled to get through the bunks, was an armed, armored man. He fell between the bunks with a thud, only one bunk's width away from the two Marines. He started forward again, only then seeing that it wasn't his target in front of him, but two Federation Marines. With a curse, he struggled to bring up his Freelancer, the muzzle catching on the bunk in front of him.

With him prone like that, not much of what was facing the two Marines was unprotected. Except for his neck. If he'd been standing upright, his neck would have been protected by his armor. However, on his belly, under his visor, there was a gap. Ryck and Wan opened up on that gap. At a meter or so, there was no way they could miss.

The man's armor was pretty good quality, from the look of it. It wasn't Federation-made, but then, pirates didn't recognize borders. Being well made, it could stop a dart. From the outside, as designed, but also from the inside. The two Marines each put several darts into the man's neck where they ricocheted back and forth inside the armor, slicing him to ribbons. He simply collapsed like a deflating balloon.

"To your right!" shouted Sparta, the circuit compensators bringing his volume down a few decibels before the two Marines heard it over their helmet speakers.

The command was not very exact, and he hadn't addressed it to anyone in particular, but both Wan and Ryck reacted, ignoring the still-tied captive as they rushed forward to a passage, then tried to force their EVA suits through it. The suits were not particularly bulky, but what they added made pushing through the bunks difficult. As they swung to the right, they flanked a pirate who was holding a man in front of him, an unrecognizable handgun of some sort to the man's head. Like the other two pirates, he also had on armor. This was out of the ordinary. From pirate culture, armor was considered coward's gear. In the flicks, pirates thought that armor was not manly. Fiction or not, flicks impacted opinion, and pirates tended to ape what was shown.

Unlike modern Federation personnel armor, which tended to be flexible plates that were attached to or inserted inside of clothing, all three pirates had outer shells. That didn't mean the armor was not effective. All that meant was that they probably acquired it outside of Federation space.

The pirate to their left had what looked to be newer armor, but either he didn't have a helmet or hadn't a chance to put it on before the four Marines burst the space. His clean-shaven face and perfectly-groomed blonde hair gave him a look far different from that of the first pirate, an indication that this group was multi-cultural.

As Ryck and Wan arrived, the man spun first towards them, then back towards Sparta and T-Rex, who had their weapons trained on him.

"Stop, or . . . " he began.

"Or" what, the Marines could guess, but never know for sure as Wan calmly put a couple of darts over the shoulder of the captive passenger and into the pirate's handsome blonde head. The tiny turn the pirate made back to Sparta and T-Rex gave the lance corporal all the opening he needed.

The captive stood still as the pirate fell back. He slowly turned around, hands still tied behind him, and stared at the dead man for a moment before taking a step forward and leveling a powerful kick at the corpse's head.

"There's three more," he said matter-of-factly to the four Marines.

"Wan, did you get anyone else?" Sparta asked.

"One down," Wan replied.

"Where are the others?" Sparta asked, his external speakers broadcasting his voice into the compartment so any captives could hear.

It was only then that Ryck really noticed the other four bodies on the deck, all with their hands tied, all executed. He hadn't been able to see them from the front hatch, and his attention had been on the pirate when they'd gotten up there.

"Over here!" a voice shouted out from within the deployed bunks to their left. "There's one of them here!"

A heavy report sounded out from that direction, followed by a cry of pain and sounds of somebody crashing around the bunks. At the same time, a finger of lightning reached out from between the bunks to their right, splashing across Sparta's EVA suit.

Someone had a plasma weapon over there, but this was a case where the EVA suits had an advantage over skins and bones. All the plasma had to do was to touch open skin, and it would essentially short-circuit the body's nervous system. It acted like it had a life of its own when it stuck, seeking out the ground through a living body. It could be devastating to Marines in just their standard combat armor. To an EVA suit, though, it had no effect.

The crewman they'd just saved dropped to the ground, whether kissed by the plasma or not, Ryck couldn't take the time to check as he and Wan instinctively spun towards the sounds on the other side of the space. They split on each side of a line of bunks, then sprinted forward, trusting the other two Marines to take out the plasma pirate.

The berthing space was not really that big. Any hanger was much larger. But with the bunks deployed and blocking the view, it seemed pretty vast. Ryck tried to keep abreast with Wan, glancing through the bunks to keep even with him. Blood covered the deck about eight or nine bunks down from the common area. Ryck took a quick glance at the bottom bunk where a man had dragged himself. A huge chunk of the man's side was simply gone. The man was struggling to breath, and Ryck knew he needed medical care ASAP.

"One friendly WIA, needs immediate care," he hit on the medical circuit, knowing the AI would add Ryck's position.

That was about all he could do for the man at the moment. A sudden boom sounded, and the rack between Wan and him simply exploded. The concussion hit Ryck, actually pushing him aside a few centimeters.

"What the hump was that?" Wan asked on Ryck's direct circuit as both Marines hit the deck.

Even though the EVA suits were not particularly bulky, they were not made for crawling around under gravity. The helmet's design made looking forward while prone difficult, and the power packs, thrusters, and oxi cells added bulk to the back. Ryck wished they had stopped to get out of the EVA suits and into skins and bones after the breach, but with the time crunch, EVA suits in the attack it was.

Another blast sounded over them, raining bits of bunks down like dirty snow. Whatever the pirate had for a weapon, it was pretty big.

"He's heading for the front hatch!" Wan said. "We've got to stop him before he gets there."

"Cpl Pallas, can you cut this guy off? He's trying to get out the front," Wan passed on the team circuit.

"Negative, Wan. We've got our hands full here. You two take him," Sparta responded.

Wan glanced over at Ryck across the bottom rack that separated the two of them and said, "You heard the man. I don't know what the hump that bastard's got with him for sure, but I think it's like our bunker buster. Whatever it is, we can't let him get away. I want you to flank him. On three, you scoot through these racks, keeping your ass low. I'm gonna get up, hit the bulkhead up ahead, and rush the arsehole. Iffen you get a shot, take him out while he's glommed onto me."

"Oh, man! You sure? Maybe we both need to rush him, so he has to choose a target, you know, confuse him until we light him up," Ryck said.

"Nah, this is the way it's gonna be. Iffen what he has is a bunker buster, you know the range is limited, and it's about as accurate as throwing rotten apples. And you know the Wan man. I can move it. I'll be juking and jiving, so no way he hits me. You just be sure to nail him."

He slowly reached up and hit the helmet release. There was a hiss as the slight overpressure inside the suit puffed out into the ship. He lifted the helmet up and placed it on the deck, detaching the comms buds and sliding them into his ears. This was against policy. If the ship suffered a catastrophic breach, Wan would have only seconds to find a pressurized space.

He shrugged at Ryck's questioning look and whispered, "Gotta be loose and light, you know."

He held up his hand, then counted down three, two, one with his fingers. On one, he stood up and rushed forward to the compartment bulkhead, five more bunk-lengths ahead. At the same time, Ryck turned to dive over the bottom rack next to him. After clearing it, he gathered his feet to dive over the next one. He barely noticed another body as he passed it. At least the guy hadn't died like a sheep at the slaughter. He'd tried to get away.

Just as he cleared the third rack, a huge boom sounded, and flames shot down the passage along the bulkhead. That pinpointed the pirate for him. He was just on the other side of the next line of bunks. Ryck slid over the next bunk and looked up.

The pirate standing in front of him was not in some hodgepodge body armor. He was fully protected with black, interlaced, external plates that looked like ceramosteel. Ryck didn't recognize the actual make, but it was doubtful that is was Federated or Brotherhood-made.

There were two main trains of thought on body armor. The Federation went with flexible inserts that reacted within a split instant upon impact, hardening to stop a projectile before reverting back to its original state. The armor was far more comfortable than plate armor and was better at stopping solid projectiles. Plate armor, on the other hand, relied on sandwiched materials that were strong enough to withstand modern projectiles. The PICSs relied on plate armor, but they were big enough and powerful enough to carry pretty heavy plates. It was easier to make plate armor, and it didn't have to be custom made for each soldier. It was actually better for protection against some energy weapons. However, it was bulky and heavy, and even with exoskeletal assists, it limited mobility.

The armor was the first thing Ryck noticed. The second thing was the stubby tube-like weapon the pirate was holding. Wan was probably correct in that it was the pirate version of the Marine's M-77 Bunker Buster. The bunker buster was designed to break or penetrate hardened targets. It sent a focused energy "shell-less shell" that would shoot forward and either re-focus that energy into a shape charge or simply explode in a blast ring. Due to the physics of energy dissipation, it had a very limited range of about 5 meters with a huge drop off in effectiveness beyond that. Within 5 meters, not much could withstand its power. It could even take out a Davis from point-blank range. Due to its power, it was almost never used aboard a ship. It could easily rupture the ship's skin, opening it up to vacuum.

Evidently the pirate was not too concerned about that. They were only a deck away from the skin of the ship, but that was far enough, along with whatever was between the weapon and the ship's skin, to keep the pirate from creating the rupture.

Bunker busters were not made for man-to-man fighting. The weapon was not very accurate, and there was a considerable re-charge time. The Marine Corps M-77, for example, carried six charges in a load, and each one took approximately 12 seconds to cycle and recharge. That was fine when taking on a hardened target, but not so fine when the shooter's target was men who were attacking him.

The pirate was looking down the passage alongside the bulkhead. Even in with the pirate in his armor, Ryck could see that he was focused on something, yet he was not scrambling to either move or fire again. The only conclusion Ryck had was that Wan had been hit.

Ryck didn't know how much time he had before the pirate's weapon would be re-charged. Just because the Marine Corps weapon needed 12 seconds didn't mean that the pirate's was the same. Instinct took over. He knew time would be tight, so he got to his feet and started charging the pirate, M-99 on full auto. He could see the impacts of the darts on the pirate's armor as they ricocheted off without effect. Ryck needed something heavier, but as the assault element with speed of an essence, they had gone in light. T-Rex had an M-72 on his back, and that might be able to knock out the pirate, but T-Rex was otherwise engaged.

Ryck kept charging as the pirate swung ponderously around to see who was attacking him. Ryck couldn't see the man in back of the dark helmet visor, but he kept pumping out rounds in hopes that one would find a crease or weak spot in the man's armor.

The pirate brought up his weapon, aiming from the hip, the 20-centimeter barrel looking huge as it pointed at him. For a moment, Ryck thought he'd be able to reach him before he fired, physically tackling the man. Just a step away, the weapon went off, a flash of light blinding Ryck as something struck him hard along his right side. He wasn't even aware of being thrown back, of his right arm and two fingers of his left hand being turned to hamburger. He wasn't aware of when his EVA, acting on the breach, closed the torn sleeve and gauntlet, slicing away the mangled flesh that used to be his right arm and left fingertips. The EVA didn't care if it was in a vacuum or on a pressurized ship. If the suit was breached, it acted to seal the breach and keep integrity.

A sense of lassitude crept over him as drugs were injected into his body, drugs meant to calm him and slow down his respirations. In space, this made sense, lowering a Marine's oxygen intake until someone could rescue him.

He looked up to see the black armored creature approach him. The huge dragon stood over him, ready to breath fire again. He settled back to watch the show, but something wouldn't let him relax.

*NO!*

He fought the pull into the cottony dreamland. That was not a dragon. That was a pirate, a man just waiting until his weapon cycled before he would end Ryck's life. Ryck had to do something. He tried to push back, to get away, but he barely moved a few centimeters before the pirate stepped forward, foot on Ryck's leg, holding him in place.

The pirate held up his weapon, looking at something, probably a gauge that would indicate when the thing was charged. Ryck reached out to grab his M-99, but there was nothing with which to reach. It was only then that he realized his right arm was gone. Surprisingly, that didn't bother him. He knew it should, but he just brushed it off. Those had to be some pretty good drugs.

Ryck was at a loss. Would T-Rex come charging in, M-77 ablazing to save the day? Or would the fire from the pirate snuff out Ryck's life.

*Fire. T-Rex. What was the connection?*

Then it hit him. As the pirate stared at his weapon's display, waiting, Ryck reached with his left hand to his hip magazine. He flipped it open and reached inside. Something was off with his touch, how his hand was working, but he wasn't sure just what. When he felt something give, though, he knew he had it.

Pulling out his toad, he thumbed the fuse just as the pirate nodded and started to lower his weapon. Ryck casually flipped the toad up into the air. Even drugged, though, he realized he'd thrown it up behind the pirate, where it would fall in back of him, not to where it would hit him. He had lost. But the pirate was not going to shoot Ryck from point-blank range. He took a step back. Ryck was looking up as the toad started its descent. It passed just behind the pirate's head and out of sight. Ryck knew the entire sequence was only three seconds from when he had thumbed the toad, but with the drugs, time was extended. Everything was in slow motion.

The pirate finished his step back and raised his bunker buster. Ryck watched dispassionately for the fire to erupt from the weapon, and when he saw a flare of light, his muggy brain thought it was from the pirate's bunker buster, that Ryck had lost. But the light was from behind the pirate's back, up around the shoulder level. The pirate hesitated and tried to turn, one hand reaching up and in back of him. The next flash was when the toad ate through the armor plate. For an instant, Ryck thought he saw the pirate's face through the man's armor visor, lit from within as a small, intensely hot star burned through his body.

Then Ryck went to sleep.

# *Alexander*
# *Camp Kolesnikov*

## *Chapter 20*

Ryck opened his eyes. His stomach was growling, crying out for food. He had to get some breakfast to quiet it down. He tried to stretch, but his hands would not move. Confused, he turned his head to his left. His hand stretched out from him, but imprisoned in some sort of restraint. Thoughts of pirates, of fighting, of death suddenly flashed through his head. He had to get out of there!

"Easy there, cowboy," a familiar voice called out as Ryck struggled to get up.

It wasn't until the person who spoke moved forward that he realized who it was. T-Rex, put a hand on Ryck's chest, calming him.

"What . . . ?" Ryck stammered as it all came back to him—the mission, the fight, him being hit.

He quickly looked over to his right arm, or at least to where his right arm should have been. Instead of an arm, the stubby chamber of the regen seeder was attached to his shoulder. A steady green light was the only sign that it was doing its job.

He looked back to his left arm. Most of the arm was intact, but the hand itself was covered by a small regen chamber. To his surprise, he wasn't horrified. He knew he was drugged—the chance for a successful regen was significantly increased when the immunosuppressants were employed. Still, he felt he should be more shocked instead of just mildly curious.

"You OK, there?" T-Rex asked.

"I . . . I guess so. Where are we? We on the *Adelaide*?"

"Not hardly! We're back on the Dirtball. Home sweet home. You've been out of it for two weeks, and they just let you wake up now," T-Rex said, nodding towards the foot of the hospital bed where a nurse stood, watching Ryck closely.

Ryck tried to organize his thoughts. Of course he would have been put into an induced coma. They'd been well-informed on what would happen if they had to go through regen. A coma during the initial stages of regen helped the process catch better and helped ensure a more complete outcome.

"A couple of the guys came to see you wake up, but you took your own sweet time with it. They went to the geedunk[19] and the head while you were napping," he told them.

"So what happened?"

"With you?" T-Rex asked. "You took on that pirate, zeroed him, but he kind of got you, too. Doc Silvestrie came in, got you stabilized, and you were zip-locked back to the *Adelaide* even before the ship was secured."

"What about Wan? Is he OK?"

Some of the spark left T-Rex's eyes as he said, "Wan Man didn't make it. Doc got him out before you, and he was put into stasis. He made it back here to the Dirtball, but he just couldn't hang on."

Ryck looked up at T-Rex uncomprehendingly. People just didn't die if they made it to stasis. "Stasis" wasn't really an actual suspension of the body, but it came pretty close. Fluids were pumped into the circulatory system, and the body was cooled, taking it down to a bare minimum of metabolic activity. If a wounded person made it that far, then he could almost always be saved once he reached a full-service medical facility. The Dirtball, as home to both a Navy fleet and a Marine division, had one of the best.

"The Wan Man fought, but the docs, they just couldn't save him," T-Rex said.

Ryck needed to change the subject until he was able to digest that, so he asked about the mission itself. T-Rex gave the nurse a pointed stare. The nurse checked Ryck's vitals, then took the hint and left. Technically, the nurse was Navy, but he almost assuredly did not have a clearance for tactical operations.

"We took back the ship," T-Rex started once the nurse was out of the room. "Two Marines KIA, Wan and SSgt Piers over in Second Platoon. Another 12 WIA, three others like you going through regen."

"The passengers?"

---

[19] **Geedunk**: Snack bar.

"312 passengers and crew out of 375 rescued. Most OK. The dead, well . . . " he began, stopping to look around to see if there was anyone within earshot before continuing. "Sgt Marc's squad from Second, they might have taken out five or six passengers, from what I've heard. The pirates had them dressed in that shitty armor, and they got zeroed when Marc took that compartment. The pirates, they got dressed like the tourists, trying to blend in. There's an investigation going on, and Marc's ass is on the line."

"They tried to blend in, to get away? That doesn't sound like SOG."

"No, it doesn't. And that's not all. Some of their combat armor, it was Alliance gear, new stuff. The scuttlebutt is that they weren't SOG at all, even if that's what's on the news feeds."

"He's awake! About fucking time," Sams said as he came in with Hu, Sparta, Smitty, and another Marine Ryck didn't recognize.

"Eat me," Ryck said automatically. "And who's that?" he asked, pointing with his chin at the new Marine.

"That's our new boot. Private Hamburger. Came in to take your place while you fuck off," Sams replied.

"I keep telling you, it's Helmesburgen, not Hamburger," the private objected.

"Shut up, boot!" the other Marines said in unison.

"You OK?" Cpl Pallas asked.

"Hungry as shit. You got anything there?" Ryck asked, looking at the burger Hu was munching.

"Yeah, don't I know it. I thought I would die of starvation when I regened my foot, but you got to eat their puke-slop to make your arm grown nice and strong. Just be glad you're not Lieutenant Badalato. He lost all his guts, everything from the belly button down Cut in frigging half. When they let him wake up, it's IVs in the arm for at least a year before his new stomach can take real food."

"You're quite the talk of the town, you know," Sams said. "Burning pirate ass with a toad. That's some freakin' shit. Most copacetic!"

"Well, he burned out his neck, at least," Hu corrected.

"No, I was there, and I saw the body. Sams has it right. Burned his *ass*. The armor that bad boy was wearing kept his stinking corpse upright enough for the toad to burn all the way down to his ass, then out the armor again. Unbelievable!" the fire team leader said.

"How did you decide to use the toad?" Hamburger asked.

"Shut up, boot!" the others chorused again.

"That was pretty bitchin'. No fucking arm, and you decide to play catch with him," Sams said.

"You didn't do too bad yourself, PFC Samuelson," Sparta said.

"PFC? You just got busted down to private." Ryck said.

"Ah, no big deal," he said before Hu cut in.

"Our esteemed dickwad here led the charge into the galley just at the pirates started to execute the captives. He took out two of them with his M77, then tackled the third, I mean bam!" Hu said, getting excited. "He's going all psycho on the guy. And this guy, he's got some of that new Alliance combat armor, but he can't do nothing, 'cause this beserker's all over him. Sams here, he saved a bunch of the passengers, and the captain, when he comes in and we show him the vid, he promotes him on the spot. Takes away his brig time, too."

"No shit?" asked Ryck in wonderment.

"It wasn't quite like that," Sams protested.

"I'll show you the vid next time I come," Hu said.

"OK, OK. We've got to get going. Someone will come back to check on you after evening chow, but you need anything now?" Sparta asked Ryck.

"Uh, yeah, but this is sorta weird. I can't move my arms now, and my nose is really getting to me. It's itching up pretty good. Could one of you, you know, give it a scratch?"

The other Marines broke out laughing, but the corporal moved forward, reaching up to gently scratch Ryck's nose.

"None of you've been through regen, so you don't know what it's like," he said.

"Just make sure that's all you do, there, corporal. Ryck never got to get that ho in Vegas, and it's been a *long* time, so don't you go getting any ideas on getting him off, what with his hands out of action like that," Sams shouted.

"Oh, man, he can't even jack off!" Hu joined in. "I bet that nurse out there, he'll do it for you, Ryck, so don't you worry. I'll go ask him now, to make sure he takes good care of you!"

That brought out howls of laughter, even Ryck joining in. He hadn't yet really thought about life without his arms for a good amount of time, but leave it to Marines to bring it up, and bring it down in the gutter.

"Something funny in here?" a voice broke through the din.

"Attention on deck" Hu shouted as the battalion commanding officer and sergeant major stepped into the room.

Despite himself, Ryck struggled to get up.

"At ease," the colonel said as he walked up to Ryck before turning around to face the others. "Sergeant Major, I think these men want that nurse out there to come in. Did we hear that right?" he asked the Marines.

There was a heavy silence as the men seemed afraid to catch anyone else's eyes.

The sergeant major glowered at them for a moment before breaking out in a laugh.

"Sorry, sir, I couldn't hold it in any longer. You had them shitting in their pants," he said to the CO.

"Just Marines looking out for each other, as it should be, Sergeant Major, as it should be. PFC Samuelson, though, seems to have a thing with the ladies, so maybe he could do better than that fat nurse out there."

There was more dead silence, and Sams snuck a look at Sparta.

"The colonel told a joke, men. Laugh!" the sergeant major said.

There was a ragged volley of forced laughter.

That elicited a hearty laugh from the colonel himself.

"OK, sergeant major, you've had your fun, so enough yanking on their chains. We're here to check on Lysander, after all," he said, turning back towards Ryck. "You've just been brought out of your coma, right? Still a bit murky, I bet, and you're probably starving."

"Yes, sir," Ryck answered.

"I've been through it myself, three times, so I know what it's like."

Everyone knew the colonel's history. He was a mustang, up from the ranks, from private to first sergeant, then to lieutenant and on up to lieutenant colonel. He wore the Navy Cross, the second highest award for valor. Earning that medal had cost him both arms and legs as well as a good portion of his torso. That the Navy docs had saved his life was something of a miracle, and he had spent a full two years in regen and therapy, so yes, Ryck was well aware that the colonel "knew what it was like."

"You'll get fed after we leave, but it won't be good. These Navy docs must think that decent taste ruins the process. Before that starts, though, the sergeant major has something for you.

"Sergeant Major, if you will, and let's bring in these reprobates here, too."

The sergeant major pulled a stack of paper cups from his cargo pocket and passed them around to the Marines. He took a tube from under his sleeve and poured something out of it into each cup. He gave another to the colonel and took one for himself before moving to Ryck and offering him the end of the tube. Just before Ryck put it in his mouth, he pulled it back a fraction of a centimeter and waited.

"Gentlemen, needless to say, this does not go beyond this room.

"Lift your glasses for a toast. To Private First Class Ryck Lysander, *Audaces Fortuna Iuvat.*"

"Here, here!" they all chorused as the sergeant major slid the tube into Ryck's mouth.

Ryck took a long swallow, the cold beer feeling wonderful as it slid past his tongue and down his throat. Alcohol was explicitly prohibited throughout the regen process, but if the colonel, with all his regen, thought it was OK, Ryck was not going to argue.

The colonel leaned forward and quietly said, "You're going to be OK, Ryck. Semper fi."

And Ryck knew it was true. He *was* going to be OK.

## Chapter 21

Ryck sat at the test bench, watching the results on the PI-530. He didn't really need to be there. The process was automated. Once the test was initiated, each PICS was pulled out of its locker, trundled over to the bench, and subjected to the tiny pulses the 530 threw at it.

The PICS was high tech. It might be over 50-year-old tech, but high nonetheless. And that required constant maintenance. The 530 was just one of the tools in the armorer's box to keep the PICS in top working condition. This piece of test equipment sent tiny pulses into the skin of the PICS, testing the kickbacks. Each kickback had to react within 10,000$^{th}$ of a second, firing back at the incoming projectile or pulse. Coupled with the integrity of the LTC array armor itself, the kickbacks helped the PICS to withstand 20mm cannon fire or 6mm hypervelocity rounds. They only helped marginally to pulse weapon strikes, but the PICS had other defenses for those.

The PICS being tested belonged to Corporal Timothy Brown in Golf Company. Golf was the "heavy" company in the battalion, with each Marine and corpsman having a suit. Ryck had been in Fox, where only one squad would be suited up if the mission required it. Ryck had seen Brownie out and about, but other than one group conversation on the NFL, he never really had any contact with him.

Ryck had been transferred to H & S, to the Rehab Platoon (the "Sick, Lame, and Lazy Platoon") once he had gotten out of the hospital, and while he still hung out with the guys, he did not train or work with them. Fox had been out on a routine show-the-flag mission to Barrow to help celebrate their Landing Day, so for the last two weeks, he hadn't even had them around. He knew they had returned the night before, but no one had stopped by. It was great when he was around them, but with new guys coming in, and with him on his eighth month since being wounded, he felt like he was being forgotten

The green light flashed, and the numbers popped on the screen. Brownie's suit was at 98.7%, good enough for government work. Ryck reached out with his left hand and hit the approve button. Brownie's suit was trundled back to its locker and another was taken out. Ryck knew he really wasn't necessary for the test. The lab was fully capable of automatically rejecting or accepting test results. This was make-work. This was a result of the psych docs who insisted that all servicemen and women in regen be given work as soon as it was feasible. It was supposed to make them feel needed. On one hand, Ryck thought that was so much BS. No one doubted that Ryck was hurt. His right arm, now three-quarters grown, was proof of that. But still, the "Sick, Lame, and Lazy" label didn't make him feel very good, nor the "gen hens" nickname, even if those undergoing regen used that term among themselves. On the other hand, he could have done worse. Some of the other gen hens were pushing papers, monitoring chow, or other thrilling, exciting jobs. At least Ryck was still peripherally associated with combat, and both CWO2 Slyth, the Fox Company armorer and CWO4 Heng, the battalion armorer, had taken him under their wings, teaching him quite a bit about not only the PICS suits, but also all the battalion's weapons. Ryck was still infantry through-and-through, but the weapons were pretty brills.

It also helped that CWO4 Heng had a prosthetic hand. It had only been his second regen, and it had gone well at first, but the regen had failed at the wrist. Hands were more difficult than arms, for reasons beyond Ryck's understanding, but still, a partial regen was rare. Heng had petitioned to remain a Marine, and it was granted. His prosthetic was pretty amazing, but still, the Corps rarely approved such requests, and only when the petitioner had a mission that he could accomplish. Of course, CWO4 Heng's four, yes, four Platinum Stars, might have helped in that.

With Heng on his mind, Ryck looked at the regen sleeve on his right arm. This was his fourth sleeve. As his arm grew longer, he went up a size. This one looked to end right about where his wrist would be. He wondered if he would have problems with the hand just as Heng had. He was scheduled for a full scan in two days. Maybe the docs would tell him something then.

Actually, his regen had progressed unremarkably. Sure, he had phantom pain and itching with his missing arm, but not to any great extent. His left fingers, though, had been another story. The itch had driven him crazy. With the regen process, the nerves re-knitting caused prickling for most people, and nothing could be done to stop the cause of the itching. Only treating the symptoms could be done, and with only varying degree of effectiveness.

His regen for his left fingers was technically completed, but he wore a special glove to protect the tips. It was skin tight, so it didn't get in the way of his using the hand. Being one-handed sure beat being no-handed.

"Happy birthday, Marine," CWO4 Heng said, sticking his head in the test lab.

"Happy birthday to you, too," Ryck said.

"You know, the pageant starts in about 20, and the armory is officially off duty now. You coming?" the Heng asked.

"Uh, yeah, sure. I just wanted to get some things finished up here," Ryck said.

In all truth, Ryck hadn't planned to watch the pageant. He couldn't get out of the mess night that was scheduled for the evening, but he figured he could skip the pageant without anyone noticing. He wasn't in the mood to watch the units march in review. While he was holed up in the hospital, Fox and Echo had conducted yet another live op, the takedown of the so-called "Kingdom of Morvania." That was three live ops since Ryck had come aboard, which was pretty amazing for a "peacetime" Corps. Joshua, who had gone to the supposedly premier First Marine Division, had yet to go into harm's way. While Joshua was jealous of Ryck's experiences, Ryck had only been on two of Fox's ops. He'd been lying flat on his back in his hospital bed when the company had answered the call to battle.

CWO4 Heng was waiting, though, so Ryck stopped the 530 and powered it down. Together, they walked down the passage and logged out.

"Happy birthday, Marines," the sailor manning Post 4 said as they came up. Post 4 was manned around the clock, but for the Marine birthday, the sailors at the Naval Air detachment usually took over some of the vital posts to let the Marines enjoy the celebration.

The gunners mate who had taken the post was huge, muscles upon muscles. His obsidian skin was in stark contrast to his Navy whites, and his smile notwithstanding, Ryck got the feeling that he could take on a Marine in a PICS even in just his skivvies. He had no doubt that the armory was in good hands.

The two Marines made their way through the various support buildings, past the regimental headquarters, and out to the parade deck. They skirted the brass, Navy and Marine, the Legion reps, and all the civilian bigwigs in the center section of the bleachers and made their way to the far right to join the other peons. In front of them, the entire regiment and attachments were waiting in formation.

Most Marines celebrated three birthdays in the course of an Earth year. The first was on February 27, commemorating the founding of the Infantería de Marina back in 1537. There had been an unbroken line of service since then, so that was considered the birthdate of the modern Marines. The celebration on Feb 27 tended to be subdued, with memorials for those who had fallen over the years. The most telling moment was when the names of those who had fallen that year were "read out," that is, their names announced as they joined the list of absent comrades.

The second birthdate was November 10th. This was the date when the Federation Marines were officially stood up. That this was also the anniversary of the date of the US Marine Corps was not lost on anyone, but with the largest contribution to the new Marine Corps, the Americans had held some sway. Politics were not absent in matters of the military. This birthday was more celebratory. The pageant was one of the main events, the mess night the other. Free flowing drink and hearty companionship were the orders of the day.

The third birthday varied by unit. With four Marine divisions, each with four regiments (three infantry and one combat support) that made 48 combat battalions in the Corps. Coincidently, there were 48 separate Marine Corps that joined to form the Federation Marines. While not official at first, each battalion "adopted" one of the old corps. They flew the colors, they kept the artifacts, and they celebrated the founding of that corps. Ryck's regiment, the Ninth Marines, were the "South East Asia Marines." First Battalion had Thailand's Royal Thai Marine Corps. Second battalion, Ryck's battalion, had the Philippines Marine Corps, and Third Battalion had Indonesia's Korps Marinir. On their adopted corps' birthdays, they would serve traditional food from that contributing nation. During the last birthday for Second Battalion, the Philippines had even sent traditional dancers for the celebration. Ryck had been still in the hospital, but the dancers had made the rounds to all the gen hens.

Of course, First Battalion, First Marines had claimed the US Marines, and 3/1[20] had claimed the Infantería de Marina, but that was a waste, as far as Ryck was concerned. It was like having a personal birthday on Christmas.

Ryck had missed the last battalion party, but no one, if it was at all possible, missed the big celebration. Several ambulances pulled up, and the most of the non-ambulatory Marines and one corpsman were wheeled out. Ryck caught the eye of LCpl Jonas Greenstein and nodded a greeting over the heads of the other spectators. Jonas had badly broken his back in a hover accident and had been Ryck's hospital suitemate for several months until Ryck was discharged back to the battalion. Even with most of his body intact, it was still going to be awhile until his nervous system re-knitted itself.

"Here we go," CWO4 Heng said as the regimental commander stood up and approached the reviewing stand, the sergeant major one step behind and to his left.

Back at Camp Otrakovskiy, outside of St. Petersburg, with the division headquarters and two of the regiments, the division commanding general would be the reviewing officer. This year, the assistant commanding general had gone all the way out to Camp Dneprovskiy and Tenth Marines to be their reviewing officer. That meant Col Pierre didn't have anyone from higher headquarters horning in on the regiment's celebration.

---

[20] **3/1**: Marine shorthand for Third Battalion, First Marine Regiment. 3/4 would be Third Battalion, Fourth Marine Regiment.

With the CO in place, the band slowly marched from behind the formed units. Only the lone drummer kept beat. When it reached in front of the formation, it wheeled about to face the CO. The band commander, who was actually a sergeant in First Battalion, raised his baton and waited.

"Regiment, atten . . . hut!" the adjutant shouted from off to the left of the reviewing stand.

There was the swish and slap of close to 7,000 Marines and sailors coming to attention.

"Sir, the regiment is formed!" the adjutant shouted out, his voice only slightly breaking at the end.

"Very well," came the reply, not as loud, but clear to those in the stands.

With that, the band commander's baton came down, and the band kicked into the Federation national anthem. Everyone in the stands stood up, those in uniform saluting, the rest with their hands over their hearts.

Next came the Marine Corps Hymn, then the Navy Hymn, followed by the Foreign Legion's Le Boudin. Finally, Alexander's planetary anthem was played. Ryck was glad when the last verse of the Dirtball anthem finished that he wasn't back at Camp Otrakovskiy. As the division headquarters, there would be many more foreign dignitaries, and each one would have his or her anthem played.

As the band finished, the adjutant marched out to the center and read the citation. Each year, the commandant sent out his message, and each year, it was read out at pageants and mess nights. Ryck tuned it out.

With the formalities over, the pageant itself could begin. The spectators sat down, the Parade of Marines led it off. This was Ninth Marines, so the Marines dressed in the uniforms of the Thai, Philippines, and Indonesian Marines were the first to march by. Ryck was surprised to see that it was Sams, LCpl Samuelson now, in the Philippines Marines uniform. Sams had been busted to private only a year before, but he was already back up to lance corporal and the new fair-haired child of the company. Sams and Ryck had two of the four Battle Citation 3s awarded for actions on the *Robin*, but then Sams had gone and earned a BC1 fighting the Kingdom of Morenvia. The so-called King had declared sovereignty for the island nation of Lesia on Glorywall. The only problem was that the people of Lesia had no intention of letting some outsider in, and "Merlin the First" had taken over 500 children hostage to ensure the cooperation of the people. Two Marine companies had gone in to secure the situation. Against only 30-40 "royal militia," it should have been and was a cakewalk. Despite this, Sams had managed to distinguish himself in the rescue of the kids, from all reports saving their lives. From women on Atacama to prisoners on the *Robin* to children on Glorywall, Sams seemed to have a thing for the civilians.

He was grinning ear-to-ear as he marched down in review, smartly saluting the CO as he passed. Following the three positions of honor, Marines marched by in period uniforms for each of the other corps that had made up the Federation Marines. As tradition dictated, once all the corps had marched by, the Federation colors, followed by the Marine Corps colors, passed in review. Everyone came to their feet and saluted again. Then, the mass of Marines started to march. A couple of companies were missing due to operational commitments, but it was still impressive. Ryck hadn't wanted to come, but he felt the pride stir within him. This was a pretty potent force.

After the infantry came the armor, artillery, transport, engineers, and the rest. Recon put on a good show. They had flown up on their one-man scoots in full stealth mode. One moment, the area in front of the CO was empty, a moment later, in unison, the recon company appeared, 15 meters in the air. The crowd broke out into applause.

The reception was even better for the air pass-over. First came the Marine air. The six Storks attached to the regiment did a flyover, followed by the Hummingbird aerial recon team. A big Navy planetary transport flew by, low and slow, looking huge. The Marine Wasps drew the oohs and aahs, looking sleek and deadly. But it was the Navy Experion fighters that caused the crowd to break out in applause again. The deadly dual space and planetary fighters were impressive, to say the least. The entire pageant took over an hour, with the band, the adjutant, the sergeant major, and the CO standing at attention, never moving except for the CO when he returned a salute. To Ryck, that was more impressive than anything else.

"Well, another pageant come and gone," CWO4 Heng said.

"How many of them have you seen?" Ryck asked.

"Too many to count," was the simple reply. "You going down there to say hello to your bros?"

Ryck looked to the right where all the equipment had been set up as static displays and Marines were already milling about.

"No, sir, I don't think so. I might need a little extra time to get ready for the mess night, so I think I'm heading back to the barracks."

"OK, but make sure you are there on time. You know how that is," the chief warrant officer said.

"No problem sir. I'll be there."

Ryck made his way out of the bleachers. He said hello to Jonas and a few of the other gen hens, then quietly slipped away. He just didn't feel up to mixing with the able-bodied Marines.

## *Chapter 22*

There wasn't a facility large enough for a full regimental mess night, so the battalions had broken off to have their own. Second Battalion had rented out the Raging River Mövenpick Resort, some 50 km outside of Rostov and Camp Kolesnikov. It was out in the middle of nowhere, but that was probably all for the best.

Ryck looked across the ballroom at the gathering Marines. Despite himself, he started feeling the esprit de corps he'd felt was missing since his injury. For some reason, he almost wanted to hold onto his feeling of isolation, but he knew that was crazy. He had to just let go and enjoy himself.

"Look, there's Captain dela Grosso," Troy Simmons said, pointing to the battalion's most decorated Marine. The captain had two Navy Crosses, one of only two Marines on active duty to be so distinguished. One of those should have been a Federation Nova, most Marines thought, but still, two Navy Crosses was nothing to sneeze at.

"He's sure got a shitload of hangers," Ryck said to Troy, watching the captain make his way to his seat.

Troy was a sergeant, but among the gen hens, ranks had a tendency to fade, and first name use between ranks was pretty common.

"Yeah, him and your good buddy, Heng," Troy said. "He's got more hangers than anyone, just no Navy Crosses."

Ryck looked over next to the bar where CWO4 Heng was standing. Troy was right. Heng had to have at least 25 hangers on his chest. Ryck looked down at his own chest. He had three. There was his Combat Mission Medal with a bronze star, his Purple Heart, and his Battle Commendation Third Class. Some of the long-time Marines had upwards of 10 or 15 hangers, but still, Ryck had more than most of the non-rates.

"Recruit Lysander! Get down and give me 20" a gravelly, unforgettable voice rang out from just in back of him.

Ryck spun around to see King Tong standing there, a grin on his face. Ryck couldn't have been more surprised had an elephant walked into the room. His heart fell.

"I, uh, I can't really, I mean, my arm!" he protested.

"Relax, Lysander! I'm just messing with you," Sgt Phantawisangtong said. "So how've you been doing? I mean, I can see you took some shit, but the word is that you've been doing yourself proud."

Ryck subconsciously covered the regen chamber on this right arm with his left hand and said, "I don't know. I guess so, but really, it was no big deal."

"That's not the word on the street," King Tong said.

"Don't listen to him. He's a certified ass-kicker," Troy said, holding out his hand and introducing himself. "Troy Simmons."

"Hector Phantawisangtong, or as Lysander here will tell you, they sometimes call me 'King Tong'".

"So what are you doing here?" Ryck asked, trying to change the subject from the King Tong nickname.

"Since this is a mess night for 2/9, I guess that means I've been transferred here."

Just then, the bugler played the call to order. The Guest of Honor must have just arrived. Marines started to move to the main ballroom where the mess night would be held. King Tong made his apologies and went his own way while Ryck followed the other gen hens to a table close to the front entrance to the ballroom where they would be sitting. Three Marines in their hospital gurneys were already there, waiting for them, as well as those in wheelchairs. Ryck took the first empty seat, next to Jonas, who was at the table in his wheelchair.

There was minimal milling about as the Marines and sailors took their seats. When the CO, who was the president of the mess, called the mess to attention, eyes craned to see the guest of honor.

"Battalion, I present Corporal Lek Gutterheim, veteran of the War of the First Reach!"

All the members of the mess applauded as the frail old man, on the arm of the sergeant major, entered the mess. He was bent at the back, but his head was held high, his eyes blazing with pride.

The adjutant's voice rang out as the three made their way to the head table, "Corporal Lek Gutterheim enlisted in the Marines on February 3, 256, Standard Accounting. His first duty station was with the Alpha Company, First Battalion, Sixth Marines, Second Marine Division. He participated in three operations, rising to the rank of lance corporal, and was a fire team leader at the outbreak of the war. During the conflict, he made two opposed landings, on G-12 and Felicity. He was promoted to the rank of corporal, and after the surrender of the CALCON forces, served out the remainder of his enlistment. He returned to his home here on Alexander where he married his wife Anna, and had four children: Paul, Sarah, Allison, and Horace. Horace served 30 years in the Federation Navy, reaching a rank of master chief."

More applause sounded as the head party took their seats. The War of the First Reach had been a full-scale, ship-on-ship, opposed-landing war, not like the skirmishes and police actions since then. Entire fleets had been wiped out. Very few vets from the war were still around, and it was a privilege to have Cpl Gutterheim as their guest of honor.

Once the head party was in place, the bugler stepped forward, along with the mess butler, and called forth the beating. A palpable sense of anticipation arose among the mess. It started with loan beat of the drum outside the ballroom. A single drummer marched into the mess. A few moments later, another drummer appeared, commencing to join the first as soon as he crossed the threshold into the room. Six more drummers made their way, one-by-one, until all eight were at the center of the ballroom, right in front of the head table. They looked like robots, their arms in perfect unison as they pounded out the beating.

Ryck especially liked it when different drummers snapped their drumsticks to eye level, horizontal, and held them there for a second, before bringing them back down again to re-join the rest. This went on for about seven or eight minutes, the drummers marching in complex patterns, their beat never faltering. Ryck found himself beating out his own tattoo with his left hand on the table.

When the drummers at last finished, the mess erupted once more into cheers and applause. This was always one of the highlights of a mess night, or most any celebration. When the Federation Marines were formed, there had been some discussion on the Marine bands. The 38 Marine bands (not every corps had a band) actually performed a throw-down. The US Marine Band, with its members having music degrees, had probably been the most technically-advanced band, and it had been chosen by the brass to form the basis of the new Marine band. The Royal Marine Band, though, and in particular, the Royal Marine Drum Corps, had been the immediate favorite of the rank and file, and by popular demand, were given a place in the new corps. A US Marine Band clone was set up on Earth at Marine Headquarters, but for the divisions, it was buglers and drummers. The leopard skin worn by some Royal Marine drummers became the uniform for all drummers, something worn with pride.

Members of the band practiced in their free time. They were not professional musicians but came out of all the jobs that Marines held. The long hours they put in, all in their free time, did not bother them, and there was always a waiting list to join.

A Marine mess night was loosely based on the old Royal Navy and Marine mess nights, but the mess beating was something that was right out of 21st Century Great Britain.

The mess butler, a civilian worker for the resort, stepped up with a silver tray and two glasses of port. The senior drummer came forward to meet him at the head table. The mess president took one glass, the drummer the other. At the colonel's nod, they both lifted and emptied their glasses. Once more, applause broke out.

The colors were then marched on. Being part of the color guard was considered a great honor, but Ryck did not really know any of the four Marines who were part of this year's guard. Of course, these were all Marines who had done well in combat, and Ryck had been bedridden or worked in the armory for the past year, so that was not surprising.

With the colors emplaced, next came the citation. This could be something from past battles to great deeds, but for the birthday, it was always the same thing, a copy of the first commandant's birthday message to the Corps on its first birthday. It was read by the junior member of the mess, in this case, Private Topol Narx, all of 18 years, 256 days old. His quavering voice went through the citation, faltering twice as he spoke before the assembled mess.

There was one more ceremony before they could eat.

The president of the mess stood up, and in a loud voice of authority, ordered "Parade the beef!"

Two servers pushed a large silver tray on wheels. The top was opened up to reveal a huge prime rib roast. To Ryck, it looked like real organic beef, not a manufactured roast. His mouth started watering as the servers pushed it through the aisles. As the cart was wheeled out, the order came to take their seats.

"That was pretty copacetic," one of the Marines at the table said, someone Ryck didn't really know.

"Yeah, brills," Jonas added. "It always gets my blood pounding. Bata-tat tat! Bata-tat-tat!"

Ryck had to admit it had much the same effect on him. He looked up at the head table. Corporal Gutterheim was sitting there, his pride evident even at this distance. The man had served only one enlistment, even if it was in a full-out war. He'd had a successful career, married, had children, even grandchildren, but he seemed hold a special place in his heart for being a Marine, to wear his old uniform, to be called "Corporal Gutterheim" again.

Ryck was proud of being a Marine, too. He'd made it through recruit training when so many others hadn't. He'd proven himself under fire. It was just that lately, he didn't *feel* like a Marine. He was missing something. Looking up there at the old man, though, tweaked something deep within his consciousness. There *was* something special about being a Marine, even if he hadn't gone on a mission in over a year.

"Hey, spaceboy! Where you at, there? You gonna eat?" Troy's voice cut through his reverie.

He looked down at the salad that had appeared in front of him. The servers were busy getting everyone fed.

"Yeah, sure. I'm starving," he replied.

And he was pretty hungry. The Mövenpick had done a pretty good job with the meal. It was all pretty delicious. He joked with the others at the table, realizing that all of them were in the same boat. All were temporarily out of action, but they would all return to it. That gave them a bond of shared experience. They were not alone in that, though. Looking up at the colonel on the head table, with his four purple hearts, that was proof that people could get through it and on with their lives.

After the main courses, the birthday cake was wheeled out. It was immense. The colonel, with his sword, cut two pieces. The first was given to the guest of honor as the oldest member of the mess. The second was given to Pvt Narx as the youngest. The Mövenpick servers then descended on the cake, and in a surprisingly short amount of time, the cake was cut up and all 2,000 + Marines served a piece. With the meal itself, all the plates were cleared, leaving only the port decanters and the glasses.

"Mr. President, the port is placed," intoned the sergeant major.

This was the cue for the pouring of the port. On each table, the decanter was poured, then passed to the left, sliding the decanter along the table, never lifting it off. Three of the Marines at their table, alongside the table, to be precise, could not move their arms, and their corpsmen attendants, in their Navy full dress, were prepared to pour for them, but before the port made it around, the colonel and the guest of honor walked up, and without a word, the colonel took the decanter and poured for the three Marines. The old Marine whispered something into the ear of Chase Hannrahan, one of the immobile men. Whatever he said brought tears to Chase's eyes.

The two men walked back to the head table and waited for the sergeant major.

"Mr. President, the port is passed."

With the port passed, the toasts started. The Corps, the Marines in the corps, the sister service of the Navy, the president, the Federation, the guest of honor, the good wives of Marines . . . pretty much everyone received a toast.

The conclusion of the toasts marked the end of the formalities of the mess. The colors were marched off, and the officers and staff NCOs made their rounds, shaking hands, before leaving. For smaller unit messes, everyone might stay together for drinking and mess games, but the common understanding was that it was a little difficult for a private to let loose and have fun when there was a colonel standing there at his shoulder. The senior Marines slowly filtered out, off to drink and do whatever officers or SNCOs did in another room, leaving the main ballroom to the NCOs and non-rates.

"Gentlemen, the bar is open for an hour, courtesy of the officers," the battalion sergeant major said, pausing at the door. "Enjoy, brothers, and *audaces fortuna iuvat*."

The cheer was deafening. Some Marines rushed the bar, ready to maximize the hour. One of the servers came over to take orders for the gen hens, which made it easier. Ryck was tempted to order a glass of wine, but after the heavy port, a beer sounded better.

He was sipping on the beer, chatting with Jonas, when a voice interrupted him with. "Is this a private party, or can anyone join?"

Ryck looked up to see Sams standing there, beer in hand. He looked good in his dress blues. The BC1 he had, along with his Combat Mission Medal and BC3, especially made him stand out. It wasn't heard to see why the guy was so popular with the ladies.

"No, take a seat," Ryck said eagerly.

"Well, actually, some of the guys sent me here to see if you wanted to join us. We don't want to take you away from your new buddies," he said, indicating Jonas, "but we kinda miss your sorry ass and want to catch up."

Ryck looked to Jonas who said, "Nah, you go. I'm about ready to call it in. The busses are going to start the runs back, and I think I'll get on one."

Ryck wished Jonas a happy birthday, then followed Sams back to the Fox Company area.

" 'Bout time you showed up, you limp dick!" Smitty shouted, already well on his way to a horrendous hangover in the morning. "Let me get you another beer!"

The others shouted their welcome as well. Hu kicked out a seat which Ryck took. There were several new Marines that Ryck barely knew or didn't know at all.

"You hanging in there?" Sparta asked.

"Yeah, no problem. All's good."

"Ryck's been fingerfuckin' all the PICS," Smitty yelled out. "He's gonna jump ship and go back to fuckin' Golf, no offense," he said over his shoulder in the general direction of the Golf Company tables, "when his arm grows back."

"Hey, Smitty . . ." Sparta began, putting his hand on the other corporal's shoulder.

"You think I'm going to Golf? No, they only take the most stellar Marines, so I guess I'm stuck here with all you asshole rejects," Ryck said.

Smitty was a good guy, but a drunk was a drunk, and it was hard to know how he would take some trash talk when seven sheets to the wind.

"Hah! Yeah, motherfuckers! Fox asshole rejects! We rejected that fuckin' dumbass king, though. Let me tell you, Ryck, you are always welcome back here to Fuckin' Fox Rejects! Here, let me get you another beer."

Ryck hadn't even opened the last one Smitty had given him only a few moments before, but he took the next one, too. Sams came back with yet another beer, saw Ryck had two unopened, shrugged, and opened the one he brought and took a swig.

"You should have been with us on Barrow. I mean, it was just for a celebration. You wouldn't need your arm for that. They treated us like kings!"

"Fuck, yeah," Smitty added.

"And there was this . . ."

"No, wait," Ryck interrupted Sams. "There was this redhead, 20 years old, about 1.6 meters, big tits, who just wanted to show you around town."

"Uh, well, she was a brunette, and she was 25," he protested as the others hooted in laughter.

"He's got you pegged, Sams," Hu shouted.

"He got her the first day, but don't forget that heavy-worlder, the teacher, just before we flew out," Mabala, one of the new Marines added.

"A heavy-worlder?" Ryck asked Sams.

"And what's wrong with a heavy-worlder?" T-Rex asked.

"Nothing if he's a Marine beside you? But what, she had to outweigh him by 30, 40 kilos?"

"Ah, just remember, my mother's a heavy-worlder. Sister, too," T-Rex said without rancor.

"Well, yeah, she was heavier than me, but only by maybe 10 kilos. Real good in the sack, though," Sams said.

That started a conversation on the relative merits of women from various worlds. Ryck sat back, just happy to take it all in. It was like he'd never been gone.

In the middle of the ballroom, some Marines were playing VSTOL. They had looped a rope around one of the ballroom's rafters (a Mövenpick staff had tried to stop that, then wisely retreated leaving the Marines to the field of battle) so Marines could grab the running end while another end, the one coming down from the rafter, was tied onto a very drunk sergeant. A table was set up under the sergeant. The goal was to lower the sergeant so he landed on the table, not touching the floor. This was the VSTOL part of it, the Vertical and Short Takeoff and Landing. Not too hard. Except that other Marines were the "crosswinds." They pummeled the sergeant, grabbed and swung him, threw drinks and chairs at him, anything to get him swinging and missing the table. The landing crew had to time the swinging in order to drop him on target. Ryck watched as the landing team almost made it, only to watch the hapless sergeant bounce off the edge of the table to land hard on the floor.

Mess games had been going on for hundreds of years, although in the days of ocean navies, VSTOL was most likely not one of them. But the mess night, the celebration of who they were and of their brotherhood, that hadn't changed over the centuries.

"Hey Ryck, you had some of those conservative religious groups on your home planet, right? Didn't you tell me that? Mabala here, he says the religious girls are conservative on the outside but tigers in bed. Is that true?" Sams asked.

Ryck laughed and turned back to his friends, his brothers. He'd been down and out, a little lost at sea over the last several months. His fellow Marines had dragged him back, and he was good to go.

"Well, it's like this. Those religious girls, in their long clothes, that gets them hot in more ways than one," he started on a sea story, one probably only 10% based on truth, which for a sea story, made it practically gospel.

# *Luminosity*

## *Chapter 23*

"Biofeedback, 100%. Tamberhall, let's get the weapons pack on and run it through. Time's getting pretty short," CWO3 William Weston, the Golf Company ordinance officer told Corporal Jasper Tamberhall, one of his enlisted armorers.

LCpl Ryck Lysander patiently waited while Tamberhall pushed the button that lifted and attached his weapons pack. While each PICS' longjohns, the tight inner, sensor-laden skinsuit that a Marine wore while in his PICS, was individually fitted to each Marine, the PICS themselves, although specifically *assigned* to an individual Marine, were still one-size-fits all. That required regular maintenance to ensure the longjohns were communicating with the PICS' brain. This was not often a problem, but the weapons pack was a little different. Weapons packs were mission-loaded, and a Marine could get any of the normal loads and some custom loads, depending on the mission and his specific task in the mission. As a Marine could get any weapons pack, the connections had to be checked and re-checked before he was sent into harm's way. In an emergency, a Marine could just suit up and go, but when there was time, a partial, or preferably, a full check was made.

Ryck, as a semi-trained armorer, had helped CWO3 Weston as the testing commenced, but now it was his turn. He had to get back to his squad and get ready for the landing.

"Pack 2, attached. Commencing analytics," Tamberhall said as the chief warrant officer walked down the line to the next testing station.

Cpl Tamberhall had all the information in front of him, but the armorers always vocalized. Mix-ups could happen, and an assaultman who showed up to blow a door with a Pack 1 instead of the EOD Pack 5 would be useless, and the mission could fail. It was up to the Marine himself to listen to the armorer and to check the readout on his visor, to make sure he had the correct pack.

Ryck was the fire team's heavy gunner for the mission, so Pack 2 was correct.

"Weapons pack check, 100%," Tamberhall said about 20 seconds later. "You are cleared for combat. Next!" he shouted out.

Ryck stepped off the platform, went to the walk-in, and popped the PICS, wiggling out the back and leaving the empty suit standing in its assigned spot. As always, Ryck pictured the empty combat suit as the shell of a cicada as the adult insect, Ryck, in this case, wormed free of it. Ryck was in the longjohns for the duration, but the PICS would sit there, an armed Navy bosun in the walk-in for security, until it was time to launch.

He checked his watch. There was just enough time to get some chow before he had to be at the final brief. He was actually a little too excited to eat, but a good Marine ate when he could, not knowing when the next opportunity would arise. He could be inside his PICs for quite some time, and the nutritional base fed to them while in the PICS, the "ghost shit," did little to assuage hunger even if it kept the body going.

He thought back to Smitty back on the Dirtball, who had accused him of wanting to go to Golf when he returned to full-duty. Ryck had been serious at the time that he wanted to come back to Fox, where his friends were. He was surprised, then, when his orders were to Golf. His time in the armory probably had something to do with it. Golf was the battalion's heavy company, with two platoons being heavy with only one being light instead of the other way around. Even then, the "light platoon" spent more time training in PICS than the lights in the other companies and could suit up if the need arose. Ryck wasn't assigned as an armorer, even if CWO4 Heng had hinted that Ryck could make the switch if he so desired. But Ryck wanted back into a fire-team. So he was with the Second Fire Team, First Squad, First Platoon. Cpl Nimoto was his fire team leader, Sgt Phantawisangtong his squad leader. At first, Ryck thought it just the worst coincidence he could imagine. But it wasn't a coincidence. King Tong had specifically asked for him. And it really hadn't turned out to be that bad. Squad Leader King Tong was not the same man as Drill Instructor King Tong. "Hecs," he was called by the other NCOs, but to Ryck, he was still King Tong.

Ryck hustled to Enlisted Galley D. This was not the little *Adelaide.* This was the *FS Praecipua,* a Prion Class battlecruiser, named for the battle during the War of the First Reaches. It was a modern dreadnaught, a huge ship, and the entire battalion was embarked. The ship itself was probably overkill. It wasn't like it could unleash its planet busters in this case. But the brass probably hoped that just the appearance of the big ship would quell the situation. If that happened, then the Marines would just have been passengers. Ryck knew he should wish for that. But after a year-and-a-half of inactivity, he hoped for some action. He knew he should feel ashamed about that, but the fact was that he didn't.

Galley D was the unofficial Marine galley. Technically, a sailor, Marine, or members of the FCDC advance party could eat at any enlisted galley, but in practice, the enlisted men and women tended to segregate themselves. The Marines took over Galley D as it was close to their main berthing. Ryck and a few others had eaten breakfast that morning at Galley B, just to see if there was a difference between "Navy food" and "Marine food." There wasn't.

There were at least 150 Marines with the same idea as Ryck in the galley, grabbing hot chow while they could. Over half were in skins. These would be the light infantry Marines, both from Golf and the other companies. The rest were in their longjohns. The longjohns were *extremely* tight and left absolutely nothing to the imagination. The Marines in their skins kept a running commentary about the various attributes, or lack thereof, of the PICS Marines. Fox was embarked on the ship as well, but a quick glance showed that none of Ryck's friends were there at chow. The company must have been in the middle of something. With only four hours before launch, Ryck thought that would have been a good guess.

"Hey, Ryck, you think we're going to launch?" LCpl Naranbaatar Bayarsaikhan, asked as Ryck sat down.

"Ghengis" was from Larudi, the extremely homogenous world settled by Mongolians, and take away his longjohns, fit him out with furs and sit him on a horse with a "larudi" on his arm, and he could pass for his ancient forebearer and nic-namesake, Ghengis Khan himself.

"Don't know," Ryck said. "Would you want to fight if you looked up and saw the *Prake* over you?"

"Well, they know we're about there, and they know what we've got. They haven't surrendered yet," Ghengis said.

"Wait until we launch," Private Courtland Prifit said. "Iffen they don't we'll kick their perking asses."

Ghengis just looked at Ryck and raised his eyebrows. Ryck shrugged. Courtland was a boot, and this was his first operation. Boots were better seen and not heard.

Their mission was to restore the government of Luminosity. Luminosity was not a corporate world, but one founded by a freespeaker society at the height of the movement some 200 years ago. Over the years, it had grown economically, but with keeping in line with their founding philosophy, had minimal government and no armed forces. Even the police were only part-time deputies.

During the planet's third immigration wave, according to the brief the Marines and sailors had received, a number of refugees from Kyber had arrived, settling in the main mountain range. When they started their own militia, the planetary authorities had objected, but as this was a "free" world, having a private militia was technically considered a matter of personal choice, and therefore legal.

That may have been a mistake, because over a month ago, that "militia" took over the government, declaring themselves in charge and the "protectors" of the citizens from both crime and outside influences. When people objected, they were arrested and thrown into hastily-constructed jails.

That created a call for assistance from the Federation. Two weeks later, the Federation voted to intervene, skirting the law by declaring that this was merely a "police action." The fact that the rare earth mines, especially the scandium and gadolinium mines, were closed by the new rulers, couldn't have had anything to do with the extremely quick response by the resource-hungry central planets of the Federation.

With somewhere close to 3,000 in the militia, the powers that be determined that one reinforced Marine battalion, with 2,000+ Marines, would be enough to defeat the militia and get things back to normal. The reports that the militia might have both armor and combat suits were largely discounted.

The battalion was assigned the mission and given two days to embark. The *Prake* was pure Navy and didn't often carry embarked Marines. But as modern bubble warships generally differed primarily in size alone, it wasn't that difficult for the ship to accommodate the Marines.

It actually took three days before they could get underway, and then another three days of bubble-space time to reach Luminosity. The ship had come out of bubble space an hour before. In another three hours, it would be in orbit around the planet.

The ship had an immense capability with more firepower than the entire Marine Corps and a good portion of the Civil Development Corps. (Not many people realized it, due to planned disinformation, but even the Civil Development Corps, which was actually an occupation army, had much more firepower than the Marines.) Using the ship's firepower on Luminosity, though, would be difficult if not impossible. Not only was the bulk of the population on the side of the Federation, but also the mines themselves could not be damaged if shipments were to commence immediately.

Marines started leaving the mess decks. Ryck looked at his watch.

"Hey, eat up. We've got to go."

They crammed down their food and got back to their staging area, a large space that they shared with crates of some sort. Then they waited. And waited. The lieutenant gathered them all together to go over their ops order, but in reality, that was busy work. They had gone over it ad infinitum, and no plan lasted past the first few minutes of contact, anyway. So it was hurry up and wait, which was par for the course.

It was a relief when the word was broadcast throughout the ship that the landing was on. Most of the Marines gave an "ooh-rah" as they scrambled to their feet and rushed to their respective walk-ins. Ryck rushed to his PICS and slithered through the back. This actually took some effort as the weapons pack was still attached, so Ryck had to get low, over the butt of the PICS, then worm his way through the opening and up the suit, then pulling his legs up until he could slide them down inside. Some of the other Marines were having problems, but there was enough assistance, Marine and Navy, to get them suited up. An armorer ran a quick check on each Marine and initiated the cold pack.

One of the problems with any type of armored suit was getting rid of built-up body heat. The old-fashioned fins that dissipated heat into the atmosphere made it easy for heat-seekers to pick up a suit's signature. The PICS were the first Marine suit to use cold packs. The packs were a surprisingly small mass of a molecularly-arrayed synthetic heat sink. To the layman, it looked like jelly. What it did was capture heat. It had to be controlled carefully, though. If left unregulated, it could literally suck all the body heat from a Marine, killing him from hypothermia. If it didn't work efficiently, it could kill a Marine from heat stroke. Any damage it received in the field could have deadly consequences, which was why each cold pack had a small jettison command that could be sent to eject it from the PICS. The same access could be used to exchange the pack as each pack was only good for 24 to 30 hours, depending on the weather and other factors.

Finally, they were ready and the lieutenant was given the OK. He ordered the platoon out and to the hanger. The Stork waiting for them was configured for PICS. It had no enclosed cargo bay. Marines and their corpsmen backed up to the overhead racks, and the back of their PICS married to the "clothes hooks." With a click, they were attached.

Within moments, the Stork lifted and flew out the hanger. The Stork was dual-purpose, but it was better designed for air operations. In space, it was a little slow. So the Storks took off before any of the support craft, the fighters and attack craft.

With no deck, the Marines were suspended "above" open space. Some Marines didn't like the "dangle," even Marines who could do EVAs without a problem, but Ryck rather liked the sensation. He'd only had two training lifts, and this was his first combat launch. Without having to fly an EVA suit, he could just sit back and enjoy the ride.

The Stork rotated and the *Prake* fell out of view behind them, the planet filling their field of vision. Ryck knew that it would be another 30 minutes until they landed. He looked around, trying to catch sight of one of the other Storks or fighters, but space was big, and he couldn't see anything.

It was obvious when they reached Luminosity's atmosphere. It started with a glow, then a burning fire that filled the space with light as the gasses of the atmosphere compressed in front of the vehicle. Ryck knew that if the diversion field on the Stork failed, they would all burn up within moments, but that really was not a concern of his, any more than if the powerpack on his PICS would explode, or if his Navy chow was contaminated. He just didn't think about odd possibilities.

"Fifteen minutes to touchdown," his comms' AI intoned.

Ryck looked, trying to see through the flaring of the atmosphere, trying to pick out some landmarks. Nothing. It wasn't for another 30 seconds that the burning died down, and he could see the planet's surface.

The bulk of the planet's population was on two main land masses. There was a small unit of the People's Army, as the militia was calling itself, on the larger mass, holding the main city there, but they would be dealt with during the second phase of the operation. Phase 1 was to take back control of the capital and the second largest city, rescue those being held as prisoners, and secure the three main mine sites. The militia was larger, but it was spread fairly thin. The Marines could concentrate their forces and have local numerical superiority. That, in addition to the Marines better training and equipment, should give the Marines the upper hand.

The Rules of Engagement were fairly stringent: minimize friendly casualties as well as damage to the infrastructure. For this reason, Fox (REIN)[21] had the point of main effort at the capital to dispose of the illegal Luminosity government and rescue those citizens held as prisoners. PICS were not particularly effective in combat in a built-up area, unless full-scale destruction was allowed, so the more nimble-foot Marines, in skins and bones, would be

---

[21] **REIN**: Reinforced with additional personnel and capabilities.

employed there, with a squad of PICS Marines in support. Weapons Company would take out the militia camp outside of the capital. Echo Company would take the first mine objective (this was a foreign-owned mine, and rumor had it that this was selected due to some very highly-placed people in the Federation government having stock in the company).

Golf's mission was the encampment located outside of Green Falls, the planet's second largest city. This was the largest encampment uncovered, and it was well-situated to react to any threat towards the bulk of the largest mines on the planet. Without friendly infrastructure or significant friendly personnel at the camp, this was more of a free fire target, where all Marine and Navy assets could be employed. Golf, with arty and armor attached, was on a mission to destroy, not rescue or save. The People's Army at the camp was to be destroyed so that none of the forces could deploy to the mines.

As the surface of the planet became visible, Ryck tried to place their own position relative to the ground below. They wouldn't be coming straight in from above, so the target was not under them. They would sweep in from southeast to northwest, supported by the two of the attached Wasps and three Navy Experion fighters. Coming in on that trajectory kept them below any anti-air defenses until the end of the approach, but it also kept them out of the way of the Navy bombardment. The *Prake* had deployed one of its monitors to soften up the rebel camp. This ball of firepower had no sailors on board; it was completely operated from the dreadnaught. It did carry a pretty solid punch, though. Parked in orbit right over the camp, so weapons had to travel through the least amount of atmosphere, it swept the camp with particle beams, disrupter fire, and explosive ordinance.

Ryck had the map pulled up on his visor, watching as they approached. At 30 klicks, though, he could actually see the flash of ionized gasses as the particle beams reached down from orbit to the camp.

Ryck ignored most of the chatter coming over the platoon circuit. It was mostly a countdown until they hit the deck. If there was anything important, he would pay closer attention. He only half-listened as he did yet one more status check on his PICS and ammo load.

As the Stork swooped in, he waited for the green light. It wasn't as if he would have to do anything. Technically, a PICS could withstand a 5 meter fall without damage, and the Stork could land on the ground so the Marines could take one step and be on terra firma. But the Storks were a valuable piece of equipment, and a land mine could take one out, so the Marines would be lowered via a hoist that was incorporated into each station. After the flare, a Stork could debark a platoon of Marines within five seconds.

The ground got closer, and a voice came over the circuit, "Fox-1, stand by!"

The go-light flashed green. Three seconds later, Ryck fell out of the sky. Five seconds was not very long, but it was more than long enough for the bad guys to take them under fire, so Ryck quickly scanned the ground, waiting to fire at any threat. They had trained to fire while being dropped, and with varying, if not very effective, degrees of success, but Ryck would go down trying if it came to that.

Nothing presented itself, though, and Ryck hit the ground, his hoist line automatically disconnecting and retracting back to the Stork, which had already begun to move out.

Ryck moved to his left, relying on visuals to get into position. His head's up display had every member of the platoon identified, and if he zoomed out, he would be able to see the entire company, but he still felt more comfortable with actual visuals.

"Fox-1, move out" the lieutenant passed.

In another time and place, the first few minutes of an assault would be taken up with getting oriented, of getting a head count, but the lieutenant's PICS-C had even more information flowing to him on each and every one of them. The common statement was that he knew if you got a hard-on and why. SSgt Grabrowski's PICS was "C-capable," which meant it had all the bells and whistles. He could view the same incoming information on each Marine, but if anything happened to the platoon commander, the AI would switch over and give his PICS the same capabilities, not only downstream but upstream as well. Ryck's PICS was the basic model with more limited upstream capabilities.

As the platoon moved out, a Navy LCC came in carrying a tank. It had to land in order to discharge its cargo, and that took a little bit of time. Still, even if it was behind them at the moment, knowing that a Davis was there was a nice security blanket.

Ryck moved forward, trying to divide his focus between what he could see in front of him and his displays. There was quite a bit of data streaming in, and he still was not totally comfortable with watching the real world out there and the electrons symbolizing the world on his visor at the same time. He could see Greg Hohn moving up just in front and to his side, but Greg was also the first blue triangle that appeared on his visor display. He knew that was Greg, but he hadn't yet made the leap to "feel" that it was Greg.

The platoon had about 900 meters of forested land through which to move, then there was another 400 meters of cleared land to cross before reaching the outer defenses of the camp. It wasn't as if this was a surprise, either. Storks in the air and PICS on the ground were somewhat hard to hide. Tactical "surprise" in the assault had to be how the Marines were employed, not in trying to hide the fact that there was going to be an assault in the first place.

He looked up to the upper-left section of his visor and blinked twice. The feed there switched positions and filled the center of his visor. It was a visual of the camp. A recon Marine out there somewhere had the camp under surveillance and was beaming the view to every Marine. There was the tiniest hint of a flicker, which was a good sign that the enemy was trying to jam the signal, but the AIs kept switching the frequency every micro-second, both for the broadcast and receiving, faster than whatever equipment the rebels had could catch up.

The vid showed a devastated landscape. There were no intact buildings. The Navy had leveled them. Ryck was not complacent, though. He knew the rebels were still there. He quickly switched back to visual, scanning the area in front of him. His PICS was moving smoothly, just an extension of his movements. He moved his leg, the PICS moved its leg. It was all done without thinking. His head being almost three meters up, his "hands" reaching out over two meters had taken a little getting used to during training, but now it was second nature.

For the thousandth time, he checked his HGL. The "Heavy Grenade Launcher" was his prime weapon, the principle weapon in any Weapons Pack 2. Greg, to his right, had Weapons Pack 1, which gave him the hypervelocity rifle, similar to the M99 Marines carried when on foot, but at 8mm, packing a much bigger dart. The HGL, though, fired a 20mm grenade. A combat load of the grenades was 250 and could be anti-personnel or anti-armor. The anti-armor could take out almost any tank if employed correctly, and the anti-personnel had an ECR of 30 meters. It could fire 60 rounds per minute, so it packed a pretty powerful punch.

Second Platoon was heading right up the gut of what had been determined to be the brunt of the defenses. They were doing this to set the defense, to get them to commit while First Platoon swept up their flank. Weapons Platoon was supporting both heavy platoons, and Third, the light platoon, was in reserve, ready to exploit any advantage.

Ryck's visor lit up with activity. Second was being hit. As a grunt, he was not privy to all the comms, but it was obvious from the display if not from the sounds of explosions a klick to his right.

"All hands, be advised that the enemy forces are employing both Boost-Assisted Anti-Armor weapons as well as anti-armor mines," the lieutenant's calm voice came over the platoon circuit.

That was a surprise. Mines were part and parcel to modern combat, but Boost Assisted Anti-Armor rounds could take out a PICS. Only one power used those weapons: The Congress of Free Worlds. The Congress was a loosely allied group of 14 planets in the Third Quadrant, a long way from Luminosity. If the People's Army had Congress weapons, that meant either the Congress was sticking its nose into Federation space or that arms dealers were supplying them to the rebels. Congress weaponology was no match for Federation, even the older Marine equipment, but still, getting hit with a BAAA round was sure to spoil a grunt's day. The Marines had to trust their PICS to deflect the rounds as they were "dumb" ordinance as the PICS' defenses could not fool a round that had no brain. All suits could do was to confuse the sighting of the weapon and hope for a glancing blow that the LTC armor could deflect.

Ryck started to blink up his scheme to change it, but the platoon sergeant beat him to it. With the command capabilities, he could switch each Marine's paint, and with visual sighting the norm for BAAA weapons, the "LSD" mode was the book answer. The LSD was the nickname for the Fractured Array. It didn't make a PICS actually invisible, but rather "fractured" the light waves, making visual sighting difficult, even causing headaches for those looking at them. An observer knew something was there, but exactly where and what would be difficult to determine.

The sounds of war to his right grew in intensity. Second was getting into it. They wouldn't be closing unless the opportunity presented itself, but that meant First had to step it up and breach the defenses.

A Wasp showed up on his readout. Ryck hoped the platoons were showing up on the pilot's readout as well. There was the incoming icon, but in flashing amber instead of the flashing red of a near miss by friendly fire. Ryck didn't hesitate in his advance as the sky lit up in front of Second's position as the Wasp's ordinance hit home.

Ryck's visor flashed green twice, signaling that Phase Line Liverpool had been reached. This was when First Squad changed their advance to a new heading, slightly oblique of the other two squads. No verbal orders were given as the new heading was centered in the nav panel.

They had reached the rise leading up to the outer perimeter of the camp. The ground was torn up from the pre-assault bombardment. This was nothing that Ryck's PICS couldn't handle, but the servos still whined a bit with each step over the rough ground as they worked to keep Ryck upright and oriented to the enemy.

Ryck didn't need the speakers to hear the blast just 30 meters to his right. The sound waves easily penetrated his PICS as Greg Hohn was lifted into the air. Ryck watched as the big PICS flew up 10 or 12 meters, then crashed back down. He hesitated a moment, then took a step to check on Greg.

"Back in position, Ryck," King Tong's voice came over the direct circuit.

The squad leader was right. Greg's fate was already determined, and he would be fine or not, but Ryck could not leave the assault. The force had to be focused. He did glance up at Greg's icon. It was still blue, but a light blue instead of the normal dark blue. He was alive and not in immediate danger, but his PICS was damaged. His weapons pack was operational, so he could still provide supporting fire if he could not advance.

The PICS were supposed to be able to locate mines, which had to be what hit Greg. Ryck wondered what happened, then started looking more closely at the ground in front of him.

They were less than 300 meters from the outer perimeter when all hell broke loose. There were at least four BAAAs facing them. They had not been sucked in to confront the frontal assault, which would have been too easy for the Marines. Going against four BAAAs with thirteen PICS should be a reasonable mission. That was, of course, unless the rebels threw something else into the mix.

The PICS could cover the 200 meters over broken terrain in about 20 seconds, and the immediate action for this would be a full charge. He started to lurch into a run as his target comp zeroed in on one of the BAAAs. He lifted the HCL and put three rounds downrange. All three hit the gun. There wasn't a catastrophic kill, but the gun went silent.

One problem with the combat visors was that there could be info overload. There were traces of incoming and outgoing fire, there were orders being given. To Ryck, though, unless he personally received a direct order to do something different, his war narrowed down to who and what was directly in front of him. Nothing else mattered, and frankly, that was about all he could take in. He had to trust his fellow Marines to take care of business on either side of him.

He fired at another position, a light automatic weapon of some sort, but nothing that could affect a PICS. And then he was inside the outer perimeter. He was within the camp. To his left was the BAAA he'd taken out, a light plume of smoke rising from it. There was an arm visible, but most of the body was hidden from sight. His original course of action was to breach the perimeter, then force his way deeper, past the outer belt of defenses. However, with Greg out, then the 60 meters or so to his right had not been cleared. Marines were not automotrons. They were trained to think. Ryck knew he had to clear the area and not leave a potential pocket of the rebels there. He veered to the right and followed the defensive line until his movement sphere intersected with that of Cpl Nimoto, who'd had the same idea with Greg's sector uncovered and had been moving to his left. As each Marine moved, the AI's determined a "cleared" area and pushed that up to the lieutenant so that he would know what areas had been cleared and what areas still had potential bad guys in them.

Cpl Nimoto pointed a big PICS arm back towards the inner defenses. Ryck didn't acknowledge, but his turning and moving out was enough. Fast dissemination of information was the key to the modern battlefield, so it was ironic that the Marines relied heavily on old fashioned-hand and arm signals. But with crowded nets and anti-comms being employed against them, the less being passed via electrons the better.

Rycks shifted back to his left top where he could cover better both his original sector as well as Greg's. He was a little behind the other Marines, so he hurried to catch up.

The turtle hatch opening up just 20 meters to his front right took him by surprise. His PICS never picked it up until it opened. The big BAAA deployed within a second as Ryck tried to bring his HCL to bear. Before he could fire, flames flew from the barrel and something big slammed into Ryck's side overpowering the PICS' servos and sending it crashing to the ground.

Ryck was stunned, certain he was in it deep. He tried to stand up, but his PICS complained as his visor started flashing different series of numbers before going dark. He tried to turn his head, and to his surprise, the PICS grudgingly complied. His comms seemed to be gone, but he could see out the visor. The BAAA was right in his sight. It was a type he'd not been briefed on before. It was obviously slaved, either controlled by an AI or by an operator off-site. It moved quickly from target to target, firing away.

"Target" seemed impersonal to Ryck. Those "targets" were his fellow Marines.

An explosion rocked the base of the BAAA. That had to be the Davis, getting into the fight. The BAAA immediately spun around and let out a string of fire, faster than Ryck had thought possible. There was no return fire from the Davis.

Ryck took stock of his situation. Despite being initially stunned, he didn't seem hurt. His PICS, though, was at 10% at best. His visor occasionally flickered on, but for the most part, he was cut off from the rest of the platoon.

The BAAA in front of him was close, only 20 meters away, and it was actively engaging the platoon, but Ryck didn't know what he could do about it. Robot gun or not, he knew a string of his 20 mike-mike grenades would do it some serious hurt.

Ryck tried to force his HCL arm forward. It edged forward before stopping, still a good 40 degrees from being on target. If his weapon wouldn't move, he wondered if his body could. He tried to edge back, hoping to drag his HCL into position. That didn't seem to be happening—all he seemed to do was to roll over on his belly.

Stuck there on his side, he was safe for the moment, but his platoon was still in the shit. He was trying to figure out his next course of action when something seemed to burn his ass. At first, he thought his PICS was on fire, but he couldn't smell anything. The pain started getting intense, and it was spreading down his leg.

Then it hit him. His coldpack had somehow ruptured!

He immediately hit the emergency eject for the pack, which had its own self-contained power source. The PICS made an odd sound of grinding, but nothing happened. The coldpack was still there, spreading down his leg. Already, the right cheek of his ass was numb, probably frozen solid.

He tried the eject again. The same grinding noise sounded, followed by a pop, then silence.

Ryck knew he had to get away from the coldpack. It could literally suck the heat right out of him. If the eject wasn't working, then there was only one choice. He had to molt.

A combat molt was a last-ditch action, used when a suit had to be abandoned. He pulled back his left hand and arm from the

PICS sleeve and wormed down his side. He resisted trying to feel around to his ass and grabbed the molt release instead. Once outside, he'd have no protection, but it was better than freezing to death. He gave it a hard pull. At first, he thought it had failed as well, but the molt was not instantaneous. A PICS was a pretty impressive machine that was designed to take a beating, so there were a number of steps to disconnect and break the integrity of it to get out. It normally took about a minute to go through the steps to get out of a suit, but an emergency molt was much, much quicker. It really only took about five seconds, but to Ryck, it seemed like an eternity. The suit split up the back, and Ryck scrambled out.

Once out, he flopped in back of his suit, expecting to feel rebel rounds hitting him. To his surprise, he seemed to be being ignored. Twenty meters from him, the unmanned B-Triple-A kept aiming at targets and firing. The way the gun seemed to pick targets, spinning from one to the other back and forth rather than from one, then to another close by, would indicate that the guns were being controlled by an AI, or at least a program that prioritized targets. When humans selected targets, they tended to go from one then to another that was close by the first target. Humans targeted in patterns while AIs ignored patterns based on location.

Ryck glanced in back of him. The Davis was some 400 meters back, a column of black smoke rising from it. He could see other PICS moving back and forth, taking cover when and where they could. The plan to bull-rush the perimeter was already by the wayside.

Ryck took stock of what he had. That wasn't much. In his longjohns, he had no protection from even thorny bushes, much less weapons. He had his small Ruger 2mm strapped to his thigh, but that was only good against unarmored personnel. His rocket launcher and HCL looked intact, but they were on the weapons pack and so, useless.

Or were they?

Ryck started thinking of the hours he'd spent in the battalion armory. Each weapons pack was powered by the PICS. However, there was a small battery in the pack that kept the electronics alive and functioning while the pack was not attached to a suit. For energy weapons, that little battery wouldn't do much. But Ryck's weapons pack was Number 2, and the pack only used power for the electronics, which included the trigger for both the rockets as well as the grenades. Both weapons were self-powered in flight to the target.

Could he jury-rig the pack to fire?

Ryck scootched forward, looking at the pack's connections. It should be easy to release the pack. Throwing the cover lever should do it. Without even thinking, he crawled up on the back of the PICS and pulled on the lever. It barely budged. In the armory, the loader mechanically opened and closed the lever. Ryck's muscles did not match that power. Mindless of the battle raging around him, he stood up on top of his PICS, reached down to grasp the lever, and heaved up with his legs. Grudgingly, the lever moved—one millimeter, two millimeters, three—before suddenly giving way. The weapons pack was free. Ryck had to kick it up and over the PICS helmet before it fell to the dirt.

He scrambled back to it, pushing it over so it "faced" up. The battery was just under the left shoulder. It seemed fine. Ryck pushed the purple test button, and the test lights lit up the armorer's panel in the correct sequence and all green. The weapons pack was undamaged. Throw in on another PICS, and it would be good to go. But Ryck didn't have another PICS.

The question was how he could get the rockets or grenades to fire. The targeting system was in the PICS, not the pack, and his PICS was out of the equation. The firing signal was also generated from the PICS. Ryck couldn't figure out a way to target a weapons pack alone, but he could bypass the firing signal.

He worried out one of his longjohns' control wires, the interface between his body and the PICS. For all the high-tech aspects of the longjohns, the controller was essentially a copper wire. He pulled off the connector, revealing the bright bare metal. Taking out his combat knife, he cut the wire in two. An explosion less than five meters away erupted beside him, showering him with dirt, but he ignored that as he twisted one end of one wire around the HCL firing input positive, and the other around the common ground in the female connector in the pack. All the prongs were color-coded, and because of his work in the armory , he knew which prong was which

He had to "fool" the pack into thinking a signal was coming from the PICS to fire. But the only power was from the pack's own battery. Taking out his combat knife, he dug through the silicon coating of the battery to reveal the terminals. He had to be careful. One slip, and the battery would short. He ended up making a small slit on the outside of both terminals. Stripping two more wires from his longjohns, he slid them into the two slits he'd made, trusting the silicon's elasticity to keep the ends of the wires in contact. He took the negative wire and twisted it around the wire that went into the firing input negative. All he would have to do, he figured, was touch the positive from the battery to the positive of the firing input, and the HTC should launch.

"Should," being the operative word.

The power from the battery was not the same as the power from the PICS. Ryck didn't know if the small output from the battery would be enough to activate the trigger mechanism.

All of this had taken a surprisingly short amount of time, maybe a minute at most. Ryck looked up in time to see a PICS off in the distance go down. One of the BAAAs was down, but there were three still in action. They were stationary targets, and Ryck didn't understand why the Marines were having issues with them, or why Marine or Navy Air couldn't take them out. He couldn't affect any of that, though.

Ryck had to get the weapons pack up and aimed somehow. The logical step would be to wear the pack, just as if it was on a PICS. The pack alone, with ammo, weighed in at a good 160 kg. That was a pretty hefty load, and Ryck wasn't sure he could manage it. He turned it around so it was facing down and slid his body in. His head went through the opening easily. Too easily. The pack was designed to sit around the collar and on the shoulders of a PICS. Ryck's shoulders were not nearly as wide, and the color ring of the pack came down right on the edge of this shoulders. There wasn't much he could do about that, though.

Ryck gathered his feet under him, and tried to stand up. He actually lifted the pack off the ground before he fell forward, his neck slamming into the hard edge of the pack. Simply standing up was not going to work. He had to get his feet under him. That was easier said than done. It took some maneuvering and using his PICS hulk as an anchor, but he finally got it done. Taking a deep breath, he stood up.

In the gym, he'd squatted more than that before. But that was on a pad with the weight being a barbell. In this case, he was standing in the dirt of Luminosity, a battle was going full tilt around him, his right butt cheek and leg were numb, and the edge of the weapons pack was digging into his shoulders. With a grunt, he did it, though. He stood up.

He expected the B-Triple A in front of him to swing in his direction and let loose. He was surprised, but quite relieved, when it seemed to ignore him. The AIs or targeting computers evidently were not particularly discerning.

He staggered forward a few steps and stopped. The pack was digging unmercifully into his shoulders. The edge of the pack came down within a couple of centimeters from the edge of this shoulder, so a lot of weight was being supported by only a little of Ryck. And that hurt.

Fifteen meters or 10 meters wouldn't make much difference, so he stopped his advance. The bulk of the grenade launcher was in the pack itself, but the muzzle was normally "worn" on the gauntlet of the PICS. Ryck didn't have the PICS there, so he simply jammed his right hand into the dangling muzzle, then strained to lift it up. A gauntlet was much bigger than a naked hand, so the fit was not right, but at least he could still reach the thumb trigger. The firing trigger itself was electronic, but the switch to open the circuit was the mechanical trigger. With his left hand, he would have to reach to the loose wire to bring it to the other one, closing the circuit and (hopefully) firing the launcher. As he raised the weapon, though, with his right arm aiming and his left trying to reach back under the pack, his shoulders narrowed, and the pack almost slipped off. He had to tense up his left shoulder, keeping it in place as his fingers quested for the wire. He should have made them longer.

He couldn't really aim, so he simply pointed the HTC at the BAAA, hoping that it was on target. His right arm trembling to hold the muzzle steady while keeping the thumb trigger depressed, he felt the wire and quickly yanked it and touched the end of the wire going into the firing controls.

The grenade launched, nearly ripping Ryck's right arm off, spinning him around and to the ground. The big PICS had the mass to withstand the recoil, but Ryck's 85 kg did not, especially when he had not been prepared for it. He should have been prepared for the recoil, but he hadn't considered that.

Ryck struggled to get up, looking back at the BAAA. The gun had stopped firing, and its movement seemed jerky. But it was still very much alive and very dangerous. Ryck managed to get up, moving towards the rear of the gun, where its armor was not as imposing. Whoever or whatever was controlling the BAAA finally figured out that there was a threat near it. The big gun turned to Ryck, but the cutout that kept the gun from firing back towards the center of the camp also kept it from hitting Ryck, who was not ten meters to the rear. The turtle hatch provided the gun with some cover from the rear, but it wasn't enough.

Ryck leaned forward, bracing himself. Carefully, he touched the wires again while depressing the thumb trigger. The recoil still felt like a mule kick, but Ryck stayed on this feet.

The BAAA started firing, the rounds whipping by five meters to Ryck's front. They couldn't reach him. Ryck fired again. And again.

After the fourth round, the BAAA canted up and to the left. The armor piercing grenades had hit something vital. The BAAA was dead.

There wasn't a huge explosion, which was all well and good. Standing a mere 10 meters away and without armor, that could have messed up Ryck's day. To be honest, Ryck thought the kill had been somewhat anticlimactic. He had expected something more dramatic. But he'd done it. Without his PICS, he'd accomplished his mission.

No rest for the weary, though. Two more BAAAs were still hammering away. The nearest active gun was a good 100 meters from Ryck's kill. Ryck tried to shrug the pack into a better position, which was more of a "less horrible" than a "better," and staggered down the perimeter, hoping that no one would notice him. A simple rebel sniper further inside the perimeter would have no problem taking Ryck out.

It took a good three minutes to just get 50 meters, and Ryck was exhausted. He had to make sure that he could hit the gun ahead, so he limped forward another 10 meters, coming up on a wooden obstacle of some kind. Ryck thought a PICS could simply smash it down, but to him, it was pretty impressive. It did, however, give him something he could use as a support. He gratefully leaned on it, taking some of the weight off of him. He laid the muzzle of the HCL across one of the logs, then fired. Pain lanced through his shoulder. He was pretty sure that he had dislocated it when firing at the first BAAA.

The grenade arched up and over the BAAA. He'd have to fire again.

Explosions started saturating the area. The rebels must have finally figured out that he was there and a threat, but for some unfathomable reason, they didn't seem to be able to pinpoint him. This puzzled Ryck, but he was not about to question his good luck.

He fired again, scoring a direct hit, but not taking the gun out. He sighed and touched the wires again. Nothing happened. There was a faint click, but the HTC did not fire. Evidently, the battery, which was not made for activating a firing mechanism, no longer had enough juice.

His only remaining possible weapon was his shoulder rockets. He didn't know if there was enough power left to fire them, but they should take less than the HTC, so it was a possibility. He pulled out the positive from the connector and twisted it around the positive from the battery.

More rounds landed around him, but he had to ignore them as he straightened up, aiming his shoulder launcher in the general direction of the BAAA. Of the 12 rockets, six had anti-personnel warheads, six anti-armor. The anti-armor rockets were semi-smart, that is, they could alter their course slightly to hit metal targets within their acquisition cone.

Ryck didn't know of a way to fire the rockets separately as he could if he was in his PICS. This would be one salvo--that is, if he could even ignite them at all. He reached around with the free wire, and started poking it into where he could feel the connector. He didn't have the time nor energy to bring the weapons pack back down, find the correct positive, and wire it. This would rely on blind luck.

Blind luck was with him. On this third poke, he touched the correct connection, the tiny rocket igniters sparked, and all twelve rockets took off. Ryck was glad that rockets had no recoil and their exhaust was too quick to burn him. He wasn't sure he could stand up to either.

Ryck wasn't sure how many rockets slammed into the BAAA, but it was enough. Flames erupted for a brief moment as the gun was blown off its gimbal. A few seconds later, a huge explosion, whether from ground forces or air, Ryck didn't see, knocked out the third BAAA another 200 meters from him. The perimeter was breached.

His shoulder was on fire, and the numbness in his ass was slowly transitioning to a pretty severe ache. Ryck looked inwards to the rest of the camp, but he knew his battle was over. He slumped against the wooden obstacle and waited.

Within moments, a PICS Marine made his appearance. From Ryck's perspective sitting down in the dirt, the suit looked immense. The Marine inside stopped the suit and turned towards him. The visor momentarily went clear, and King Tong's face looked out at him. The squad leader winked at Ryck before the visor went dark again and he continued his assault into the camp.

# *Prophesy*

## *Chapter 24*

"You be lookin' for a good time dere, sailor boy?" a heavily accented male voice came from behind him as he entered the passenger pickup.

Ryck spun around, took in the dark blue shirt of a Torritite, and took a step to hug the man.

"Hey sailor, we must be agreeing to price afore we be getting cozy-like," Joshua Hope-of-Life said, but returning the bear hug.

"Josh, good to see you. I thought we weren't going to get together until next week, though," Ryck said as they broke their hug.

"Eh, I've already been back for a week, and my sibs are driving me crazy. It's crazy and boring at the same time, so I told your sister I'd come into Williamson to pick you up. It gave me a good excuse to get out of the house for a bit," he said, back in the accent and manner of speaking he'd cultivated in the Marines, all trace of his Torritite drawl gone.

"Looking copacetic, there, Marine," he continued, eyeing the Silver Star on Ryck's chest.

Ryck was still self-conscious about the medal, which had been approved seven months after Luminosity. The citation read that Ryck's "ingenuity" and "courage" while "wounded" had cleared the way for the stalled assault to continue. Ryck had only participated in the war for an hour, really. He'd been picked up by a corpsman while sitting at the wooden obstacle, all fighting much further inside the camp. He'd been casevac'd back to the *Prake* where they immediately began the regen on his dislocated shoulder and frostbit ass. The fighting on Luminosity took a little longer than expected due to the arms the rebels had acquired. Ryck tried to rejoin his platoon while they were supporting the recovery of the main mines, but even with his shoulder basically set, the Navy docs wouldn't clear him. The dead skin on his ass and leg evidently took longer to regen for some reason, and so he was stuck on the ship while the rest of the platoon fought.

It was a minor miracle, from Ryck's point of view, that no one from the squad was killed. Four PICS had been knocked out, but only the boot Prifit had been seriously hurt and put into long-term regen. All told, the battalion had lost 21 Marines and one Navy corpsman with 28 Marines, mostly from the light platoons, going into long-term regen. The fighting in the mines had been the most fierce of the operation, and the light platoons, in the skins and bones, had been the go-to Marines for that.

Two men, one of the Marines from India Company and the corpsman from Fox who had been killed, had been put in for the Federation Nova, which had been approved only a couple of months ago, while another two Marines had been approved for the Navy Cross. One of those was Sgt Homer Phantawisangtong, King Tong, who had single-handedly blown the central bunker. Along with the two Platinum Stars, four Silver Stars, a Legion of Merit for the colonel, and more than a few Battle Commendations of all three classes, that made the battalion one of the most decorated for a single operation since the War of the Far Reaches. And Ryck missed most of it.

This was not false modesty. Ryck realized that what he'd done was pretty grubbing copacetic. But when the war stories on the two-week battle were brought out in the galley, at the club, out in town, he could just listen in. When they gushed over King Tong's one-man assault, with "Did you see when he . . ." or "What about when he blasted that . . . ," no Ryck hadn't seen. When they described the Helicon Mine going up, a suicide by the rebels inside of it just before the Marines of India entered, no, he hadn't seen that, either. He was already on his way back to the *Prake*. He stayed on the ship, getting three hots and a cot, while the Marines slugged it out on the planet below.

"Nice stripes, too," Joshua continued, pointing at the corporal chevrons on his sleeve.

"Shit, just in the right place at the right time," Ryck said, uncomfortable under Joshua's gaze.

Joshua had served his entire enlistment without one actual operation. He'd gone to First Division, yet nothing had happened. Ryck had three combat stars while Joshua had none.

"Hey, no more Marine shit for now. Let's get you home to your sister. You've got to see your nieces, cute as a grub in a rug. The big celebrations don't start for another two days, so you've got to get out of the uniform and decompress."

This was Ryck's first time home since he enlisted. "Home," though, didn't really fit anymore. It was where he grew up, and it was where his sister was, but not much else tugged at him. Barret had let him know that there was a place for him in his company, a well-paying job with room for advancement. If Ryck got out in another three months, he knew he could be set with a comfortable lifestyle. That was one of the reasons why he took his leave back on Prophesy. The timing also coincided with Incorporation Day. Even with PCDC bankrupt and out of the picture, the people of Prophesy still celebrated Incorporation Day, the anniversary of when they became a legal entity. This was a time for family and friends.

Ryck followed Joshua out into the parking and up to a brand new, shiny red Hyundai Tonora.

"Holy gubbing shit! This thing yours?" he asked.

"Hell no! You know my lowly lance corporal's salary. This is my baby brother's. Only 21, and his processing company is going gangbusters. The company is not even a year old, and look at this baby," he said, pointing at the Hyundai.

"Damn! Sure looks like we picked the wrong line of work," Ryck said, stepping back to take in the sleek lines of the sports hover.

"Yeah, sure did. Caleb says he's got a job for me in the company if I don't re-up. I could get one of these for myself."

Ryck went quiet for a moment. Talking about re-enlisting was something generally off the table. But Joshua was his friend.

"You going to take him up on that?" he asked.

"Me? In an office? Nah, I don't grubbing think so. I'm not a grubbing combat hero like you, but still, I like it, and if I stay in long enough, I'll see some action. Show you what a real warrior can do!" he said, punching Ryck in the arm.

Ryck was both relieved and disappointed to hear that, and he wasn't sure why. Ryck wanted to re-enlist, and he had a good tour, but he wasn't sure yet. He'd lost friends, he'd had a miserable year plus in regen, but he had actually made a difference. On the other hand, if he took Barret up on his offer, he could make a good living, find a wife, settle down and start a family.

He dumped his pack in the Hyundai's small trunk and slid into the passenger seat. It felt decadent, and Ryck was in love. That love deepened as the Tonora lifted off the pavement and slowly moved to the exit. He knew that the hover could be almost silent, but the sound engineers for Hyundai created a low rumble, more felt than heard, that reflected the power in the car. Lysa's home was on the other side of Williamson, so Joshua took the ring road around the city, opening the hover up at 240 KPH. This was better than a Stork!

Too soon, Joshua pulled off the ring road and was on the surface streets to Elysium Hills, the subdivision where Lysa and Barret had bought a house the year before. Ryck had been to their previous home, and he thought it had been rather nice. But with two kids, Lysa told him they needed someplace bigger, and Barret wanted to be in the capital city.

Bigger was an understatement, Ryck thought as Joshua pulled in front of a, well, a mansion. There was no other way to describe it. Easily twice as large as Barret's old home, it had all the architectural extras currently in fashion. The front yard was stately, with two huge trees of some sort as the main features. The water tax on those two trees alone represented a huge chunk of Ryck's corporal's salary. From one tree, a rope swing hung, out of place in the new construction, but a nice touch. Above the side wall, Ryck could see the tops of what looked like a jungle gym. This wasn't Barret's old bachelor pad. This was a family home.

"Here you go, my man," Joshua said as he pulled up.

"You coming in?"

"Nah, this is family time. Do your duty. We're all getting together on I-Day to watch the fireworks, so I'll see you then. Don't worry, we'll have some time together, just you and me," Joshua told him.

Ryck took his pack, watched Joshua pull out, and walked up to the front door. Before he reached it, the door opened and Lysa ran out, colliding with him in a hug.

"Little brother, it's so good to see you. Come in, come in!"

"Uncle Ryck, Uncle Ryck, come here," a little voice said in back of Lysa.

Ryck had spoken with Kylee on the cam, but this was the first time he'd seen her in the flesh. She reached around Lysa to take his hand.

"Kylee! What did I tell you! Give Uncle Ryck a chance to breathe first. He'll see your room later," Lysa told her daughter. Lysa took Ryck's hand and led him into the house. Barret was waiting there, a beer in his hand that Ryck gratefully took, giving his pack to Barret in exchange.

"You look good, there, Ryck. I don't know what all those ribbons mean on your chest exactly, but your friend Joshua says they are pretty important. I know the girls want you to stay in your uniform, but I bet you'd like to get into something more comfortable," Barret said.

Ryck was towed to his room by Kylee as she pulled on his arm. He managed to get into the room alone and changed into shorts and a 2/9 t-shirt. As he opened the door, Kylee was waiting, and grabbing his arm, she dragged him back into the living room. Barret was sitting down, another little girl peeking out from behind his chair.

"Hi, Camyle," Ryck said to his youngest niece.

The two-year-old retreated back a little further behind her father's chair.

"Don't worry about her. She's a little shy, but she'll warm up to you," Lysa told him.

The next few hours were pure domesticity. Lysa cooked up some katsudon and yakisoba, Barret talked about the job he was offering Ryck, sports, and asked about Ryck's military operations, Kylee dragged him to her room for an introduction to over 30 stuffed animals, and Camyle even said a few words to him.

Ryck didn't have much time alone with Lysa. He managed to catch her while she was making the noodles for the yakisoba. She had flour on her forehead as she kneaded the dough. She was different. Not just the weight, which had crept on during the last four years. This woman was not the woman who left the house in skin-tight dresses for a night in the bars and night-spots. This was a woman who was at home.

"You look happy," Ryck told her, knowing it was true.

"Like this?" she said with a laugh, brushing the hair back off her forehead, leaving more flour.

"Yeah, just like that."

"You're right. I am happy. I'm not sure I deserve it, but I thank God every day for my two little girls, my husband. The only thing I am missing is you. If you take Barret's job offer, then that would complete me. Of course, then I'll be bugging you to find a wife and give me some nieces and nephews."

"And I'm happy for you, big sister. Really, I am."

Dinner was great, and conversation was surprisingly interesting, even when initiated by a three-year-old. Three-and-a-half, that was, as Kylee took pains to remind everyone. Ryck had to watch his language a bit as some phrases and words almost leaked out. Little girls should not be faced with the same language as salty Marines and sailors.

To his surprise, Ryck was tired, and he went to bed early. He had to show up at his high school the next day to receive an award. He'd have liked to skip it, but he got three extra days of leave for what the Marines considered a recruiting trip. In the afternoon, he promised he'd visit Barret at his office to check out the position being offered.

He had never been in Lysa and Barret's house before, and never in the guest bedroom. But as he lay down, with the little-girl shrieks of laughter coming from downstairs, it was feeling much more like home than he would have imagined.

## *Chapter 25*

"This is your office," Barret told him, as they stepped into a good-sized, if barren room. "Of course, you can personalize it as you want when you get here. But you can see it has a pretty good view. You don't get a private bathroom, I mean 'head,' but who knows?" he said with a laugh.

Water, or water reclamation and prospecting, had been good to Barret. With PCDC off the planet, water was scarce, and those who could find it were at a premium. Barret's company had done very well since the PCDC's charter was revoked. Barret was offering Ryck a position as vice-president of operations. Ryck didn't know the first thing about the water business, or any business for that matter, and he knew this was an offer based entirely on Barret's love for his sister. Still, as Barret said, the discipline Ryck had gained as a Marine would enable him to quickly grasp the ins and outs of his job.

The day had turned out better than he'd expected. Going back to school, this time in his dress blues, had been a rush. He felt like a flick star with all the attention. He was even moved by the Distinguished Alumni Award he'd received, much to his surprise. He'd received an extra three days of leave for meeting with his school, but frankly, he'd do it again even without the extra leave.

Barret had picked him up after lunch and taken him out to one of his projects in the area, which proved quite interesting. The company had dug several "lead wells" around what had once been a producing well but was now dry. With modern technology, the lead wells were able to "suck," as Barret explained in not so technical terms, the residual moisture from the area. The science was beyond him, but Barret assured him that the understanding would only take a bit of time.

During the long drive back to Williamson, Barret did most of the talking, and most of that was family-related. Barret would never fit in with a Marine platoon, and he had no idea of what Ryck had experienced, but he was a good man. Ryck felt guilty for not liking him at first. He would never be Ryck's best buddy, but he was good for Lysa and good for the girls. For that, he deserved Ryck's respect.

"Well, what do you think? I mean, do you like it?" he asked Ryck.

"I have to admit, it's kinda interesting. You've certainly done well with it," he said.

"You will, too. We'll talk about salary and perks later, but be easy on me, OK? No Marine combat attacks here. I'm not the enemy!" Barret said with yet another laugh.

Barret's sense of humor was not the most developed, and that fact alone made Ryck smile.

## Chapter 26

"You ever get to Goa?" Charles asked as they looked out over the crowd.

"No," Joshua and Ryck said in unison.

"You've got to get there," Charles said. "Grubbing amazing! Better than Vegas or Pattaya, and I've been to both of them. We pulled into Goa, and as soon as you get off the spaceport, there's this line of bars with hot, and I mean hot mares . . ."

Ryck and Joshua had met up with Charles at The Park while waiting for the fireworks. He was obviously military, and he could tell both Marines were military, too. After introductions, they found out he was Navy, a petty officer second class. His ship was in the same sector as with First Division, and the talk drifted to bases in the area, then liberty ports. Ryck listened with half an ear while he watched Joshua's and his families. Joshua's dwarfed Ryck's in size, but for the little kids, Kylee was making her presence felt, bossing the other little ones around into playing her games.

*She'd make a good DI*, Ryck thought.

Ryck turned back to the two others. Charles was in the middle of a description of a very perverted, obscene, and frankly funny escapade he and another sailor had on Goa. Ryck found himself laughing along. Even Joshua got into the flow of it, with a few somewhat-risqué stories of his own. Ryck knew better now, but before he enlisted, he thought the Torritites were all pretty up-tight prudes. In fact, he doubted that his family would be sitting there together with a Torritite family, sharing food and companionship, if Ryck and Joshua had not become friends. If nothing else, the Marines gave him the opportunity to have his eyes opened. If he got out of the Corps, he promised himself to stay in contact with Joshua's family.

His eyes roamed over the crowd. There were a lot of eligible women there, and Joshua had assured him that it was a good time to be in uniform. There was a new romance-flick that was all the rage, and the little-understood-but-noble-hero was a Marine lieutenant. Usually, the heroes, if they were military, were Navy or Legion, so this was something new, and Joshua was more than willing to take advantage of the current popularity if he could.

Joshua's own sister, Hannah, had grown into a fine-looking young woman. She had talked with Ryck for about 30 minutes as they set up the picnic dinner. Whether that was out of politeness to her brother's friend or something more, Ryck had no clue. He wouldn't mind finding out more about that, though.

He shifted his gaze to his sister just as Barret leaned over and kissed her. She accepted his kiss and laid her head on his shoulder as they sat on the blanket, waiting for the show.

Joshua's laugh brought him back to where he was. Charles had finished the sea story, and Joshua was hurriedly launching into his own. Ryck didn't really have any of his own such escapades. He had combat stories, but those were usually only shared with those who were there, too. He could discuss regen, but that was for other gen hens. Still, the very nature of the military made him part and parcel to the stories, even if he hadn't actually been there. If Ryck decided to get out when his enlistment ended, he would miss that. He would miss the brotherhood.

Down in front of him, there was family. Beside him was the brotherhood of the uniform. He had to make his choice.

His train of thought was interrupted when the first explosion showered the sky with color. The show was on.

# *Tarawa*

## *Chapter 27*

"Enter!" the voice ordered.

Corporal Ryck Lysander opened the hatch, then marched in to center himself in front of SgtMaj Huertas.

"Corporal Lysander, reporting as ordered."

"At ease, Lysdander, at ease. You know why you're here. Your enlistment is up in seven days. It's declare time for you. As you know, you've been approved for re-enlistment. It's yours if you want it. You can stay infantry, but there have been by-name requests for you from the armory and armor. Have you made your decision?"

"Yes, sergeant major, but first, can I ask you something, if I can get personal?"

That seemed to take the sergeant major back, but after a moment, he replied, "Sure, son. What is it?"

"Well, and please accept it if I'm getting too personal, but you never married. Why?"

Ryck half expected a blast with a "None of your fucking business!"

Instead, the sergeant major looked down at his fingers as if checking the nails for dirt, then said "I was married to the Corps, son. It wouldn't be fair for some young honey to be waiting for me, to wonder what was happening, to sit with me while I was going through regen. Hardly seems fair to me."

"Do you regret it?"

"Oh, I like women, you can be sure of that. And I've had my fun. Maybe I've had some regrets, but I made my choice."

"Was it worth it, though?" Ryck asked.

"Yes. Absolutely. You know I'm retiring next month. But if I could I would switch places with you in a heartbeat. To be a corporal in the Marines again. Things are happening now, things are heating up. If the shit hits the fan, I would want to be at the tip of the spear, son, the tip of the spear.

"But I'm just an old fart now, regened three times, and ready to be put out to pasture. Maybe I'll hook up with some honeywa and see what all those civvies think is so great about marriage. Maybe I'll just whore around until they bury me. But my time has passed. Now it's your time. So it is up to you. What is your decision?"

"You know I went to my home planet two months ago, right? I saw my sister, her kids. I got a great job offer. I'd make more money in a year than I would in an entire career in the Corps. I could find a wife. I could have a family."

"And so . . . ?"

"But that was not my home. My home is here. My family is here. In the Corps. I want to re-enlist."

# BOOK 2: SERGEANT

# Soreau

## Chapter 1

"Look sharp, Tizzard! Keep your team up," Sergeant Ryck Lysander sent to Cpl Rey, his First Team leader.

Ryck knew that was easier said than done. The squad was moving down a wide boulevard to the Tylarian government house, but with thirteen Marines in the squad, all in Personal Integrated Combat Units, or PICS, they easily filled the road. Add in the civilians lining the edge of the road, and it was a pretty tight fit.

Those civilians were none too happy, and they didn't hesitate to let the Marines know that. The locals didn't appreciate "foreign mercs" in their country, which seemed ironic to Ryck as the Marines themselves were not mercenaries, but they were there to get mercenaries out of a jamb.

The Foreign Legion might be semi-official, but in this case, they had been hired on as mercenaries no matter how it was cut. A negotiating team from the Legion had arrived to work out a contract with the Tylarian government, evidently without the support of the people.

A flash on his visor grabbed Ryck's attention. After four years in a PICS, the electronic displays on the visor were second nature to him, but this signal was different. He swung his head and looked past the images to the real world beyond. Something trailing smoke had arched up and was coming back down. Ryck spun around, weapon ready, as the Molotov cocktail registered in his mind. It hit LCpl Teung in the back with a burst of flames as a blanket fire spread over him.

"Keep it steady, keep moving!" Ryck sent over the squad circuit, anxious to avoid a violent reaction.

Marines were not good at inaction. They were trained to react and react with extreme prejudice. However, a Molotov cocktail wasn't going to do anything to a Marine in a PICS, and their ROEs[22] were very clear. No action against the locals unless it was

[22] ROE: Rules of Engagement

life or death. A few flames did not fit the bill. Teung didn't even falter. He just kept marching as the flames burnt themselves out.

Ryck wondered what the people would do if they knew that, Teung, their first target, was actually a native of Tylaria. Would they have held back, or would that have inflamed them even more?

The Navy intel officer had laid out the political situation on the planet during their briefing aboard the *FS Chappa*. Tylaria was one of three countries on the planet Soreau. The nation shared a 1,650km-long border with New Guangzhou, a border where skirmishes had broken out over the last several months as New Guangzhou was making noises about a "reunification" of the two countries that comprised the planet's main land mass. With only a small militia, the Tylarian government called upon the Legion for help. The arrival of the negotiating team was widely broadcast in both countries, probably to both bolster the Tylarian public resolve and lessen the resolve of the New Guangzhou people.

That might have made sense, but the government was obviously out of touch with public opinion. If the masses around Ryck's squad were any indication, the people of Tylaria wanted reunification, and they didn't want anyone from off-planet there to force their hand one way or the other.

Ryck watched his visor display. Each Marine was identified as a blue avatar. He wanted to see a nice, even pattern. What he saw was a bunched-up group, almost a gaggle. With a blink, he zoomed out, and Second Squad's avatars appeared, displayed on the next street over where they moved parallel to his Third Squad. They were even more bunched, given they had a much narrower avenue of approach. The lieutenant was with them, too, and the Marines in the squad looked like they were forming around him almost as bodyguards even if it wouldn't be obvious to someone outside of the platoon to identify him as anything other than a Marine in a PICS.

"Grubbing Legion," Ryck muttered under his breath.

Ryck actually had nothing against the Legion. Sure there was the Marine-Legion rivalry, but on the whole, they were good guys. They might have had better equipment, and they certainly were paid better than the Marines, but a grunt was a grunt. He just didn't understand why a Marine company was being sent in to rescue a Legion negotiating team.

From a practical standpoint, it made sense. Golf Company had been going through routine jungle training on Ho`oku`i on the other side of the globe. When things started getting dicey for the Legion team, the Legion brass on Camerone made a request to the Federation Council for assistance, and here they were. Ryck didn't object to breaking from training, and he didn't object to an operational mission. What he did object to was the principle of the thing, which was, using government assets for the Legion's benefit. More than that, the ROEs were not only limiting, but also downright dangerous. The aggressiveness that gave the Marines their effectiveness was taken away.

If a government organization had to react, it should have been the Federation Civil Development Corps. The FCDC handled civilians, not the Marines. Marines were trained to close with and destroy the enemy, not to play riot police.

As if to buttress his thoughts, a woman rushed out in front of the squad point man, LCpl "Lips" Holleran. Lips was a busted-down corporal, but one of the steadiest Marines in the squad. Ryck wasn't sure what the 50 kg woman thought she was going to do against the 945 kg PICS, but it looked like she was going to try and latch herself onto Lips' left leg.

The Marines had been briefed to keep movement slow and steady and not to stop. Lips didn't stop. The woman was flung to the ground as he walked his suit forward.

"Uh, I think I squished one," Lips sent to Cpl Beady, his team leader.

Ryck, as squad leader, had ears on all the circuits.

"One-six, this is one-three. We've got a civilian woman down. She looks pretty bad, over," Ryck passed to the lieutenant.

If one of his Marines had gone down, the lieutenant, in his PICS-C, would have known immediately, but the civvies were not in the system other than as featureless grey avatars, and the PICS' sensors couldn't even determine an accurate count when they were bunched up so closely. Ryck knew the platoon commander had to pass up the incident immediately so the JAG[23] could get involved as soon as the situation was secured. If she were still alive, she would be in for a pretty hefty payment. All for being a grubbing idiot! What did she expect?

A hail of rocks came over the edge of a roof to shower the Marines. One rock bounced off Ryck's helmet. He blinked to an infrared scan and saw several signatures. If any of them had something more powerful than a rock, they were in a pretty good position in which to employ it. Ryck ached to call in a Wasp strike. He had been trained to take out potential threats instead of waiting for them to strike.

He couldn't call in a Wasp, though, even if they were under a real attack. The initial plan cobbled together was for the two Marine Wasps that were part of the combined unit going through the jungle package at the Mona Loa National Park training area to come in hot and heavy, leading the way for the PICS Marines. A Navy Experion fighter would have been better, but to civilians, the Wasp would still be pretty intimidating. The powers that be, though, nixed that. "Too aggressive."

Instead, the company's two heavy platoons were walking to the government building uncovered, or at least as uncovered as a Marine in the Corps' most modern fighting suit could be.

"Uh, Sergeant Lysander, do you see what I see?" Lips passed over the squad circuit.

Technically, LCpl Holleran should have used standard radio procedure, but with the circuit's frequency jumping and scrambling, and with the displays indicating who was sending, communications tended to slide to a more normal speech pattern at the squad level.

In front of Lips, beyond the people lining the road and the scattering of people milling about in front of them, approximately 50 or 60 civilians were shuffling to block the Marines way to the square in front of the government building. Lips, closely followed by his team, was closing fast. Their orders were to keep moving, but not to hurt anyone. As far as Ryck could tell, the two orders were diametrically opposed to each other. He had to make a decision.

---

[23] JAG: Judge Advocate General, the "lawyers" of the military.

"Third Team, halt! Form in a line, but do not push into them yet. First and Second, get on line with Third. It's going to be tight, so squeeze it in."

Ryck took a second to blink up the larger picture. To the south of the building, but still 500 meters away, the three squads from Second Platoon were making their way forward. To his left, Second Squad was stopped, and beyond them, First Squad was still moving forward.

"Push it forward, Stillwell," he sent to the PFC in Second Fire Team. "Don't hit anyone, but use your bulk to get in line with Peretti.

"OK, now, elbow-to-elbow, slowly, and I mean *slowly*, shuffle forward. Do not raise your feet. We don't need to be making pancakes out of any of them," he said to the rest of the squad as they came online.

The squad had managed to fill the entire street. About 20 meters ahead of them was the square in front of the government building. Between the square and the squad, though, were 60 or so shouting civilians. Ryck had a sudden urge to sound a charge and scatter them, but orders were orders.

"Form on Holleran. I don't want any space between us. Cpl Beady, give us a cadence, slow and steady."

Ryck was standing one pace behind Lips, and with Beady giving a cadence, he could focus on what was happening.

"One, two, one, two, one, two . . ." the team leader intoned as the Marines did a shuffle step forward.

The PICS were not made for elbow-to-elbow formations, nor were they designed for shuffling. The Marines were clanging against each other as the line lumbered forward.

"Cpl Rey, what do I do with this negat?" PFC Hartono asked his team leader over his comms.

Ryck switched to put Hartono's visor view on his own visor. A young man with a red bandana across his face had taken a few steps into Hartono's path, then launched himself up with a spinning kick to the Marine's chest. What he expected that to accomplish other than maybe breaking his foot, Ryck didn't know. What happened was that the man bounced off Hartono's carapace, not even budging the Marine.

"Ignore him. He's going to fall flat on his arse," Rey replied.

The man tried to take a few steps back for another go at Hartono, but the mass of people kept him from getting too far. He ran up to level another kick, but just as Rey had predicted, he slipped and fell to the ground. Hartono switched from a shuffle to lift his feet and carefully step over the stunned man.

Ryck switched off Hartono's viewpoint. They were only 10 meters now from the square. The press of people was such that the first rank of civilians was right up against the Marines. They were being pushed back by the advancing Marines, but more Tylarians back of them were pushing forward. Some were trying to turn around and get out of the way, but that was not going to be happening.

An obese man in what looked like old-fashioned lederhosen tried to lower his shoulders to stop Lips as if he were a rugger joining a scrum, but as he put his legs back to push, they buckled. He went face first down on the pavement. Lips shuffled over him, the man's big body bouncing between Lips and LCpl Martin off Lips' right side. He was dragged forward a meter or so, his body too big to easily slide between them, but like toothpaste in a tube, the man finally squeezed past to lie motionless on the road.

To Ryck's right, a body came flying forward. It was Hartono's bandanaed nemesis. Now in back of the line of Marines, he had a cleared area in which to run, and he had built up a head of steam before launching himself once again, kicking out against the PFC's weapons pack.

Despite himself, Ryck was pretty impressed. The guy really had no chance to rock a Marine in a PICS. The gyros kept the PICS upright, and it would take more than a 70kg martial arts wannabe to overcome that. But the guy had sure jumped up pretty high to slam his kick on the Marine's weapons pack.

Ryck was tempted to slap some sense into the guy, but as the civilian wasn't armed, Ryck decided that ignoring him was the best option given their ROE.

Ryck quickly toggled to a wider view. Second Squad had been delayed in their movement: they were still a good 50 meters from the square. First Squad, on the other hand, had already entered the square and looked to be forming to advance on the government building itself.

"Squad, listen up," Ryck began. "We're going to push out into the square two meters and halt. Keiji, you're going to refuse our right flank. Peretti, you've got our left. Between you and Stillwell, don't let anyone get in our way on the left. We need to look like the crowd has stopped us, let them relax even just a bit. When I give the order, we're going to give it a military left face and move our asses, and I mean *move them*, in a column to join up with First Squad. We need to surprises these people, then leave them in the dust. Peretti, that means you're going to be leading us. Get us past these rock-apes, but steer clear of the civvies who are holding up Second Squad. We need to get past them before they realize we're coming. All of us, keep it tight! Assholes to belly buttons! Got it?"

A green check appeared under 11 of the avatars on his visor display. Ryck waited another few seconds.

"Khouri, do you understand?" he asked his 12th Marine. "We're waiting!"

A green check belatedly appeared under the lance corporal's avatar.

"Sams, this is Ryck" he passed to the First Squad leader, knowing that the lieutenant, SSgt Hecs, and Sgt Pope Paul, "Popo," would be listening in. "In about two mikes, we're going to hightail it to your position to link up. I'm hoping there will be some scatter when the civs see a PICS squad rushing them, so that should give us an opportunity to present a more formidable front and maybe get up into the objective. You copy that?"

"Roger than, Ryck. Sounds copacetic. We'll mill about smartly here until you arrive, then let's push it forward," Sams replied.

"Good thinking on your feet, Sgt Lysander," Lieutenant Nidishchii' passed on the circuit. "SSgt Phantawisangtong, you've got command of the two squads. We're kind of bottled up here, so I don't think we can get there to join you until after the fact. Remember the ROE, though. No civilian casualties."

"Aye-aye, sir," the platoon sergeant acknowledged. "Get your butt in gear, Ryck. More rock-apes are on their way."

The lieutenant was new to the platoon, and his enlisted time was in the Second Marine Division, so he was somewhat of an unknown entity. Both Sams and SSgt Hector Phantawisangtong were well known to Ryck, though. Sams was Sgt Bobbi Samuelson, and Ryck had served with him when they were both privates over in Fox Company. SSgt "Hecs" had been Ryck's heavy hat at recruit training back on Tarawa. Despite the years that had passed, Ryck still thought of him as "King Tong."

The squad pushed into the square. Lips went slightly deeper than two meters, but along the edge of the square, tables and chairs were cluttered in front of what had to be restaurants. Even though a Marine in a PICS wouldn't notice crushing a table, there were people grouped there as well, and his squad needed to have a clearer shot to First Squad.

The squad halted. In front of them, the crowd, which had been slowly retreating in the face of the Marine advance, eased to a stop as well. A few of the braver sorts took a step or two closer to the Marine line, but staying out of arm's reach. In back of the squad, more civilians gathered and began to press forward. Ryck knew he had to move before they pushed up against the Marines.

"On three," he passed over the squad circuit, "left face and move out."

All twelve Marines acknowledge the order by activating their check marks.

"One . . . two . . . three! Move it!"

A PICS was not an extremely nimble piece of equipment. It had significant mass, and even with each Marine's physical movements augmented, the suit was not as agile as a Marine not meched up. However, once they got going, they were surprisingly fast. Within a few steps, the Marines were running at almost 60 KPH, far faster than any human could match. They left the protesters facing them and were able to dodge in back of the protesters surrounding Second Squad before those civilians could react.

Just as Ryck had hoped, when the protesters around First Squad saw the advancing Marines coming at full tilt, they scattered like a covey of quail. First Squad immediately started moving forward.

Stopping a PICS from full speed was an exercise in physics. Nine-hundred and forty-five kilograms at 60 KPH created beaucoup momentum. There was a trick to bringing the beast to heel. Ryck leaned back and thrust one foot forward, the LTC coating on his PICS heel digging a furrow through the stone cobbles of the square, individual stones dislodging to fly through the air. He pulled up to a stop exactly where he had intended.

Hartono was not as skilled. As the newest member of the squad and new to his PICS, he didn't get enough braking resistance, and he crashed into Keiji. Ryck knew the PICS' gyros would keep their suits upright despite some pretty serious impacts, and the suit's themselves were pretty sturdy, but a collision like that could damage sensors or even the weapons packs. Ryck had no time to check out either Marine's PICS, though. First Squad was on the move, and they had to get up to the objective before the protesters could shift with enough mass to impede their progress.

The square was covered in cobblestones, which didn't impede the progress of the Marines as they trotted up to their objective, but it slowed down the ability of the protesters to react to the Marines' movement. Ryck could see several small civilian groups trying to interspace themselves between the Marines and the building, but they were not going to be able to close in time. Nearly a hundred people were at the bottom of the steps, but the vast majority of the protesters had previously flooded out to plug up the streets and were now out of the Marines' path.

It took about 30 seconds to cross the big square. A single line of protesters tried to stop them, but the Marines slowed down and easily pushed their way through the crowd. The civilians didn't even try hard. They seemed to have given up, at least for the moment. Ryck knew they hadn't thrown in the towel, though. Getting into the government building was only part of the mission.

The Marines had to get out again, with the Legionnaires, and the protesters were undoubtedly going to try and stop them. To the protesters, the Marines reaching the government house was probably considered only a temporary setback.

SSgt Hecs led the two squads up the many steps to the main entrance. About 20 nervous-looking local militia manned two crew-served weapons which were sandbagged on either side of the big bronze doors. One soldier raised his rifle to aim at the Marines before another soldier knocked the muzzle back down.

SSgt Hecs moved forward and addressed the soldier who had stepped out from behind the sandbags.

"Staff Sergeant Phantawisangtong, Federation Marine Corps. I think you are expecting us?"

"Yes, sir! Lieutenant Xie, uh, militia, uh, Tylarian Militia, I mean. Yes, we're glad you're here. Please, come inside," the flustered militiaman managed to get out.

He nodded at another of the soldiers who picked up a landline and quietly spoke into it. A few moments later, the big doors pulled open. The 27 Marines almost casually walked through them and into a very large, ornate rotunda.

Ryck listened with half an ear as SSgt Hecs reported in to the Lt Nidishchii'. Ryck was in awe of what he was seeing. Back on Prophesy, the government building was more of an office building, perhaps befitting a planet that was colonized by a corporation. This was more in the lines of an old-fashion capitol building, with statues in the cornices and an intricate tile mosaic covering the vast floor. Ryck took a step further into the room, then stopped, conscious of his big PICS crushing some of the tiles underfoot.

They waited only a few moments before a Legion captain, wearing his T34 Parade Dress uniform, came hurrying down one of the large staircases. SSgt Hecs had activated his rockers[24] on his PICS arms and went right to him.

SSgt Hecs opened up the input to his speakers to the two squad leaders.

---

[24] Rockers: slang for the insignia of a staff sergeant. The "rockers" are the curves lines under the "stripes."

"Staff Sergeant, I am Capitaine Pichon. Thank you for your arrival. I understood, though, that a full Marine Company was coming?"

"Sir, SSgt Phantawisangtong here. The company commander has been held up outside by the mass of civilians. Our ROE is very clear that we are to avoid civilian casualties, so for the moment, we are the only forces to reach this building."

"Ah, just so. Well, if you could, please follow me to meet Commandant Gruenstein, our senior negotiator."

The captain started for the sweeping stairway before stopping and looking back at the Marines.

"Ah, perhaps you can evacuate your Personal Combat Systems? They may not be so maneuverable upstairs," he said.

Ryck tried to decide if there was a condescending note to his voice. It was taken for granted that the Legion's Rigaudeau-3s were better combat suits than the Marines' PICS, but Ryck didn't think the legionnaire was in a position to dismissive of Marine Corps gear.

"Ryck, strip and join me," SSgt Hecs told him, already starting the procedures to release the back seal so he could get out of the PICS.

It took almost a minute before Ryck could perform the Cirque du Soleil maneuvers necessary to hitch his legs up, then back down outside his PICS. He disconnected the hood interface, and he was free of the big beast, feeling naked, and not only from shedding his PCS, but also because his longjohns were so tight and thin as to leave nothing about him to the imagination. He checked his small Ruger 2mm, holstered it, and followed his platoon sergeant up the stairs.

An armed militiaman guard standing outside the door leading into Conference Room A came to attention and presented arms. The captain made a cursory salute and entered the room.

Inside, Ryck saw four more legionnaires and two men in civilian clothes. The civvies looked relieved at the sight of SSgt Hecs and Ryck. The legionnaires showed no reaction one way or the other.

With their longjohns on, neither Ryck nor Hecs had on any indication of rank. Without hesitating, though, the tall, hawk-nosed commandant stepped forward, hand outstretched.

"Major Nicholas Gruenstein. It is good to meet you."

The major could have come from central casting for a new Legion flick. Ryck noted that he used the Standard "major" instead of the Legion rank of "commandant," unlike the captain who had insisted on using "capitaine" for his rank.

*Score one for the major*, Ryck thought.

"Happy to be here, sir," SSgt Hecs told him. "Staff Sergeant Phantawisangtong and Sergeant Lysander. We've got two heavy squads inside this building. My commander, Lt. Nidishchii' is outside holding a few hundred civilians in place. Captain Davis, our company commander, is directly behind this building with another platoon of Marines. I've been tasked with preparing your team for evacuation so we are ready to move out as soon as Captain Davis arrives."

He looked around the room before continuing, "I was lead to believe that there were going to be more Tylarian personnel to evacuate?"

One of the two civvies looked embarrassed as the major said, "I'm afraid that Mr. Gelan and Mr. Liu are all that are left. Their, uh, *superiors*, decided that after the first group of protesters made it in the building, they didn't want to draw any more here to put us, their guests, in any danger."

"So you are saying they diddiho'd out of here, sir?" SSgt Hecs asked.

"Yes, I think that phrase is an apt description," the major said, only a slight hint of scorn in his voice.

Ryck wouldn't have done so well in hiding his opinions of the officials who had fled.

"If you think it feasible, we can move to the rotunda, sir, so we can prepare for the evac. We've got about a klick to go to our pick-up point," the platoon sergeant told him, careful not to make it sound like an order.

"Sounds good, Staff Sergeant Phantawisangtong," the Legion major said, actually doing a pretty good job with the platoon sergeant's name. "Lead on."

The five legionnaires, two civilians, and two Marines walked out the room, down the hall, and back down the stairs, but not before the major told the lone guard to rejoin his unit.

In the rotunda, Sams was taking some uniforms out of LCpl Andersen's buttpack. The PICS buttpack, which was actually more of a small-of-the-back-pack, allowed a Marine to carry cargo with him. The problem with them, in typical Marine logic, was that there were impossible to reach while inside the PICS. The pack could be dropped and then accessed, but the fingers of the PICS were a little big to handle smaller items that might be carried. Once dropped, the pack could not be re-attached without outside help. Most Marines simply used them to carry some extra chow and an emergency coldpack, the small gel piece of gear that kept a PICS from overheating on the inside.

Sams brought the uniforms from Andersen's pack over to SSgt Hecs.

"Sir, please have your men change into these utilities. They will offer you some protection as we leave," the staff sergeant told the major.

Major Gruenstein reached out and took one of the skins tops, fingering it before asking, "You've already inserted the armor protection in these, correct?"

The armor, what was called the "bones," was 23 separate pieces of what looked to be cardboard or feltboard that instantly hardened upon impact of a projectile. They were lampreyed onto the trousers and blouse, the skins, and rendered the uniform system proof against most small arms.

"Yes, sir," SSgt Hecs answered. "They're ready to go."

"As I understand it, your armor is custom made for each individual, correct?" the major asked.

"Well, yes, sir, they are. But we took a bunch of different sets, and with most of the Tylarian negotiators gone, we have plenty to pick and choose."

"I appreciate the consideration, but I hardly think that wearing ill-fitting clothing leaves a good impression. I think we will remain in our parade dress. If that leads to an injury, that will be on my head," the Legion officer said with an air of finality.

Either Mr. Gelan or Mr. Liu (Ryck never got which one was which) stepped to face SSgt Hecs and hurriedly spoke up, "Um, officer, we would like to put on your uniforms."

The platoon sergeant nodded to Sams, and the two Tylarian functionaries began to paw through the skins and bones looking for a close fit.

"If you will wait a moment, sir, let me get back into my suit so I have full comms and can report back to my command for an update," Hecs said, stepping back and moving to where his empty PICS stood like an empty insect molt. "You, too, Sergeant Lysander."

Getting back into a PICS was easier than getting out of one, but it still took a bit of dexterity. Ryck had to connect his hood, then push his arms in first and squirm up until he could bring up his legs to clear the opening. There were two handles inside the PICS up near the shoulder that made donning the PICS much easier. Some enterprising armorer had installed a set some years back when the PICS was first introduced, and now they were standard to the combat suits. Ryck grabbed the handles, pulled up, bringing his knees up past his belly, then slid his legs back down inside the PICS. He hit the closure button, then watched as his lights indicated the check process. Twenty seconds later, he was combat-ready.

He checked on his platoon sergeant. SSgt Hecs didn't look much different from the other Marines as they stationed themselves near the entrance and around the rotunda, but from the slight forward tilt of the platoon sergeant's PICS, it was clear that he was in intense comms with the lieutenant or the skipper.

The two Tylarians had selected their skins and stripped down. One was in his skivvies, the other was going commando. Ryck couldn't help but hope that it wasn't his set of skins that the skivvie-less man had selected.

There was the ever-so-slight click as SSgt Hecs came on the open circuit and activated his speaker.

"Sir, our drones are showing thousands of people converging here. Captain Davis, our commanding officer, has been ordered by higher headquarters that we need to move now. With thousands of people out there instead of hundreds, they don't think we can extract you without harm to the civilians, and they do not want to bring in air assets to the city proper to try and extract from the roof," SSgt Hecs said.

"Captain Davis is going to push forward to just short of the rear of this building, trying to attract as many of the protesters as possible. Lieutenant Nidishcii', our platoon commander, will move into the square to the northwest in an attempt to draw those right outside the entrance to them. As soon as we see the ones outside begin to draw away, clearing the entrance, we're to move out and run directly to the northeast as fast as we can go. There will be ground transport about four klicks away that will take you to an LZ[25] outside of town where you will be lifted off and taken to where a French packet ship, the *Améthyst,* is waiting in orbit. Mr. Gelan and Mr. Liu, you will be met at the LZ by one of your own representatives."

Ryck saw one immediate problem. There was no way five legionnaires in parade dress and two Tylarian politicos were going to keep up with PICS Marines. Major Greunstein had evidently realized the same thing.

"Staff Sergeant Phantawisangtong, I am afraid that 'as fast as you can go' is much faster than we will be able to go. How do we get around that?" he asked.

"Yeah, that's the thing, sir. It's been discussed, and with the concurrence of the captain of the *Améthyst*, who has taken command the French side of the operation, you are going to have to ride us," SSgt Hecs, said, waiting for a response.

"Capitaine de corvette Blanchard is in command? I am senior to him, but that is not your problem," the major said, sounding miffed. "We will *ride* you? How?"

"The best we can come up with is piggyback, sir," SSgt Hecs said sounding unsure.

---

[25] LZ: Landing Zone

"'Piggyback?' Like a child on papa's back?" came the incredulous response.

"Yes, sir, like that."

As if in punctuation, a large rock crashed through one of the windows of the rotunda. One of Sams' Marines moved to cover the new opening. Chanting could be heard outside.

"Piggyback," the major said with a shrug. "*C'est la guerre, mon* staff sergeant. If you can show us how we will ride you, then that is what we will do."

They needed seven "mounts." SSgt Hecs took three from First Squad and four from Ryck's Third Squad. This wasn't the first time PICS had been used to carry people. A PICS was a pretty good platform from which to go into the line of fire to take out besieged Marines, so this was something almost everyone had trained for at least once.

SSgt Hecs had them drop their weapons pack, leaving each of the Marine's back bare of anything extra. The clips on the shoulders to which the tops of the weapons packs were attached functioned as handles, even if they were not designed with that in mind. Below the PICS chest carapace and above the girdle, the waist narrowed, making a natural place around which a rider could latch his legs. It took only a few moments before the method became clear to the seven passengers.

"The ride will be quite rough. You will be jolted around, so you have to hold on tight. We haven't seen anything out there that can damage a PICS, but you are not PICS, gentlemen. A rock thrown off a roof can kill you, so we need to get you out of the area as soon as possible," SSgt Hecs told them.

"Jolted" was an understatement, Ryck knew. The one time he had ridden a PICS in training had shown him that. The seven men would be hard-pressed to stay on, and they would undoubtedly suffer bruises and cuts as they bounced around the hard-backed PICS.

"Are you ready, sir?" SSgt Hecs asked the major.

"This is not quite as I would have wished, but yes, we are ready."

Ryck would have felt more comfortable if all the passengers were in skins and bones, not just the two Tylarians. He hoped the major's vanity, if that was what it was, would not result in someone getting seriously hurt.

"Sergeant Samuelson, I want just one Marine watching outside. Everyone else step back out of sight. We don't want to play our hand too early," the platoon sergeant said.

"Lieutenant Xie," he called out to the militia commander. "The word from your higher headquarters is, I'm sorry to say, that you are on your own. My commander suggests that you leave with us. You won't be able to keep up all the way to the rally point, but you should be able to get out of the square, at least, before we pull away."

And if anyone had to fire on possible pursuers, Ryck realized cynically, it would be better if it were Tylarian militia rather than Federation Marines.

SSgt Hecs passed to Capt Davis that they were ready. The men in the rotunda stood around, doing nothing, basically waiting. Within a few minutes, though, the noise from outside shifted somehow.

"Some of them civvies is moving to the right," LCpl Jurić from First Squad said as he watched out the window.

"Your right or their right, Jurić?" Sams asked his Marine.

Jurić, inside his PICS, moved the big suit back and forth, arms out, as he tried to figure out which direction was right and which was left.

"Our right," he said after a moment.

"Captain Davis is in position, and he says he can see the crowd gathering in front of him," SSgt Hecs reported.

Suddenly, Ryck's comms with the company opened up. SSgt Hecs must have switched both squad leaders onto the company command net.

Ryck knew both SSgt Hecs and Sams could see what Jurić was seeing, but as their lone set of eyes was in First Squad, not Third, Ryck didn't have that capability.

"Sams, can you slave me to Jurić's visuals?" he sent on a P2P[26] circuit.

"Sure thing," Sams said, and a moment later, Ryck was able to see Jurić's vids displayed on the upper right quadrant of his visor.

There were still about 50 people right outside the front entrance of the building. One man was talking to several other, pointing back at the entrance. He had the posture of someone in authority. Capt Davis' plan, if it was even his and not something higher headquarters was throwing at him, had not drawn everyone away from the building.

In the distance, more people were gathering, but those should be the protesters around the lieutenant and Popo's squad. Ryck wanted to tell Jurić to pan and zoom in to focus on them, but that wasn't his place to do that.

"Sams, Ryck," SSgt Hecs said over the command net, one linked to just the three of them.

"These civvies aren't moving. We can push through them, but our cargo is going to be at risk. Until we get everyone out and we can get up to speed, those yahoos out there can do some serious hurt to them. If they have any small arms, they really can't miss at that range, and rocks, or even just yanking their asses off of us could be pretty serious. We need a distraction, for at least 20 or 30 seconds. Any ideas?"

"What about sending a team, like out to join the lieutenant," Sams offered. "Think they would follow the team?"

"Nah, I don't think so. The team would be through them and gone," SSgt Hecs said.

Right then, Ryck knew what would work, but he hesitated to say it. As a new private on Atacama, in his first engagement, Ryck had seen the results of when miners had managed to knock down several PICS Marines and cracked them open with LTC drills. The sight of those Marines, opened up like a can of sardines, had stuck with Ryck through the ensuing years, a phobia that Ryck tried to suppress.

"We need someone to take a dive," Ryck said reluctantly.

"A dive?" Sams asked.

---

[26] P2P: Person-to-person, a direct communication line between two people.

"Yeah. If a team runs through them out there, the staff sergeant is right. No one will follow. But what if two or three Marines make a dash, like they are making a break for it, but one Marine falls down? They'll swarm him, jump all over him."

"Shit!" Sams said, his opinion of the suggestion clear even over the circuit.

"No, I think Ryck's right. We need a distraction that'll keep their attention," SSgt Hecs said. "That would probably do it. We just need a few moments. I don't think they could actually do anything to us in that amount of time."

"What about if one of them has a toad?" Sams asked, referring to a hand-held incendiary that could slowly burn through about anything, including aPICS.

"That's a chance I think we have to take. We haven't seen anything to suggest that they might have something like that, and if they do, then our bait will just have to get up and out of there."

"So who's going to do it?" Sams asked. "Who's going to take the fall?"

"I will," Ryck said immediately.

It was his idea—it was his responsibility to take the risk.

"No," SSgt Hecs said. "You're a squad leader. I need to you for control. You need to bring up the rear, keeping everyone together, and trying to keep Marines between the bad guys and our cargo. Who else you got?"

Ryck thought for a moment. Ling, Stillwell, Khouri, and Hartono were "mounts" for the dash out of there. Peretti would be a good choice, but Ryck wanted him to help cover the rear. That left Holleran as the best choice. Knowing him, he would probably even think it was fun.

"Sams, give me one guy to go with Holleran, like two are making a break for it. Holleran will take the fall," he said.

"You gonna ask him if he volunteers?" Sams asked.

"Don't need to. He'll do it. And sometimes, you just need to pick the best person for the job anyway," Ryck said.

"That's it, then," SSgt Hecs said. "I'll tell Lieutenant Xie to bring in his men outside the door to encourage the civvies to focus on Holleran. Let me pass this up the chain, and you go tell Holleran. Sams, who're you sending?"

"Lopez. That mother can really get his PICS flying."

"OK, good. Get ready. I want to leave in two mikes," he said before flipping back on the command circuit.

Ryck could hear him reporting to Captain Davis their plans as Ryck grabbed Holleran and briefed him. As expected, Holleran was up for the idea. He thought it would be "fun." Ryck couldn't help but think of Sgt Nbele lying out on the ground on that Atacama mine pit, his PICS opened up and half of his guts spread out all over the dirt.

It was closer to three minutes before the seven passengers were mounted up and everyone was in position. SSgt Hecs gave the command, and Holleran and Lopez pushed out the main doors while the five militiamen slipped back inside. Ryck had Holleran's visuals on his visor. The lance corporal bounded down the steps in front of him, startling the surprised protesters who then started to move back. Suddenly, the projection tumbled, making it hard to tell what was going on.

"Falling" while in a PICS was actually pretty hard to do. The gyros kept PICS upright through most forces thrown at it. The gyros had to be bypassed, and with them off, controlling the PICS took much more skill, skill Ryck hoped Holleran really did possess.

A loud "fuck!" sounded out as Holleran yelled, making sure his speakers were on. For a moment, the visuals steadied with a view of the sky. Then images started crowding forward as they shouted for the Marine's blood. A couple of men actually jumped on Holleran's chest, making the visuals too jumbled to make much sense from.

"Now!" SSgt Hecs passed, and Sams' first fire team and then the mounts-with their cargo onboard—pushed out the door to start running along the broad walkway that ran along the front of the building.

One of the legionnaires shouted "giddyup" as they started to move, to Ryck's annoyance.

Ryck had to wait several moments before he, as the second-to-last one to leave, got outside. About 20 meters beyond the bottom of the steps, a mass of people was attacking the prone Holleran. Several of the crowd, though, had stopped when they realized more Marines were pouring out of the building. A few were starting towards them.

To his left, Ryck saw that the way was clear all the way to the end of the building. Marines had already reached the edge and were disappearing down the stairs to ground level. He counted the seven mounts, their piggyback cargo still secure on their backs. As he took that in, a couple of the militiamen scooted past him and started running pell-mell after the lead elements.

"OK, Holleran," he passed. "Get out of there now!"

ROE be damned. If Holleran had any problem, Ryck was going to charge, his 8mm hypervelocity gun ablaze. Bodies were going to fall.

A few of the protesters who were still focused on Holleran seemed to lose their footing. The welcome sight of a PICS Marine rose from the mass of people. It lurched forward, looking like at least one protestor was under its bulk. A few steps forward, and Holleran broke free and started into a lumbering run along the bottom of the stairs parallel to the route Ryck was now taking. Two protesters tried to stop Holleran, but they went flying like pinballs after colliding with him.

At the end of the building, Ryck ran down the steps into the square. Along with the rest of his squad who were not acting as mounts and joined by Holleran, they formed a rough arc in back of the last of the cargo.

"Vehicle at our two o'clock!" Cpl Mendoza passed.

Ryck looked to see a hover picking up speed as it crossed the square, heading for where the Marines were entering the street that led deeper into the city. A quick mental calculation, and Ryck knew the hover could crash into the last of the Marines carrying the legionnaires and the two civvies before they could get out and into the street. A hover at speed could probably only damage a PICS if it crashed into it, but the same impact could be deadly to any unprotected passenger.

He was about to tell Prifit, one of the squad's heavy gunners, armed with the 20mm HGL[27], to take out the hover when a burst of fire sounded behind him. He didn't have to look back. His visor identified the outgoing fire as coming from two of the militiamen. The sparks flashed off the hover, then it fell to the ground sending even more sparks as it slid along the cobbles.

"Rey, Prifit, Keiji, slow down a little. We're going to cover those militia until they can at least get out of the square," Ryck passed to First Fire Team.

They might not be highly trained, but the militiamen, already being left in the dust, had stopped to remove a threat to the Marines. Ryck was not going to abandoned them.

It seemed like forever, but it probably only took another minute until the militiamen, with the four Marines covering them, made it to the edge of the square. Lieutenant Xie gave Ryck a sloppy salute, then followed his men as they disappeared into the warrens that surrounded the area to the northeast of the square.

Ryck immediately sped up his team and caught back up with the rest. The same warrens that gave the militiamen cover provided the same cover for anyone trying to stop the Marines, so all senses were on full alert.

Ryck only half listened to the recall of Capt Davis and Lt. Nidishchii's groups to turn and move to their respective rally points. They didn't have unprotected people riding Marines.

An explosion sounded in front of Ryck, and he caught a glimpse of a body being blown off one of the Marines. It wasn't much of an explosion, probably a home-made grenade of some sort, but Ryck's heart fell. Losing one of his charges was not supposed to happen. But much to Ryck's surprise, the passenger got back to his feet. It was one of the Tylarians. The skin and bones he had put on had saved his butt. He shakily got back up on Hartono, and the group was back on the move.

Despite the confined route to the rally point, they were able to move pretty quickly, only having to stop twice for one of the legionnaires who was having a hard time staying on his Marine.

Eight minutes after leaving the square, they arrived at the rally point, which was a parking lot for a large Tesco store. Two

---

[27] Heavy Grenade Launcher

Tylarian armored personnel carriers were there waiting. The five legionnaires and two Tylarians climbed off their Marines—gratefully, Ryck thought. The legionnaire who had fallen, a captain whose name Ryck hadn't caught, had messed up his uniform pretty badly. It was torn, and one sleeve was hanging off. Major Gruenstein was rumpled, and his nose was bleeding where he had probably slammed it into the back of his ride, but he had somehow managed to keep the blood off of his uniform. None of the legionnaires looked good, uniform-wise. Looking at the two Tylarians, even the one who'd been blown off Hartono, Ryck thought the legionnaires would be looking much more presentable if they had put on the skins.

"Well, Staff Sergeant Phantawisangtong, this was, shall we say, an adventure?" Major Gruenstein said, walking stiffly to the platoon sergeant.

"Glad to be of service, sir," the platoon sergeant said. "You should be at the LZ in another 10 or 15 minutes, so in less than an hour, you'll be on a French vessel."

"Yes, and in the arms of dear Capitaine de corvette Blanchard," he said dryly.

Ryck laughed, despite himself. The major had escaped what could have been a serious situation. He'd been beat up on a long run riding piggyback on a PICS. He looked like shit. But still, inter-service rivalries and personal dislikes trumped all of that. It was good to know that the Legion was just like any other service.

The major might have a feather up his ass, but Ryck found he kind of liked the guy. He wished him well, at least.

Major Gruenstein loaded up his four legionnaires, then turned and saluted the Marines before getting in himself. A moment later, the personnel carrier roared out of the parking lot and disappeared down the road in a cloud of black smoke.

"Good job, everyone," SSgt Hecs said. "We accomplished that part of the mission, but it's not over yet. We've got another five klicks to the rest of the platoon before we can get out of here. The ROE is still in effect. We will avoid any situation that can get ugly. Any questions?"

"Yeah, anyone got any charge on them?" Sams asked Ryck and SSgt Hecs on the command circuit.

"What?" SSgt Hecs asked.

"Charge. On your PA. Money."

"What the grubbing hell for, Sams?" Ryck asked.

"Coke. That's a Tesco there. They've got to have Coke. I want a Coke."

Ryck started laughing, choking it off as SSgt Hecs flipped them back to the platoon circuit.

"If no questions, let's get the hell out of here," SSgt Hector Phantawisangtong, Federation Marines Corps, passed on to his men.

# Alexander

## Chapter 2

"You ready for this shit?" Sams whispered out of the side of his mouth to Ryck.

"Quiet in the ranks," Lieutenant Nidishchii' hissed, shutting Sams up.

The entire battalion was formed up in front of the nine of them: Capt Davis, the lieutenant, Lieutenant Lauer from Second Platoon, SSgt Hecs, Sams, Ryck, Lips Holleran, and Fab Groton, one of the squad leaders from Second.

The PA system was not working well. With galactic travel a long accepted fact of life, Ryck thought a simple PA system should not be beyond their capabilities. At least the battalion adjutant was able to project his voice.

"Personnel to be recognized, front and center . . . march!" he called out, his command clearly reaching them in back of the formation.

"Detail, right face," Capt Davis ordered. "Forward, march."

The eight Marines marched to the far right side of the formation, in back of H & S Company, then performed a column left and marched up alongside the formation. They conducted another column left after clearing the battalion, marching along its front to the center before halting.

"Detail, right, face. Present, arms!" the captain ordered.

Nine Marines saluted the three men in front of them. One of the men was the battalion commander. The second was none other than Major General Praeter, the division commanding general. The third was a *Général Denis* Bellerose, a Legion three-star. *Général* Bellerose was short, wiry man. His grayish dress uniform was understated despite the colorful medals on his chest, but the scrambled eggs adorning his kepi was pretty impressive. Ryck tried to keep his eyes locked forward, but he kept looking at the legionnaire through the corner of his eyes. He'd read the general's bio on the ceremony program, and it was pretty impressive. He'd served in seemingly most Legion conflicts over the last 30 years, commanding everything from a platoon to a division.

The fact that the Legion had sent a three star to Alexander for the presentation was a message in and of itself. With the current tension between Greater France and the Federation, the Legion was showing that civilian leaders aside, there was a brotherhood of warriors. The cynic in Sams kept insisting to Ryck and Popo that the French were just trying to win over the Marines for political purposes.

The three officers returned the salute and the captain brought them to order arms. There was a pause, then the adjutant's voice rang out .

"The *Commandant de la Légion Étrangère, Général Alain Plessey, takes pleasure in authorizing the Croix de guerre des théâtres d'opérations extérieurs* with bronze star to the following United Federation Marines for service in Tylaria on the planet Soreau on June 14, 366 Standard Reckoning:

"Captain Prentice K. Davis."

Ryck had been told that the award was the equivalent to a Federation Battle Commendation Second Class. If a Marines was awarded a BC, even a Third Class, a citation describing the action was read before presenting the medal. Not so with the TOE, which was the nickname of the French medal. Each recipient was mentioned by name in the battle dispatch, but not to the detail as in a Federation award citation.

A Legion lieutenant stepped up and presented the medal in a platinum box to the general as the flag officer stepped up to the captain. He pinned the white and red medal to the captain's dress blue blouse. As he stepped back, Capt Davis saluted, which the general returned. The French general took a step to his right to stand in front of SSgt Hecs while General Praeter slid in front of the captain.

"First Lieutenant Robert Lauer," the adjutant called out as the same procedure was followed to pin on the medal.

"Second Lieutenant Bertrand Nidishchii'," "Staff Sergeant Hector L. Phantawisangtong," "Sergeant Fabio Groton," and "Sergeant Bobbi Samuelson" followed. Ryck had to keep from sniggering at Sams' real name. Sams detested having a "girl's" name, and only answered to "Sams." It was as simple enough procedure to change a name. He could be "Duke," "Butch," "Rock," whatever, but he refused, saying Bobbi was the name his father gave him. He wouldn't let anyone use it to call him, though.

"Sergeant Ryck Lysander," the adjutant called out.

The Legion general took a step to stand in front of Ryck. He took the medal and started to pin it to Ryck's chest.

"That was aggressive thinking, sergeant. Major Gruenstein was quite impressed. Rumor has it that you were originally planning to join the Legion back on your home planet of Prophesy," he said quietly in his French-accented Standard.

*How did he know that?* Ryck wondered. Standing at attention, he stared straight ahead at the general's forehead, not responding.

"If you ever have second thoughts, I imagine we would have a place for you," the general said.

With the medal pinned on his blouse, Ryck saluted. A salute was an all-encompassing action, one that forced the officer to stop what he was saying to return it. It was the simplest thing for Ryck to do to change the subject.

"Lance Corporal Laste R. Holleran," rang out as the general took another step to his left.

Ryck let out a breath he hadn't realized he was holding. One general might have passed him, but now his division commander was in front of him. Ryck saluted, figuring that was usually a safe move.

General Praeter had started to reach to shake Ryck's hand, then when Ryck saluted, had to reverse course and bring his hand up in a salute. That done, he stuck out his hand once more.

Ryck didn't think he could shake hands while in the position of attention, but when a general officer offered his hand, it was best taken.

"Good job, Ryck. You made the division proud."

*What is with these flags? One knows about when I enlisted, and here another is calling me by my first name?*

The familiarity was making Ryck uncomfortable. General Praeter's attempt seemed forced, and that was even more disquieting. Ryck was glad when Lips' medal was pinned and the officer's stepped back.

"Detail, present, arms!" Capt Davis ordered.

The three brass returned the salute, and the captain had them order arms, left face, and forward march. They got back to behind the formation, and within minutes, the battalion commander had turned the formation over to the sergeant major who dismissed the battalion.

The formalities were not over, though. The Legion was hosting a social at the O-Club, and each awardee was to attend. A number of Marines wandered over to take a look at the French medal and offer congratulations, and the platoon sergeant had to remind everyone to get to the club. He addressed the enlisted, but made sure the three officers heard him as well.

"So, Ryck, what do you think?" the staff sergeant asked once everyone was moving towards the club. "This legion medal mean as much as your Silver Star or BCs?"

"I don't know, Staff Sergeant. I mean, its kinda zap, I know, what with not many Marines having one."

Even after all these years, Ryck still had a problem addressing his former drill instructor. The staff sergeant was low-key, not at all like he'd been on the drill field. He called Ryck by his first name on a social basis. But to Ryck, SSgt Phantawisangtong was still "King Tong." His actual name was too unwieldy, and Ryck didn't feel comfortable calling him just "Hecs," so it was usually "staff sergeant" or rarely "Staff Sergeant Hecs."

"Still, we got the froggies out without too much damage to the locals, right?"

"But it isn't like we were really in too much danger. Not like on Luminosity," Ryck countered.

Ryck had earned a Silver Star on Luminosity as well as his second trip to regen. SSgt Hecs had earned a Navy Cross. A Navy Corpsman and another Marine had been awarded Federation Novas, one posthumously, the first time since the War of the Far Reaches that two Novas had been awarded for the same battle.

"True," Hecs replied. "But we saved lives, and sometimes, that is our mission."

"If you two can stop jabbering, we're here. The caic[28] is that the Frenchies have brought some real French wine and cognac, and I'm itching to try some of that," Sams said, pushing past the two to climb the steps to the club.

Ryck had never been in the O-Club. It was forbidden territory, not open to mere NCOs. As they entered the big double doors, he looked around eagerly—and was a bit disappointed. There was more wood than in the NCO Club and a fancy carpet at the entrance, but it was basically the same layout. Dining tables were off in a room to the left, a more open room with high tables at which they could stand was directly forward, and the bar, with lower tables and chairs and a pool table was off to the right—just like the NCO Club. Even the Enlisted Club was laid out in the same pattern. Ryck hadn't really thought about it before, but it seemed as if officers hung out, drinking beer and playing pool, just like the enlisted Marines. Officers and enlisted might not be as different as Ryck had assumed.

"Gentlemen, may I interest you in some of this '56 Chateau Latour?" a familiar French-accented voice asked from behind them, the major's hand grasping the neck of a partially drunk bottle of wine.

"Major, it's good to see you," SSgt Hecs said to Maj Gruenstein. "You kinda left us with the impression that the Legion was gonna slap your wrist some."

"True, I did say that. But good for me that my father is a schoolmate of our president, so after a short investigation, I was absolved of any wrongdoing. I was, how you say, whitewashed?"

He grabbed three empty glasses off a passing waiter, handed them to the three Marines, and sloppily filled the glasses.

"No disrespect, sir, but are you drunk?" Sams asked before taking a tentative sip of the wine.

"Ah, very astute of you. Yes, I most certainly am drunk. I am *bourré*. Do you say that? 'Buttered?' No, you don't," he

---

[28] Caic: rumor, scuttlebutt.

answered for himself. "'Smashed,' yes, that is what you say. But this is very fine, very expensive wine, so it matters not."

Ryck took a sip of the wine. He had always liked wine, even the cheap stuff back on Prophesy. This was decidedly not the same. It was intense and complicated. He wasn't sure how much he liked it, but he knew he should like it, so he swirled it around in his mouth, sucking in some air, just as he'd seen on the food vids.

Sams made no pretense.

"Whew! Don't like it none. Maybe I need to try that cognac stuff instead," he said, pronouncing it "cog-nac."

"So what's next for you, sir?" SSgt Hecs asked, talking over Sams. "You still getting your command?"

"That, my dear staff sergeant of Marines, is why I am buttered. Our dear *général over there," he said, pointing with his glass at the Legion flag officer, "is not so much a fan of our president. And with the present situation growing between Greater France and your Federation, he seems to feel that we need a bigger liaison with you Marines and your Navy. As someone who has now performed combined operations with you, I am his logical choice. I found out this morning that I will be staying here on Alexander."*

*"Sorry about that, sir," SSgt Hecs said, reaching out to take the almost empty wine bottle. "But you'll get your command billet soon, I'm sure."*

*"C'est la vie, mon sergeant, c'est la vie,"* he replied, refusing to relinquish the bottle, tipping it up instead to drain it into his mouth.

Ryck wasn't sure how, or even if, he should respond. He looked up at the two generals on the other side of the room. Both men were watching them, and the Legion general didn't seem happy as he said something to General Praeter.

"Uh, Staff Sergeant, check your six," he said quietly, worried for the major.

SSgt Hecs casually glanced about, immediately realizing what Ryck had meant.

"Sams, why don't you take the good major and try and find that cognac you said you wanted. Ryck, grab Holleran and Groton, and let's go make nice with our honored guests."

The rest of the evening dragged on. Ryck was bored after 15 minutes, but he put up with the congratulations of the legionnaires, Marines, sailors, and civvie bigwigs. The deputy mayor wanted to drag Ryck into a discussion on what whether Greater France and the Federations would ease tensions between them, but Ryck begged off comment, saying that was for the civilian government to decide.

He finally decided that he did like the Latour, as well as several other nice vintages. The Le Bleu champagne was particularly nice. Sams, on the other hand, tried the cognac and immediately switched to beer. When Ryck spied Lips standing alone behind one of the buffet tables, he took that as an excuse to make his getaway.

"You ready to blow?" he asked as he walked up.

"Oh, cement it, sergeant! I've been ready!"

"Let me get Sergeant Samuelson, and we'll diddiho."

Sams wasn't ready, though. He was in deep conversation with and cleavage-peering at an attractive member of the governor's entourage. She seemed to be welcoming his attention.

*Typical Sams*, he thought as he went back to pick up Lips.

He stuffed a couple more pieces of *saucisson*, the label called it, but seemed like normal salami to him, in his mouth and grabbed a half-full bottle of wine that someone had left on a table as he took Lips and got out of there.

## Chapter 3

"You coming? It's your brills-bro, after all," Sams said after sticking his head in the small squad leaders' office.

Ryck looked up from his screen to where Sams and Popo waited, both in their PT gear with their MCMA belts on.

"MacPruit's not my anything-bro, dipwad," Ryck responded sourly.

"Come on, Rycky-my-boy, you and him, you're tight, recruit buddies, and all," Sams went on as Popo laughed.

For the hundredth time, Ryck wished he hadn't told the other two squad leaders about the beasting the recruit platoon leaders had given MacPruit when the recruit had refused to acknowledge his recruit squad leader's authority. It had been Ryck's rabbit punch to the back of the neck that had knocked MacPruit to his knees, but not before he had taken down two of them. Seth MacPruit had been an MMA planetary champion before enlisting, and he was one tough customer. Against eight other recruits, though, he had taken a pretty serious beasting. It had brought him around, at least. He hadn't questioned recruit authority, and by the end of training, he had even started assisting other recruits in need.

Given his background, it wasn't surprising that he'd eventually been grabbed from a line company to coordinate the regiment's Marine Corps Martial Arts program. Ryck just wished that MacPruit hadn't gotten orders to Ninth Marines. It wasn't bad when MacPruit been in First Battalion as a regular grunt. Ryck only occasionally saw him around camp. But when he made sergeant and became the MCMA instructor, Ryck was going to have to enjoy his company once a quarter.

"OK, I'm coming. Just let me log off," Ryck said.

"You should thank your buddy, there. What Marines wants to have his nose stuck in his PA studying when he could be out kicking ass and taking names?" Popo asked, punctuating his question with a series of lame air punches and a side-kick. "Pow, pow! Take that, motherfuckers!"

"If that's the best you can do, Popo, then maybe you'd better be doing some studying, too, 'cause you aren't going to be advancing based on that weak shit," Ryck said.

He saved his notes and bookmarked the site he was reading, then powered down his screen. He'd been working on his degree in his free time, much to the delight of the other NCOs who accused him of wanting to become an officer, something he vociferously denied. He was just interested in history, something that had bloomed in him during Dr. Berber's classes back at recruit training. As long as he was studying, he figured he might as well earn a degree while he was at it.

If he could ever keep on track, that was. He had a paper on the background leading up to the War of the Lost Surrender due by 2200 that evening, and he hadn't even started writing it yet. He had started the research, but he'd gotten lost on a tangent reading about one of the true Marine heroes, First Lieutenant Ian Cannon, Jr., who was awarded the Federation Nova for taking command of the *FS Ponce* when the entire navy command had been wiped out, and instead of retreating, took the heavily damaged ship into the fray, destroying two enemy corvettes.

"Uh, forgetting something?" Sams asked, pointing down to his own waist at his blue belt.

Ryck had already changed into his skin trou and t-shirt PT gear before sitting down to study, but he hadn't put on the yellow belt that signified his MCMA level. He went back to his locker and grubbed around until he found it. He put it on.

"Satisfied?" he asked Sams

"Now we're talking! Let's diddiho. They're already out there, and Hecs and the lieutenant'll be out there soon," Sams said.

The three of them left the squadbay and made their way to the large, sawdust-filled pit where MCMA was conducted. MacPruit was already waiting, looking assured in his skin trousers, red shirt, and boots. Around his waist was a black belt, of course. He nodded at Ryck, but didn't approach the other three sergeants.

"See you two on the bounce," Popo said as they split up to join their squads ringing the outside of the pit.

Keijo and Prifit had been wrestling around, with Khouri egging them on when Ryck came up. He didn't have to say anything, though. They both stopped and started a more appropriate warm-up. Within a few minutes, the platoon commander and sergeant came out, signaling the start of the instruction.

"Marines of First Platoon, you ready to kick some ass?" MacPruit called out as he stepped into the training pit.

He was greeted by a chorus of "oo-rahs."

"As all of you know, you NEED your MCMA belt to get promoted. Iffen you don't have it, you ain't gettin' that next rank. Sose you all better pay attention. All you white belts, you ain't safe, neither. Iffen I think you don' rate that measly white belt, I can take it back right now," MacPruit yelled out as he strode back and forth in the middle of the ring.

Ryck wondered if he could take a yellow belt away, too. Not demote it to a white, but take it completely away. He decided he better keep that thought to himself. No use giving anyone any ideas.

"But you are not here jus' to qualify, jus' to get promoted. You are Marines, an' you want to close with and destroy the enemy. This is what you're made for! Am I right?"

There was another chorus of "oo-rahs," but not quite as enthusiastic. Ryck thought MacPruit might have gone a little heavy with the demotion threat. Three of his Marines--Stillwell, Peretti, and Rey--were white belts, and they had to be a little nervous. The previous regimental MCMA instructor had never mentioned demoting Marines, so for most of them, this was a new concept.

"Some of you ask why MCMA? Am I right?" MacPruit went on.

*Damn skippy!* Ryck agreed. Golf Company was a heavy company. They fought in PICS. All this hand-to-hand stuff was so much horseshit. Ryck knew it was to foster the warrior spirit, but in reality, just like pugil stick training, it offered nothing for a Marine in combat.

"Well, you aren't always gonna be in your PICS, you know. You could go in light, or you can lose your PICS. Your own Sergeant Lysander over there, he lost his PICS when you guys were fightin' on

Luminosity, right? Without his PICS, he even got a Silver Star, right? So you never know, you never know."

Ryck was surprised that MacPruit singled him out. He wondered what game the sergeant was playing. Yes, Ryck's PICS had been disabled, and yes, Ryck had continued the fight, but not as some kung fu master. He'd just figured out how to engage his weapons without the PICS' interface.

"So let's get goin'. First, let's do some warm-ups. I wanna see where you all are. Give yourself a little room," MacPruit told them before leading them in some basic forms.

He wandered through class as he barked out commands, stopping to critique a few Marines. Ryck wanted to puke when MacPruit complemented the lieutenant on his form. As MacPruit moved on, the look on the lieutenant's face led Ryck to believe that the platoon commander had not been taken in by the brown-nosing.

"OK, Marines, OK," MacPruit shouted out. "Good job. But that's the boring part, am I right? You want combat, am I right? We'll get to that now, but first, I'm gonna demo it. I need a partner for that. Who's it gonna be?"

Ryck felt his heart sink. He thought he knew where this was leading. He was right.

"How about Sergeant Lysander? Me and him go back a long way, an' let me tell you, he's one tough hombre. An' he's already got combat experience without a PICS, without his skins and bones. Am I right?"

There was clapping from some of the Marines, and a "Kick some ass, Sergeant Lysander!" was shouted up from someone in Sams' squad.

Neither the reference to recruit training nor the combat was lost on Ryck. MacPruit, despite the ensuing years, had not forgotten that beasting in the showers that night. It also sounded like he resented Ryck's combat record. All MacPruit had done during his first tour with 1/9 was one show-the-flag-in-force to intimidate a case of social unrest. The unit had earned a Combat Mission medal, but Ryck doubted that MacPruit had even fired his weapon in anger.

There wasn't much Ryck could do, so he plastered a smile on his face and moved to the center of a pit. He stood in front of

MacPruit, trying to look at ease. The other sergeant reached into the cargo pocket of his skins trou and pulled out a training knife. He tossed it to Ryck, who managed to catch it.

"OK, sergeant, show me what you've got. Come at me," MacPruit told him.

*This is stupid,* Ryck thought. *When am I ever going to come at someone with a freaking knife?*

He couldn't hesitate, though. He raised the knife over his head and started forward with a yell.

MacPruit pulled an eGun out of his pocket and shot Ryck in the chest. Ryck looked down, staring at the slowly fading "hole" in his chest.

*No shit, Sherlock. You've got a grubbing gun while you give me a freaking knife,* he thought.

"That's not how you do it," MacPruit said to the platoon. "You don' need a knife. You don' need a rifle. You don' need a PICS. You, the Marine, are the weapon, whether you are naked or in a battle cruiser. But you need to know how to fight."

"Here, sergeant, give me the knife," he said, turning his attention back to Ryck. Ryck tossed it to him and caught the eGun tossed back. It was only a training aid, but it felt good in his hand. He checked the setting. I was set as a generic handgun. This was a standard training eGun, so it could be set to simulate all Marines ballistic small arms as well as several of the pulse weapons. It worked by calculating the range to a target, then sending a small electrostatic charge that simulated the effects of a specific weapon. The charge ionized at the target, leaving a glowing "impact" to show where a real round or charge would have hit. They were limited in range. The further out, the less accurate the simulation, but close in, they were a pretty fun training tool.

"OK, Sergeant Lysander. This time, I'm comin' at you."

Ryck held his eGun out. He was going to nail MacPruit and shut him up.

MacPruit turned to sweep his gaze around the pit at the Marines in the platoon before continuing, "Before I show you this, though . . ."

MacPruit suddenly spun, dropping down almost to the sawdust before springing up at Ryck. Ryck fired the eGun, but he was aiming at where the other sergeant's chest had been a moment before. The charge went right over MacPruit's head as the instructor crashed into Ryck, taking him down. Almost immediately, Ryck was stretched out, held captive by MacPruit, his right arm stretched out over his head and slightly behind him.

" . . . I should remind you never to give your enemy a warning. Hit him, and hit him hard."

MacPruit leaned back, stretching Ryck out further. Ryck tried to resist the pressure, to muscle through it, but the pain on his arm was too great. As much as he hated to do it, he tapped out with his left hand.

"Another thing. Iffen you ever get into combat with someone, neutralize him. See, this is hurtin' Sergeant Lysander's arm. See him trying to tap out, his hand flappin' like a beached salmon? But iffen I let him go now, he can still turn on me and do me damage. So I got to make sure he can't do nothing anymore."

He pulled back even further, and the pain made Ryck scream out. Something in his elbow popped, and MacPruit finally let up.

"See? Come in low, and never give an inch," he said as he got to his feet. "Let's pair up. I've got knives here in this box. Sorry, no eGuns, but we don' need them for this."

Ryck was still down in the sawdust, his arm on fire. He struggled to sit up.

"You ready to try it again?" MacPruit asked innocently. "I can be your partner."

"You mother grubber," Ryck hissed. "You broke my fucking arm!"

"Break it? Nah, I would've felt that. Maybe just sprained. Nothing a day or two in regen won't fix up, right? No harm, no foul," MacPruit said quietly.

"Doc, can you come over here?" he called out to the corpsman. "Looks like Sergeant Lysander hurt himself."

The corpsman did a quick check of Ryck's arm. MacPruit had been right. It was a sprain, and it would take two days of regen to heal it.

"Payback's a bitch," MacPruit said to Ryck as he was led off to sickbay. "Am I right?"

# BHP Billiton B-19

## Chapter 4

Ryck snuck another glance a Major Laurent standing across from him. The legionnaire barely fit inside the Stork, the top of his combat suit grazing the bird's overhead. It was not without a twinge of envy that he took in the legionnaire in his Rigaudeau-3s, the Legion's version of the Marine PICS. Ryck was proud of being a Marine, but still, every comparison between the two combat suits seemed to favor the Rigaudeau-3s as the better piece of gear.

It may have been a better piece of gear, but it did not marry well with a feet-in-the-wind Stork. Normally, when deploying in a PICS, Marines were lifted by an MV63-C, the Stork variant without a cargo bay. The PICS were slotted into cradle hoists which could quickly get two squads of PICS Marines onto the ground and into the fight. However, the Legion suit didn't have the coupling, so in order to accommodate Major Laurent, they were in an MV63-D, the latest model of the "normal" Stork. The web seats on which a Marine would normally sit were neither big enough nor strong enough for combat suits, so the seats were folded up and the pax[29] were all standing. With only the exit ramp as an egress, it would be more difficult and time-consuming to get the one embarked squad of Marines offloaded and the Delta on its way.

"What do you think of our friend, there?" SSgt Hecs asked him over the direct comms.

"I don't know. He seems OK, but his rank is screwing with me. 'Major Laurent,' but he's really an SNCO, a sergeant major?" Ryck answered back.

"Yeah, and they call their gunnies '*adjudant*.' I don't mean that. I mean how are you with this guy following us, watching what we do?"

"I'm not copacetic with it, Staff Sergeant, to be honest. I still don't know why all of these observers, all of a sudden. At least we don't have the capitaine, like Sams and the lieutenant have with

---

[29] Pax: Passengers.

them. You said you were going to keep him off my ass, anyway," Ryck told his platoon sergeant.

As relations deteriorated between Greater France and the Federation, there had been a flurry of initiatives between the Marines and the Legion, fully supported by the brass. Ryck wasn't sure how the brass expected these initiatives to improve anything. The civilian politicians were going to do what they were going to do no matter what their military arms thought.

Not everyone was on board with the increased interaction, though. A plainclothes member of the Navy Office of Information, accompanied by the battalion S2 officer, had briefed the Marines prior to embarkation. The Legion observers were to be treated with respect, but care was to be taken with regards to technical information or other operations. It was pretty obvious that the Marines were supposed to keep their mouths shut while around the observers.

Still, despite the fact that he wished the legionnaire was not with them, that Legion R-3 was one sexy piece of gear. A good head taller than a PICS, it had highly advanced stealth capabilities which rendered it virtually invisible to most sensors, at least until is started firing its weapons. It supposedly used a different cooling system that didn't have to be changed out like the Marine's coldpacks. The armor, too, was supposedly better, especially against energy weapons. It was more effective and somehow more flexible at the same time. Ryck had spent a number of months in the battalion armory while a genhen, and he would have loved to get into the guts of a Legion suit and see what made it tick.

*Enough of the R-fucking-3,* he thought. *Eye on the prize!*

In this case, the "prize" was a command base for the Soldiers of God. BHP Billiton, the huge resource conglomerate, owned B-19. There were three major mines in operation, although exactly what they were extracting was a trade secret. The planet had never been terraformed, but it had plant life and an atmosphere, albeit one that could not support human life for long. Trace gasses would have a person coughing out his lungs within an hour after exposure.

About three months ago, the planet managing director informed their lone Federation liaison that they'd had odd fluctuations in their survey readings. He was suspicious that there could be poachers mining the other side of the planet. The Ministry of Resources looked into it before quickly turning it over to the Navy. Something was there, and it wasn't illegal mining.

A Navy Information Analysis Team, the NIS super spooks made up of ex-SEALS and techno wizards, was sent it. Within weeks, they had located the shielded station and confirmed it was SOG.

The location made sense for the criminal gang. The planet was very lightly populated and all on the other side of the globe. There was no military presence. If the MD hadn't decided to send out survey drones to see what could have been missed during the initial assessment, they could have remained undetected for years.

Ryck had a history with SOG, and when his platoon had taken down the *Robin*, an SOG-held hostage ship, Ryck's experience with them cost him over a year in regen. At least, the official report was that it was SOG. Most of the Marines involved thought it hadn't really been SOG but a copycat. Too many things didn't add up. But as the official version was that it was Soldiers of God, no one was going to go public and say anything different.

SOG was a criminal organization, nothing less. They acted under the guise of religious righteousness, but they were simply in it for the money, seeding their path with unspeakable acts of terror. Every government known to man had proclaimed them pariah, not covered by treaties of human rights. The Federation, acting hand-in-hand with the Brotherhood,[30] had thought it had cut off the head of the organization, but instead, many new heads had sprung up, far more decentralized. Wherever one of those heads showed up, it was immediately stomped.

This time, it was Second Battalion, Ninth Marines, with the *FS Toowoomba*, that would be doing the stomping.

Golf Company was the lead element, each platoon going in heavy. Echo was setting a perimeter, Weapons was in support, and Fox, going light, but with breathing gear, was in reserve, waiting to exploit success or move in if the complex was too tight for PICS.

[30] Brotherhood: The second largest confederation of planets. It has a religious basis and is a sometimes wary ally of the Federation.

The attached Frog Team, with their Ratcatcher missiles, was deploying to knock down any escaping craft. The *Toowoomba*, in geosynchronous orbit above the target, with its array of weapons and Experion fighters, was more than capable of taking out a SOG ship, but if they were going to be in a fight in the first place, the Marines wanted credit, either with the Ratcatchers or their Wasp attack craft.

Ryck checked the readouts of each of his Marines, checking biostats and power levels. The upgraded command information system gave him ammo counts as well and would calculate rates of fire and depletion. It was a good add, but it was just one more thing to monitor. As a sergeant, Ryck was beginning to think he was getting to be more of a resource manager than a fighting Marine.

At five minutes out, he toggled the countdown warning. He could have passed it on over the comms, but they didn't need to continually hear his voice. A simple data message would suffice.

Like it or not, Ryck was feeling a bit nervous, and he couldn't let his Marines know that. Whether that had been SOG or a copycat on the *Robin*, memories of the misery that was regen kept creeping back into his mind. He looked at his rising pulse rate and tried to will it down. If SSgt Hecs or the lieutenant looked at their readouts, they would see his stress levels rising.

*Get a hold of yourself. This isn't your first time to the party!* he told himself.

He knew he just had to focus on the mission. Second Squad, with the EOD[31] team and heavy weapons team, was in a Charlie Stork, so they would be first in the zone, getting out and deployed within 15 or 20 seconds. The two Deltas, carrying First and Third, would flare in right after. Marines in PICS could actually damage a Stork if they weren't careful, so they couldn't bumrush out the back. They had rehearsed deplaning back on Alexander, like the riffle of a pack of cards shuffle in reverse, Ryck imagined it, the port aft Marine followed by the starboard aft Marine, followed by the next port Marine, and so on. It would take at least a minute to deplane. That was when they would be the most vulnerable.

---

[31] EOD: Explosive Ordinance Disposal

There were three eyes on the target as they approached. The *Toowoomba* had her planetary sensors, battalion had a butterfly drone, and there was a recon team out there, all streaming in data. With the naked eye, their target looked like a rock face to a hill. Under different spectrums, seeds to which Ryck could switch, he could tell there was something off with it. There were odd lines visible on the display, and the rock's ambient temperature was slightly different from the rest of the rocks. The SOG had made a pretty elaborate and extensive effort, and it might confuse a casual sensor, but not the Federation's best equipment. It was SOG's bad luck that the original BHP Billiton drone was designed for deep ground analysis and not surface observation. Good luck to the Federation, though.

The go-light turned amber, indicating one minute. A matching amber icon flashed in their helmet face shields. Ryck shifted to look out the back to where the ramp was already lowering. When in skins and bones, Marines could start out a Stork before the ramp was fully lowered: with them in PICS, this wouldn't be possible. The Stork crew was going to be over the LZ much longer than normal as it was, so they were already lowering the ramp. There was no intel on anti-air, but with the ramp lowered, the Stork's stealth capabilities would be far less effective, and if spotted, their shielding wouldn't be as strong, either.

As if to emphasize that vulnerability, a flash of light from the outside illuminated the cabin of the Stork. Ryck felt his heart drop as he tried to see out the back.

There was a surge of chatter on the comms. Ryck didn't have ears on higher headquarters circuits, but he could hear the platoon circuit. A missile, probably part of an automated defense system, had been launched at the other Stork carrying the lieutenant and Sams' squad just as they lowered their ramp. Luckily, it never hit the Stork. One of the *Toowoomba's* monitors, parked at the edge of space over the target, and taken the missile out with its ARG, the Atmospheric Rail Gun. A split second later, the jacketed round delivered its kilo-joule pulse to the missile's launch site.

Atmosphere dissipation was the bane of space-based energy weapons, requiring huge amounts of power to get that energy focused on the target on the ground. The ARG got around that by using railgun technology to send shells at amazingly high speeds through the atmosphere, each shell, a self-contained pulse generator. The jacket of the round would slough off at the target, and the pulse would initiate, focused at the target, and taking it out. A kilojoule was not as effective against hardened targets, but it should have been enough to put the launcher out of action.

Ryck hoped, at least.

Lieutenant Nidishchii' passed that one of the Wasps was coming in for a strike at the launch site, but Ryck knew the monitor's crew back on the *Toowoomba* would be watching the site closely, and at the first sign of electronic stirring from enemy weapons systems, would hit them with something a little more effective.

Worse than the scare of the missile attack was the fact that if they ever did have the element of surprise, it was gone now. Whoever was in the hidden complex had to know that they'd been discovered.

The Storks had continued their approach while the incoming missile had been destroyed. The first Stork, carrying Second Squad and the Weapons team, had already reached the LZ and was lifting back out of the LZ. Ryck's Stork flew in fast, flaring at the last moment, its ramp slamming a little harder than normal.

Cpl Mendoza's team started the deliberate shuffle to get out of the bird. Ryck wanted to scream out to hurry, but that was just his nerves wanting to get out of the bird and to where he had more control of his situation. Peretti led, then Khouri, Mendoza, and Stillwell. Ryck was next, and he followed Stillwell out, ducking down as well as he could to make sure the helmet of his PICS didn't hit the top of the Stork's cabin at the lead edge of the ramp. He hoped his pet legionnaire wouldn't have an issue with The R-3's added height.

As soon as Ryck's feet hit the ground, he pushed forward, running a good 15 quick meters before turning to make sure everyone else debarked OK. Major Laurent was only a step or two behind him, and Ryck's abrupt stop and turn obviously took him by surprise. He nimbly dodged to his left and scooted past Ryck.

"Scooted" seemed like an odd term to Ryck to describe someone in a combat suit, but that is what it seemed to him. The legionnaire was remarkably nimble in his R-3. While the armor on an R-3 was termed "flexible" by many, it wasn't as if it was just a shirt and trou. However, there was some give to it, and the globe joints, which were small hardened spheres actually imbedded into the armor skin, offered a far more realistic range of motion than the PICS GT joints. If Ryck ignored the size and shape of the R-3, just from the movement, Ryck could almost imagine that the legionnaire was not in a combat suit at all as naturally as he was moving.

Ryck had to get his attention off the legionnaire. It was crunch time, and he had to focus on the mission. He waited until his squad had debarked, then got the Marines moving out of the zone and out of the path of any possible incoming that had targeted the LZ. He toggled up the route overlay on his display, then nudged the icons for his lead team over another 30 meters. Peretti, on point, would see where Ryck had positioned the command avatar for him and then move to the right until he was where Ryck wanted him. It was a very simple, yet effective method of troop placement.

Ryck quickly zoomed out his display view. Echo was already forming the perimeter around the target, even placing a platoon behind the small mountain in case their targets had a rabbit hole that had not been identified. Ryck could see the Navy shuttle approaching with Fox, ready to land two platoons in the LZ Golf had just left. Golf's Second Platoon was moving forward in line with Third and First Platoon followed in trace. Things were going according to plan—so far.

The Marines moved through the five-meter tall fern-like vegetation. This was the first planet Ryck had been on that had vegetation but had not been terraformed. He'd seen alien plants before at a few botanical gardens, but never in their natural state. There was an odd homogeneity to the forest with none of the variation in height or variety found in terraformed worlds.

The two platoons moved at a fairly good clip through the fern-tree-things, simply pushing them aside. As the Marines approached the target, though, the terrain worked to pinch the two platoons together. This was the reason that only Golf was going in as the point of main effort. There simply was no room for any more units within the confined area.

As they passed one of the hillocks to their right, Ryck took a quick look with full sensors. He knew the recon team was on that 40 meter-tall rock jumble, but he couldn't pick up a thing on them. That always impressed Ryck. Going out into bad-guy territory pooping and snooping with minimal armor seemed risky, but if the bad guys couldn't see them, then Ryck figured it was a risk worth taking. He sure appreciated having actual human eyes on a target, not just sensors. He gave the unseen team a nod of respect despite knowing they couldn't see it.

There was a surprising lack of comms chatter. As a rule, Marines were supposed to keep talking to a minimum. Even with frequency shifting and scrambling, the enemy could pick up the fact that communications were taking place, and with good AIs, could calculate potential courses of action based strictly on the amount, duration, and direction of voice comms being made. The less said over the net, the less there was to analyze. Still, voice comms were sometimes needed. So far, though, not much had been necessary during the movement to contact.

As the squad moved around another outcropping, about 300 meters from its target, a small yellow flashing number on Ryck's display caught his attention. Martin's PICS was running slightly hot. It wasn't into redline territory, but that was something that needed to be monitored. He made a mental note to have it checked.

Ryck toggled Martin's readout to the top of his display so he could keep an eye on it when the world around him erupted into a flash of flames and smoke. Ryck was thrown to the ground, banging painfully against the inside of his PICS. His display disappeared, leaving him with only a clear visor through which to see the dust cloud forming around him.

*Mother grub!* was all he could think as he tried to get his thoughts straight. He could taste blood where he'd bitten his tongue.

Everything was down. No comms, no data display. He couldn't even move his PICS. Ryck's immediately thought of his first mission when a squad of PICS Marines had been put out of action through a Trojan that had been wormed into the combat suit's control system. Four of the Marines had been killed. Despite this flashback, he was surprised at how calm he was as he hit the reset. To his tremendous relief, the status lights came on and the suit's AI began the start-up check. A set of PICS feet stepped into view, then the PICS ponderously bent over to reveal Cpl Rey's face. Ryck had no comms nor movement yet, but he winked back at his team leader. Rey gave him a thumbs up, then moved out of Ryck's narrow range of vision, probably moving to check on someone else. Yancy Sullivan had been just to Ryck's left where the blast seemed to have originated. Ryck needed to know if his PFC was OK.

Ryck was confused as to what could have hit them. Nothing was picked up by the sensors as incoming, and their sensors should have identified any mines.

The dust cleared, but Ryck couldn't see much. Marines were moving back and forth in front of him, but Ryck was facing away from the direction he wanted to face, that towards Sullivan. Two more of the squad bent down to check Ryck, turning him onto his back.

Ryck tried to take stock of himself as his PICS started coming back online. He'd banged his left arm pretty good, and he knew his tongue was bitten, but other than that, he seemed in one piece.

Lips put his face shield against Ryck's and shouted out "Are you OK?"

Ryck could hear him clearly, but muffled, through his face shield, so he shouted back "Yeah. How about Sullivan?"

As he yelled, he splattered blood across the inside of his face shield. It started to form into droplets and drip back down on his face. Instinctively, he tried to shift his body, and his PICS responded. It was coming back online. The display on his visor came to life—covered in blood splatters.

"Sullivan's out of action. Doc's got him stable though, but his leg's pretty fucked up. That blast twisted it like he was some sort of doll," Tizzard Rey said, his shout coming both through his PICS and over the comms.

"What the fuck was that?" Ryck asked. "How come we didn't pick anything up?"

"Don't know yet. Sergeant Kyle is doing a scan," Rey told him.

Frank Kyle was the EOD team leader. He would have some basic analyzing tools in his PICS-E, but Ryck knew they had to keep moving, and Frank might not have time to do a full scan. Knowing just what had exploded might have to wait for the Navy Seabees to come down and determine what had hit them.

Ryck slowly stood, checking all the readouts he could. He bent his knees and flexed his arms. He seemed to be moving OK, but he couldn't check the actual readout figures. Much of his face shield display was obscured by the blood he'd spit out. For all the advances in battle suit technology, something as simple as blood inside was a big problem. He couldn't just reach up and wipe it, after all. Not only did it block his view of some of his readouts, but it blocked some of the small micro-scans embedded in the face shield that read the eye commands used to activate the PICS' various display functions.

He turned to where PFC Sullivan had been and took his first steps to see if his PFC was OK.

"Sergeant Lysander, you back online?" the lieutenant asked over the person-to-person circuit.

"I think so, sir, but I can't really tell. My display is sort of covered in blood. I'm OK, though," he said, his words slightly slurred as his tongue was already swelling. "Can you wait one, though? I need to check on Sullivan."

The platoon commander said nothing else as Ryck arrived at where Sullivan was down, Doc Grbil working on him. The blast had wrenched the PFC's right leg, actually bending it at the knee at about a 70-degree angle. The joints were the weakest part of a PICS, but still, that had to have been one hellacious blast. Luckily, the PICS leg had not completely detached, so Sullivan's leg had not been amputated. The angle was gruesome, but Ryck thought a couple of months in regen would make him as good as new.

"Yancy, how're you hanging?" Ryck asked as he approached the Marine.

The PFC's face shield was on clear, and Ryck could see Sullivan's face, a goofy-looking grin plastered across it.

"Oh, copacetic, Sergeant. No pain at all. Doc's hooked me up," he said as if he hadn't a care in the world.

"I've given him somamine," Doc Grbil passed to Ryck on a person-to-person. "He's not going to be feeling a thing."

Somamine was one of Pfizer's newest painkillers. It worked by changing the pain impulses into something the brain recognized as a warm feeling of contentment. The science of it was beyond Ryck, but it was a favorite among the Marines. They called it "happyland." It couldn't be used for too long as it could permanently re-program the brain as to what was pain and what was pleasure, but it was very effective in situations such as this.

"Is he going to be OK?" Ryck asked.

"Yeah, he'll be fine. He's going to have to go through decon, though. The blast broke through his armor, and he got some of this toxic atmosphere that leaked in. I've gunked the break, and that should hold for now. As for his leg, it'll probably take some surgery to repair the damage, then regen to heal it. I think a couple of months, tops."

"Sergeant Lysander, I can see your stats even if you can't. All your readings are in the green. Are you effective? We've got to keep moving," the lieutenant asked.

"Uh, roger, sir, I'm still effective," Ryck responded.

He could hear the slight click that told him the platoon commander had switched back to the platoon net.

"PFC Sullivan has been WIA'd but is in no danger. He will be picked up by G-One for a casevac. We've still got our mission, so move it out. We don't know what ordinance was used against us, so until we identify it and devise countermeasure, watch your dispersion. Gee-Three-Six, out."

As Ryck turned to go back to his squad, he caught sight of Major Laurent standing 20 meters off to the side, clearly studying Sullivan. Ryck was suddenly washed over by a feeling of foreboding. Laurent was an observer, so he was bound to observe. Ryck couldn't help but feel, though, that he might be too interested in a weakness in the Marine PICS.

Within moments, as a team from First Platoon arrived to take charge of Sullivan, the platoon was back on the move. Ryck's

PICS was moving normally. His problem, though, was visibility. Back on Prophesy, when the PCDC declared bankruptcy and pulled out, the economy had shattered with many people finding themselves out of work. A number of people took to standing at intersections and washing the windows of hovers for a few credits. Ryck would have paid 100 credits at the moment if one of those men or women was there now and could reach inside his PICS to clean off the blood.

The top of his face shield was clear. Ryck was using this section for visibility as he moved forward. This was where the anti-fogging vents were, though. In certain conditions, such as when out of direct sunlight in open space, the outside of the visor would be bitterly cold while the inside was kept warm. This could lead to fogging, so a simple vent system blew warmed air over the inside of the face shield. This was a basic, old-fashion method that worked surprisingly well.

On a whim, Ryck activated it. He didn't want to dry the blood where it was. That would make things worse. But he turned up the vent to its highest speed anyway. It worked. With the fan pumping out the air, it blew the droplets down the inside of the face shield to where it caught on the edge of where the face shield met armor. There were still streaks of blood which started to dry, but Ryck could see through his visor. More importantly, he could see his displays again.

The lieutenant had told him his numbers were good, but Ryck ran a quick check anyway. Other than a still slightly elevated pulse rate, everything was normal. Less than five minutes had passed since the explosion, so that was probably adrenalin still coursing through his body that had shot up his heart rate.

He ran a quick check on the rest of the squad. Sullivan's avatar had turned to the light blue of a Marine out of the fight, but still alive. Everyone else had normal readings.

This had been an unexpected delay, one that had cost the platoon a Marine, but the mission was still in place. Ryck forced his mind back on point, pushing the blast to the back of his mind.

He expected another blast, though, all his senses on the alert. However, they made it to Phase Line Rat without further incident.

This was the final phase line before the Final Coordination Line, the FCL. Rat was in defilade to the final objective, out of any direct fire weapons. From Rat, the EOD team moved forward, supported by First Squad. The boomboom boys and Second Squad crossed the FCL and moved carefully to a point about 100 meters from the disguised entrance to the hidden depot. Ryck watched through piggybacking Popo's visuals as Sgt Kyle unlimbered his DSD[32] and sent it trundling up to the doors. The small robot extended the first of its sensors, sending the readings back to Kyle. The EOD team leader shook his head, then deployed the drill, trying to take a core sample. The drill easily moved through the outer, rock-like covering, but when it hit the actual door beneath, it stopped its progress. The little robot's front tracks lifted off the ground as it applied more pressure to the drill.

Sgt Kyle stopped the drilling and deployed the laser. He had the DSD fire it where it had been drilling. Ryck remembered from his classes that the laser was not intended to penetrate but merely ablate off some of the surface so the robot's spectrometer could get an analysis.

Kyle shut down his DSD, and a moment later passed to Capt Davis on the command net "G6, these are some extremely hardened doors. They look to be a LTC variant and are around 3 meters thick. I don't have anything in my bag of tricks to breach this. We can look to bypass the doors and go through the rock face itself, but there's no telling yet how much rock we'll have to blast through. Waiting further instructions, over."

There was a moment of silence, assuredly as the company and maybe battalion leadership discussed what Frank had told them.

The nets crackled with Capt Davis' voice, "Give me a degree of assuredness on that. What's the chance that you can breach the doors."

"Uh, I'd say about zero to no chance. These things are massive. If you want me to blow our way in, we need to find a better spot to do it," the EOD sergeant replied.

32 Drug Sniffing Dog, slang for the E-334 EOD Remote Analytical Robot.

"Roger that. I understand. Wait one, out," the company commander passed.

Only Ryck was able to access the command circuit, and he knew his Marines would wonder what was going on, so he passed, "There seems to be a problem. The doors at the entrance might be too big for the boomboom team. So we're waiting for further word now."

"Shit, stand by to stand by. Typical shit," Lips said.

Lips had been a corporal selected to sergeant when he'd been busted back down to E3 for taking a swing at an MP while drunk. He might have been Ryck's most capable Marine, but he did tend to exhibit a degree of cynicism. Ryck didn't know if he blamed him for his cynicism, given his history. And this time, Ryck agreed with Lips' sentiment.

SOG knew they were there. Delaying the assault just gave them more time to prepare whatever they had planned for the Marines. Sgt Kyle and his team couldn't get in, but there were other resources available to them.

"Sergeant L," PFC Stillwell asked on the P2P, "Is Yancy really going to be OK?"

Ryck realized that Stillwell had never seen a Marine WIA'd. Most of his squad had never seen combat. Their operation on Soreau wasn't combat, and it hadn't prepared them for their first taste of fighting. They still hadn't fired their weapons in anger, and to see one of their own taken down was a gut-check.

Stillwell and Sullivan were also buddies, he knew. They'd gone through boot together, been assigned to Fox together, then transferred over to Golf together.

"He's barely hurt. Two months in regen, and he'll be back good as new, Jeb," he told the PFC.

"Is it going to hurt? Regen, I mean. I mean, you've been there, and they say it hurts," Stillwell went on.

"It fucking sucks, to be honest. The itch is the worse 'cause you can't scratch it. And the Navy docs can't give you anything for it. They say that can affect the healing. But Yancy's a tough mother. He'll handle it just fine."

Ryck was about to continue in that vein when the command circuit came alive.

"All hands, get your men turned around and move back to your platoon rally points. The Navy's going to drop a GD-1905," Capt Davis passed. "The ship's monitor is getting into position for the correct drop aspect. We've got four minutes, I repeat four minutes, before the drop."

Ryck looked at his display. The captain had lied. His display already read 3:47.

"I want to see heels and asses, now!" the skipper ordered.

Ryck didn't wait for the lieutenant to pass it down.

"We've got a Tungsicle coming, in 3:42 and counting. Everybody, form up now! Squad V, and move it back to Rally Point Isaacs. The captain wants heels and asses!"

The Gravity Dropped-1905, the "Tungsicle," was a simple four-meter long column of crystallized ceramic-covered tungsten. One end was pointed, the other flat. At 80 centimeters wide, it was a hefty 155,000 kg of unstoppable penetration power. It was too big for the monitor's main railgun, so a modified railgun with far less power was mounted on the exterior of the monitor to get the weapon moving. It left the monitor at "only" 2000 mps. Ryck didn't know the correct calculations for how fast it would be moving when it hit based on BHP Billiton B-19's 1.2 G gravity well and 90% atmospheric density, but with a heavy sectional density and a low ballistic coefficient, it should still be at over 1,000 mps upon impact.

That impact would be huge, in the giga-joule range. The crystallized ceramic coating not only kept the Tungsicle from burning up in the atmosphere as it fell, it also helped internalize the KE upon impact. The weapon was designed to penetrate into a target, not expend all that energy in a surface blast. However, that much energy could not be completely contained. There was going to be a pretty big bang when it hit, the equivalent to maybe 15 tons of TNT.

Navy gunners had the motto *Velocitas Eradico*, or "I, who am speed, eradicate." The Tungsicle put fact to that motto.

The Marines were in full, if controlled flight. Ryck was proud to see that their formation was holding well, and that they were in line with the other squads. Rally Point Isaac was the platoon rally point, some 1550 meters away from the target and back towards the LZ, just past a flat-topped rocky outcropping. The original rally point was to the side of the hill, but as he watched his display, it was shifted to the back of the hill.

*The lieutenant's on the ball*, Ryck thought approvingly.

The hill would give added protection to the Marines.

On open terrain and at a flat out run, a Marine in a PICS could cover that much ground in a little mover a minute and a half. Over unknown terrain, Ryck thought two and a half minutes was more reasonable. That would give them a minute to take whatever cover they could get.

"Khouri, keep up," he sent on a P2P, almost automatically.

Part of his mind was focused on running, on picking the right path. Another part of his mind, the analytical part, watched the 11 blue icons that represented his men. Watching the display could tend to reduce them to pieces of a game. They were not electrons, though. They were his men, his Marines, and he was responsible for them.

His display read 1:03 when they reached the rally point. Ryck knew he had the far sector of their position, but his display helpfully highlighted just where his squad was supposed to be. His Marines fanned out, achieving good dispersion.

"Everyone, down on the deck," he told them.

Ryck activated the gyro shutdown, then had to wait the five seconds before he could actually kneel first, then fall forward onto his face. His display looked brighter with the dark dirt as a background.

Just as he was almost prone, he caught sight of his pet legionnaire. Major Laurent was kneeling, not lying flat on his face. Ryck wondered if that was by choice or if his R-3 could not switch off the aspect control of his combat suit. That was food for thought.

Flat on the deck, Ryck contemplated sending off one of his two dragonflies. He wanted to watch the target. He'd seen vids of the Tungsicle, even of the larger ship-based Doric, but he'd never witnessed the real thing. As if reading his mind, the lieutenant slaved the recon team's eyes to the entire platoon.

"The second it hits, we are up and moving," Lt. Nidishchii' passed on the platoon circuit. "Treat the impact the same as if EOD had blown the doors. Everything else remains the same as planned."

There was a short pause, then the lieutenant came back on the circuit with, "SSgt Phantawisangtong has reminded me that there could be significant debris flying through the air. I will coordinate with the rest, but keep your heads down and don't move until given the order."

Ryck watched the display count down: . . . four . . . three . . . two . . . one . . . .

There was a brilliant flash that temporarily burned out the recon team's feed and lit the sky above the platoon. Ryck was face down, but the light made it to his face shield.

A moment later, the shock wave travelling through the ground hit beneath him, lifting him up 10 or 15 centimeters. Still another few moments later, the atmospheric shock wave rolled over them.

"Keep down," Ryck reminded his squad.

The feed from recon stabilized. It showed the rock camouflage over the doors in rubble, the heavy metal of the doors revealing their size. A huge hole had been torn into the left side, leaving it twisted and glowing orange. Surprisingly, the right side was still up, even if canted outwards. Dust and smoke poured up into the sky while heavy pieces of debris fell between the recon team's eyes and the target.

A loud whump sounded behind Ryck as something fell from above. There was a small patter of tiny bits of debris, but only that one piece that had made the whump was heavy enough to have posed any danger.

Ryck's action icon on his display flashed green.

"Up and at 'em," he passed to his men as he got up, reactivating his gyro stabilization system.

The overall plan had been loaded into their AIs. These worked well as an initial plan, but the AIs had only limited capability to make corrections with regards to the rest of the force as the assault progressed. This broke down the initial plan during the fog of war and the Marines had to rely on their training and ability to react to events.

Ryck didn't need his display, though, to show him where to go. The dark column of smoke ahead of his was a beacon. This was the squad's third time over the exact same ground, so they were able to cover it quickly. It was important to reach and enter the complex as soon as possible. Intel thought the initial chamber would be a warehouse or receiving station. At least two cloaked shuttles had arrived while the target had been under direct observation, and some large pieces of equipment as well as pallets of supplies had been offloaded and muled through the doors and into the complex. Anyone directly inside the doors would probably have been killed when the Tungsicle hit, but there were tunnels and other areas that had been identified, and any SOG deeper inside the facility could have survived. If the enemy was making their way to the first chamber, it would be better for the Marines if they beat the SOG there.

Ryck monitored his squad's progress as each Marine got their PICS up to speed. The squad was moving in good order, each one keeping the proper dispersion. He felt a surge of pride. These were good men.

Ryck's squad was designated to enter the complex first. As they approached, Ryck activated one of his dragonflies, sending the small drone up and zooming it through the smoldering doors. He'd already programmed it to scout out the entire interior, and his AI took over control of the drone. Ryck could manually take control, but the AI was pretty good at this function, leaving Ryck with one less thing on his plate.

It took a lot of training to multitask in a PICS. Ryck had to move forward in a tactical method, monitor his squad, and observe what his dragonfly revealed. Watching the dragonfly's feed while reacting to what was in front of him as he moved was the most difficult part. It was as if his two eyes were looking in different directions at the same time.

The Tungsicle had blown through the big doors before penetrating the ferrocrete floor of the warehouse, a four or five meter hole its signature. Despite the crystallized ceramic coating, this had released a huge amount of energy, and the entire deck of the warehouse had cracked and buckled. What looked to be a complete Viceroy-class fighter had been destroyed, as well as a number of ground vehicles. The warehouse had been full of supplies and equipment. Now it was full of junk.

Ryck wasn't seeing a real visual. There was too much dust and smoke inside. But the AI was taking the visual, the infrared, and the radar image from the dragonfly and compiling it into one view that made sense.

There was only one signature of a human body. At least it was half of a body. There could be more hidden in the rubble, but that was the only one evident from the scan.

The lieutenant was watching the same feed, so Ryck didn't have to report it up. Ryck tended to rely on speech too much, and it sometimes was difficult for him to step back and let the displays do their job. In many cases, a quick glance at the display could tell someone what they needed to know when trying to explain it would take four or five times as long.

Still, he couldn't resist the simple "Go" he passed to Cpl Rey to move into the complex.

Cpl Rey's team skirted the glowing edges of the destroyed portion of the door and disappeared into the warehouse. The AI noted the movement and focused the dragonfly on the team as they entered. Now, Ryck's face shield had Rey's visuals, the dragonfly's compiled display, and the actual visuals of what was in front of him. It took a lot of focus to keep things straight in his mind.

Rey signaled the all clear, and Ryck and the rest of the squad followed inside. He closed Rey's feed and reduced the dragonfly's to a small screen on the upper right side of his face shield. This was better.

Intel had been right. This was a warehouse, a monster one. To Ryck, it looked like the preparation for a major offensive, not just the typical ship pirating for which the gang was known. This looked similar in scale to when a Marine battalion was getting ready to deploy.

Third Squad pushed to the back of the warehouse, making room for the rest of the platoon as well as First Platoon to enter.

"I've got the main passage here," Cpl Beady passed.

Ryck moved to meet him. He and Lips were standing in front of a large passage, five meters wide and three high. Down the middle was the shiny surface of a magnostrip,[33] a sure sign that supplies were floated along it to other parts of the complex.

Ryck did a quick re-program, and the dragonfly zipped past the three Marines to enter the passage. Ryck followed the feeds as the drone flew in about 30 meters before encountering blast doors. The shock of the Tungsicle had bucked the deck even this far back, but the doors appeared to be solid.

Ryck could see that the lieutenant was no longer on the feed, so he brought him up on a P2P.

"Sir, we've got a major passage out, but it's got a blast door barring our way. I've got my dragonfly on it now."

The small dark blue light that flashed on let Ryck know the lieutenant had slaved onto his dragonfly's feed.

"Hold your position. I'm sending Sgt Kyle in now," he passed after a few moments.

Sgt Kyle and his team arrived. Ryck switched over control of his dragonfly to Frank and let him fly it across the face of the door. The EOD sergeant gave the drone back, then took the DSD off its harness on his back, and sent it forward.

"Just checking for little surprises," The EOD sergeant told Ryck.

They hadn't sensed the mine or whatever that had taken Sullivan out, so Ryck was not totally confident that the DSD could sniff out any other booby traps.

As soon as the DSD hit the door, instead of having the robot analyze it, Kyle moved his team forward. Ryck motioned Cpl Beady to move his team forward for security as well.

SSgt Hecs came up alongside of Ryck and asked, "What have we got?"

---

[33] Magnostrip: A positively charged strip laid down to facilitate the movement of pallets, which were also positively charged. The repelling forces elevated the pallet, making it quite easy to move up and down the strip.

Ryck shrugged the best he could while in a PICS and ran a 10 or 15 seconds of the dragonfly's previous feed.

"Frank Kyle's in there with his team. I sent Beady's team in, too. I think I'm going to tag along," Ryck told his platoon sergeant.

"Lead on, then," SSgt Hecs said.

Both Marines walked down the passage. The overhead was low for a PICS, so low that Ryck could have jumped up and hit the top of his PICS on it. But it was plenty wide enough for two PICS Marines to walk in side-by-side.

At the corner of the door, Frank Kyle and Cpl Zhou, one of his team members, were gesturing along its breadth, obviously in deep conversation. They quickly seem to come to a course of action. The three Marines, in their PICS-Es, brought out their jack-off hands. Like corpsmen, sometimes EOD Marines needed more dexterity and control than offered by the normal arms and hands of a PICS. When that happened, they could open their PICS' arms, then slide their real arms out the bottom, protected by a much thinner PICS "skin." The jack-off arms provided nothing other than atmospheric protection, but they Marines could use their real arms almost as if they were in a regular uniform. Ryck always thought that they looked like insects molting when they used the jack-off arms.

The three EOD Marines began placing their shaped charge limpets in a pattern. It took less than a minute to get all six charges placed. A small red light on each limpet indicated that they were ready for detonation.

"Gentlemen, I suggest we move back out of here," Kyle said matter-of-factly.

The Marines moved to the warehouse proper, stepping to the side of the passage as they reached it. Kyle reported back to the lieutenant that they were ready to blow the door.

"You holding up, Ryck?" SSgt Hecs asked him on the P2P.

"I'm fine. I might be a bit stiff tomorrow, but no problem now," he answered.

Lieutenant Nidishchii' and Capt Davis lumbered up to them. The captain took Kyle's report, then had a P2P discussion with the lieutenant, after which, the platoon commander brought up the three squad leaders, Sgt Kyle, and SSgt Hecs on the command circuit.

"We think there's another staging area on the other side of that door. We know there's at least 20 SOG here, maybe more. We've seen only one body. That leaves no fewer than 19 others, and we know they don't meekly surrender. We've got to anticipate that at some point, they are going to fight. Capt Davis thinks the staging area might give them cover to put up a defensive position, and I agree. We've got to get in and hit them hard, but this passage is a choke point. They can Horatio at the Bridge it and make it tough for us. What we're going to do is at the moment the door comes down . . . " he paused. "You've got that covered, right Sergeant Kyle?"

"I abso-fucking-lutely guarantee it, Lieutenant," Kyle responded.

"OK. Then, as I was saying, the second the door comes down, Weapons is going to pulse and HE down the passage. Third, you're still the tip of the spear. I want you moving right on the ass of the HE rounds. Sgt Samuelson, you're on Sergeant Lysander's ass, and Sergeant Paul, you're next. I'm moving with Third Squad, SSgt Phantawisangtong will be with First. I'm loading a movement plan on where to go once we hit the room, but as always, use your judgment.

"This will be a very confined area, so watch your displays. I want no friendly fire casualties. Got it?"

The five Marines all acknowledged their orders, then split to bring their Marines up to speed. As Ryck was briefing his squad, two teams from Weapons came up with their heavy guns. Ryck raised a hand in a half salute to Sergeant Xander Kubasaki, the heavy guns section leader, who was a friend of his.

Xander's team set up two weapons just inside the start of the passage. The M232 was a small, multipurpose artillery piece. It fired a 70 mm shell and could be adjusted for mortar, artillery or direct fire. The P-996B was a self-contained pulse weapon. The gun itself was smaller than the M232, but with the power-pack attached, the system was bigger. It fired a two-joule EMP charge.

With the players in place, the lieutenant signaled Kyle to detonate he charge. Kyle took out his Marine Corps-issue Samsung

PA. This being the Corps, the PA was rather obsolete, and Ryck always thought it was funny when EOD initiated huge amounts of destruction and mayhem with a 30-year-old telephone. They might as well bring back semaphore to send messages, or light smoke signals.

With a simple press of this thumb, Sgt Kyle set off the charges. There was a flash as the shaped charges, programmed for cutting, detonated. The explosion that reached the waiting Marines was subdued. Kyle was not trying to destroy the door, merely get it open.

Ryck had recovered his dragonfly to his sleeve, where it was recharging in case it was needed again. But the weapon's team had deployed another, and Ryck was slaved to it. For a moment, it looked as if Kyle had miscalculated. Then the door began to lean before falling back in a cloud of dust.

Immediately, the M232 opened up with two rounds. Those rounds impacted on the wall another 15 or 20 meters beyond the now flat door. A simple curve in the passage had defeated a modern piece of artillery. From his schoolwork, Ryck knew that even castle-makers in medieval times understood this defense and built ogees like this, as they were termed, to slow down attacks.

The P-996B had better luck. The pulse charge took off in a flash of blue, hit the far wall, and bounced past. Whether it reached the far compartment or not, Ryck didn't know. Whether it did or didn't, though, the assault was on.

Ryck followed right on Keiji's ass, two steps back and up against the left-had wall. That made five Marines forming an interlocking front as they rushed down the passage. The weapons team's dragonfly preceded them, and Ryck tried to glance at its feed, but the Marines were already in assault mode. They passed the door, stepping on it as they ran. Moments later, they rounded the curve in the passage—and were immediately taken under fire.

A PICS relied on its armor to protect the Marine inside, and that armor was pretty effective against kinetic weapons up to a certain size and velocity. For energy weapons, the armor helped deflect the waves, but the Marines relied on small, portable shields that both repelled and absorbed the energy thrown at them.

Ryck's shield took on the blue glow which indicated it was activated by incoming fire. With the dried blood still on his face shield, the light blue glow took on a darker more sinister tone.

Ryck's display flashed with the warning, and the intake gauge began to rise. Whatever was being fired at them was pretty powerful, and he could see the numbers flash as he approached critical. If he redlined, he was done for. The suit, at best, would shut down. At worse, the situation would go critical with potentially fatal consequences. At the rate at which the gauge was climbing, that point could come as soon as ten seconds.

Ryck let loose a string of his 8mm high-velocity darts. He wanted to send in this shoulder rockets as well, but with Keiji bobbing just in front of him, it was too risky. Keiji let loose with his rockets, though, four salvos of three each, one after the other. Then he let loose with his 20mm cannon. He had a full combat load of 104 shells, and he looked bound and determined to expend them all by the time they closed with the enemy.

The little dragonfly had been knocked out of action at the first pulse fired. Ryck's AI tried to make sense of just where their targets were, but huge amount of energy flying around the confined area, the sensors were struggling to gather any meaningful data.

It didn't matter. Ahead of him, behind a barricade of some sort, the faint green flashes of pulses being fired at the Marines pinpointed their adversary. The green flash was indicative of a Confederation[34] weapon system, something Ryck noted despite the urgency of their situation.

Ryck shifted his darts to the green flashes. At immense speeds, the darts could actually penetrate armor given lucky circumstances. They could also mess up the circuits of EMP weapons if they hit right.

Ryck was almost redlined. They had to get out of the kill zone, but the only way out was forward.

His exterior sensors failed, burnt out. Those gave him atmospheric readings, so they wouldn't stop him from fighting, but the rest of his sensors couldn't be far behind.

[34] Confederation: The Confederation of Free States, a small loosely-aligned group of planets.

"You mother grubbing toad suckers!" he shouted as he pushed to the end of the passage and his system alarm went to a single, ominous tone. He was in the red, past the manufacturer's tolerances.

To this right, another salvo of rockets went off while Keiji kept pumping 20 mike mike grenades. Explosions filled the 30 x 30 meter room, and suddenly, the incoming blasts of energy stopped. What had taken the weapon out, Ryck didn't know nor care at the moment. He was still redlined–how far into the red, he didn't know. It was beyond the gauge's ability to measure it.

He rushed with the other four Marines to where the incoming had originated. Two shattered, armored bodies, hung down over the barricade they had been using while firing the pulse cannon, which was now canted upwards. Another man was still alive. He was getting to his feet and unlimbering, amazingly enough, a honest-to-goodness sword. Technically, a mono-molecular edged blade could do damage to even a Marine in a PICS, but with five PICS Marines bearing down on him, he had no chance. Whether he died as a result of the 8mm darts fired into his chest or when Lips simply ran him over, Ryck couldn't tell. He was definitely, 100% dead, though, Ryck knew that.

The rest of the platoon was there in seconds. Ryck stood there, heart pounding. He didn't need his readouts to know he was hyperventilating, which was good, as all his readouts had flickered, then failed. He forced himself to calm down, to center himself.

The lieutenant barely looked at the three dead SOG before going on his exterior speaker and asking for status checks. That puzzled Ryck for a moment before he realized that his comms were out, too. With First Platoon entering the room, it was getting crowded, but they took up positions while Third took stock of themselves. Without comms and displays, it was pretty confusing. It shouldn't be, Ryck knew, but they were pretty much married to their electronics. Ryck would have to think on that later. War should not be so reliant on electrons.

It took about five minutes to tally the damage. Of the squad, only Peretti hadn't redlined. Ryck and the lieutenant and three Marines from First Platoon were also redlined. Once redlined, a

PICS was combat ineffective until the armory gave it a full check and repair. Somehow, no combat suits had suffered catastrophic failures, and no Marines were WIA. All five of the first Marines in the assault had taken their suits well past their tolerances, which would interest the brass back in the head shed.

Captain Davis took arrived and took over, but not for long. He told SSgt Hecs, who still had comms, to take over the platoon, which must have galled the lieutenant. A quick look at the passages leading off from the scene, though, made it obvious that the PICS Marines had done all they could do. The passages were just too small for combat suits. Fox Company was called forward, to take the fight on to the remaining enemy.

As Ryck waited to move out, he thought that his squad had fought well, especially given the fact that this was the first combat for a good chunk of his platoon.

Corporals Rey and Mendoza, Lance Corporals Keiji and Martin, and Private Peretti were the only Marines who had faced combat before. Caesar Peretti was the only one who even had a bronze star on his Combat Mission Medal, earned before a drunken spree out in the ville had gotten him busted back down to private. Yet the squad had faced an armed, determined enemy and had not blinked. Ryck felt honored to be a part of the squad, part of this group of men.

His reverie was broken as they started to form up. The platoon, using the hand and arm signals Ryck had thought were obsolete back at Camp Charles when the recruits had to learn them, rallied up and started moving back down the main passage to get out of the complex and where they could get picked-up for their ride to the ship. They filed past Fox as the light company made its way in. They would be fighting in their skins and bones against a foe that had managed to take out one Marine in a PICS and almost disabled an entire platoon of PICS Marines.

Ryck had been in Fox when he first joined the battalion, and he had friends there. When he saw his old running mate T-Rex filing in with his squad, Ryck gave him a thumbs up. Even if his squad had led the initial assault, he felt guilty about leaving the field of battle before the battle was won. Now his friends, his fellow Marines, would have to go in and finish the job.

*Fair winds and following seas, brothers*, he sent his thoughts out to them as his fight was done.

# Prophesy

## Chapter 5

Ryck looked in the mirror. His medals hung straight, his dress blues sharp and creased. Everything looked right with his uniform. Today, everything *had* to be right.

"Looking good, little brother, looking good. You're going to make the ladies fall hard," Lysa said from the bathroom doorway.

"None will be as good looking as you, sis," he said.

"Ha! Like this?" she asked, pointing at her very pregnant belly.

"Men on Prophesy like their women fertile. You know that," he said with a laugh.

After seeing the look on her face, he protested, "Just joking, just joking!"

"Well, that's me, fertile, despite the misogyny inherent in your statement," she said, punching Ryck in the arm. "When your new nephew arrives on the scene, I'll be up on you three to zero, so maybe you can use this opportunity to find your own wife? Women get the nesting instinct at weddings, after all, and you, little brother, more than most, need someone. And speaking of weddings, Barret and the girls are already in the hover waiting. You about ready?"

"Yeah, just trying to make sure I look OK," he answered.

He followed his twin down the stairs and out the front door to where Barret had the Lexus idling.

"Uncle Ryck, sit with me!" Camyle called out from the back seat.

"No, your Uncle Ryck is going to sit in the front seat. He has to keep his uniform nice and clean," Lysa told her four-year-old.

"But he never sits with me!" she cried out.

"Yes he did. This morning, to go to the store," Kylee told her.

"That doesn't count!"

"Should I?" Ryck whispered to his sister.

"You kidding? You may be a Marine, but you'd stand no chance with those two. No, you get in front. We've got an hour before we get there."

As soon as they got in, Barret lifted the big hover off the pavement and pulled out of the development. This was the fourth Lexus Barret had since Ryck had known him. The water reclamation business was very kind to him. Ryck knew he could have the same kind of life. Barret had offered him the position of vice president of the company, but Ryck had decided that he wanted to re-enlist in the Corps. He didn't regret his decision, but still, this was one sweet ride.

The hour drive flew by quickly with Camyle teaching Ryck *The Popcorn Song*. Kylee, with her 6-year-old sense of maturity, didn't join in.

Ryck had only been to the Hope-of-Life family compound once, and he had thought it crowded then with his friend Joshua's large family. This time, it was a zoo. A teenager was directing traffic, and he waved Barret to park the Lexus right up against a corn field along with what had to be 30 or 35 other vehicles.

They got out of the Lexus and walked over to the barn, each of his nieces taking one of his hands in hers. Joshua's mother was in the yard in front of the barn, giving instructions. She saw Ryck and waved him over.

"Do you know my Uncle Ryck is a Marine?" Camyle asked Joshua's mom.

"Of course she does," Kylee said in an exasperated tone. "Uncle Ryck and Mr. Joshua are Marines together, and Mrs. Hope-of-Life is Mr. Joshua's mom."

"Ryck, it be good to see you again," Joshua's mother said, giving him a hug and a kiss on the cheek. "Joshua be in the house in the guest bedroom. Why don't you go in and see what he be needing. Tabitha here will take care of your family."

Before Ryck could reply, she shouted out "No, no! Those are to go under the tent!" to some unseen worker.

"Sorry, Ryck, I must be going," she said before hurrying off to take care of whatever emergency she had discovered.

Ryck left Lysa, Barret, and the girls and walked over to the main house. People were streaming in and out of the main doors on various missions. Most of the women and men were wearing the plainly-colored clothes typical of a Torritite, but there were a few splashes of color, and more than a little cleavage and leg exhibited by some of the women. Not all the guests were part of the Torritite community.

Ryck walked into the foyer, barely getting out of the way of a young girl rushing out carrying a pitcher of some sort of drink. He spied the stairs and started to them when a familiar face caught his eye. Hannah, Joshua's sister, had come out of the large kitchen, wiping her hands on the little white apron that most single Torritite women wore. Ryck made a beeline to her.

"Hi Hannah. You busy?" he said as he came up, immediately regretting his choice of an opening line.

Busy? Really? That was the best he could do?

Hannah's eyes lit up when she saw him.

"Ryck, welcome! Joshua's going to be happy to see you. He be afraid all week that you weren't going to make it, and he be so happy afta you called last night," she said, giving him a hug and a kiss on the cheek. "Oh, it be good to see you!"

She reached up and flicked his Silver Star.

"Joshua, you know, he be always talking about you. 'Ryck be a hero, Ryck be going to make sergeant major.' But if you don't be showing up here, I think I be tracking you down and let you have some."

"Have some what?" Ryck said, trying to inject a playfully suggestive quality to his voice.

"Oh, don't you be trying that stuff with me, Ryck Lysander," she said with a laugh. "No way I be getting with a soldier boy, no sir. Not like poor Hope, the dear girl."

Hope was Joshua's soon-to-be bride.

"What do you mean? She's marrying your brother," Ryck asked.

"Well, aside from her new name, Hope Hope-of-Life, she be marrying a Marine. A Marine be like any soldier. He be gone from home. And the wife be worrying, waiting while her husband fights, waiting for the chaplain to come a'knocking on the door to tell her that her man won't be coming home. No, not for me, thank you very much. Not for me."

Ryck felt deflated. He didn't know Hannah well enough to have any serious intentions with her, but to be knocked out of the race before even leaving the gate was a little rough.

"Oh, listen to me, rattling on. This be a joyous day," she said, reaching out to take one of Ryck's hands in hers. "You go on upstairs and see Joshua. He probably be about ready to pass out by now. And after the ceremony, come see me. Mayhaps we can get together some evening while you are here."

"You and me? Like on a date?" he asked stupidly. "I thought you didn't want to date a Marine."

"I don't want to be with a Marine, as in marry one. But I want to see if men in uniform be really as fun as the other girls say, and you be cutting a rather fine figure, if I do say so."

That was fine with Ryck. More than fine.

"OK, then. It's a date. I'll catch up with you later," he said, reluctantly pulling away and rushing up the stairs.

He should have known better by now. The Torritites dressed conservatively, and they followed the teachings of the Bible as they understood them, but they were not prudes. Joshua liked to lift a pint or two, and he was no stranger to the ladies. Why would Hannah be any different?

Never having been upstairs in the Hope-of-Life household, he didn't know which was the guest bedroom. He opened one door to see the bride, in her long white gown, getting help with her veil. A dozen female voices screamed at him to get out.

He did.

The next room was empty, but he felt a sense of relief when he saw Joshua in the third room he tried. He was leaning up against a dresser, talking to several other men both in uniform and out. As soon as he saw Ryck, he broke out into a huge smile.

"'Bout time you showed up, bro," he said as he strode over to Ryck and gave him a bear hug.

They pounded each other's back a few times, then tried to disengage. Ryck's medals, though, hung up on Joshua's shooting badges, hooking them together.

"Oh, snark. You're hero shit's trying to mess me up. A little help here!" he called out.

Another Marine stood up and reached between them to unhook the two.

"Kellen Krupt. You must be Ryck Lysander," the Marines said. "Josh's told us all about you since we left Tarawa."

"I swear I'm innocent. Don't believe all his BS," Ryck said as the others broke out into laughter.

There were eight men in uniform, all wearing sword belts. Six were Marines, Joshua's friends from Camp Charles where he was a DI. One was a Navy corpsman, also one of Joshua's drill field friends. The eighth was a legionnaire. That had to be Joshua's older brother, Ezekiel. The eight were to form the sword arch to welcome the new bride into the military family. The last man in the arch would swat Hope on the butt as they passed through the arch.

"Hey, come help me with my SGA,[35]" Joshua told Ryck, leading him to the guest bath off the main room.

Ryck made a show of checking the alignment of the Marine Corps emblem on Joshua's collar, but he realized that had just been an excuse to talk to him.

"You OK?" Ryck asked.

"I be stressed but good," Joshua said, momentarily reverting to his Tortie speech patterns.

"Seems normal to me. I'd be stressing, too, if I be getting married," Ryck replied, mimicking Tortie speech.

"But, I'm glad you're here, bro. You and I go back. Remember when we were sitting there, ready to enlist in the Legion? Then your friend, what was his name?" Joshua asked.

"Proctor. Proctor Miller."

"Yeah, that's the guy. He convinced us to go see the Marine recruiter, and that sly cat hooked us. Your buddy didn't even make it. DOR'd[36]. But we did. Now we're Sergeants of Marines."

"And why the history lesson, bro?" Ryck asked.

---

[35] SGA: the Star, Globe, and Anchor, the emblem of the Federation Marines

[36] DOR: Dropped on Request. Quit the training program.

"I don't know. Just been thinking. About life, you know. I had my tour with 1stMarDiv as a grunt, then re-upped and went to the drill field. Never saw any action, though, not like you. I don't know how I would have reacted," Joshua said matter-of-factly.

"You would have been fine, kicking ass and taking names," Ryck assured him.

"Maybe, but I was single then. Now, I'm gonna have me a wife and kid, and they're gonna need me."

"No hurry on the kid, there, big boy. Take it a step at a time," Ryck told him.

"Already took that step," Joshua admitted.

"You mean you knocked her up," Ryck asked, surprised.

"You'll see in about seven-and-a-half months," Joshua told him. "Hope came out to visit me on Tarawa, and well, you know how that goes."

"Yeah, I guess I do now!" Ryck exclaimed.

"So, what I mean is, I still gotta prove myself in combat. You've been there. You've proven the temper of your steel. We've never talked about it, but I gotta know if I can do the same. But now, I'm going to be a husband and a father. Hope thinks she's gonna like the military life, but only if I redesignate into a pogue billet."

"You want to do that?" Ryck asked his friend.

"Fuck no. I need to prove myself first. Maybe after, but not now."

"Well, you're just going to have to tell her," Ryck said.

"Hey, you two done making out in there? They're calling for the groom!" a voice shouted out accompanied by a pounding on the door.

"Just a freaking minute!" Joshua shouted back.

"Hey, don't stress out now. This is your happy day. We'll talk later, OK?" Ryck said.

"OK, OK. We'll talk," Joshua said, taking a deep breath. "Thanks, bro, though, for coming."

"Wouldn't miss it for the world. And I am honored to be your best man. Surprised, though. Your brother is out in the next room, and you've got your Camp Charles buds."

"What, Ezekiel? Nope. He's married, and Kellen, he's married, too. According to tradition, a best man has to be single. The other guys, I just needed eight for the sword arch."

"So I'm your third choice? Suddenly, I'm not feeling so honored," Ryck said with a chuckle.

"Hey, at least you made the list, bro!"

"Before we go, here," Joshua said, taking a slim package from his trouser pocket. "I think it's traditional, right, for the Best Man?"

Ryck took it, admiring the clean packing for a moment, then tried to slide off the ribbon without breaking it."

"For goodness sakes, just open the grubbing thing!"

Ryck broke the ribbon and slit the paper. His heart caught when he saw the name on the box. He opened it, and yes, there was a Rolex Adventurer, shiny and beckoning.

"Shit, Joshua, that's amazing, but it's what, a month's pay?"

"A month-and-a-half, but who's counting?"

"I can't take this!" Ryck protested.

"Yeah, you can. This is from me to you, brother."

"I don't know what to say."

"You can say thanks. And you can make sure I don't grubbing faint out there. No viral vids making the circuit of me passing out, OK?"

"Sure thing, and well, thanks. I think your blushing bride is waiting for her prince." Ryck told him.

They hugged one more time before opening the door and stepping out to where the others were waiting.

"Enjoy your last few minutes of freedom, there, Sergeant of Marines. Let's go get this thing done," Ryck said as he escorted his friend to change his life.

# Pannington

## Chapter 6

The Stork flared above the LZ, the ramp coming down to half a meter above the grass. Ryck was up as the light turned green, pushing forward to debark and deploy into a defensive position.

Ryck was nervous despite his previous combat experience. Over the last five years, he'd gotten used to his PICS. He hadn't gone into a hot zone in skins and bones since Atacama, his very first operation. Still, he was a Marine, and every Marine was a rifleman. It was the man inside the PICS that wrecked havoc amongst his enemies, not the hardware itself.

He kept telling himself that.

He rushed out, immediately moved to his nine o'clock, and took a knee at the edge of the zone. Glancing down at his forearm, he saw avatars that told him the rest of the squad and the automatic weapons team from Weapons Platoon had deployed in textbook fashion. The LZ was not that big, maybe 40 meters across, so he could have just lifted his eyes, but old habits died hard, and even if the display was on his sleeve and not on his visor, he now trusted the electronics more than actual visuals.

For the zillionth time, he wished the Corps had not moved away from the combat face shield he'd first used in recruit training. He didn't' believe the tests that concluded that having a face shield made each Marine ever-so-slightly less efficient and reactive. As a squad leader, having the displays in front of his eyes seemed more natural than having to look down at his forearm.

Ryck felt somewhat naked, but with only a squad of mercenaries guarding the complex, this was not expected to be a serious action. Navy intel had told them Luminosity was going to be a cakewalk, too, though, and Ryck remembered how that had turned out.

The wind kicked up by the departing Stork died down, so Ryck told the squad to move out. They were to marry up with Second Squad 200 meters to the northwest, clearing the zone for First. Sams' squad would be in their PICS, but they would be acting as the heavy reserve. The point of main effort was Third and Second.

The squad formed into a wedge just inside the treeline, then moved through the low canopy. Pannington had only been terraformed for 50 years, so the forest didn't have any old growth. The tallest trees were perhaps 20 meters. A newly populated planet or not, there was a myriad of animal life, mostly birds, flitting about them as they moved to the link up.

Popo and the Lieutenant met him as they took position off Third's right flank.

"Nothing new from the company," Lt. Nidishchii' told him. "Third Platoon has met up with the NIS agent, and they'll be moving to the cargo bays on schedule. Second Platoon has landed at Parkerville and has deployed, making its presence known by inspecting the legitimate warehouses. We don't have an exact location for the mercenaries, but intel thinks they will be deployed around the main entrance. Our guide is about five minutes out, and we've got 45 minutes to get to the emergency exit, breach it, and take the escape tunnels. No one, and that means *no one*, is to get through us."

Ryck tried to catch any flicker of uncertainty in the lieutenant's voice. The wiry Marine had been with the platoon for over a year now, and he'd been promoted to first lieutenant. This was their second real action as platoon commander and squad leader.

Ryck didn't know what to make of the lieutenant. He didn't seem to have much of a personality one way or the other, but his reputation was stellar. Evidently, as an enlisted Marine, he'd built up quite a name for himself, earning two Silver Stars and a Purple Heart. He'd gotten an appointment to the Naval Academy, and came out a new second lieutenant. During the last year, though, Ryck hadn't seen anything noteworthy in his platoon commander. Nothing bad about him, but nothing noteworthy. He done OK on BHP Billiton B-19, but hadn't really stepped out to match his rep, in Ryck's humble opinion. Maybe Ryck would see something now that they were in the real deal.

The platoon commander's voice was steady, no hint of uncertainty. Ryck hoped his own voice didn't reveal the uncertainty in his mind, though, uncertainty rooted not only because the squad was going in light and not in their PICS, but in the mission itself.

Golf Company's mission was to take out an illegal warehouse complex, a hub of black-market trading. At the same time, Fox would be taking out another complex located deep underground on the larger of Pannington's two moons. Echo would "occupy" Robbinsville, the planetary capital, showing the flag with PICS Marines.

The assault on the SOG warehouse made sense. SOG was a terrorist gang who attacked and killed Federation citizens. This mission was different, though. As far as he knew, the people running this operation were not terrorists. They did not kidnap and kill. Ryck knew that black-marketing was illegal. He'd downloaded a few vids without paying, of course, but didn't everyone do that? That wasn't wholesale commerce. He understood the need for the government to regulate commerce, to collect taxes. Some of those taxes paid for his salary, after all.

But why the Marines? Since when had they become Commerce Cops? The Marine Corps' mission was defense, not being policemen. The Federation Charter forbade armed Marines from even stepping foot on Earth, so strong was the concept that the Marine Corps was not an instrument to use against the general populace. Yet here they were, being cops.

All that was above Ryck's pay grade—way above. He had a mission to accomplish, and he was going to get all his Marines through it and back home. That was a mission that he understood.

This was Ryck's sixth combat op, seven if he counted the NEO[37] on Soreau. Of the six, this would be the third time he was going underground. He'd done a paper on the war in Vietnam back in the 20th Century, old time, and he'd been fascinated by the tunnel rats of the US, Australian, and Korean forces. It looked like he was turning into a modern version of them, though, and he wasn't sure

[37] NEO: Non-combatant Evacuation Operation

he really wanted to be. He wasn't claustrophobic, but fighting underground could give anyone the jeebies.

Their guide, a local whose name was withheld, contacted the lieutenant. Three Marines from Second went out to meet him, then escorted him back. He was wearing a ski-mask, which had to be hot in the muggy, late morning heat. With no name and a mask, Ryck did not get a warm and fuzzy about the man. Supposedly, he worked in the complex, but NIS had turned him (for what had to be a tidy sum.) He could just as well be leading them into a trap, though.

The two squads broke into columns. With Ryck's squad 50 meters to the left of Second, they made their way through the forest. A column was not a secure formation for a movement to contact, but it did allow for a smaller front to any observers. There were sensors guarding the exit and surrounding area, of course, but the Marines had been assured that they had been deactivated.

First Squad, in their PICS, would follow in trace, staying out of the complex itself while securing their rear. Any belligerent who somehow made it past the other two squads would be picked up by them.

There was not much undergrowth, which surprised Ryck. Normally, with younger forests, thickets and other vegetation made movement difficult. Here, it was pretty clear. Evidently, many of the different kinds of plant life which could fill the forest floor had either never been introduced, or more likely, given the biogenesis teams penchant for a full bio-diversity, they just hadn't established themselves yet. Terraforming was not like engineering. Nature had a way of asserting itself despite centuries of mankind's experience.

The two squads stopped 150 meters short of their objective to wait out the final 10 minutes. Ryck pulled up the map of the complex one more time on his display. His mission was to follow Third through the exit, then take the right-branching tunnel. They would move forward to the next intersection, secure it, then sit and wait for the ants to come scurrying out.

There was no telling how accurate the map was, though. The best ground penetration sensors, both from space and from atmosphere drones, had only been able to discern the larger passages. NIS had acquired some hand-drawn maps as well, but who knew how accurate they were?

At five minutes to go-time, the boomboom team from Weapons Platoon crept forward, covered by one of Second's fire teams. Sergeant Kyle led them as they placed their charge on the door. Ryck half-expected someone to come out shooting, but all remained quiet.

Second Squad crept closer while the boomboom team retreated back. They would not be detonating the charge. It was slaved to the charges that Third Platoon would be placing on the cargo bays. Once armed, the charge would detonate at the same time as Third's.

"Get ready," Ryck sent on the squad circuit needlessly.

His Marines would be watching the same timer as he was. When it got to 10 seconds, he gathered his legs under him and got into a crouch, ready to move. At exactly zero, a muffled explosion sounded in front of him.

Second Squad was up and moving before the smoke and dust had cleared. Ryck gave them ten seconds, then sent off Cpl Rey's team. He followed next with the other two fire teams and the automatic weapons team in back of him.

Ryck should have waited another ten seconds. Rey's team ran into the tail end of Popo's squad, and they had to stop. Within a few heartbeats, though, the last Marine in Third was in and LCpl Keiji led the way for Second.

Sweat was already pouring down Ryck's back, faster than his skins could wick it away. His PICS was temperature controlled. Skins were not, unless a heavy environmental pack was carried.

He scooted past the big steel door that hung ajar. The boomboom boys knew their stuff. Just enough explosives had been used to breach the door, but not enough to destroy it.

The lieutenant had stopped at the Y in the main corridor. He was playing traffic cop, motioning Ryck's squad off to the right. With Keiji on point, they moved quickly down their assigned corridor. A small room on the left slowed them down. The room was not on the map, but it had to be cleared. The room had a half-dozen drums, and each one had to be checked to make sure it was empty. That took time, at least 30 seconds. They still had another 50 meters to go before they reached their objective. Ryck had Mendoza's team cover Rey's as First sprinted the last interval.

"We're at Blue Whiskey," Rey passed as he set his team.

Ryck jumped up and moved forward. The intersection was too small for his entire squad. The main corridor was about three meters across, the side corridor two. He had 15 Marines, the 13 in his squad and the two in the heavy machine gun team attached to him. He sent the machine gun team to join with Rey's team, told Mendoza to cover the side corridor, and told Cpl Beady to cover their rear.

"We've got movement to our front," Keiji passed before the machine gun team could get their M449 deployed.

Ryck could see their renewed efforts to get the gun ready as other Marines took whatever cover they could find.

"Halt! Put your hands up!" someone, probably Prifit, shouted in front of Ryck.

A three round burst sounded, at least one round winging past Ryck's head as it ricocheted along the wall of the corridor. Ahead of him, Ryck could see shapes hitting the deck as the M449 opened up.

"Cease fire! Cease Fire! We surrender!" a panicked voice called out.

"Push your weapon away from you, slowly. If you make one move, so help me, I'll ghost you right there," Prifit called out.

Ryck was already moving. He slid past the M449 team, leaving them a field of fire in case they had to open up again. Prifit and Keiji were standing in the middle of the corridor. Cpl Rey and Hartono were hugging the wall, but covering the 10 or so people lying on the ground 10 meters in front of them. One man was on his back, leg twisted under him, one hand still grasping his Lancet. His dead eyes stared at the ceiling while blood pooled rapidly to his side. Two more men in military-looking utilities were slowly, ever so slowly, pushing their own Lancets away from them.

Ryck touched Keiji's shoulder and motioned him to move to the side. They had to leave the middle of the corridor open in case the gun team needed to engage again.

"John, get your team up here," he passed to Cpl Beady.

"That's far enough, you two. Hands behind your head," Prifit told the two living gunmen.

It took only seconds before Third Team was there. Ryck had Beady send two men, Holleran and Ling, to pick up the three Lancets, then slap zips on each of the prisoners. Once the last man had his hands secured behind his back, Ryck could finally turn down the stress a notch.

Shots rang out, momentarily bringing the stress back until Ryck realized they were sounding from off to the left of his Marines, out of their area. Second Squad sounded like they were in it, but within 20 or 30 seconds, the firing died away. The last shots sounded like M99 reports, not Lancets, though it was hard to tell with all the echoing.

Ryck had reported their catch to the lieutenant and was ordered to sit tight. One of the prisoners asked to have his zips adjusted. Ryck ignored him.

It only took about 30 minutes for the all-clear to sound. The lieutenant told Ryck to move back, taking the prisoners out of the complex. A few of them had to be helped to their feet. Two had pissed in their pants, and the smell was getting ripe. That was another advantage to PICS that Ryck missed: filtered air.

He released the zips on two of the men in overalls, then refastened them with their hands in front. They had to drag the body of the dead merc. The younger of the two, a heavyset man, looked like he wanted to throw up as they picked up the merc's arms. The blood trail, which looked dark brown under the fluorescent lights, seemed to mesmerize him for a moment of time before the gag reflex took over him. Ryck heard Holleran bet Martin that the guy would lose it before they made it out. Ryck pushed to the front, and he never did find out who won the bet.

Two Marines in PICS stood outside at either side of the exit, looking like ancient statues guarding a temple. Several of the prisoners tried to crowd the center, trying to keep as far away from the motionless Marines as possible. The two surviving mercs didn't give the Marines a second glance.

For once, Navy intel seemed to have been right. This had been an easy mission, all things considered. A Marine in Third Platoon had been slightly wounded, but that was the only WIA from Golf. Two Marines in Second Squad had been hit, as had Hartono, but their bones had hardened as they were designed to do, and none of the three had been hurt. Ryck looked over at Hartono who was showing the boot, PFC Ling, where he had been hit.

Ryck thought Ling didn't show enough gumption as a member of the squad. He wasn't sure how the PFC had even made it through boot camp. To Ryck, this mission was barely worth mentioning, but to PFC Jeb Ling, this was a pivotal moment in his career. He had been blooded. Maybe that would stiffen up his backbone.

The mercs and workers had not fared as well as the Marines. Ryck didn't know how many had fallen before Third Platoon, but a three had died facing Second. There was the merc killed by the M449 with Ryck, and Third squad had killed two of the workers. A merc with them had been gut-shot. Doc Steuber was working on him, and he didn't seem too concerned, so the merc was probably going to pull through.

"Good job, Sergeant Lysander. Your Marines did well. We'll wait for recall instructions, but meanwhile, work on your after action report. I'd like it by 2200," the lieutenant told him, cool as could be.

This was the lieutenant's second combat action as an officer, discounting the rescue of the Legion officers on Soreau, and he acted like this was simply another training exercise. With two Silver Stars, he'd been in the shit before, and this was nothing to compare with that, but still, Ryck expected a little more emotion.

"Aye-aye, sir," Ryck responded. At first, he'd hated the after action reports he'd had to draft up after every training evolution. When he started treating them like homework for his academic classes, though, they became less of a burden, just one of those routine things he had to do.

"Hey, what unit are you guys?" one of the mercs asked from where he was sitting.

Ryck caught his eye, then looked away.

"Come one, what harm is there? Let's see, one heavy squad, two light. From where we are, you're, what Third Marine Division? Ninth Marines maybe? So not a heavy company. I'm guessing Alpha, 1/9," he went on.

"Shut the fuck up," Holleran told him, stepping up and bending over to address the merc.

"Calm down there, Joe. Just making conversation," the merc said, seemingly nonplussed by Holleran's aggressive stance over him.

"Name's not Joe, worm, and I said shut up," Holleran said, leaning over further to put his face right in the merc's.

"Remember Paragraph 2002. You don't want an international incident, do you?"

"Lips, stand down," Ryck said, putting his hand on the lance corporal's shoulder and turning him around. "Go wait by Doc and bring him here when he's done. This guy's been hit, too."

"But what about what he said?" Lips protested.

"Go," Ryck told him, giving him a light shove.

"Lips? That's precious," the merc said as Lips strode off.

"What do you know about Paragraph 2002?" Ryck asked.

Paragraph 2002 was part of the Harbin Accords, the agreement in which the interplanetary rules of combat were delineated. That paragraph specifically prohibited any maltreatment of civilian prisoners.

"I used to be a Marine. LCpl Jerry Damien, at your service," he said with a smile. "I'd offer you my hand, but I'm kind of tied up at the moment."

Ryck just stared at him, mouth falling open.

"Yep, thought that might surprise you," the merc said.

"You, what, you deserted to become a mercenary?" Ryck asked, still stunned.

"What? No, of course not. I did my time. Didn't get recommended for re-enlistment, though, so I got out. Thought about the Legion, but got picked up by Phoenix Security, instead. They sent me here."

"But you're a mercenary," Ryck protested.

"And you are . . .?" the man asked, waiting for Ryck to reply.

"I'm not a grubbing mercenary, that's for sure!" Ryck answered.

"Really? So what mission of 'defense' are you on right now? Who are you saving? At least I know what my job was. I was hired to protect a legitimate business enterprise. You, on the other hand, were sent to close it down. Sounds like a corporate mercenary to me," he said.

Ryck had noted this very point to himself earlier, so the merc's statement hit him hard. He could not admit that, though.

"Sorry, you're all fucked up. I'm a Federation Marine," he stated with conviction. "and this 'business,' as you call it, is not legitimate. It's a smuggling operation."

"Smuggling? Because it doesn't pay Federation protection money--excuse me--tariffs? Who do you think runs this operation?"

Ryck shrugged.

"Greater France, that's who. They're not part of your vaunted Federation."

"But the Mutual Defense Treaty. They have to kick in for that, right?" Ryck asked.

"Do you know your history, Sergeant? The American Revolution? 'No taxation without representation?'" the merc asked, continuing before Ryck could reply. "Well, Greater France doesn't feel that they have to kowtow to the great Federation. I know you've been following the news. You've seen the goings on back on Earth. Things are coming to a head, and I wouldn't be surprised to see war break out."

*War, with France? No, it'll never happen*, Ryck thought. *What am I doing arguing with him?*

" Enjoy your time in prison, asshole," he said.

"Prison? Won't happen."

"Yeah, right. You attacked a Federation military force. You're going to a POW camp somewhere in the far reaches of space. Enjoy the rest of your life," Ryck told him.

"Attacked? No, as bonded security guards, we reacted to what we thought was a criminal action taken against our clients. When we realized that you were Marines, we laid down our weapons. No, I'll be back out on the street within a week," he said confidently.

Ryck went over the events in his mind. With a sinking feeling, he realized that this merc was probably right. The lawyers would get them all freed.

"On the other hand," he said, looking around to see if anyone else was listening in, "I don't really want to spend a week as a guest of the Federation, so if you could see to let me walk, I could get a cool 10k to you, more if you walked with me. When you and the Legion go head-to-head, no one's going to win, so you might as well look out for yourself, and we pay much, much better."

Ryck just stared at him for a moment, not believing what he'd heard, before answering, "Are you freaking high? You think you can offer me anything at all? Look at you. You've been shot in the arm. Your buddy over there, he's dead!"

"He was an asshole anyway. Good riddance. But this is about you. What's it going to be?"

"Fuck you," Ryck said as he turned away and walked off.

"What was did that guy want?" Popo asked as Ryck joined him.

"He wanted someone to put a round through his grubbing brain, and I came close to granting him that," Ryck said. "Forget it."

But Ryck couldn't forget what the guy had said. He was afraid it might be true.

# Alexander

## Chapter 7

With one simple click, Ryck closed his exam—his last exam. What had started as a means to combat boredom while going through his first regen had somehow grown into a full student status. With this exam, Ryck had completed the requirements for a degree—if he passed, that is. The school was pretty quick on letting students know their grades, so Ryck should know within a couple of days.

He got up from the testing station and walked up to the proctor. This was McBored, the proctor who always seemed to wish he was somewhere else. The identities of the two proctors for Camp Kolesnikov were guarded, as per SOP. Ryck thought that was pretty funny, as if this was some top secret spy mission. Someone had to know who they were just to give them base access, after all. Instead, they were anonymous figures who were supposedly above corruption and who monitored both military and civilian testing on the base. McBored and Goat, two nameless cogs in the Federation bureaucracy.

Ryck smiled as he handed McBored his ID and put his thumb on the reader. Unlike Goat, who at least made a show of checking the pic to the face, McBored simply waited for the green light over the thumb reader before leaning in for his own retinal scan. Once that was done, the outgoing was unlocked, and Ryck's exam was off to the University of Phoenix for grading.

Getting a degree would mean nothing to Ryck as a Marine, but in the civil service, any certified education meant an increase in salary, and after several grand corruption schemes were uncovered, the exam processes had been changed. The military had been caught up in those changes. It didn't really matter to Ryck one way or the other, but he usually had to withhold a laugh at the super-spy-like procedures. It was just an exam, not the plans for a new bubble space projector.

He left the testing center feeling pretty good. A degree! He'd never really considered any schooling after high school. Glancing at his watch, he picked up the pace back to his IBC. As an NCO, he rated an Individual Berthing Compartment rather than the Dual Berthing Compartment of a non-rate. He had to get ready for the Camerone Day reception and had less than an hour before the bus left.

The Legion only had a small detachment of about 30 legionnaires on Alexander, including the embassy staff. They handled liaison with both the Navy and Marines. But no matter the size, every Legion post celebrated April 30. Larger units had parades, but all units read the story of the battle where *faire camerone* became embossed in the Legion psyche. After the ceremonies, "receptions," or authorized excuses to get drunk, were usually the order of the day, and it was to the reception that Ryck was invited. All the members of the two platoons who had been on Soreau were honored guests, along with the military and civilian bigwigs. Last year's reception, which had been the first to which the Golf Marines had been invited, had started slow, but by the early hours of the morning, had turned into something the Marines only blurredly remembered, but remembered as a smashing good time.

He checked his watch. It wasn't Camerone Day back in Paris yet, but by the time they got to the Westin in St. Petersburg, it would be.

He got into his room and gave his underarm a sniff. Unfortunately, pit juice wasn't going to cut it. He jumped into the shower, ignoring the autocycle in order to manually zip through it. He used his old t-shirt to dry off as he took his blues out of the closet. Luckily, he'd prepared them the night before. He gave them a once over, but they looked fine. He dressed and was about to leave when his PA chimed. He looked at the desk screen to see if he could ignore it. He couldn't.

He hit the accept, and Hannah's face appeared. She had a big smile which morphed into a look of grudging admiration.

"Wow, you be looking smart, there, Ryck. Very impressive! Makes a poor girl's heart flutter!" she said with a laugh.

"Right. I know you can hardly contain yourself," Ryck said, pleased to see her, but knowing he had to cut the cam short.

"What girl can resist a handsome wolf in uniform?" she asked.

"Well, as much as I'm happy you cammed, I need to leave. I've got a reception I have to get to," Ryck told her.

She looked puzzled as she asked, "Reception? What time be it there? I installed the app like you told me, and it says it be 3:15 your time."

With all the planets in the Federation, each rotating at different speeds, each with different landmasses, keeping track of local time could be confusing. All Federation planets and countries, as well as many independents, kept Greenwich Mean Time as the official time and date. But night and day, not to mention planetary years, varied, and Hannah, for all her scholastic achievements, continually got confused on what local time it was for Ryck. The app Ryck had her download was so she wouldn't keep waking him up in the middle of the night.

"No, you're right, it's after three here, but I have to take a bus into St. Petersburg, and we're leaving in 15 minutes."

"Oh, too bad. I tried to get a hold of you a few hours ago to wish you luck on your test, but it's been hard getting a line out. How did you do? Did you take it?"

Hannah was working on her masters and had been a big supporter of Ryck's attempt to earn his own degree.

"Yeah, I took it. All good, I think. I'll find out in a day or two," he told her.

"OK, that's copacetic. Well, that be all I wanted to know. You have fun at the reception. Don't let those local girls snare you, though," she said.

"Nah, all they want are officers, not a lowly sergeant like me," he said. "I don't make enough to keep them in the lifestyle they want."

"A handsome wolf like you? You'll have your pick."

"Hah. I think you need to get your eyes adjusted again, young lady. They seem to be failing you," he said. "Uh, I . . . I really have to go. Thanks for camming. Tell your family hello, OK?"

"Oh, sure. Don't let me be keeping you," she said.

"OK, well, goodbye!"

Ryck turned off the cam and looked at his watch. He needed to move it. He grabbed his cover and rushed out of his IBC, then hurried to the battalion CP. He didn't want to run and start sweating under his blues, so he kept it to a speed walk.

SSgt Hecs was standing at the door to the bus, his PA out.

"Glad you decided to join us, sergeant. We keeping you from anything important?" he asked, checking Ryck off the list on his screen.

"Sorry, Staff Sergeant," Ryck told him, climbing up into the bus and sitting down in the seat Sams had saved.

SSgt Hecs followed him and told the gunny everyone was aboard. Gunny Smith told the driver to take off. The big bus rose on it air cushion, then eased out of the camp before opening up on the highway.

Ryck dozed off during the three-and-a-half hour ride to the capital city. He woke up when Sams punched his arm as they pulled into the Westin.

"Some company you've been," Sams said sourly.

"Sorry, I was up late studying for my exam," he said.

"I still don't know why you've been putting in the time for that," Sams said. "Popo and Brett swear you're gonna be putting in to be an O."

"An officer? No I work for a living," Ryck said with the time-honored reply. "I just like history, and Hannah thinks it's a good idea?"

"Crispus! It always 'Hannah this' and 'Hannah' that lately. You getting serious?"

"Oh, good God no. She doesn't like the military. She's just a friend," Ryck protested.

"Yeah, that's what everyone says before they're hitched."

As the officers got off, Gunny Smith stood up and said, "This is our second time here as guests. We want no liberty incidents. Enjoy yourselves, but remember, this is not just a drinking binge. You are representing the Federation Marine Corps. General Praeter is there, the governor is there, Admiral Yost is there, the French ambassador is there. I don't have to tell you what's going to happen to the negat who spills some of that fancy French wine over one of those esteemed gentlemen."

"Won't be me, Gunny. I'll be drinking beer!" SSgt Gordon, the First platoon sergeant said amidst the laughter.

"I'll be watching you most of all, Gordon!" the Gunny replied as the laughter intensified.

"OK, OK! We're all in a good mood. Last year was brills, so have fun. One more thing. The CO, that's the battalion CO, says no politics. No matter what, no matter who asks you, especially some civvie who's probably a reporter looking for a tag line, you say nothing about what's happening back on Earth. This is a social gathering, so keep it social. Any questions? OK, no? Then let's go have some fun!"

The Marines trooped off the bus and wound their way into the huge lobby of the Westin. Ryck had been there a year ago, but it was still pretty impressive. About 50 meters across, it reached up to the hotel's roof, some 20 stories above them. Hanging from the roof was a sculpture that had to be 40 meters tall, given that it covered eight stories of rooms. Ryck wasn't sure what it was supposed to be, but he liked it.

A Legion lieutenant was standing to the right of the lobby, and when the Marines came in, he started ushering them to the ballroom. It would have been hard to miss even without their guide. A French flag was beside the doorway, and a huge bunting of the same blue, white and red was hung over the door. Not many people were there yet: Marines being Marines, they had gotten there early. Major Gruenstein, though, was there, and he hurried over.

"Welcome, sir," he said to LtCol Adeyemi, the battalion CO, as he shook his hand. "As always, the Marines of Golf, 2/9 are eternally welcome. I hope you enjoy our hospitality."

He looked behind him, then turned back around and continued, "I see the receiving line hasn't started yet, but if you and Captain Davis would follow me, I'd like to introduce you to Colonel Giraud, our new head of mission. I don't believe you have met him yet, no?"

Sams nudged Ryck as the CO and company commander were led off, gesturing at the two bars in the back of the ballroom. Unfortunately, Gunny Smith put a kibosh on any immediate libation.

"No drinking until after we make pleasant with the brass. Just hold steady for now," he told the gathered Marines.

"Well, might as well check out the chow," Sams said. "The gunny said nuttin' about that."

Ryck and Rey followed Sams to the buffet line. There was a huge ice sculpture of a hand in the middle of the line, between a huge ice bowl of peeled shrimp and an equally huge bowl of small cracked crab claws. Ryck knew that had to represent Capt Danjou's wooden hand. The real wooden hand, recovered from the battlefield at Camerone and then bought by the Legion a few years later, was probably the Legion's most sacred relic.

The spread was pretty impressive. It was mostly finger food, some on crackers, some in little glasses. Sams grabbed a puff ball of some sort and popped it into his mouth.

"Hey, you heard the gunny!" Ryck said.

"Yeah, no drinking he said. Last time I checked this was eating, not drinking you Alice," Sams replied, speaking around the puff ball still in his mouth. "Hey, not bad!"

"What is it?" Ryck asked, inching closer to snatch one for himself.

"Hell if I know. Where's Henri?" Sams asked, referring to Cpl Henri, a Marine in Second Platoon. "Rey, go get him, OK?"

Sams grabbed another and popped it into his mouth. Ryck glanced about, only to see Gunny at the other buffet table, filching something for himself. That was good enough for Ryck, so he took one of the same fried balls and bit in. It was pretty good; a little fishy, but light.

Cpl Rey returned with Henri in tow.

"What are these?" Sams asked the corporal.

"Hors d'oeuvres. Appetizers," Henri answered.

"No shit, Sherlock. I mean what kind?"

Henri looked over the spread, then said "I don't know. Just hors d'oevers," before taking a small glass with what looked to be a bite-sized piece of chicken and avocado inside. "Tastes good, though."

"What do you mean, you don't know. You're French, right?" Sams asked.

"French-Ergat, yeah, but I don't know shit about cooking. I'm a fucking Marine, not a chef. We're BBQ people, anyway, big hunks of meat."

Ergat was one of the French worlds, out there in Second Sector. France populated all or the bulk of nine different planets. Three, like Ergat, were technically part of the Federation."

"You might try LCpl Paddyfoote. He's from Clercy," Henri said, scanning the waiting Marines. "There he is," he said before waving the Marine over."

"What's cracking, *mon corporel*? You feeling your blood here?" asked gesturing at the French-themed decorations.

Paddyfoote was one of the darkest Marines Ryck had seen, his skin almost black. Ryck didn't know much about him other than he was one of the strongest Marines in the company. He knew Henri was ethnically French, but he hadn't realized Paddyfoote was, too.

"Sure, *oui* and *liberté, égalité, fraternité* and all of that. But Sergeant Samuelson here is asking me about these hors d'oevers, and I can't answer him. You know what this shit is?"

"Shit? You wound me, *mon corporel*. This should be your lifeblood," he said with a laugh. "Let me see . . ." he said as he looked around the table.

"Theese eeze *a ballotin*," he said with a comically exaggerated French accent, pointing at pieces of asparagus wrapped in some kind of ham. "And theese, theese eeze *accras*, what you say feesh balls, from lovelee 'aiti," he told them, pointing at the puffball Sams had just taken.

"In zee glass, we call theese *verrines*, but for 'eaven, you must try zee *beignets*," he said, bringing his fingers to his lips and kissing them before pushing them out while making a popping sound, then grabbing what looked to be a fried doughnut ball.

Several other Marines had gathered and were laughing at Paddyfoote's over-the-top performance. Six or seven did grab the beignets, though, at his suggestion.

"Gents, the receiving line is about to start. I would suggest we all get in line and pay our respects before it gets too long," SSgt

Hecs said, pointing back to where the French Ambassador, the Legion colonel, and some other men and women were lining up.

The quicker through the line, the quicker to the bar, so the platoon sergeant didn't have to tell them that twice. It wasn't actually a rush, but still, no one took their time as they got into position.

The line started moving as each guest was introduced, shook hands with the ambassador and her husband, then the Legion colonel and his wife. Each person was asked his or her name by a resplendent legion lieutenant, who then repeated it to the ambassador.

SSgt Hecs followed Lt. Nidishchii' and was right in front of Ryck. The poor Legion lieutenant had a hard enough time with Nidishchii', but he completely mangled "Phantawisangtong." He seemed relieved when Ryck told him his last name.

The receiving line was, well, a receiving line. The ambassador smiled and thanked the Marines for coming. The ambassador's husband seemed friendly, but a strong smell of mouthwash did not completely hide the aroma of alcohol in his breath. Evidently, his celebration had already started. The Marines filed past the colonel and his wife, then most made a beeline for one of the two bars. The few teetotalers headed back to the buffet line to start loading up on food.

Ryck headed for the bar. It was well-stocked, but Ryck thought it was only fitting that he try some wine, first. The bartender gave him a glass of beaujolais noveau, something Ryck had never heard of much less tried. It meant "new beaujolais," and it was light and a bit sweet, OK, but not great. Ryck thought Hannah might like it, though.

Sams was drinking single-malt scotch from New Halifax, pleased to see not only Greater French booze, while Popo, Rey, and Corporals Henri and Stenski from Second Platoon were drinking beer while they munched on the various appetizers. It wasn't too long before Sams drifted over to chat up a young lady in a long, blue gown.

Their little core group shifted with the three corporals drifting off, SSgt Groton drifting in, PFC Ling coming over and trying to impressed his NCOs with some sort of questions on tactics. The boot was a certified butt-kisser. Several of the legionnaires came over to make them feel welcome, but mostly, it was Marines mixing with Marines, which was fine with Ryck and the rest. The booze and food were good, and that was what mattered.

Shortly after it turned April 30 back in France, the ambassador gave a speech full of praise for French history and brotherhood between France and the Federation. Everyone dutifully applauded, then got back to his or her drinks.

"Fucking Sams," Popo said, pointing to where the young lady, obviously in her cups, was now leaning against the tall Marines, laughing at something he had said. "How does he always manage to pull a dove wherever we go?"

"Yeah, it got him busted to private once, back on Atacama. He'd be a staff sergeant now, maybe a gunny if not for that. He says it was worth it, though," Ryck told him.

"Looking at the ass on that girl, yeah, it might be worth it," Popo said.

When the busybody Legion lieutenant came and whispered into Colonel Giraud's ear, no one seemed to notice. The two legionnaires left, then the lieutenant came back a few moments later to fetch the ambassador, who stopped socializing with the governor and hurried out of the room.

"Wonder what's up with that," SSgt Hecs said. "Hope nothing cuts this party short. I'm just catching my stride."

"Shit, don't worry. You ever see a froggie leave with booze still in the bar?" SSgt Groton said before lifting up his glass in a wordless toast before downing the rest of his glass. "Time to get recharged," he added before staggering ever-so-slightly off to get more beer.

Talk drifted back to Sams and his magic touch with women when Ryck noticed General Prater getting a call. He didn't think much about it until the Division commander's posture changed and he held up his hand to get the officers around him to stop talking. When the Legion lieutenant came back into the ballroom one more time and evidently asked both the CG and Admiral Yost to follow him, Ryck knew something was up. The CG said something to Col Pierre and the others, then followed the legionnaire out of the room.

The regimental sergeant major waved over the gunny as the officers put down their drinks. Gunny Smith listened, then nodded. Ryck felt the tension build as the gunny came back to them first.

"The bar is closed. Quietly and calmly, get everyone to dump whatever drink they have. I want everyone to move to where Captain Davis and First Sergeant Peale are heading. Be ready for an order to move out," he quietly told them.

Most of the Marines and other party-goers hadn't noticed anything, and a few Marines thought it was all a joke. One look to the company staff, though, brought it into focus. Something was going on, something big.

SSgt Groton tried to ask what was happening as the company gathered, but Capt Davis motioned him to be quiet. Ryck thought the captain was in the dark as much as the rest of them.

With the Marines in one corner of the room and the small Legion detachment gathering back near the bar, the civilians slowly coalesced across from the Marines. The governor started walking over, and Col Pierre met him, whispering in the politician's ear. The two of them stood there for a few moments, discussing what was happening, before the CO came back to the rest of the Marines.

A long 15 minutes later, Admiral Yost, the Legion colonel, and General Praeter, came back into the ballroom, somberly marching to the center of it.

The admiral cleared his throat and began, "Ladies and gentlemen, please listen up. Colonel Giraud, General Praeter, and I have something to say. At 0100 Paris time, the Greater French president formally revoked the Mutual Defense Treaty with the Federation, declaring themselves divorced from all Federation laws and agreements. At 0115. FCDC troops began to move into France and the French Lunar base."

*Fifteen fucking minutes to invade? This was no surprise*, thought Ryck.

"At 0120, Greater France declared an opening of adversarial relations and appealed to the independent states as well as the Brotherhood for support. For those of you who are not familiar with the legalese, this is not a declaration of war, but one step below. What this means, we don't know yet. Can the politicians fix this? Will war be declared? We don't know. We are now on Class 1 Alert, and all military hands are to return to their bases for further orders.

"I have given Colonel Giraud my assurances that he and his detachment, that all French embassy personnel, will be allowed to depart Alexander unmolested. Ambassador Basel is already making preparations. All Legion personnel in this room are requested to follow your colonel. Transport off Alexander is now being procured."

There was a stunned silence as everyone digested the news. Things had been dicey back on Earth, but very few people could have imagined the situation could disintegrate so thoroughly.

Ryck thought back to the ex-Marine merc back on Pannington. He had said it would come to this, so clearly, some people , though, had been aware of the oncoming storm.

Col Giraud stepped forward and said, "Admiral Yost, I want to thank you for your chivalrous gesture. You have my respect," before switching over to French.

Ryck couldn't follow what was said, but there was obviously a lot of emotion in the telling of it. When he finished, the legionnaires in the back of the ballroom slowly started moving forward, eyes to the front. Not only the legionnaires started moving, though.

From the corner of his eye, Ryck caught movement from within the Marines. He turned his head to see LCpl Paddyfoote making his way out of the mass of Marines. He made it to the front of the crowd, then marched up to join the legionnaires.

Ryck stared at him in shock. It was obvious that he was deserting the Corps for the Legion. Ryck looked around to see who was going to stop him, to arrest him. When someone else started moving, he thought that was the person who was going to grab Paddyfoote.

"What the fuck you doing, Marc?" Sgt Temper from Second Platoon was shouting, grabbing Cpl Henri by the arm.

"Those are my people, Devin. I gotta go," Henri said with tears welling in his eyes.

"No, Marc, we're your people. Think about it. What about Hermone, saving your ass at the mine? What about that?" Devin Temper shouted as the other Marines around them moved back a step, giving the two friends a buffer.

Marc Henri looked up at the retreating legionnaires, then back at Devin, before saying, "You, all of you, have been there for me, and I'm proud to be a Marine. But if this is war, do you expect me to fight my family? The family who welcomed you, Devin, when you came to visit , the family who fed you. What about Giselle? You met her, took her out for dinner, for God's sake? I've known her family for all my life, you really expect me to fight them?" he asked, a tear making a track down his cheek.

"But you can't! This is desertion! I won't let you do—" he started before LtCol Adeyemi stepped up to them. He took Devin's hand and gently pulled it away from Henri's arm.

The CO simply shook his head, effectively telling the Marine to leave it be, and Devin slumped back, defeated. LCpl Marc Henri, UFMC, shook his head, then turned and marched forward to join the last of the legionnaires leaving the room.

What had just transpired was beyond Ryck's comprehension. War with France? Marines deserting? It didn't make sense. He scanned the Marines to see if anyone else was going to leave. Col Pierre, the regimental commander was French, wasn't he? His brother was a Legion colonel. Ryck had seen him at the change of command when Col Pierre had taken command of the regiment.

Col Pierre stood emotionless in with Capt Davis. He wasn't moving.

With the last legionnaire gone, the room broke into a hubbub of chatter. The civilians went right for their PAs, some as they hurried out of the ballroom, their devices glued to their ears. The Marines were no different, bringing out their PAs and connecting until the sergeant major yelled out that they were in a Security Status 2, which meant no unauthorized communications.

Within moments, the SNCOs had taken charge and were forming the Marines up. The General and his aides left first, his staff car whisking him back to division headquarters. Col Pierre and LtCol Adeyemi took Capt Davis and the sergeant's major with them in their van, leaving Lieutenant Patrick, the company XO, in charge of the movement to camp. The two busses arrived, and the Marines were quickly embarked.

Within minutes, the busses were on the way back, but back to what, Ryck just didn't know.

# PART 2

# *FS Ark Royal*

## Chapter 8

Ryck settled into his cradle in the 14-man PVS-14, or Personnel Vacuum Sled 14. The "reki" looked more like a roller-coaster car instead of the old-time Finnish reindeer sleigh from which it took its nickname, and Ryck had the temptation to lift his arms roller-coaster-style if they did in fact deploy out of the *Ark Royal*. This was the fourth time the Marines had been loaded into the rekis since the beginning of the interdiction, but each previous time, the target vessel had turned back and the Marines stood down without any action.

A state of war between Greater France and the Federation did not technically exist, at least at the moment. The FDCD officers (always referred to as "officers," never "soldiers") had moved into France shortly after the Mutual Defense Treaty had been abrogated. They stopped well short of Paris, though, leaving the city itself in the hands of the French government. The FCDC had moved in to "protect the integrity of the Federation borders." The six planetary republics in Greater France filed grievances, as had governments of seven other worlds. Three of those worlds had been colonized by French companies but were members of the Federation; the other four were independents. The Federation responded by employing exclusion zones around each of those 13 planets. The only exception was a narrow "elevator" over the nation of Guildenhaus, a Federation member-state located on the otherwise independent planet of First Strike.

The *Ark Royal* was the flagship for the small task force enforcing the exclusion zone around Tel Aviv. Tel Aviv had never been a member of the Federation but had generally worked within the Federation sphere, which made sense as the Federation bought the bulk of its exports. Upon the incursion of the FCDC into France, though, Tel Aviv quickly sided with Greater France and pledged its support. The planet was immediately slapped with the exclusion zone by the Federation.

The *Ark Royal* task force was small with only three ships. But the *Ark Royal* itself would have been enough to enforce the blockade. The ship was, in a word, huge.

Bubble ships, by design, were spherical, so from the outside, the *Ark Royal*'s primary difference from other bubble ships was its size. In this case, that size difference was immense. A full 800 meters in diameter, the ship was not a dreadnought in the sense of an offensive weapons platform like the Prion Class Battle Cruisers. It was a more direct descendant of the old wet-water Navy aircraft carriers. The ship's huge hangars housed three full squadrons of Experion fighters, a squadron of Griffyn monitors, four orbit-to-ground assault craft, each capable of carrying a company of PICS Marines or 400 pax, and all the assorted support, ECM, recon, and comms craft necessary to support any mission given to the ship. The embarked Marine battalion, complete with the attached Wasp flight and Stork squadron, was easily lost among the 16,000 sailors onboard the ship.

With all the sailors, the Marines almost seemed an afterthought, shunted aside. They were in Ancillary Hangar 3A, a small (in comparison) hangar located off of B Deck. At 30 meters across, there was more than enough room for the 12 rekis in it, all loaded with Marines. The rekis were in two ranks, six abreast. Ryck's squad was in the third reki, ready to deploy in the first rank if the call came through. Squeezed in beside the first reki was a small PVS-2, the small two-man version of the larger 14-man reki. Two Recon Marines, in their slicks, stood by, leaning up against the PVS-2's nose.

Ryck took a quick look behind him. Two of the rekis in the second rank had four PICS Marines each, ready to act as heavy hitters if needed. Ryck wasn't too confident on how the two fire teams from Second Platoon would fare if anything happened to them on an EVA. Each PICS had been outfitted with both an external oxygen tank and a small auxiliary thrust pack. The thrust packs, though were really not very effective. "Space farts" was the commonly used term for them, able to nudge a PICS Marine in a vacuum, but not really move the combat suit with any degree of authority. If anything happened and one of the Marines separated from his reki, then he could easily be lost for good. PICS were just not designed for EVA work.

Ryck never felt completely comfortable in his Marine Corps EVA suit, but at least they were designed for the mission of open-space operations. He went through his checks again, and all lights were green. He would have already known, though, if anything was wrong, given that the hangar doors were open and he was sitting in the vacuum of open space.

The small, dull blue numbers in the lower right corner of his helmet face shield counted out the seconds as time passed. They'd been in the suits for almost 45 minutes so far. The mission would probably be another scratch. What commercial carrier was going to risk destruction at the hands of the *Ark Royal*?

Since the interdiction was declared, military action was primarily Navy. As on Alexander, Legion troops had been generally give free passage off Federation worlds, and the small Federation attachments on the Greater French worlds had been accorded the same courtesy. It was only on Pallidyne IV, an unincorporated planet in the Third Quadrant, that fighting had broken out. A Marine expeditionary company and a Legion light battalion had gone into battle with the Legion emerging victorious. This surprised no one given the much smaller numbers of the Marines and the superiority of the Legion weaponry.

The Legion had reported to the press that the Marines had attacked and the Legion post was forced to defend itself. No Marines believed that. There was no logical reason why an expeditionary company, only lightly armed and there to provide security for a Navy scientific team, would take on a Legion combat battalion, even one with only two companies. Even in the best of times, the Legion had better war-fighting equipment and weapons. The Legion always bought the most advanced gear available while the Marines relied on old technology, preferring half-assed upgrades than a full acquisition of the next generation gear. It wasn't actually that the Marines didn't want the newest and best—it was the Federation that didn't want to pay for it. Military funds in the Federation went to the Navy first and foremost with the Marines and, to an extent, the FCDC sucking hind tit.

"Heads up," the lieutenant passed on the command circuit. "The target is making a run for it."

The target had been identified as the New Chilean-registered freighter *Marie's Best.* It was an old hull, laid down over 120 years ago. It had gone through a full retrofit some 40 years earlier, but this was still old techno. How its captain thought it would be able to evade the *Ark Royal*, a frigate, and a destroyer was beyond Ryck. It had been trying to sneak in, approaching Tel Aviv directly from the system's sun. That plan had little to no chance in succeeding against the Navy ships, so it was no surprise that the attempt failed. What was a surprise was that the ship didn't surrender when the captain realized they had been compromised.

"Listen up," Ryck passed on the squad circuit. "The target ship is making a run for it. There still won't be much for us to do if the Navy blasts it out of space, but . . . hold on, I'm getting something else."

"The target has been hit by one of the *Ark Royal's* monitors. Scans indicate that it has not, I repeat, has not been destroyed. There are life readings on board. We are a go," the lieutenant passed before remembering to open the platoon circuit and repeat the message for all hands.

Ryck looked to his right where the two recon Marines were scrambling to board their coffin, the nickname given to the PVS-2. It didn't really look like a coffin but more like a large cigar. Like the reki, it was basically a simple powered platform open to space, but where Marines in a reki were sitting side-by-side, in the coffin, one man lay on top of the other. Their slicks were a dark, slate grey rather then the lighter-colored EVA suits of the grunt Marines, and they allowed a wearer to remain in space for longer, but many of the other differences were classified.

Within moments, the two recon Marines had launched, moving out to provide eyes on the target. It took a bit longer for the rest of the Marines to launch. The lead reki had a Navy cybo on board to provide navigation. The rekis could be put on automatic nav, but for the distance to be covered, the Navy felt better with one of their own in control.

In this case, the lead reki was #2. The other 11 of them would move out to a pre-determined distance from #2, then move to the target in tandem with the lead sled. Only as they approached the target would the connection be broken and a Marine, acting as a coxswain, would navigate to the appropriate spot on the target.

Ryck keyed in his three fire team leaders, "We've trained for this. There shouldn't be any surprises, but if there are, just keep your heads and react. Any action is better than inaction. Any questions?"

When there were none, he isolated Cpl Beady, his Third Fire Team leader, and asked, "John, how's Ling?"

PFC Ling was the second junior man in the squad and Ryck's headache. Even after their last op, he still seemed to be more bark than bite, somewhat of a kiss-ass, but he had been uncharacteristically quiet while they were forming for the possible mission. Ling had been with the squad on Pannington and so was technically blooded, but for all intents and purposes, he was still a combat virgin, and there was no telling how he would react under fire. Ryck didn't want to have to worry that one of his Marines would be ineffective.

"He's nervous, but not too bad. I think he'll be fine," Cpl Beady answered.

If they were in their PICS, Ryck could be monitoring the vitals of all the Marines in the squad. The EVA suits didn't have that capability, so Ryck had to rely on his unit leaders.

"Ok, but keep an eye on him," he said.

Ryck looked back at the *Ark Royal* as his reki moved into position. The ship was even more impressive from the outside. The Marines had boarded the ship from an enclosed shuttle, where the lack of portholes had kept them from seeing the ship. Here, in the openness of space, the ship glistened in the harsh sunlight.

Too quickly, though, all the rekis had been launched, and they were moving away. The *Ark Royal* dwindled and vanished behind them as the small reki fleet picked up speed.

*Dashing through the space, on a one horse open sleigh . . .* Ryck couldn't help but sing to himself as they accelerated at five g's, the vast openness of space surrounding them.

Without the compensators, Ryck knew they would be pulled against the harnesses, struggling to breathe. As it was, they only felt a slight tug as they zipped over to their target.

The EVA suits did not compile as much combat-related information as a PICS or even a sleeve display on skins, but it did provide better data in other areas. Ryck had a location of the target, approximately 10,000 klicks away. At 5 g's, accelerating half way before beginning deceleration, they should arrive at the target in about 26 minutes. The cybo navigating #2 would have more exact data, taking into consideration that the target, even if hit, would still be moving, but the Ryck's guesstimate was good enough for government work.

"Settle in for the ride. We've got about 25 more minutes until we arrive on the scene," he passed to the squad, keying in the lieutenant and SSgt Hecs as well and hoping he entered the correct input.

When the lieutenant didn't correct him, the figured he had done the math right.

Ten-thousand klicks was more than most EVAs, but the rekis could handle the distance, and EVA suits were generally good for up to 18 hours. In the back of his mind, Ryck also knew that the Marines were far more expendable than the *Ark Royal* or the other two ships in the task force. Years ago, the *FS Mumbai* had been destroyed when it moved in to facilitate the rescue of a damaged Western Alliance frigate. It had never been proven that the frigate had suicided to take out the *Mumbai*, but that was the general consensus. Consequently, losing a few Marines and EVA sleds was a risk the admiral would feel far more comfortable taking than putting any of the capital ships in harm's way.

The recon team arrived at the target within 11 minutes of leaving the *Ark Royal*. That was smoking fast, and the best compensators couldn't completely neutralize the g's it would have taken to get there that quickly. The two recon Marines would have had to fight the g's the best they could.

The team started with passive surveillance, and they feed they sent back was forwarded to each Marine's face shield. The *Marie's Best* had the characteristics cigar shape of an ion-tube ship. The side facing the recon Marine's cameras was dark, the edges of the ship framed in the sunlight. The damage to the front of the ship was evident, but looked to be isolated to that small section. Ryck had to admire the Navy gunnery skills. The monitor that had taken down the *Marie's Best* was unmanned, controlled by a team on the *Ark Royal*. This had been a surgical strike, not the wholesale destruction Ryck had expected. The skill of the gunnery team, to take down a ship while basically leaving it whole, really impressed him.

Instinctively, Ryck peered ahead of the reki, but they were still way too far to be able to pick out the target. He paid more attention to his data stream on his face shield. More input was coming from the team as they employed a fairly impressive array of passive gathering processes. The ship was essentially dead. A cloud of gasses surrounded the ship, indicating that the ship's atmosphere had been vented. There were no sustained emissions in any of the normal spectrums, only flickers as the ship's emergency systems tried to come back online.

Captain Davis was in command of the operation, and he ordered the recon team to move to active surveillance. This was a moment of truth. The stealth capabilities of the PVS-2 would have kept the team invisible to anyone on the *Marie's Best*. As soon as they went active, though, their position would be revealed. There wasn't much a coffin could do against incoming missiles or energy weapons.

A few moments later, new data started streaming in. It was too much for Ryck to grasp, so he blinked his AI to make some sense of it. The AI put that results in what it determined to be in order of importance to a combat Marine. Foremost among this was that none of the ship's weapons systems were operational. Second was that there were 133 living humans aboard. Third, there were working, active personnel weapons on the ship.

The scans couldn't determine if the survivors were armed with any of the active weapons. It couldn't tell the intent of the survivors. But the mere fact that there were people alive on the ship, a ship that had tried to run the interdiction, and that there were functioning small arms on the ship, was something Captain Davis had to take under consideration.

Captain Davis, the two platoon commanders, the gunny, and the Navy engineer were massaging the plan as the small flotilla approached the *Marie's Best.* The engineer had no command authority, but he was the Navy rep, answering directly back to the admiral, and his mission to secure the integrity of the ship was second only to the overall security of the task force. Ryck listened in as the company commander made the adjustments. Several times, the captain's local command circuit was cut, probably when the battalion CO or even the admiral stuck their noses into things.

As a young private, Ryck thought captains, if not gods, were at least saints, doing what they pleased. It took him awhile to realize that they had the same pressures and "input" from above. Private or captain, all Marines answered to someone else.

At five minutes out, the plan had gelled. Of course no plan survived the first few moments of combat, but at least Ryck knew where his squad would be breaching and what their task would be. That was a start.

Ryck took a minute to relay the word to his squad. Only three Marines in the squad had ever done any actual ship takedown ops. For the rest of the squad, their only experience had been in Phase IV of recruit training. Since embarking on the *Ark Royal*, the OpsO[38] had scheduled an immediate action drill, but without actually going EVA, that was only moderately useful. It would have to be enough, though.

The entire platoon was going to breach the *Marie's Best* amidships, close to the galley where the bulk of the survivors were

[38] OpsO: Operations Officer. This is the individual who creates and runs an operational plan.

gathered. Each squad was going to breach at about a 120-degree angle from each other so that they would be essentially encircling the galley and coming in from different directions. With no artificial gravity working on the ship, there would be no up or down, so the Marines could not think in a two-planed battlespace.

At two minutes out, the company got a "good luck" from the recon team. The Marines couldn't pick the team, but the team could pick them up as they approached the *Marie's Best*. Ryck wondered about the recon Marines for a moment. When Ryck went into battle, he had his Marines around him. The two recon Marines just had each other as they drifted out there in space somewhere.

The *Marie's Best* registered on their sensors before they could actually see her, but finally, Ryck could pick her out with his zoom panel. Technically, he wasn't seeing her but rather an image captured by his shoulder cam and displayed on his face shield, but for all intents and purposes, she was in view.

The Navy cybo released control of the rekis, and LCpl Keiji, the squad coxswain, took over, "diving" below the x-axis to come up on the other side of the ship. They passed under it, "under" only because their orientation within the reki made them crane their heads up to see the ship as they went past. "Under" and "over" had little real meaning in space, so the terms were used within a personal perspective connotation. Marines on the other side of the ship could also be passing "under" the ship as well.

Ryck half-expected fire to reach out from the ship to rake the reki, but the *Marie's Best* remained quiet and unresponsive.

Something did hit the reki, though, as they moved in. They couldn't hear it, of course, but all the Marines could feel the vibration. Some of the debris from the monitor strike had not been blown away. With no atmosphere to slow it down, the debris keeping alongside the ship as it continued through space. The reki didn't seem damaged, but whatever hit the sled might have been able to put a serious hurt on the unprotected Marines.

"Slow it down, Keiji," Ryck ordered. "Let them wait up for us, if they have to. No use getting one of us zeroed by pieces of dead ship."

He started to report their speed change when he heard Sams pass the same thing. The debris field surrounded a good portion of the ship. Ryck could see some of the larger pieces closer to the bow of the ship, but even around the center, glints of reflected sunlight caught his eyes as pieces and shards tumbled. It was as if space fireflies had gathered around the ship.

Keiji slowed them down to a crawl. They were a good 200 meters away when they passed a piece of cloth, probably part of a blanket. Ryck had to push it out of the way. At their relative speed, it wouldn't have done any damage, and Ryck was glad they'd slowed down instead of coming in blazing.

The reki had a very simple console. An image of the ship was displayed on it, with their breach-location highlighted with a narrowing yellow square. LCpl Keiji was using it to guide the sled to the correct spot. He brought the reki to a stop just 20 meters from the skin of the *Marie's Best*.

That was a relative stop, Ryck reminded himself. It was a little hard to grasp that they were still hurtling through space at a pretty good clip. If the Navy engineer team couldn't get the ship under its own power, or if task force couldn't get a tug on the ship, it would probably plunge into the planet's atmosphere and burn up, at least most of it. Some pieces would undoubtedly make it to the ground.

At his signal, the squad released their harnesses. Third Fire Team flew to the back of the reki where their breaching chamber had been loaded. In space it didn't weigh anything, but it still had mass, and once moving, its momentum could make it dangerous. The other Marines and Doc Grbil gave way, leaving the team plenty of maneuver space to get the chamber up against the skin of the ship.

It took almost five minutes of slow maneuvering to get the chamber in placed and locked. This would be a simple breach. With no atmosphere inside the ship, there was no need to create an airlock. If the damaged area could be sealed off after the ship was under Navy control, the breach could be sealed once again.

"Golf-three-six, we are in position and waiting to execute," Ryck passed on the platoon circuit.

Ryck used the lieutenant's call sign to indicate he was speaking to the platoon commander. He could have gone on a direct P2P circuit with him, but he wanted everyone else to know their status. Third Squad itself was "Golf-three-three," but as his identity was indicated as soon as he keyed his mic, passing that merely took up unnecessary time.

"Roger that. Wait for my command," the lieutenant passed.

Ryck checked the feed from the recon team. The blobs that indicated living people were still grouped inside. There was nothing to indicate a marshalling of forces. The recon team was at the wrong angle to give a clear indication of what was right inside Third Squad's planned breach, but it looked like the area might be empty of life.

First Platoon would be entering the ship through the damaged nose. Ryck didn't envy them that task. There was much more debris up there, and inside, maneuvering around wreckage in an EVA suit could be a stressful undertaking. The suits were tough, but not indestructible. However, the Navy engineer needed to check that area first. Only if it was totally destroyed would he take his team to the aft control center.

It took longer than expected, but First Platoon finally picked their way through the debris. Capt Davis gave the command, and the Third Platoon started breaching. Sparks flew from the end of the chamber as the LTC blades bit into the ship's skin.

Breaches could be made by either blowing their way into a breach or by cutting. Given the age of the Marie's Best and her hallo aluminum skin, cutting was the least catastrophic method of breaching. Within twenty seconds, the breach was made, and the Marines poured into the ship.

The ship was dark where they breached. Each EVA's AI recognized that and turned on the infrared lamps located around the face shield. Ryck didn't like having to rely on them. He could see with them on, but the EVA's night vision capability left him with a flat, almost two-dimensional view that left him feeling out of sorts.

The EVA suit displays, while not as detailed at those in a PICS, did display ID avatars, so when one Marine lost control and slammed into another, sending the second one cart wheeling to the far side of the room, Ryck could see it was Ling who slammed into Beady. Null-G movement had to be controlled. Being too hyped made it difficult to gain that steady control. Ryck wanted to remind Cpl Beady that he had to keep an eye on Ling, but he knew that Beady knew that, too. No use harping on it.

"First, move it out. Second, cover them," Ryck passed.

He hooked a strut with his M99 and pulled himself forward. Outside or inside a ship, the EVA suit's thrusters would work. But in the confines of a ship, the exhaust of the thruster could impact other nearby Marines. So movement became a series of jumps with tiny adjustments from the microjets to keep steady. Controlling the foot pads to grip when needed, but to let go when jumping was an exercise in timing that did not come easily. The six centimeter hooks that some Marine had designed to slip over the muzzle of their M99s was a godsend. With them, a Marine could reach out and pull himself along without having to ground his feet.

Greg Prifit had his usual assignment as the fire team's heavy gunner. Instead of a 20mm grenade launcher, though, he was armed with a M51 plasma gun. Set on full dispersion, he could fill a ship's passage with blue death, sending it out over 20 meters before its effectiveness started to diminish. He cautiously pushed out of the compartment, peering down the passage. The retrans from the recon team indicated there were no life forms in the passage, but there were a number of ways to counteract or spoof sensors. He paused only a moment before pulling himself through the hatch and down the passage, the rest of his team on his ass. Ryck followed, and behind him were the other two teams.

First Team was hugging the sides of the passage, one Marine on the deck, the overhead, and each bulkhead. All were oriented with their feet towards the outside of the passage, their heads toward the middle. This allowed for better fields of fire, and would allow for easier support from the rest of the squad. Realistically, if they hit the shit, only two or three of the other Marines would be able to support with fire without too great of a risk of friendly fire casualties.

The squad moved like a disjointed snake down the passage, making their way to the galley. There were compartments along the way, but there was no time to clear each one, so Hartono used the weldmaster, a small gun that "flowed" a small area of the metal hatches, bridging the seam between the door and the jamb and sealing them shut until an engineer could come by and opened them.

First Fire Team had only moved about 30 meters through the curved corridor when they saw their first person. Ex-person, that is. The young man was in the grey overalls popular with many fabrication factories. He was floating a few centimeters off of the outer bulkhead. His eyes were glassy and bulging, his mouth open. Around his nose and from his mouth were bubbles. Ryck knew they would be red under normal lighting. He'd obviously been without access to an EVA suit, and when the ship was breached, he would have had only 20 or 30 seconds until the air was expelled, leaving the ship in a vacuum. Clearly, he had tried to hold his breath while he struggled to reach safety.

Back at boot, one of the things drilled into recruits was that holding the breath in a vacuum was tantamount to a death sentence. The air in their lungs would quickly expand, causing embolisms that would kill within seconds. This could be avoided by immediately expelling all the air from the lungs and keeping the mouth open. A human could remain conscious for up to 15 seconds in a vacuum and could remain alive for up to a minute or more. People could be revived even after longer than that. A Brotherhood sailor had supposedly been brought back after six minutes in a vacuum with no signs of permanent damage.

This young man undoubtedly never had that type of training, though. He was probably the factory worker he seemed to be. What he was doing in a ship trying to run a Federation blockade was a mystery to Ryck. Whatever the reason, it ended up killing him.

The man was drifting in front of Keiji, and the lance corporal tried to avoid the body. He just nudged it, though, as he passed, sending the body slowly tumbling. Ryck tried to scoot past the body, but the body's tumbling took up a lot of space, and it rotated into him. This could slow down the squad it every Marine was trying to avoid the corpse. Ryck took a hold of it and planted his feet on the corridor's overhead. Slowly turning, he steadied himself, and with a sure push, sent the body down the very center of the passage. With the Marines around the corridor's periphery, the body floated past them, making it beyond the last Marine before hitting the far overhead as the corridor curved.

"The passage to the next deck isn't here," Cpl Rey passed. "It's supposed to be here."

Ryck turned back and moved forward, switching to the ship's plan on his readout. Every ship moving through Federated space was required to have complete ship's blueprints registered. Rey was correct. He was right at the spot where the passage to the inner decks was supposed to be, and the galley was two decks in. There was a fine seam in the bulkhead where the entrance to the ladder should have been. The ship had been modified, and the new plans had never been submitted.

"There has to be a way," Ryck said, checking his readout.

"Sams, is your access to Bravo and Charlie decks there?" he asked the First Squad leader.

There was a pause until Sams came on the circuit and said, "Roger that. We're just passing Bravo. What's up?"

"They've modified the ship. Our ladder is sealed off. There's not another passage on the plans until we reach yours, but there is a compartment, Alpha-One-Six, between us, and it looks like it opens on both decks. If it's sealed, though, or doesn't open to Bravo, then we're going to have to move on and use your route in," Ryck said.

"OK, just give me a heads up if you are going to be coming up our butt," Sams said.

Ryck reported the issue to the lieutenant, who told Ryck to keep moving and try that compartment as a passage to the inner decks.

"Rey, do you see Alpha-One-Six on your plans?" he asked.

"Not really. How far down is it?" Cpl Rey asked.

With a PICS' more advanced display capability, Ryck could have highlighted the compartment and activated that highlight on Rey's display. With the EVA suits' less-capable displays, that wasn't possible.

"Thirty meters ahead, proximal," Ryck told him.

"Oh, proximal, I was looking at the regular compartments. Yeah, I see it," Rey said.

The *Marie's Best* had artificial gravity, and that oriented the ship so that down was proximal, towards the center of the ship. The overhead was distal. For ships that used rotation to simulate gravity, this was reversed. With both methods, the larger compartments tended to be medial, on the horizontal axis, surrounding the corridors. In between decks, though, there was space, valuable space. This was primarily used for conduits, air tubes, and the like, but wherever small compartments could be jigsawed in, they provided extra storage space, control rooms, or even hydroponic farms.

"Head for that. Let's see if we can get through to Bravo. According to this ship's diagram, it should," Ryck said.

"Yeah, but it also showed this ladder going though, and this is one of the main ones," Cpl Rey said.

Ryck snorted, then replied, "Got that right. Well, let's see if it's right on this.

Cpl Rey led his team down the passage, pushing with the grip-tite toes of his EVA for forward momentum and the hook on his weapon to keep him close along the bulkhead.

Ryck liked to use the hook more than anything else. If someone hit them while the hook was latched onto something, he knew the split second it took to release that and bring his weapon to bear could be the difference between getting shot and shooting the enemy. But First Team was in front of him, so he felt simply using the hook kept his eyes steady and gave him a better picture of what was going on. The grip-tite that was on the toes of the EVA suit did as advertised, gripping most any surface and giving traction, but the push and dolphin motion it took to move forward without drifting out interfered with his line of sight.

It only took a few minutes before First Team reached the round door on the deck that led to the compartment. Ryck pulled Second Team up, then gave Cpl Rey the signal to open it up.

Hartono slid the M99 into the magholster on his thigh and grabbed the door's wheel, bringing his legs under him and flat on the deck. Braced by holding the small, recessed wheel, he could exert as much force on the door as his hands could maintain their grip. He spun the wheel, and the door immediately opened without resistance. With his right hand, he grabbed his weapon; with his left, he pulled himself into a dive down through the door and into the compartment. Keiji and Prifit were on his ass.

Cpl Rey was about to follow when Keiji told him to stop. Ryck crowded up, ready for anything, but Keiji's head appeared through the open door.

"It's kinda tight here. This is some kinda bunkroom. Harts is ready to open up the door to Bravo Deck, so me and Tip are gonna cover. That's all the room there is."

"Wait one," Ryck said, pulling himself over to the door so he could see inside.

Keiji was right. Inside the cramped space were six racks, three on a side. This had to be crew's quarters. Ryck had heard that some lines were tight-ass stingy, using all bigger compartments for cargo or paying passengers, but this was the first time he'd ever run across this shoehorning in crew wherever they could.

Ryck called up Cpl Mendoza's team, arraying the Marines the best he could around the small round door. It would be extremely difficult to provide supporting fire if there was anyone right there at Bravo Deck as First Team would be in the way, but at least they were closer and could get down there quicker if need be.

"OK, hit it," Ryck told PFC Hartono.

Hartono spun the wheel on the door, and it silently opened into Bravo Deck. Ryck could just see the overhead past him as Hartono's infrared torch lit up the area.

"Oh God!" the PFC exclaimed as he pushed into the corridor.

"Go, go!" Cpl Rey shouted at his other two Marines who quickly pulled through the door to join Hartono.

Ryck was already diving through, right on Rey's ass. In front of the two NCOs, Keiji was motionless just inside the door.

He held up a hand and quietly said, "All clear."

Letting Rey go first, Ryck followed through the door and into the Bravo Deck corridor. He twisted and landed feet-first on the deck. He immediately saw what elicited Hartono's exclamation. In front of him, illuminated in the infrared, were six people, all dead.

Two adults, four children. The man looked to be in his early 30's. All he had on a pair of dark shorts. The man was facing the others, one arm reached out towards them. Facing the man was a woman. Ryck couldn't see her face, so only her close-cropped hair and unitard registered. With one arm, she was reaching out for the man. Her other arm was crooked, holding the baby. In death, her arm was still positioned to hold the baby, but her grip had slackened, and the infant's legs could be seen protruding to the side of the woman. Ryck was suddenly glad he couldn't see the baby's face.

He could see the other three children's faces though. The closest victim to the Marines was a young boy, possibly 10 or 11 years old. He had on a Thunder Bluster t-shirt, the band's skull logo catching the infrared beams and looking as if it was lit. He would have looked like any other kid scoping the mall after school—if it weren't for the look of utter agony frozen on his face. His eyes were protruding and dark with petechiae, his mouth opened in a silent scream. One arm was obviously broken, probably from being slammed against something as the air rushed out of the ship. The kid had not gone easily into the night.

In front of him and up against the overhead were the two girls. They looked like twins, around five or six years old. Each was locked in the other's embrace, faces against each other's. At least their eyes were closed, and while they had to have suffered, they seemed more peaceful.

In a complete vacuum a person would lose consciousness in less than 15 seconds. However, when the ship this size was breached with the degree of destruction the *Marie's Best* suffered, it would have taken 20 or even 30 seconds for the ship's atmosphere to be vented. That meant this family would have known what was happening. They would have suffered as the air pressure dropped towards zero.

Airtight bulkheads could have kept pockets of air inside, but for some reason, they had not been activated. The crew had probably felt the AI would take care of that, but the AI could have been destroyed in the initial strike. That was why on all military ships, at least, the AIs had several secondary "brains" located throughout the ship, and all ships going into battle had airtight bulkheads sealed.

The family was stretched out over about 20 meters. They must have been bounced through the corridor as the air evacuated, trying to stay together. With the artificial gravity fading, it would have been even harder. Ryck tried not to imagine what it must have been like.

He swallowed trying to keep the bile from rising in his throat. Vomiting in an EVA suit was not a good idea, but this scene hit him hard. He tried to block it, but images of Lysa and his two nieces floating in the cold vacuum of space flooded his imagination

The rest of the squad slowly made their way into Bravo Deck. Everyone was silent as they took in the scene.

Why hadn't the family been in evac suits? They had to have known they were running a blockade. And why run a blockade in the first place? These were not combatants. They were just people. Why was it that important to get them to the planet's surface?

Ryck knew that warfare was dirty, that civilians got killed. He'd been on ops where he knew that had happened. This was the first time, though, that he'd really seen the effects right before his eyes. This was the first time he'd really seen "collateral damage." He'd cheered when he'd heard the *Ark Royal's* monitors had scored the hit. He'd felt pride when he'd seen the damage to the *Marie's Best*. He wasn't feeling so enthused now.

"Three-six, this is three-three" he passed on the platoon circuit, "we've got six dead civilians here. Looks like a family."

"There's quite a number of bodies throughout the ship," Lt. Nidishchii' passed back. "They'll be taken care of later. What's your progress now? I can't get a good fix on you."

"We're on Bravo, heading back to see if we can make it to Charlie," Ryck replied.

"Three-two is already at the objective. We will be there momentarily. You need to get a move on."

"Roger that. If we have a ladder, it shouldn't be more than five mikes," Ryck said.

"Understood. If you have any problems, keep me informed. Three-six, out."

"Let's move it. We're behind schedule," Ryck passed through the squad circuit.

"Which way?" Cpl Rey asked.

Trying to see if the original ladder connected Bravo and Charlie meant passing through the family, and Ryck could hear the strain in Rey's voice as he asked. Going the other way, though, meant they would be using the same ladder as First Squad. Ryck didn't want to disturb the family as they floated in the corridor, but that was the direction they had to take.

"Forward," was all he passed.

Ryck tried to keep his gaze forward as they moved between the bodies. The twin girls were blocking his route, so he jumped across the corridor to use one of the bulkheads. He also made pretty heavy use of his microjets to not only maintain attitude, as they were designed for, but to bend him around the bodies. He determinedly refused to even glance at the woman's face or the infant still in her arm as he passed her.

Thankfully, they reached the clear corridor ahead. A few moments later, Cpl Rey passed that the ladder between Bravo and Charlie was in fact there. Whatever modification had been done to the ship had only affected the space between Alpha and Bravo.

They went down the ladder, one at a time, to emerge in a cleared Charlie Deck. No bodies rose to greet them. From there, it was only about 25 meters to their assigned entrance to the galley. Ryck let the rest of the platoon know the squad was entering, then when given the all clear, the squad filed inside.

Emergency lights lit the galley, bringing color back to their view. The four lights in each corner cast harsh, but sufficient illumination. The galley was about 20 meters across, and there were probably close to 100 people from the ship there. With the 40 Marines there as well, it was somewhat packed. However, with no gravity, groups had drifted in all three axis, making it a little less crowded.

Doc Grbil, with the red cross illuminated on his shoulder, was easy to spot as he worked on one of the civilians. The much taller Doc Francis, one of the battalion aid station corpsman attached to the platoon for the mission, was there assisting. From the civilians waiting, it looked like many of them needed help.

The civilians were in "walmarts," the cheaply made but effective emergency suits that were never intended to be worn for long. By Federation law, there had to be at least one temporary emergency evacuation suit for each and every soul on board. Ryck wondered why the first man they'd seen and the family hadn't gotten into their walmarts. The recon team had reported 133 people alive on the ship. Take away those killed in the bridge and close to it, and there still would only have been a little over 200 people. A ship this size would be able to provide emergency suits to that number and more.

*Unless more were killed*, Ryck thought soberly.

There were a few commercial evac suits being worn, so it looked like some of the crew had survived. They were sized for each wearer, not like the one-size-fits-all walmarts. Ryck could see at least two baby bubbles, so at least some infants had made it.

This was a deflated group, and they didn't look to be offering any resistance. Only one crewman, in the far corner of the gallery, had a defiant posture that suggested different. He had stationed himself in front of three bodies, all in walmarts, but obviously dead. The walmarts were actually a pretty good piece of gear, but they seemed to have failed with the three dead people in front of the man. In the maelstrom of the air rushing out of the ship, they could have been breached when the three had been pushed up against something hard or sharp.

The crewman reminded Ryck of the vids of dogs, guarding over their dead masters. None of the Marines were bothering him.

Ryck made his way to the lieutenant and SSgt Hecs, who were with the Navy chief from the engineer division as they discussed what could be done to make conditions better for the civvies. Most of the work was being done by Capt Davis and the head engineer up in the destroyed bow as they evaluated the damage done to the ship.

"Sgt Lysander, spread your teams out. There doesn't seem to be a threat here now, but keep alert. We're awaiting orders at the moment. If we get them, I'm going to want you to escort Senior

Chief Han here to aft engineering. But for now, just spread out, keeping it low key. I want eyes open, but no aggressive posture," the platoon commander said as Ryck came up.

"Aye-aye, sir," Ryck acknowledged as he turned and went back to where the squad waited.

He'd wanted to get more of the scoop as to what was going on, but orders were orders, and he figured that whatever he needed to know, he would be told. Keeping the "no aggressive posture" part of his orders, he broke the squad into teams, sending each team to a position towards the back of the galley. He put each team on a different plane, one on the overhead, one on the deck, and one on the bulkhead. This would give them a better view on the people. This was right out of the training pubs, as people tended to process things better when what they were observing was on the same plane as they were.

Ryck decided to move around his little claimed sector of the galley. There were around 20 or 25 people crowded in the back. Most seemed to be ignoring him, but that could be just shock. They'd been through a lot.

Doc Grbil popped a zip-lock out of his med-pack and deployed it. Normal zip-locks were simply clear bags that could hold a person and maintain an atmosphere for a number of hours while people were transported to safety. The corpsmen had special zip-locks that had small stasis units that could slow down the metabolism of whomever was inside. These were not the same stasis units as those which were in a ship's sickbay. They were portable units that slowly lowered the metabolism, never reaching full stasis. Still, the time they gave a patient could make all the difference between life and death.

The civvie was unresponsive, and he was probably fading, but Doc must have thought the zip-lock could help. He and Doc Francis maneuvered the civvie inside, then partially closed the zip-lock. Doc Grbil reached in with a scalpel, and with a quick slash, slit the man's walmart before pulling his arm out and sealing the zip-lock. Almost immediately, the zip-lock puffed out.

Ryck wondered why he'd compromised the walmart. Maybe it would have interfered with the stasis? He'd have to ask Doc later.

Ryck turned back and pulled himself along, using the galley tables as anchor points. Three civvies, a man and two women were sitting at one of the tables, their legs under the tabletops and keeping them in place. These walmarts were the basic ones, without comms, so they weren't talking but just keeping each other company. As Ryck pulled himself past, he gave them a thumbs-up. The man and one woman stared at him blankly, but there was a flicker in the eyes in the second woman as she inadvertently glanced over to the recessed fabrication nook of the galley.

Ryck looked over in that direction but didn't see anything out of the ordinary. There were three fabricators, a double sink for clean-up, and cupboards for plates and utensils. He glanced back at the woman, but she was once again staring blankly ahead.

Ryck pushed off towards the nook, pulling his legs under and thrusting them in front so he hit the sink area feet-first. He couldn't see anything that caught his attention. He felt eyes on him, though, that weird, tingling feeling that he could not explain. Casually glancing back into the galley seating, he could see one of the crewmen carefully avoiding looking at Ryck, in a way that told Ryck the man had seen Ryck's interest in the nook. Ryck moved to his right, and he thought the crewman relaxed slightly. He then reversed and moved back to his left. He could swear the crewman tensed up again.

There was nothing there, though. The nook ended. There was the small access hatch through which the bases for that meal's recipes came. But that was only a passage leading up from storage. It wasn't a compartment. But that small compartment they'd taken from Alpha to Bravo deck hadn't been designed for people, either. On the *Marie's Best*, it had been crew berthing. Ryck casually left the nook and approached Cpl Beady.

"John, bring your team and follow me. There's something fishy about the fabrication nook. I don't know what it is, but at least two people out there seem to be very interested in it. Could be something there. All I can see, though, is the feed tunnel for the food bases, but let's take a look."

Cpl Beady motioned for his team to follow. All five Marines looked over the nook, which was only about five meters long and two meters deep. Ryck pointed at the small hatch, about one meter square, though which supplies were delivered. If this was like any other delivery chute, when the hatch was opened, a small tray would slide out on which the supplies would be loaded. As one carton was lifted up, another would slide in to take its place.

Ryck took a look back. The crewman who'd been so studiously ignoring him before had abandoned all pretense now. He had moved closer and was staring at them.

Ryck pointed at the access hatch with the muzzle of his M99. Cpl Beady motioned Ling to the overhead, where he would be looking down at the hatch. He positioned LCpl Martin to the sink, just to the side of the access hatch. Martin put his feet in the sink, his grip-tites keeping him in place. He motioned Lips Holleran to get ready to open the hatch.

"First and Second, it may be nothing, but we're checking out the supply access hatch here. Keep an eye on anyone who might not want us to take a look," Ryck passed on the squad circuit.

He joined Cpl Beady, oriented on the deck, facing the hatch. They had three of the four directions around the hatch covered. The fourth was the nook bulkhead, and there wasn't room for anyone to fit in given the half-meter between the edge of the hatch and the bulkhead.

"OK, Lips, let's see what we've got," Ryck passed.

Just as LCpl Holleran started opening the hatch, Ryck couldn't help but turn slightly to see what their crewman friend was doing. The crewman had edged forward, but had stopped and was simply watching. Ryck knew he should have put one of the other Marines on him.

Holleran had opened the hatch, which opened outwards to the rest of the nook. Ryck turned his head just as the hatch was forced open quicker, pushing Lips back. A small blue light flashed in the dark recesses of the tunnel, followed by a shape erupting out of it. Ryck felt more than saw Cpl Beady getting hit.

In front of Ryck, coming out was a man in a white, military EVA suit. It was Legion design, Ryck realized, and the Legion Sallie Gun that had hit Beady was swinging right at him, the hypervelocity darts making a stream that could easily puncture his EVA suit.

In null G, it is impossible to quickly turn and dodge. Ryck had shifted his attention to the *Marie's Best* crewman, moving him out of position. Martin was out of position, too, on the other side of the open hatch and with Lips tumbling between him and the legionnaire. Ryck started the kip-around to get his own M99 deployed, but he knew he wasn't going to make it in time.

Just as he expected to feel darts impacting on him, something big and heavy hit him from above, sending him flying. He started spinning, bouncing him off the deck and back up. He tried to get a grip with his toe, but his momentum was too high.

As he spun, though, his M99 was out, ready to fire. In null G, the M99 automatically shifted from the Roeniger Display scope to old-style "iron" sights. The Roeniger scope inputted drop from gravity, coriolis, wind, and any other influences that could affect the trajectory of a dart. In null G, those forces did not exist, so what you saw is what was hit. As he bounced off the deck, Ryck caught a flash of white through his peep site. It wasn't a good sight picture, but at a meter-and-a-half, it was good enough. He depressed his trigger, sending three or four darts into the legionnaire before he spun past. Martin was clear by that time, and he also fired a burst into the man.

Cpl Mendoza and LCpl Khouri bounded in just then.

"Cease fire!" someone shouted, but Ryck was too busy regaining control to pay attention to just who passed that. He kipped his legs under and absorbed the shock as he hit the overhead. His grip-tites kept him in place.

"Doc, get over here. Man down!" he shouted into his mic.

Above him, he could see Cpl Beady, arms barely moving as he drifted slowly backwards. A small pink mist was coalescing in front of his chest. It looked like he'd taken two hits, through and through, but his suit had already sealed the holes, the bright blue sealing patches very visible.

Ryck's helmet speakers exploded into a cacophony of talk. That suddenly quit as the lieutenant over-rode the circuit, switching Ryck to the command circuit.

"Report!" he commanded.

Ryck could see the lieutenant pulling himself over the tables, rushing to the scene.

"We've got one man down. There was what looks to be a legionnaire hiding in the supply tube, and he came out firing. We took him out," he said, glancing to where the legionnaire floated lifelessly.

Oddly, for a moment, all Ryck could notice was that legionnaire EVA suit patches were red, not the blue of Federation suits. Ryck could see half a dozen or more red patches on the front of the man's suit.

It was only then that Ryck noticed the blue patch on Ling's arm. Suddenly, he realized that it was Ling who had hit him. Ling had seen that he was out of position, and he'd launched himself at Ryck, knocking him out of the line of fire. Ling had taken at least one round as a result. This was the brown-noser who Ryck thought might be a liability. The kid had saved Ryck's life.

"Correction, two down. Beady and Ling," he sent to the platoon commander.

By then, the lieutenant, SSgt Hecs, and the two corpsmen had gotten there. More Marines would have come, but the lieutenant had ordered them to maintain total security. Hecs immediately checked the access tunnel for anyone else, something Ryck should have done, he realized.

Doc Grbil went right to Cpl Beady, checking his vitals on the readout. The EVA suits recorded O2 consumption, pulse, and perspiration, less than what a PICS monitored, but things that were valuable to a corpsman. Doc Francis went to check Ling, but after a cursory inspection, came back to Beady. That was not a good sign.

Ryck pushed off the overhead, spun around, and came down to where the two corpsman were working on John. The fire team leader was not doing well; even Ryck could see that. Blood had frothed up against his EVA suit face shield.

Grbil and Francis were pretty obviously on a medical circuit, one Ryck could not listen in on. By their gestures, Ryck could tell they were arguing. Ryck was getting frantic.

*Quite arguing and save him!* he shouted in his mind.

Doc Francis reached out and put his hand on Doc Grbil's shoulder, only to have the platoon corpsman knock it away. Francis seemed to deflate, and Ryck could swear he saw the moment when he capitulated to Grbil. What that meant for Beady, Ryck didn't know.

"OK, this is what's going to happen," Doc Grbil passed on the platoon circuit while Doc Francis got out another zip-lock and started preparing it. "Cpl Beady is bleeding out. There is no way he will make it back to the *Ark Royal*, and I don't think the portable stasis will be effective enough, fast enough. I need to stop the bleeding, first."

How could he do that? If this was on solid ground or in a pressurized ship, it would be easy. Doc could take Beady out of his suit, close off any arteries, and give him a spray of skin-in-a-can. But in this situation, it was the same as in open space. If Doc was going to take him out of his suit, Beady would die anyway.

"The only thing I can do is go in there with him, stop the bleeding, then start stasis," Doc passed.

The zip-locks were not that big, Ryck knew. Two men in EVA suits just weren't going to fit. If they did manage to squeeze in, there would be no room for Doc to work. And even if he did, once sealed, the zip-locks could only be opened in a sickbay, so how was Doc going to get out once the stasis generator was turned on?

"What I need is for two Marines to hold the zip-lock opening, half closed. I'm going to have Doug here cut off my suit, and I've got to get inside immediately. I need the opening closed and air pumped in right then if I'm going to remain conscious. If— " he started.

"No way!" Lieutenant Nidishchii' shouted over the net. "That's too dangerous. I'm going to canc that plan right now!"

"Sorry sir, but you can't," Doc Grbil told him.

"The hell I can't! I'm your commanding officer, and I say no!"

"You know better than that, lieutenant. You are in tactical command of me, true. But in medical matters, my authority trumps yours. We can argue this. We can send back to the *Ark Royal* for confirmation, but time is wasting. I need to do this right now if Cpl Beady is to have a chance," he said, looking at the lieutenant.

The platoon commander stared back for a moment before passing, "All right. Two Marines, up here now."

Ryck was right there, so he took the edge of the zip-lock that Doc Francis held. Lips and Keiji started to join him, but as Lips was in Beady's fire team, Keiji backed off. Doc Francis gave them a 15-second brief on what to do. It wasn't difficult. They all been in zip-locks back at recruit training, and Ryck had been in one in an actual medical situation, even if he was unconscious at the time. The seal was a simple groove-in-slot, just like the old-style zip-lock bags from which they got their nickname.

The two docs maneuvered Beady into the zip-lock, pushing him towards the back. Ryck saw no movement from the corporal and hoped he was still alive, still hanging on. With Doc Francis assisting, they closed the opening half-way, leaving the top half unsealed. Doc threw in a medical kit, then stood in front of the opening. Doc Francis stood in back of him with a scalpel in his hand.

Ryck could see Doc Grbil's EVA suit expand as he took several deep breaths. Doc wanted to get as much O2 into his system as possible before he tried the transfer. He held up one hand, then exhaled as much as he could, bringing down the hand as a signal to Doc Francis.

The battalion aid station corpsman quickly sliced down the side of his fellow corpsman's suit, from shoulder to calf. With a quick reverse, he slit Doc Grbil's left sleeve.

With several shakes, Doc Grbil tried to free himself from the suit. He was already in vacuum, and time was ticking. His hand seemed to be sticking, so Ryck reached out with one hand and gave the glove of the suit a jerk. That seemed to work, and Doc Grbil was diving forward into the zip-lock, blood globes spinning off from where Doc Francis had cut him while slicing the suit. Doc went in head first, but his feet hung up on the opening, and Lips and Ryck had to grab them and push them in.

Doc Francis had hit the switch that started the air flowing into the zip-lock even before the two Marines had sealed the opening. SSgt Hecs and the lieutenant jumped up to help, pulling the seam out straight so Lips and Ryck could get it sealed.

It took a few long seconds before the zip-lock began to puff out. Doc Grbil was crumbled in the bottom of the lock, not moving.

Had it taken them too long? Ryck wondered.

If Doc was unconscious, the increase in pressure brought him around. He shook his head once or twice, then squirmed around to face Cpl Beady. He checked Beady's breathing. Ryck could not see his corporal's chest rising, but he must have been breathing as Doc Grbil went on to the second B in triage, "bleeding."[39] Reaching into his kit, he took out a fabric cutter, which was nothing more than a scalpel with a curved guard that kept it from slicing into the person whose clothing was being removed. He inserted it into the suit at Beady's waist, then ran it up, cutting the fabric away from his torso. Underneath the suit, Beady's white cottons were soaked red with blood. Doc Grbil cut the cottons away, exposing the wounds to the torso.

Ryck wanted to turn away, but he had to watch as Doc quickly inserted the cauterizer into the holes made into Beady's body when the darts burst through him. The little tool sought out major arteries and veins, automatically sealing them off. Quickly, but with a sure hand, Doc Grbil took out the *siliderma*, the skin-in-a can, and closed off all the outside wounds. Turning Beady around, he slit off the rest of the corporal's EVA suit, then repeated the process.

Ryck watched the entire process, willing Doc to hurry. He knew his team leader had to get into stasis quick. Field expedient first aid was great, but Beady needed surgery.

Doc gave Beady the once over, sealing shut another wound in his arm and checked Beady's breathing again. He didn't seem satisfied, so he intubated the corporal, then started oxygen. He looked out through the clear sides of the zip-lock to his fellow corpsman. Doc Francis pointed at his wrist as it to a watch. Doc Grbil nodded, and Doc Francis started the stasis generator.

Ryck felt a surge of gratitude towards the corpsman. He put his life on the line to try and save John. Even going into stasis had a degree of danger. On occasion, people in stasis were damaged in the process, and some even died. Doc Grbil was putting himself at risk.

---

39 Triage's Three B's: A simple way to triage patients with "breathing" the highest priority, then "bleeding," and finally "breaks."

While waiting for stasis to take over, Doc Francis went back to work on PFC Ling. He looked at the readings, then applied a broad, low-pressure bandage to the area. Blood would still flow, but at a reduced rate, thereby slowing any bleeding.

The portable stasis generator was slow, and it took several minutes for it to take effect on Beady and the doc. Ryck could see no change in Beady, but Doc's head began to loll, and his mouth opened. Within moments after that, he was out. It still took another ten minutes for Doc Francis to be satisfied that full stasis, and least as full as the portable generator could reach, had been attained.

"Cpl Beady was still alive when stasis took over. Harris is fine, too. We need to get them back to the *Ark Royal* ASAP, though," Doc Francis said.

"Captain Davis has a reki waiting right outside Finland," the lieutenant said, referring to the operational name of the breach where Second Squad had entered the Marie's Best. "If he's ready, let's get them there. PFC Ling goes, too. Sgt Lysander, get a team together and get it done."

"Aye-aye, sir," he replied, then to his team, "First, take point and clear the way. Just because it was cleared on the way in does not mean someone else hasn't moved in afterwards. Stillwell, you help Ling, Peretti, you've got our rear. The rest of you, you've got Cpl Beady and the Doc. I shouldn't have to say it, but be careful!"

He switched to a direct circuit and asked, "Joab, how are you doing?"

"I'm fine, sergeant. No problem," Ling answered.

His voice did not sound fine, though. It sounded shocky.

"If you feel nauseous, if you are having any problems, let me know. Cpl Beady and Doc Grbil are in stasis, so a few more minutes won't matter much. One more thing, though," Ryck said as they moved out to take Beady, Grbil, and Ling to the reki and then back to the ship.

"What's that, sergeant?"

"Thanks. You saved my ass back there," he told his PFC .

## Chapter 9

Ryck entered the lieutenant's stateroom. He shared it with four other lieutenants, but it did have a small table and four chairs that he could use as a workspace.

The platoon commander motioned for Ryck to take a seat. SSgt Hecs was sitting there, but none of the other squad leaders had been summoned.

"You about done with your after action report?" the lieutenant asked.

"Uh, not quite yet, sir. I've been in sickbay to check on Cpl Beady and PFC Ling, then getting the squad back in the squadbay," he answered.

They had only been back to the *Ark Royal* for a couple of hours. What did the lieutenant expect? He knew the platoon commander had to get his own report up to Capt Davis, but still, Ryck needed more time, and unless the lieutenant could read gibberish, he really needed some shut-eye before writing it.

"No problem, just get it up to me when you can. I just wanted to ask a few questions so I have it straight in my mind and give you some intel. First, the man you killed was in fact a legionnaire, a Lieutenant Colonel Tolbert. He had his full ID with him, and in his stateroom, his full compliments of uniforms. We don't know why he was attempting to land on Tel Aviv, but N2 thinks he was the reason the *Marie's Best* was trying to run our blockade," he told Ryck.

Ryck sat back in surprise. A man was a man, a kill a kill, but still, it was a shock that the man he'd shot was so high-ranking.

"But why did he fight? He had to know he couldn't win?" Ryck asked.

"Have you ever heard of the old phrase, suicide-by-cop?" the platoon commander asked.

"Well, yeah, when a guy wants the cops to kill him, and he goes after them. I've seen it in some old flicks."

"Well, N2 is pretty sure this was suicide-by-Marines. Whatever Colonel Tolbert was doing, it was pretty important, and he did not want to be interrogated by us, so he went out fighting."

"And almost took Cpl Beady with him," Ryck said sourly.

The lieutenant seemed almost to admire the guy's actions. Ryck was still pissed that two of his Marines had been hurt, and now to find out it was just so the guy couldn't talk, well, that torqued him even more. *Grub the guy!*

"Well, yes, there is that. But you took care of him, so I would say it evens out."

*No, it never evens out*, Ryck thought. *Not when you hurt one of mine.*

"Yes sir," he said instead.

"Speaking of which, I've already spoken to Capt Davis. I want to put you in for another BC3 and Doc Grbil for a BC1. Congratulations," he told Ryck.

"Uh, sir, if you wouldn't mind, I mean, if you could withdraw that, I would appreciate it," Ryck said. "Not Docs, but mine."

The lieutenant's eyes seemed to cloud over just the slightest and a steely tone took over his voice as he asked, "What, with your Silver Star, a BC3 isn't worthy?"

"Oh no, sir, that's not it at all. It's just that, well, I made a mistake, and I almost paid for it. I was looking the wrong way, and if it weren't for PFC Ling, I don't think I'd be here, or at the least, either Cpl Beady or I wouldn't have made it. Ling saw I was in trouble, then launched himself to get me out of the way. He took a round for that. I just think he deserves it more than me," Ryck said.

The lieutenant turned to SSgt Hecs and asked, "Had you heard this?"

"No, sir. This is the first time I've had to talk with Sergeant Lysander," the staff sergeant replied.

"Well, that puts a different light on it. And others will back that up?" the lieutenant asked.

*No, I'm grubbing lying*, Ryck thought. *Geez!*

"Yes, sir. Lance corporals Martin and Holleran were there," he said.

"But you shot Lieutenant Colonel Tolbert, right? I am sure I saw that," the lieutenant went on.

"Yes, sir, but only because PFC Ling had already knocked me out of the way of the legionnaire's fire," Ryck answered.

"PFC Ling, the kind of, well, squirrely Marine? One-point-six meters? Maybe 65 kg?" he asked Ryck.

"Yes, sir, that PFC Ling. Joab Ling."

"Wow, I would never have guessed that," SSgt Hecs said. "Pretty fantasmagorical, if you ask me."

"So, sir, my point is that if anyone is going to get a medal, I think it should be Ling," Ryck said.

"Well, OK. I guess it would be deserved. I wish you had told me before I went to the Captain, though. It's going to make me look bad, but there's no getting around that," Lieutenant Nidishchii' said.

*Well, wait until you talk to me, or wait until you get my after action before you go run to the captain*, he thought.

That probably wasn't fair, he knew. He was tired, dead tired, and stressed with two hurt Marines. Ling was going to be fine, nothing a week in regen wouldn't cure. John was more seriously hurt, and he had some rehab coming, maybe a month or so in regen. The lieutenant was running on even less sleep than Ryck, and he had his own stressors. The fact that he would even go up to the captain and admit he had been wrong about something was a big point in his favor.

"Thank you, sir. I appreciate it," Ryck said.

"Look, I was going to ask you how you knew there was someone in that stores access, but I can see you're dragging. Your squad is racked out?" he asked.

"Yes, sir, about an hour ago."

"You look like you need a clear head. I'll go see the captain now, but I want you to go get showered and hit the rack. Don't get up until, say, 0430 GMT," he said after looking at his watch. "You, too, staff sergeant. We can't do our jobs if we are falling asleep on our feet."

"And you too, lieutenant," SSgt Hecs told him.

"I will, after I get a few more things done."

"No, sir, as soon as you speak to the skipper. Nothing more than that. You're not superman, and you need your sleep, too." SSgt Hecs told him.

Ryck was surprised at Hec's tone. This was not just to get his platoon commander out of his hair. He sounded like he really cared for the lieutenant, the man himself, not the platoon commander. Ryck filed that away for when he was more alert to figure out what that really meant.

"OK, OK, I promise. Fifteen minutes with the captain, then I'm hitting the rack."

"And not getting up until when?" SSgt Hecs asked.

"Zero-four-thirty," Lt. Nidishchii' said with a laugh. "No putting anything past you."

"And that's why I'm a Marine staff NCO," Hecs said.

"Yeah, I guess it is. OK, both of you, get out of here. Get some sleep, and that's an order!"

That was one order Ryck would be very, very happy to obey.

## Chapter 10

Ryck was in the mess decks, eating breakfast, when the world was passed over the 1MC.[40]

It was War.

[40] 1MC: The generic term for the ship-wide speaker system over which word can be passed.

## Chapter 11

Hannah looked worried as she tried to go on, "I just want to know . . . I mean . . . well, Joshua be still at his, you know, and you?"

Hannah was being careful. All comms were being monitored by the censor bots, and if they picked up any security breach, the line would be cut, and the military side of the conversation could face punishment.

Ryck thought it was amazing that the Federation even allowed personal comms in time of war. But the powers that be thought a happy sailor or Marine was a good sailor or Marine. Self-serving or not, Ryck appreciated it.

Ryck knew what Hannah was saying even if she couldn't be too direct. Joshua had expected to be set to a line unit, but all DI positions were frozen as draftees started arriving en masse at the recruit depot. He was out of any fighting, and she wanted some assurance that Ryck would also be safe. He couldn't say that, and not just because of the censor bots. He didn't know if he would be safe. He was on a capital ship of the Navy, going into harm's way. The Federation Navy was far stronger than the coalition Greater France had gathered, and would still be even if the Confederation decided to join with the French.

Thankfully, The Brotherhood had declared its neutrality. Their Navy could match the Federation's, and their Army was much larger than the Federation's Marines.

"This will all be over soon, and I'll be back for I-Day, just like I promised," he told her.

She looked at him with a small frown causing her forehead to wrinkle up.

"How do you know that? I be wanting that more than you can imagine, and I've prayed for your safety, but the news is . . ."

Ryck held up a finger to silence her. He didn't want the conversation cut off.

"So, Lysa says you've been accepted for the Ph.D. program? I thought you said you didn't have a chance," he said, trying to change the subject.

She sighed, then took the hint.

"I guess I just wowed them with my proposal. You know me, Miss Sunshine," she said, her demeanor anything but sunshiny.

"I knew you would. You are the most capable woman I've ever met. No, the most capable person," he said.

It was true, he realized. The two of them had gotten quite close since Joshua's wedding, and despite his protestations to his friends, he was thinking about a future together with her. If she would take him, he constantly reminded himself. He was proud of being a Marine, but he was hardly in her class. Extremely intelligent, athletic, and very personable, she could have whomever she wanted. It amazed him that she seemed attached to a dumb grunt.

"Quit the sugar-mouth, Ryck, always thinking you can sweet-talk me," she said, but Ryck could see her soften up. She always protested his compliments, but Ryck thought she secretly liked them.

"OK, then get this. I'm getting better at Five. I challenge you to a best two out of three as soon as I get back."

"Hah! You be dreaming if you think you can beat me. I accept, and I be spotting you five points per game. Deal?" she asked, her smile making a return.

Ryck, the big tough Marine, had suffered a humiliating defeat to Hannah on the Five court. She didn't have his strength, but she had a knack for putting the small ball to where he had to lunge and struggle just to reach it. It was all in good fun, but Ryck's competitive nature had risen, and he had kept playing whenever he could, trying to get better. Truthfully, he still might not be able to beat her, but at least he could make a better showing at it.

"I don't need your points — " he began when the connection was cut.

*What? I didn't say anything*, he thought.

"All hands, report to your stations. This is not a drill," came over the 1MC.

"Stations" was not "battle stations." For Marines, that meant go to their berthing decks and staying there, out of the way of the sailors. "Battle stations" meant going to their ancillary hangar and combat up as ordered.

Ryck joined the 20 or so sailors and Marines who had been camming. This was the smallest cam center with only 25 consoles, but because it was smaller, not as many people used it, and the wait to get on was usually not as lengthy. It was a long way to the Marine berthing, though, so Ryck and two other Marines had to dodge sailors rushing to their stations and they made their way slowly across the bulk of the ship. The Marines always gave way—the sailors had jobs to do, while the Marines' job was to stay out of the way.

Ryck was the last one to reach their compartment. He hit his thumb on the register, and the report went up. Golf Company, Third Platoon, was present and accounted for.

The entire platoon, minus the lieutenant and SSgt Hecs, was berthed in the compartment. The NCOs had partitioned off the far end of the space, but with bunks four high, it was rather crowded.

Ryck made his way down through the other Marines, pulling back the curtain to the NCO's quarters.

"Son of Cain, Sams, you stink like rotten ass!" he exclaimed as he sat pulled himself into his rack.

"Can't help it none if we get stations while I'm in the gym. Which reminds me, where were you? You promised to meet us there."

"Got held up. There wasn't a line at the cam shop, so I took advantage of it . . ."

". . . to call your Hannah, yeah, we figured," Sams interrupted. "You are seriously PW'd[41], my man, seriously."

Ryck was about to retort when the vid screens lit up. While there were real holos in the ship's lounges, space in berthing was limited, and there were only two-dimensional screens installed for the Marines.

Admiral Starling, over on the *Bismarck*, was whistled onto the screen first. It sounded like a real boatswain did the whistling, maybe even the *Bismarck's* bos'un. Ryck guessed admirals didn't use recordings.

"All hands, we have located the rebel fleet," he began.

---

[41] PW'd: Pussy-whipped. A man controlled by a wife or girlfriend.

*French fleet*, Ryck thought. *Isn't "rebel" a bit dramatic?*

"We are now on a course to intercept it. We have superiority, both in numbers and in the moral righteousness of our cause. If we all do our duty, we can end this war before it ever really starts, saving countless lives. I trust every single sailor on every ship, and every Marine, to perform his mission with utter devotion."

He went on in that vein, mostly a pep talk. He gave no details, which Ryck wanted. How many ships were opposing them? Which kind? More of this would make its way down the pipeline, but Ryck hated being in the dark.

The admiral signed off after only five minutes, something of a record as he tended to be a bit longwinded. It made sense, though, as planning the mission should take priority.

Col Petrakis came on next, at least on the Marine vids. Other Navy staff would be addressing different Navy divisions. The colonel was Colonel Pierre's replacement as regimental commander. The official word was that Col Pierre had been promoted to a higher staff billet, but even the newest boot private smelled the shit emanating from that line of bull. No one was "promoted" from a command to a staff billet before his command tour was over. "Pierre" was just a bit too French for the current climate.

Col Petrakis had a good rep, but Ryck disliked him on principle. It wasn't fair, but Ryck thought Col Pierre hadn't been treated fairly, either, and Ryck was loyal to the man.

Col Petrakis didn't add much in the way of more specific info, just to stay ready for any call. Ship-to-ship was the Navy's game, though, and the Marines didn't expect much except possibly to take damaged vessels. If that happened, though, it would be long after any battle. He did mention the *Jean d'Arc*, though, and that caught Ryck's attention.

It caught everyone's attention.

"Admiral DeMornay," Cpl Revis, one of First Squad's team leaders, said in a hushed tone.

As the colonel signed off and the vid screen went black, most of the NCO's swung about so they were facing the center.

"Who the fuck is Admiral DeMornee?" Teller Simms, Cpl Revis' squad leader asked.

"DeMornAY," Ryck answered. "Celeste DeMornay. You mean to say you've never heard of her?"

"'Celeste?' Like in a woman's name?" Simms continued. "No, never heard of her. Why should I have?"

"Only because she's the most famous French admiral. She was awarded the Légion d'honneur *and* the Federation Nova during the War of the Far Reaches," Popo added.

"Shit, a woman? And in the War? She's got to be an old biddy now. So what?" Sams asked.

"You too? Don't any of you negats read any history?" Popo asked.

"I'll read the history of your dick," Simms said. "Better yet, I'll give her mine," he added, grabbing his crotch.

Simms' attitude was somewhat typical, Ryck knew. For over 150 years, women had not been allowed to serve in the Federation armed forces. The original proclamation came after the devastating Tenner War, when a huge percentage of the population was either killed or suffered extreme chromosomal damage. Women were deemed "too vital" to be put in physical danger and were relegated to breeding up a new generation. That was what the history accounts said, at least. Whatever the reason, women effectively became second-class citizens and had been so ever since. There wasn't any regulated second class status; it was just that many paths were closed to them.

Ryck wasn't about to start a revolution to bring about social change, but thought that if there ever was a need to "protect" women, that time was long gone. It was ironic that one of the heroes of the Tenner War, and of the Marine Corps, was Major Melissa "Missy" Walters, one of only two people to have been awarded two Federation Novas. The second one was awarded posthumously.

Ryck didn't know many women well, but he thought either his sister, or especially Hannah, could serve admirably in the military. The Brotherhood, the Confederation, and most other planets had women serving in all walks of life. Gender equality was a fact of life. And if it was Admiral DeMornay facing them, and if her abilities were only half that of her reputation, then Admiral Starling might be facing much more than he expected.

Cpl Revis tried to give his squad leader a short history lesson on the admiral, but Simms was making light of it. Ryck just sighed, lay back down on his bunk, and did what all good Marines did when given the chance. He caught some z's.

## Chapter 12

Every Marine's eyes were glued to the holo display in the lounge. With the Navy at Battle Stations Bravo, the lounge was empty, and the battalion CO had gotten permission for the Marines to watch the feed in the lounges rather than in their berthing spaces. Trying to watch on the 2D screens in berthing did not convey the true breadth and depth of a battle in space.

Battle Stations Bravo meant the Marines were in longjohns or cottons, as their mission required, but not in full battle gear, be that PICS, or EVAs. That would be Battle Stations Alpha.

The *Ark Royal* was on the periphery of the probable battlespace, providing security along the Z-axis, several million kilometers from the *Bismarck*. That was why the crew was only in Battle Stations Bravo. If she was with the main force, they would already be at Alpha.

The Y-axis was always parallel to an arbitrary line running through Earth and along the galactic center. During fleet ops, one ship, in this case the *Bismarck*, was the reference point, with the X, Y, and Z axes radiating from it.

The display had the 41 Navy ships in the task force identified, 29 in the main assault force, the remainder in peripheral security. A few platoons of Marines had been cross-decked to other ships, but the bulk were on three ships: the regimental headquarters and 1/9 were on the *Bismarck*, 2/9 was on the *Ark Royal*, and 3/9 on the *Chakri Naruebet*, which was on the other side of the Z-axis as the *Ark Royal*. If things continued as being announced, only 1/9 might see any action, much to the dismay of most of Ryck's fellow 2/9 Marines.

This was history in the making. TF-207, with Admiral Starling in command, was the first Federation fleet to locate a French task force, and the upcoming engagement would be the first Navy full-fledged action since the War of the Far Reaches. If things went as forecasted, a quick defeat would force the French to capitulate and be absorbed into the Federation. Careers would be made in this battle, and it could even pave the way for Starling to assume the Federation chairmanship.

"This sucks the big one," Sams muttered beside Ryck as they watched the slowly shifting display. "1/9's going to get all the glory."

"You've got that right," Ryck whispered back.

Ryck had nothing against the French, and truth be told, he thought Greater France might have had a legitimate beef with the Federation, although he knew better than to ever express that opinion. He'd even almost joined the Legion before enlisting in the Marines. But he was not involved with the politics—he just did his duty as ordered.

Ryck doubted that 1/9 would really get any glory, anyway. This was going to be a Navy fight. But still, to be there in the thick of things in what would be a pivotal moment in history, that would be something special.

"Sgt L, why is everything moving so slow?" asked Tipper Prifit.

Keeping his voice down, Ryck answered the lance corporal, "What you see there covers millions of kilometers of space. The ships aren't moving slowly. They've just got to cover a long ways."

Prifit seemed to consider that for a moment. "But I can see the French ships right there. Why doesn't the admiral just go get them?"

"Well, first, we don't exactly know where they are or even how many there are," Ryck said as a few other Marines sitting close by turned to listen.

"But we can see them. Right there!" Keiji said, pointing at the display.

"No, we can see where we *project* some of them to be. It is a calculated position, not a real-time position," PFC Ling put in.

"What?" several Marines asked in unison.

"Ling's right," Ryck said. "We don't really know exactly where they are. We've caught some signatures as we keep trying to pierce their cloaking, just little hints, and the AI's on the *Bismarck* use those to calculate probable positions. Those . . ." he paused, counting the small red icons, ". . . 11 ships might actually be all of the French ships. There might be more, there might be fewer. And their positions might be close or pretty far from what we see represented here. As far as what specific ships, their names, all we know for sure is that that one," he said, pointing at the only red icon with a designator, "is the *Jean d'Arc.*"

"Sergeant Lysander, for all those still confused, why don't you come up front and repeat what you've been saying," Lt Nidishchii' said from the other side of the lounge.

Ryck hadn't known the platoon commander was listening in to him. Ryck stood up and moved to the holo. Both Third and Weapons Platoon were in the lounge. He knew all the Marines in the two platoons, and they knew him. He glanced up at the two platoon commanders, his own and 1stLt Baca, the Weapons Platoon commander. Both of them looked at him expectantly.

Ryck cleared his throat to buy him a few seconds of time. He'd taken a class in Naval Strategy while earning his degree, so the constant battle for supremacy in cloaking and spoofing and piercing the enemy efforts at the same was something he'd studied. The rest of his knowledge, though, came from a class at boot camp, a class every single Marine had taken, so they should have known all of this. Looking out at the Marines, though, a good half of them looked confused.

Ryck glanced back at the display. Not much had changed, which didn't surprise him. The distances covered were just too great for the scale to show anything in greater detail.

"OK, well, as I was saying back there, to put this into perspective, first, you gotta keep in mind that this small display is set to represent a huge pocket of space. I can't see the legend . . ."

"Down on the base, that second button," Lt. Nidishchii' said.

"Sir? Oh, OK," Ryck said, reaching down to push the button.

Immediately, a scale popped up along with the three axes, oriented on the *Bismarck*. It took Ryck a moment to orient the scale in his mind.

"OK, this is the flagship," he said, pointing to the largest blue icon. "This, is us," he added, pointing to another blue icon, this one slightly down and a good distance towards the bulk of the Marines in the lounge.

"Right now, we're about 6,200,000 klicks from the *Bismarck*. Up here," he continued, this time pointing to the red icons above the *Bismarck*, "are the calculated positions of the

French ships. That's at about 10,000,000 klicks away from us. If we were in bubble space, that would be nothing, but we're combat deployed, in real space, so even at top speed, it would take us, I don't know, maybe an hour to close the gap? So forget that we look close to them now on the holo. We're really a long ways apart.

"The second thing is that really, what you see is not what's really there. These are all calculations," he said, waving an arm at the red icons. "You have to remember that all the time, both fleets are cloaking and spoofing each other."

Several of the Marines had blank looks on their faces.

"OK, the difference is that cloaking means hiding where you are, like what we do with our comms, when we shield our transmission so the bad guys don't know we are there. Spoofing is telling the enemy that you are somewhere else, like when you activate the Fractured Array in a PICS. Given enough time, we can penetrate both of those, so all the time, they are changing frequencies and methods, bouncing back and forth and hoping we don't catch up to them. We do catch up to them, though, even if only for a split second, and that is enough to grab a data point. Given enough grabs, and our AI's can start predicting where the ship actually is."

He looked over at the lieutenant, who had a slightly pleased look on his face. Ryck figured he hadn't made a mistake yet.

"During all of this, ships try to disguise themselves, so when we get a data point, we still don't know exactly what we face."

"Then how do we know that's the *Jean d'Arc*?" one of the Marines from Weapons asked.

"Well, I'm not sure in this case. Maybe the Navy scout that spotted them got that before the fleets came together and managed to paint her specs. Or, maybe she just screwed up," Ryck answered.

"Screwing up" did not sound like something Admiral DeMornay would have allowed to happen, given her rep. It was more likely something in line with his first guess.

"So we don't know their positions, but they know ours?" Cpl Johnson, from Sams' squad asked.

"What do you mean?" Ryck asked.

"There, all our ships are there, so the froggies know where each of our Navy ships are."

Most of the Marines groaned, and the corporal sitting next to him reached up, grabbed the back of his head, and pushed Johnson down.

"We know where we are 'cause we don't spoof ourselves, you dumb negat," the corporal told his buddy.

Johnson looked suitably sheepish when he was let back up.

Ryck tried to think of anything else. He wasn't an expert, but he hoped he'd explained things correctly. Then something else hit him, a pet peeve of his.

"One last thing. Forget about every war flick you've seen. When our ships actually start shooting, they are not going to be firing from a few kilometers away. They won't be able to see each other with the naked eye. They'll still be tens of thousands, probably hundreds of thousands of kilometers apart. When we boarded the *Marie's Best,* remember, the *Ark* was over 15,000 km away, and it was only that close so we wouldn't take forever getting there on rekis.

"Lieutenant, that's all I've got, I think. Is there anything else I should say?"

"No, good job, Sergeant. I think that was helpful," he replied.

As Ryck move back to his seat, he realized that the platoon commander hadn't only been looking for a field expedient class in naval warfare. He'd wanted to break the tension that had been building since the Marines had gathered around the slowly evolving display.

Sams had his hand in a fist, and was slowly rotating in back and forth around his nose as Ryck walked up.

"Fuck you, too, Sams. It ain't brown-nosing unless you volunteer. I was just following orders."

"If you say so," Sams said as he and Popo laughed.

Even Cpl Rey was smirking.

"I can't do anything about these negats," Ryck said, pointing at his two fellow sergeants, "but I've got power over you, Corporal of

Marines. I've seen corporals stand fire watch, and who knows, that might be a good idea."

At that, more Marines broke out into laughter. If the lieutenant really had been trying to break the tension, then the trash talk and laughter showed he had succeeded.

It was a temporary respite, though. There was a battle building, and after a few more jabs back and forth, the Marines slowly settled down and focused their attention back on the display.

After about twenty minutes during which the blue and red icons inched together, a voice came over the feed.

"Sailors and Marines, this is Lieutenant Commander Huang, the task force PAO.[42] As we close in with the rebel fleet, Admiral Starling has given me permission to narrate what is happening, so even those on ships not actively engaged will be able to follow the battle to our inevitable victory."

That perked Ryck up. He was cynical enough to think that the "narration" was more aimed at furthering the admiral's ambitions after the battle, but that didn't mean he couldn't enjoy being more in the know.

The PAO started with more comments on history in the making without giving out very many details. Ryck started to tune the officer out, instead, watching as the *Bismarck* and the two frigates *Monty* and *Decatur* adjusted their track to close in on the *Jean d'Arc.*

The *Bismarck* was one of the most capable ships in the Navy, but Ryck thought it slightly odd that it looked to be the admiral's tip of the spear. Both the *Ark Royal* and the *Chakri Naruebet* were, on paper, at least, more than a match for the *Jean d'Arc*, and the task force's three cruisers were at about par with the French flagship. Sending in two cruisers would put fewer men at risk while still projecting enough firepower for a victory. Sending in two cruisers and a couple of frigates or destroyers would be extra insurance in case Admiral DeMornay had a few tricks up her sleeve. It probably wouldn't make any difference, though, as the *Bismarck* could handle herself. The cynic in Ryck rose once again as he realized that a

[42] PAO: Public Affairs Officer

personal victory would stand the admiral in much better stead than if he'd just ordered other ships into the fray.

Technically, he wasn't the captain of the *Bismarck* and wouldn't actually be fighting her. The *Bismarck's* captain would be giving the tactical orders. Admiral Starling was the task force commander, in charge of the overall picture. But the public wouldn't make that distinction.

The PAO's voice rose in excitement, bringing Ryck back to the battle. First blood had been drawn, and not by the *Bismarck*. Two frigates, the *Madras* and the *Tehran*, had fixed a French corvette's position and fired their big plasma guns. The corvette's shields had collapsed within seconds, imploding the ship.

The Marines in the lounge cheered, drowning out the excited PAO. Ryck cheered, too. In the back of his mind, he knew over 200 men and women had just been wiped out, but on the holo display, they were just electrons.

One concern had been whether energy or kinetic weapons would be more effective. Ship defenses had improved dramatically since the War of the Far Reaches, and while tests and calculations had been continuously made, things could be different in real combat.

Kinetic weapons were harder to bring on target, being slower than energy weapons, and smaller ships could carry only so many of them, and the rounds or missiles could be shot down or deflected. They packed a big punch, though, much bigger than an energy weapon. There were also a very wide array of kinetic weapons from which to choose, ranging from point defense auto-cannons to huge megaton warhead missiles.

Energy weapons acquired targets easier, and in the vacuum of space, had very long effective ranges. However, they were easier to shield against and usually took awhile to break through defenses. The speed at which the French corvette was destroyed, though, boded well for the use of Federation energy weapons, especially as the frigates used plasma guns. Several of the ships in the task force, to include each of the cruisers, had the more effective hadron cannons, and the *Bismarck* had the Navy's newest energy weapon, the terajoule P2-Meson Cannon.

All three energy weapons had about the same degree of effectiveness in knocking out a target once they hit it. The plasma, which fired in near-continuous pulses, was bulkier and more of an energy hog as it required an electromagnetic "jacket" to keep the plasma charge from dispersing as it traveled through space. Hadron cannons bypassed the inverse square law, so they didn't need a jacket. They focused an unbroken beam on the target. The cannon itself, which was actually a type of projector, was smaller and more efficient than a plasma gun, but it built up charges on the hull of the ship firing it, which interfered with cloaking and sensors. The new meson cannon, never before fired in actual combat, was the most efficient and could theoretically be fired without pause, as long as the ship's engines could supply the juice.

During their class on ship-borne weapons systems, Ryck thought it bass-'ackwards that the smaller ships had the larger, energy-hogging weapons while the huge capital ships tended to have the smaller, more efficient guns. He thought a small corvette, maybe only 50 meters long, armed with one meson cannon, would be one über-nasty weapon.

Within minutes, the *FS Pretoria*, one of the cruisers, launched two SCAT missiles. They passed through where the display indicated a large French ship of some kind was, but there were no detonations. The *Pretoria's* target acquisition AI had been spoofed.

Things in the battlespace were quiet for a few moments as the red and blue icons did a slow ballet in the display. Then the *Pretoria's* sister ship, the *Cairo*, launched another SCAT. The SCAT flew at over 20,000 km per second, so the Marines on the *Ark Royal* could actually see its icon move. Three, four, five seconds. Then the display flashed to represent an explosion. The Marines cheered again, but the SCAT had not detonated on a French ship. It had been destroyed by a French anti-missile battery.

The French ship had knocked out the SCAT, but by firing its weapons, the ship had given up its position. Within moments, three Navy ships concentrated their weapons, two firing plasma guns and one firing a hadron cannon, on where their AIs calculated the

French ship to be. After ten seconds of intense fire, the French ship went up.

The PAO was going crazy, announcing the battle as if it was a football game.

"Did you see that? Did you see it? Oh my God, we're kicking ass!" he shouted, forgetting his officer-like decorum.

They all had seen it. Actually, they had seen a representation of it. Humans could not see energy weapon beams, could not watch a SCAT fly across space. The display AI created representations of the beams, missiles, and explosions so human viewers could make sense of what was happening.

The excitement level in the lounge was high, but then for almost 20 minutes, nothing much happened. The blue icons maneuvered smoothly in the display; the red icons jumped here and there as the AIs calculate new probable positions.

From a spot without a red icon, a beam of light flashed to envelope the *Madras,* one of the two frigates that had drawn first blood. Firing had given up data points to the French, and the cloaked ship had opened up on the Federation frigate from less than 50,000 kilometers away, almost spitting distance in space battles.

The AIs calculated with a 76% probability that the French ship was the *Giraud*, a cruiser. This ship was more than a match for the *Madras*, and as the fire locked on the frigate, Marines in the lounge stood up yelling for another ship to come help.

The *Madras* couldn't even escape to bubble space. The enveloping energy being thrown at it made generating the bubble space field impossible.

In the same way that the *Madras* had given away its positional data by firing, the *Giraud's* firing pinpointed its position as well. Beams of energy and at least two SCATs reached out to the French ship. It was a race to see whose shields would last the longest. The *Giraud* had the stronger shields, but it had at least four Federation ships focused on it. Just as the *Madras*' shields started to redline, the French ship imploded.

Another cheer rang out in the lounge. It had been a close thing, though. The *Madras*' icon shifted to a light blue. She was alive, but no longer effective.

Three French ships destroyed, one Federation ship out-of-action. Ryck wondered how many French ships were actually out there. The French Navy had 98 capital ships—only 95 now—and another 20 from their allies, bringing their total fleet to 115. The Federation had almost 600. TF-207 had 41 ships, and there were seven other task forces aggressively patrolling Federation space at the moment. How many of the French fleet were opposing the task force? The display showed nine ships left, but it had shown eleven prior to the first engagement. The *Giraud* had never registered on the display. What other ships were there lurking, unseen?

The Federation had the numbers, but when the French-allied forces made the strategic decision not to protect any French or allied planets, their Navy had the initiative. The Federation was forced to protect all Federation territory. The French could consolidate their forces and engage when and where at their choosing.

"Now they're gonna pay," Sams said as the *Bismarck* maneuvered closer to the *Jean d'Arc*, which looked to be swinging up to engage. The *Monty* and *Decatur* were pulling back, leaving the field of battle to the two flagships, which had closed to just under a million klicks.

*This is medieval*, Ryck thought. *Since when do flagships square off like jousting knights? It just isn't done this way.*

He was fascinated, though. It may not have been what was taught in any military tactics book, but two giants lumbering at each other was something of note.

Of course, "lumbering" was not an apt description. They were closing at extremely high rates of speed. Ryck kept watching for the *Monty* and *Decatur* to pounce, thinking that made the most sense. They kept station, though.

The PAO was excited, obviously thrilled to be part of an epic clash. He started speaking quicker, trying to describe what he was feeling. What he wasn't doing was offering any concrete info that the Marines couldn't already see from the display.

At 800,000 klicks, the *Bismarck* reached out with its meson cannon. It splashed the *Jean d'Arc*, which kept coming at the Federation battleship. The display didn't show the soft orange glow it gave to active enemy shields, but the French ship kept coming, so she was still in the fight.

Ryck would have thrown in a few missiles, maybe the huge HYNA-3's that battleships and dreadnaughts carried, but he thought the ship's commander might want to register the first-ever kill with a meson cannon. It might be a footnote in history, but Ryck was more in the better-safe-than-sorry camp.

"How come the froggie isn't firing back?" Cpl Mendoza asked.

*Good question*, Ryck thought.

The two ships kept closing and the *Jean d'Arc* had yet to fire anything.

*She couldn't have already been crippled, could she?*

The seconds ticked away as the ships came closer together.

*Was she going to try and ram the Bismarck?* Ryck wondered.

That didn't make any sense. If she tried, the *Bismarck* had the kinetic weapons that would not only stop her, but also blow her apart into tiny little pieces.

And then it was over.

The energy signature of the French ship disappeared. She was dead.

It was easier for Ryck to think in terms of the entire ship. "She" was dead. Not that over 8,000 men and women were dead. They were the enemy, but the sheer numbers of casualties were staggering. That was the same as two full regiments of Marines, gone, just like that.

The lounge erupted into cheers as LCDR Huang shouted himself hoarse over the comms. It hadn't been the epic battle that it might have been, but from both a tactical and strategic standpoint, it had been a major victory.

Something caught his attention, and he listened into the PAO.

" . . . so with that in mind, Admiral Starling has ordered the *Bismarck* to match trajectories with the rebel flagship. If in fact our sensors are correct and the ship was not totally destroyed, we will rescue any survivors and stabilize the wreck for salvage."

That was a new wrinkle. The "survivor" comment was a throwaway for public consumption. Unless someone was in a heavily shielded, self-contained capsule, they could not have survived the bombardment of the meson beam. However, energy weapons did not in and of themselves destroy ships. When a ship imploded or exploded, it was because of the rupture of its own fields, weapons, and energy supply. A ship could actually shut completely down to avoid that, but, of course, that would kill the crew and leave the crewless ship defenseless against a KE weapon. More than a few times, though, ships "killed" were left basically intact and could be salvaged. At least 14 Federation ships had once been acquired that way, either in the War of the Far Reaches of through anti-piracy actions.

"Shit, those 1/9 mothers are going to cash in!" SSgt Groton shouted out.

IF the *Jean d'Arc* was intact, or partially intact, and IF she was salvageable, not only would that be a huge propaganda victory, but each member of the Ark Royal crew would get a prize bonus, and that included the onboard Marines.

The Marines erupted into chatter, mostly expressing disgust at their lack of luck. Not only was 2/9 out of the action, it would not share any prize money their 1/9 brethren would receive.

The battle was not over, but there was a subtle shift in the disposition of the icons in the display as the remaining red icons began to leave the battlespace. The *Chakri Naruebet* moved to intercept one French ship, opening fire as the *Bismarck* was still matching trajectory with the carcass of the *Jean d'Arc*. Even 3/9 was getting in on the action, despite the fact that the AIs could not confirm the kill to give the Federation cruiser.

On the *Bismarck*, 1/9 would be getting ready for an EVA. Additional readings had indicated that the *Jean d'Arc* was probably in small pieces. There just wasn't enough there do indicate an intact ship. But it had not exploded, so there could still be good intel to be gathered. The Marines and a Navy boarding team were still on. Dreams of huge prize money were shattered, but there was still the potential for a nice bonus.

The "battle" such as it was, was on the far side of the battlespace from the Ark Royal. After an hour, the ship downgraded to Battle Stations Charlie. A few of the Marines trickled out to get some chow, but most stayed, watching the display.

The *Bismarck* positioned itself 40,000 km off the *Jean d'Arc*. The two ships were motionless in relative terms, but like the entire task force, were hurtling through space at tremendous speeds. LCDR Huang signed off, giving way to a JG, as the 1/9 Marines loaded their rekis, and with a Gryphon monitor and several Experion fighters in support, started the long journey to the French ship. Forty-thousand klicks were nothing to a warship, but to a reki, that was an hour-long journey. Forty-thousand klicks was also the by-the-manual minimum safe distance for a warship to maintain when approaching another. The *Ark Royal* had gotten closer to the *Marie's Best*, but that had been a civilian ship. The *Jean d'Arc* was a warship, and if she somehow blew, either by design or by accident, the stand-off safe distance was greater.

The *Jean d'Arc* didn't blow. What it actually did, though, was confusing. Just as the Marines started their journey, there was a flicker on the display as sensors detected some sort of energy emissions.

A warning icon flashed, and the JG stopped mid-sentence. Ryck knew the meson cannon as well as other weapons would be trained on the *Jean d'Arc*, but he knew the meson cannon would need approximately five seconds to activate the electron and positron collisions that resulted in the mesons. More importantly to him, the Marines were outside the ship, now almost 500 km away, between the *Bismarck* with its meson cannon and the French ship.

Time seemed to slow down, but it was actually fewer than the five seconds needed to fire the meson cannon when a number of yellow streaks took off from the *Jean d'Arc*.

Immediately after that, the *Bismarck* opened up.

Ryck jumped up, his heart in his throat as the small blue icons for the rekis immediately faded to grey. The embarked Marines had no chance. The meson beam had swept through them. A battalion of his fellow Marines had just been killed, something that seemed unimaginable.

Ryck was numb as he watched the yellow icons rushed to the *Bismarck* at a blazing speed, undeterred by the meson cannon. The icons switched from the yellow of an unknown object to the orange of a KE weapon of some sort a second after the *Bismarck* fired, but the meson beam had no effect on them. Another two seconds, and the battleship's point-defense auto-cannons opened up, their stream of rail-gun projected depleted uranium rounds making a ribbon on the display as the rounds rushed out to meet the incoming weapons. The yellow icons split up into nine separate— rounds? Missiles?—as the AIs analyzed the readings. Six of the French weapons were knocked off their course by the intense fire, but three made it through the *Bismarck's* defenses and pierced the shields, slamming into the battleship.

The anonymous JG's voice was cut off, then the display went out.

Each Marine was on his feet, staring at the dead display in shock.

*What the fuck had happened?*

The display flickered, then came back on as the *Ark Royal's* AIs took over from the *Bismarck's* feed. The *Bismarck* was still there, but the icon was light blue. Then a new red icon appeared about 500,000 km to the *Bismarck's* upper right, an icon with full identification.

The *Jean d'Arc.*

It fired its own weapons at the *Bismarck*, more kinetic rounds. Almost immediately, the *Decatur* opened up on her, followed by the *Monty*. Neither ship was the match for the *Jean d'Arc*, but that didn't stop either one. They started rushing to attack, to protect what was left of the *Bismarck*.

Battle Stations Alpha sounded on the *Ark Royal*.

"To your stations, now!" Lieutenant Nidishchii' shouted, the first Marine to utter a word since everything unfolded only 15 seconds ago.

As Ryck rushed to leave the lounge, he glanced back to see the *Chakri Naruebet* and several other ships converge on the French flagship when the icon for the *Jean d'Arc* disappeared from the display.

## Chapter 13

Twenty-two hours after the battle, Ryck was with the rest of the battalion NCOs and Marines in Hangar B while the senior chief briefed them. All over the ship, the all hands were getting their first explanation on what had happened.

The Navy was a political animal, the forward projection of the government's power. But it was still a professional fighting force that believed in transparency in after action reports and keeping all hands informed.

The ship had stayed at Battle Stations Alpha for almost twelve hours before standing down. As soon as the *Bismarck* was hit, Commodore Weinstein, the assistant task force commander, took full command from the new flagship, the *Chakri Naruebet*. He initiated rescue operations, started analyzing what happened, and sent ships, including the *Ark Royal*, after the fleeing French fleet. Other than a few data hits, though, the French slipped away, and the commodore recalled his ships, not willing to disperse his forces.

Marines and sailors were fed and put to the rack, but not many really got much sleep. Hours later, exhausted and still in emotional shock they gathered to hear the brief.

" . . . and remember, these are only initial findings, but we have put engineers on what we thought was the *Jean d'Arc*. As I said, it wasn't even a ship. It was a construct of tubing, propulsion, and launch rails that gave off the same signature as the real ship. We were spoofed into thinking this was the French flagship. I don't need to tell you that this is some pretty sophisticated cyberwarfare, something beyond our present capabilities given the nature of existing sensors.

"The best that we can determine is that the decoy ship was turned off prior to the *Bismarck* opening fire. Only very heavily shielded switches remained, and in the quiet mode. When the meson beams struck the ship, they flowed around the framework, causing no damage as there really wasn't anything to react with.

"When the meson cannon was turned off, the switches remained intact, ready for activation. The *Jean d'Arc*, cloaked but nearby, or possibly another platform, reactivated the switches and powered up their rail guns, which were actually part of the structure of the ship. They waited until the Marines launched, knowing that the AIs would need an override to fire with the Marines between the ship and the target."

There was a rush of murmurs as the Marines took this in.

"At ease, at ease," Gunny Greuber said, holding up his hand. "Let's listen to the senior chief."

"As I was saying they wanted that split-second advantage as they needed the rail guns to power up. Nine inert, non-conductive missiles were launched. We have recovered particles of one from the *Bismarck* and are analyzing it, but it looks to be a dense synthetic. Each one was approximately 40 meters long and massed 350,000 kg. Being non-conductive, the meson beam had no effect on them. They were essentially big rocks being thrown at the ship.

"Travelling at 10,000 kilometers per second, it took five seconds to reach the *Bismarck*. Point defense deflected six off course, but three hit the flagship. Serious damage was done to these three sections," he said as a holo appeared over his head.

Ryck sucked in his breath. This was the first image of the *Bismarck* after the battle that he'd seen, and huge chunks of the ship were simply gone.

"Immediately after impact, the *Jean d'Arc* deliberately uncloaked and fired two BC-8 anti-ship missiles at the *Bismarck*. With her defenses compromised, both missiles struck the ship here," he said as the holo rotated, showing two more chunks taken out of the ship.

Inside the *Bismarck,* all compartments were sealed and fire-fighting measure taken. Within five minutes, the ship was secure, but non-effective. Overall, we lost 9,787 men in the attack. We believe that 6,000 were lost in the initial strike, another 3,000 in the missile attack, and the rest due to exposure to vacuum within moments after the strikes. We should note that most of the remainder could have survived had they been in the correct gear.

"As to the casualties, almost all of the command was taken out in the missile strike, to include Mr. Starling."

"Mr." Starling was telling. The Navy was a fighting force, but it was political, and blame had been laid. "Admiral" had been stripped from him even in death. It was just as well that he had died, though. He would have faced execution had he managed to survive the battle.

“As to Marines,” the senior chief continued, and here he stopped to look up and the men facing him. “I, uh, I regret to inform you that only three embarked Marines survived: Sergeant Mark Tillhouse, Lance Corporal Sig Poulson, and Private Spencer Hamilton. These three were bedridden in sickbay on the other side of the ship. Most of the Marines were killed when the *Bismarck* fired on the launch platform. Your Marine command was located with the Navy command when they were hit, and the rest were at the launch hangar when the first strike hit them. I’m sorry to pass that to you.”

Some Marines sat in stunned silence, others broke out into exclamations.

*Only three survived?* Ryck asked himself.

Ryck knew the toll was going to be high. He’d seen the lights turn when the rekis were in the way of the meson cannon. But more than that had to have survived. He knew Mark Tillhouse. They had attended the NCO course together. And he was grateful that he had survived. But that was all? Only three Marines?

They had all been so jealous when they heard 1/9 was going to help salvage a warship. But that mission had been their death sentence.

Ryck was barely aware that the senior chief was continuing, and he had to focus to catch what he was saying.

“ . . . a lack of leadership, a failure to follow established operational procedures, and most of all, a sense of individual ambition that overcame Navy policy and put his command at risk. Any one of a number of steps would have kept this from happening. The decoy ship was unable to maneuver once it had been set on its final course, so simple course change would have revealed the plan. One kinetic missile could have destroyed all the launch rails. Even after the decoy seemed destroyed, sensor readings were off, and a simple recon could have discovered that this was, in fact, a decoy, but arrogant pride wanted there to be a prize to capture, and by wanting it, the command ignored normal warnings.

"This is not the Navy way, and such actions will not be tolerated. Rest assured that procedures will be implemented to ensure this will not be repeated.

"That is all I have for now. I will not be able to take any questions at the moment, but we will issue a more detailed report available for download onto your PAs. The commodore wanted all of you to get an update, though, before we issue our complete findings."

The senior chief and the sergeant major stepped of the platform and walked through the seated Marines. Not taking questions was probably a smart move. He would have been there forever.

Ryck was impressed with the senior chief's candor. There was no question that the blame was on the admiral, but to tell the enlisted so with such candor was rare. Ryck wondered if the officers had gotten the same brief, or if theirs been even more candid.

He stood up, mentally and physically exhausted. Sams was still sitting on the hangar deck, head down. Ryck grabbed him under the armpit and hauled him up.

"Head up, Sams. We've got to get our heads on straight. We're going to get a chance for revenge, mark my words, and we've got to be ready for it when it comes."

# FS Intrepid

## Chapter 14

Ryck looked across the hold to where SSgt Hecs was waiting. Their visors were clear, so Ryck could see that the platoon sergeant was in dreamland. Ryck could almost hear the snoring. He nudged Cpl Winsted, more of a bump, given that they were mounted in their PICS, and pointed at their fearless leader.

"How the hell can he do that?" the Third Fire Team leader asked on the P2P.

"Beats the hell out of me," Ryck admitted.

In the midst of a naval battle, where they could be reduced to their component atoms in a second, not many Marines could drift off to sleep. It was an admirable skill, but not one Ryck possessed.

Many things had changed since their last disastrous fight. The battle was broadcast to the populace as a victory, and with three French ships destroyed to one Federation ship, that claim could be made. However, no one in the military thought it was anything other than an ass-whipping. Out-numbered and out-gunned, Admiral DeMornay had managed to take out a Federation battleship. More lives were lost on that one ship than in all three French ships combined. Complacency may have been the order of the day before, but the foe was taken much more seriously now.

Now, the forces were ordered to follow naval doctrine more closely. Of course, the French fleet knew Federation doctrine, but with the Federation's much stronger fleet, there wasn't much the French could do with the knowledge. Only a week prior in the First Quadrant, TF-202 had met and destroyed five French ships without a loss of its own.

One of the changes was that the Marines had been cross-decked to smaller platforms. The loss of an entire battalion, although only a percentage of the total loss of life on the *Bismarck*, had hit the community hard. There were to be no more units that large together on any one ship. Golf Company, along with two Storks, had been embarked about the *Intrepid*, an old destroyer.

Another change was that during any action, or possibility of action, all hands were to be in EVA suits, or in the case of Golf Company, two platoons were in PICS. Over two hours ago, the call for Battle Stations Alpha had gone out, and Third Platoon had donned their PICS and entered one of the ship's shuttles. First Platoon was in their PICS hooked up to the two Storks, ready to go if the need arose. Most of Second Platoon were in EVAs, sitting in two 14-man rekis.

In the hangars, the Marines had no idea what was going on. If Ryck stood perfectly still, though, he could feel the subtle "pull" along his body that signified the ship was doing some serious maneuvers. The compensators, arrayed around the ship, kept the men inside the ships alive through the huge G-forces that would crush an unprotected crew. However, G-forces worked along one axis. The compensators reacted in concert, "pulling" to counteract the effect of the G-forces. At any given time, several of them would be working on the body, and that counteraction varied with the distance to the various repeaters. So the counter-force would be slightly different on one side of the body as the other. Most people said they couldn't feel anything, but Ryck was positive he could. To him, it felt like skin drying with an almost-itch.

About ten minutes earlier, he had noticed a very slight dimming of the ship's lights, something that repeated two more times. Ryck was pretty sure that meant they had fired their plasma guns.

The first time they had gone to Battle Stations Alpha, the Marines had stood in the shuttle for almost seven hours before the all clear was sounded. It had been a false alarm. Ryck was almost positive that this time, they were all in the middle of another battle.

As if reading his mind, Cpl Winsted said on the P2P, "I think the ship fired her guns a while back. Did you notice it?"

Cpl Winsted was John Beady's replacement, joining the squad when they were cross-decked. He had never seen combat before.

"Yep, sure did. But not everyone noticed it, I'm sure, and as there is nothing we can do about it one way or the other, then no use bringing it up, right? No use getting your team stressed."

"Oh, yeah, right, of course. I didn't mean that. It's just, you know, kinda hard to sit here not knowing what's going on," the corporal said.

Ryck closed his eyes and said, "Well, I'm going to follow in our leader's footsteps and catch some z's."

There was no way Ryck was going to sleep, but he had to exude a sense of calm. What he had said to Winsted was right, there was no use in stressing out his Marines, and if they knew he was stressed, then they would stress.

Ryck was amazed when, sometime later, he was jolted awake by the skipper's voice. He had no idea how long he'd been out.

"We've got a potential mission. While we've been waiting, there has been an engagement," Captain Davis passed. "A French gunship has been damaged and is trying to escape. The AIs put its probable destination as the planet Weyerhaeuser 23, an uninhabited corporate holding. The *Intrepid* has been ordered to give chase and destroy the ship if possible. If it turns out she is heading to the planet, it will be to offload the crew as the ship itself is too damaged to attempt an atmospheric re-entry. Or entry, I guess, would be more correct. If that happens, First and Third will land and attempt to force a surrender, eliminate them if they don't accept. I will be the operation commander. The XO will be the contingency commander and will be ready with Second Platoon for any possible ship-to-ship boarding. Commander Sukishi has given us possible launch time of 50 minutes. I know there is not much we can do while we wait, but squad leaders, I want one more check of your Marines' readouts. Gunny Greuber will be downloading the planet specifics, and I want everyone to make themselves familiar with them. Platoon commanders and sergeants and company headquarters, over to the command circuit for your orders. This is Captain Davis, out."

Even with the Marines in their PICS, there was a palpable sense of alertness, if not excitement. Within an hour and a half, maybe two, they could be in action, where they could influence what they did, not just sitting like cargo, wondering if any moment could be their last. Anything was better than not having any control over their destinies. Ryck knew that most of the Marines would be remembering 1/9 and wanting to extract some revenge.

Ryck did a quick check of the squad's readouts. Other than a bump in heart rate and breathing, nothing had changed. They were ready.

The planetary specs came over the link, and Ryck toggled them up. Weyerhaeuser 23 was another corporate holding, this one uninhabited. The huge galaxy-wide conglomerate had seeded vast tracts of the planet with various genmodded tree species some 30 years ago, then left. It wasn't scheduled for a first harvest for another 10 years. Atmosphere was 18% O2, 81% N2, and the remainder trace gasses, and pressure was 95% ES, or "Earth-standard." Gravity was .96 ES. Planetary rotation was 22.4 hours. Temperature ranged for -10 degrees at the poles to 40 at the equator.

These were all very close to ES, and Ryck wondered why the planet was not open to human colonization. He knew that Weyerhaeuser was not in the people business, but comparing this planet to Prophesy, where his family had struggled to scrape crops out of the parched soil, this looked like paradise. It hadn't even needed any terraforming. From what he read, the trees had minor genmods to be able to out-compete the native flora (which had been infected by the company biologists to clear them to help make room for the earth species), the symbiotic-type insect life was released, and that was about it. Seed, then leave until the trees grew into a commercially valuable crop.

There was more to the report, but Ryck had the gist of it. The atmosphere was not going to kill them, they would not burn up nor freeze, and they could move around without issue, even outside of their PICS.

"Everyone ready?" he sent to the squad circuit. "Looks like a nice vacation spot, right?"

"Sure, Sergeant L, I'm ready for some libo[43]," Lips responded.

---

[43] Libo: short for liberty, when military personnel are off-duty and off base enjoying free time.

It really wasn't that funny, Ryck knew, but most of the squad laughed, if somewhat nervously.

Ryck knew the company staff was furiously hammering out a basic plan, adjusting from hip-pocket ops orders that had been developed long before. But for the Marines in the squad, it was sit and wait until the word came down. And that wasn't good. Just being inside their PICS tended to psychologically isolate the men psychologically, making them feel alone. Simple chatter helped combat that feeling.

"Uh, Lips, I don't think libo is your strong suit. Why don't you tell the rest of the squad about the Monster Hut?" Ryck told the lance corporal.

There were hoots from some of the other Marines, those who had been in the squad for a while. Lips had been busted for a drunken liberty incident at the bar. Already selected for sergeant, the then-Corporal Holleran was demoted to lance corporal. He was salty enough to understand Ryck's intentions, though, so he launched into a rather exaggerated tale of his demise, bringing in the bar owner, her husband, and two FCDC officers. Even Ryck was laughing, despite knowing that only 20% of the story at best was true.

It was almost disconcerting to be pulled back into reality when the lieutenant came back from the command net to give them their orders, but the tactic had been effective. Almost 20 minutes had passed, 20 minutes when the men were not standing there like statues with only their own thoughts for company.

Their orders were pretty basic, about what Ryck had expected. Until the situation on the ground became clear, it was hard to plan anything concrete or too elaborate. If they launched for the planet, The two Storks with First Platoon would lead the way with Third in the *Intrepid*'s shuttle coming in behind. The Storks were transports, but they were armed, and without dedicated Navy air support, they would take the air cover mission. Depending on where anyone might land, the skipper would decide on whether to split up or to remain one unit. The opposing forces would be given the opportunity to surrender. If they refused, they would be attacked.

This wasn't really an ops order, Ryck realized as he listened to the lieutenant. At best, it was a vague concept of operations with a list of coordinating measures. But until they knew more, any detailed plan was probably a waste of time.

A few minutes after the lieutenant was done, the skipper came back up on the company circuit.

"All hands, I have an update. We were not able to close with the enemy gunboat in time, and they have reached Weyerhaeuser 23. Two shuttles have been launched and are descending to the planet. Given the class of the gunboat and the listed crew, either each shuttle is only half full or there was a Legion platoon on board. We are now operating under the assumption that we will be facing the legionnaires. The *Intrepid* could knock the enemy shuttles out of the sky, but we have been ordered to attempt to garner a surrender first, so we will be launching as soon as we get into range, in about six minutes. Second Platoon, you will launch immediately after us and board the gunboat as it orbits. The XO will issue your specific orders in a few moments.

"I charge all of you to be ready, remain flexible, and do your duty. If in fact there are legionnaires among the enemy, they represent a real threat, so it is imperative that we work as a team. We still outnumber them, and we have the *Intrepid* at our backs."

Ryck perked up when the Capt Davis mentioned legionnaires. If the legionnaires chose, they could put up a fight. Still, the Marines outnumbered them, and the *Intrepid* was a pretty big stick to wield.

"Platoon commanders, make ready. Let's kick some ass," the skipper said.

Six minutes was a short time in the grand scheme of things, but it stretched out while the Marines waited. Ryck wondered if the French shuttles had landed, and if so, were they preparing to surrender or fight. They would know the *Intrepid* was on their tail, and sitting out the rest of the war sure beat being blasted by a plasma gun. The Legion R-3s might be a great combat suit, but they couldn't stand up to a Federation destroyer.

A Navy sailor in a bright yellow EVA ran up the back hatch of the shuttle, took a reading at a gauge, then scrambled back out as the hatch closed.

"What was that about?" Cpl Winsted asked.

"Just routine. You know the Navy," Ryck responded, even though he was wondering the same thing.

The *Intrepid's* main hangar was a far cry from that of the *Ark Royal's* five hangars. The *Intrepid* was designed to fight, not carry Marines. It barely fit the two Storks along with its two shuttles. In the ancillary hangar, where Second Platoon was loaded on their rekis, the ship's skiff had been pushed to the side just to prep the rekis to launch. With a limited launch crew on the *Intrepid*, launching shuttles, Storks, or rekis wasn't the synchronized ballet that characterized the bigger ship's launch ops.

The Marines were blind in the shuttle's cargo compartment, but a vibration was their hint that they were ready to go. When the artificial gravity disappeared, they knew they were out of the ship and on their way.

After travelling so far in such a short amount of time, it was frustrating for the Marines to know they were so close to the ground, yet they had to wait another 40 minutes until they landed. The physics of atmospheric entry could not be denied. At least the French would face the same timeline.

After ten minutes of uneventful flight, updates began to flash on Ryck's face shield. Both French shuttles had landed close to each other, about 30 km apart. One looked to be in bad shape, making it a miracle that it had even remained in one piece upon landing. The other looked fine. It the French did surrender, only the second shuttle could be used to bring them up to the *Intrepid*. The ship's own two shuttles would be necessary as well.

The glare of atmospheric entry illuminated the hold, coming in from the pilot's station. It was not a steady light, and it made shifting shadows from the Marines across from Ryck. If they were coming through the atmosphere, then they should be landing in less than five minutes.

Their landing points were selected and relayed to each Marine's display. The Storks would land approximately 15 km from the intact shuttle. The *Intrepid's* shuttle would drop Third platoon another 12 kms on the other side of the intact French shuttle.

A message flashed across their displays. The French commander had been contacted by the crew of the *Intrepid*, and the offer for them to surrender had been made. None of the details of the comms was passed, only that the French needed time to consider it. The Marines were ordered to land, but not advance until given the word to do so.

"Looks like there might not be any action," Ryck passed to his three team leaders. "Keep alert, though. Talks could break down."

Despite what he told his team leaders, Ryck throttled back his intensity a bit. It was just as well, really, better, in fact, if the French surrendered. There was no use wasting lives if it wasn't needed--not just French lives, but his Marines' as well. Even a platoon of legionnaires could prove a formidable foe, and if it came to that, not every Marine would be likely to make it home.

They were skimming over the planet still some 200 km from their target. The long route in was actually much quicker and took far less energy than descending straight down from the perpendicular as soldiers and shuttles always did in the flicks.

Ryck pulled up an overlay and placed it over the tactical map. They were coming in over the largest plantation on the planet. If they were going to land, Ryck wouldn't have minded seeing the native plants, but it looked like it was going to be genmodded walnut and teak, two high-value wood species.

The shuttle broke away from the two Storks and started sweeping around to land behind their target shuttle. The back hatch started lowering flooding the cargo hold with light. Outside, Ryck could see a bright green landscape, undisturbed by any sign of humanity.

"Here we go," Ryck passed to his squad. "We've got the 12 to 4, so move it out and stop. Form on me as to how far to go. Then we just sit and wait while the commands negotiate with each other."

The shuttle was slowing, less than a km out when all hell broke loose on Ryck's face shield display. Four tracks appeared from some three km from the French shuttle, reaching out for the two Storks.

The Stork was a big transport, not a fighting craft. It was armed, and it had defenses, but it was not a fighter. In the second or two it took the hyper-velocity missiles to reach the two aircraft, the lead Stork juked to its right and ejected flares. It wasn't enough. While one missile missed, the other three hit. The lead Stork took one, the trail two. Both icons went immediately grey.

"Get us down!" Lieutenant Nidishchii' screamed over the circuit to the shuttle pilots.

Ryck's adrenaline level surged as he realized what was happening. First Platoon had been knocked from the sky, along with the Captain Davis and Gunny Greuber. That would sink in later, if there was a later. Now he had to take care of his men.

"Move to the ramp," he shouted into his mic.

They were about 30 meters above the ground, coming into the LZ. This was probably too high to fall without injury, but it would be better to try that than be inside the shuttle if it got hit. And to protect that shuttle, the Marines had to get out of it immediately.

Ryck saw the plasma signature on his display. The *Intrepid* was answering back.

"All Marines, I want you out in ten seconds so I can fight," the pilot passed on the open circuit. Evidently, he didn't want the weight of a platoon of PICS Marines while he took action. If the Stork was not a fighter, the shuttle was even less of one, but the pilot was going to try.

Ryck led the way, feet at the edge of the ramp, holding on to the hydraulic ramp lift to keep from being pushed out. Someone was on his ass, pushing against him.

The LZ was below them, maybe 15 meters away, when the explosion rocked the shuttle, lifting up her nose, dropping the ass end another five meters. Ryck slid out, falling to the ground with a thud. The shock of the ground was followed by Marines in PICS landing on top of him. There were three or four shocks before Ryck was able to look up. They shuttle was settling, Marines still falling from the ramp. As the shuttle fell, it kept moving forward, so the

Marines were not all on top of each other. The bottom of the ramp hit the ground, Marines still jumping out, while the bow was levered into the ground with a vicious slam. The shuttle didn't explode, but the force of the impact collapsed it upon itself.

Ryck tore his gaze away to check his display. An entire platoon was gone. Some of his platoon's icons were light blue, a couple already grey. They were on a planet with an enemy force of an unknown size and strength.

They were in the shit!

# Weyerhaeuser 23

## Chapter 15

"That's it, then" Lieutenant Nidishchii' said on the command circuit. "The *Intrepid's* down to 70% effective, but it is in pursuit of the French destroyer. We're on our own for now."

"What the fuck?" Sams said. "They're just going to leave us here?"

"They've got over 100 of their own dead, too. The ambush took them by surprise while they were taking out the two shuttles and the first missile launcher. Despite their damage, they've been ordered by the commodore to pursue and finish off the enemy ship. Evidently it's more damaged than the *Intrepid* and is trying to flee."

"What about Second Platoon?" Ryck asked. "They can't survive for long in EVAs."

"There's been no contact with them for over an hour. Our command is assuming they are lost, too."

"'Assuming? Without proof? Sorry sir, but that is fucking bullshit," Sams said, his anger evident.

"Yes it is fucking bullshit, sergeant. So what do we do about it? Sit here and cry, or get on with our mission? Get a fucking grip on yourself," the platoon commander shouted back.

Ryck had never heard the platoon commander raise his voice, much less use profanity. It took him by surprise.

"Now, I want a complete inventory of what we've got, and I want it in five minutes, no longer. They know where we are, and I don't know what else they've got up their sleeves, but we're getting out of here."

"What about the WIAs, sir?" Doc Grbil asked.

"What's their status?" the platoon commander asked him.

"Roskins, Singh, and Patani are hurt but ambulatory. I've bandaged them up, but they can get back in their PICS and function. Smythe, Tally, Portono, and Justice are pretty bad. Justice isn't going anywhere with that leg, and I've got the other three in ziplocks. Oh yeah, there's the crewchief. He's probably got a concussion, but he's cognizant."

The lieutenant didn't have to ask about the KIAs. Both pilots and five Marines, including Sergeant Paul Pope, Popo, had been killed. Ryck wasn't letting himself think of his friend for now. He would grieve later.

"Staff Sergeant, any way we can get that sailor inside a PICS?" the lieutenant asked.

"We can get him inside one," SSgt Hecs began.

Each one knew that "one" meant one of the dead Marine's PICS.

". . . but can he operate it? Why don't we leave him here with the KIA and ziplocked WIA? We can move them over there under the trees in case someone lobs something at the shuttle hulk, but I don't think anyone is going to attack one sailor and the wounded. Leave him and LCpl Justice to watch over them."

"OK, do it. You two," he pointed at the two surviving squad leaders, "go get me that report."

As Ryck hurried off, SSgt Hecs grabbed him and said on the P2P, "Make sure you take the cold packs from the dead."

Ryck momentarily recoiled, but then common sense kicked in. They had no idea on how long they were going to be stuck on the planet. Each Marine had the coldpack in his PICS, then one spare. A coldpack was good for a little more than a day, maybe up to 30 hours. After that, even if the PICS was otherwise battle-worthy, it could not be used. Within 20 or 25 minutes at the most, the Marine inside would go into heat exhaustion. In another five minutes, he would be dead.

"Roger that," he said, calling Rey forward.

He told Rey to collect the packs, both the ones in the PICS and any spares. He then took Third Team and went back into the shuttle to see what could be salvaged.

The door gun on the shuttle was a 300-round-per-minute 25mm KE gun. Without the shuttle's targeting system, it would not be accurate, so Ryck wasn't sure how they could use it, but he told LCpl Martin to take it out of the pintle. It was bulky, and the ammo box added more weight, but it was nothing a PICS could not handle.

Ryck was much happier to see the crate for the M229. This was a small, but compact artillery piece. It could be horsed around by a single Marine, so it was even easier for a Marine in a combat suit. There were only ten rounds for it: five anti-personnel and five anti-armor. Ryck was expecting more rounds, but he couldn't find any.

He was also hoping to find one of the pulse cannons. He knew the company had one, but not where it had been loaded for the operation. The pulse cannon was their only crew-served energy weapon, and if they were going to face legionnaires, and those legionnaires were in R-3s, then they really needed that weapon. He had to get back to the lieutenant, so he gave up the search and moved back out of the wreck.

With comms, a command meeting did not have to take place with each person in a circle facing each other. In fact, that was not tactically sound. Yet that is what usually happened. Ryck, SSgt Hecs, Sams, and the lieutenant came together and met where they could clear their visors and see each other's faces while they talked.

SSgt Hecs started it off. "Without counting the four WIA and the Navy crewchief, we've got 26 Marines, 25 from the platoon and Cpl Evans from EOD, and Doc Grbil. All PICS are functioning, but ten are at less than 90%. LCpl Khouri's right arm is inoperable, and his HGL broke right off when he fell out of the shuttle. However, the rest of his PICS functions. Power levels on all suits are still above 95%. All told, I'm amazed the damage to the suits was as light as it turned out to be. We are still combat effective as a platoon."

Sams told the lieutenant that Cpl Evans had only a partial EOD kit, and Ryck reported the status of the M229, which caught their attention. None of the Marines in the platoon were artillery, but the gun was pretty easy to fire.

"Well, it is what it is," the platoon commander said when Ryck finished. "This is what we have to play with. I want to move over to here," he said, as a spot appeared on their display map. "I want a good defense put in, then we're going to try and recon what we're facing. After that, we're going to pay them a little social call. We owe them that."

## Chapter 16

Ryck lay flat on the ground, his face shield in the dirt. Ahead of him, over a small rise and about 500 meters away, was where they had determined the French were.

PICS were not made for lying down. Once on their bellies, they were not made to rotate the helmet and neck to the right or left. So once down, the Marines inside the PICS were essentially blind.

Ryck would rather have been on his back. At least that way, he could see something. But if they had to move quickly, with their attitude systems turned off, it was quicker and easier to stand up while face down than while face up.

"OK, Ryck, launch it," the lieutenant said beside him.

Ryck, the platoon commander, Cpl Evans, and Cpl Rey's team had left the rest of the platoon some three hours earlier, carefully advancing forward. Judging from where the French shuttles had landed, a few data captures by their sensors, and pure gut instinct, they figured the French had to be close to the position they had identified.

In order to plan an assault, the Marines had to know what they faced—hence, the recon. The lieutenant's AI gave it a 82% probability that there was a Legion platoon there, in combat suits. SSgt Hec's AI came up with a 77% probability of the same thing.

The other group of French another 15 kms away were almost assuredly the Navy crew of the gunship. The Marines were able to capture many more data points and all pointed to that fact. Of course, Admiral DeMornay had spoofed an entire Federation task force, so spoofing a single Marine platoon was not something too difficult to imagine.

Ryck toggled the dragonfly loose. It rose in the air, then started making its way through the trees. The forest was thick, but somehow sterile. Normal forests had a variety of species, but this one had three plant species: the walnut and teak Ryck had read about online and a hanging moss covered vine that helped regulate water flow to maximize tree growth. The vine-regulated water system must have worked, because the trees were pretty huge for only being 30 years old.

The dragonfly was programmed to flit around like its namesake, but that would only fool a casual observer. It was shielded, so it should escape sensor detection, but anyone seeing it would understand what it was.

The dragonfly could have covered the 500 meters in less than 20 seconds, but that speed would probably give it away to any observers, so it slowly made its way through the forest. It wasn't until it was 30 meters away that it detected movement. Ryck slowed it down and gave it the command to latch itself to one of the trees.

What it captured wasn't good. There was about a platoon of legionnaires there, all in R-3s. They were getting ready for something. That something was most likely an attack on the Marines. The Marines had been using their best shielding technology, but if they picked up slight data points on the Legion, it was likely that the Legion had picked up the same points, if not more, on the Marines.

A platoon of R-3 legionnaires was a very formidable opponent for a platoon of PICS Marines. This was not just in theory. In war games, back when relations were better, the computer referees almost always gave the Legion victories over the Marines when numbers were equal and it was PICS Marines versus R-3 legionnaires. The current PICS was slightly better than those used during the war games, but the R-3s were probably better now as well.

Ryck wanted to be able to assess the full strength of the legionnaires. He counted 12 within view, but he knew there were probably more. He never had the chance for a full count, though, as all the legionnaires in view of the dragonfly suddenly turned to look up at it. One legionnaire pointed up, his arm gunport cover retreating to reveal a snub barrel projector. Then the dragonfly went dead.

"Let's get out of here," the lieutenant said.

All five Marines got up, turned their attitude stabilizers back on, and started to move. They weren't heading directly back to the rest of the Marines, but off at a tangent. Above them, rounds exploded in the canopy. At the second set of explosions, something pinged of Ryck's PICS, but whether that was shrapnel or a piece of shattered wood, Ryck didn't know.

Looking at his display, he could see ghosts appearing behind him. The R-3s were very good and were shielded quite well, but when they were moving, the shielding was less effective. This was opposite from the Marines fractured arrays. They were not as effective when still, but worked better when moving. With the legionnaires in hot pursuit, the Marine AIs could pick up more data points, but as they were still approximations, the icons were not the bright colors of identified objects or people, but wavering off-white circles. Ghosts.

The rounds exploding in the canopy stopped, either because the legionnaires firing them were out of mortar rounds or they just realized that the rounds were not very effective. A few moments later, though, there was a huge blast in back of the Marines, and suddenly, a light red icon appeared on Ryck's display.

A legionnaire was down, his suit's shielding compromised.

"Holy shit, Evans, it worked!" Ryck exclaimed.

They had brought along the EDO Marine because Evans had been sure he could booby-trap their route back for just this situation. Evans had placed five mines, all with passive firing mechanisms. When the Marines ran through the minefield, the mechanisms were bypassed. If anything else lumbered by, the vibrations of the footsteps set off the explosion. The theory was sound, but Ryck had figured that the legionnaires would be able to sense the explosives, if not the mechanism. He was wrong.

"Oohrah!" Evans exclaimed.

The ghosts stopped advancing. The legionnaires had been caught up in the chase, and it had cost them. First blood had gone to the Legion when they shot down the Storks and the shuttle. Second blood went to the Marines, and even if the two were in no way equal, it was a good morale boost for the Marines to strike back at all.

## Chapter 17

"OK, Staff Sergeant, you've got them. We'll meet you at the new site in about four hours," Lieutenant Nidishchii' told SSgt Hecs.

The platoon commander hadn't liked where the platoon had formed up and wanted to move them to something more defensible. There was one piece of high ground that looked promising, but it was too close to where the second group of French was located. Instead, the lieutenant had selected another small rise about 20 k from their present position. It was covered in trees, so it was not much better in terms of visibility, but any advantage had to be taken.

While the platoon was moving, the same group that had reconned the Legion platoon was going to confirm that the second group of French were actually sailors and not combat troops. This was to be a quick recon. The lieutenant didn't want to split his forces, but he had to make sure he understood just what they faced.

Keiji took point. Normally, the HGL gunner would be second in the movement as the HGL itself was not as quick a weapon to deploy as the normal M114, but if they were to face combat-suited legionnaires, then the HGL gave the Marines their best chance to take one of them out.

Reports on the effectiveness of the armor on the Legion R-3s were not conclusive at best, contradictory at worst. The armor was interspaced with circuits that created intense fields whereas the PICS had two field generators that created a sort of bubble around the Marines. The consensus was that the circuit method of generation made for a more effective shielding, particularly against energy weapons.

How effective it was against KE weapons, on the other hand, was not as well known. Some analysts felt that the lighter, more flexible armor of the R-3 was better against physical KE rounds as well. Others felt it gave an advantage in surviving the effects of concussive shock waves. But still others felt the armor was too light and not strong enough to match the older techno PICS in as far as brute ability to withstand KE strikes.

The PICS M114 was a great weapon against softer targets. It fired a stream of 8mm hyper-velocity darts that would pierce ordinary body armor without too much of a problem. However, it would not pierce a PICS. A lucky shot might damage sensors or weapons, but it would not make it through the armor of a PICS to the Marine inside. With that in mind, the Marines could not count on it to be able to take down a legionnaire in an R-3.

When the platoon had been loaded onto the shuttle, they had been given a standard combat load, not one designed to take on other combat-suited soldiers. This had been rather shortsighted given that the Legion possessed combat suits. Since even before the War of the Far Reaches, Marines hadn't faced anyone who had combat suits in their forces, and tactics had evolved without taking combat suits into much consideration. Always fighting the last war, however, was a good way to lose the next one.

With their weapons mix, the Marines had a few weapons that could be effective against a legionnaire in an R-3. The HGL might need multiple hits, but it could work. Their shoulder rocket launchers, with the 7.5cm rockets should be effective. Each Marine, though, had a total of only 12 rockets, six anti-personnel and six anti-armor, and the box could not be reloaded in the field. They had the M229, which would undoubtedly mess up a legionnaire's day, and if they could figure out how to use it, the shuttle's 25mm gun.

Each PICS also had its plasma gun. In an atmosphere, the plasma dispersed quickly, so the distance had to be close, and they took up a huge amount of energy. A fully-charged PICS could maybe fire three times before the suit went dead. With the R-3's effectiveness against energy weapons, and the fact that they had no way to recharge the PICS until back on the ship, those were pretty much a non-starter against the Legion troops.

On the other side of the battlefield, the legionnaires had weapons that could take out a PICS. The weapons of an R-3 remained inside the skin of the suit until fired. This helped with the stealth techno that made the R-3s so hard to acquire with the Marine sensors. Their own version of the hyper-velocity darts wouldn't do much against a PICS, but instead of a plasma gun, they had a hadron gun, miniaturized enough to carry. It was far more efficient than a plasma gun, and it could probably fire for at least a minute, if the Federation math was accurate. It wasn't as powerful as a ship-based hadron cannon, but it didn't have to be. The Marines had been briefed that the R=3's hadron gun would probably take from eight to twelve seconds to "burn" through the PICS' shields.

The legionnaires also had larger KE weapons, and the recording from Ryck's dragonfly revealed what looked to be a portable field gun. Other than that, though, the Marines didn't know with what the Legion platoon was equipped.

Ryck scanned his display as they moved through the trees. He had to watch where he was going, but still focus on his display, looking for the slightest aberration that might indicate a legionnaire was out there. Somewhere in the back of his mind, he marveled at the trees, the spongy surface of the ground. They didn't have forests on Prophesy where he grew up. They didn't have forests like this on Tarawa, either, nor on Alexander, where the division was based.

The lieutenant stopped them several times to stand and scan, but they still made good time to their rally point. All was quiet. SSgt Hecs reported in from the new position, and LCpl Justice with the WIA and AT3 Fodor, the shuttle crewchief, reported in as well. The legionnaires were nowhere on anyone's scanners.

At least the French crew was showing up on their sensors, about 500 meters ahead of the small recon force. Ryck had taken one of Popo's dragonflies, so he was back up to two. It seemed to synch all right to his PICS, but he decided to launch his remaining original drone.

This far back and in the forest, the lieutenant kept them standing, which was easier. With the others providing security, Ryck was able to concentrate on his dragonfly. He slowed it down as it approached the French, sending it higher into the canopy. This close, it could pick up 15 separate heat signatures. Ryck edged it forward, and the view suddenly opened up to a small clearing. It looked like a tree had fallen, leaving a crease in the otherwise uninterrupted forest.

Fifteen men and women, all sailors were in the clearing, three lying together seemingly injured. Several lean-tos had been built from branches and deadfall, and another few sailors were sitting under them. Ryck counted two sailors, armed with the small French slurp guns, standing guard at either end of the clearing. The rest were engaged in small tasks. There was no sign of heavy weaponry of any kind, either energy or KE.

The little dragonfly had basic sensors, but the PICS, in particular the lieutenant's PICS-C, had much more sophisticated ones, so after the preliminary scan, the Marines moved forward. They walked their PICS as "stealthily" as they could, which was somewhat of an oxymoron when describing movement in a PICS. Ryck doubted that the sailors had much in the way of sensors, but they had their eyeballs and ears, and they would be able to see and hear a PICS coming through the trees.

At 200 meters out, the lieutenant stopped them. Ryck had the platoon commander's data feed slaved, so he could see the readout. The dragonfly had gotten most of the info already. The French were what they seemed to be: sailors, not legionnaires.

"What do we do?" Ryck asked the lieutenant.

Their mission was still intact. They were to accept a surrender or destroy anyone who refused to give up. There were 15 French combatants up ahead, and with seven PICS Marines, they would stand no chance.

Ryck knew their orders, but he had no stomach to launch an attack. These were shipwreck survivors, in his mind, and the treaties were clear as to how they should be treated. The fact that the two forces were at war, the fact that they were armed, didn't make a difference to him. Ryck didn't know, though, how anal the lieutenant would be with regards to their orders. And if the lieutenant ordered an assault, he would obey.

"They're no threat to us," Lieutenant Nidishchii' said. "Let's leave your dragonfly to watch over them, but let's leave them be. Once we've dealt with the legionnaires, then we can take the crew's surrender."

That was a relief to Ryck. He turned to the lieutenant just as a flicker appeared in the platoon commander's scan feed. An amber warning icon flashed on Ryck's display, indicating an anomaly, but not the red icon of a positive threat identification.

Both Ryck and the lieutenant turned just as a flash illuminated the trees to their right. Their face shields lit up as their PICS identified a Gazelle, the small, man-packed anti-armor missile hurtling at them. From only 100 meters out, barely within arming range, they had no chance. This missile was designed to take out tanks.

Their AIs flashed on each Marine's fractured arrays, but that didn't matter. The missile knew where they were and had locked into their position. Ryck started to lurch to the side, knowing there was not enough time. There was a bigger flash as the missile hit—Prifit.

The missile's exhaust made a cloud from which two legionnaires emerged. The Marines' scans started pulling in data points, but the two were right there in front of them, in plain sight. To Ryck's left, Keiji started pouring his grenades at the legionnaire closest to him. Ryck's first instinct was to open fire with his M114, but he pulled that back and toggled his rocket launcher.

Before he could fire, his alarms screamed as a hadron beam touched him. Immediately his shielding gauge popped up on his display and started to give the numbers as his shield began to disintegrate. Ryck jumped to his right, and his alarms turned off. The legionnaire was targeting the lieutenant, and Ryck had only been caught in a side lobe.

He started to turn back around to take the legionnaire under fire, but to his amazement, Lt. Nidishchii' was running, not away, but right at the legionnaire firing at him.

Ryck's display registered an explosion on the arm of the second legionnaire, but he was more focused on the one firing at his platoon commander. He started to fire his rockets, but with the lieutenant between them, he couldn't. He ran to his right further to get a clear line of fire.

At about 50 meters, the lieutenant started firing his rockets, bam, bam, one after the other. The air around him started to glow as his shields approached failure, but he didn't stop.

The anti-armor rockets had limited self-guidance towards metallic objects, but the R-3 wasn't made of metal. The lieutenant was firing his rockets from the hip while running. Each rocket, though, hit the chest of the legionnaire. When the first one hit, Ryck could see the armor actually ripple. When the second one hit an instant later, the rippled became more pronounced.

The lieutenant didn't stop running forward or firing. The third rocket hit in the legionnaire in same spot, but the fourth went over the man's shoulder.

Ryck didn't know how much time had elapsed since the lieutenant had been taken under fire. Seven, eight seconds? His shield was a bright orange, a sure sign of imminent failure.

The lieutenant was only 20 meters from the legionnaire, but he didn't stop. Ryck aimed in on the soldier, who had taken a step back when faced with the charging Marine. Just as Ryck fired, the fifth, or maybe the sixth rocket fired by the lieutenant hit home, this time penetrating the R-3 and blowing a 10-centimeter hole in the R-3's chest. Ryck's rocket skimmed past the lieutenant's head before slamming into the legionnaire's shoulder, but his round was unnecessary. The legionnaire was dead, his R-3 trying to maintain a vertical aspect. Sparks flew out of it, and it slowly collapsed upon itself.

Ryck wheeled to face the other legionnaire, but he was retreating, barely visible through the trees.

"Lieutenant, are you OK?" he shouted into his mic.

There was no response, so Ryck ran forward as the lieutenant turned around.

Ryck shouted out his question again, but the lieutenant pointed at where his ear would be, then shook his head back and forth.

His shield was still glowing, a couple of centimeter cloud around him. It wasn't glowing as brightly as before, but with all that ionized air, it was affecting his comms.

He could see the lieutenant's smile through his face shield, so Ryck knew he was OK. Ryck turned back to check on the others.

Prifit was on his back, and Ryck hoped for the best. Instead, he saw the worst, and that staggered him. The entire carapace section of Prifit's PICS had been blown away. Above the shoulders, the PICS looked normal, as it did below the gut plate. Where Prifit's chest had been though, was a bloody, mangled mess. The anti-armor round, designed to take out tanks, had passed right through his Marine.

Without power, Prifit's face shield was dark, and Ryck was relieved that he couldn't see the lance corporal's face for the moment. He had to prepare himself before he did that.

Ryck turned from Prifit and ordered Keiji to provide security in the direction to which the other legionnaire had fled while he went to checked over the dead soldier. The legionnaire was slouched on the dirt in a way a PICS could not. The armor of the R-3, while not pliable, was not as rigid as it was when the man was firing at the lieutenant. From reading published articles in various journals and blogs, Ryck knew the R-3 armor was powered, but it looked like that power gave the suit at least some degree of support as well. Ryck reached out with his foot and gave the legionnaire a shove, knocking him flat to the ground. The feedback sensors let Ryck know the R-3 was still a pretty heavy piece of gear, probably right at the 825kg reported in the general specs.

The rocket that had blown the hole in the legionnaire's chest did not cause as much damage as the missile that had hit Prifit, but it had done enough. His time as an armorer while still in regen gave him some expertise in combat suits, so he kneeled to examine what the damage revealed. The R-3 armor was thinner than PICS armor, which was to be expected, but Ryck couldn't see any of the circuits that powered it.

"Ryck, are you there?" SSgt Hecs voice came over the net.

"Yeah, I'm here."

"What the hell's going on? We've got Justice in a panic saying he's heard fighting, and I can't raise the lieutenant. My display's got LCpl Prifit down," the platoon sergeant said.

"We were hit by two legionnaires. Prifit's KIA, but the lieutenant's fine. He friggin' charged one of the legionnaires while taking full fire, but his rockets took the guy out first. His PICS is pretty fried, and I think it's going to need a reset."

There was a moment of silence, then "Prifit's KIA? No chance of bringing him back?"

"Staff Sergeant, no way. His entire chest is gone."

The lieutenant was making a circle in the air with his gauntlet. Back at boot, Ryck had wondered why they spent so much time on hand and arm signals. He never would have thought he would be in the field with a platoon commander who couldn't communicate, though.

"Staff Sergeant, the lieutenant wants me. I'll keep you informed," he told SSgt Hecs as he went up to his platoon commander.

It wasn't textbook hand and arm signals, but the lieutenant made his intentions clear. He wanted Prifit taken out of his PICS, anything salvaged, then for the Gazelle launcher and the PICS to be destroyed. Ryck grabbed the launcher while Rey and Hartono pulled the pieces of what was left of Tipper Prifit out of his PICS. Ryck tried to avoid looking at what was left inside the PICS, but he managed to take the shoulder launcher and helmet off. He was sure the coldpack was destroyed, and he didn't want to feel around in the bloody mess that was left to confirm that. When he was done, he put the launcher on top of Prifit's destroyed PICS.

Hartono had a buttpack, and what was left of Prifit fit inside of it. Cpl Evans took two of his bullfrogs, the EOD version of the toads[44] each Marine carried, and put one on top of the Gazelle launcher, one on the PICS' codpiece. He lit them off, and the Marines stepped back. All of them stood watching in silence as bullfrogs ignited and burned their way through the armor. Packing two or three times the punch of a normal toad, it didn't take long.

It wasn't until the bullfrogs flickered out, leaving a smoking pile of junk, that they turned and left to rejoin the rest of the platoon.

---

[44] Toad: Slang for the E-559 Self-contained Slow Breaching Device, a high-intensity heat weapon that can be attached to an object and burn through it.

## Chapter 18

Ryck sighed with contentment. He felt naked, his visibility was low in the darkness, and something was digging into his back, but it felt good to be out of his PICS. With power levels down for all the Marines, particularly for the seven who had made the two recons, the lieutenant had ordered a rotating watch, with those off watch out of their PICS.

More vital than the power levels, though, were the coldpacks. With the two per Marine, they had about 50-60 hours of operating time before the PICS became unusable. The lieutenant hoped that the *Intrepid* would be back by then, but it was better to be safe than sorry.

Getting out of the PICS was a calculated risk. If they were hit, it would take up to 30 seconds or possibly longer for the Marines to get back in, sealed, and ready to fight. If the PICS were completely powered down instead of on standby, it would take even longer, but while that would save more power, it increased the risk dramatically.

The lieutenant had sent out three OPs[45], Marines without their PICS and under tarnkappes.[46] Simple vibration sensors were placed to fill in the gaps between the OPs. Even under a full charge by R-3 legionnaires, the platoon should have the time needed to be ready to meet the threat.

Four Marines were in their PICS and on full alert around them—the rest of the empty PICS stood like sentinel statues, ready to come to life.

"Thanks for getting my PICS back up to speed, Ryck," the lieutenant said as he took a seat beside his sergeant.

*Ryck? That's a first,* Ryck thought.

---

[45] OP: Observation post. One or two Marines sent out in front of the unit's lines to give early warning of approaching enemy.

[46] Tarnkappe: slang, taken from a Grimm's Fairy Tales description of a cloak of concealment, for the S-77 Shielding Blanket. The blanket shields against most sensors as well as from vision.

With the lieutenant, it was always rank and last name. Ryck wondered if sitting there in the dark in their longjohns affected the degree of formality between the two Marines.

"No problem, sir. It wasn't hard."

Ryck didn't mention that it hadn't been difficult from a technical standpoint, but he had cannibalized the controls from Tipper Prifit's helmet, which had been a bit rough emotionally.

"I guess your time in the armory paid off, huh?" he asked, then continuing before Ryck could respond. "My time as a genhen was in admin, so I can help unscrew a pay problem, but that's about it."

From what he'd heard, the lieutenant had spent almost as much time as Ryck had in regen. He wondered if his platoon commander had hated it as much as he did. Not the discomfort and pain--everyone hated that--but being away from his unit, away from his fellow Marines, and most of all, the feeling of uselessness. At least Ryck had been with weapons while he was a genhen. With all respect and gratitude to the admin types who kept things running smoothly, Ryck thought he would have died had he been locked up in an office somewhere, shuffling papers.

"This might seem odd, given the circumstances, but I've been watching you pretty closely," the lieutenant continued.

*What now*? Ryck thought.

"What I mean is that you are a good Marine, a good NCO. You think on your feet. That's why I wanted you with me today on the recons. I knew I could count on you."

"Uh, well, thanks, sir," Ryck answered, unsure of where the conversation was going.

"You finished your degree, right?"

"Yes, sir. I received my diploma two months ago."

"Yes, I saw the message. Well, I just wanted to tell you that it's not just me, but Captain Davis had taken note of you, too."

*Captain Davis? He's hardly said ten words to me since I've been in the company, and now he's gone.*

"My point is, and I just want you to think of it, if you ever want to apply to be an officer, I would endorse you, and Captain

Davis told me he would have endorsed you. I can write that endorsement from him as well."

"I . . . I don't know what to say, sir. I mean, it's an honor to hear you tell me that, but I've never even thought of applying for a commission."

That was a lie. He had thought about it, but he kept denying it to the rest of the Marines. For some warped reason that Ryck didn't understand, Marine culture ruled that enlisted Marines who wanted to be officers were suspect, not full members of the "brotherhood."

"Just consider it, OK? The Marines need leaders like you in the officer corps. Anyway, that's all I wanted to say. You make sure to catch some sleep. We don't know what tomorrow will bring, right?"

"Right, sir," Ryck said as the lieutenant stood up and excused himself before walking over to where SSgt Hecs had bedded down.

"You should be an officer," Sams said quietly beside him, his voice several octaves higher than normal. "Oh really, sir? You mean that? Of course I want that," he went on, answering himself.

"Fuck you," Ryck said. "I can't help what the lieutenant thinks."

"Sure. You are such a fucking brown-noser, Ryck. I didn't hear you tell him no."

"Eat me," Ryck grumbled.

Despite himself, the lieutenant's words had piqued his interest. In order to become an officer, a Marine had to get recommended by his unit, even if he met all other qualifications. To know he had one, or two, if what the lieutenant had said about Capt Davis was true, opened the door.

He wasn't sure he wanted to become one, though. Sure it was an advancement in responsibility, not to mention pay, and it would take care of one of Ryck's constant frustrations, that of not knowing what was happening all the time, of being kept in the dark. On the other hand, it would take him farther from his Marines, and there was all the other BS that officers had to deal with that had nothing to do with leading Marines.

Ryck generally liked it as a sergeant, and becoming a platoon sergeant would be pretty awesome. Why take the BS of being an officer when you could get all the good parts as a SNCO?

"Eh, what does Lieutenant Personality know, anyway."

"You know, Sams, you keep calling him that, but the guy is good. Look at us now. He's put in for every contingency. That's pretty copacetic, if you ask me."

Sams was one of his closest Marines in the platoon, and with Popo dead, there were only two sergeants. Ryck loved Sams like a brother, but his cynical attitude sometimes pissed Ryck off.

"Sure, I'll give you that. But any manual-reading bozo could do that. I don't think he's got the fire that, say, Lieutenant Hargrave's got, or the skipper," he said.

That put an immediate damper on things. Both officers had been killed this morning.

"He had fire today," Ryck muttered.

"What do you mean?" Sams asked.

"You should have seen him. When we both got hit by the legionnaire with his hadron gun, here I am diving to get out of the line of fire. Does the lieutenant do that? Fuck no. He charged the motherfucker. Charges like some knight with a lance. No fucking hesitation."

"He charged *into* the fire? I thought you were supposed to get further away, 'cause the beam dissipates," Sams asked.

"That's for a plasma gun, like ours. But I said hadron gun, which you know the Legion uses. The beam's not going to dissipate for a long, long distance."

"Oh, yeah."

"So I'm getting out of the way, Keiji's shooting like some rabid wolf, and he even hits the other legionnaire's gun port, knocking it out of action -- "

"He hits the gun port?"

"Didn't you listen to the debrief? Yeah, one of his grenades hits the gunport that this asshole is using to fire on us, and that knocks his weapon offline. That's why he took off. No weapons."

"Pisspot froggie. Running away," Sams said.

"Yeah, well anyway, I'm trying to get a shot in, and I can see the lieutenant's shield glow, I mean, I can really see it. He's going all orange. But he doesn't stop. Five rockets, no fucking guidance on them. Four hit the legionnaire, and the fourth does it. Bam! He's smoke-checked. And let me tell you, when I worked on his PICS, if that last rocket hadn't hit, the lieutenant would be KIA now. One more second, and his PICS would have been fried. It's because he didn't hesitate, that he went into the attack, that he lived, and maybe the rest of us, too. So don't tell me he's got no fire, OK?"

"Shit, OK, OK. Back off. I meant, with us, at least, he's like a robot. Never excited. Just does his job."

"He's a good officer. Made his ancestors proud, I bet."

"Something special about his ancestors?" Ryck asked.

"Yeah, he's Navaho," Ryck told him, wondering why Sams had to ask.

"And . . . ?"

"Saint Harry on a rope, Sams, don't you keep track of anything? The lieutenant's from Dinétah,"

"Again, and . . .?"

"You know about Dinétah, right?"

"It's a country on Manitoba. Some of them join the Marines. So? Lots of planets send more than their fair share to the Marines."

"You've never heard of the Code-Talkers?" Ryck asked.

"No, I've never hear of the Code-Talkers," Sams responded, his voice inflected to show his lack of interest.

"You really should. They're part of Marine Corps history. Back in WWII, the Navaho people sent their young men into the U.S. Marines to fight the Japanese, and they were vital in keeping Marine comms secure from being compromised by the Japanese."

"Ancient history, my friend, ancient history. I'm not the one trying to get a history degree."

"It may be old, but it is our history, and when the Navajo relocated to Dinétah, they re-established their warrior culture. So guess where their best and brightest go? Yep, to the Marines. Like the old-time Gurkhas, only the very top few were able to join the Marines."

"Gurkhas, I know about them. We had a Gurkha gunny before you got here. He had this wicked knife he took everywhere, a cokry or something," Sams said.

"A kukri," Ryck corrected him. "The Gurkhas were big in the old Royal Marines, the Navaho in the U.S. Marines. They both still serve in our Marines. My point is that the lieutenant comes from a long line of warriors, and they only let the best enlist. So he's made his ancestors proud, today, not just for what he's done when he was an enlisted slob like us."

"Ah, whatever. He may be some kick-butt warrior, but I still think he's got a stick up his ass. He needs to lighten up a schosh. Now, you heard your hero. We've got the get some sleep."

With that, Sams laid back, turning away from Ryck. Within a minute or so, Ryck's friend started snoring.

## Chapter 19

The next day, the Marines spent time preparing their position. The hadron comms had been with the skipper, so the platoon had nothing with which to communicate with a ship out of planetary orbit. But the lieutenant assigned LCpl Vargas out of First Squad to monitor all the ground-to-orbit frequencies. When the *Intrepid* returned, the platoon commander wanted to know immediately.

The lieutenant, SSgt Hecs, Ryck, Sams, and Cpl St. Cyr, the new Second Squad leader, met several times in a mini-war council, going over their options to take the fight to the enemy. It was during one of these that a mass of explosions sounded off to their southwest, possibly 30 km away. The firing kept up for almost two minutes before dying off. Ryck knew there were no Marines there—Justice and the WIA were almost 40 km away to the northeast, and they were the only other Federation forces on the planet. He turned to ask the lieutenant what was going on, but the platoon commander was high-fiving SSgt Hecs.

"And that, sir, is how it's done," SSgt Hecs said.

"What was that?" Ryck asked.

"Oh, our good platoon sergeant set up a little decoy last night. It seems like it's not only the French who can spoof."

"And it looks like you owe me 20, sir," SSgt Hecs said.

"Duly noted, there, Staff Sergeant Phantawisangtong."

The lieutenant got down in the dirt and pushed out a quick 20 pushups.

Ryck hadn't even realized the platoon sergeant had slipped out during the night. If that was 30 km away, then that was 60 km back and forth, quite a trip even in a PICS.

About 30 minutes after the "attack," a voice came over several frequencies at once. The Marines outside of their PICS heard the message over the external speakers of the active PICS.

"Federation Marines, let's avoid any further bloodshed. First Lieutenant Nidishchii'" the voice went on, stumbling a bit over the name, "we are offering you our full guarantee of humane treatment if you surrender your force to us. No one will be hurt, and all needing it will receive medical care. The war is almost over, so let's sit it out. That was a nice feint you pulled, but we have your position locked now. You and your 32 surviving Marines have no air support, no supporting arms, and without those, I am sure you can do the math. You really don't have much chance against a larger Legion force. We outnumber you and outgun you."

There was an explosion of protest from the Marines.

"No need for an immediate reply. No one is doubting your courage. Lieutenant, you have proven your courage time and time again, and several of your men, notably Staff Sergeant Phantawisangtong," the voice said, making even more havoc over the name, "Sergeants Samuelson and Sergeant Lysander, Lance Corporal Westminster, Lance Corporal Laste Holleran, and Private First Class Ling, are well known in the Legion, so this is not a matter of whose balls are the biggest. Most of you have even been of service to the Legion, and you have our gratitude. This is a matter of simply living without needless bloodshed."

While the voice was going on, SSgt Hecs had wormed into the back of his PICS, and the voice was cut off. He wormed back out and went up to the lieutenant.

Ryck, Sams, and several others came as well.

"How do they know my name," Ling asked with a worried tone to his voice.

SSgt Hecs held up his hand, forestalling him, then looking up to the lieutenant.

"Well, that's a nice ni hao," the lieutenant said to them. "Interesting in what they gave away."

"Sir?" Sams asked.

"Well, first, they were specific on us being 32 Marines, and they mentioned every Marine in the platoon who's been awarded a BCS-1 or higher. What does that tell you?" he asked the group.

"Well, Westminster was KIA from the crash," Ryck said.

"Yes, and they have not taken into account that we have seven WIA still alive, and no mention was made of Cpl Evans and HM2 Grbil. Grbil's been decorated, so it they knew about him, they would have mentioned him. What they have is partial intel, and they are guessing the rest. You could have found out most of that from our battalion facebook.[47] By telling us too much, they are revealing their limitations."

"They don't have more men than us, either, right sir?" SSgt Hecs said.

"I doubt it. We know they lost one and probably two others. If you count the Navy sailors, then yes, they probably have more, but as far as legionnaires, I am guess we are about even-strengthed."

"But they've got R-3s, and we don't have air now," Vargas said.

"True, but I don't think the R-3 is really that great. I took one out yesterday, and I'm still here, right? And if we make them come to us, maybe we can even out the odds."

"So do we answer?" asked SSgt Hecs.

"Can we get a mic out here, out of the helmet?" he asked.

"Sure, no problem," Cpl Evans said.

He took a length of ignition wire, then crawled half-way inside his own PICS. A moment later, he emerged, holding the small chin mic in his hand, the wire trailing from it back to inside the PICS. He handed it to the lieutenant.

"Turn back on the broadcast," he told SSgt Hecs.

Since SSgt Hecs had overridden the broadcast from his PICS-C, he had to turn it back on from either his or the lieutenants. He squirmed up inside the back of his, and a few moments, the French voice came back on.

" . . . too long before we will be forced to take offensive action."

"Our French friends, if I may interrupt, I do have a response for you. This is First Lieutenant Nidishchii', UFMC."

The voice stopped for a moment, then said, "Uh, yes, Lieutenant. Please go on."

Every Marine and Doc Grbil had stopped what they were doing and stared at the lieutenant. Slowly, the lieutenant lowered the mic to his ass, and after a moment, let out a tremendous fart, amplified to its max.

[47] Facebook: a generic reference to any public relations media information for an organization or personal information for an individual.

There was dead silence before the Marines erupted into howls of laughter, “oohrahs,” and “get some, Lieutenant!”

Ryck, trying to control his laughter, looked to Sams and said, “The lieutenant’s got no fire, Sams?”

## Chapter 20

"Steve, when we attacked the SOG back on Billiton, they used a mine to take out one of my Marines," Ryck told their EOD Marine.

"Yeah, Yancy Sullivan. I remember," Cpl Evans replied.

"What was the result of the investigation, something about them using wood and an organic explosive?"

"Yeah, the mine body was wood, of all things. For the explosive, they used simple fertilizer. A pressure plate was the trigger. Yancy was pretty unlucky. He stepped right on it."

"Is that something we could do here?" Ryck asked.

"Oh, wow. I don't know. I could if we were back at battalion, no sweat. It wouldn't be as good as one of our issued mines, but it would work. This is real old technology."

"If it was that old, how did it work against us?"

"Because we aren't looking for wood with our PICS. We're looking for all the latest and greatest weapons, not bows and arrows or leather slings," Evans said.

"Do you think it's possible, though?"

"Well, I can take the M887 round casing. They're an organic pulp. Shouldn't be too hard to make a mine casing from them. I can probably come up with something to put inside. All my igniters, though, the legionnaires would be able to pick them up and jam them. I might be able to rig up a pressure plate, but the chances that someone would actually step on it are about nil. The SOG set up over 50, and only one was triggered. So I'm not sure how we could set them off. A wire is out of the question. I guess we could attach a string or something and try and make it manual, but they could probably see it, and I'm not sure any string would be strong enough to activate any sort of trigger I could come up with. I think we would need a timer of some sort, to activate. Yeah, that would do it. We could activate a timer with a string, for say, a 20 or 30 or whatever second detonation we want. Yeah, that would work!" he said, his voice getting a little excited as he spoke.

"You mean, like a watch?"

"No, that wouldn't work. Watches are electronic, no moving parts. It would have to be a mechanical timer of some sort, and we don't have any," Evans said, sounding deflated.

Ryck sighed, then took the Rolex off his wrist. This was Joshua's gift to him, intended to be a lifetime treasure. He knew his friend would understand, though.

"Like this?" he asked, holding out the hand-made timepiece.

"Ooh, that's psycho," Cpl Evans said as he reached out to take it. "Yeah, that'll work, but man, that's a shame. This is one beautiful watch."

"Let's do it. As soon as you get the smoke pots up, I want this done. I'll brief the lieutenant, and we'll tell you where we want it."

"No problem, Sergeant L. I'll get on it."

Ryck really, really loved that watch, but not as much as he valued the lives of the Marines around him.

## Chapter 21

We've got movement," LCpl Denny sent back on the landline they had rigged from the OP back to the lieutenant's foxhole.

They had set up simple vibration detectors, something very difficult to pick up on a scanner until it was too late and had already been activated, and the landline was pretty much impossible to jam. It could be cut, but that was about it. Between the two sources, the platoon knew the Legion was on the march.

"OK, cover up and wait this out. Do not try to come back," the lieutenant passed.

Ryck sent a quick message out on the squad circuit, "Here they come, from the north."

They had decided if the legionnaires were going to attack, they would come from that direction. It was the most logical avenue of approach, and for that reason alone, Ryck would have picked something different. But the legionnaires evidently had a lot of confidence in their abilities. Ryck hoped that confidence was misplaced.

Unless this was yet another spoof, the Marines were well-arrayed for the incoming assault. They had prepared alternate positions, but the main ones were in a slight horseshoe around the crest of the high ground. If it had been a real hill, that position would not have worked. But by varying the depth of each fighting hole, each Marine had a clear field of fire down below them. Clear except for the trees, that was. They'd knocked down a few, but if too many were down, the legionnaires would simply bypass the area and attack from the flanks where it would be harder to mass fire on them.

The M229 was emplaced towards the right of the line, where a subtle amount of tree removal gave it just a hair more of a field of fire. On the left side of the line, the shuttle's 250mm gun had been lashed onto a tree trunk they had knocked over. Ryck didn't give the gun much credit. There were no working sights, much less a target acquisition control, so it would be blindly firing forward, but at least it was something.

Modern warfare was not supposed to be like this anymore. It was fluid actions across a battlefield with interlocking support and assaults. Marines just didn't go on the defense, either. Sams, for one, had been advocating taking the fight to the legionnaires, not sitting and waiting for the enemy to come to them.

Marines didn't go into the defense, but it had been decades since they had faced a force even equal to them.

The lieutenant merely said "Whoever is first in the field and awaits the coming of the enemy, will be fresh for the fight; whoever is second in the field and has to hasten to battle will arrive exhausted."

Ryck recognized that from Sun Tzu, and while he didn't think it really fit the situation, it seemed weighty enough to shut up Sams.

"Get the pots going," the lieutenant told Evans.

Evans in turn told Pvt Holderstead, who'd been made his assistant. The private jumped out of his fighting hole and ran forward to the line of makeshift smoke pots Evans had managed to rig up. One smack on the top of each pot and it ignited, sending grey smoke out which rose a meter or so off the ground as it slowly spread. Cpl Evans had tried to explain that it wasn't actually smoke, but it acted like smoke and looked like smoke, so to the rest of the Marines, smoke it was.

It might seem counterintuitive to send out any agent, smoke or not, that blocked visuals when an assault was expected. However, Ryck knew that the legionnaires would not be low-crawling up to their positions, and the lieutenant's reason for the smoke seemed sound. Only time would tell if the lieutenant was right.

The Marines couldn't tell how many legionnaires they faced. Their vibration sensors did not indicate direction, so there was no way for the AIs to triangulate and make an estimate. There had to be over 20, but probably fewer than 40. That was a pretty big range.

When the legionnaires were at 200 meters, Ryck felt his excitement rise. There might have been a touch of fear in there, too, but nothing overriding. He tried to see through the trees, but the legionnaires were still too far away to spot. His sensors were picking up nothing. They probably would continue to pick up nothing until the legionnaires' weapons ports opened, breaking the stealth profile of the R-3's.

Then he saw it, the slightest swirl in the smoke some 120 meters away. The fire team assigned to the M229 saw it as well. In direct fire mode, the gun opened up. A split second later, the anti-armor round impacted, and a R-3 flashed into view as it was blown back.

The battle was on. More swirls in the smoke appeared as unseen legionnaires rushed forward. The M229 fired again, but the round exploded against a tree.

Cpl Evans had laid out ten of his issued mines, but as expected, the legionnaires were able to detect them. They sidestepped them, three coming together and heading right towards Evan's field expedient mine. Ryck reached down and pulled the string, an unraveled piece of Evan's longjohns. His Rolex started its 10-second count down.

The M229 opened up once more, and it looked like it took another legionnaire out. Then all sensors went crazy as the legionnaires opened fire. The first casualty was the M229 team. Something big hit them, and a column of flames lit up the area.

The fractured array shielding should have made the first shots fired at the Marines miss them, but the artillery piece itself didn't have the shielding, and once it fired, it gave up the gun team's position.

With the sensors locking in on the legionnaires, the displays started placing them, and the Marines started to get visuals on them as well. One of the three legionnaires being funneled into the blast area of Evan's filed expedient mine stopped, probably to fire, but the other two kept advancing. The timing couldn't have been better. The mine erupted, a slow, powerful blast that lifted the two legionnaires into the air at least 20 meters before sending them crashing back down.

Another Gazelle fired, but it went over Cpl Rey's head to impact on the trees well behind the Marines. Immediately, at least 20 rockets were fired at the point of launch for the missile. Ryck couldn't tell if they hit anything, but no more Gazelles were fired.

To his left, the shuttle's 25mm gun opened up. It was not aimed, but it created a stream of fire a meter and a half above the ground. A few trees had been strategically knocked down, so the gun was able to cover the entire platoon front. At least one legionnaire was hit, although Ryck couldn't tell if it was a lethal strike or not. A number of hadron beams reached out to it, too many for Ryck's display to number, and ten seconds later, the gun stopped firing.

The legionnaires had something else, something bigger. From way back, there was a blast, followed by an explosion not 10 meters from Ryck. Khouri and Stillwell's icons went grey.

"Khouri, you OK?" he asked, knowing he wouldn't get a response.

The lieutenant was shouting orders over the circuit, trying to get frontage covered as Marines were knocked out. Ryck fired his remaining rockets at the far weapon, whatever it was. The moment it fired, though, it was withdrawn behind a tree, and all of Ryck's rockets impacted on the trees between them. Ryck knew it would take timing and luck to take the weapon out with a rocket. It fired again, but the same trees that protected it gave it a limited field of fire of its own, and it nicked a tree, enough to throw the round off target. It impacted into the dirt in front of one of Second Squad's position, showering the Marines with clods of dirt.

Martin's icon went grey. There hadn't been an explosion, so a hadron beam must have gotten him. Three of Ryck's squad were already gone. Ryck couldn't keep track, of the entire battlefield, but he only knew of three legionnaires down.

The legionnaires' headlong rush had stopped. They had thought to run over the Marines, but the defensive fire was too heavy. However, using the trees as protection, they started a war of attrition. Their big gun, whatever it was, kept pounding away, taking out five Marines from First from the center of the line.

Ryck kept watching the ammo counts of his squad dwindle. Hartono fired his plasma gun, but the distance, coupled with the smoke which lingered, dissipated the beam, and if it hit anyone, the legionnaire's armor was more than able to withstand it. To make matters worse, Hartono's power supply dropped to 38% after firing.

"Hartono, no more P-guns. We're too far. That goes for everyone, only at point-blank range!" he passed.

Ryck leveled his M-77 and chewed up a tree in back of which a legionnaire stood. It was only 50 cm across, so it couldn't give the legionnaire complete cover, but it offered a degree of protection. Ryck's 8mm darts quickly chewed through the wood, dropping the tree, and the legionnaire ran to the next one. Ryck knew his darts hit him, but they didn't slow the man down.

Keiji scored another hit on a legionnaire 80 meters away. This was the second hit at the same spot, and it blew off the arm of the R-3.

"The arms are not as strong as the torso," Ryck passed on the platoon circuit. "Try for that!"

"You heard him," the lieutenant followed up. "Aim for the extremities."

With the Marines firing, it was difficult for the legionnaire's to hold their hadron guns on target long enough to take out a Marine. The effect was cumulative, though, if they could hit the Marines often enough in a short period of time. Twice now, Ryck had been hit, but each time for only seconds before answering fire made the legionnaire firing at him break off to take cover. His shielding was down to 82%, though.

Their most effective remaining weapon was their HGL. There were only six Marines, though, with functional HGLs, and they were running low on ammo. When those rounds ran out, there wasn't much that would keep the legionnaires from concentrating their hadron guns on them. Ryck didn't know how many charges the hadron guns had, but they could fire much, much longer than the Marines' plasma guns.

"Lieutenant, Keiji and Holleran are down to a 10% load each. Do you think it's time?" Ryck asked?

"They're still too far away," the lieutenant replied. "Too much time exposed."

Another explosion sounded down the line, and two more icons went grey.

"I've got two more down," Cpl St. Cyr passed, his voice fast and excited. "We're getting slammed."

The lieutenant had put Second Squad in the middle, thinking the two squads with more experienced squad leaders could help support him. Instead, the squad had been taking the brunt of the fire.

"Lieutenant, we didn't figure they'd have some sort of big gun, and it's going to eat us up. Maybe we've just got to go for it?" SSgt Hecs said.

There was a pause, then the lieutenant answered, "Maybe you're right. OK, Third, tell your two HGL gunners to cease fire. First, tell one of yours. Maybe they'll think they are out of ammo and advance. The rest of you, you know the plan. Get ready. I'll give the command, but it will be soon.

*This is crazy*, Ryck thought, *but who the hell knows?*

Standing pat was a sure path to defeat, he knew. In previous engagements over the last 50 years, the Marines always had the technological advantage. But this time, the difference in energy weapons was the deciding factor. The R-3 might not be as good as they thought, but the hadron gun was light years ahead of the Marines' P-guns.

Ryck took out his six toads. Ryck was perhaps the only living Marine who had ever taken out an enemy with a toad. They were not designed for fighting but rather burning through things, but watching Evans burn the Gazelle launcher and Prifit's PICS had convinced Ryck that they would burn through the R-3 armor. After getting a close-up look at it, Ryck couldn't believe the R-3 armor itself was stronger than the PICS LTC[48] armor.

Cpl Evans had given him two of his much more powerful bullfrogs. Now all Ryck had to do was to somehow get them on the legionnaires. Both the toads and bullfrogs were sticky lumps of synthetic pyro, and once put on something, they stuck, so even tossing them at a legionnaire would work. But it was a fair bet that a legionnaire wouldn't just stand there and play catch.

Ryck coated his right gauntlet with the silicon spray that would keep the little hellfires from sticking to his hand. He was ready. Another icon, this one in First Squad, went grey.

---

[48] LTC: Lutetium Tungsten Carbide

"You ready, Ryck?" the lieutenant asked. "I think you'll appreciate this."

Ryck wondered what his platoon commander meant.

"Come on you sons-o'-bitches! Do you want to live forever?" the lieutenant shouted as en masse, the bulk of the platoon got out of their fighting holes and charge forward.

Despite himself, Ryck laughed out loud as he left the slight safety of his hole. They were going "over the top," so what better quote? Dan Daly would be proud. And just as in Belleau Wood so many years ago, the Marines answered the call.

Immediately, hadron beams lanced out at them. If the legionnaires had been surprised at the charge, the certainly recovered quickly. Ryck was aware of the beam, aware of his shields going down, but he pushed forward. He angled to where Evans had set up his own mines, where the legionnaires were avoiding. Then he angled back. He had to get close. It took him only five seconds once under fire to close the distance, and suddenly, there not five meters in front of him, was a legionnaire, stepping backwards, gunport open, and covering him with fire.

Ryck leveled one blast of his plasma gun, and the legionnaire collapsed. Ryck felt a thrill run through him. He had been sure the more powerful plasma gun would knock out an R-3 if they could only get close enough.

"P-guns will take them down" he shouted on the circuit as he ran forward.

A shape formed to his left, and as he turned, he saw another legionnaire pouring fire downrange. His plasma gun hadn't recharged, and firing it again might deplete his power, so he tossed the toad in his hand at the unsuspecting legionnaire. The man didn't seem to even know the toad landed, but as it sparked and started to burn, he would soon enough. Ryck just hoped that it would be before whichever Marine the legionnaire was firing at went down under the man's beam.

Something hit Ryck in the arm, hard enough to actually jerk it out of position. Ryck was still functioning, so he kept moving.

His display gave the alarm at another touch of a beam, but it stopped as Ryck ran farther, whether from that legionnaire being taken out or because Ryck just ran out of the line of fire, he didn't know. What he did know was that he was down to 28% on his shields.

Then he was past the bulk of the legionnaires, much to his surprise. Of course, that meant that any security forces there would focus on him. Another Marine had broken through, as well. It took a second, but Ryck realized it was the lieutenant. Behind them, more and more Marine icons were going light blue or grey. But in front of them, the only identified red icons were on the gun team that had been wreaking havoc on the platoon.

"Let's get them, Ryck," the lieutenant said as they matched stride in rushing ahead.

Then they got a visual on the gun and two Legionnaires manning it. It looked like a fat mortar, even if it was leveled in direct fire mode. Ryck didn't recognize it, but he didn't have to. All he had to do was destroy it.

With his power down, Ryck didn't know how well his fractured array would be working. He could see that the gun team knew they were coming. They were physically yanking the gun around to face them. Ryck knew they would be able to fire before the lieutenant and he could reach them, and it was still too far away for a P-gun shot.

From beside him, the lieutenant let loose four rockets. He'd rationed his out better than Ryck. Two hit one of the gunners in the chest, the other in the left arm. The legionnaire immediately wheeled around, clutching his arm. He was not out, but down for the moment, at least.

Ryck had nothing, so he continued his charge. He could see the other legionnaire touch something, and Ryck knew this was it. There was a flash, but Ryck kept running. He felt a moment of elation until he realized that the lieutenant was down.

The gunner was furiously trying to reload another electrostatically-jacketed round. If this had been an auto-fire gun, Ryck would be dead. But this was a single-shot gun, probably to make it more portable. Whatever the reason, Ryck was able to close the distance.

The gun was the first priority, so Ryck slapped one of the bullfrogs on it as he jumped over the gun. He collided with the gunner, who had just started to deploy his personal weapon. Stupid move. If he had done that sooner, depending on what weapon he had, he might have been able to stop Ryck before he reached the man. Instead, the collision with Ryck sent the man flying. Ryck just had to reach over to put a toad on the man's chest. He turned to the one with the damaged arm, who had started to run around his downed buddy. He grabbed another toad just as the screams of the first legionnaire reached him over the man's speakers. The first man heard the screams too, and before Ryck could react, he turned and took off. Ryck threw the toad, but he misjudged the lead, and he missed the man by centimeters. He started to give chase, but it was obvious that among other strengths, the R-3 was also faster. Ryck gave up after less than seconds.

The circuit was alive with messages. It was only then that Ryck paused to give himself an update. What he saw made his heart fall. He could see that 14 Marines had been greyed out, another eight were light blue. In less than five minutes, 14 Marines had died. He couldn't take time to identify each one.

He ran back to the lieutenant. The platoon commander was down, one leg gone mid-thigh, the other canted at an awkward angle. The bulk of his PICS was intact, and it had started treatment. He was out cold, but alive. Ryck looked back at the now-destroyed gun. Depending on the type of round, the fuze may not have had time to arm, but the sheer velocity of it was enough to cut down the lieutenant.

There was no time to tend him. He had to get back to the fight. He started running forward when he realized that the fighting was slowing down. The legionnaires were pulling back!

There was an explosion as one of them ran too close to one of Evan's mines, but Ryck couldn't tell the amount of damage the mine might have inflicted. Several legionnaires appeared in front of him. Ryck tossed two of his toads. One missed, but the other struck one of the legionnaires on the lower leg. Both fired at Ryck as they passed, and his alarms went off, but they were not going to stop to keep Ryck under fire.

Ryck turned to see the toad ignite, and the legionnaire started kicking out. A chunk of his R-3 went flying, taking the toad with it. The man went to one knee, then got back up and limped off. Ryck watched all of this from less than 40 meters away without interference.

The battle was over, and Ryck went back to survey the carnage. It was more than he expected. Even when faced by a better-armed force, he had expected to come out victorious. And even if the Marines had "won," if they had carried the field, it was a Pyrrhic victory. Fourteen Marines were dead, including Sams. Sams! From his own squad, Cpl Rey and Cpl Mendoza, Hartono and Martin were dead. With Khouri and Stillwell from earlier, Ryck had six KIA just today. Add Prifit, and he'd lost seven Marines, seven friends. Cpl Winsted and Keiji were down, but alive, but Ryck didn't know how bad they were.

Only Ling, Holleran, and Peretti were combat effective. With Ryck, only four men, just a fire team, were left.

Ryck vomited in his PICS. He gut heaved until there was nothing left.

"Sgt L, what are your orders?"

Ryck managed to look up, vomit dripping from his chin. Cpl St. Cyr was on a P2P with him.

"What?" he asked stupidly.

"What are your orders? You've got the platoon now."

He'd been so concerned with his squad that he'd barely noticed the rest. SSgt Hecs was light blue. HM2 Grbil had the same rank as Ryck, but as a Marine, command fell to him. He was the senior man. He did a quick check. Including the four of them from Third Squad, he had eight Marines and a corpsman. Nine Federation fighting men to hold off a larger Legion force.

He didn't know what to do.

## Chapter 22

"So, what do we do about them? Both are probably going to die unless they get into stasis," Doc asked him.

Ryck looked at the two legionnaires. One was missing an arm and was thankfully unconscious. The other was terribly burned, from the shoulder down through his chest and into his gut and hip. Ryck could see organs exposed in amongst the blackened flesh. The smell was overpowering, and it threatened to make Ryck vomit again. The legionnaire was conscious, and he stared blankly up at Ryck.

Using the toads had been Ryck's idea, and it had seemed so logical at the time. Now he was seeing the effects, what it meant on a personal level.

"You can't do anything else for them?" he asked Doc, who was waiting for a decision.

"Not really. I've cleaned around the damage, but they need help, fast. Especially Gary here," he pointed at the burned legionnaire. "Sorry man, but you should know," he said directly to the man.

*Shit, Gary? He knows the guy's name?* Ryck thought.

"He's got a falling hemoglobin count, renal failure, and is going into dehydration. The pain is manageable because the nerves have been burnt, but I can't keep his fluids going. He needs intensive care and a long bout of regen, and he needs to get in stasis now," Doc went on, addressing Ryck again.

"And we've got only those last two ziplocks?"

"Yeah, that's it. We never, I mean, before . . ." the corpsman started.

"Not your fault. You've took your combat issue. If you hadn't split them up and put those in the bottom of your hole, all of them would have been fried," Ryck assured him.

Before the battle, Doc had broken up his kit, putting half in the bottom of a fighting hole, the other half he carried. When he rushed out to pull back LCpl Dodson in the middle of the fight, he'd been taken under fire. He'd been under the hadron beam for about five seconds, enough for his PICS to survive, but it had fried the ziplocks in his pack. Only the ziplocks he'd had in the hole, out of the reach of energy beams, had survived the battle.

Ryck stopped to survey the scene in front of him. Ling and Denny, the Marine who'd been on OP duty and so had missed the fight, were in their PICS and providing security. Cpl St. Cyr was supervising the Peretti and PFC Stamos, one of the surviving Second Squad Marines, in the gathering of the dead legionnaires. Despite the low energy levels in everyone's PICS, the lifting required strength, so the two Marines were in their combat suits. Six legionnaires were lined up to the right of the platoon flank. There were five more, including the one Ryck had killed back at their field piece, left to gather.

On their left flank, 14 Marines were laid out. Cpl Rjils, who had survived the fight, had died before he could get into stasis. Ryck knew Doc blamed himself for that, but LCpl Truth in Means had been just as badly off, and Doc picked Truth in Means first.

In back of the lines, just over the slight crest, eight Marines were in ziplocks, stasis units on. Ryck turned to look at them. Each Marine had his longjohns cut away, and some showed signs of Doc's field treatment. The lieutenant was in the third ziplock, one leg gone, the other in a pressure bandage. He looked small in the bag, not like the warrior he'd proven himself to be. Ryck knew that could have been him in that ziplock just as easily.

SSgt Hecs had most of his left shoulder gone, as well as the arm. The white bandages stood out in stark contrast to his dark skin. Two of the Marines looked undamaged, but the other five showed obvious scars from the fight. They reminded Ryck of photos he'd seen of fetuses in the womb--fetuses who'd been roughed up, that was.

Two Marines were walking wounded, which was somewhat rare. In modern warfare, anything that could take out a PICS usually took out the Marine inside as well. Stefan Wilz' PICS had started to fail, the shielding on the arm giving out just as the hadron beam quit. Stefan's arm had been immediately paralyzed, but the last gasps of the rest of his PICS shielding had protected his vital organs. His arm was going to have to come off and be regened, but he wasn't in pain and could function for the near term.

Wilz' fellow First Squad Marine, LCpl Cashew, had taken a huge blow to the head that the PICS had withstood, but even with the cradling, his head had bounced back and forth, giving him a concussion. He was groggy and had a headache, but he could manage.

Two legionnaires were also seriously hurt and had been recovered by the Marines, and Doc wanted to know if they should use their last two precious ziplocks to save their lives.

"On the *Marie's Best*, you went into the ziplock with John. Can you do that here?" Ryck asked.

Doc stood back and looked at the two men.

"How much do you weigh, Gary?" he asked the legionnaire.

"Seventy-eight," the man mumbled.

"And let's say another 80 kg for this guy? Yeah, that should be within limits," Doc said.

"OK, we can't let these guys die, so just put them both in one, and that leaves one for us," Ryck said, coming to a decision.

*One for 11 men*, he reminded himself.

"Roger. I'll get on it," Doc said.

"Thanks, man. I appreciate it," the legionnaire, Gary, said to Ryck, his words slurred, but clear.

Ryck didn't want the guy's thanks. He just hoped that he hadn't put the rest of the Marines in danger.

He went back to where his PICS stood in silence. He'd managed to clean up most of the vomit, but the inside of the suit still smelled. He was down to 22% on his PICS. There wasn't much he could do about that. He could change out his coldpack, though. A suit that overheated was combat ineffective just as much as one that had been fried. This was his last coldpack, but with the casualties, that wasn't something he had to worry about. There were more than enough coldpacks available now for all the surviving Marines. That macabre thought threatened to take over, and Ryck had to force his mind back to the task at hand.

His M77, though was a total loss. That was what had been hit during the battle, and something had actually broken the barrel, making it hang at an odd angle. Even if he could find a way to reload, that rifle was not going to be firing again.

He could putter around his PICS, but his real task was to decide what to do now. He could strengthen the defenses the best he could. He could move men to somewhere else and try to keep out of contact. Or he could take the fight to the legionnaires.

He knew what Sams would have done. Sams would have rushed into the attack. He couldn't help but glance to where Sams' body was lying on the ground. He wanted to go over there to tell him the joke was over, to just get up and get back to business. Irreverent Sams, ladies' man, and one hell of a Marine. More than that, Sams was his friend.

Frankly, Ryck wasn't sure what was the correct action. Honoring Sams' wishes could get them all killed. Maybe attacking was the right course of action, but maybe not. His lack of intel was frustrating. He had to know how many legionnaires were combat effective.

Ryck knew for certain that twelve legionnaires had been killed: 11 here and one back near the French sailors. Two more were ziplocked and out of the fight. At least three more had been hurt, and Ling had reported seeing another three being helped out of the area. So there were possibly 20 out of the fight, but at a minimum, 14. But how many had they started with? The lieutenant had guessed they'd had close to the Marines' own 32 before the last fight. That meant they could have anywhere from 12 to 18 left. Ryck had nine effectives and two walking wounded left to face them.

"Lieutenant Nidishchii', Capitaine de corvette Benyamina is offering a temporary cease-fire in order to take care of our dead and wounded. If you agree to this, please respond," came over Ryck's PICS' speaker.

Ryck had powered down most of his energy-eating functions, but the comms had been left open.

*Capitaine de corvette?* That was the Navy equivalent to a Marine major or Federation lieutenant commander. That was probably the correct rank for a gunboat captain, but why was the Navy getting involved? They were out of the fight as far as Ryck knew.

He reached his PICS and toggled the mic. He almost gave his rank and name then thought better of it.

"You've reach the Federation Marines. What are you proposing?" he sent.

"During today's . . . " there was a pause, " . . . *conflict*, 13 legionnaires did not return. We proposed a three-hour truce so we both can recover our fallen. We are open to your terms, of course."

Ryck looked around at their position. Doc caught his eye and began pointing towards their wounded. They had placed the WIA in back of the slight crest of the high ground in an attempt to keep them out of the line of any energy weapons fire. Just one touch, though, and the ziplocks would fail, the stasis fields with them.

"Wait one, Legion," Ryck said.

"What do you think?" he passed on the open circuit to the rest of the Marines.

"If we can get the WIAs out of the line of fire, I'm all for it," Doc responded.

"Vic?" Ryck asked Cpl St. Cyr.

"It's your call, but if they're sincere, we can use the break and take care of our people," the corporal answered.

*Aye, there's the rub,* Ryck thought. *Is this a trick?*

In all this dealings with the Legion, they had acted honorably, even if they were at times arrogant. Ryck made his decision quickly. He went back onto the frequency the Legion had used.

"We agree in principle. We have eleven Legion dead here, two severely wounded and in stasis. You are welcome to come get them. We want to move our own WIA to a safe location out of the way of any potential areas of *conflict*," he said, stressing the same word the legionnaire on the other side had used.

"You have two of our wounded? May we know their names and condition?"

Ryck knew he only was required to give the names of enemy prisoners to the Red Cross, but he didn't hesitate.

"One answers to Gary. He was severely burnt. He was conscious before going into stasis, but he's in pretty serious condition. We don't have the name of the second man. He suffered a traumatic amputation of his arm and is in stasis now as well."

There was a pause, then, "We thank you for the care of our wounded. Will you be moving your own wounded to the same location as the rest of your wounded?"

*Shit! They knew where the others were.*

Ryck would've liked to get all of the WIAs together, but there wasn't any way he could move eight Marines and two legionnaires that distance with the men he had. That didn't even take into account the dead.

"That's a negative. Are you able to take a grid coordinate?" he asked.

Grid coordinates were just arbitrary points, and there was no guarantee that the French used the same ones as the Federation.

"Yes, we can," came the reply.

Ryck picked out a point about 700 meters off the left flank of their position and sent the coordinates. He couldn't transport the wounded far, but he didn't want to give the French any opportunity to view their defenses. And if the French agreed to his next condition, that would close off one potential avenue of approach.

"We will have your wounded and dead at this position in two hours. We require that there is no maneuver on your side until that time. You may approach with whatever size unit you need to retrieve your men, but no shielding will be engaged. The truce will remain for two hours after that. We will be leaving our own casualties at that spot, so after you withdraw, this area, bounded by the coordinates I sent, will remain a no-fire zone. I am sure you can appreciate the effects of energy weapons on our medical stasis units."

Ryck waited until the response came.

"We agree with your terms but wonder on the position. We think it might be close to your present position and possibly within range of collateral fire."

They realized what Ryck intended, he knew.

*Tough shit, take it or leave it.*

"We have the ability to honor a no-fire zone. I am assuming you have the same ability. This is the area which we have designated," he said.

There was another pause, then the voice came back, "Very well. We agree to your terms. It is now 0245 Paris Time. We will be at your coordinates as 0445. *Merci.*"

Ryck switched to the platoon circuit and passed, "OK, you heard that. We've got a four-hour truce. Everyone, into your PICS. We've got a lot to do and not much time."

He organized the platoon into work details. A PICS had the strength to carry all of their wounded but not the grip. To keep integrity on the ziplocks, to keep the life-saving bags from getting damaged, each Marine could carry only one ziplocked Marine at a time. With Doc trailing like a mother hen, each of the other eight healthy Marines picked up one of the WIAs and followed Ryck, who had the two legionnaires, to the spot he'd picked. It was just a coordinate chosen at random, nothing special from the map, and when they arrived, it looked no different than any other stretch of forest. Once the set down the WIAs, Ryck left Doc and Cashew with the wounded and jogged his Marines back to their position.

He half-expected that the legionnaires would have taken over the position while they were gone, but it was quiet. Each Marine, including Wilz, took the dead man's handle[49] on the back of those PICS that still had them, or if they didn't, on anything they could grab, and lifted their dead comrades to carry them to the no fire zone. They had to help Wilz hoist Cpl Franks to his shoulder, but once up, the one-armed Marine had no problem. It took two trips, but all the Marines had been moved. Ryck looked at the time. They had an hour left.

The legionnaires, with sleeker armor on their R-3s had less to grab onto, and several times, the dead legionnaires were dropped, but once again with two trips, each legionnaire was carried to the spot.

Ryck took a look at his Marines. They were a grubby lot, the fighting marring their PICS. Ling and Denny looked the best of them, and Denny had the greatest charge on his PICS, so Ryck told both of them, along with Cashew, to stay. He gave Sgt St. Cyr his

---

[49] Dead Man's Handle: the slang term for a handle on the back of each PICS that is used to pick up and carry it should the PICS become immobilized.

orders. He concluded with what St. Cyr should do if this was a Legion trap.

"If that happens, you're in charge. I'm not going to tell you what to do then. You're going to have to make that decision."

The corporal looked like he was going to say something, but he stopped and followed the rest back to their position.

Ryck looked around him. He had three Marines with him, to face who knew what. He was going to do this in good faith, though. No surprises, no hidden Marines. He checked over the WIAs, then took a position in the center of them. He had the other three Marines stand in back of him. Cashew was wobbly and not totally with it, but all he had to do was stand.

At 0425, Ryck's sensors went off, indicating movement in front of him. The contacts slowly made their way forward, slower than expected. He counted three R-3s, then readings for two more people.

At 0446, the group came into view. One legionnaire led the rest. Two sailors, a man and a woman, followed. Behind them were the last two legionnaires.

Ryck stood still as the first legionnaire walked up to within five meters of him. His face shield was clear, as if he had nothing to hide. A ruddy, round face stared at him. Freckles were plastered across his nose and cheeks.

"Lieutenant . . . " he started, then obviously noticed the sergeant's chevrons Ryck had illuminated on his combat suit's shoulders.

"I'm representing the Federation here," Ryck said.

Ryck could almost see the legionnaire's thoughts as the man's eyebrows scrunched together. He would be wondering if the lieutenant was out of action, or if he was back there somewhere, waiting and watching.

"Very well. Capitaine de corvette Benyamina would like to have word with you."

He stepped to the side, making way for Ryck. Ryck walked forward to the older sailor standing there and waited for the man to start.

It was the woman who spoke, and Ryck had to turn and face her. He felt embarrassed. He had often thought that women could serve just as well as men in the Federation military, and here he was, assuming that the gunship's captain had to be a man.

"Do you have a name?" the woman asked.

Ryck hesitated, but as they already knew his name as one of the platoon, he replied, "Sergeant Ryck Lysander, sir."

*Sir? Is it supposed to be ma'am or something like that?*

Capitaine de corvette Benyamina didn't seem to notice as she went on, "Sergeant Lysander, thank you for agreeing to this truce. And thank you especially for taking care of our wounded comrades. You and your commander are men of honor.

"With your permission, I would like to check our wounded?"

Ryck gave his consent, and the male sailor, who had on what Ryck only now noticed was the caduceus of the medical service on his collar, walked forward to where the legionnaires, both WIA and KIA, were laid out. If he thought it strange that two legionnaires were in a single ziplock, he said nothing. He peered at them through the clear walls of the bag and checked the stasis readout. He seemed satisfied and said something in French to his commander.

"We will be removing our two wounded men first, then return for our fallen. If time becomes short, may we contact you for an extension?" she asked Ryck.

"Let's see how the time goes. We will be leaving LCpl Cashew here," Ryck said, pointing at the Marine.

That seemed to take her aback, and she said, "This is new to me. I thought this was to be a no-fire area."

"LCpl Cashew has a concussion. He will not be returning with us," Ryck said, keeping his voice steady, and with what he hoped sounded like conviction.

"Yet he is in your combat suit, which you must acknowledge is an offensive weapon," she countered.

"And as I am sure you have been briefed, our PICS have some basic medical capability. Our corpsman has stressed to me that it would be best if LCpl Cashew remain in his PICS."

"If you keep an armed soldier here, I will have to re-evaluate our position for this area at the conclusion of the truce, Sergeant.

You may tell your commander that. Our soldiers will not purposely fire on your wounded, but we would have to treat this area as a potential for combat operations. Would you reconsider your position on that? For the good of your wounded?" she asked.

Ryck thought about it. Cashew, although ambulatory, was in no condition to fight. He barely knew where he was. There was a hard and fast rule in the Marines, and that was not to separate a Marine from his weapon. Cashew's rockets were all expended, though, and while he had 52 rounds left for his M77, those had shown to have little to no effect on the Legion's R-3s.

"If I removed his M77, that gun on his arm, would that satisfy you?" he asked.

The Navy officer went silent, most likely listening to what one of the three legionnaires was telling her over their comms. Ryck wondered if one of them would call Ryck on Cashew's P-gun.

He was relieved when she turned towards him and said, "If you can remove it, that will be satisfactory."

Ryck nodded, something that the PICS read and moved the suit up and down in an approximation. He turned and walked up to Cashew.

"Sergeant Lysander, what was that? You're taking my M77?" Cashew asked on the open circuit, his speech still slurred.

Ryck switched both of them to a P2P. "Look, uh, Spence," he said, after checking Cashew's readout to get his first name. Ryck had forgotten that.

"You've got 52 darts left, and they won't do anything against the R-3s. We need to keep our WIAs safe, and that means here out of the line of the line of fire. I want you to guard them, OK?"

"But how, without a weapon?"

"You've got your P-gun, right? They don't realize that," Ryck said.

"Oh, right. But I can go with you and the lieutenant and fight. I'm good to go."

"I know you are, but I need you here, Spence. I need you to watch over everyone. The lieutenant's here, not back there. He needs you here."

Cashew didn't like the idea of not going back, but orders were orders. Ryck went to remove the M77, but realized he hadn't any armorer tools. The Marines didn't know what to do, but finally went with brute force. With Ling and Denny holding Cashew's arm steady, Ryck grabbed the M77, barely getting his gauntlet fingers under it, then gave it six good yanks. On the sixth, the M77 broke free, the barrel breaking off the receiver embedded in the arm of the PICS.

The gunship commander watch closely, and once Ryck held up the barrel of the M77, she nodded. She signaled the two quiet legionnaires, and they moved forward to their KIAs.

"Taking a Marine's weapon, that's a keister kick circus," someone said.

Ryck turned to see that the legionnaire, the first one to speak, had spoken to him through a directional speaker, which from the look of things, could not be overheard by the rest of his team.

"Don't worry, though, I didn't mention his plasma gun. It's a piece of shit, but a man's gotta have something, you know?"

Ryck didn't know how to respond.

"It's not like he's gonna need it. The captain is by-the-fucking-book, but would never go back on her honor, so no matter what happens, we won't be back here. We've left your guys back at your shuttle alone, too. That's some sailor-boy you've got there, though, by the way. The guy was about shitting his pants when we came up, but he stood up to us, telling us we had to go through him to get at your wounded. No weapons, and he's gonna hold off a bunch of us in our Rigs?"

*The shuttle crew chief?*

Ryck didn't even remember the guy's name, but he'd have to find that out if they ever made is through this. The guy evidently had balls.

Ryck looked at the legionnaire, wondering just what the man's game was. He seemed sincere, though, and that was surprisingly disarming.

"Hey, where you from?" Ryck asked for lack of anything better to say.

The others turned towards him when he said that. Ryck didn't have a direction speaker, and his voice went out in surround sound.

"Why you askin'?" the legionnaire asked, voice suddenly wary.

Ryck did a quick scan of available nets and directed his AI to initiate a P2P with the legionnaire. To his surprise, a direct connection was made.

"You there?" he asked.

"Yeah, so again, why you askin'?"

"It's just, my dad, he always said that, a 'keister kick circus.' He said it was an Ellison thing."

"No farting? You from Ellison?"

"He said that, too, 'no farting,'" Ryck said with a laugh. "No, my parents were from Ellison, but they immigrated to Prophesy before I was born."

"Got out when they could. Smart folks, your parents. Yeah, Ellison born and raised. Took the Legion route out of town, and I've never looked back. Lots of guys do that."

"Not too many Marines from Ellison, though," Ryck said.

"No farting, Castor. We all go Legion. It was the Marines that broke the general strike in '24. Killed lots of folks. So the Marines are persona non grata."

Ryck vaguely remembered reading about that. Ellison was a true corporate world, and there had been a worker uprising, not a strike, as this guy was saying. Ryck's grandparents on both sides had been alive then, but he'd never heard any family stories of the time from his parents.

"But that's old news. It's a new age. Who ever thought that GF and the Fed would be at war?" the guy said.

Ryck was suddenly struck at how surreal this was. Greater France and the Federation were at war. A few hours ago, Ryck and this legionnaire had been doing their best to kill each other. Now this guy was chatting as if they were long-lost cousins.

He had an urge to ask the legionnaire how he could still be fighting for the Legion. Whatever the Federation did in his grandparents time, Ellison was still a Federation world.

"Well, the captain is calling. Looks like we're gonna start hauling the cargo. Nice meeting you," the guy said.

"Hey, you know Ezekiel Hope-of-Life?" Ryck asked.

"No, not really. He a friend of yours?"

"My girlfriend's brother. He's Legion."

"No, sorry. But it a big Legion, as they say. Look, I gotta run. Hope we don't meet again until the politicos get their heads out of their keisters and end this cluster."

"Sure. Uh, good luck," Ryck said to the legionnaire's retreating back.

"Name's Meyers. Coltrain Meyers. Look me up sometime when this is over, and I'll buy you a beer."

## Chapter 23

The truce was officially long gone, but through the night and next day, there had been no sign of the legionnaires. Ryck wracked his brain for a way to take the fight to the Legion, but he couldn't think of anything that would give them even a 10% chance at success. He convened a "war council" of the rest of the Marines and Doc, but no one else had any decent ideas, either.

He kept hoping that the Navy would get back, taking the matter out of his hands, but the airwaves remained silent. He had no idea what was happening out there in the space lanes.

Ryck was a Marine, and now in command of a fighting force. He was supposed to be aggressive. Yet, he was secretly wishing that the legionnaires had been hurt badly, too badly to want to tangle again. On one hand, his emotions threatened to take over when he thought about the Marine dead and wounded. He wanted to extract revenge. On the other hand, the rational part of him realized that the legionnaires were just doing their job. Coltrain Meyers was no different than he was, and his comment was telling. The legionnaires and Marines were not fighting each other because of some deep-seated hate. They were fighting because the politicos were playing statesmanship games, maneuvering for a better hand. This was about economics and who was able to pocket the most.

Just because Ryck couldn't come up with a decent plan to attack the Legion, and just because he hoped the two groups would not clash again, did not mean he could just sit there on his butt doing nothing. He had to plan for the worst. And once he decided to stay in their present position, that meant coming up with a better defensive plan. He didn't have much in the way of resources, so he had to out-think any attackers.

They didn't much in the way of intel. They didn't know where the legionnaires were. They didn't know how many there were or what they had left in the way of weapons. But Ryck had formed several opinions that, if correct, might be put to use.

First, the vaunted R-3's, or "rigs" as Meyers had referred to them, were not as invincible as they were made out to be. They had hadron guns, true, and those were as advertised. However, the armor on the R-3 was not as good as that on a PICS. Their stealth capability disappeared when their gun ports opened, and that capability only worked when they were out of visuals, anyway. The fractured array of the PICS seemed to work even when in line-of-sight, leading Ryck to believe the R-3's relied on electronics even when using visuals, unlike the PICS where the eyeball saw what was through the face shield.

Second, the legionnaires seemed pretty confident in themselves. They had hurt the Marines in their attack, but a frontal attack was something you only did when you knew you had overwhelming superiority of numbers or capability. Ryck had been on a number of frontal assaults, but always when they could overwhelm the enemy. He had to think the Legion worked the same way. But the fact that the Marines had taken out so many legionnaires was a good indication that even without air, even without Navy support, man-for-man, the Marines were a match for the legionnaires. His short chat with Meyers wasn't all revealing, but the man had sounded confident.

How Ryck was going to make use of those guesses and observations, he wasn't sure, but he had to come up with something.

The issued mines were still emplaced surrounding their position. They hadn't worked in the first assault, but they still formed a barrier by their mere presence. Ryck had Evans make two more of his improvised mines, but without a timer, he had to rig up simple pressure plates. That meant a legionnaire would actually have to step on a mine to set it off. There was only a small chance of that, but any chance had to be taken. Ryck had the position of the two mines entered into the PICS of the Marines so that even in the heat of battle, if it got to that, each member of the platoon would know where the mines were. These mines had no way to distinguish between friend or foe.

Ryck had managed to salvage two more dragonflies. He sent these, along with his last one, out to the most probable avenues of approach. The dragonflies had limited power, normally good for about two hours of total flight time, so he landed them on high branches and powered them down, only using enough juice to send back feeds. It wasn't a perfect warning system, but with the vibration sensors still out there, he thought they would get a good warning in case of someone approaching.

The shuttle's 25mm gun was still working. When the legionnaires had fired on it during the fight, they had used their hadron guns. That had killed Cpl Stuyvestent and PFC Bokaw, but the beam had no effect on the gun itself. It would have taken a shipboard hadron gun to put out enough power to slag metal, and as they didn't even have any electronics for the gun, nothing was affected. At the base level, it was just an iron sight gun, like an old WWI machine gun. Without its advanced targeting system, it was, in a sense, too primitive to be hurt by the most modern weapons technologies. Of course, that old Vickers gun was designed to be fired with the technology of the time, so it would have been more accurate than the 25mm being fired as the modern gun no longer had any targeting capability. Still, the round itself was deadly to anyone in an R-3. If the Marines could hit them, the legionnaires would go down.

The shuttle's gun was still functional. The same could not be said of the M229. Its firing electronics were fused, so even if the barrel and breach were sound, it could not send a round downrange. Ryck had six rounds for it, but no way to use them. With their electrostatic jacketing, Evans couldn't even come up with a way to jury-rig them into something more useful.

Power reserves on each PICS were woefully low. Without the proper tools, Ryck couldn't even switch out powerpacks with those from any of the fallen Marine's PICS that still had some degree of functionality. Technically, there was a way to vampire power from one suit to another, but that required cabling that Ryck didn't have. Ryck kept everyone out of the suits as much as he could, but some of the preparations required the strength of a PICS, and there was no getting around that.

By the middle of the next night, Ryck had a good deal of his preparations completed. He half-expected an attack during the night. With both the Marines and Legion's equipment, night and day made little difference. But his men were dead on their feet, and Ryck needed them combat effective. He put six men asleep at a time, keeping up a three-man watch. Ryck took the first watch along with Ling and Perreti.

When he awoke the next morning, the sun was already climbing high in the sky. The night had been quiet. Today, he thought, would be an important one.

Ryck had read in the civilian military journals, which seemed to be enamored with all things Legion, that the R-3's could operate for four days on a single power charge. This was the fourth day. True, the legionnaires could have been getting out of their R-3's and spending time with the suits powered down, but if they were within 60-70 km, the Marine's own sensors should have been able to pick up the cycling of the suits before the shielding was up to power. Ryck was betting that they were closer than that given the speed at which they had met him to retrieve their two WIA's. In addition, they had been in combat, and that would have depleted their power reserves as well. Ryck knew they had field generators, just as the Marines had, but just as the Marine's generator had gone down with the skipper, he thought any generator would have been destroyed when the *Intrepid* took out the French shuttles.

If there was going to be an attack, Ryck was sure it would happen today. Anything after that would be Marines in longjohns attacking legionnaires in their version of combat suit underwear with pointy sticks.

Ryck looked at their position. It was good, he thought. Possibly enough. But he had to do more. He just couldn't think of what.

"Evans, come here a sec," he called out.

The EOD corporal walked over and asked, "What's up?"

"I was just thinking, could we take those arty rounds and hoist them up in the trees over there? Then if they come, drop them on top of their heads?"

"Sure, I could rig something up. But we could do that with rocks, too. All it will do is piss them off."

"But the 889 can take out an R-3. We saw that two days ago," Ryck protested.

"Yes, and armed M889 round will destroy an R-3. An 887 would probably, too. But it takes 10 g's of pressure after the breach initiates the sequence to arm one of them, and dropping one from five meters high just won't do it. Sorry, Sergeant L, it just won't work," Evans told him.

"Oh, OK. I'm just trying to think out loud here."

"Look, Sergeant L, me and Nance, we were talking this morning. You've done a great job here, and we think we've actually got a chance if it comes to that. None of us two would've come up with half of this. So no matter what happens, even if the worst, well, we, I would say all of us, we're proud to be here with you."

Ryck was floored. He'd been feeling like a failure for not coming up with anything better. If the others were counting on him, well God help them with that, but it made Ryck feel honored. If this was going to be his last day, at least he was with men he respected, men about whom he felt proud.

"I . . . it is me who is proud. All of you," he said, speaking louder and addressing the rest of them. "All of you, I couldn't wish for a better group of Marines, of brothers. I am proud to be here with you."

There was a chorus of oohrahs from the Marines, from *his* Marines.

As if on cue, the alarm sounded from his PICS. Ryck ran over to it and clamored inside. The feed from one of the dragonflies was dead. Ryck ran back the recording, and just a few moments ago, it picked up the slightest movement in the trees before going dead. Ryck went back and froze it at the last second it was live, then had his AI enhance it. He couldn't see anything concrete, but he didn't have to. They were on their way.

"OK, Marines, enough of this mutual love fest. They're on their way. Everyone into your positions, now!"

There was the slight, almost inaudible hum as his PICS powered up. Ryck checked his power level first: 14%. This was going to be it, whatever *it* turned out to be, with this particular PICS. He checked the other suits as the powered up. None were over 22%.

PFC Ling and Pvt Peretti stopped in front of him and saluted. Ryck brought his PICS to attention and returned he salute to the two Marines standing in front of him in their longjohns. They were not going to be in their PICS. They had volunteered to man the 25 mm.

Each had a tarnkappe. A dead PICS had been dragged over in front of the gun, hopefully providing cover from any Legion sensors. In back of the gun, the two Marines were to hide under their tarnkappes, and when they had targets, they were to fire. Without their face shield displays, though, their AI's could not get enough data points to form an image of the legionnaires, so they would have to wait until the legionnaire's gun ports opened, spoiling their stealth profile. With the naked eye, though, even when under full stealth, the R-3's gave enough hints so the two Marines should be able to pick up something.

If they made it out of the fight, Ryck would make sure Peretti regained some of his lost rank and Ling got a meritorious promotion as well. If *anyone* made it out of this, Ryck would fight for meritorious promotions.

The Marines had no surprises downrange, unless someone stepped on one of the mines. They just had to sit and wait. A surprisingly few number of vibration sensors sounded—Ryck hoped that meant that the legionnaire numbers were few.

From over 500 meters out, Ryck's display started picking up readings. The AI's quickly identified them as two R-3's. There was no way they should be able to pick them up. That meant that either this was part of their cyberwarfare games, or more hopefully, that those two R-3's were damaged. Even if that were the case, Ryck still didn't know how many undamaged R-3's were out there.

They were not coming in from the same direction, into the teeth, such as they were, of the defense. They were working from the flank, evidently trying to roll up the Marines. Ryck had guessed correctly, but that still didn't ensure anything. He'd had two other contingencies depending on the legionnaire's approach, but this way, none of the Marines had to move to alternate positions.

*Keep it steady,* he silently thought to his men.

The legionnaires didn't stop their advance. Previously, their field piece had taken a deadly toll on the Marines, and if they had another, Ryck's plan would be stillborn. However, nothing was fired, and as the legionnaires closed to within 300 meters, Ryck let out a breath he hadn't realized he was holding. He now doubted they had another field piece.

Ryck's AI picked up another R-3. It's shielding was obviously in better condition, but not good enough. That was at least three legionnaires, by his count, all with some degree of damage, or at least degradation, to their suits.

Ryck watched his display closely, looking for any surprises. If the three in front were a feint, a force attacking from either side of them could be disastrous. With the legionnaire's this close, the Marines could not move to their alternate positions without giving themselves away.

A few moments later, the first legionnaire opened fire, suddenly appearing on Ryck's display. That was the fourth legionnaire identified. One of the previously noted legionnaire's opened fire, too.

*Steady!* Ryck willed on the rest.

Nine seconds later, the PICS 20 meters to Ryck's right front started to send up sparks before dying.

"Hell yeah!" he whispered excitedly to himself as the two more legionnaire's opened fire, one, someone brand new.

Five legionnaires were in the attack, firing at Marine PICS unheeded. The current target lasted only five seconds before going up. That was longer than Ryck had hoped. That had been SSgt Hecs' PICS, and it had been a miracle that they'd even been able to get the thing powered up. It had to have been leaking like a sieve, so the legionnaires couldn't have missed it.

Within moments, seven legionnaires were advancing, firing their hadron guns. In quick succession, four empty PICS were fried. The Marines only had three more that they'd managed to power up, or at least make them seem to be powered up, and then the seven of them that had the Marines and Doc inside, so Ryck was relieved when the legionnaires quit firing. They'd finally noticed that no one was firing back.

*Come on, baby, come one*, he thought. *Just a little closer.*

Ryck watched them on his display. They had stopped about 50 meters out. He wished he could listen in, but he imagined them trying to figure out what was up, what trick the Marines had planned.

After a few moments, two of the legionnaires retreated, as if to provide security.

*Grubbing shit!* thought Ryck.

He wanted them together, checking out the apparently abandoned position.

Five of them did come forward. Ryck crouched in his fighting hole, waiting. They were on complete passive sensing. They couldn't talk. Ryck knew there was no way the legionnaires could listen into one of their circuits, but the mere fact that there was a transmission would be enough to alert the legionnaires that not all of the PICS power emissions were from empty combat suits.

*Come on guys, it's up to you,* he pleaded with Peretti and Ling.

He was tempted to open up a comms link. They were the ones to initiate the attack.

When the 25 mm gun opened up, despite expecting it, Ryck about jumped out of his skin. With more of a scramble than a leap, he was out of the extra deep fighting hole he had dug.

In an instant, he saw that two of the legionnaires were down, the rest darting out of the way. Ryck threw the toad he had ready at the legionnaire nearest him, not even 15 meters away. The toad struck the legionnaire on the shoulder before bouncing off.

*What the . . . ?*

They'd adapted. They knew what a toad was, and had applied some sort of lubrication, like what the Marines used on their gauntlets to handle the toads, to their R-3's.

Their adjustment wasn't perfect, however. To his left, a toad was burning a hole in the hip of another legionnaire. The R-3 started to split open as the legionnaire inside initiated an emergency molt.

Ryck's alarms went off as a hadron beam touched him, but then the beam was gone.

The 25 mm continued its chatter, but unless the targets were already in the line of fire, it was hard to horse the thing around and aim it. One of the legionnaires leveled his arm at it, but instead of a beam, the muzzle of a KE gun appeared. It looked too big for the Legion version of the M77, so it was probably their 10 mm gun. The legionnaire fired a burst at Peretti and Ling, but then the guy took a direct hit from Cowboy, LCpl Manteo Silver, their last HGL gunner.

The legionnaire spun around, quicker than Ryck thought possible in a combat suit, and returned fire. Ryck started sprinting forward, but another hadron beam touched him, and he had to stop to throw his last toad. He missed the 20 meter throw, but the legionnaire saw the toad coming and stopped firing to get out of the way.

Meanwhile, the Cowboy and the legionnaire traded shots like old-time duelists until one of Cowboy's grenades broke through, and the legionnaire fell back, smoke pouring from what used to be his belly.

Things were happening quickly, and it was hard to keep track of events. Ryck saw Ling jumping over the PICS that had been used to mask the 25 mm, his gloved hand holding one of Evan's bullfrogs. In his longjohns, even the slightest touch of a hadron beam would kill him. Ryck wanted to tell him to get back, but Ling had taken matters into his own hand and had launched the bullfrog. Ryck couldn't see where it landed or even who was the target.

Ryck tried to find another target when beside, him, LCpl Denny exploded, blood and PICS parts pelting Ryck. Ryck stared for a moment in shock. One moment, Denny was there, the next, he was in pieces. One of the legionnaires, one of the two who had retreated to provide security, had charged back into the fray. He had another KE gun deployed, but what did they Legion have on its R-3's bigger than their 10 mm?

Anger flowed through Ryck. Denny was gone, just like that, and this mother grubbing fucker was to blame. The legionnaire had swung about to take another Marine under fire, and Ryck charged.

He had one weapon left, his plasma gun. His energy charge was at 9%. That had to be enough, he hoped with all his might. But he had to close the gap. He was too far away. He flipped off his attitude stabilizers to be able to coax the last bit of speed out of his tired PICS.

It took only seconds, but time slowed down. Twenty meters, fifteen. At 10, the legionnaire realized what was happening. He started to swing his gun around.

*Too late mother fucker!* Ryck thought with glee as he triggered his plasma gun.

And nothing happened.

Ryck's PICS simply didn't have enough power, which meant that without a weapon, Ryck was charging a fully armed legionnaire in an R-3.

By instinct, Ryck's training kicked in. MacPruitt's MCMA class flashed through his brain. He dropped down, almost to the ground as the legionnaire fired, the round going off over his head. From that position, he lunged forward as hard as he could as the legionnaire took a step back, another round going high.

Ryck hit the legionnaire in the chest with the force of a small tank. The R-3 had pretty powerful stabilizers of its own, and they increased power to keep the legionnaire upright, but they were not designed with a charging PICS in mind. Ryck and the legionnaire crashed to the ground, Ryck on top of his enemy.

"You mother fucker!" he screamed in almost inarticulate rage as he pulled back his gauntleted fist and smashed it into the legionnaire's face shield.

The legionnaire tried to struggle, to throw Ryck off of him, but his own R-3's attempts to right him back to his feet interfered with his efforts.

Ryck reared back and hit again, his mind losing itself in animalistic, single-minded violence.

"This is for Denny!" he screamed, hitting again.

"This is for Rey!" he shouted as he struck.

"This is for Hartono, for Priffit, for Khouri!"

*Bam, bam bam.* The face shield began to crack.

"Mendoza, Martin!"

The face shield shattered. As Ryck pulled his gauntleted hand back again, a ruddy, freckled face looked up at him, bloody and in sheer terror, mouth open to plead for his life. Ryck didn't hesitate.

"And this is for my friend Sams!" he shouted, driving his fist through the face shield mount and through the head of Coltrain Meyers, pulverizing it. Hunks of brain matter, bone splinters, and blood spattered over him, covering his own face shield and blocking most of his view.

Ryck didn't stop, again and again he struck, each time, going through the list of men, of brothers, who had fallen, not just here on this godforsaken planet, but since he'd been in the Corps.

Davis, Wan, Nbele, Smith, Peale, Popo--damn it all—Coudry, Rjils, Greuber , Dodson, even going back to recruit training with Yount and Hyunh. Stuyvestent , Bokaw. With each name, he pounded the legionnaire's corpse.

"Sergeant L, Sergeant L, it's over. You can stop," a voice finally registered.

The voice had been yammering on for a while, an incessant whine, but it only then started to coalesce into something her recognized as human speech. Ryck finally paused in his assault and looked up. He tried to wipe some of the mess on his face shield, but mostly just pushed it around. He could see Ling standing there though, in his longjohns. Two Marines in PICS stood beside him, but Ryck's face shield was too smeared to make out who they were.

"Huh?" he said in a daze.

"It's over Sergeant L," Ling told him, speaking slowly and clearly as if to a child. "It's over, and we won."

Ryck rolled off the dead legionnaire and slowly got to his feet. Tears and snot were flowing down his face.

It's over?

Ling said they'd won, but it sure the hell didn't feel that way, that anyone had won.

## Chapter 24

Ryck stared at Doc Grbil. The corpsman's face had finally relaxed. It had been a rough hour, and watching Doc pass had been painful, but Ryck was numb. He had no more tears to shed.

The son-of-a-bitch didn't need to have died. Three Marines had been killed in the final battle: Denny, Stamos, and Yuan. Peretti had been hit by shrapnel and suffered a serious head wound, and he needed stasis. One of the two surviving legionnaires, the one who had molted from his burning R-3, had also been seriously hurt with third-degree burns over a good portion of his body, and much of his flesh had been burnt away. Doc and the other legionnaire had also been wounded, but Doc assured Ryck that they would make it, and he needed to double up Peretti and the burned legionnaire in the last remaining ziplock. Despite his misgivings, Ryck gave the OK, not that Doc needed it on medical matters, where he could overrule Ryck if he so chose.

Several hours after the two were put into stasis, Doc had collapsed. He had hidden the extent of his wounds. His gut had been torn apart. He had to have known how serious his wounds were, that he had to get into stasis if he was going to have a chance to survive, but he hid that, giving up his own life to save a grubbing legionnaire. That was not a fair trade by any stretch of the imagination. The four Marines stood by helplessly as Doc suffered until he couldn't take it anymore and agreed to a pain block. Doc's last hour was better, if only in a relative sense. He took one final breath, then no more.

Ryck had boarded the *Intrepid* as part of a Marine company. Of that company, over the last few days, Second Platoon probably died abandoned in space. Third, First, part of Weapons platoon, along with company HQ, had launched for the planet's surface. Only Third actually landed with the rest blown out of the sky. Of those who made it down, Ryck had managed to keep only three other Marines alive and unhurt. Four, if he was counted. Four Marines out of an entire company.

A Marine company was nothing in the grand scheme of things. When entire ships the size of the *Bismarck* were lost, with thousands of sailors and Marines onboard, what was one company? Third Platoon had been trapped on Weyerhaeuser in their tiny slice of the war while hundreds of Navy ships slugged it out. He looked over at the legionnaire, Legionnaire de 1ere classe Khalid Ramzy. One of the 25 mm rounds had pierced his R-3, creasing his chest and cutting his pecs open. Doc had sprayed the gouge shut and told Ryck the wounded man would survive. The legionnaire had seen what Ryck had done to Coltrain, though, and now refused to look him in the eye. His fear was almost palpable.

The legionnaire's fear was misplaced. Ryck's anger was spent.. He knew Khalid was just someone trying to get by, just as Coltrain had been. He'd used the Legion to escape the corporate madhouse of Ellison, never imaging that someone with Ellison roots was going to smash his brains out on yet another corporate fiefdom.

Ryck regretted it now. If he could take it back, he would. But there were no mulligans in war.

Of the four Marines, only one PICS had any power left. They had only their small 2 mm Rugers. If the French sailors mounted an attack, Ryck wasn't sure they could fend them off.

Ryck was tired. He gave Ling, who seemed to be a fountain of energy, the first watch. He lay down on the dirt and had drifted off to a dreamless sleep when Ling shook his arm, waking him.

"Sergeant L, we've got company," Ling told him.

The other two Marines were groggily waking up when a huge shape passed over them, instantly wiping away any dregs of fatigue.

At first, Ryck thought the *Intrepid* had made finally returned and had sent down a shuttle to pick them up. That momentary flash of joy was dashed, though, when the make of the shuttle became clear. It was French.

"Shit," Cpl St. Cyr simply said, succinctly reflecting all their feelings.

They looked to Ryck. If he told them to fight, he knew they would fight. But to what end? He'd probably get court-martialed when all this was over, but he wasn't going to waste the three Marine's life on a futile gesture.

"Hey Khalid, it looks like your buddies are here," he started, before a voice poured down from the above.

"Federation Marines, we are from the Greater French ship *Forbin*. Please do not fire upon us. The war is over. We repeat, the war is over. We are here to retrieve all French personnel. We already have retrieved your wounded and dead from the other site, and we've been informed that you have more in this area. We offer you the same courtesy. If you have any French personnel with you, please make them available. Please acknowledge this on Universal."

Ryck stared in shock as the shuttle kept circling, moving in and out of his line of sight because of the trees. The voice started repeating the same message.

"Well, what do you think?" he asked the other three. "Is this a trick?"

"If it is, I'm not sure we can do anything about it," St. Cyr said. "I think a squad of girl scouts could probably handle us about now. We're out of any real weapons, and almost out of supplements. Besides, I've heard the French Navy chow is pretty good," he said bitterly.

The three waited for his decision. There really wasn't any decision to make, though. Circumstances had made it for him.

"Khalid," he said again, "if this is another French trick, I hope you remember that we gave you medical treatment, you and your buddy there."

He walked over to St. Cyr's PICS, the only one with any power left, reached in, and toggled the Universal.

"French shuttle, this is Sergeant Ryck Lysander, United Federation Marine Corps. We have two legionnaires here, both wounded, one in stasis. You are welcome to land and pick them up. As for us, if we can hitch a ride back to a Federation ship, we would sure appreciate it."

# Alexander

## February 27, 311 (Standard Reckoning)

## Chapter 25

Ryck stared at the Navy Cross, hanging crookedly on the chest of his dress blues blouse. He was torn about it. As he'd said during the ceremony after the commandant had pinned it on him only an hour ago, this was for those who hadn't made it. In that manner it was a fitting tribute. However, Ryck knew the award had also been a political statement.

At the conclusion of hostilities, the Federation had rushed to declare victory. Buckets of medal had been awarded, and all in record time. No less than 18 Federation Novas had been awarded, mostly to Naval commanders, but Doc Grbil received one posthumously, and a living Marine captain in 2/3 had been awarded one. Normally, the Nova took up to two years to be vetted and awarded, but those 18 had flown through the process in less than five months.

Lieutenant Nidishchii' had been awarded the Navy Cross, too, presented to him earlier in the morning at his bedside in regen. Every other Marine in the platoon had been awarded a Silver Star. Ryck had done a quick search, and never in the history of the Corps had an entire unit been awarded Silver Stars. Now, his platoon and the entire company from 2/3 had received them. The whole thing reeked of politics.

That was not to say that Ryck didn't think his Marines deserved to be commended. They had kicked ass in a very trying situation. They deserved whatever they got. It was just the political grandstanding tainted the awards, Ryck thought.

The Federation declared victory, and merely going by numbers of men and ships lost, there was a basis for that claim. The Federation had lost 12 capital ships, the largest being the *Bismarck*. Over 20,000 sailors had died, as had 1,914 Marines. The Greater French alliance had lost 38 ships, 25,000 sailors, 2,400 legionnaires, and a handful of allied soldiers and Marines. The numbers were heavily skewed to the Federation, which wasn't surprising given their overwhelming superiority in naval forces. Actually, it was surprising to Ryck that the numbers weren't even more lopsided.

But what had been gained? Greater France was still not a full-member of the Federation. They still had their government in Paris. Not only that, but they had also managed to extract a concession on tariffs. Only they could place import or export tariffs on goods going into or out of their territory. This had been one of their key complaints that had led to the conflict.

The French had remained mostly quiet about the terms of the peace agreement, just issuing the obligatory comments about regretting any misunderstandings and hoping for a prosperous and cooperative future. The blogosphere was live with accusations of the Federation "capitulating," but from Greater France itself, the media was mostly quiet.

Ryck knew the real reason that the war had ended so abruptly, though. When the Legion suicide team had taken the Siren Corporation's mine on New Lancashire, the Federations largest source of erbium, the vital rare earth needed for the manufacture of ship hulls, fighter craft, and even parts of Marine PICS, they threatened to set off a dirty bomb, which would somehow chain react, contaminating the resource. Without a source of erbium, commerce would dry up as shipbuilding would cease, and those already in service would eventually lose their ability to use bubble space.

Of course, it didn't help that Siren Corp was owned by retired and current admirals and a few other high-ranking government officials. The Council was willing to spend Navy and Marine lives to "bring Greater France to the negotiating table," but threaten their individual financial bottom lines, and the war was over, just like that.

There had never been a way for the French to win a conventional war with the Federation. But they had figured out how to hurt the men in charge, and that was enough to get their basic demands met.

The legionnaire who had led the assault on the mine, breaking through the FCDC officers protecting it, was none other than Commandant Nicholas Gruenstein, the ex-liaison to Third Marine Division. Ryck guessed that the major had pretty much erased any black mark the Legion had given him for the failed negotiations on Soreau .

Ryck removed his medal bar and the free-hanging Navy Cross medal that had just been pinned on his chest. He needed to switch to a medal bar which held each award in place. He'd already had two of them made, with all his previous awards as well as the new Navy Cross, both different in only the last medal on the bar. He considered both for the hundredth time, then chose the second one, pinning it to his blouse. The bar was getting a little crowded. Any more medals and he'd have to go to two rows.

He checked the time. He was tempted to try a quick cam with Hannah. Things had been a little strained after they found out that Ezekiel had been killed on some unnamed moon in the Second Quadrant, but things between them were getting back to normal. He wanted to make a stop before the ceremony, though, so he figured he didn't have enough time.

He took the blouse off the hanger and put it back on, checking himself in the mirror. The rocker under his chevrons looked good, he had to admit to himself. Staff Sergeant Ryck Lysander, meritoriously promoted, turned and left his quarters.

He had to stop as other SNCO's offered their congratulations as he walked, or tried to walk, down the passage. The SNCO barracks, the "Holiday Inn," was packed as Marines were getting into their own blues, and it seemed as if each SNCO had something to say to him. It felt weird to have gunnies, even the master and first sergeants, treating him like that. He made it through their gauntlet and out into the quad. Passing between C and D barracks, it was only 50 meters to Franz Hall, the home of the gen hens.

It felt like he'd never left as he entered the front hatch. He'd spent over a year as a guest there, and it held mixed memories--mostly bad though. The corpsman on duty looked up, then when he saw who it was, went back to his PA. Ryck had a routine that he tried to follow each day. He checked on each of the Marines from the platoon. Peretti was still in an induced coma and back at the hospital, and Justice and Tally had finished regen and had been released back to their units. The rest, though, except for the lieutenant who was at the officers' quarters, were there.

Ryck started his rounds. Most of them had already left for the ceremony. Keiji was going to be standing in formation, by his special request, but the rest were going to be in the bleachers with the rest of the gen hens. Cpl Winsted and LCpl Cashew were there, though, and Ryck chatted with them for a few minutes. Both had their Silver Stars mounted, and both commented on Ryck's Navy Cross.

Checking the time, Ryck made his excuses and took the elevator to the fifth deck. This was the SNCO's deck, and seven of the twelve quarters were occupied. Two men, a gunny and another staff sergeant, had been discharged only this morning to get them back with their units for the ceremony.

He knocked on one of the hatches.

"Come in!" a voice shouted.

He opened the hatch and walked in. SSgt Hecs was getting ready to put on his blouse. The left sleeve of his blues had been removed due to the heavy regen cage that surrounded his growing arm, but still, getting the arm and cage through the sleeve opening could be difficult.

"Hey, good timing. Can you help me with this thing?" he asked Ryck.

"Sure, Staff Sergeant," Ryck answered stepping up to help.

"What the hell, Ryck, what have I told you? Two weeks already with your rocker, and it's still staff sergeant to me?"

Ryck hadn't too much trouble with the other SNCOs, but even after fighting side-by-side with the man, Ryck still tended to see SSgt Hecs as his hard-ass heavy hat DI.

"It's Hecs, Hector, Asshole. Even 'King Tong.' Just not 'Staff Sergeant.'"

Ryck grimaced. No matter what, "Hecs" was still, in many ways. "King Tong" to him.

"Of course I knew what you called me. You think you were the first to come up with that oh-so-clever name? You've got to remember, you were my fifth platoon, and each one thought they had come up with it."

"Well, uh, it kinda fit. You were rather, uh, animal on us," Ryck said sheepishly.

"Of course I was. You negats needed it. You seemed to have come out OK," Hecs said, before continuing. "You know what, though? None of you little wannabes knew something. You called me King Tong, but you know I am Thai, right?"

Ryck didn't know, but he nodded.

"In Thai, 'ting tong' means crazy. So Ting Tong King Tong. I just thought that was pretty freaking funny. Hell, I called myself that. I had to keep from laughing anytime I overheard you guys. Did you ever see my I Love Me Wall?"

Ryck had seen it, of course. He'd never really looked at it in any great detail when he was a sergeant. NCO's didn't pry into SNCOs' lives.

"Go take a look at my drill field plaque."

Ryck walked up to it, saw the drill field emblem, then below it was his name:

*Sergeant "Ting Tong King Kong" Hector Phantawisangtong*
*Feb 22, 306 to July 3, 309*

"See, we even had it put on the plaque. We all put our nicknames on them. If you make it there, and I am recommending that you do, you'll get your own, I'm sure."

"Really? You think I should go to Camp Charles?"

"Damn right I do. You would do great there, and frankly, it's a stepping stone you need if you ever want to make sergeant major."

"I don't know. I've got my best buddy there, and he hates it. He keeps wanting to get into combat."

Hecs eyeballed Ryck's chest and said, "I think you've got enough combat for now, Ryck."

Hecs looked closer at Ryck's ribbon, then said, "I see you went with your *Croix de guerre.*"

"Yeah, I had two bars made up, one with and one without. I was torn. We just fought them, for God's sake. We lost good men. But, I don't know. It wasn't like the legionnaires chose to fight us, just like we didn't choose to fight them. We all were just following orders. Orders that were there for grubbing bank accounts, not for freedom or defense."

"Oh, sounding cynical there, Ryck. I think Sams would have approved. He always thought you accepted too much, you know?"

"Yeah, fucking Sams. He was a cynic, that's for sure. I miss that bastard," Ryck said quietly before asking Hecs, "You think I shouldn't wear it?"

"Look at mine."

Ryck only then really looked at Hecs' blues. There, the last medal in his row, was his *Croix de guerre.*

"Fuck them if they don't like it," Hecs said. "So, you here to gab, or are you going to help me get this thing on?"

Ryck held the blouse, maneuvering it around so Hecs could slide his arm through. They checked each other's uniforms, making sure each was squared way, then left to attend the ceremony.

The Birthday Remembrance was held on February 27 each year, the anniversary of the forming of the *Infantería de Marina* back in 1537, Old Reckoning. While the November 10 Birthday Celebration was just that, a celebration, the February 27 ceremonies were more somber occasion. While a toast might be lifted to fallen comrades, drunkenness was frowned upon. The most important activity during the day was the reading of the fallen. Each and every Marine who had died during the year had his name read aloud in front of those still left behind.

This year's reading was going to take a long time. Ninth Marines had lost 1,214 Marines and sailors, most in 1/9 and the regimental headquarters. That would take about an hour and a half to read the names.

As they arrived in back of the parade deck, Ryck said goodbye to Hecs and started walking to where 2/9 was forming. A face in the regimental headquarters caught his eye, a Marine who had not deployed but who had stayed back with the rear party to assist in sending forward replacements.

Ryck walked up to the sergeant and stood there until the sergeant noticed him.

"Staff Sergeant," he said to Ryck, looking stiff and uncomfortable.

"Sergeant MacPruit. You can be a royal asshole. You know that, right?" Ryck asked.

MacPruit locked his eyes over Ryck's shoulder, focusing on nothing.

"But, and I say this with all sincerity, you saved my life on Weyerhaeuser. "

MacPruit broke his escape gaze to stare at Ryck in confusion.

"I know you were getting back at me back in your class when you broke my arm. But the class was effective. I don't know how much you were told about what happened, but when I was weaponless and faced with an armed legionnaire, of all people, it was you who came to me, telling me what to do. I reacted, just as you had taught. And because of that, I'm here today. I just want to thank you."

Ryck held out his hand, and MacPruit hesitantly took it.

"You're still a grubbing asshole, but I would be proud to serve with you anytime," Ryck said, and he meant it.

MacPruit colored, his face turning red, and he said, "You made us all proud. The whole Marine Corps knows you. And if you say I helped at all, well, thank you. I am humbled. I may be an asshole, like you say, I know. But I do respect you, and thank you for your words."

He seemed to want to say something else, but then let it go. He could imagine MacPruit's guilt, alive only because he had been left in the rear with the gear. Ryck hoped MacPruit would realize that he had contributed after all.

"Well, we're forming up. I've got to go," Ryck said, then hurried back to Golf Company.

Captain Quartermain was the new company commander, but commander of a gutted company. Second Platoon was at full strength. Not one of them had died. They had boarded the abandoned French ship, then basically sat out the war after managing to return life support to the aft crew spaces and holing up there until rescued. Ryck had thought they were all dead, and to find out that each Marine had survived had been a welcome piece of news.

With five new Marines, Third Platoon's formation was up to nine with Keiji joining them again for the ceremony. Ryck was the acting platoon commander. There had been talk about disbanding the platoon, even temporarily, but Ryck had fought that, saying both the platoon commander and platoon sergeant were still alive, as were a number of the rest. As a "war hero," his opinion had actually carried some weight.

First Platoon, though, had been disbanded. It would be reinstated later, once the personnel situation had stabilized.

The regiment formed up, and led by a single drummer, his leopard skin draped in black, marched onto the parade deck.

The regimental headquarters led the way. Following them was 1/9. Sergeant Mark Tillhouse carried the battalion colors, a black streamer joining the other battle streamers, signifying their unit awards over the battalion's years of service. Behind him, the other two surviving Marines marched. They were in turn followed by the new cadre staff of about 30 Marines.

Slowly, the rest of the regiment marched in. No music was played. Only the steady beat of the drummer kept a lonely cadence. When the regiment was formed, the Commandant of the Marines marched forward, taking the new regimental commander's salute. With the *Bismarck* Marines constituting the single largest loss of life, the commandant had travelled to Alexander for this year's ceremony. He was accompanied by a large news contingent that was anxious to film the reading of names. Rumor had it that the commandant had wanted to make this a closed ceremony but had been overruled. It took someone very high on the pecking order to overrule the Marine commandant on something like that.

Without an order being spoken, the regimental sergeant major's voice rang out with "Ninth Regimental Headquarters: Jerome William Able."

For a last call, ranks were never given. A Marine was a Marine.

Master Gunnery Sergeant Teleste was next with "John King Accord."

Then it was back to the sergeant major with "Antonio Salcedo Pious Accounte."

Back and forth, one after the other, they took turns, solemnly reading out each name. Ryck recognized a few. The colonel, of course. The sergeant major. Several of the NCO's. When they got to 1/9, Ryck could feel the tension increase. He knew the news hounds would be salivating, the reading of the Marines of the "Lost Battalion."

Ryck's back started to bother him, but he stood stock still. He hoped Keiji was doing OK. Regen took a lot out of a person.

The list of name went on: Kellen Lin Huang . . . Francis Kipriyanov . . . George Victor Lodgepole.

Finally, the sergeant major intoned "Second Battalion, Ninth Marines."

Ryck and the rest tightened up their position of attention.

All the Marines in the headquarters and 1/9 had their names read out in alphabetical order as they had died at the same instant, more or less. With 2/9, things were different. It started the same, with the company headquarters and First Platoon Marines' names being read in alphabetical order, then those killed when the shuttle went down.

Ryck had to swallow when he heard the master guns call out "Paul Pope."

After "Francis Sylian Westminster," the last of those who had died on the shuttle, though, each name was read in the order in which he had fallen.

"Tipper Prifit," the sergeant major said, the first of Ryck's squad.

Ryck felt dizzy as he heard the name. He wanted to take a knee. It took an extreme amount of willpower to remain at attention.

"Botros Khouri."

"Jeb A. Stillwell."

"Uriah Sampson Martin."

Those were the first three to fall in the first battle.

"Priest Randall Hennesy . . . Giant Luck . . . Griffin L. Holderstead . . . Lin Chan Ho. . . Rosario Gambino" from First and Second Squads.

Then, "Bobbi Samuelson."

*Rest in peace, brother*, Ryck thought, the tears that had been welling in his eyes now streaming down his cheeks.

"Tizzard Fu Rey."

Ryck could see his corporal, sitting in ships berthing laughing uproariously at one of his own stupid jokes.

"Hartono."

Hartono was always a boot to Ryck. The guy only had one name, for goodness sake, and fervently avoided any nickname. It was against his religion, he maintained.

"Albert Gomez Smith," from First Squad.

"Jorge Jesus Jacamba Mendoza."

The last of his squad to fall. But all the Marines were his, not just those in his squad. He was in command in command when the next five fell.

"Jan Rjils."

"Pacscal Stamos."

"Evan John Denny."

"Lawrence Peter Yuang."

And finally, "Harris Theodore Grbil."

These were men that Ryck had led, led them to their deaths. Ryck swore to himself that he would etch their names in his memory. As long as he remembered them, they were not gone.

Ryck felt a surge of guilt, guilt that had been building up since he had been taken aboard the French shuttle and flown off the planet. Why had he survived, without really a scratch, when so many had died? Was he really meant to be a leader? Everyone was telling him he was some sort of hero, but he'd just been lucky. Only he wasn't so sure that was a good thing.

He'd killed human beings. Not crazed terrorists like the SOG. Just normal guys. If Ezekiel Hope-of-Life had been facing him, Ryck would have cut him down in a heartbeat. The brother of Joshua, the brother of Hannah. He'd have killed the man, simply because Ezekiel had turned right instead of left into the Legion office back when he'd enlisted.

He'd killed men, beating one to death with his fists. Civilized people just didn't do that.

More damning, he'd gotten his own men killed.

Lost in his thoughts, Ryck hadn't noticed that the long list had finally reached the end. The sergeant major and master guns, their voices hoarse, stood back. A lone Marine marched onto the parade deck.

The classic Amazing Grace reached out as the Marine bagpiper poured his soul into his music. The mournful sounds reverberated among the Marines, and somehow, they cleansed Ryck's thoughts. When the last notes faded away, Ryck stood up straighter. He would miss his men, his friends. But the best way to honor them would be to become a better Marine, a better leader.

Could he have done a better job? Could he have brought home more of his Marines? He was sure of it. And if it ever came to that again, he was going to be better prepared, he would make better decisions.

There was no march in review. The regimental commander saluted the commandant, then turned to dismiss the regiment. There would be six services at the two chapels, a service for each recorded faith of the fallen Marines and sailors, and Ryck decided he was going to attend each one.

# Prophesy

## Epilogue

"You don't want to see your sister first?" Joshua asked.

"No, I cammed her before we landed. She understands." Ryck said.

"OK. I just thought you'd want to get cleaned up first."

"I'm grubbing nervous enough as it is. Waiting any longer will just make it worse," Ryck told his friend. "Do you really think this is the right thing to do?"

"You kidding me? Of course it is."

"Yeah, but now? With, you know?"

"Look, Ryck. Shit happens, and this has been a horrible year. Not your fault, not my fault. The guys on top, they play their games, and it's the troops in the trenches who pay the price. It's always been that way, from the Greeks to us here now."

"Yeah, but . . ."

"But nothing. Life goes on. If things are meant to be, they are meant to be," Joshua went on.

They sat in silence as the cab brought them closer. The taxi driver was studiously ignoring them, but Ryck could catch him glimpse at them in the mirror every so often.

Both men were in civvies. Ryck hadn't even brought a uniform with him. But they had the air of soldiers about them. Prophesy was behind the Federation, and most people had bought the Federation's grand claim of victory. The driver had to be wondering if the two were Marines, Navy, or Legion. If he said the wrong thing, he could be jeopardizing his potential tip.

"So, what do you think?" Ryck asked, pulling his thoughts away from the driver.

"Don't rightly know," Joshua said matter-of-factly.

"But she's your sister. Hasn't she said anything to you?"

"Hey, she likes you. But after that, who knows? She's pretty strong-willed, and she doesn't come running to her big brother with every little thing."

"Big brother" sobered them up. With Ezekiel gone, Joshua was in fact the big brother of the family, something pretty important in Tortie culture.

"What about you, you ready?" Ryck asked.

"Born ready. No matter what happens, don't come knocking on my door for at least a day. I'm taking Hope, and we're locking out the rest of the world."

Joshua had spent the war at Camp Charles, but all dependents had been required to leave Tarawa and go back home for the duration. The recruit training surge had continued after the war as the new recruits cycled through training, and this was his first opportunity to see his wife. The fact that it coincided with I-Day was a happy coincidence as it meant he could travel with Ryck back home, but Ryck knew Joshua's only goal was to spend time with Hope, not attend I-Day celebrations..

"You guys in the war?" the taxi driver asked, his curiosity overcoming his common sense.

"Yep," Ryck said, offering nothing else. For once he wanted to leave the Corps behind him for a few days.

The taxi driver was waiting for more details, but Ryck turned back to Joshua and asked, "So are you happy being a married man? Last time we were here, you were a little nervous."

"Yeah, I am. I think of her all the time. I think of little Ester, too. She's growing by leaps and bounds, and I can't wait to see how big she's grown."

"I'm married. Me and the wife's got three," the driver said.

Joshua keyed up the privacy screen.

"It was the best move I've made. If I make staff sergeant, I can get married quarters, so Hope doesn't have to sit in some apartment out in the ville. Maybe we can start on number two, a little guy?"

"Holy shit! If you do, you better hope he takes after Hope and not you!" Ryck told him.

That started a smack-talk session that hadn't ended by the time they reached the Hope-of-Life compound. Ryck only had his backpack, so he took the driver's meter and swiped it while Joshua grabbed his suitcase, full of presents for his family.

The driver's surly attitude at having been cut off changed when he saw the tip Ryck keyed in.

"When you want to leave, you call me, OK?" he said, slipping Ryck his card.

Ryck absentmindedly pocketed it as he followed Joshua to the main house. A rocket streaked out, slamming into his friend, knocking him back a step. Hope clung to his neck, her face buried into his shoulder. They both were crying.

Joshua's mother followed at a more leisurely pace, a small girl on her hip. When Joshua opened his eyes, he saw her, then reached out for the small girl, who recoiled slightly at the strange man hugging her mother.

"It's OK baby, that be your papa," Mrs. Hope-of-Life said.

"Papa?" the little girl asked, clearly getting excited.

She squirmed down from her grandmother and rushed to hug Joshua's leg.

Ryck felt out of place, like an intruder.

"Why don't you come on inside," Mrs. Hope-of-Life suggested. "Leave these three for a piece. I imagine you be thirsty. I also imagine you be wanting to see Hannah?" she asked, a twinkle in her eyes.

"Uh, yes ma'am," Ryck said.

"Yes to what?"

"Uh, both?"

She laughed, a deep throaty laugh.

"Of course, I just be teasing. Come on in. I'll fetch Hannah."

Ryck left the small family in front of the house and followed Mrs. Hope-of-Life inside. She got him a home-made lemon squash, telling him how much better it was for him than what he could get at the stores. She left him there nursing it.

*This really is pretty good,* he thought as he sipped the drink before a slender form moved in front of him.

"Ryck, Joshua didn't tell me you be coming. I . . . where be your sister? I think Joshua will be a mite busy to be socializing with you. Maybe you should be with Lysa?"

"I didn't come to be with Joshua, and Lysa knows where I am," he said.

Her eyes narrowed.

"And why be you here?"

"It's I-Day in two days. I promised you I would be back to see you this I-Day."

"That you did, Ryck."

"Did you forget that?" Ryck asked, suddenly less sure of himself.

"No, of course I didn't. But soldier boys make many promises to girls. Most promises are not kept."

Her face clouded over while she said that. Ryck wondered if Ezekiel had made a promise to come back.

"Well, I'm here," he said.

"So you are."

She didn't seem talkative. Ryck wondered if things had changed between them. Her brother had been killed by Marines, after all. Did she blame him for that?

"Well, so what will you do now that you be here?" she asked.

"I wanted . . . I wanted to talk to you. I wanted to ask you something."

"OK, then ask," she prompted.

"Uh, not here in the kitchen," he said, pointing out her sister who had just come in and opened the fridge.

"How about the library?" she asked.

He followed her to the library, where she sat down, pointing to a plush chair for him to sit. He sat, but it was very deep, pulling him away from her. He scootched forward and sat on the edge of the chair.

"I'm . . . I mean, I, well, this has been a very rough year, for both of us. I'm sorry I couldn't get here for Ezekiel's funeral, and all."

*Shit, this is hard!*

She sat silently, waiting.

"Anyway, I've been thinking of you. Of us. I really like when we're together. I feel comfortable with you."

"Comfortable?" she asked, arching her eyebrow.

"No, not like that. I mean, I care for you. I mean, I love you, and I want to marry you."

*That's not how I wanted it to go!*

She sat there, not saying a word.

He started to panic. She wasn't jumping up to agree, like the women did in the flicks.

"Ryck," she began. "I care for you, too. Maybe I love you. I never meant to. I was just going out for fun. You be Joshua's friend, and I wanted to see the kind of man he would love. Somewhere in there, I think I fell a little in love with you myself. You are strong, yet kind. You have a gentle heart. I've watched you with your nieces, and I know you would be a good father."

His heart gave a little jump of hope.

"But I told you long ago that I am not a soldier's girl. I am not like Hope, bless her heart, ready to follow her man from base to base, sitting in apartments, waiting for him to show up."

"But I'm a staff sergeant now. I can get base housing."

She held up her hand to stop him.

"I be a little more than a year away from my Ph.D. This has been my goal since I was a little girl. I am going to make something of myself. I love and respect my mother dearly, but I am not going to be the matriarch of some household. I have my dreams. And I will not marry someone and have them taken away from me."

"Why would they get taken from you?" Ryck asked, heartbroken in the direction this was taking.

"You be not a Torritite. That be OK, and I respect your beliefs, but your kind do not suffer women to make their own way in life."

"Why do you think that?" Ryck asked, confused.

"Because of the laws. Making women little more than chattel. You don't have women in your precious Marines, right?"

"Hannah, I think you are mistaking things here. Sure, the Federation is behind the times on things, to include women in the service. But that's not what all people think. Of course, you should finish your degree. And whatever you wanted to do in your life, I would support you. I can't promise that I will be home every night. I can't promise that I wouldn't be gone for long periods of time. But if I am going to be gone, do you think I would be attracted to a woman who needed me every minute of the day to make every single decision? Part of the reason I love you is that you are so capable. You are strong."

Hannah looked at him in shock, surprised by his outburst.

"I . . . I'm sorry I threw this at you, especially now. Maybe I should have waited. Or maybe it was never going to be. Just don't say no just yet. Think about it. If you do love me, like you said, we can work out anything. If not, then I will always wish you well. And if you change your mind, if you want to marry me, then I will be waiting for your yes."

He stood up then, looking at her for a moment before bending over and kissing her forehead. He left her there, sitting in the library. Mrs. Hope-of-Life was waiting in the kitchen. Her eyes lit up when Ryck appeared, but that faded when she saw his expression. She didn't say a word as Ryck opened the door and walked outside.

Joshua was just coming in, one arm around Hope, the other hand holding Ester's little hand. He looked at Ryck, eyes questioning.

Ryck shook his head and gave a thumbs down. He didn't bother to say anything.

He felt the taxi driver's card in his pocket. He hadn't expected to need it so soon. He pulled it out and called the man who happily said he'd be right back.

This had been one shitty year. He'd lost friends, close friends. He'd fought against men with whom he had no beef, and in doing so, had revealed a savage side to him that he hadn't know he'd had. A side of him that shamed him. And now, just when he'd hoped for an anchor for all his troubles, he'd been cast adrift.

Maybe that was the problem. A marriage should be because of love. A marriage shouldn't be because a man, or woman, needed something, be that financial support or emotional support. That was a contract, not a marriage.

The taxi driver appeared down the road, his fans kicking up dust as he turned and made his way down the drive. Ryck would call Lysa as soon as he got in to tell her the news. She'd be disappointed, of course, but she'd hide it and try to make him feel better. Lysa might not have a degree, might not ever set the world on fire, but she was strong in her own way, too.

The taxi pulled to a stop and sank down. Just as Ryck was opening the door, he heard his name called in back of him. Turning he saw Hannah, hair streaming in back of her while running pell-mell after him. She was shouting one word.

"Yes!"

# BOOK 3: LIEUTENANT

"Push right, Third!" Second Lieutenant (T) Ryck Lysander keyed over the platoon circuit. "I want you to anchor us up against that rock face. Don't let anyone flank us."

"Roger that," Sgt Bonnyman, his Third Squad leader responded.

Ryck watched his visor display as the avatars representing the Marines in the squad slowly started to spread out. Ryck couldn't afford to get his men too dispersed, but he thought the threat of getting flanked took priority.

Ryck's primary background was in the Marine Corps PICS, the Personal Integrated Combat System, and those combat suits had far more information processed and available to him. In his skins and bones,[50] the helmet visor display was fairly detailed, but it didn't seem as responsive to his commands as his PICS display. He had to make a greater effort to focus his eyes on whatever he wanted to pull up, and that somehow took him away from the battle. He wasn't looking at the real world past the display readouts.

Ryck needed the direct visuals. It had been bad enough as a squad leader, processing all the data being fed him. Now, with three squads and the company commander feeding him information, it was all he could do to process the information and lead the platoon at the same time. By focusing on his readouts, he felt he was losing touch with what was actually happening on the ground.

"One-Six, we have lost air support. Your requested mission has been denied," the company commander passed over the command net.

*Mother grubbing shit!* Ryck thought. *How in St. Chuck's hell am I supposed to hold them off now?*

"Roger," he passed instead, trying to keep his voice steady.

In front of his platoon's position, a reported mechanized company of the Canolian militia was massing. If they made it to the LZ,[51] where the rest of the company was evacuating the civilians,

---

[50] Skins and bones: slang for the Marine combat uniform. "Skins" are the utility blouse and trousers. "Bones" are the armor inserts that give ballistic and a degree of energy weapon protection.
[51] LZ: Landing zone.

they could make mincemeat of the shuttles, stranding civilians and Marines alike. Ryck's mission was to buy the company time, at least another 45 minutes, keeping the Canolians out of range of the LZ. Ryck didn't think the Canolian commander was going to give him that time.

Ryck had called for an air strike against the oncoming forces, but that had been denied for some unfathomable reason. Without air, Ryck's anti-armor capabilities were limited.

The platoon had six Banshee missiles, something newly acquired from the Legion. Ryck knew their lethality from a personal perspective. He had lost three Marines to them during the battle with the Legion on Weyerhaeuser. But friends became enemies and then friends again, and experiencing their effectiveness first-hand, the Marines had bought them, renaming them from the French "Gazelle" to the Marine "Banshee." The six missiles would be effective against anything the Canolians could throw at them.

After that, it was more of a crapshoot. He had nine Marines with the M72, an 18mm grenade launcher. Although not as powerful as the PICS-mounted 20mm HGL, it should be able to take out anything lighter than a full tank or "Patty," the PTY Armored Combat Vehicle. The attached heavy gun team with their M76 bunker buster should be able to handle any Patties, but Ryck had only one team. He had to place them where he thought they could best employ their weapon, but that didn't mean the Canolians would cooperate and approach where Ryck had thought they would.

As far as the rest of the grunts, himself included, he didn't think their M99's would have much effect on any of the expected armored vehicles. The high-velocity darts were extremely effective against dismounted troops and even normal vehicles, but the armor available to the Canolians would be proof against them.

For the hundredth time, Ryck wished he had requested another heavy gun team, or even some of the extra Harpy missiles, the less capable man-packed missile the Banshee had replaced. But when he'd been sent out on his blocking mission, no one had expected the Canolians to have armor assets. Navy intel had screwed up again, and this time, Ryck's platoon was going to pay the price.

Still, with four "Tamika" tanks and four Patties facing the platoon, he should technically have the firepower to hold them off—if he could emplace his forces correctly.

He checked the map readout once again. He'd emplaced the heavy gun team just to the west of the center where the natural draw and surrounding rocks might funnel the advancing armor. The Banshee gunners, with the weapon's longer range, were spread out over the 900 meter platoon front. Nine hundred meters would be nothing to a PICS platoon, but to ground troops, that was a pretty big frontage.

The far right flank worried him. There was a small, but real avenue of approach there, one that a Patty might be able to use. He had only one Banshee gunner on that flank, and if more than one Patty came up that way, it could be disastrous.

Ryck wracked his brain to come up with a solution. In his infantry officers classes, he was taught to use a hierarchy of supporting arms. Space assets could pound threatening armor from hundreds of kilometers away. Air would take over from about 30 kilometers out. Artillery was next, from 15 km out, and only then, would the infantry-based weapons engage the enemy from 3,000 meters right up to the defensive lines. That was great on paper, but Ryck had no space support, no air, and no arty. It was up to his infantry Marines to stop the Canolian advance.

Ryck wondered if he could somehow block the far right avenue of approach. He had no engineer assets, but it wouldn't be hard to at least knock down a few trees to impede the Patties.

"Cpl Halliday, take your team out and cut three or four of the biggest trees that you can find amongst the rocks. Make sure they fall across the open area between the trees and the cliff face," he sent to the Second Fire Team leader from Third Platoon.

"I don't have any axes or demo," the fire team leader responded.

"Just use your M99's," Ryck told him, knowing the darts would have little problem chewing through the trunks.

As the fire team left the line, he tried to blink up the orbital feed again. No go. It was still down. He wondered how close the

Canolians were. Looking down at the dragonfly mini-drone in its case, he decided he couldn't wait any longer. He had to know.

The dragonfly was the same as what he'd used when in his PICS. This one didn't deploy from his combat suit's arm, but rather out of a small carrying case. Ryck pulled it out, initiated the connection, and then let the small drone take off. It was quickly out of sight as it raced out in front of the platoon. Ryck blinked the feed from the far right of his face shield to bring it to a more center position.

The feed showed the drone flying over the rock-strewn slope, copses of trees scattered about. At the base of the slope, the trees got thicker. The trees would channelize the enemy armor, and it was along those paths through the trees that Ryck would have targeted the arty and air if he had them. He had briefly considered stationing a few ambush teams in the trees, but the weapons the platoon had at its disposal had minimum arming distances, and the proximity of trees might not give them those distances. A Banshee missile is a pretty potent weapon, but if its warhead hadn't armed, it would just make a bang and clatter as it bounced off the Canolian armor.

At 3,800 meters out, a puff of black smoke rose from the trees. The Canolian vehicles were Gentry-made. Gentry was part of the Congress of Free Worlds, a semi-independent coalition outside of the reach of the Federation but dependent on Federation planets to buy its products. Gentry specialized in sturdy, dependable, low-cost weaponry. The vehicles the Canolians bought had decent armor given their low price, but they used old fashioned diesel engines, no different than so many 20th Century tanks. Hundreds of years had passed since then, but the old tech was reliable and economical for carbon-rich worlds. The Marines didn't use diesel fuel for anything, but it wasn't how the engines were powered that concerned Ryck—it was the 90mm cannon on the Tamikas and the short-barreled 50mm chain gun on the Patties that worried him. These were pretty basic weapons in the grand scheme of things, but even a stone axe could kill a Marine if it hit him on the head.

Ryck zoomed in on his tree-cutting fire team. With the Canolians fewer than 4,000 meters out, he couldn't leave them exposed.

"Cpl Halliday, what's your status?"

"We have one tree down," the fire team leader responded over the P2P.[52]

*Shit, that's slow*, Ryck thought.

"How long to cut down a tree?" he subvocalized into his throat mic.

"Ten minutes for trunks up to 50 centimeters in diameter," his AI responded.

Ryck knew he should have checked that before he sent out the fire team. One tree wasn't much of an obstacle, nor would two be. The forest would slow down the advance, but he wasn't sure if the team could get another tree down before the Canolians arrived. He couldn't take the chance.

"Corporal Halliday, return to your positions," he ordered.

He turned his attention back to the dragonfly feed. The drone was at treetop height, its little AI guiding it to where it could observe an opening along the main path. Despite the distance and the fact that it was only an image, Ryck jumped as the first Tamika emerged from the dark forest into the sunlight. It looked huge. Ryck knew it was nowhere close to a match to the Marines' M1 Davis, but Ryck didn't have a Davis in his back pocket, so the Tamika looked pretty impressive.

The left side of the tank's tracks stopped for a moment as the other side kept going, lurching the tank around the bend in the path and in a new direction. The left tracks started up again as the tank kept advancing. Another Tamika came out of the trees and into the opening. Two more followed, and to Ryck's relief the next vehicle was a Patty. There were only four Tamikas.

*ONLY!* Ryck thought to himself sarcastically. *Yeah, there are ONLY 27 billion people in the slums of GFA, too.*

After two more Patties, something else lumbered into view, something that made Ryck's heart drop. It took a moment for his AI

---

[52] P2P: person-to-person direct communications

to identify the actual vehicle model, but Ryck immediately recognized the gun design protruding from the turret.

His AI flashed the designation on his display: TNY-P Tank Destroyer, codenamed "Tonya."

Ryck ignored all the specs that flashed on his screen. He focused on the gun, which gave the Tonya the "P" designation. The blue rings along the barrel gave it away. This was a plasma gun.

Plasma energy weapons have the inherent liability of dispersion in atmosphere. However, more than 150 years ago, CWO5 Terrance Sukerson came up with the idea to put a plasma charge into an artillery shell which would carry the charge through the air to the target, where the charge would be detonated.

As its name implies, a tank destroyer was designed simply to destroy tanks. To Marines in skins and bones, even a touch of the charge would be fatal. He scrolled through the data until he found the information he was looking for: with an eight kilojoule shell, it had an ECR[53] of 23 meters for unshielded ground troops. Even if they'd been issued the new personal shields—which of course, they hadn't—the shields wouldn't stand up to that much power.

Ryck looked around at his platoon line. He'd had them all dig in, and that would protect them to a degree. But while Ryck didn't know what type of fuzes the plasma rounds had, a fuze that could detect when it was over fighting holes was very old tech.

"All hands, listen up," he passed on the platoon circuit. "We have a new threat. In addition to the armor you were already told about, they have a Tonya-P. The 'P,' as you know, means it's a plasma gun. Your fighting holes will give you some protection, but all Banshee, M72, and M76 teams, this is your prime target."

He belatedly switched the feed to the entire platoon, rewinding it 15 seconds so they could see the Tonya emerge. After a few moments, he fast-forwarded it so the platoon could watch the feed in real time.

Ryck only had one dragonfly. He was tempted to direct it to follow the lead element, but he wanted to see the entirety of the force opposing him. He counted the four Tamikas, four Patties, the

[53] ECR: Effective Casualty Radius

one Tonya, four lightly armored trucks, and two command vehicles. He tried to calculate the militia being carried. The Patty, according to his AI, carried a squad of 13 men. That meant a platoon+ if the Canolians were organized in the same manner as the Marines. The trucks, though, could easily carry 30-40 men each.

If the platoon could neutralize the armor, then Ryck wouldn't be as concerned about the trucks and militiamen. Ryck's platoon was dug in, and he couldn't imagine any militia having the same degree of discipline and tactical ability as the Marines. The platoon's M99's would tear the militiamen to pieces. The problem was the armor.

Ryck re-directed the dragonfly to head back up to the head of the column. The lead vehicle was about 2,600 meters away with the drone hovering above it when the dragonfly suddenly quit broadcasting.

*What now?* Ryck asked himself as he tried to reconnect with his forward eyes.

Nothing doing. His dragonfly had been knocked out. It wasn't a complete disaster, though. The Canolians most likely knew where the platoon was, and Ryck would have eyeballs on them soon enough. Already, his AI was beginning to pick up noise and electromagnetic signatures and translating that to probable vehicles and positions on his display. As they got closer, the platoon's AIs would have more data points, and the order of battle would become clearer.

To the rear of their lines, another 300 meters back, Ryck had some alternate positions dug. If it got too rough, he could order the platoon to fall back to those positions. That would give the high ground to the enemy, but it would also highlight any vehicles as they crested the pass. The AI's best-guess positions on the enemy, though, had them getting closer. If Ryck did decide to fall back, he'd have to do it before the armor arrived. They would be sitting ducks if they tried to fall back while under fire.

It was almost too late for that. Ryck could hear the approaching Canolians, and a few tree tops swung violently as vehicles hit them from below. The AIs were firming up their projections.

"Get ready, here they come," Ryck passed needlessly.

Each Marine was getting the same feedback from the linked AIs. They could see the avatars just as easily as he could.

The trees started opening up at about 800 meters away, just as the slope started to rise. Ryck strained to see the first Tamika, but it wasn't he who made the initial spot. From the left flank, from LCpl Finich's position, one of the Banshee's took off. The telltale *bop, bop, bop* of the guidance rockets sounded in the three seconds it took the missile to cover the 800 meters, then an explosion rocked their front, just out of Ryck's view. He could see the flames shooting up, though, over the intervening trees.

*Hell yes!* he shouted to himself.

"One-six, one confirmed kill of the lead tank," Cpl Yurong, the First Squad's Second Fire Team leader passed.

The Canolians broke out from the trees and spread out over the slope. Two more Banshee's took off, but instead of hitting two separate targets, they both converged on the same Tamika.

*Shit!*

"First Squad, all anti-armor to the left 300 meters, Second, the middle 300 meters, and Third, the right" he passed as the third Tamika opened up on the platoon's position.

The AIs should have been coordinating, making sure two missile gunners were not targeting the same vehicle, but even without the armor emerging at about the boundary between First and Second, Ryck should have made their targeting priorities more clear.

"LCpl Dowell, your target is the Tonya. I repeat, the Tonya. Do not fire on anything else. Do you understand?" he passed to one of his remaining Banshee missile gunners.

"Roger," came Dowell's flat voice.

The second remaining Tamika rushed into view, moving quickly to the right. Another Banshee took off, but just before impact, it exploded in a shower of sparks. Ryck thought the missile had hit, but the tank emerged from the smoke unscathed, its 90mm canon firing.

Just like that, Barnum and Lumsden's icons went grey. The two Marines had taken a direct hit. Ryck wanted to stand up to look, to see if they were really KIA, but he had to focus on what was happening.

The Bunker Buster was not a long-range weapon, and the team had to wait until a target was within about 400 meters. Ryck had guessed right, and they were in position to take out either of the two remaining Tamikas, but they couldn't fire yet.

"Wait, Corporal Zakharchuk, they're still too far out," he said, even if he hadn't seen the M-76's tracker engage.

Ryck knew that the Weapons Platoon heavy gun team leader understood that if he was tracking the Canolians, they would see that and most likely target him, but Ryck figured it didn't hurt to remind him.

"There! The Tonya! Dowell, take it!" he shouted into his mic as the plasma tank came into view.

The Tonya got off one shot before the missile hit it head on. The turret flew up lazily, turning over and over before it fell back to the ground. The plasma round hit short before detonating, the plasma field just reaching out over two Marines, but their icons remained a healthy dark blue.

Ryck felt a wave of relief sweep over him. There were still two Tamikas facing them along with the rest of the company, but at least the big threat was gone.

As the first of the Patties came into view, several of the M72's opened up. It was a long shot for a moving vehicle, but they had plenty of grenades, and as cold-blooded as it sounded, they gave the enemy targets other than his last Banshee and the M76 team. The two Tamikas were lumbering up the slope, guns pounding as the first Patty opened up.

Ryck waited for the last Banshee to open up to take out one of the tanks, but then he remembered that he'd just ordered the weapons team with Third to hold their fire unless their target was in the right 500 meters of their frontage.

"Park! Weapons free! Target the tank on the right," he shouted as he realized his mistake.

Almost immediately, the Banshee took off. This time, the missile hit true, and the Tamika stopped dead in its tracks.

Ryck was out of missiles, and there was still one tank, but it was almost within range of the M76 team. For the rest of the armor, which was now pouring onto the slope, they would have to use their M72 grenades. If it came to that, then their hypervelocity rifles could take the trucks with the mounted militia under fire.

Ryck ducked as a round impacted just in front of him, pelting him with a shower of dirt clods. He wiped the dirt off his face shield as another explosion sounded a few meters t to his right. Another Marine, PFC Reem, was down.

"Riflemen, keep your heads down!" he shouted over the platoon circuit. Until the trucks got there, or if the Patties dismounted their troops, there was nothing they could do.

"Alpha-Six, we're getting pounded. Any change in the air support?" he passed back to the company commander.

He could see the orange slave light blinking in the corner of his display. The skipper was watching everything in real time, so he knew what was happening. If he had air, he would have told Ryck, but Ryck couldn't keep from asking.

"That's a negative, One-Six. No change. You have to stop them with what you have," the entirely predictable and disappointing reply sounded in his ear.

The problem was that Ryck didn't have much. The lone Tamika was raking the line with fire, and it was by sheer luck that no one else had been killed yet. All of the Patties were deployed and firing.

A grenade managed to penetrate the engine block of a Patty, stopping it. She wasn't moving, but her gun hadn't ceased firing.

One of the 50mm short-barreled guns scored a direct hit on Sorenson, silencing his M72. His icon went light blue: he was out, but not KIA—yet.

Finally, the M76 powered up and started firing. The Tamika started to swing its cannon at Zakharchuk and Tsung, Zakharchuk 's A-gunner. Ryck could see what was happening through the other Marines' feeds, but he couldn't help himself. He raised his head over the edge of his fighting hole to watch the duel. Three, four, five grenades hit the tank as the 90 mm cannon swept at them. One of the grenades hit something vital just as the cannon came to bear. There was no catastrophic kill. The tank simply stopped.

He pumped his fist in the air as something caught his eye. The immobile Patty was disgorging troops.

"All riflemen, get your heads up and take the troops *here* under fire," he ordered, toggling the location of the Patty to display on their face shields just where "here" was.

Within moments, the M-99 fire started, cutting down a full half of the militiamen who had left their vehicle. The remaining men hit the deck and took whatever cover they could find.

Three more Marines—Medvedev, Vargas, and Portuno—were killed in quick succession before another Patty was taken out. The fog of battle started taking over, and Ryck lost his focus. This was a battle of wills, with the remaining M72 Marines taking on the two Patties and the trucks that were now deploying. When he saw the first truck, he lowered his own M99 and started pouring fire into it. This was something he could do, something he was used to. The trucks armored glass spiderwebbed, but didn't break. Ryck's darts penetrated the cargo bed of the truck, though, surely hitting militiamen.

"One-six, we've got vehicle sounds in front of us," Sgt Bonnyman passed, breaking Ryck's rhythm.

Ryck's heart dropped. In the heat of the fight, he'd forgotten about that second possible avenue of approach.

"What does it look like?" he asked, afraid of what he might hear.

"Wait one," the sergeant passed as another Marine from Second's icon went grey.

LCpl Payute. Another Marine killed.

"One-Six, we've got at least another Tonya and two Patties," Sgt Bonnyman passed at the same moment that Ryck's AI put them on his display.

The lead vehicle, the Tonya, was still in the trees, about 150 meters from where it could deploy its gun. Ryck had no more Banshee's, and Zakharchuk was toward the left side of the platoon, well out of range from where the Tonya would emerge. He had to get someone down there before that occurred so they could get close enough to lay a bullfrog on the vehicle. The good thing was that if they could get close, the Tonya's gun would be ineffective against them.

He started to give Bonnyman an order, but addressed it to SSgt de la Cuadra, his platoon sergeant, instead. De la Cuadra was his best Marine, and Ryck trusted his abilities more.

"SSgt de la Cuadra, take Hakkenberg with you and whatever bullfrogs you've got. Get to the second avenue of approach before that Tonya gets here and do what you can. We will cover you," he ordered.

Ryck had a reputation for liking the toads and the larger bullfrogs, small limpet breaching devices that could burn through about anything. His reputation was deserved, given his past, and here he was, trying to employ them again as an offensive weapon. Ryck hadn't planned that, but he was out of options.

Without hesitation, the two Marines jumped out of their holes and started running. The massed fire of the Marines had little effect on the Patties, but another truck was stopped. Somehow, the two Marines kept going, going, going. The Tonya emerged, and the first plasma round reached out, graying out two more Marines, Carlotto and Schwab. The Tonya didn't seem to notice the staff sergeant and corporal as it cycled another round and waited for the barrel to recharge to send it downrange.

The Tonya's crew might not have seen them, but one of the remaining Patties' did, and its coaxial cut the two Marines down less than 100 meters from their target. One moment they were running—the next they were flopping bonelessly onto the dirt.

"No!" Ryck shouted.

He jumped out of his hole and started charging, fumbling for his own toad. Normally, a Marine would use a special glove to handle it so it wouldn't stick to the skin, but Ryck grabbed it barehanded.

He barely noticed as another Marine, one of HIS Marines, was killed. All he could think of was to close with the Tonya. The blue lights on the barrel pulsed, and the gun swung to Ryck. With the flicker that indicated a round was fired, the shell zipped past Ryck, detonating behind him.

He had gotten past the kill zone!

By the time the tank cycled again, he would be too close.

Ryck never saw the militiaman who cut him down as everything went black.

# EARTH

## Chapter 1

"You did it again, Mr. Lysander. Don't you think it's about time you got it right?" the flat voice cut through to Ryck.

With a sigh, Ryck reached up to detach his helmet feed. He blinked as the cavernous studio of one of NSA Annapolis' RCETs[54] flooded his view. The fictional planet of Canolia, the enemy vehicles, his Marines, even his rank of Second Lieutenant (Training) had disappeared back into the electrons that had created them. What didn't disappear was Gunnery Sergeant William Meader, UFMC, much to Ryck's annoyance.

Gunny Meader was the bane of Ryck's training. The man seemed to have it in for him, but Ryck didn't know why. Ever since Ryck had moved to Phase 2 of the Naval Officer Training Course, the gunny had been on his ass, never letting up.

Phase 1 had been easy. Ryck and the other midshipmen had taken courses on military law, leadership, history, military theory, and political science, and his college courses had prepared him well for those classes. Wearing the Navy uniform had been the oddest thing he'd experienced. Mixing with the Navy-appointed midshipmen had been interesting, and he'd even known one, Midshipmen Terry Halsted, who'd been a snipe[55] on the *Adelaide* back when Ryck was aboard her. But along with the other Marine-appointed mids, he felt out of place wearing the Navy dress blues.

Phase 2 (Marine) had been a different story. Along with the Marine-track mids from the Academy who had joined them for this phase, the training had been more specific to being a Marine officer. Classes were more detailed, the PT more strenuous. These things didn't bother Ryck, though—it was the practical applications in the RCET that was killing him. It was hard to believe that as a recruit, he had loved RCET training: now, he dreaded it.

---

[54] RCET: Realistic Combat Environment Trainer. This is a huge simulator used to train Marines and sailors how to fight.
[55] Snipe: a member of a ship's engineering division.

"I don't think you are ever going to learn, Mr. Lysander," the gunny said. "Nope, I don't think so. It takes more than being able to fight to become an officer, and you just don't have it. You're just a barroom brawler, sir, not officer material."

A midshipman was technically an officer, ranked between a WO1 and a CWO2, but the gunny made his "sir" sound like an insult. During a Phase 1 history class, the mids had been told the tale of Midshipman William Sitgreaves Cox, from back in the old wet-water navy days. Midshipman Cox was court martialed for dereliction of duty for taking his commanding officer, Captain James Lawrence, of the "Don't Give Up the Ship" fame, below decks when the captain was wounded. As a midshipman, though, he had then been technically in command of a ship in battle and had left his post, so he was convicted of the charges and dismissed from the Navy in disgrace.

The lesson had been meant to instill a sense of being an officer into the mids, most of whom had just come up from the enlisted ranks. No mid, though, was stupid enough to think that a simple appointment gave him any degree of authority or respect. The chiefs and Marine SNCOs held all the cards and could make or break any one of them. They may call them "mister" or even interject a "sir" into their speech every now and then, but that didn't fool anybody.

Ryck just stared at the gunny. He knew he'd failed the task—just as he had failed every other RCET assignment so far. He didn't need the gunny to remind him.

He was a freaking combat Marine! He'd succeeded in real life battles. Why the hell couldn't he get through a simple simulation?

"Give your slug to Mr. Uttley, sir, and report back to the master guns," Gunny Meader told him.

The "slug" was the simulated M99 which was used for RCET training. As per the Charter, sailors and Marines were not allowed on earth's surface while armed, so for the training at NSA Annapolis, they used a basic game wand that looked nothing like a real M99. Ryck walked back to the prep area and gave it to Hank Uttley before marching through the hatch and up the stairs to the observation room.

Prince Jellico caught his eye as Ryck came in and gave a sympathetic shrug. The midshipmen who had already finished had all been watching Ryck's feeds and knew what had happened. This session had been particularly brutal. Only Jorge Simone had managed to accomplish the mission so far. Jorge, a no-neck heavy worlder might look dull, but he had managed to succeed in all six RCET missions they had been assigned. Ryck, on the other hand, for all his reputation as being a fighter, had failed each and every one.

After the last session, the only other mid to have failed every task, Pietr Hartman, had been called into the Captain's office. He never returned, and his stateroom was emptied by the BOQ[56] staff. Ryck didn't know if Pietr had opted to revert back to his previous rank of corporal or if he merely resigned from the service.

Ryck straightened his back as he marched up to the small hatch leading into the control booth. Inside, Master Gunnery Sergeant Kofi Ghanaba was watching the screen as Hank Uttley began his simulation. He didn't even glance up as Ryck entered.

"Mr. Lysander, please go to the company office. I will meet you there after the final two ranks go through today's training. We have a meeting with Captain Klein," he said as he watched over the RCET training staff.

"One-Six, we have lost air support. Your requested mission has been denied," a rat-faced civilian kid, barely out of his teens, spoke into a headset from where he was sitting on the other side of the master guns.

*So this kid was my so-called company commander?* Ryck wondered.

Ryck knew they worked off a script and had canned responses for most contingencies, but this kid had probably never even gotten into a school-yard fight. Now, he was having an input into whether Ryck would make it through training. It didn't seem right.

---

[56] BOQ: Bachelor Officer's Quarters.

The master guns said nothing else, so Ryck turned and left. He felt the eyes of the other mids on him as he made his way down the steps and out the hatch. When he got outside, the muggy August afternoon breeze carried more than a hint of the Chesapeake in it. The planet was the birthplace of humanity, but to Ryck, it was a foreign world.

He stood for a moment, knowing these few hours were probably his last as a midshipmen. He felt defeated, but other than his pride, he was relieved. He could go back to his previous rank where he belonged. Other Marines would know he had failed, and that might affect his ability to lead Marines, but that couldn't be helped. Gunny Meader was a right royal dick, but he was correct. Ryck wasn't officer material. He didn't belong.

Looking over the Severn River, he could see Bancroft Hall nestled between old, but still more modern buildings. For hundreds of years, midshipmen had lived in that huge dormitory while the Academy molded the men (and women, for the bulk of its history) into the leaders of first the United States, and then the Federation. How many midshipmen had slept, eaten, studied, and lived there?

Ryck wasn't an Academy mid. He'd been appointed from the ranks. Most Marine-appointed mids were like him. Only a few spent the four years at the Academy proper. There was a higher percentage of Navy officers who attended the Academy, but still, the majority were just like Ryck, appointed out of the ranks.

Phase 2, though, included the Academy mids training with the "peons." That gave Ryck a connection, tenuous as it might be, to the Academy. Ryck could feel the history flow out from Bancroft Hall and seep over the Severn to the Naval Support Station. He knew, though, that storied history would not include him.

Ryck made his way to Alderman Hall, the headquarters for naval officer training. It occupied a prime piece of real estate right on the Severn with views of the entire Academy, part of the city of Annapolis, and the Chesapeake Bay, with Maryland's Eastern Shore a hazy shadow on the horizon. A two-star blue flag flew beside the Federation's black and silver—the blue flag indicating that the Commander, Officer Training Command was in the building. Not that it mattered to Ryck. He was so far down the pecking order that the great man would neither know nor care that Ryck was on his way out the door.

Ryck walked through the main entrance, then up the main ladderwell one deck and to the right where midshipman training was developed and monitored. The Academy itself had its own staff, to include a three-star superintendent, but the Midshipman Training Division technically even monitored the Academy.

Ryck made his way past the desks of the civilian staffers and few Navy ratings who kept the office humming and then to the left to where the training class staffs had their offices. He spotted the placard "The Naval Officer Training Course" and walked through the open hatch.

"Mr. Lysander," the middle-aged woman at the desk greeted him. "Please have a seat. Captain Klein will call for you shortly."

Ryck took a seat, studying the woman who had returned to her screen and to whatever task she had been doing. He'd never met her, and he was sure she'd never met him, but she recognized him. Granted, she probably knew he was coming, but there were over a thousand mids going through courses at the time.

The leather couch looked good, and it had a nice cushion, but it was slick. Ryck kept sliding on the seat, and he had to keep hitching his butt back up. He wondered if that was some sort of psychological tactic.

After at least 30 minutes, Master Guns Ghanaba walked in.

"Grace, is he ready?" he asked the woman behind the desk.

"Yes he is, Khofi. You're to go in first, then come back out to get Mr. Lysander," she told him.

The master guns didn't even look at him before walking to his right and into a hatch with "59-2" identifying it as the office for the staff of Ryck's class. As the minutes dragged on, Ryck's nerves got the better of him. He had already accepted that he was getting the boot, but waiting for confirmation of that was excruciating. Finally, the hatch opened back up and the master guns motioned him in.

Ryck took a deep breath, and only hesitating a second, marched in and centered himself on Captain Klein's desk.

"Midshipman Lysander, reporting as ordered, sir!"

"Take a seat, Mr. Lysander," the bull-necked officer told him, indicating one of the two chairs that were placed in front of the desk.

Ryck took the one indicated and sat on the outer six or seven centimeters of the seat while MGSgt Ghanaba took the other.

The captain studied his PA for a few moments before looking up at Ryck. Ryck tried not to stare, but the captain's eyes were two different colors. One was blue, the other green. He'd heard that, of course, but seeing it up close was different. Ryck had to focus on the subject at hand, not the captain's eyes.

"Mr. Lysander, I have here the results for PA-06.[57] As you know, you did not perform particularly well. In fact, while you did well in Phase 1, you have not done well in any assignment for Phase 2, starting with your first assignment."

Ryck grimaced. On their first day in Phase 2, the instructor had given them a pop quiz. They were given a list of resources—including Marines, tools, cement, a pole, equipment, and sensors—and were asked to write down what they would do to get that pole erected as a flagpole. Ryck got into the problem, calculating the amount of cement required to hold the pole steady, the necessary supports, the time for the cement to cure—details in that vein. He was the last midshipman done, and when he'd uploaded his response, he was sure he'd aced it. Instead, he'd been one of only five to fail. The only acceptable answer was anything along the lines of "Staff Sergeant, erect that flag pole." Ryck had made the fatal mistake of getting down into the weeds.

The captain went on, "I want to find out why this has been a difficult transition. You've got an exemplary record as an enlisted Marine, but that has not translated to NOTC.[58]"

He paused and simply looked at Ryck for a moment before asking, "What do you think of your men?"

Ryck couldn't help but to look confused. His men? The computer generated men assigned to him? He thought carefully, wondering what the captain wanted to hear.

---

[57] PA-06: Practical Application Zero Six. All practical application training events are numbered in the order in which they are taken.

[58] NOTC: Naval Officer Training Course.

"Um, sir, well, I respect each one of them. They are part of our history."

Each "Marine" was named for a hero of one of the old Marine Corps or the Federation Marines. They had been awarded Federation Novas, Medals of Honor, Victoria Crosses, Heroes of the Soviet Union or Russian Federation, the Military William Order, Philippines Medals of Valor, Taegeuk Cordons, even a Laureate Cross of Saint Ferdinand, the one that Ryck found the most historically interesting.

"You know as well as I do that naming them for old heroes is part of the Marine way, to keep tradition alive. I don't mean the historical figures, but the men attached to you for each exercise. What do you think of each one of them as individuals? Who is your strongest Marine?"

"Staff Sergeant de la Cuadra," Ryck answered immediately.

Each Marine had been given an extensive bio, complete with schooling, experience, and evaluations by those senior to him. Each midshipmen had to study those bios to get to know their platoon as if they were flesh and blood Marines.

"De la Cuadra?" the captain asked. "Are you sure?"

"Yes, sir," Ryck responded without hesitation.

"Then why during the course of the exercise, did you fail to address him until sending him on that suicide mission?"

"Of course I–" Ryck started automatically before thinking back.

*Did I really ignore my platoon sergeant?* he asked himself.

"The only time you initiated contact with him was to order him and Cpl Hakkenberg to charge the Tonya. Do you really think an attack with so little chance at survival was the best use of your self-determined strongest Marine?" the captain asked him.

"I thought that if anyone could take out the Tonya, it would be him, sir," Ryck said, trying not to sound defensive.

"You basically ordered him to run at a Tonya to place a toad on it. Couldn't any of a number of Marines have done that, maybe even better than de la Cuadra? Say, maybe, Kroon?" the master guns suggested.

Ryck started to reply, but then thought about LCpl Marco Kroon. He'd been on the Marine Corps track team, representing the Marines at the Federation games as a 440 man. For a task that was basically run to a tank and throw a toad on it, maybe Kroon would have been a better choice.

"You were in some pretty deep shit, Lysander, and as it turned out, you didn't survive because you wanted to be the hero. By sacrificing your so-called best Marine, your own platoon sergeant, you significantly decreased the chances of your platoon being able to accomplish its mission when you were taken out," Capt Klein told him.

"So I need to protect my platoon sergeant?" Ryck asked, confused now.

"No, that is not what I said. You need to use him where he can best contribute as a leader, not as cannon-fodder."

Ryck tried not to show any emotion at the term. He'd been "cannon-fodder" before, and all Marines were equal in terms of life and death.

"It might come down to sacrificing your platoon sergeant if he is in a position where he can do the most good and keep more of your Marines alive," the captain continued.

"OK, let's leave that for now. At the 7:43 minute mark, you ordered Corporal Halliday to take his team out and try and construct some obstacles, correct?" the captain asked.

"Yes, sir. I knew that was a possible avenue of approach and I—" Ryck started before the captain held up a hand to stop him.

"I am not questioning the decision. You might have started earlier, but it was a sound tactic. I am questioning the manner in which you went about it. Who is Corporal Halliday's squad leader?"

"Sergeant Bonnyman, sir," Ryck told him.

"So why are you jumping your squad leader to give orders to a fire team leader? You were a squad leader. How would you have felt if Lieutenant Nidischii' kept bypassing you and giving orders to your men directly?"

"Well, sir, since I know my men the best and who would be suited best for each task, I wouldn't like it," he responded.

Captain Klein just stared at Ryck until what he'd said finally registered with him.

"Oh," was all Ryck could say as he realized the captain's point, a point he hadn't had to vocalize.

"You're thinking like a sergeant, Mr. Lysander," the master guns told him. "You've got to let that go. Remember the flagpole lesson. You shouldn't, you *can't* do everything. You've got to let your NCOs do their job. Train them, lead them, kick their asses when you have to, but let them perform."

"You've had a habit of micromanaging, of trying to do everything yourself. You cannot be a successful leader as a micromanager. Look at the word itself: "Micro-manager." We aren't government bureaus, we aren't GE. We want leaders, not managers.

"Only when it is absolutely necessary for clarity or timeliness should you be issuing orders to your riflemen. You had an example in this exercise when you stepped in and allocated target responsibilities, but whenever possible, even if you have a valid reason for a specific Marine to perform a specific task, go through the chain of command. Get your NCOs involved."

"Yes, sir, I will," Ryck said automatically.

*Am I getting another chance?* he wondered. *Do I even want one?*

"I won't even begin to address your John Wayneing it here, leaving your platoon without leadership. That will be covered in the full debrief with your instructors. But we need to talk. Normally, as I am sure you are aware, with your performance so far, you would be getting dropped," the captain said.

Ryck swallowed the saliva that suddenly started to build up in his mouth.

"But while all midshipmen are equal, some are a bit more equal. You've created quite a reputation in the Marines, and not just the Marines. The politicos are aware of you. They want you to get your bars."

Ryck just sat there, listening.

"And, when I called Lieutenant Nidischii', he was adamant that you would make a 'great' officer, in his words."

*Why was the captain calling Nidischii', and why would he even listen to just another lieutenant?* Ryck wondered.

"Against the better judgment of many here at NOTC, you are being retained. But have no doubt, Mr. Lysander, that your support from high places, your Navy Cross, and even your former commanders aren't going to be enough to save your ass. Only you can do that. And if you don't cut it, you will be dropped. Our Marines are too important to give them an incompetent officer to lead them."

Both men sat and stared at each other. Ryck kept the captain's gaze, but inside, his guts were in turmoil.

"Any questions?" the captain asked him.

"No, sir," was Ryck's response.

"OK, then. Keep in mind what I've said this afternoon. You're dismissed."

Ryck came to attention, paused, then performed an about face and marched out into the room. He kept his posture until he left the division offices. Out in the passage, he lost his composure and leaned against the bulkhead.

"You OK there, Mr. Lysander?" Master Gunnery Sergeant Ghanaba asked.

Ryck hadn't even realized the master guns was following him.

"Uh, yes, sir, I mean, yes, I'm fine," Ryck said, gathering himself.

"Look, the captain's right. You need to quit thinking like a grunt and start thinking like a leader. It isn't easy now, and it certainly doesn't get any easier, but you've got people in your corner, and I'm talking Marines, not political hacks. Marines who know you."

"Captain Klein said he called my old platoon commander. That threw me. I guess that's who you're talking about?"

"The captain and Lieutenant Nidischii' were at the Academy together. Captain Klein was Nidischii's firstie,[59] and they've both made names for themselves, so I was not surprised that he'd call up

[59] Firstie: a first class midshipman, a senior at the Academy.

the lieutenant. I had just arrived on station here when Lt Nidischii' came through, and that was one squared away mid. He's going places, and with him as a godfather, you sure could do worse. But you've got to get through this course and get commissioned, first."

Ryck hesitated. He was technically the master guns' senior, but that meant nothing. Ryck was a boot compared to the older Marines, and he needed the more experienced man's opinion.

"Do you think I can?"

"I'm not going to bullshit you. I don't know. Some amazing warriors never make it through. Gunny Meader thinks you have it. As far as what I think, you have the potential, but you have to learn to tap that," the master guns told him.

"Gunny Meader thinks I can? I thought he hated me."

"Oh shit. Belay my last. I wasn't supposed to let that out. But yeah, he does. He rides you because he wants you to succeed. But don't let him know I slipped up and told you that."

That was a strange turn of events. *Gunny Meader*?

"I won't. But it's hard to believe. He was on my ass hard today when I fucked up the prac ap.[60]"

"Since I seem to have diarrhea of the mouth today, I might as well tell you that you didn't do half bad today if you forget your penchant for going at it alone. I mean, at least as far as enemy killed, you did better than most. If you can learn to lead, you've got the instinctive ability to fight in you."

"But I got killed, and I got my Marines killed," Ryck protested.

"That's the way it was designed, Mister. What, you think no air, no supporting arms, and surprise plasma tanks are normal?"

"But Mr. Simone passed the test."

"Yeah, and we're going to have to look at that and close that opportunity off for the next class," the master guns said. "Mr. Simone is a tactical freak, the first midshipman to succeed in this particular exercise since I've been here, at least."

"So you wanted us to fail?" Ryck asked.

---

[60] Prac Ap: Practical Application Test

"Sometimes, we can learn more about the temper of a man's steel when all is lost than when things go well, Mr. Lysander. What a man does when his back is against the wall can tell us his true mettle."

Ryck thought about the master guns words as he walked back to his quarters. He'd been ready to get kicked out and had accepted it. He had tried to convince himself that he was happy about it. But now that he was given a second chance, a last chance, he knew he'd been lying to himself. He wanted this more than anything, even if self-doubts had started to crumble his confidence. If he had others who thought he would succeed, then he had to have that same resolve. He would take this last opportunity and seize the moment.

He *would* become a lieutenant of Marines.

# Tarawa

## Chapter 2

"We have the hostage in hand, and she is unhurt," Cpl Halliday passed over the platoon net.

"Roger that," Ryck responded before the scene faded and his face shield went dark.

It only took a moment before the lights came on, revealing the same RCET in which he'd trained as a recruit. Ryck looked up to see Gunny Meader looking at him.

Ryck had never let on that he knew the gunny thought he had potential. He'd endured months of "gentle" abuse at the gunny's hands, but it had been pretty easy to take. Now, with their final prac ap in the books, and with Ryck succeeding in the mission, he was sure he saw just the slightest gleam of satisfaction in his instructor's eyes.

"How'd I do, Gunny?" Ryck asked.

Gunny Meader harrumphed before answering, "You got Sung killed, so let's wait until the debrief before we go puffing out our chests, OK sir?"

Ryck knew he'd done well. The mission had been difficult: breaching a ship and rescuing four hostages being held in different locations. He'd rescued all four with one friendly KIA. Sung had been killed by a booby-trap, but no one else had been hurt. It was still difficult for him to just coordinate a mission, letting his Marines do the bulk of the actual fighting, but this was simple gaming, not real combat, and he finally understood the "rules," so-to-speak. It might be different in actual combat, but electrons were just electrons, like any commercial game. Every other mid had passed this final prac ap so far, but only Simone had performed better than Ryck had, at least on paper.

Phase 3 (Marines) had taken place at Camp Charles, the same place where Ryck had attended boot camp. Life was *much* different as a midshipman, though. No DIs were there screaming in his face. The MTIs[61] took more time to explain things, and while they didn't hold back on their criticism, there was none of the abuse and profanity that DIs used during recruit training.

Phase 3 could not be conducted on Earth due to the Charter. Prospective Marine officers had to use weapons, and that had to be done off-planet. Ryck had wondered why their entire training hadn't been done at Camp Charles, but Prince Jellico had pointed out that the Federation wanted their undying loyalty, so their hajj to Earth, and to the Academy in particular, was designed to imprint the new midshipmen with a renewed sense of dedication. That made sense to Ryck, and it had probably worked. Ryck was a provincial from a backwater planet, never really considering Earth one way or the other, but spending time there, especially on the battlefield tours of Iwo Jima, Gibraltar, Fallujah, Inchon, and Belleau Wood had somehow forged a link with the planet and those Marines who had served so long ago.

Ryck let Gunny check his weapon. He hadn't been issued any rounds, and this was an RCET evolution, not a live-fire exercise. But while NOTC was different in most ways than boot camp, some things never changed. Ryck had carried every type of ordinance he could into combat, but here, at Camp Charles, he was not trusted to have a safe weapon on his own.

Ryck left the theater and walked into the observation room. Prince raised a fist which Ryck dutifully bumped.

"Not bad there, devil dog," Prince said. "Looks like your sorry ass might make it after all."

"And how did you do, oh great one?" Ryck asked as he slid into the seat beside Prince.

"Rescued all four, but two KIA and two WIA," Prince admitted.

"Hah! I slammed you!" Ryck crowed.

"Yeah, even a blind squirrel finds a nut every now and then," Prince grumbled.

Ryck had done well during Phase 3. He had been one of the best during the live fire training exercises, getting the highest score on the arty and naval call for fire. He'd done well in the tank

---

[61] MTI: Midshipmen Training Instructor

training, and not surprisingly, he'd scored among the highest in PICS –related exercises. But his dismal scores in Phase 2 relegated him in the middle-of-the-pack. Middle-of-the-pack was good enough for government work, though. Unless he really screwed up somehow in the next week, he'd get his commission.

Derrick Ohu reached over with his own fist and asked, "So, is your self-appointed exile over? You going to join us for a celebratory drink or three tonight at the class time box dedication?"

Ryck bumped Derrick's fist and said, "Of course. Count me in."

Ever since his last warning from Capt Klein back at Annapolis, Ryck had self-imposed a monastic regimen. He hadn't gone out with the other guys, hadn't had a drink. His life had been attending classes, studying, and exercise. Midshipmen were not under the same restrictions as recruits, and most of the other mids went out into town on the weekends, but Ryck had demurred. Gunny Meader had noticed it and had even hinted that socializing with the other mids now would help strengthen the base for the bonds among the officer corps in later years. Ryck didn't think he needed the distractions, though, and when Kyle Brown had gotten into a bar fight only three weeks before and dropped from the program, that confirmed to Ryck that his decision was the right one.

But now, there were no more tests, no more evaluations. Ryck thought he could relax, and he really could use the downtime. The time box dedication was traditional as well, and he should really take part in that.

"So, is Hannah coming to the commissioning?" Prince asked.

"I hope so. I'll cam her this afternoon. I've got reservations for her, but I'm not sure of her schedule," Ryck said.

"You mean, you haven't even told her yet?" Prince asked incredulously.

"Well, you know, I wasn't sure, and I didn't want to jinx anything."

"Shit. You knew you were going to make it. All of us knew you were going to make it. You are a bonafide, sure as shit hero, and the Corps was going to commission you no matter how fucked up you were," Prince told him.

There was dead silence for a moment as Prince realized what he'd said.

"Oh, man, I didn't mean it like that!" Prince said.

There was a pause, then Ryck quietly asked, "Is that what the other guys think? Is that what they think of me?"

"Fuck no, Ryck. Sure, you messed up during Phase 2, but a lot of us messed up there, too. Here in Phase 3, you kicked ass. No one thinks your lieutenant's bars are being given to you. You earned them."

Ryck knew he had performed well enough to make it through training, but he'd had the nagging concern that many of the other mids had thought he was being given his bars because of his combat record, not because he was qualified to be an officer. He had gotten his degree through a correspondence course, and from a school that while legit, was not high on anyone's list of academic excellence. Some of his fellow mids were Academy grads. Many had gone to real campuses before enlisting, or had been sent by the Marines to campuses after performing well while enlisted. One was even an Oxford grad, another a Bicam Tech grad. Academically, they were all out of Ryck's league.

"What about you, Prince? Do you think I'm qualified?"

"Hell yes. Look, some of the other guys don't know you as well. You didn't hang out at the club or go out into town with them. But you and me, we've spent a lot of time together, in study groups, in the gym, playing B-Ball or Five. I know you, and so do a bunch of us. There is a drive in you, one that pushes you to succeed. Tonight, you know, at the Globe and Laurel, we're dedicating our class time box. You need to pitch in, especially as a bunch of us think the champagne has your name on it."

That took Ryck aback. Others thought the champagne would be his?

No one knew how long the tradition had existed, maybe even before the Corps moved to Tarawa. Each class bought three bottles: one of port, champagne, and sherry. The bottles were placed in small climate controlled boxes which were then hung on the walls of the pub. The port was taken out on the first Marine Corps birthday following the death of the first classmate to fall. The champagne was taken out when the first stars were pinned on a classmate. The sherry was saved for the final two living classmates to share when all their brothers had passed.

Ryck had been in the Globe and Laurel after recruit training, and all the boxes on the walls had impressed him. Almost all had the port missing, a testament to the danger of their chosen profession. Most had the champagne missing, with a lone bottle of sherry a symbol of the old Marines living out their lives. The remaining empty boxes, with a simple brass plaque with the class number engraved on it, somehow spoke the most eloquently of the years of service to the Federation.

"Of course I'm going to be there, and I'm going to pitch in, but Simone's going to be our first flag," Ryck said, protesting Prince's inference.

"Could be," Prince agreed, "but I'm placing my bet on you."

Ryck didn't know what else to say, so he said nothing. He felt uncomfortable with Prince's confidence, and he wasn't sure that confidence was well-placed. He watched the screens where Kipper Johnson was going through his prac ap, but his mind wasn't focusing on his classmate's actions. His mind wandered to the future, to what it would bring.

Glancing about the room, he studied the other 67 mids there. Some of them would be killed, serving the Federation. No, not the Federation. Except for a few of them, the Federation was some amorphous, distant organism. Ryck, at least, didn't fight for the Federation. He fought for the Marines—for the Marine Corps, and for his individual brother Marines.

Who among them would die in combat? Who would become "heroes," whatever that meant? Who would earn their stars and lead the Marines into the future?

"Hey, wake up," Prince said, interrupting his reverie. "You with us?"

Ryck smiled sheepishly, then said, "Yeah, I'm here. Just thinking."

"Dangerous practice that—thinking. We're done here. A couple of us are going to the gym for a game. You up for it?"

"I think I'm going to pass. I want to check up with someone, and I've got to let Hannah know what's happening," Ryck said.

"OK, but you're coming to the Globe and Laurel, right? We're meeting around 2000. Don't back out, OK?" Prince said.

"Sure thing. I'll be there. The first drink's on you, though!"

## Chapter 3

Ryck was in a good mood as he got off his bike and put it in the rack, locking it never crossing his mind. It was an old Reimer mountain bike passed down from class to class. He'd only paid 150 credits for it, and he expected to get another 150 from someone in the next class for it. Some of the guys had bought old hovers the same way, but most mids stuck with bikes.

He'd just ridden over from the base where he'd stopped to pay a call on Dr. Berber, his Marine history instructor during recruit training. It was Dr. Berber's classes that had germinated Ryck's interest in history, and that had led to his earning his degree. In no small way, it was because of Dr. Berber that Ryck was now about to accept his commission. To Ryck's surprise, Dr. Berber not only remembered him, but also knew of Ryck's combat record. Ryck had spent an hour with the instructor, and he could have spent more time if he hadn't needed to get to the Globe and Laurel.

As he opened the pub's door, a small group of recruits came barging out, almost knocking him over. No, Ryck corrected himself, they couldn't be recruits—recruits were not allowed out in town. They had to be part of the class that had graduated that morning, and these four seemed to have gotten an early start on their celebration.

One of them put a forearm up, hitting Ryck in the chest and pushing him aside.

"Out of the way, oldster," the new Marines said, eliciting a laugh from the others.

"You just graduate?" Ryck asked.

"Yeah, we're fucking Marines now, ooh-rah!" one of them said, staring at Ryck a little blurrily. "What's it to you?"

Ryck wasn't about to cause a scene or get them into trouble, but someone else might not be so lenient.

"What's your name, recruit?" Ryck barked.

The four hesitated, trying to focus. One started to object to being called recruit, but another seemed to suddenly take in Ryck's haircut, military demeanor, and obvious older age, and he stepped forward, coming to attention.

"Private Rage MacHarris, sir. Sorry sir, we don't mean anything. We're just celebrating."

"Well, Private MacHarris, no problem with celebrating, but you're a Marine now, so act like one. The Globe and Laurel is popular with officers and staff NCO's, so do you really want to start your Marine career getting office hours?"[62]

Three of the new Marines were at attention, only the one who had pushed into Ryck being too drunk to realize what was happening.

"Sorry sir, we didn't mean to come to an officer's area, and we didn't mean to offend the officer, you, I mean, sir," MacHarris said, struggling to conquer his booze-befuddled mind and sound somewhat coherent.

"This is the ville, and there are no areas reserved for officers. It's just that if you are going to push the envelope tonight, a smart Marine, and I assume you four are smart, would go to where there weren't any NCOs or officers around. I might suggest the Pelican's Beak, over on 12th Street," Ryck said.

"Uh, yes, sir! Sounds like a great idea. Begging the officer's pardon, then, but maybe we'd better move on," MacHarris said while he and one of the other new Marines started to push the other two past Ryck and down the Globe and Laurel's walkway. "Have a great night sir," the private called out.

Ryck watched them hurry to the street before he called out, "Hey, Marines!"

The four stopped, and with a look of resignation, slowly turned around.

"Yes, sir?" three of them chorused.

"Congratulations, devil dogs!" he called out, holding up his PA. "Have a round on me."

"Aye-aye, sir!" all four shouted out with much more enthusiasm while MacHarris held out his PA.

Ryck zapped 12 credits to the private's PA, enough for four steins of beer.

---

[62] Office Hours: Non-judicial punishment used for minor offenses.

Ryck watched the four hurry out of sight. They seemed so young. The "oldster" the private had called him was hardly appropriate, but seeing how young they were, Ryck guessed it was all relative.

Ryck turned back and entered the pub. The Globe and Laurel reeked of history. It was mostly wood and barely lit with old fashioned faux incandescent bulbs, giving it a feel of age. Photos and holos of various Marine commanders, commandants, sergeants major, and heroes were on the walls, some being signed command photos, some being taken with the pub staff. Memorabilia hung on the walls, but the entire back wall and part of one side wall had the class time boxes, the boxes with the three bottles in them.

Ryck made his way back to one of the dining rooms where the class was gathering. At least half of the class was already there. A few looked to have been tapping the kegs that Mr. Geiland had put out for them while others were munching on the small snack line. The Globe and Laurel put on this little party for each class gratis, but the three bottles were paid for by the mids themselves. All three bottles were there on the table. Ryck had to remind himself to find out who was taking the collection for them.

"I see you made it," Prince said, handing Ryck a stein of beer.

"Wouldn't miss it, my friend. Wouldn't miss it," Ryck said.

Ryck spent the next hour drifting about, touching base with most of the others. More than a few toasts were called, and after three beers, Ryck was beginning to feel the effects. He knew he was being a lightweight, but he slowed down. He didn't want to be completely plastered before the time box was locked.

It was good to relax. For once, he didn't have to worry about whether he would make it or not. He could listen to sea stories, even tell a few of his own. It felt good to be with his class, and it was not lost on any of them that they would be the first generation of new lieutenants for a long time to have been blooded in a real war.

The last full-fledged war had been the War of the Far Reaches, and there weren't any Marines left on active duty who had served in that conflict. Granted, the latest war with Greater France was not termed a war for political reasons, and most of the fight had been between the navies, but still, Marines had fought a well-armed, well-trained force. Another all-out war was almost unthinkable, so it could very well be that his generation of officers would be the last to have real war experience.

When Jorge Simone, as the class honor graduate, clinked the side of his glass for attention, everyone in the room stopped their conversations and turned to him. Jorge looked brutish, to be blunt, with a bullet-shaped head seemingly sprouting up directly from his broad shoulders. He'd proven, though, that he had a keen intellect, and Ryck acknowledged Jorge as his tactical superior.

"Gentlemen, we are gathered here for comradeship, for one last gathering before we are sent out to serve our Corps. We have been forged from the same crucible, though, so we will always share that connection. We are brothers of the blood," he said, not bothering to refer back to the written words given to him by Colonel Jimjim Stacy, the oldest retired Marine on Tarawa.

"To keep this connection, we now place three bottles of elixir in this sacred case, three bottles to be taken out when the time is right.

"If you can all create the chain, we will dedicate our box."

At that, each midshipman put his hand on the shoulder of the man next to him, until all were connected. The mid closest to the class time box reached out to put his hand on it. Another mid reached out to touch Jorge, keeping him in the chain.

"The port, the drink of remembrance, will be opened on the Marine Corps birthday following the first of us to fall. Any of the class present will open the bottle and toast our fallen brother."

With that, Jorge picked up the bottle of 298 Quinta do Vesúvio and almost reverently placed it in the first cradle in the box.

"In remembrance," the rest of the mids intoned.

"The champagne, the drink of celebration, will be opened when the first of us earns his brigadier's star. All who are present for the promotion will join in the toast as the stars are a reflection of not only an individual, but our entire class."

"In celebration," the class intoned as Jorge placed the Krug Clos d'Ambonnay in the second cradle.

"The sherry, the drink of loyalty and service, will be opened by our last two surviving classmates on the Marine Corps birthday following the passing of our third longest surviving classmate," he said as the placed the bottle of 302 Massandra in the last cradle.

"In retrospect," the rest of the midshipmen finished.

They stood there, all of them, knowing that after commissioning, they would never be together like this again. Some would spend a career in the fleet, leading Marines. Some of them would die. Others would leave the Corps and make their way in the civilian world. But right then, at that moment, they were all the same. They were a band of brothers.

The midshipmen kept their hands on each other's shoulders for longer than necessary, none of them wanting to be the first to break the connection.

## Chapter 4

Ryck opened the door to Room 246 at the Escalante, dress blues in hand. He had to admit, they looked good, even without his staff sergeant chevrons on the sleeves. They should look good. He'd had to pay over 4,600 credits for them, and that didn't include his other uniforms or sword. As an enlisted man, his uniforms had been provided: as an officer, he was expected to pay for his. The problem was that he wasn't an officer yet and wasn't receiving officer pay.

*Oh, well. That's what credit is for*, he reminded himself.

He placed the uniform carefully on the bed, then looked around. He heard something in the bathroom, his senses on alert. Stealthily, Ryck moved to the side of the room and inched his way along the wall to the bathroom door. He could hear a male voice.

As quietly as possible, he eased open the door.

"Well, Mrs. Lysander," he said to the woman in the tub, bubbles covering her up to her neck, watching the holo. "I trust you had a relaxing morning."

Hannah had kept her last name after they had gotten married just before he'd left for NTOC, but Ryck enjoyed calling her Mrs. Lysander.

"Well, since my big strong husband be decidin' to leave our nice warm bed and abandon me, there wasn't much for me to do now, was there?" Hannah replied.

Although they had been married for over a year, they had only spent a handful of days together, and the thoughts of their reunion the evening before (and the night, and the morning), still had the power to arouse him. He sat down on the edge of the tub, looking at his wife.

*His wife.*

The thought still amazed him.

"I would never leave you, madam, but duty called," he said as he leaned over to kiss her.

Hannah reached up, took him by the collar of his polo shirt, and dragged him into the big tub. He only put up a token resistance before sliding into the warm water.

"Duty be not just to the Marines, but there be a concept called marital duty, too. You know that, right?" she whispered into his ear.

"Yes ma'am, and I tried to fulfill those obligations last night. And this morning."

"'Obligation?' Be that what you call it?" she asked with a laugh.

Ryck didn't answer, but took the PA out of his pocket, shook off the water and bubbles, and placed it on the sink beside the tub. He turned back to his wife and slid an arm around her, marveling at her supple skin.

From an objective standpoint, Ryck knew his wife was not some holo-star. She was a few kilos heavier than what was considered optimum, and her nose had a decided crook courtesy of a fieldball game, one she refused to get corrected ("It's my battle scar," she would say). But to Ryck, she was his Helen. Smart, funny, and capable: she fit him. He couldn't understand what she saw in him, though, but he wasn't going to press that issue.

She snuggled up against him, but in the way a cat snuggles against a person, not in a "I need more sex" way. Ryck might have been capable of another round, but the simple closeness reassured him, that she was comfortable with him. He was still unused to being married and being with her, and the quiet moments of normalcy made him feel more secure.

"So what are you watching?" he asked her, pushing some bubbles out of the way so he could see the holo at the foot of the tub.

Ryck had been surprised to see the holo when they'd checked in. The Escalante was a new chain of luxury hotels—this one, the first on Tarawa, had only opened four months before. It was full of little surprises, and a bathtub holo was just one of many.

"G.K. Nutrition," she said. "The SPCA be tryin' to bring charges up on those farmers."

Three talking heads were discussing the situation. One was backing the farmers, one was backing the environmentalists and religious groups, and the moderator was obviously trying to set the other two on each other. Behind the three people were images of the dead trinoculars.

The trinocluars were the only multi-celled vertebrates yet discovered on another planet. They looked like meter tall capybaras, but seemed mindless. G.K. Nutrition Six was an extremely fertile world with lush vegetation, and the trinocluars were the top life-form. The initial planet surveys had somehow missed them, something that still was a minor scandal and the fertilizer for endless conspiracy theories. They had ambled out of the forests a few years after the initial indentureds had established themselves, eating through the crops that had been planted.

Their discovery had rocked the net, but the trinoculars, nicknamed "capys," had turned out to be extremely dull, and most of the public quickly lost interest. There had been some indication that their DNA did not match what should have evolved on G.K. Nutrition, but even that had died out after a few weeks. It wasn't until the wholesale massacre by the farmers that the capys were back in Prime Time.

Fed up with destroyed crops and without the promised Federation compensation, the farmers had simply slaughtered all the known herds of capys, over a million individual animals. This had raised an outcry, but the farmers had been adamant as to their rights to defend their crops, and legally, they were correct. Federation laws protected business interests more than individual, but the farmers were all corporate indentureds, and without a way to grow crops, they would not be able to pay off their servitude.

In back of the talking heads, the scene changed to one that had been going viral—that of two laughing farmers pulling chunks off a capy being roasted on a spit, then taking huge bites, mugging for the holo recorders.

That holo had come out a few days ago, much to the outcry of certain groups. Even some doctors got their 15 minutes in, discussing if it was even safe to eat the foreign flesh.

"What do you think?" he asked Hannah.

Hannah had recently earned her Ph.D., and Ryck respected her view on life in general. He wasn't too proud to admit that her academic intellect was on a higher plane than his.

"We've got specimens throughout most research facilities, and they've recovered cells from the dead animals for cloning, but still, it seems like a waste. Those animals were there long before we humans arrived on the scene, so I think something should have been worked out," she said, snuggling closer, her Torritite accent fading as she shifted to a more academic subject.

As she moved, some of the bubbles opened up to reveal a long expanse of smooth skin along her side. Ryck tried not to notice as he attempted to come up with something that sounded astute.

"What do you think of the claims that the capys never evolved on G.K. Nutrition?" he asked.

"I'd have to see more results, but if they evolved elsewhere, then how did they get to the planet? That would be a rather intriguing question," she said.

"So how long do we have?" she asked, changing the subject as a questing hand reached to his belt.

"About two hours," he said, reaching over to cup her breast.

"Two hours?" she screeched, suddenly standing up, bubbles and water streaming off her. "Why didn't you tell me? I've got to get ready!"

She stepped over Ryck, getting out of the tub. Ryck had a glance of a lovely rounded ass as she darted towards the bedroom, continually complaining that she had no time.

Ryck looked down at himself, fully clothed in a bathtub full of rose-scented bubbles. His capable, accomplished wife had changed in one second from professor to high-school girl getting ready for prom. He sighed, then got up, water streaming from him as well. He pulled off his sopping clothes and stepped into the separate shower to rinse off. It would take him 15 minutes, 20 max to get ready, so he toweled off, slipped on one the Escalante's terry cloth robes, and went out to see what he could do to help.

He knew there wasn't much he could do, but even he knew he should at least ask.

## Chapter 5

The commandant's voice boomed out over the gathered midshipmen and guests, "I, state your name . . ."

Each Marine in the class repeated after the commandant, right hand raised.

> *. . .do solemnly swear, to support and defend Articles of Council of the Federation of United Nations, against all enemies, foreign and domestic; that I will bear true faith and allegiance to the same and above all others; and that I will obey the orders of the Chairman of the Federation of the United Nations and the orders of those appointed over me, according to the Uniform Code of Military Justice. So help me God.*

"Congratulations, lieutenants," the commandant said as he lowered his right arm. "I look forward to serving with all of you. You are dismissed."

"Ooh-rah!" burst out of 67 throats of some very happy second lieutenants.

"Refreshments are under the canopy," a civilian staffer shouted out over the rising clamor.

Ryck took a punch in the arm.

"Congrats, devil dog," Prince said, his smile beaming.

Ryck pulled him into a back-pounding hug.

The class had sat through two speeches: one from the commandant, and another even longer one from the Tarawa governor. The day was hot, and the dress blues made it even hotter. The high collar had dug into Ryck's neck as he had sat at attention. But finally, the commandant had given them the oath, and that was that. They were second lieutenants of Marines.

They milled about, shaking hands and pounding backs. The 26 Academy Marines among them had spent five years together—four at the Academy and one with the rest of the class—but even the direct commissioning lieutenants had been together for a year. That was more than enough time to forge bonds.

A few of his fellow lieutenants started to drift off to meet with family. Ryck looked back to the spectators and caught Hannah's eyes. She blew him a kiss, then nodded her head. He had told her what he had to do next, and she understood.

The commissioning had been on the lawn in front of Marine Headquarters. As the newly commissioned Marines started to leave their seats, there was a slow maneuvering of the enlisted staff as they tracked down their prey. Ryck caught a glimpse of a petty officer closing in on him and barely avoided the man. His eyes searched until he finally caught a familiar face standing off to the side, under General Salizar's statue. Ryck almost nonchalantly walked over, only speeding up when his peripheral vision caught sight of another Marine sergeant closing in.

As he walked up to Gunny Meader, the SNCO came to attention and gave a drill field salute.

"Congratulations, sir!" he said, this time with none of the dismissive tone he had used so often before.

Ryck came to attention and returned the salute with as much precision as he could muster.

"Thank you, gunnery sergeant," he said before reaching into his pocket and taking out a silver dollar and handing it to him.

Gunny Meader started to pocket it, but he couldn't help but glance at it first. His eyes lit up as he recognized it, and he faltered.

"Well, I mean, that's, well, uh, thank you, sir," he said, stumbling for words for the first time since Ryck had met him.

The Federation used electronic credits as individual currency. Several planets and nations issued commemorative coins, including Tarawa. Most new lieutenants bought the United Federation Marine Corps 300th Anniversary Commemorative Silver Dollar to give to the first enlisted Marine or sailor to salute him. These were not inexpensive, and enlisted Marines and sailors scrambled to collect as many as they could when each class was commissioned.

Ryck wanted something special, though. He searched the net and found what he wanted: a 2123 O.R.[63] Australian Kookaburra

Dollar. Gunny Meader was from Earth, Perth, Australia, specifically. The Kookaburra dollar cost Ryck quite a bit more than if he had bought a Tarawa commemorative, but he wanted his first salute to be special.

"Thanks for everything, Gunny," Ryck simply said, letting the dollar express his gratitude more than words.

"You're going to do well, sir," Gunny added. "Just remember you don't have to put the world on your shoulders. Use your NCOs. Let them do their jobs."

"I will, Gunny. I promise you that," Ryck said as he turned to find his wife.

She was in deep conversation with some colonel's wife, by the look of the woman. All trace of Hannah's Torritite accent was gone as she spoke. Ryck rather liked the way she spoke—it was endearing. But in social occasions, she shifted to Federation Standard mode.

"If I can interrupt, ma'am," Ryck said to the woman, "I'd like to steal my wife."

"Certainly, young man. And congratulations," she added.

"Let's make the rounds, here" he told her as they walked toward the canopy and refreshments. "We've got that dinner with Prince and Fera and some of the other couples, but after that . . . ?" he left it hanging.

"Afta that, lieutenant," she told him in a throaty voice, "I be goin' to give you a real commissionin'."

This was turning into one great day.

---

[63] O.R.: Old Reckoning. The method of numbering years until the Federation was formed. After the Federation, years started again from the Year One, and are designated by N.R., or New Reckoning.

# Zephyr-Hadreson

## Chapter 6

"Sergeant Timothy, get in here!" Second Lieutenant Ryck Lysander shouted out for his acting platoon sergeant.

"Yes, sir?" the sergeant said as he entered the small, cramped office from which Ryck was trying to organize his platoon.

"What's going on with the Class B[64] issue?" Ryck snapped out.

"Sir, supply's holding out. We've got First squad camped out at the issue bay, but the supply chief says the chain of custody tags haven't been inputted yet."

"Come on, Sergeant! Get your ass down there and get it unscrewed. The skipper's going to be inspecting tonight, and he can't inspect anything if we don't have the gear, right?"

"Uh, right, sir, but–" his sergeant started, only to be cut off by Ryck.

"No buts! Just do it!"

"Aye-aye, sir. I'll get down there again," the harried sergeant said before hurrying out of Ryck's office.

Ryck knew he was being unjustly harsh towards Sgt Timothy. The supply chief was a staff sergeant, and there wasn't much Timothy could do to speed up the process. This might have been a time for Ryck to head over to the supply shed and see what he could do, but his plate was just too full at the moment. Timothy would just have to get it done.

Ryck had hoped to be assigned to First Marine Division, the unofficial premier division in the Corps. Instead, he'd received orders to Second Mar Div on Zephyr-Hadreson, where he took over Second Platoon, Kilo Company, Third Battalion, Sixth Marines. Not only was Second Mar Div considered out in the galactic boonies, 3/6 was only now being reconstituted back from cadre status. Most of

---

[64] Class B: a class of issued gear. Class A is clothing and boots. Class B is equipment not to include weapons and ammunition. Class C is weapons. Class D is ordinance.

the Sixth Marines had been pulled during the conflict with Greater France to fill up the T/Os[65] of units closer to the action. Now, almost two years later, the Sixth Marines were finally being brought back up to full strength.

3/6 hadn't always been considered a second-class status. It had been in the midst of the fiercest battle in the War of the Far Reaches, and no less than nine 3/6 Marines and a corpsman had been awarded the Federation Nova for their actions in that battle. The battalion had adopted the Dutch Royal Marines as their historical ancestor, taking the Dutch Marines' *Qua Patet Orbis*[66] motto as their own. Storied history or not, though, the battalion was now in a state of rebuilding.

Technically, Sgt Timothy was his First Squad leader, but as the senior enlisted Marine, and as the only NCO who had been with the platoon for more than six months, he was Ryck's go-to guy.

Ryck hoped Timothy could unfuck the supply situation. His Marines needed time not only to receive the gear, but they had to prepare it and display it for the skipper's junk-on-the-bunk scheduled for the evening. Why Capt Portuno felt he needed to inspect tonight was beyond Ryck. The skipper knew the situation with supply, and it wasn't as if the battalion was on a deadline for a deployment, after all.

Ryck couldn't make up his mind about the skipper. Capt Portuno looked the part of a Marine officer—tall, square-jawed, physically fit. There just seemed to be something missing in the man, something that Ryck couldn't quite put his finger on. Ryck had only been with the platoon for two days, though, so he had to admit that he could be misreading his company commander. He'd thought that Lt. Nidischii' had been somewhat reserved when he first met him, after all, and Ryck now had undying respect and admiration for the man.

Ryck sighed and got back to his report. He had less than an hour to get it compiled and submitted.

---

[65] T/O: Table of Organization. This is a list of what Marines and in what ranks were allotted to each unit.

[66] *Qua Patet Orbis:* "As far as the world extends"

"Request permission to come aboard," a voice sounded off from outside the platoon office.

"Enter," Ryck answered, looking up to see who it was.

"Holy grubbing shit!" Ryck said, jumping up to rush the staff sergeant standing in front of his desk.

Staff Sergeant Joshua Hope-of-Life was not only his oldest and closest friend in the Corps, he was Ryck's brother-in-law.

Ryck pounded on the larger man's shoulder, then wrapped him in a bear hug.

"What are you doing here?" Ryck asked as he released Joshua. "I'm up to my ass in alligators, but take a seat. I can spare a few minutes."

Joshua looked around the tiny office and said, "Nice hole you've got here. I had more room just with my desk and locker back on the drill field."

"Well, this is the real Corps here, devil dog. Not all that spit and polish BS," Ryck responded.

He wanted to take that back, though, when he saw the slight darkening of his friend's eyes. Joshua had initially been assigned to First Mar Div, but due to the vagaries of timing, had never seen combat while Ryck, in Third, had gotten more than his fair share of it. Joshua had been on the drill field when the war with Greater France had broken out, so he had sat out that conflict as well. Just when he'd thought he could get back into the fleet, he'd been placed on a special task force to re-evaluate recruit training. As a staff sergeant, Joshua had to be one of a small percentage to SNCOs never to have heard a shot fired in anger.

"So, what the heck are you doing out here?" Ryck asked, anxious to change the subject. "Your task force send you out to get feedback from the field?"

"The task force is finished. I'm finally off Tarawa, finally going back to the fleet," Joshua told him.

"No shit? And you're here, with Third? We're both in the same division?" Ryck asked. "What unit are you in?"

"That's the thing. Right now, I'm tentatively assigned to Kilo, 3/6. That is if the Second Platoon commander accepts me as his platoon sergeant."

It took a moment for that to register.

"You mean me?" Ryck asked.

"That's right, sir, you."

*Sir? Joshua's calling me sir now?* Ryck wondered.

"Uh, I mean, how did this happen? It can't be a coincidence," Ryck said.

"No, no coincidence. I really did get orders to Second Mar Div, which wasn't surprising given that the Corps is bringing the division back to T/O. But I banked a lot of favors with that task force, so when I found out I was coming here, I sort of called in some of those favors and got assigned to Kilo, and then to Second Platoon. If you'll have me, I mean," Joshua said, his voice flat, but with a hint of uncertainty to it.

Ryck looked at his friend, his brother-in-law for a moment before asking, "Why do you want to serve with me?" he asked.

Joshua shrugged before saying, "Shit seems to follow you. If I want to see some fighting, being with you seems like the best course of action. I talked to Hannah today before coming over to report in, and she told me I need to watch out for you, too."

Ryck stared at Joshua. He didn't think he could do it. Ryck was a lieutenant and Joshua a staff sergeant, but they were friends, they were family. How would that affect their working relationship? This just wasn't going to work.

"Joshua, do you think this is a good idea? I mean, we go way back together. How are you going to feel when I have to give you an order? How am I going to feel? I think I can swing you another platoon sergeant billet with Fifth Marines, and no one will wonder why you changed units. Don't you think that'd be better?" Ryck asked him.

Joshua's eyes clouded as he stood up and assumed the position of attention, eyes focused straight ahead and over Ryck.

"If the lieutenant doesn't believe I can do the job, he just has to say so. He doesn't have to do me any favors with other units. I will go where the Marine Corps tells me to go."

"That's not what I meant, Joshua, and you know it. It's just, well, don't you think it would be weird?" Ryck asked as he stood up.

"A Marine can either perform his mission or not. Nothing weird about it, sir. I know I don't have combat experience, and I know your platoon has to get trained up. So if you need a combat vet to assist you, if you believe I cannot do the job, then I request permission to be dismissed, sir," Joshua said, voice steady.

Ryck stood there, looking at Joshua, who refused to meet Ryck's eyes. He knew Joshua was a capable Marine, combat or not. Just to be one of the few DI's on the recruit training task force was proof enough of that. Ryck also knew that Joshua's lack of combat experience gnawed at him. Joshua needed to prove himself in combat. If Ryck refused him, that would only verify the inadequacy that Joshua unfairly placed on himself. As a friend, as a brother, Ryck didn't want to do that.

*This is really a bad idea,* he thought. *I need to say no.*

Instead, he said, "Well, who am I to question orders? We've got a junk-on-the-bunk in four hours, but the supply chief won't release the Class B gear. I trust that you can take care of that?"

Joshua finally looked down and caught Ryck's eyes.

"You mean, I'm in?" he asked, relief evident in his voice.

"You've got it, staff sergeant. And times a-wasting. I need you down at the supply shed now. There's a young sergeant, Sergeant Timothy, there who's going to be very happy to see you."

"Aye-aye, sir!" Joshua shouted as he started to turn to leave the office.

"Joshua," Ryck said, stopping his new platoon sergeant in his tracks.

Ryck held out his hand, which Joshua took.

"Welcome aboard, devil dog. It's good to have you with me."

# Killington Industries

## Chapter 7

"I can't believe Killington authorized the arty," Joshua said to Ryck as they lay side-by-side on the ridge a klick from the plant.

"Well, they've designated where we can fire, and most facilities are off limits, but yeah, that's pretty flash," Ryck responded. "We'll see how much good it will do in about a minute," he said before checking his face shield readout. "Make that 52 seconds."

The entire battalion had landed on Killington Industries five days before and had been cooling their heels waiting to either forge ahead with the mission or pack up and go back home. Most Marines thought their mere presence would goose the negotiations between Killington and Fukimoto Corp, with the Federation negotiating team assisting. But things had broken down last night past the point of no return, and the mission was given the thumbs up around midnight local time.

Killington Industries Co., Ltd. and Fukimoto Corp were industrial competitors of the first rate. When Killington had been granted the charter for the planet, Fukimoto had been thrown the bone of a right-to-operate license by the Federation. Killington had erected massive conversion facilities, while Fukimoto stayed small, with only a token facility. This had worked out for almost 70 years until Fukimoto decided to expand their factory. Killington, as the planetary authority, began to stymie Fukimoto by throwing roadblocks at the spaceport for the importation of machinery and equipment, making it difficult to hire construction workers, and refusing to authorized the increased power supplies.

Fukimoto sued Killington, claiming unfair impediment to business. Federation courts sided with Killington, acting as the Federation authority, though, stating that the Killington Industries charter only allowed for Fukimoto to operate on the planet, not for Killington, acting as the company, to have to support Fukimoto in that business. As Killington paid for the spaceport, paid to operate it, and paid for the infrastructure, they had the right to withhold services to a competitor or at least not work to improve them.

This raised a pretty heavy outcry throughout the Federation. A majority of Federation planets were under corporate charter, charters held by a tiny select group of corporations. Other companies needed freedom to operate on all planets, and this was setting a bad precedent. Fukimoto appealed the decision.

Ryck thought Fukimoto, and by inference, all the companies siding with their legal battle, had a good case. Federation charters granted wide powers to corporations, but they also incurred obligations, not the least of which was the requirement to be neutral representatives of the Federation itself on all planetary matters.

Then Fukimoto upped the ante. One of Killington's largest facilities, Killington Industries Plant #5, was located about 30 klicks beyond Fukimoto's own factory, and the power lines ran from the generation plant to Fukimoto's factory and then on to Killington's. Fukimoto threatened to shut down the power, and Killington responded by deploying corporate security into the Fukimoto plant, physically taking control of the power substation. Fukimoto was not going to simply accept that, so they hired a company from Kracivik's Battalion that not only cleared out the Killington jimmylegs[67] at the Fukimoto facility, but took over Killington's factory for good measure.

Fukimoto issued a press release that this was only to "protect" the power grid until the appeal process made its way through the court. The Federation stepped in, ordering both corporations to the negotiating table. The Marines were brought in to emphasize the Federation's resolve in the matter. When Fukimoto walked away, the Federation ordered the Marines to take back Factory #5.

Ryck had been in more than his fair share of conflicts, but never as a fully organized battalion landing team: 3/6 was only the infantry element. The landing team had two sections of arty, a tank platoon, a composite air squadron, and assorted combat and logistics attachments. Ryck glanced over to his right where an M1

---

[67] Jimmylegs: a somewhat derogatory term for hired security teams

Davis sat in defilade, its big Chrysler engine idling. A factory was not a great battleground for tanks, and Ryck had witnessed an M1 get taken out on Luminosity, but still, having it there gave Ryck a feeling of confidence.

As the countdown on his display reached zero, Ryck heard the crump of outgoing fire as the 160mm section opened up. The section had five tubes, each capable of putting out 10 rounds per minute. This time, though, the arty only fired only round apiece.

All eyes were focused downrange on the factory, waiting for the impacts. Ryck knew the targets, and with GPS sensors in each round, accuracy was not going to be an issue. Despite knowing where and when the rounds were going to hit, Ryck still flinched when the five explosions rocked the first five targets. One of those was a chemical storage tank which erupted in an impressive fireball, sending flames, then black smoke roiling 150 meters up into the air.

"Oo-rah" and "Get some" burst out of the Marines around him.

"Think the message got through?" Joshua asked him.

"Oh, I think they got the message. Killington's willing to sacrifice the factory," Ryck answered.

"So, they gonna surrender?" Joshua asked.

Ryck took a deep breath before answering, "That's the thing, right? I hope they do, but that's Kracivik's company. You know their rep."

Theodyne Kracivik had been a Congress of Free Worlds army officer before forming his own mercenary company. Over the years, it had grown into a battalion, one with a reputation of professionalism and loyalty to its employers. The mercs in the battalion were among the best paid of any military unit.

"All the money won't mean rat shit if they're dead. They're only a company, and we've got a battalion landing team with Navy support. They can't win," Joshua countered.

Joshua was thinking with logic. He hadn't been in combat and hadn't seen how men reacted when under fire, sometimes defying logic or reason.

"I hope you're right, but Kracivik's mercs get paid so well because of their rep. If they just give up, their rep goes out the door, right? So even if they can't win, they have to make a good show of it," Ryck told him.

"Good for the company bottom line, maybe, but if we zero the mercs, what about that? They won't be around for more campaigns to enjoy that rep."

"How many will be actually zeroed? Lot's of WIAs, lots of regen, but they can afford the best regen, and each merc gets that regen bonus. I just don't know what they'll do. But I guess we'll find out soon enough."

When the 160mm section opened up again not two minutes later, they had the answer. The mercs had evidently turned down whatever the CO[68] had offered them. The Wyvern missile section also fired, the big missiles showing up on Ryck's display. These were probably overkill given the targets the arty was authorized to engage, but Ryck knew they wanted to play too, and the arty det commander would have pushed hard for them.

A series of explosions lit up the factory, demolishing storage tanks, pipes, chimneys, and warehouses. Ryck could track the kinetic rounds on his display, but when the Wyvern arrived, he could actually see the two missiles with his naked eyes. One flew right in the front door of the factory headquarters, bringing down the entire building in a cloud of dust and smoke. The other Wyvern flew through the dust and hit a target out of Ryck's sight.

"OK, Josh, time to get going. Take your position," Ryck told his platoon sergeant as the warning light flashed on his display.

"Roger that. Keep your head down," Joshua said as he stood up and rushed to take his position.

"You too," Ryck sent on a B2B before checking his display again.

Ryck really would have rather been in a PICS again. He was most comfortable in them, but Kilo only had one PICS platoon, and that was First. Donte Ward was the First Platoon commander, and he'd never fought in PICS before, but the skipper told them he felt each lieutenant needed to expand his experiences. Consequently, Donte, who had fought well in skins and bones was in PICS, and

---

[68] CO: Commanding Officer

Ryck, who was highly decorated for actions in PICS, was in skins and bones. It didn't make much sense to Ryck, though. He felt Marines should maximize their strengths. Unfortunately, it was Capt Portuno's call.

Most of the factory compound was a mass of flames and smoke. The heart of the factory, though, where the fabrication took place, was untouched. There were corporate reps with the battalion CP, the arty sections, the assault section, and with the *FS Holle* in orbit above the battle area to make sure that the most valuable part of the factory did not suffer damage.

Lima Company was ordered to move out. It was to advance through the trees to a position north of the factory. Lima would then provide a base of fire for Kilo and India to move forward into the assault.

"Ten minutes," Ryck passed over the platoon net.

He'd hated it when his own commanders had stated the obvious, but he'd hated it more when he didn't know what was happening. Giving his Marines a countdown was not really necessary, given that they had the same countdown on their own displays, but Ryck was bound and determined to keep the comms open and flowing.

"Grizzly-two-five, give me a status check," he sent to Joshua.

Capt Portuno had insisted on using "Grizzly" as the company call sign. "Two" was second platoon, "five" was his platoon sergeant. Ryck liked the cleaner, more traditional method of call signs, in this case, a simple "Kilo" instead of the fanciful "Grizzly."

Ryck could have done the status checks on each Marine himself, but this was Joshua's first taste of combat, and he wanted his platoon sergeant to be busy with routine functions instead of imagining what might happen. It took a little longer than he would have expected, but finally Joshua reported that everyone was up and ready to go.

Ryck watched Lima move into position. The arty kept up intermittent fire: they had pretty much leveled all that they were allowed to hit, but the rounds served to keep the mercs' heads down as the two line companies started to move out. Kilo was on the left flank with India on the right. India was the heavy company, so they had two PICS platoons and one light platoon. Kilo had First Platoon in PICS and Second and Third, flanking First, in skins and bones.

Flanking the two assault companies were two tanks, their 75mm hypervelocity railguns seeking a target. Ryck had been offered tanks for his first reenlistment, but he had chosen to remain infantry. That didn't mean the big machines didn't impress him. They were mean and very threatening, but not for him.

The tanks' target acquisition systems were slaved into various sensors, both automatic and organic. The unseen recon team, for example, was hidden somewhere with eyes on the targets, and Navy spotters had the factory under full surveillance from up in orbit. The fact that the tanks never opened up was a pretty good indication that no mercs were showing their heads. With no enemy to engage, the company kept a steady pace, covering the 1,000 meters in just over 10 minutes. The arty suppressing fire tapered off as the two companies entered the campus, PICS in the lead, the light platoons following.

The data the suborbital sensors were gathering were analyzed up on the *Holle* and sent back down to the Marines as intel. There were organic remains from four humans within the wreckage at the plant. A few of the mercs, at least, would not be making it to regen. Their shields had kept them invisible as they waited, probably there to keep the Marines under observation. An arty round, though, doesn't care much about shields. It just pretty much blasts everything in sight. When the round hit, the shields were destroyed, so the human remains then became visible to the Navy sensors.

First Platoon, in their PICS, made their way through the outer walls and into the campus. They encountered no hostility. Ryck's platoon followed in trace, clambering over the ruins of the outer walls. His face shield display indicated that two of the dead bodies were just to his right. Ryck took a look, but the only thing he could see was a severed hand, dusty, but surprisingly intact, in the dirt. The rest of the mercs were under the rubble. Ryck watched his display first as LCpl Fielder, PFC Meung, and finally Joshua passed the hand. None of the three had been in combat before, and Ryck monitored each of their bioreadouts. Meung had almost no reaction, and Joshua only had a slight one, to Ryck's relief. Quite a few of Fielder's bioreadouts, though, had spiked, his pulse and blood pressure jumping as he gagged. Ryck started to switch to a P2P with the lance corporal

"Concentrate, Fielder," Sgt Timothy, the Marine's squad leader passed on his squad's circuit before Ryck could key in. "Nothing to see there."

Ryck grimaced. It wasn't his job to monitor each individual Marine. By focusing on the Marines behind him as they approached the merc's severed hand, he was not looking forward to where live mercs were certainly lying in wait. Gunny Meader's continual mantra of letting his NCOs do their job came back to him.

"All clear to Crazy Horse," SSgt Mourka passed back to Ryck. Mourka was the First's platoon sergeant, and he had half of his platoon clearing the way to Ryck's platoon objective, the QC Lab, designated Objective "Crazy Horse." Donte Ward was leading the rest of the platoon to Third Platoon's objective, the power station, designated "Light Finder."

As far as Ryck was concerned, the PICS Marines could have stormed the objective. The building, consisting of offices and a number of labs filled with quality control equipment, was where all of the factories products underwent quality testing. The ceilings were high, the labs large. A PICS Marine would have no problem maneuvering inside. However, the Killington reps had nixed that. It seems they didn't want Marines in PICS "blundering about," as they put it, "destroying valuable testing equipment." So First Platoon, with limited weaponry, was to go in and root out any mercs who had taken up position in the building.

A quick look-up on Janes[69] revealed that the Kracivik Battalion had recently bought Farnham CYL Plate armor for its soldiers. The "lobster" armor consisted of a tough, one-piece torso shell with strap on arm and leg plates. The main shell was fairly impervious to kinetic small arms, including the Marine's M99s. It could even deflect larger man-packed rounds, such as the M76

---

[69] *Janes*: the short name for a civilian data base of all things military. They often have more quality information on unit weapons and equipment than government intelligence agencies.

"bunker buster" that one Marine in each fire team carried, although a direct hit would pierce it.

The relative weakness in the armor was in the extremities. The arm and leg plates never seemed to fit well, leaving areas of vulnerability. Kinetic rounds could find those seams and joints, while energy weapons had even an easier time breaching the armor's protection. Against poorly armed fighters, and that included most militias, the lobster armor was quite effective. Against the better-armed Marines, it didn't match up to the Marines' skins and bones.

The lobster armor couldn't protect the four mercs who had been out in the arty barrage, but it should keep most of the mercs alive, if missing limbs, in a battle with infantry Marines.

"Grizzly-six, this is Grizzly-two-six. We are now passing through Grizzly-one and are assuming point of main effort," Ryck passed back to the skipper.

SSgt Mourka gave Ryck a nod as Ryck passed him. In the PICS, it was more of a lean than anything else, but the intent was clear. The field of battle had been passed to him.

"Sgt Timothy, send up your team," he passed on a P2P, foregoing the "Grizzly" call signs.

Their comms were shielded, encrypted, and employed frequency hopping, which made listening in by the enemy almost impossible, and Ryck wanted to leave no room for misunderstanding. On a simple P2P, he felt he could be more direct.

The Killington liaison team had given the Marines the combinations for all entrances, assuring the battalion that they would still be valid. They were confident that their codes could not be breached.

Ryck couldn't see any damage to the lab building, and if the codes could not be breached, then there couldn't be any mercs inside, right?

*And if you believe that, I've got some great beach-front property for you on Deseret*, he thought sourly to himself.

Ryck watched as Sgt Timothy sent forward his second fire team. Ryck slaved Cpl Goddard's feed to his own display, and he watched as LCpl Pannata keyed in the combination. Instead of a steady green light of an open door, the lock display went to a flashing amber. Pannata tried again, but no green. He turned to look right at Goddard, his hands raised, palms up, in the universal "I don't know" gesture.

*Grubbing hell!* Ryck thought.

He knew the codes would have been broken. This was a professional merc company in there, not some half-assed hackers.

His alternate plan had been to call the skipper to request a demo team, but that would take time, and he would have to explain why he couldn't open the doors to the lab. He looked up to see SSgt Mourka standing there, a huge hulk in his PICS.

"Staff sergeant," he keyed on a P2P. "Seems like the combos we got are not worth a rabbit's hop. I could call back for a boomboom team, but seeing as you guys are just standing around, you want to see if you can crack that door open?"

Ryck couldn't see inside the staff sergeant's visor, but he swore he could see the Marines posture change, the big PICS seemingly more alert.

"Uh, blow it open?" he answered back, holding up his attached HGL.

"Well, if we have to. But first, let's see if one of you can just ram your way through."

Ryck didn't think highly of the Killington reps, and if it came down to it, he'd level the lab if he had to, but still, sending a grenade through it might mean a ton of paperwork to explain why he'd dared to damage some piece of shit lab equipment.

"Well, it's not like that's some sort of military installation," the staff sergeant said. "Yeah, I'll give it a shot myself. Clear me with the company, though, will you, sir?"

"I've got you covered," Ryck said as the platoon sergeant left the P2P to coordinate with a few of his Marines.

"Grizzly-six, this is Grizzly-one-six. The combination codes were not valid. I repeat, they were not valid. I am commencing my own breach," Ryck sent back to his commander.

Ryck thought the captain might want a longer explanation, or worse, tell Ryck to wait until he could come up to the position.

Instead, the captain merely told him to go ahead and report back when he got the door open.

If there were mercs inside, they had to know the Marines were there, ready to come in. The delay was frustrating, and it gave any mercs more time to prepare. If Ryck had his way, he would have had a team from Weapons Platoon, and they would have blown open an entrance right through a wall with a Banshee. Never enter where an enemy thought you would was one of the prime lessons taught at recruit training. When he'd suggested this, he thought the Killington rep was going to have a heart attack. The rep had gone on about how the company was "allowing" the Marines to destroy the outer facilities, but Killington would not stand for any of their core facilities being damaged.

"Sgt Timothy, move two teams up to cover Staff Sergeant Mourka, then back to the plan. I want your squad in and in fast. Secure the front office. Second squad's going to be on your ass," Ryck told his First Squad leader over the platoon command circuit. "All three of you squad leaders, get your Marines moving. We don't know if there's anyone in the lab, but we need to mass our forces if we meet resistance. Watson and Ariana, no gap."

Then, over his platoon circuit, "We've got a slight delay here. As you can see, the combination we received is worthless. We've got Staff Sergeant Mourka now about to create a breach. As soon as he does, we're back on track."

"Joshua, I really need you to push. Make sure Ariana gets Third in. Keep an eye on him, and let me know after this is over if you still think he's got what it takes," Ryck passed to his platoon sergeant after switching to a P2P.

Ryck wasn't sure Sgt Tand Ariana had it in him to be an effective combat Marine. Joshua, though, wasn't ready to give up on the squad leader. This was Ariana's chance to prove himself. If he fell short, Ryck was ready to get Ariana transferred. Ryck felt that Cpl Kerrick Howell, the squad's Third Fire Team leader, was more than capable of leading the squad if it came to that. A gung ho aggressive corporal was better than a weak sergeant any day of the week.

Ryck turned his attention back to SSgt Mourka. The PICS Marine, flanked by four others, was at the double doors leading into the building. He stood there a moment, studying the entrance. Taking a step forward, he put his gauntleted arms, one on each door, and pushed. To Ryck's surprise, the doors crashed in. He'd expected the SSgt to be able to break them down, but these didn't offer even a hint of resistance. Then again, this wasn't a military installation. A simple retina scan and lock would have been more than enough to keep unauthorized people out of the building.

SSgt Mourka stumbled in, probably surprised the doors had collapsed so easily as well, followed immediately by his security.

"Go First!" Ryck sent, even though Sgt Timothy had his squad right on the PICS Marines' asses.

There was a burst of automatic fire, then several answering bursts and one explosion. Ryck was slaved into Sgt Timothy, but by the time his squad leader made it into the building, the fight was over. Icons appeared on Ryck's display as the AIs analyzed what the PICS and First Squad Marines were able to pick up. There were four more mercs inside the office: all were down, but only one was zeroed. Sgt Timothy was already calling for Doc Camp.

One of the PICS Marines was out of action. LCpl Vance was unhurt, but he was out of the fight with a fried PICS. One of the mercs had taken him out with what the AIs identified as a DIF-3 "Diablo" rocket.

Ryck had heard of Diablos, but he was not completely familiar with them, so he popped up the specs as he ran forward to the building. The Diablo was a small, relatively inexpensive 6mm rocket, a semi-smart fire-and-forget. It was dual-use, with both a small shape charge and pulse warhead. The shape charge could pierce armor, depositing the pulse warhead inside the outer layers of defense of its target. The little rocket had taken a PICS out of action. From what Ryck read off the specs, just the shape charge alone could wreck havoc on a Marine in skins and bones. Ryck flashed the spec summary to the platoon. He hoped the mercs wouldn't have too many of the rockets, but his Marines had to be aware of them.

Ryck dashed through the smashed entrance. Sgt Timothy had his squad deployed to cover the entire outer office. Two of the

PICS Marines were at the entrance to the lab floor while two more were assisting LCpl Vance out of his PICS. The office itself was in shambles. The Killington rep was going to be royally pissed.

*Fuck him*, Ryck thought. *Take it up with the lawyers after all this is over.*

"Hold on Sgt Ariana," he passed to his Third Squad leader. "It's getting crowded in here, so secure the entrance for now."

This was a 180 from Ariana's previous orders, but flexibility was a key to combat. Nothing went according to plan, and Ariana had to be able to adjust.

"What about me?" Joshua asked over the P2P.

Ryck knew that Joshua was itching to get into the fight. But he needed his platoon sergeant with Third.

"Stay with Ariana. Make sure no one comes up our ass here. Once I get my bearings, we're pushing on, and I'm going to need you to bring up the rear," Ryck passed.

"Sergeant Timothy, get a probe through the hatch into the lab, then I want you and Sergeant Watson over to me," he sent on the platoon circuit.

"Lieutenant Ward wants to know if you still need us," SSgt Mourka asked him.

"Hey Donte, Mourka was a big help," Ryck said after switching to a P2P with the First Platoon commander. "You need them back now?"

"Is Vance OK? Mourka says he's fine, but he'd say that no matter what," Donte asked first.

Ryck looked over at the lance corporal, who was laughing at something one of the other Marines had said. He looked naked in his longjohns, but he had his Ruger out of the leg holster and in his hand.

"He looks fine. I'll have Doc check him out, though, after he stabilizes the mercs."

"OK, that's good. About Mourka, I'm in a holding pattern now. The Killington rep is on my ass not to let my guys get too aggressive. But if you need him, you got him," Donte said.

Ryck's display suddenly lit up with more data. Cpl Goddard had run a probe through the entrance to the lab floor, and it was picking up more data. The AIs were trying to analyze that and decipher it into usable intel. The mercs inside were shielded, but there were enough tiny leaks to be able to start to form a picture of what awaited them.

Ryck was tempted to ask Donte to task Mourka and the squad to him to assault the lab, but the ROEs were pretty clear. Like it or not, he had to minimize damage.

"No, I don't need them to be taking anything out of my salary to pay for stuff they destroy. A year's pay probably wouldn't take care of the broom and shitcan they use to clean up the place. If you don't mind, though, I'd like them to secure our six so I can use all three squads to assault," Ryck responded.

"You got it, bro. Let me tell Mourka. This is Donte the Great, out."

Ryck had started to key in the platoon command circuit but stopped as he broke out in a laugh. Donte was still Donte, whether back at the O-Club or here in combat.

"Doc, how are the mercs?" he sent to HM3 Campomanosi, Doc "Camp."

"We've got three WIA. One is a Code 3, but the other two are Code 1s. Lots of regen for all three, but the Code 1 needs to get casevac'd ASAP," Doc told him.

Ryck didn't have the merc's bioreadouts, of course, but Doc uploaded his own findings. Ryck had basic first aid training, but not much of what Doc sent really meant a lot to him. That is, except for the Code 1. Code 1 meant a life-and-death situation where a WIA needed immediate evacuation and advanced care. The UCFMJ required that all prisoners receive medical care as required.

Tactically, Ryck didn't want to give the mercs inside any more time to prepare or plan. Waiting for a casevac would give them that time. On the other hand, the mercs inside knew they had a KIA and three WIA, and they probably knew that one of the WIAs was serious. They would counter-attack when it wouldn't put their comrades in danger.

There was also the moral side of the issue. These were men, just like his Marines. Ryck would hope that if the situation were reversed, any wounded Marines would be afforded proper care. The moral issue trumped tactics.

"OK, call it in," he told Doc.

He wasn't just going to call a timeout in the battle, though.

"Staff Sergeant Mourka, can you get parole from the two Code 3s, then stand by with the Code 1 until he can get casevac'd?" he asked the First Platoon sergeant.

Ryck knew a Kracivik merc would honor his parole, even if he wasn't wounded. The two Code 3's would pose no problem.

"Roger that, sir," SSgt Mourka responded. "I've got the rest of Second Squad providing security now, and I'll leave two Marines in here with the mercs."

It would still be crowded inside the office, but that freed up Ryck's Third Squad and Joshua. Ryck called them in. The AIs kept trying to firm up the intel, but things were still hazy. They estimated that there were between eight and 15 mercs inside the two main QC labs. They seemed to be pretty spread out, probably around the major pieces of equipment. The mercs would have guessed that Killington would try and protect its assets and make sure the ROIs were limited.

Ryck needed to keep up the momentum. He couldn't let the mercs adjust to the flow. But Capt Portuno had given him a direct order to get into the building, then assess the situation. This screamed against all of Ryck's instincts, but orders were orders.

With his four key Marines, he quickly went over the newest intel, sparse as it was, and their original plan. Not much of the plan had to be adjusted, which was both surprising and frustrating. It was surprising because no plan survives the actual start of a battle, and frustrating because they could have flowed right into the second phase of the assault without hesitation.

Ryck's "assessment" took all of 45 seconds. The captain may have wanted a more detailed assessment, but Ryck had at least obeyed the letter of the law. The only change Ryck made was that after First and Second cleared the two main labs on either side of the building with Third in the middle acting as a reaction force, he tasked Third, with Joshua, to clear the environmental lab at the far end of the building. The sensors were not picking up anything from that area, and Ryck thought that might be a safer opportunity to see how Ariana—and Joshua—would react.

He was about to give the order to blow the doors into the lab floor when he had a change of heart.

"SSgt Mourka, I think I need two of your Marines for a little breaching. Can you spare them?"

The staff sergeant readily agreed, and a few moments later, two PICS Marines lumbered up, their heads almost touching the ceiling. Ryck told them what he wanted, and both moved into position. Ryck put First and Second Squads right off the PICS Marines' hips. At his signal, both PICS Marines simply punched out two entries into the lab, then stood aside as Ryck's two squads poured in.

Always make your own entrance was the rule, and with simple, non-structural walls separating the office from the lab floor, Ryck knew the PICS Marines would have no problem creating new entrances, and that with no real resistance, there would not be damage to any equipment on the other side.

For a moment, as the Marines poured in, there was no response. For only a moment, though. Just as Ryck was following First in, the mercs opened up. An automatic weapon opened fire from an elevated position and in back of the lab. Several Marines were hit before they could get in among some of the bigger pieces of equipment in the room, but no one was taken out. Their bones had worked as designed.

Shadows flitted between the testing equipment as his Marines took them under fire. Ryck could see sparks as darts rebounded off of plate armor, but enough found their way through, and several mercs went down. One was down hard in the middle of an opening, yet at least one Marine continued to pour fire at the merc. Ryck checked his display to see who that was, but Sgt Watson cut in on the net, telling PFC Julian to cease fire. Ryck held no love for the mercs, but he hoped the man hadn't been killed after being put out of action. Marines weren't supposed do that kind of thing, but Ryck was also experienced enough to know that in a firefight, some things just happened. Julian was a newbie, and as Ryck saw when he checked Julian's bioreadouts, was hyped up on adrenaline.

"Sgt Timothy, I want someone on that automatic weapon," he passed.

Now that they were in among the huge pieces of testing gear near the entrance, the machine gun was more of an annoyance than a danger, but as they progressed to the smaller banks of equipment, they would move back under the gun's fields of fire. Someone had placed the weapon well, and it had to be taken out. Unfortunately for the gun team, the Marines had the means to do that.

A few moments later, a HGL off to Ryck's right fired. Ryck caught a glimpse of the grenade as it arched to the far back, then exploded low on the far wall. The gunner adjusted his aim, and fired again. This time, though, the grenade hit the overhead as it arched up, exploding right there, only half way to its target. Maybe the merc commander had been smarter than Ryck had initially thought. The low overhead precluded anything like a grenade launcher from traversing the length of the lab.

"M76, Timothy," Ryck passed.

The M76 Bunker Buster had a flatter trajectory. It would also cause more damage. But grub that. Ryck was not going to move his Marines forward into a line of automatic fire before he could employ an HGL. He didn't care if it brought down the entire far side of the lab.

A round of some sort ricocheted off the pulling arm of the machine Ryck was using as cover. He felt a small piece of something hit him in the chin, stinging him. Jumping back, he had to remind himself that the mercs were still out there, trying to bring him down. He wasn't invincible.

"Watson, Timothy, get ready. As soon as the machine gun is taken out, I want you two to move itt. Rush the bastards before they can react," he passed.

He turned around and caught Joshua's eyes. With Third Squad, he'd moved up and was right in back of the other two squads, ready to go. He leaned out to give Ryck a thumb's up, only to jerk back as two rounds impacted on his bones.

*Stupid shit!* Ryck thought. *Hannah will kill me if I let you get hurt!*

He had to laugh, though, when Joshua made an exaggerated face, holding his forefinger up to his temple, mimicking shooting a handgun. The near miss hadn't even fazed him.

There was the sharp report of the M76, then a second later, a blast reverberated from the far side of the big lab. A huge hole appeared where an office or storeroom had been and from where the machinegun had been firing.

Immediately, the two Marine squads rushed forward firing as they went. Ryck got caught up in the moment, and he rushed as well, his M99 in the assault firing position. He didn't have a target, but simply by firing, he was helping keep the heads down of any mercs. On his display, one of his Marine's icons went light blue. Cpl Keisen was down, but not KIA. Keisen was only a couple of meters to Ryck's right, but out of Ryck's line of sight.

Ryck made it across the open area in the middle of the lab where overhead cranes and rails carried larger items to be tested from the loading bays to the test machines. Ryck wasn't sure why his mind noted this. To a Marine, it was simply an open area. Its purpose was really immaterial.

Ryck stopped to kneel beside what he recalled was a tensile strength tester, something that came unbidden to his mind from the list of equipment he'd studied before the assault. Running and firing interfered with his ability to process his display. He focused on what was happening. Two Marines were down, but not seriously hurt. At least one merc was KIA, and another three looked to be WIA. That was not counting the automatic gun team. AI's were notoriously inaccurate in assessing enemy information without more sophisticated sensors than infantry Marines carried into combat, and the gun team was not registering yet.

There was a flicker of red in his display which corresponded with a position just off to his left. Timothy's squad had just passed through that position, so Ryck figured it had to be another merc casualty, only now showing up on the sensors. He glanced over his shoulder and was shocked to see a merc who had obviously just climbed out of the base for a mandrel bend tester. He had a smile on his face as he leveled a Diablo rocket at Ryck. From this distance, the merc couldn't miss. Ryck tried to spin around to take the merc under fire, but he knew he would be too late.

A line of darts hit the merc just as he fired, jerking him up just enough so the Diablo blew over Ryck's shoulder, the heat singeing his cheek as it passed. More rounds impacted the merc, who dropped his launcher and fell to a sitting position, one hand raised up in surrender, one arm rapidly become a bloody mess.

Ryck touched his chin which tingled from the rocket's blast past him, his heart pounding from his close call. He looked back up to see Joshua covering the merc while he sent Pvt Gilliard forward to disarm the man. It wasn't until the private signaled the all clear and zip-tied the merc's hands, wounded arm and all, that Joshua looked over to catch Ryck's eyes.

He had a huge smile on his face, and he pointed at his chest, then at Ryck. He had Ryck's back, he was saying. Ryck had been so concerned about keeping Joshua alive, so concerned about Hannah and Hope and little Ester, but it had been Joshua who'd saved Ryck's life.

Ryck gave Joshua a little salute, then got back to the task at hand. He'd thank Joshua later. He'd almost gotten killed because he'd reverted to being a fighter, not a leader. He'd gotten caught up in the fight, and he'd lost sight of his job. When he'd tried to get back on track, it had been too late. He'd been targeted. Gunny Meader would have his ass on a plate if he knew what had happened.

*Time to act like a leader of Marines, not some grubbing super warrior! Shitcan that ego!* he admonished himself.

He motioned for Third Squad to move up, giving him a bit of security as he brought his display back up so he could take control of the platoon again. But suddenly, more and more red icons appeared on the display. For a moment, he thought they were under a counter-attack, and he got ready to issue orders. But then it became clear. The mercs were surrendering. They had turned off their shields and were coming out. They had done enough to honor their contract, but now it was over.

Nine mercs walked forward, hands in the air. Coupled with three KIA, two being the automatic gun team, and seven WIA, they had only started with 18 men to face a better-armed Marine platoon. Make that 14 men and four women. Ryck had been surprised to see that one of the WIA, two of the ones who surrendered, and the merc leader were all women. Ryck knew that many merc companies had women in their ranks, but as a Federation Marine, he was not used to the idea. Yet the mercs, as they were both given medical treatment and giving their parole, treated each other, men and women, seemingly without regard to gender.

The merc captain had thanked Ryck for their treatment and accepting their surrender and parole. She asked about the three who had been in the outer office. She acted as any officer would. And if Ryck was honest with himself, given her resources, she had actually led her company quite competently. The only difference was her gender.

"Well, Ryck, looks like we got out of this one pretty light," Joshua said after the merc captain took her leave of Ryck to rejoin her men.

"Two wounded, neither one pretty bad. Yeah, I'd say that's pretty light. It could have been worse, you know, if not for you."

"I've got your back, Ryck. I promised Hannah, that I would."

The two Marines, brothers-in-law, fell into silence. That was all they said about the incident. That was all they needed to say.

# Zephyr-Hadreson

## Chapter 8

Ryck took a long swig of Poison Amber Ale, draining his bottle. The O-Club had Poison both on tap and in the normal pressure packs, but the last CG[70] had a liking for his beer in real bottles, so the O-Club started stocking them. Ryck really liked the bottled beer, too. He knew the taste was the same, but the feel of a cold bottle in his hand made drinking a more visceral experience for him. True, the pressure packs were more practical and could cool a beer within five seconds of activation, but they never felt as good in his hand.

He let out a loud burp and said, "Well, I'm off. You guys take it easy."

"You leaving, you lightweight?" Donte asked. "We're just getting started. Let me get you another round."

"No, I really have to go," Ryck protested. "Hannah's got this dinner thing going, and she'll kill me if I'm late."

"You are so whipped," Cal Anderson said, taking a slow sip of his cider. "That's why you'll never see me tied down with a wife."

Cal was the Third Platoon commander. He was younger than both Donte and Ryck, having gone straight to the Academy without serving as an enlisted Marine first. Ryck thought he had a pretty high opinion of himself, but Ryck was honest enough to realize that might just be his personal opinion of officers who had never been enlisted. Donte, Jeremiah Benton (the weapons platoon commander) and Unger Tately (the company XO) had all been enlisted before being commissioned and had fought in the last war.

Most of the lieutenants in the battalion were there at the club. The battalion had just had their new star on their battle streamer awarded at a ceremony an hour before, and the officers had gathered at the club to hoist a celebratory drink (or two). The action on Killington had barely deserved a star, Ryck thought. Of course, to LCpl Godfrey of India Company, or more correctly, to his

[70] CG: Commanding General

family, dying during a quick police action or in a major conflict didn't make much difference. Dead was dead.

"That's assuming you could ever find anyone who'd want to marry you, dickwad," Donte told Cal.

"They all want to, and can you blame them? I mean, look at me," Cal said, one hand sweeping to take in his frame.

"Well, I'm outta here, guys. Don't get too plastered. We're still the secondary alert battalion," Ryck interrupted their trash talk, knowing he could be there for hours if he waited for it to subside on its own

He ignored their cat calls and walked out of the club. It was a brisk evening, making him feel invigorated. He felt even more invigorated as he walked up to his brand new Hyundai Vulture. It might not match his brother-in-law Barret's Tonora, but it was more car than he'd had ever hoped for. Hannah had surprised him with it when he'd gotten back from Killington. He'd balked at the price she'd paid, but only half-heartedly. Hannah had gotten a job at the Federation lab on base, and as a FS-15, she not only outranked him, but she made almost twice as much as he did. Besides, the Vulture was one sweet ride.

The Vulture recognized him and the driver's door swung up. Ryck slid inside, the nanos in the seat molding it around him. He'd only had one beer, so the hover allowed him to take control. The hover was almost silent as it rose off the deck, only the low, almost subsonic rumbling giving any indication of the horsepower under the hood.

Ryck eased the Vulture out of the parking lot. He carefully kept to the speed limit on base. The MP's were extremely strict, and they seemed to like nothing more than to give officers, especially lieutenants, citations. Once out the gate, he opened the Vulture up a little. The hover leapt forward like a racehorse released from the bit.

Ryck almost wished he lived further away. He was in base housing, though, in Januzek Manor, only three klicks from the main gate. He slowed back down, passed through the gate, and barely puttered down the street to his home. With Hannah's new job, they, as a couple, rated a single home with the senior officers. But they'd decided to stay in the junior officer housing. Hannah and Ryck had half of a duplex. It wasn't large, and Hannah had been used to better back on Prophesy, but for Ryck, it was fine, more than fine, actually.

He carefully pulled the Vulture alongside Hannah's Creighton B50, then set it down. It looked like he was the last one there. Joshua's old Ford Flamingo was parked in front. Joshua had been at the same ceremony, yet he'd obviously not stopped for a drink, first, before heading over. Score one for the brother-in-law.

"'Bout time you made it," Joshua said from the couch as Ryck entered.

Joshua was in his civvies, a cider in one hand, the other reaching into a bowl of chips. Technically, there was nothing wrong with him being in officer country. Ryck and Joshua were brothers-in-law, after all. But still, he always came over in civvies if it was a social call.

"Duty calls," Ryck responded, reaching for his own handful of chips.

"I thought I heard you," Hannah said, coming into the room followed by Hope, Joshua's wife.

Hannah was a very competent, independent woman who had a pretty high-flying job. But Ryck was sure that she appreciated having Hope around. They were both Torritites from Prophesy, and that common background kept Hannah grounded.

"Have I told you how beautiful you are?" Ryck asked, putting his arm in back of her, pulling her close for a kiss.

"Not be often enough," she responded after coming up for air, playfully reverting to her Torritite speech pattern what with her brother and sister-in-law there. "But you sayin' that now won't be getting' you out of trouble. I be smellin' the beer on your breath. Joshua and Hope be comin' more than 30 minutes ago, and I be left with entertainin' them."

"Well, it was worth a try," Ryck said with a laugh. "But you are beautiful."

"Why be you not more as Ryck," Hope asked her husband, her Torritite patois much more pronounced than Hannah's. "He be havin' the best sugar mouth around."

"Thanks a lot, Ryck," Joshua said with an overacting tone before turning to Hope.

"Thou be the fairest maiden in all the land, love of my life," Joshua said, one hand sweeping towards the floor as he bowed his head.

"OK, OK, it be getting' deep in here," Hannah said, trying not to laugh. "If you two gentlemen can set the table, Hope here has prepared somethin' special for us."

"You heard the ladies," Ryck told Joshua. "Let's get at it."

"And what will you be doing?" Joshua asked when Ryck didn't join him.

"Let me get out of this uniform, and I'll be right back down."

The two men quickly set the table after Ryck returned, and a few minutes later, the two women brought in the food. Hannah was right about the meal. She had bought a real prime rib, and Hope had spent the day at the house slow-roasting it. With fresh veggies, mashed potatoes, and a garden salad, the meal was prime alpha. Ryck stuffed himself to bursting. He stayed to clear the table as the other three went to the front room where Hannah had prepared a pitcher of sangria.

Sangria was not really an after dinner drink, but Ryck was pleasantly surprised to find it was a nice, crisp balance to the heavy meal. He had three glasses before it was gone and he switched to cider. The four sat around, mostly listening to Hannah and Joshua telling tales about each other when they were kids. At one point, when Joshua was relating when an eight-year-old Hannah had gotten her hand stuck in a toilet, Ryck laughed so hard that cider came out of his nose, burning as it came. That made all four of them laugh even harder.

It took a few moments for Ryck to realize the recall was being sounded. The four of them were singing a love song popular when they had been in high school, and it wasn't until Joshua's wrist PA started chiming in with its own recall that the singing stopped.

"What's going on?" Ryck asked stupidly, more than a little tipsy.

"Oh, man. We've got to get back to battalion. It's the sergeant major, I know it is," Joshua slurred in disgust.

The sergeant major was a reformed alcoholic, and his opinion of Marines who drank was well known. Ryck thought it was within the realm of possibility that the sergeant major had convinced the CO to sound a recall. The battalion was the secondary alert battalion, and technically, they should be ready to take off on a moment notice. That had never happened without prior warning, though, at least as far as Ryck knew.

Ryck shook his head, trying to clear it.

"Baby, can you get us both a cup of coffee?" he asked Hannah. "If it really is just a drill, we'll be back in a couple of hours, but we should sober up a bit if we can.

"Well, Joshua, you ready? Get some water on your face, and we'll head on back."

Hannah came back with the coffee, and both Marines drained the cups. It really didn't help. Ryck kissed Hannah before he noticed Hope seemed worried.

"Nothing to it, Hope. It's probably just a drill, and we'll be back in a shake."

The two men went to Joshua's Flamingo. The hover's AI detected the level of alcohol and refused to relinquish control. Joshua keyed in the battalion, and the hover lifted off in automatic mode and took them back to the gate where a line of hovers slowly made it past security. It looked like the entire division was on the recall. Whatever this was, it wasn't the sergeant major checking to see how many Marines had been drinking.

When they finally pulled into the battalion area, Ryck told Joshua to go check on the platoon to see if everyone was making it back. Ryck made his way to the battalion CP to see what was up. Donte, still in uniform, saw him and motioned him over.

"All officers are supposed to be in the conference room in ten. You hear anything yet?" he asked Ryck.

"I just got here. What about you?"

"Nothing. We were still at the club when the recall came," Donte said.

They both made their way to the conference room where most of the officers were already gathered. The majority of them were in civvies. Capt Yu was even in coat and tails. Ryck knew the captain and his wife were champion ballroom dancers, and he figured the suit had to be related to that. There was surprisingly little talking as the Marines waited. The sheer number of people streaming back onto base was indicative that something, probably something big, was up.

"Attention on deck!" the XO shouted as he and the CO burst through the hatch.

The CO was in PT gear, so this had evidently caught him unawares as well. He strode to the head of the conference table before putting them at ease. He nodded to Terry Olney, the commo[71], to start the holo.

The image was only 2D, obviously from a security camera.

"This was just received at Franklin Station from G.K. Nutrition Six about an hour ago," the CO intoned. "I have not seen it yet, but I've been briefed by the CG. I will withhold comment until I see it with all of you first."

Ryck shifted his position from where he was standing behind the company commanders and senior staff so he could see the display better. The image seemed to be a gathering of some sort, a picnic or fair. People were eating, kids were darting back and forth. It was a scene probably repeated hundreds if not thousands of times each day throughout the Federation—nothing remarkable.

Then things changed. People started falling to the ground while others started screaming and running. More fell, and the panic grew to encompass all the people.

"What the hell?" someone said from the far side of the room as they watched.

"Who's attacking them?" Capt Yu asked, voicing something each of them was probably thinking.

The CO held up his hand, palm out, and the muttering ceased. He focused on the screen.

When the attackers appeared in view, even the CO couldn't quiet the gasps. Shockingly, the attackers were not human. They looked like something out of a scifi flick. Standing about five or six feet tall, the, well, *creatures* were bipedal, walking upright. Covered

---

[71] Commo: Communications Officer

in hair or fur, they looked like odd, vaguely familiar teddy bears. There was no mistaking the weapons in their hands, though. The short, squat guns had glowing balls at their fore, and the creatures launched the balls forward at the few people still left alive.

Then it hit Ryck why the creatures seemed familiar. They were walking upright, were larger, and had weapons, but it was unmistakable. They were larger, deadlier versions of the capys, the smaller creatures that the farmers had been trying to exterminate.

Humanity had finally run into intelligent life, and the capys' big brothers were back for revenge.

# G.K. Nutrition Six

## Chapter 9

"The *Shetlands* just got destroyed. No survivors," Ryck passed to Joshua as they moved across the abandoned fields to the salt mine where a pocket of survivors were hopefully still hanging on.

"How the hell did that happen? The entire ship?" Joshua asked incredulously.

"Looks like it. I'm not getting everything, but an alien ship appeared and took out the *Shetlands*. It's been either driven off or destroyed, but I can't get clear word on that."

"A capy ship?" Joshua asked.

"Has to be," Ryck responded.

Ryck was monitoring the command circuit which was understandably on fire. He glanced up as if he could see what was happening in space around G.K. Nutrition Six, but the heavens were quiet. The day was sunny, the breeze light. Genmodded bees were the only sign of animal life as the Marines moved through the knee-high wheat.

Despite the situation, Ryck reached down and took a handful of soil. Before enlisting, he'd been a farmer on Prophesy. This planet's soil was excellent, which was not surprising given GKN's experience and resources. If the soil on his farm had been half this good, he might still be back on Prophesy, tilling the fields.

"Grizzly Two, this is Grizzly Six. You need to pick up the pace. We've been ordered to be ready for evac in 90 mikes. Get that salt mine checked out ASAP, then report back. I'll try to get a flight of Storks in to pick you and any civilians up at your position, but don't count on it. If I can't get one, you've got to be at LZ Diego at 1430. You copy that? Over" Capt Portuno passed on the command circuit.

Ryck checked his display. They were still a good klick-and-a-half from the entrance to the mine, then another klick to the open field designated as LZ Diego. He'd originally been given a pick-up time of 1800.

"Roger, Grizzly-Six. Understood. Any reason given for the change? Do we have signs of capys in my AO?[72]"

"Negative to the enemy here. But up there and with 2/6, things are heating up, and the Navy has been ordered to withdraw," the captain said. "Keep me informed. Grizzly-Six, out."

"Listen up," Ryck passed on the platoon circuit. "The situation has changed, and the Navy's got to pull out sooner. The *Shetlands* has been hit hard, and 2/6 is already being evacuated. We've been ordered to get to our objective, rescue any civilians, and get back to the LZ for pickup by 1430. There's no way we'll make it in a platoon V, so we're switching to a column—First Squad, then Second and Third. Sgt Timothy, send a team out ahead 100 meters to precede us, then everyone move it. I want to be there in 20 mikes."

"Twenty mikes?" Joshua asked on the P2P. "That's almost at a double time. What happened to the tactical security you were harping on?"

Ryck hated leaving the V, which provided optimum security. While there were no known capy soldiers in the area, something had caused the local settlement to go to ground. He wished he could contact them, but the salt mine in which they had taken refuge blocked all comms. The group of 36 settlers had passed that they were going in, then once in, they were out of contact.

"No choice here. I hate it, but we've got to make time. The Navy's going to pull out, and I don't think we want to be here alone when they do," Ryck told Joshua.

"No, not with what happened to 2/6," Joshua agreed. "I guess there's no helping it. You move on up with First. I'll bring up the rear, kicking ass to keep everyone going."

Second Battalion, Sixth Marines had formed one half of the NEO[73] task force sent to rescue any surviving civilians. While the Federation Council hemmed and hawed and tried to come to an agreement with the Brotherhood, the Congress of Free Worlds, the Liberty Alliance, and the major independent worlds on how to react to the attack on GKN, 2/6 and 3/6 were dispatched, along with four

---

[72] AO: Area of Operations

[73] NEO: Noncombatant Evacuation Operations

Navy ships of the line, to evacuate the planet. Recon teams had been sent in first while the ships scanned the planet's surface. Pockets of humans had been located, but none of the soldier capys. 2/6 had been tasked with the main population center of Peterbund while 3/6 was given the scattered settlements across the main growing region.

When 2/6 entered Peterbund, they found thousands of people—all dead. Fewer than 30 were discovered hiding out in the sewers, in a bank vault, and in building crawlspaces. What they didn't find was capys—no sign of them at all. The Marines' and Navy's sensors were quiet.

Two hours earlier, though, the capys found them. They appeared suddenly among the Marines, attacking. Ryck wasn't connected to the 2/6 or MEB command circuit, but from what was being passed, 2/6 was in the shit. Casualties were mounting fast. Ryck had told Joshua all he had been able to glean, but as no good specific intel was being disseminated, all he'd told the platoon was that contact between 2/6 and the capys had been initiated.

The Navy had insisted that the 3/6 AO was clear, but they hadn't detected the capys in Peterbund, either. Now Ryck was forced to move into a column. If they got hit, it wouldn't be pretty.

Ryck slid in behind the First Squad's Second Fire Team. Cpl Ibrahim, the Third Fire Team leader, led the point team out in front of the column. The four Marines were trotting ahead, eyes and sensors scanning the fields for any threat. One hundred meters behind them, Second Fire Team led the rest of the platoon.

The terrain consisted of slightly rolling wheat fields, broken up by low hedgerows of a native vegetation, genmodded to coexist with the Terran crops. It was pleasantly warm, and their skins' cooling webs had no problem keeping the Marines comfortable as they trotted along. Even with the bones inserted, they moved freely. Take away their weapons, and they could be back on Zephyr-Hadreson running an afternoon PT on a nice spring day.

Their stress levels, though, were not the same as if back home. The enemy was out there somewhere, an enemy with unknown capabilities. Ryck felt exposed, moving through the fields.

He kept flicking his viewfinder to max magnification, trying to spot any movement.

Up ahead of the main body, the point team held up. They had reached the mine head. This wasn't a huge working mine as on Atacama, where Ryck had first tasted combat. The opening to the mine was simply a hole going into the low hill. The door to the mine was simply two pieces of corrugated metal, tied shut with wire. A dump truck and a pickup hover had been set down in front of the doors as if to provide more of an obstacle.

"Check them for keys," Ryck told the Marines in First Squad as he came up.

LCpl's Thomas and Sutarno checked out each cab but ended up empty-handed.

*That would have been too easy,* Ryck thought.

With a PICS, he could have simply shoved the vehicles aside. Even breaking out their muscles—the strength-augmenting framework each Marine could attach to their skins— the dump truck would be a tough move.

Ryck walked over to the far side of the two vehicles. There was enough room between them and the door for the Marines to squeeze by.

"What do we got?" Joshua asked as he came up.

"We can get by these, but single file," Ryck told him. "Have Ariana form a perimeter around the door. No, belay that. Make it Watson. I want you inside with me, and Doc. I'd rather have Watson handle the security. And I want his sensors on max gain. Give him one of your dragonflies, and get it up in the air."

"Roger that," Joshua said before striding off to brief the two squads.

Ryck turned back to Sergeant Timothy and said, "I don't think the capys are here, but that doesn't mean squat. I want that door blown, then get your squad in as fast as you can. I'll be on your ass, but make contact with any civilians. We've got to get them and get out of here ASAP."

Ryck looked back, and Sgt Watson was getting his Marines deployed around the mine opening. Within moments, First Squad was in a file between the truck and the doors. LCpl Pannata was watching his squad leader.

Ryck didn't want to wait until Second Squad was fully deployed, so he gave Timothy the go-ahead. The squad leader nodded at his lance corporal, who raised his M76 and aimed it at the twisted wire that was acting as a door lock. The bunker buster was probably overkill, but it would ensure a quick entry.

With one blast, the door blew open, one piece of corrugated metal blown completely off its hinges, the other one askew. Pannata stepped aside as Pvt Hueber, M99 at the ready, started to dash inside. A single shot rang out from the mine, and Hueber jumped back out.

"Hold your fire, hold your fire! We are Federation Marines!" Pannata called out.

There was a pause as the Marines stopped in their tracks. Ryck wanted to push ahead to the door, but there was no room unless he climbed on top of the truck and clambered over.

Finally, a voice called out from inside the salt mine, "Prove it!"

*What the . . .* Ryck wondered.

The Marines in front of Ryck started looking around in confusion.

"What do we do, L/T[74]?" Sgt Timothy asked on the platoon command circuit. "Prove it?"

Ryck changed his display menu, pulled up LCpl Pannata, then took over the Marine's comms, switching his speakers to external.

"This is Second Lieutenant Ryck Lysander, United Federation Marine Corps. We have been sent to evacuate you. Your planet is under attack, and it is not safe here. Do you understand?"

There was another pause, then "How do we know you ain't one of them," the voice called out.

*Mother grubbing shit! We don't have time for this!*

Ryck made up his mind. He might get his ass in a sling for this, but he couldn't sit here arguing with the man.

---

[74] L/T: A common form of nickname for a lieutenant, pronounced "el -tee."

"Sgt Timothy, get your men in there and rush the guy. Don't hurt him, at least too seriously, but secure his weapon."

Ryck hoped there wasn't anyone else armed, but Timothy's Marines would react to whatever they encountered. Sgt Timothy took a few seconds to brief his men, then on his command, Cpl Goddard's team rushed inside with the other Marines on their tail. One more shot rang out, then someone shouted.

Ryck was pushing up Sutarno's ass, and by the time he got into the mine, Goddard's team had the man down on his face.

"You sumbitch," Pannata was yelling. "You fucking shot me!"

Pannata's bios read fine, so if he'd been hit, his bones had protected him.

"Don't kill me!" the man was crying out, his face pushed into the mixture of salt and dirt that covered the entrance floor.

"No one's going to kill you, you dumbshit," Sgt Timothy told him. "Didn't we say we were Marines? You think we're the friggin' capys?"

"I didn't know," he whined. "All we know here is something big's going down. I don't know nothing about no capys. None of them here. 'Sides, they can't hurt no one."

"Let him up. Pvt Hueber, you take that rifle, though," Ryck said as he came up, pointing to the man's old Winchester that was lying in the dirt. "No use tempting anyone.

"What's your name, sir," he asked the man who was now sitting up, spitting out dirt and salt.

"Morrison Tahoe, sir."

"Where are the rest of you? We need to get moving," Ryck told him.

The man hesitated, and Ryck, exasperated, had to keep from yelling as he said, "Look, we've no time for this shit. If you don't get your people out here, there all going to die. Do you understand that? We're going to leave you here and you're all going to die!"

Ryck wouldn't leave them, but he was not above telling a lie to get them going. It seemed to work and the man's will broke right then. Whatever suspicions he had evaporated.

"Back in the chamber, sir. We've got 35 more of us, mostly women and children. We didn't know what was going on, only that it was bad. So me and Tyrone, Tyrone Sukito, that is, he's the—"

"Sorry, sir, you can fill me in on the details later. Just get us to your people now," Ryck interrupted.

"Oh yeah, sure. This way," the man said, leading them down the only passage, a low, meter-and-a-half wide cut in the salt. The air in the passage was dry as a bone. The hairs in Ryck's nose clumped together as the moisture was sucked away. A naked wire looped along the ceiling, LED's hanging every three or four meters. Within 30 or 40 meters, the passage opened up into a chamber. The Marines pushed by a hover cart, something obviously used to transport salt to the entrance.

The chamber was well lit and the white salt walls reflected a somewhat eerie glow. Twenty or so barrels were stacked up against one wall. An old beat-up metal desk was along the far side of the chamber, and several benches had been carved right out of the walls. Sitting on the benches and cross-legged on the deck were the civilians.

"Give me a head count, Joshua," Ryck passed as his platoon sergeant entered the chamber.

He was pretty sure all of them would be there, but he wanted to be certain of that. Several passages led away from the chamber, and it was possible someone had wandered away.

"Who's your commander?" a voice asked in back of him.

Ryck turned to see a large, broad-shouldered middle-aged man asking Cpl Howell the question. Howell silently pointed to Ryck. The man caught Ryck's eye, then strode over, with a younger man who just as big and carrying a cricket bat, one step behind.

"Supervisor Sukito. I'm in charge here," he said, a smile on his face and his hand out.

Ryck took the hand and shook it. He was surprised the man had to ask who was in command. Ryck had his bars illuminated, and anyone who went to the movies or watched the holos should recognize Marine, Navy, or Legion ranks.

"Second Lieutenant Ryck Lysander, sir. We're here to evacuate your group."

"Yes, about that. Can you tell us what's going on? We got the emergency beacon, then some garbled message about an attack before all communications were cut off. Did the French start up again, or maybe Soldiers of God?"

"You didn't get any information on what was happening?" Ryck asked.

"Nada. We received the beacon, and company policy is to take refuge until we receive a recall. Whatever it was, it sounded bad, though, for the few moments we had a connection," the man said, seemingly completely at ease.

Ryck looked at him, then at his sidekick. He looked physically fit and moved like a man who could take care of himself. Yet he was back in the deeper chamber with someone who had an air of a bodyguard about him. Mr. Tahoe might be filling the billet of village idiot, but at least he was out there at the entrance to the mine, ready to defend the others, even if from friendly forces.

"Supervisor Sukito, Peterbund has been attacked with the population essentially wiped out by capys. A Navy ship has been destroyed, and our mission is to rescue any surviving civilians before we abandon the planet," Ryck said without preamble.

The supervisor looked stunned.

"Capys? Impossible. They're imbecilic eating machines, nothing more," he sputtered.

"Not the capys you settlers have been killing. These are larger, soldier varieties. We don't know anything about them, but we have a few images of them attacking your fellow settlers."

"We've got all 36 here," Joshua said over the P2P.

Ryck nodded, but didn't reply. He was waiting for Sukito.

"I really find that hard to believe. As far as leaving here, I think I need those orders from my superiors back at company headquarters," he finally said.

"I'm not sure you heard me. Peterbund has been emptied. Everyone back at your headquarters has been killed," Ryck said as he got closer to losing his patience.

"Someone must have survived. I'm going to convene our branch council. I'll get back to you with my decision," Sukito told Ryck, turning away.

Ryck reached out and grabbed the man by the shoulder, spinning him back. The bodyguard, who had to be Sukito Junior, took a step forward, but wilted under Ryck's glare and stopped.

Ryck knew the man had to be in a state of shock, but there was no time for him to baby the pompous fool.

"You are not going to convene anything. You are not going to wait for orders from your company. This planet is under interdiction, and as the senior Federation representative here, I am in complete control. What I say, goes. And what I say now is that you and your people have five minutes to be ready to move out. Do you understand me?" Ryck said, his tone leaving no room to doubt his resolve.

Behind him, both Joshua and Howell stepped up to flank him, lending their physical support. The supervisor gaped like a fish out of water, looking from one Marine to the other.

"Uh, well, of course. Let me get everyone ready. You have to realize this is quite a shock. Capys, you say? That's hard to believe, but if you say it, well—"

"I do say it, and I'd suggest you quit explaining and get your people together. We've got an extremely tight schedule, and none of us want to be left behind."

Supervisor Sukito started to say something else, but evidently thought better of it and turned to get his people together.

"What a piece of brown," Howell muttered.

Ryck totally agreed.

"Sgt Timothy, Sgt Ariana, come here," Ryck passed on the command circuit.

Both squad leaders ran up within seconds. Ryck pulled the two, along with Joshua, aside.

"What state are the civilians in? See any problems?"

"Doc Camp is checking them out," Joshua told him. "I saw a couple of oldsters and at least half-a-dozen kids. It'll be slow going if we walk."

"What about that truck out there? That could hold the kids and anyone else who had problems. Can we ask someone for the key?" Ryck asked.

Joshua held out one hand. The key dangled from it.

"Done and done."

"Damn, staff sergeant. That's why you get the big bucks," Ryck said with a laugh. "OK, then how about—"

"Lieutenant!" Cpl Saul, Second Squads Second Fire Team leader shouted, running into the chamber. Another Marine followed him, breathing heavily.

The new Marine had no helmet. His monocle display was pushed to the side. That was enough to identify him as a recon Marine.

What's he doing here? Ryck wondered.

"Sir, you need to hear this," Saul said excitedly.

"Sir, Staff Sergeant Hills, Fourth Recon Battalion. We're your eyes and ears for this AO. To make a long story short, the capys are on their way, and they're close," he gasped between breaths.

"Here? What's their ETA? How many of them?" Ryck asked.

"Don't rightly know sir. They didn't show up on any of our sensors. If we hadn't been in their path, we'd never have seen them."

"You saw them?" Ryck asked, confused. "With your eyes? But your sensors never picked them up?"

"That's right, sir. We saw them plain as day, but nothing registered. We tried to raise you, but all the comms were out, so I took off running to get here before them."

Recon had some mighty high-speed, low-drag electronics. If their sensors couldn't detect the capys, then nothing Ryck had would, either.

"How far did you run?" Ryck asked.

"About 20 minutes. Maybe seven or eight klicks. From what I saw, they looked slow, so you've got another 15 minutes, 30 max. The rest of the team's supposed to be flanking them, but without comms, we can't find out where the capys are."

"Joshua, give the key to the truck to Abbas. He worked construction before enlisting, so he's driving it. I want you to be in charge of getting these people out of here. Five minutes. Everyone out of this mine and moving. You two," he said to the two squad leaders, "spread out your Marines. I want them where they can kick butt to keep the civilians moving."

Within moments, shouting broke out as the Marines turned into shepherds. A baby started crying, and a number of civilians started protesting. Ryck ignored them. His Marines could take care of the situation.

Inside the salt dome, he had no connectivity. But he'd downloaded the route to the LZ, and he went over it. There was a route from the mine to the LZ, taking two paths. The dump truck should be able to handle it, Ryck thought. Unloaded, it would rise up a little higher, clearing the one or two hedgerows between the two locations.

"Staff Sergeant, where was the last location you had the capys?"

The recon Marine, who was rapidly regaining his breath, pulled down his monocle, then tapped over the coordinates. They appeared on Ryck's display.

It wasn't good, but it could be worse, I guess, Ryck thought.

It all depended on how fast they moved. From where SSgt Hills had them last, if they angled to their right, they could cut-off the Marines and civilians. If they came straight for the mine, Ryck thought they could reach the LZ, and if the Storks were on time, they could be gone before the capys could get there.

"Joshua, get these people out of here. I'm going to the entrance to raise the company."

He spun around to leave when the supervisor rushed forward and planted himself in front of Ryck.

"Lieutenant Alexander, your sergeant here is trying to tell me we can't bring our vitals. Will you please correct his thinking?"

Ryck looked over to where two young men had attached hover clamps to one of the barrels. It hovered six inches above the deck. While the barrel was essentially weightless, it still had mass, and maneuvering it took care. If it got going too fast, it could get out of control, and even a gentle turn would be out of the question. Something like that would slow down the movement to the LZ.

"I believe Sgt Ariana, is correct. You can't take it. And the name's Lysander, not Alexander."

"But you don't understand," he protested. "Those are our vitals. Without them, the company can't calculate out how much each of us have left to fulfill our contracts. For those who are employees, we need that for our bonuses. You may be technically in charge, but GKN will hold you responsible once all this blows over if the vitals don't make it back.

Ryck lowered his M99 and fired a long burst into the barrel, the two handlers diving to either side as it splintered.

"They'll know where to find me," Ryck said as he turned to leave.

Any "vitals" would have been able to fit in a hard drive, and those could be transmitted as soon as they left the mine. Something else had been in that barrel, not that Ryck cared. He didn't even bother to look through the splintered pieces, still held aloft by the hover clamp, to see what was inside. It didn't matter.

Ryck ran down the passage and out into the sunlight. Immediately his comms lit up.

"Grizzly-six, this is Grizzly-two-six. We've got 36 civilian pax[75], but we've got capys about to arrive at our position. What is the status on a pick-up here at our objective?"

"Grizzly-two-six. Say again your last. You have enemy at your position, over?"

"Negative. They are not here yet, but we expect them soon. They do not show up on any sensors, but we have recon eyes on them. Please advise, over."

"Wait one."

Ryck stood at the front of the mine, looking out over the fields of wheat. It seemed so peaceful.

"Grizzly-Two-Six, we can get three Storks at your position in 30 mikes. Will that do?" Capt Portuno asked over the comms.

Ryck looked at the track he'd created, showing the possible advances of the capy force. Thirty minutes might have the capys right at the mine.

"That's a negative. In 30 mikes, I expect this location to be hot. Request the pick-up remain at LZ Diego," Ryck passed.

---

[75] PAX: passengers

"Roger that. I understand keeping the pick-up at LZ Diego, but moving it up to 30 mikes from now."

"That's affirmative, Grizzly-Six."

"Roger. Keep me informed on any developments. Grizzly-Six, out."

LCpl Abbas ran out of the mine and climbed into the truck.

"You can handle that thing?" Ryck asked.

"In my sleep, sir," Abbas said.

Ryck sent forward the route he'd mapped.

"No matter what, you get that truck to the LZ. You've got the countdown on your display. You have to be there when our ride out of here shows up."

"No problem, L/T. I'll get this beast there or die trying," Abbas said as he powered up the truck and turned it around, dump bed facing the entrance. PFC "Prez" Prezuluski jumped up into the bed, ready to assist getting people up into it.

The first of the civilians started trickling out. A woman with two children in hand were Prez' first customers. Prez reached down and took the proffered children, one after the other. The little blonde girl seemed excited, calling out "Truck!" over and over, running from one side of the bed to the other so she could look out. The boy was not so sure, and reached out to the woman. She tried to assure him, but he started crying, his face screwed up in righteous anger.

"Ma'am, why don't you hop onboard for now until we get more people in here. He'll be fine then, I bet," Prez told the woman, who gratefully accepted his hand to be pulled up into the bed.

Ryck made a mental note of how easily Prez was interacting with the civilians. He wanted to make sure he mentioned that to him once they got back.

More people, most escorted by Marines, came out of the mine. Joshua was everywhere, getting them organized. The man was a fount of energy. He'd had plenty of experience running recruits, but this had to be of a magnitude more difficult than that.

Ryck toggled over to the dragonfly feed. It was blank. There was no connection.

"Sergeant Watson, what's wrong with the dragonfly? Do you have a feed?" he shouted at his squad leader standing 15 meters away.

"Uh, negative, sir," Watson answered, hurrying over to Ryck. "It just quit about a minute ago. I've been trying to re-connect."

"What was its last position before it went off the net?" Ryck asked needlessly as he pulled up the track himself.

A sense of foreboding came over him. If the dragonfly had been taken out by the capys, then that might mean they'd shifted their approach. They could be moving to cut off Ryck's line of advance.

"Joshua, we need to move now! The capys have changed their advance, and that might cut us off if we stay here any longer. I don't want any panic, but we leave now!" he said over the P2P.

Joshua was only 20 meters away, and Ryck could have shouted out, but he didn't want any panic. Joshua caught his eye and gave him a thumbs up before going into DI mode.

"You've got 30 seconds to get those people up in the truck. Thirty seconds, Thallicker!

"Sergeant Timothy, move it out now. Head out on the bearing I gave you. You civilians, the ones I assigned to Green Team, follow First Squad. You, the one in the grey shirt, you're the first one in line, and I want you on Lance Corporal Sutarno's ass. Sutarno, raise your hand. See him Grey Shirt? Yes? OK, head 'em out!" Joshua shouted out at the milling people.

"Lieutenant? I'm going to head out to see if I can't link up with my team. If I can get you any info, I will," SSgt Hills said as he walked up.

"Sure, and good luck. First, though, you said you could see them with your eyes, but nothing showed up on any of your scanners?"

"That's right, sir. They were plain as day when we saw them, but the scanners still showed nothing."

"OK, thanks. And Godspeed. I really appreciate your efforts. I'll make sure to tell your command when we get back," Ryck told him.

"Just doing our job, sir," the recon Marine said, but Ryck could see he was pleased.

Ryck pulled up the Navy supporting arms net, bypassing the Marine FSCC.[76] He knew he would hear about it later, but he didn't have time to go through channels.

"*Ashland*, this is Lieutenant Lysander of Kilo 3/6 at the coordinates I'm sending. I've got a flash EIR[77] for you, over."

"Roger, lieutenant. But why send an EIR to us? We're fire support," came the reply.

"No time, *Ashland*, and you've got the scopes. Can you scan the coordinates I'm sending for any sign of enemy forces? This has to be done visually, and Lieutenant (JG) Juarez showed me your old optic tracking scope. Can you get that online?" Ryck asked.

"Uh, wait one. Let me ask someone," the voice on the other end said, clearly out of his comfort zone. "I'll get back to you."

"Hurry on that. We need that info right now," Ryck said.

LCpl Abbas beeped the horn behind Ryck as he put the truck into motion. Ryck moved to the side to let it pass. An old lady sat in the back of the bed, and her flat, dull eyes focused on Ryck as the truck moved past. Her grey hair was escaping the bun that had previously held it, and strands blew back and forth across her face, but her eyes never left Ryck. It was a little creepy.

Ryck took a look behind him. Joshua was getting the last group of civilians moving with Sgt Watson's squad ready to bring up the rear.

*Shit!* Ryck thought. *I've got to get moving, too.*

He ran back alongside the truck, the old lady thankfully blocked from his view. He wanted to follow First Squad, but 15 or so civilians were between Ryck and Sgt Timothy, so Ryck just merged in behind the civilians and joined Cpl Goddard's team.

"Marine officer calling, this is *Ashland* fire control. We've approved your EIR and are bringing the J80 online. Anything particular we're supposed to look for?" the voice came over Ryck's net.

---

[76] FSCC: Fire Support Coordination Center

[77] EIR: Essential Information Request. These are high-priority requests for tactical intel.

"Affirmative, *Ashland*, anything that looks like a bunch of capys on the move," Ryck responded.

*Dipshits!* he thought. *What grubbing else would you look for?*

He checked his display. Sgt Timothy and his lead two teams were about 200 meters from the salt mine. They had another 300 meters until they reached the first hedgerow, then they would take the dogleg left, following the hedgerow for 400 meters until the intersection with the next one. Then it was over that hedgerow, where the truck would have its only difficulty, then down the hill, alongside the marsh and into the LZ.

Ryck wished they could have designated a closer LZ, but with the marsh on two sides of it, the battalion S3[78] felt it would be more defensible than anywhere else in the immediate area. Ryck though, and he assumed the pilots as well, did not like that there was high ground around the LZ.

Ryck looked back. The final group of civilians was on the move, and Second Squad was just leaving the front of the mine. It would be close, but Ryck thought they could get everyone to the LZ just as the Storks arrive.

He zoomed back on his route display, overlaying their positions so he could get a better idea of where they were and where they had to go. Everyone was on the long line creeping forward. Two Marines from Sgt Ariana's team were off to the flank closest to the last known location of the capys, and one team was providing flank security on the other side of the column. Those three teams were tramping through knee-high wheat, but with the slow speed of march of the civilians, they would have no problem keeping up.

Sgt Timothy's team, in the lead, reached the first checkpoint and had bent the column around to the left to follow along the hedgerow. Ryck checked the time on his display—they were doing OK. If they kept up the pace, they could be at the LZ in 15 more minutes.

"Lieutenant Lysander, this is the *Ashland*, we . . . pick . . .ter . . ." the call came, flickering in and out before fading.

---

[78] S3: Operations Officer

"*Ashland, Ashland*, do you read me?" Ryck asked as his AI searched the waves to re-connect.

*What now?* Ryck wondered. *Good grubbing time for comms to fail.*

There was a flash of light behind Ryck. He spun around to see the truck settle down to the ground, digging a furrow as it lurched to a stop.

"I thought you said you could drive that thing, Abbas!" Ryck shouted, running back to jump up on the passenger side running board.

*He's asleep?* was all Ryck could think as he looked inside the cab to see LCpl Abbas slumped against the instrument panel.

Ryck glanced into the bed of the truck. Every passenger was down. There was no visible damage, but with certainty, Ryck knew they were dead. The image of the little girl who had been so happy to get in the truck, the little boy and his mother, the old lady—all of them, motionless, was seared into his mind.

He spun to yell out when another flash, this time subdued, hit Cpl Goddard's team where Ryck had been walking only ten seconds before. Three of the Marines simply collapsed in boneless heaps while Pvt Hueber wheeled and went down, only to start to stagger back up. There was no explosion, no gouts of dirt being flung up. One moment, the Marines were looking up at him, the next moment, they were down.

Shouts and screams erupted along the line. Ryck looked to the right, and there, about 800 meters away, a line marched steadily towards them. The capys had found them.

## Chapter 10

"Ughar, target to your right!" Ryck shouted from his higher vantage point on the truck's running board.

LCpl Ughar and LCpl Keith made up the heavy gun team from Weapons Platoon that had been attached to Second. They had one of the brand new M665 man-packed hadron guns. This was the most powerful man-packed weapon in the Marine's arsenal, new to all of them. Three of the guns had arrived only hours before they had lifted off on the mission.

Ughar had just made the dogleg, but as Ryck shouted, he came rushing back. The big M665 looked like an old WWII flamethrower on his back.

"Everyone else, move it!" Ryck shouted, all his comms gone.

If he could get people on the other side of the hedgerow, he hoped that would provide some degree of cover.

By now, pretty much everyone had seen the capys. The group of 15 civilians froze, wondering what to do.

"I said move it. Get forward!" Ryck yelled, pointing the way for his charges.

The capys, what looked to be 40 or more of them, were slightly ahead of the column as well as far to the column's right. The bunched civilians hesitated, obviously not wanting to move forward when all their instincts screamed for them to turn and go back.

There was a dim flash from in front of one of the capys to the left of their line, then an instant later, a larger flash 20 meters in front of Ryck. Five civilians, three men and two women, fell to the ground.

That broke their trance. They turned and started running back towards the mine.

In back of Ryck, Joshua was running forward.

"Turn those mother-grubbing idiots around! Ryck shouted at his platoon sergeant. "We need that cover in front of us!"

M99 fire reached out to the oncoming capys. Ryck couldn't tell if it was having any effect, but the capys didn't seem to stop their steady movement. LCpl Ughar moved into a clear field of fire, leveled his beam generator, and fired.

Ryck had only seen an M665 fire on a training holo. The shielding on the gun was extremely heavy. It had to be in order to be man-packed. But the side-lobes of the beam generation made Ryck's hair stand on end. The beam lanced out to impact among the capys.

Technically, the beam itself was invisible, but the designers had created a sympathetic laser which could be used to walk the beam onto the target. When that beam hit the capys, there was a blinding flare of actinic blue—and the capys emerged from the glare unharmed.

A beam like that could take down a ship, for God's sake, and these creatures were untouched?

Ryck wasn't sure how long the M665 could fire with the charge Ughar carried, but the Marines danced his beam back and forth among the enemy.

"Concentrate on one of them!" Ryck shouted.

If LCpl Ughar heard him, he gave no indication, and it wouldn't have mattered. Another flash of light, and both Ughar and Keith were down, the M665 inert.

Somehow, Joshua had stopped the flight of the ten civilians and turned them around. Ryck finally jumped off the truck and sprinted forward to Sgt Timothy's squad. Two Marines were down, face-first in the wheat. The rest were moving to shield the civilians, firing every weapon they had.

"That got one of those wind-up fucking hamsters," LCpl La Garza shouted, still firing his M76.

The M76 was the man-packed version of the PICS M77 bunker buster. It was a nice weapon, with a slow-moving 8mm rocket designed to penetrate hardened targets, but it didn't have nearly the destructive power of the M665. Yet several of the Marines were cheering the downing of one of the "wind-up fucking hamsters," as La Garza called them.

The description was apt, Ryck thought as he looked over at the capys. They'd all seen the images that had been broadcast, so the general physiology was not new. But as they advanced over the wheat fields towards them, they walked in an almost disjointed manner, extremely upright. They reminded Ryck of when Hannah had dragged him to see the ballet, *March of the Teddy Bears*, the classic story of wind-up toy teddy bears coming to life for Christmas Eve.

The ballet teddy bears, though, didn't march with a deadly purpose.

Two more Marines in front of Ryck fell. It was all very surreal. The Marines were yelling, the civilians screaming, but whatever weapons the capys were using were silent. One moment, LCpl Thomas was firing his M76, the next moment, he collapsed, dead.

Ryck rushed to grab Thomas' weapon, then wheeled to fire. He took one shot at a capy still some 700 meters away. If he hit it, the thing didn't drop. He started to sight in again when Gunny Meader's admonition cut through his rising berserker mindset. He had to lead them out of this mess, not fight.

"Hogger!" he shouted, using PFC Highsmith's nickname. "Use this! It's got a bigger punch!"

He tossed the weapon into the air at Highsmith, not even watching to see if he caught it.

He spun around to check on the civilians. The last of his charges were rushing past him, being forcibly pushed by Joshua and a few of Second Squad's Marines.

Ryck swept along side of them.

"Timothy!" he shouted.

*Fuck this no comms shit!* he thought.

"Timothy!" he shouted again as he rushed forward, finally catching the squad leader's attention.

"Pull in behind and cover our rear. Keep your squad between the capys and the civilians," Ryck shouted, using hand and arm singles to emphasize what he wanted.

Sgt Timothy raised a hand to acknowledge and started to turn back as another subdued flash of light illuminated him. He dropped to a heap under the wheat tops.

"Mother fucking pigs!" Ryck shouted, firing off a burst of his M99 darts at the capys.

He pushed forward as the air crackled with pent up energy in the direction of the capys. It was the *Ashland*, firing in support!

That seemed to buy them enough time to get everyone left alive behind the hedgerow. It wasn't high, and it didn't provide much cover, but it was something.

"Squad leaders, keep moving, but give me a headcount!" he shouted out, his voice beginning to go hoarse.

He made a quick mental tally, and his heart fell. Barely 10 or 12 civilians seemed to have made it, and it looked as if only half of the platoon was combat effective. Pvt Hueber had made it, dragging one useless leg behind him. Two Marines were carrying Cpl Saul, who hung motionless between them.

Ryck looked back to where they had been hit. The truck sat there motionless, and Ryck could just make out Abbas, still slumped in the cab. Several other bodies were visible, but others were hidden by the wheat.

*Could some of them still be alive?* he wondered.

Marines don't leave their dead, and that gnawed on Ryck. He wanted to rush back, but *Ashland* or not, he had to get the civilians out of there. That was his mission. If he'd seen anyone alive out there, he would have gotten them, but the way most of the people had fallen, with his combat experience, he knew that they were KIA.

The crackle of the air as the Navy ship fired died away.

"Think the ship got them all?" Hueber asked as he hobbled forward.

That was what Ryck wondered. Joshua had the civilians moving, so it was worth a look. Just intel, Ryck rationalized, not fighting.

"Private Lin, come with me," he said to the nearest unhurt Marine.

Ryck ran back to where the dogleg started. He slowly edged around the hedgerow only to dive back, every hair on his body on end from a near miss. Less than 300 meters away, the capys were still advancing. Ryck couldn't even tell if their numbers had been pared down.

"Move it, Lin!" he shouted, breaking into a run to catch up with the others.

"Move, move, move!" he implored them, willing them forward.

"Who's got a claymore on them?" he yelled out.

"I do, sir!" Cpl Howell answered.

"Halfway to the next checkpoint, I want you to wait until the last person passes, then set it for motion detection. Got it?"

"Roger that, sir. Got it," Howell said as he fell back to the rear of the ragged procession.

Looking up ahead, Ryck could see the first of the civilians and a few Marines turning the corner. They were only 200 meters or so from the LZ, which was down a short but steep hill and around a marsh at the bottom.

Four civilians, one who seemed wounded, were hobbling along, each one assisted by a Marine. Ryck and the remainder of his Marines flowed just behind, slowed down but unwilling to pass them. The four were their charges.

"Howell, here!" Ryck said, pointing out a spot on the ground.

Howell and Weiss, his grenadier, stopped and knelt. It would take Howell about a minute to employ the claymore, but the powerful mine could make all the difference between success and failure. Ryck kept moving, knowing the two Marines could sprint up to catch them before they made the turn.

As Ryck got within 50 meters of the checkpoint, he turned to see if Howell and Weiss were coming. They were just getting up and beginning to run when far in back of them, the first of the capy soldiers marched into view around the end of the hedgerow.

"Cover them!" Ryck shouted, stepping off to the side and opening fire. Ryck could see the darts impacting the blue shielding of one of the capys, little flashes of light bursting as the darts hit. The capys didn't seem to try to take any cover or make any evasive action. They just kept coming. Ryck's target, though, seemed to falter. It didn't go down, but it certainly looked like it was falling back, slower than the rest.

Someone fired an M72 HGL[79], and this did have effect. One capy went stiffly down to a knee, then toppled over backwards.

---

[79] M72 HGL: A man-packed 18mm grenade launcher: Heavy Grenade Launcher.

Then the capys opened fire. The first two to fall were Howell and Weiss. They were lit up, and down they went.

"Die you mother fuckers!" someone shouted to Ryck's left.

Marines didn't run from a fight, and every emotion shouted at Ryck to attack, to charge the mother-grubbers. But he had his mission, and that was to evacuate the remaining civilians. The fleet was leaving, and they had to get off the planet.

"Bounding overwatch, now!" he shouted.

The platoon was in shambles, the organization shot. But Marines were Marines. Without any more guidance, the eleven of them broke into three teams, each one with at least one M76 or HGL, the Marines' only two weapons that seemed to have any effect on the capys. Ryck was in one team, Joshua in another, and Sgt Watson in the third. Ryck labeled them, and off they went.

"Watson, back, now!" he shouted while he and his team poured fire at the capys.

Sgt Watson's team got up, ran back 15 meters, then wheeled to cover the others.

"Staff Sergeant, now!"

Joshua, with three others, ran back, passing past Watson's Marines, and turning to face the capys.

"My team, now!"

Ryck felt a now-familiar tingle of a near miss. Doc Camp, who was running beside and just to the front of him, stumbled and went down. Ryck grabbed him by his harness and pulled him along.

He got past Joshua's team as Joshua took over, shouting, "Watson's team, now!"

Ryck dropped Doc, then looked back to fire. The capy's were still coming, more and more appearing around the edge of the hedgerow some 400 meters away. But they didn't seem quite so rotely organized anymore. The Marines' fire had to be having an effect.

Ryck was only ten meters from the checkpoint. A couple of Marines had stopped there and were covering their movement. Sgt Watson ran by, scooping up Doc and taking his team around the corner of the hedgerow.

Joshua yelled out his command, and his team got up, rushing through what was left of Ryck's team and into cover.

"My team, let's go!" Ryck shouted.

Ryck spun around and sprinted for safety. Pvt Hueber, despite only one side of his body working, had stopped at the edge of the hedgerow and was firing, one-handed, back at the enemy. Ryck felt pride at that, and he started to smile when his world erupted into light. He fell to the ground, unable to move.

He took a deep breath, then managed to get one arm out to push himself up. Right in front of him, not a meter away, Hueber's lifeless body stared up at him.

Ryck wanted to scream, but his lungs wouldn't obey his commands. Arms grabbed him and roughly pulled him back out of the line of fire.

"You OK?" Joshua asked him, panic in his voice.

Ryck gasped twice, then managed to get out a weak, "Yeah, I think."

But he wasn't OK. His left arm and leg, along with a good deal of his body, were numb and paralyzed. He could barely keep breathing. His heart was fluttering, but it still managed to beat.

Ryck tried to sit up, but hands kept him down.

"Get me up," he managed to gasp out. "Can't breathe."

The hands that were keeping him down now lifted him up. He was still in trouble, but that eased his distress somewhat.

At the top of the hill, he could see the LZ, just 200 meters away. A few of the civilians were on the LZ, covered by a handful of Marines. And beyond them was a beautiful sight. Three Storks, more than they needed now, he realized with a sense of sorrow, were inbound, coming in low.

Ryck had hated the fact that the LZ was on the low ground, but it turned out to be fortuitous. By coming in from the northwest, the birds would be in defilade to the oncoming capys.

Marines were darting out beyond the cover of the edge of the hedgerow, firing, then darting back. As Ryck watched, trying to gather his thoughts, Pvt Lin darted out, only to fall in a flash of light. Several sets of hands reached out and grabbed him by his legs to haul him back.

Ryck's mind cleared. He knew what had to be done, but this would be the hardest order he'd had to give. He would be sentencing someone to death by his decision.

"Joshua," he croaked out. We've got to get those four civilians down to the LZ," he said, nodding his head to point at the four who were halfway down the hill and stumbling forward.

"And we've got to give the Storks time to land, get the people on board, and get out of here. We don't know what the capys have against air, but we can't chance it. We need to leave a blocking force here to cover the LZ. If we don't, the capys will overrun it before we can get the people off."

"I understand, Ryck. Give me a moment to get a team together," Joshua said.

"No, not you! I mean me. I need three Marines, all with M76s. You take the rest and the civilians and get out of here."

"That be not happening," he said, dropping back into his old accent for a moment. "Look, you can't even hold a weapon. You'd be a liability."

"I so too can hold a weapon, you grubber!" Ryck said, trying to shout but ending in a coughing fit.

When he stopped, he looked up into his friend's face. He was about to pass out, and he realized he would be that liability Joshua had said he'd be.

"OK, maybe not me. But not you, either," Ryck insisted.

"Really?" was all Joshua said.

"Yeah, maybe Ariana. You said he's coming along," Ryck said, grasping at anything to avoid the finality that logic demanded.

"Come one, Ryck," Joshua said quietly, leaning close. Beyond his head, Marines continued to pepper the oncoming capys.

"I'm the only choice, and you know it. Give the order. Forget about our relationship. If you really think Ariana or Watson is better qualified for it, then give that order, and I'll follow it. But if I'm the best for the job, as I'm sure you'll realize, then give the order now."

"But, but, you're . . . ah, fuck it, I can't do that. What about Hope? What about Hannah? What about Ester? She needs her father.

"I knew this would happen when you showed up and asked to be in the platoon. I knew it!" Ryck said, choking back a sob brought forth from pain, frustration and a sense of loss.

"Give the order, Ryck. Do what's right."

Back at Annapolis, Capt Klein had said that ordering men to die was the hardest thing a leader could do. But the captain couldn't have had something like this in mind.

Ryck looked up, catching sight of Sgt Ariana, who was nervously waiting for Ryck's decision. Ryck could take care of it right then, just give the sergeant the orders. But in his heart, Ryck knew that while willing, Sgt Ariana was just not as capable as Joshua. Neither was Watson.

If Joshua wasn't his friend, his brother-in-law, he would still dread giving the order, but he would do it. Lives were at stake, and the more he hesitated, the greater the chance that everyone would die.

He knew what he had to do.

"Joshua," he said loudly, so the rest could hear. "I'm giving you three Marines with M76s, and stay here while we get everyone loaded. Do not let the capys past, or we're all lost. Once the Storks are loaded, get your asses down the hill and into the last bird. You understand ?"

"Aye-aye, sir. Who do I keep with me?"

Ryck looked at the waiting Marines, Marines waiting to hear if they would live or die. He chose those with M76s.

"Take Jones, Felicity, and Hogger."

*Shit, Hogger! I threw him the M76, and now he dies because of that!*

"The rest of you, let's move it!"

"You heard him," Sgt Ariana yelled out. "Let's go!"

Pvt Gilliard lifted Ryck up, ready to carry him to the LZ.

The Marines started down the hill, but before Gilliard stepped off, Joshua reached over to hug Ryck.

"I'm so sorry, my brother. I'm sorry," Ryck whispered in Joshua's ear.

"Don't be. You gave me the chance to prove myself, and I hope I'm doing that."

"You be doing that, my brother, you be doing that. Just make sure you get your ass down the hill and onto the birds, you hear?"

"Sure thing, Ryck," Joshua said, but they both knew it would never happen.

Joshua wheeled to join the other three Marines who were sending a volley of fire down the hedgerow to the capys. All four began screaming like banshees.

"We gotta go, sir," Gillaird said, pulling Ryck away.

The private pulled and mostly carried his platoon commander down the hill to the LZ. Two of the Storks had landed and were embarking civilians and Marines.

Behind Ryck, the crescendo of outgoing fire kept rising. He could barely make out the shouting as he was half-dragged around the edge of the marsh. One Stork was already lifting off, and the other waited, ramp down, a crew chef waving them to hurry up.

Ryck was fading. Breathing was getting almost impossible as he labored to draw in air. Just as Gilliard dragged him up the ramp, behind him, the sound of Marine fire faltered, then stopped.

Ryck grabbed the crew chief by his flight suit as he was pulled past, a deathlock that the crewchief couldn't break.

"We've got four more Marines out there. We have to wait!" he shouted.

The Stork lurched into the air.

"Let me go!" the crewchief shouted, trying to pull off Ryck's hand.

"No, go back! That's an order!" Ryck gasped out.

The Stork leaned forward and started to gather speed. Ryck looked back, and in the gap between the ramp and the fuselage, he had a momentary glimpse of the checkpoint where Joshua and his three Marines had given the rest enough time to take off. Capys swarmed the hedgerow and were moving down the hill.

The inside of the cabin went momentarily white. The capys were firing at them, and if the decreased engine noise was any indication, the Stork's shields wouldn't hold up under many more hits.

The crewchief managed to pry Ryck's hands off of him.

"We aren't going anywhere, lieutenant except back to the *Rio Pacure*. If we make it, that is. If you got men back down there, sorry, but they're dead now."

Pvt Gilliard helped Ryck down into a seat as darkness took over and Ryck knew no more.

# Zephyr-Hadreson

## Chapter 11

Ryck groaned as he started to surface, the familiar itch/ache cross of regen pervading his senses. He thought he was almost through, almost finished, but this felt like when he first started. Did he have a relapse?

Then his thoughts coalesced. He wasn't on Alexander, where he'd first endured regen. He was with Second MarDiv, now, a lieutenant.

"Joshua!" he shouted, opening his eyes.

He was in a darkened room. His left arm and leg were immobilized, and tubes ran from his body into an assortment of monitoring machines. The flowers in a vase beside him, as well as the sunlight that fought to make it into the room past the blinds, were enough to let Ryck know he was back on a planet, probably Zephyr-Hadreson, and in regen once more. The thought made him shudder.

He looked around for his call button. He had to know what had happened. Had Joshua and his three Marines made it off the planet? Who in his platoon hadn't made it?

He caught sight of a figure sitting in a chair in the corner, deep in the shadows. Ryck tried to raise his body to get a better look, and the person stirred.

Hannah stood up, coming forward until she was standing beside him, saying nothing. Ryck wanted to reach out, to hold her, but he couldn't reach across with his good arm to touch her.

"Joshua?" he asked.

Hannah simply shook her head.

The tears came unabated then. They were not just for Joshua, but for all of his Marines. For Jones, Felicity, and Hogger. For Lin, Timothy, Abbas, Howell. Prez. Ughar, Keith. For the children in the back of the truck, for the old lady who had stared at him. For everyone. He didn't even know yet who had made it and who hadn't. But he grieved for them. They were his Marines and his charges, and he had let them die.

Hannah stood beside him, hand on his wrapped left arm, and let him cry until he was too exhausted to cry anymore. Ryck tried to control his breathing, to gather himself.

"Do you want me to call a nurse?" Hannah asked quietly. "The doctors said you might be thirsty when you came to."

"No, not yet. I just need you here now," Ryck said.

He was thirsty, which was a side-effect from the induced coma in which regen patients were placed. He looked to his left to see his arm bandaged. It wasn't in a regen cage, so the arm had not been amputated. He tried to lift his body to look down to his legs.

"Lay still," Hannah said, leaning forward and placing a hand against his chest. "You've got complete nerve damage in your left arm and upper leg. One lung was damaged, as was your heart and liver. You're going to survive, but you've got some time in regen to endure. The doctor says maybe a year until the nerves have knitted."

"A year? That's not so bad, I guess," Ryck said, although he dreaded the thought of the process. Regen sucked, to be blunt, with constant pain and itch.

"So, you know about Joshua," Ryck said.

*Stupid thing to say. Of course she knows!* he berated himself.

She slowly nodded. Ryck knew his wife, and he knew she was trying to marshal her thoughts to say something. Ryck just lay there, waiting for her.

"I . . . I read the report of the battle. And I've talked to Stu Watson," she began.

*Watson made it? Good.*

Ryck had thought the sergeant had made it on one of the Storks, but in the end there, he was out of it and he wasn't sure what he remembered and what he imagined.

"I need to ask you something," she said, moving around the bed and bending down so she could look into his eyes.

"Did you order Joshua to stay back while you escaped?"

Ryck was stunned. The intensity of Hannah's eyes scared him, and her use of "escaped" was like a dagger to his heart. It wasn't like that, was it? He didn't sacrifice Joshua and the three Marines just to save his ass, right?

But maybe he did. He got out, he was back home with his wife. He had a rough year in front of him, but wouldn't Joshua do anything for that year, even in regen?

"Maybe he's still alive? The capys, they don't move fast, and Joshua, you know him, he can run. When we go back, maybe we'll find him and the rest," he offered, grasping at straws.

"You don't know. Of course not. The planet was interdicted two days after you escaped."

*Interdicted?*

That was planet death. The Federation had only done that twice, once in conjunction with the Brotherhood to wipe out the Soldiers of God home base. If the Federation had cleansed GKN with its planetbusters, nothing would have survived. Nothing. The planet was dead.

As Ryck tried to absorb that, Hannah leaned in closer and asked once again, "Did you order Joshua to hold them back so you could escape?"

Ryck stared into his wife's eyes. Ryck had given the order because it was the right order, and Joshua had known it. He had expected it, almost begging Ryck to give it. He had done it because that was what he'd been taught to do. He had to ignore the personal and act the professional. But as Ryck tried to read inside Hannah's mind, he knew she didn't want to hear that. She didn't want reasons.

"Yes," he said quietly.

A cloud seemed to form over her eyes, but that could have been Ryck's imagination. She stayed there a moment, still bent over, before slowly straightening out. Ryck waited in the silence that took over the room.

"I be goin' home," she finally said, quietly reverting to her Torritite accent.

"Sure, I understand. You're probably exhausted, waiting for me to come to, and you need to absorb that. I'm going to be stuck here for awhile, but we can talk after you've gotten some rest, OK?"

"No, I be goin' home. To Prophesy," she said.

Ryck's heart lurched as her words fell on him.

"But . . . uh, sure. When will you be back?" he asked.

"I don't know. Probably never. I don't know what I feel now," she said, facing away from him.

"But, we're married," he said. "We are a team?"

She wheeled on him, anger making an appearance by her demeanor.

"I've lost two brothers to your precious Marine Corps. Two *alderbruten*.[80] And my lovin' husband be the one who killed our Joshua," she hissed, venom dripping from her words. "I want no more of your death machine, no more bein' the hired enforcer for a corrupt Federation. I be done!"

Ryck sat gaping as his wife wheeled about and stalked out of the room.

---

[80] *Adlerbruten*: a Torritite word meaning the eldest son in a family. This has an important cultural significance in Torritite society.

## Chapter 12

"Congratulations, there, Lieutenant," Major General Han said, shaking Ryck's right hand. "You're getting a habit of making a name for yourself. Pretty soon, you'll have more fruit salad on your chest than me!" he said.

The other Marines in Ryck's ward room dutifully laughed. When the big man jokes, everyone reacts.

"Well, duty calls. I'm sure some of your friends here will want to stay and help you celebrate. No alcohol for you, son. I know you young guns like to lift a cold one, but your buddies will have to drink up for you!"

Again, everyone laughed, even though the general's words really weren't funny. Ryck, while undergoing regen, was not allowed to drink alcoholic beverages as they could affect the regen process.

The general, followed by his aide and his civilian photographer, left the room. Ryck could hear the aid giving him the background for the next Marine on the ward who was getting a medal today. Ryck didn't even recognize who that Marine was. He'd been stuck in his hospital bed for almost two weeks since Hannah had left, and he had no interest in trying to find out who else was going to be one of his fellow genhens as they started therapy.

LtCol Montrose came up first and shook Ryck's hand. Lying on his back, the angle was a little awkward with the colonel having to lift up his elbow and reach down.

"The general's right. That was a damned fine job you did. You deserve the medal. You need to concentrate on getting better so you can rejoin us before we take the fight to the capys. We need you," he told Ryck.

"Thank you, sir," was all Ryck said.

The entourage followed: the battalion XO, the sergeant major, Capt Portuno and the other captains, the battalion's lieutenants. The members of his platoon were also there to watch the ceremony. Doc Camp and Cpl Torrington were alive but in regen, but all the rest of the survivors, all who had gotten off GKN, were there. It was a very small number. Including Urghard and

Keith, Ryck had gone ashore with 40 other men. Nine Marines were there in his ward room. Nine.

When Sgt Watson came forward to shake his hand, Ryck had to control himself. He wanted to ask Watson just what he'd told Hannah. Deep inside, he knew he just wanted to blame someone, but still, he felt what he felt, and he was angry with his sergeant. Well, not his anymore. Ryck had been transferred out of the platoon and was officially assigned to the WWB.[81]

While Ryck's platoon had been devastated, the battalion as a whole had gotten off pretty lightly. There had been no other contact within the battalion's AO, although the capys had been closing in on India Company when a flight of Navy shuttles had swooped in to pull the company and over 50 civilians to safety. They had taken capy fire as they were flying off, and one shuttle, with over 100 people crammed aboard, had almost been disabled. From all accounts, it had been a miracle that the pilot had kept the shuttle aloft and flew it back to the ship.

Second Battalion, Sixth Marines, though, had been almost wiped out. Details were still sketchy given the capys' ability to block electronics, but from accounts given by the last few shuttles to leave the area, the capys had come in along three major axis of approach, completely surprising the battalion when they suddenly appeared on the city outskirts. What happened after that was somewhat of a mystery, but one in which rumors ran rampant. The *Rio Pacure* sent in its flight of four Experion fighters, but all four were lost as soon as they swept in over the city. The sensors on the monitor stationed over the city could discern nothing, and the drones it controlled all fell off the circuit.

Admiral Hennesy, Commander in Chief, Third Quadrant, monitoring the situation from back on New Halifax, ordered the withdrawal after consultation with the Federation Council. Two days later, with full approval of all the governing authorities of the human worlds, GKN was interdicted, the hulk placed under quarantine. A fleet of 30 ships patrolled the area, trying to locate the capy ship that had made an appearance before disappearing.

---

[81] WWB: an acronym now used for an old term first used in the 21st Century, the "Wounded Warrior Battalion."

There was a strong rumor, which Donte assured him was more than just a rumor, that when the four battle cruisers surrounded the planet to drop their planetbusters, a message was seen, cut out of the wheat outside of Peterbund, asking for a pickup. Marines from 2/6 had fought their way outside the city. That became moot, though, when the Navy killed off the planet.

Ryck put up with all the well-wishers, just waiting for them to leave. He was not in a socializing mood. Finally, it was just Donte and Unger left.

"Glad that's over?" Donte asked as he sat down, pulled off his shoes and put his feet up on another seat.

"I was about ready to scream, if you really want to know the truth," Ryck admitted.

"I know what you mean, man," Donte said.

"You need anything?" Unger asked. "Do you want to be alone?"

"No," Ryck said, surprised that that was the truth. He didn't want to be alone.

"How about that kiss-ass with the general. I went to NOTC with him, and he was a kiss-ass there, too. Acts like he's this big war hero and such, but that ain't how it went down, as I hear it," Donte said in a conspiratorial tone.

"No shit? What'd you hear?" Unger asked.

"Funny you should use that word, shit," Donte started.

Despite himself, Ryck perked up and listened to Donte relate how one Second Lieutenant Hawk Pfiser had a malfunction in his PICS absorbing gel and had to take a dump. He had exited his PICS, taken off his longjohns, and was squatting in the bushes when a Legion platoon attacked. Pfiser's NCOs saved the day while he was running around, bare-assed naked, his Ruger in his hand, trying to direct the fight.

For the first time since GKN, Ryck laughed. He and Unger couldn't contain themselves while Donte pranced around the room, acting out what he thought Pfiser would have been doing.

Finally, Ryck had to hold up his good hand, crying out "Stop! You're going to set me back a month if I disconnect myself from this Frankenstein contraption."

"Oh, I haven't gotten to the good part. The mother-fucker gets put up for a BC2[82], and the wormhole accepts it!

That quieted Ryck, obviously not what Donte expected.

"Hey, what's going on," he asked, concerned.

"Um, can you come over here a sec," Ryck asked.

"Sure," Donte said, getting up and walking to stand by Ryck's side.

"Can you lift that thing up so I can see it?" Ryck asked, pointing to the medal case on the side table next to his rack.

Donte picked it up and flipped it open, tilting it so Ryck could see the silver Distinguished Meritorious Service Medal hanging from the maroon and green ribbon. There was a gold combat "V" pinned to the middle of the ribbon.

Ryck studied it for a moment. The medal was given to him for getting his men and civilians off the planet. The citation lauded his "tactical acumen" and "fierce resolve." This was his reward for losing over half of his platoon.

"Toss it," he told Donte.

"Excuse me?" Donte asked, confused.

Unger got up and came to stand by Donte.

"Toss it. In the shitcan."

Donte and Unger looked at each other, concern on their faces.

"Look, Ryck, we know how you feel. But why shitcan the medal? You earned it, man," Unger said.

"Earned it?" Ryck said with a sarcastic-sounding laugh. "Earned it? How? I got 29 Marines killed. We were sent to rescue civilians, and I lost 21 of them. There were kids, little children there, for God's sake. And you say I earned it?"

"You also brought back eleven of your men and fifteen civilians," Unger said quietly. "Against the odds. No one else has faced those fucking rats and brought back anyone, so yeah, you earned it."

"Do you know I ordered my own brother-in-law to his death? I ordered three Marines to die with him. One of them, fucking

---

[82] BC2: Battlefield Citation, Second Class

Hogger, I picked him just because I had already given him Thomas' M76 when Thomas went down. It was pure fucking chance, but I still gave the order."

"And if you hadn't, none of you would have gotten off that fucking planet alive. You had to do it," Unger said while Donte nodded his agreement.

"I don't care. That grubbing piece of shit is for killing my men. Whether I had to or not, that's what it means. Shitcan it."

Both Donte and Unger were combat vets. Both had lost men. They understood. Donte held his arm out, parallel with the deck. He waited a moment, then dropped the medal, case and all, into the plastic trash can alongside Ryck's rack. It landed with a thud.

"I will never wear that medal," Ryck promised.

And he never did.

## Chapter 13

"I already told you a thousand times. When the M665 fire hit the capys, there was a flash of blue light, light blue, but bright, and they just kept coming," Ryck said, frustration evident in his voice.

This would be the sixth time he'd been debriefed. A Marine captain, a Navy lieutenant commander, a civilian, and a petty officer made up this team. Each team asked the same questions over and over, as if he were a criminal, and they were waiting for him to mess up his story.

To make matters worse, this time, they'd actually let some information slip. The claymores that Howell and Weiss had set up at the cost of their lives had evidently never detonated. That was two more men added to Ryck's butcher's bill.

"OK, Dr. Telluren, why don't we give Lieutenant Lysander a breather," the Marine captain told the civilian, who had been particularly interested in the shade of the glaring light. "Say, five minutes?"

Ryck shot a grateful look at the captain. He wasn't doing much of the questioning, and Ryck knew his command had sent the Marines to watch out for him.

Ryck completely understood why he was being questioned. The capys, or *Tricnocular majoris*, as they were being officially called, were an unknown entity. Not many humans had observed them and lived to tell anyone about it. The Federation was on a full push to take the fight to the capys, but they didn't know yet just what they were. All they had were specimens of the *Trinocular minors*, the ones the farmers had slaughtered. The current thinking was that the smaller trinoculars served some sort of livestock function, although there was a good deal of disagreement about that. If the similarities in appearance were an indication of similar evolutions, then the big capys might be vegetarian.

What the brains had been able to glean was that the soldier capys have an unknown but highly effective form of shielding against energy weapons, seem to be more susceptible to kinetic weapons, and have shielding against detection better than anything known to man. They didn't seem to have armor or supporting arms, but were essentially somewhat slow light infantry. That didn't mean they were inferior to Marine units. They had devastated 2/6, after all.

The one silver lining was that despite the capy ships seeming to have superior shielding, the Navy intel types thought the Federation ships might have a weapons edge over capy ships, based on their analysis of their brief encounter.

All over human space, the governments were in deep talks on Arrival, the Brotherhood's capital planet. Humans were gearing up for a conflict, and every scrap of intel on the capys was being processed. The little capys were being analyzed in an attempt to design weapons that might be effective against the soldier capys. Deep space scouts had been dispersed to try to find capy worlds, or hopefully, their homeworld. Ryck knew he had to contribute any way he could. But it was frustrating, to be stuck on his back in a hospital ward, being asked the same thing over and over.

The captain stuck his head back in the door, and asked "You ready for some more."

Ryck sighed quietly, but spoke up and answered, "Yes, sir. Bring them in and let's see what they can pick out of my tired brain."

# Alexander

## Chapter 14

Ryck stood in the office, looking at the photos on the wall. There were Marines in small groups, on underwater sleds, in re-entry pods (Ryck knew they were referred to as "goose eggs), airborne on powered wings, and firing all sorts of exotic weapons. This was high-speed, low-drag stuff. Despite himself, Ryck was impressed.

"Hey, Ryck, sorry I'm late. I was out on a run when you got here," Captain Bertrand Nidischii' said, coming through the hatch. "Pull up a chair."

Bert looked good, Ryck thought. He was in running tights and a form-fitting shirt, and to Ryck's eyes, there was no sign of the injuries that had put the captain in regen for almost two years.

"You need anything to drink?" Bert asked while reaching in his small reefer to pull out a Kick Ass.

"No thanks," Ryck started automatically, then, "No, wait a minute, yeah, maybe I can use one."

The captain tossed his Kick Ass to Ryck, and then grabbed another for himself before sitting down and looking across the office at his former sergeant.

"So, how're you holding up?" he asked Ryck.

This could be a simple question about his regen status, but Ryck knew what the captain had meant.

"Not much better. We cam about once a week or so, but only for small talk—how's my regen, things like that."

"I wish I could say something about that, but I'm at a loss. I hope she comes around. She's an intelligent woman, but she doesn't seem smart enough to know you two need to be together," Bert said.

Ryck had needed a shoulder during regen, and not the chaplain or the Navy psychs. Not his fellow lieutenants, either. They were all fine, but he needed someone out of his chain, out of his unit. Captain Nidischii' had been through two regens himself, so he had a personal feel for the stress that created in a man. The fact that Ryck had saved his life was not a small factor, either. They had fought and bled together, and that created a strong bond.

At some point, the captain became more than a mentor to Ryck. He had become a friend, and with Joshua gone, Ryck thought that Bert might be his closest friend, the one in whom he could confide.

"Hey, Warpath, we've got the reports . . . oh, sorry. Didn't, know you had company," another Marine in PT gear said after sticking his head in the door.

Bert held up a hand and said, "Leave it on Grease's desk. I'll get to it in a bit."

"'Warpath?" Ryck asked, raising his eyebrows after the Marine had closed the door behind him.

Ryck knew that in recon, it was the norm that each recon Marine went by a nickname, but "Warpath?" For a Navajo?

Bert, or "Warpath," looked down and laughed before saying, "Well, you know how it is. Almost none of our names are PC, and most are not very complimentary, to be honest. But you get what you get, so I could have done worse."

"You like it here? I mean in recon?" Ryck asked.

"Yeah, sure. As a captain, I might be too senior for the teams, but these are great guys, really the top one-percenters. I'll be putting in for a rifle company when this is over, but it's been a great tour. And with the capy situation, we're a resource that's getting a lot more attention."

Ryck had heard that while the Federation geared up, recon teams had joined Navy picket-skiffs stationed at strategic points around Federations space. It sounded like a necessary, but lonely job.

"And you need to get back into the infantry if you want to make stars someday," Ryck added.

"Hey, no jinxes. But yeah, recon for officers really is considered career limiting."

The two Marines stared at each other for a moment before Bert asked, "So you pulled your growing reputation to wangle a flight out here, while still in regen, to see me. What couldn't you say on cam?"

"Hey, I'm almost done with regen," Ryck said, holding out and stretching his left arm.

The captain just stared at him.

"OK, well, I'm thinking about resigning my commission," Ryck admitted.

There, he'd finally said it to someone.

To his surprise, Bert didn't seem shocked, nor did he recoil in horror.

"And do you think it'll be accepted? With the state of emergency?" Bert asked.

"I've gone through major regen twice now. That's been the bottom line for over a hundred years now. If we want, we can opt out, even with a commitment left."

"I'm not so sure about that. A state of emergency might take precedence. But say you can resign. Why? I mean why now? Is it Hannah?"

"No. Yes. I don't know. I mean that isn't the only reason. It's a big one, though. She hates the Corps now. It cost her two of her brothers, and both were *aldrebruten*, which is—"

"I know the term," Bert told him. "Go on."

"OK, well, she hates the Corps, so that means she hates me, right? If I were out, maybe we could work things through, you know?"

"So that's part of it. But what's the real reason?" Bert asked calmly, no judgment in his voice.

"Ah, OK. Here's the thing. I think I'm done, mentally done. Both times I've been in charge of a platoon, I lost almost all of my Marines. With you, on Pannington, I lost 13 men. Then, on GKN, I lost 29 men and 20 civilians. I couldn't keep them alive. Worse than that, I ordered men, more than I can count, to their deaths. It was my decision on who lived and who died. I made it out, but they didn't."

Bert didn't rush to protest, something for which Ryck was grateful. He didn't want platitudes. He wanted someone who understood.

"You know," Bert said after a few moments," on Pannington, I didn't even make it far enough to fight with you. I left you to pick up the pieces. It's taken me a long time to come to grips with that."

Both men sipped their drinks. Ryck studied the label on the can, not wanting to look anywhere else.

"Germaine Highsmith," Ryck said.

Bert didn't respond. He just waited for Ryck to continue.

"That's his real name. They called him Hogger. I don't know why. Nineteen years old. From New Northumberland. Went to Public School 5670. Graduated 486 out of 561. Mother, Tessa. Father, Derek. Brother, Roger, died in 309 in a hover crash. He liked billiards and BBW porn."

Ryck listed each piece of information, each piece of Hogger's life, as if reading a checklist.

"And he's dead now. Why? Because I gave him Corporal Thomas' M76. That's why. I gave him the weapon, and he had it when I was picking who had to die. If I'd given the 76 to Private Joinovic instead, Hogger would be alive and Joinovic dead. But I didn't, and Tessa and Derek lost their last son, because of my decision.

"I see him, you know? Hogger comes to me at night. Sometimes the others come, too. But always Hogger."

"What about Joshua?" Bert asked.

"No, Joshua doesn't come to me in my dreams. Never him."

The two men sat in silence for a long minute before Bert asked, "Have you lost your nerve?"

Some men might have bristled at this. Ryck took it as it was intended.

"No, not really. Hell, I think I would welcome going like that. Like them. I haven't lost my nerve. It's numb, maybe. But I am not afraid of the fight, and I'd love to get some payback on those grubbing animals."

"Then what are you afraid of?"

"I can't take the responsibility. I can't face playing God, deciding who lives and who dies," Ryck said.

"That's about what I figured. And so I'll ask you, have you considered going recon?"

"What? Recon?"

"Yeah, recon. I'm not going to sit here and psycho-analyze you. I know the psychs have told you about survivor guilt and all of that, how you saved some of your men and civilians. I know what you're feeling. I lost men on Helvelle, and on Pannigton. Those were my men, and I was in a damn ziplock for most of the fight.

"I just think you're wrong, and I don't think your resignation is going to be accepted. So what can you do about it? You can sit and refuse to accept orders, and you'll be in the brig, war hero or not. You can accept the orders, but you won't be as effective, and you could get more men killed. Or you can change jobs. You could probably swing a desk job somewhere. You've earned it. But if you've got fight in you, why not go recon? You'll have some of the best Marines around, and you won't be making tactical decisions. As a lieutenant, you'd be running interference with the infantry command staff and making sure your team is prepared, but when it gets down to it, you would be a fighter. At the most, you would have seven Marines with you, and in the field, you would probably only be with one other Marine. You'd be a fighter, not really a commander making command-type decisions."

"But lieutenants are team leaders," Ryck protested. "That means *lead.*"

"Listen to me. Not everything is by the infantry bible. In recon, you are in charge in training, you help form the reconnaissance plan, but once inserted, you are a fighter. The teams are too small for it not to be that way."

Despite himself, Ryck felt a stirring of interest. He didn't really want to leave the Corps. Yes, he wanted Hannah back. But he was a Marine. It was in his blood. He just needed a break. He couldn't face ordering men to their deaths. If it really was as Bert described, then that horrible decision would be out of his hands. He could focus on fighting, on killing capys.

"But," he started, lifting up his left arm, "I'm still in regen."

"I used my own rehab time to get ready for the Sifter. It's tough, no lie, especially coming off regen. But you've got two more months, right? Start getting in shape. Take your month's convalescent leave and see to Hannah. Then get back and get in the next Sifter platoon."

Ryck considered what his friend had said. It made sense. He still had two months left on regen, and he could put off any decision until then. Meanwhile, he could put in the papers for recon. If he still wanted to resign, he could do it after he was back on full duty. If he didn't want to resign, then he had an option that just might work.

# Tarawa

## Chapter 15

Ryck was wheezing as he got to the top of Mount Motherfucker. He bent over at the waist, hands on his knees. Most of the class had already made it up, but at least three were still behind him.

Reconnaissance Training Course had been a kick in the proverbial ass. It was doubly difficult for Ryck as he hadn't even finished his regen therapy, and his left side was still weak. But he had made it. The final run up the mountain was a tradition on the morning of graduation.

Ryck wasn't dumb, though. Physically, he hadn't been up to his own previous standards, much less that of recon. He knew he'd been cut some slack in that regard, given his medical condition and his proven combat track record. His ability to be creative had been particularly valued as something necessary in recon. He'd been pulled along where someone else, someone not wounded or someone without his record might have been dropped.

"You OK, L-T?" Sergeant June asked, coming over to stand beside Ryck.

Sgt June was a bright, earnest Marine. He was also one heck of a runner, and had probably been the first one up the mountain.

"Sure . . . I'm . . . OK. Just let . . . me catch . . . my breath."

"Here, have some water," June said, holding out his canteen.

Ryck waved him off. He had his own canteen, but he needed to control his breathing before he'd be able to drink. Ryck turned and flopped on the ground. As SSgt Lipsieg huffed his way to the top, Ryck clapped, but didn't get up. It was still zero-dark-thirty, the sun only beginning to make its rosy presence visible off in the horizon. The 19 remaining members of RTC 315-03 would watch the sunrise and have a breakfast that was being brought up before trudging back down and getting ready for the 1100 graduation ceremony.

Ryck looked at the other 16 Marines who had finished the run. Bert had been right. These were the cream of the crop. It wasn't that they were all superstuds. Yes, the course screened out those who were not fit, but Ryck had had more fit, better gym rats or runners in his infantry platoons before. But each one of the surviving classmates had a sense of drive, or purpose, of self-discipline that transcended the average Marine, much less the average civilian.

These elements had been necessary to get through the course. The academics had been difficult for many of the Marines, but they were really not that bad. The PT had been brutal at times, but certainly achievable. It had been the mental discipline that was the toughest thing to master. All the days without sleep, without food, in the cold, the heat, the most miserable conditions the staff could throw at them. Of the 49 drops in the class, 41 were DORs. They just quit after shivering in the cold for two days, or marching across the desert heat with 70 kg packs.

The physical discomfort had been easier for Ryck to endure. He had found a place to go where he could almost observe the situation without experiencing it. It was like he was having, not an out-of-body-experience, but an inner-body-experience, where he could wall off the cold, the heat, the hunger, the weariness.

Ryck's two moments of truth were in the pool and in the medical facility. The one in the pool should not have been surprising. There were very few pools on Prophesy, and Ryck had never swum before getting to bootcamp. He was a mediocre swimmer at best, and when they had undergone shark training, he'd almost lost it. At the bottom of the pool, breathing through his BA,[83] he had watched warily as the "sharks," the RTs[84], circled above the class before diving down to tear off the BAs, pummel the candidates, and generally make life miserable for them. Ryck had to fight down the welling panic when he was the target, and he'd almost lost it twice. It had only been by an extreme force of will that he hadn't shot for the surface.

---

[83] BA: Breathing Apparatus. A small diaphragm device that mixes oxygen from a small tank with oxygen from the water, rendering breathing possible.

[84] RT: Reconnaissance Trainers. The training cadre at Reconnaissance Training Course at Camp Prettyjohn.

The second precipice had been at the medical facility, of all places. Ryck was leery of medical facilities in general, given his misery during his two major regens. The antiseptic, mediciny smell of the places alone was enough to raise his stress levels. But the procedure that was to be done on him gave him the creeping jeepies.

Recon Marines were supposed to be invisible. No matter how proficient they were as warriors, they were out in two-to-eight-man teams, and even an eight-man team could not hold off an enemy company. They had the finest cloaking technology available to them, but the best cloaking was to have nothing that could be picked up. Their special skins and chest carapace were both designed to deaden the tiny electrical emissions from the body. The heartbeat, in particular, was passively shielded. Recon Marines didn't have normal AIs nor even normal displays. The small display monocle was a super-low emission screen that stayed off most of the time, with a mechanical on-off switch. The data it could display was not pulled from the net. It was downloaded before going into bad-guy country. One of the results of this was that the normal navigation system Marines employed was unusable to a recon Marine.

The mad scientists had come up with a solution: they would make recon Marines better navigators. First, the hippocampus would be stimulated to develop. This would allow recon Marines to have a much better sense of direction. Second, two Neulife bridges, one for each hemisphere, would be inserted from the hippocampus to the rest of the brain, to enable the Marine to make use of that input in a more cognitive fashion.

The bridge was essentially a bundle of KD crystal connectors, bundled much like dried spaghetti in the hand before putting it into the boiling water. But KD crystals cannot connect into brain cells. So on each end of the KD bundle, Neulife "caps" were attached which could take the input from the hippocampus, transmit it to the crystals, then interface back into the entorhinal cortex, bypassing the fornix, in a usable format.

Ryck had been almost petrified of having Neulife inserted into his brain. The thought of the artificial life sucking nutrients out of him, attaching to his brain, almost made him sick. The doctor assured him that this wasn't a genmod, that it was related to what the Navy navigators had done to them, which didn't help. He had even shown Ryck one of the bridges under his operating screen, and that was even worse. The Neulife caps looked like small, moldy, white worms.

Ryck had come close to DOR'ing right then and there. It had taken all of his self-discipline to go through prep and get on the table for the surgery. He might have had a change of heart as the anesthesia took over, but he wasn't sure if he had actually objected or only thought he had in the cotton-effect of the drugs just before he went under.

When he awoke, he really didn't feel different. He knew it would take awhile for the hippocampus to fully develop, but he did seem to have a better feel of where he was with relationship to his surroundings.

Not all of RCT had been onerous. Some of the training had been downright fun. Recon had lots of sexy toys for movement, fighting, and concealment, and learning to use them had been a blast. For example, while mastering the hover sleds Ryck had first seen back on Alexander during the birthday pageant, the class had been divided into teams to play world football against each other. Ryck's team, Giant Ballbusters, had lost to the other team, Up Your Mamma's, and had to run up Mount Motherfucker as punishment. Up Your Mamma's along with all the RTs had joined in the run in a show of solidarity.

The rest of the Marine moved to the edge of the mountaintop, cheering and clapping. Ryck pulled himself up and joined them where First Sergeant Poulson was just arriving. The first sergeant was pretty old to be only now going through RCT, and he'd had the added handicap of going through regen for both legs and a good portion of his pelvis. But he had a steel will, and he never quit.

Several Marines ran down the last 150 meters to where, Capt Horsvatch, the Course Director, and Gunny Jiminez, the class senior RT, paced alongside the first sergeant. The rest of the class quickly followed.

"Ooh-rah! First Sergeant!" Marines called out as the entire class fell alongside him and escorted him up the final climb.

They got to the top, and the first sergeant yelled out, "If you ain't recon, you ain't shit!" much to the delight of the rest.

In his heart, Ryck was an infantry Marine, in particular, a PICS Marine. But as he looked around at his classmates, who were in a circle surrounding the first sergeant, chanting the "if you ain't recon" mantra over and over, he knew this was a good crew. He could serve with them.

Ryck was back in the fight.

# Zephyr-Hadreson

## Chapter 16

First Lieutenant Ryck Lysander subconsciously straightened his gig line,[85] then pushed open the hatch to his new office. He'd already been welcomed aboard by everyone from the Division CG on down to Captain Sverge, his platoon commander.

In an infantry company, a captain was generally a company commander. Recon tended to be rank heavy, though, with only experienced Marines being accepted. Captain Sverge had already commanded an infantry company, but instead of taking a staff job, he had volunteered for recon, where he was back to platoon commander.

Ryck, as a first lieutenant, was a team leader, in charge of seven other Marines. That was more than fine with him. Seven Marines, especially experienced Marines, was more than enough.

He'd been assigned to Fourth Team, Second Platoon, Charlie Company, Second Recon Battalion, back in his old Second Marine Division. The division had been beefed up since Ryck had gone to regen and then off to RCT. It was on a war footing, and the undercurrent was that action was imminent. The rumor mill had it that two planets had been found to have capy "infestations," as it was being termed. The Navy and both Second and Fourth Division, with attachments from the Legion and with the Brotherhood Navy augmenting the Federation Navy, were to be tasked with eliminating the capy threat on those planets.

After the initial confrontation on G.K. Nutrition Six, the public had been up in arms demanding an immediate retaliatory strike, and the Federation powers-that-be would have ordered one, if there had been a target. The capys had simply disappeared from sight. With GKN on the edge of Federation space, the picket-skiffs

[85] Gig line: A line from the front edge of a shirt, running through the belt and down the zipper of the trousers. All three should be in line.

and recon teams had been sent out further into the galactic arm. Several picket-skiffs had simply disappeared, but whether to the capys or to the normal perils of very deep space, no one knew. But after two-and-a-half years, two skiffs had returned with information of capy infestations. At least according to rumor. All of this was classified, so all or none of it could be true. The division temp, though, had risen to almost a fever pitch, so bets were heavily in the this-is-a-no-shitter camp.

Ryck felt nervous as he entered the office space. He hadn't received a team list, so he didn't know what to expect. Four Marines were lounging on the couch in front of his new desk, and one Marine was standing in the corner.

There was none of the "Attention on deck" that occurred elsewhere in the Corps. The four Marines on the couch simply stood up.

"Welcome aboard, Toad," a gunny said, holding out his hand. "Klepto here."

Ryck only slightly grimaced at the nickname. It would still take some getting used to. It could have been worse. His class had been relatively gentle, naming him for the E-559 "Toad" combustion devices he'd used as weapons in combat.

"Good to meet you, Klepto."

A huge chested, short-necked staff sergeant, obviously a heavy-worlder, held out his hand and simply said "Buttercup."

Ryck tried to choke back a laugh and failed miserably.

*Buttercup?*

Buttercup rolled his eyes, and Klepto offered, "That's Staff Sergeant Honor Gilroy," and when Ryck didn't indicate comprehension, added, "Homer Gilroy, and *You are My Buttercup*?"

Then it sunk in. Homer Gilroy had written that sappy love song that had somehow become a hit four years ago.

*Wow, sucks to be Buttercup*, Ryck thought, his own nic seeming much better now.

"Shart, Toad. Glad to meet you," a sergeant said.

"You don't want to know, sir," the gunny said.

Ryck did want to know, though. "Shart" had an old, but specific meaning.

Ryck looked at the other gunny and held out his hand.

"Rabbit, sir."

It was only then that Ryck turned to look at the Marine still standing in the corner.

"My grubbing shit! Sams!" Ryck shouted to Staff Sergeant Bobbi Samuelson, one of the Marines in his very first unit.

Sams walked over to shake his hand, but Ryck pulled him into a bear hug.

"I didn't expect to see you here, Sams," he said, surprised but happy.

"It's Bobbi," Sams said.

"Yeah, I know your name, Sams. What the fuck? You think I forgot?"

"No, my name. Now. It's Bobbi."

Once again, it took a moment for Ryck to understand, and he started laughing. Sams' real name seemed strange enough that his RCT class had kept it as his nic.

"Who's the top shirt?" Ryck asked, still laughing.

"That'd be me, sir," Klepto said. "I've got the personnel records on all of us on your desk. We've got one on emergency leave and one in at sickbay right now."

"Emergency leave?"

"Having his first baby. That'd be Cpl Caruthers, Crutch. Wife's local, so he can be here in an hour if need be," his team sergeant, or "first shirt," said.

Klepto had an odd, clipped way of speaking. Ryck couldn't quite place from what planet the gunny might be. It would be in his records, though.

"How are the teams organized? I mean, who's left out for now?"

"Uh, Ryck, I mean lieutenant, I mean Toad, you've got me for your teammate, if that's copacetic. I'm the orphan now," Sams said.

Sams—Bobbi—was an irreverent, cynical smart ass. He was also a helluva Marine.

"Well, I guess we're stuck with each other, then, *Bobbi*!" Ryck told him, a smile on his face.

Things were looking up.

# HAC-440

## Chapter 17

Ryck came out of the head, glad his "Navy's Revenge" seemed to be over.

"Everything come out OK, Toad?" Gunny Heang asked, the rest of the team dutifully laughing at the old joke.

"Yeah, Rabbit, everything came out just fine," Ryck answered.

With a long drop ahead of them, and in very, very close confinement, each Marine had been given an impact laxative to evacuate their bowels as well as a glucose bomb to raise caloric levels without bulk. The shit buster injection started working within five minutes and usually completed its function within 30. Ryck was pretty sure he had run the course and was now squeaky clean, at least on the inside.

Except for Sgt Rogers, the rest of the Marines were in the holding space, ready for their drop. Ryck put his back against the bulkhead and slid to a sitting position. As team leader, he'd been busy in briefings and mission planning. Now, with the drop imminent, he was just one more team member. Each two-man team had a separate mission and drop location, and it would be essentially impossible for him to exert any command control on the other teams.

Rogers finally came out of the head, still pulling up his flight suit trou, showing the team and Navy crew that he was going commando.

"Hell, Jolly, how about covering up that thing before coming out?" Gunny Heang asked. "We don't need that flapping in our faces before a drop."

Sgt Rogers didn't say anything, but slowed down, slowly zipping up, leaving himself exposed until the last moment. He had to wheel away suddenly and finish as Sams threw a glove at him, aiming for his crotch.

There had always been a degree of grab-ass and smack-talk before any of Ryck's previous operations, but this time, his team seemed pretty calm and relaxed. Ryck was outwardly just as relaxed, but inwardly, he had a few butterflies. He wondered if his last regen had affected him, making him a little more nervous.

Finally, the Navy chief gave the signal. The Marines got to their feet, did one last weapons check, then wandered over to the duck eggs. Ryck and Sams were in the second egg. Ryck let his teammate slide in, giving him the husband position.

As Sams wiggled in, Ryck felt he should say something, but the men knew their mission, and wishing good luck was bad juju according to recon tradition.

He settled for yelling out, “Get tight, but don’t do anything we wouldn’t do!” before starting to slide into the wife position in the egg.

The hoots and hollers from the others, with “What we do in private ain’t no one’s business,” and “But Buttercup is just so girly-cute,” let Ryck know he’d hit the right note.

Ryck slid into position, his face just centimeters away from Sams’ crotch and his crotch in Sams’ face. When they hit the planet’s atmosphere, Ryck would be head down with regards to the planet’s surface, hence the term “wife position.”

The Inert Atmospheric Insertion Capsule, the “duck egg,” was a very small capsule designed to insert one or two men from space to a planet’s surface. Inside, it was tiny, barely big enough for two men to fit. They could be configured back-to-front, or “spooning,” or facing each other, but face-to-foot. This, not surprisingly, was “69’ing.”

The four capsules for the insert would be inserted into a larger inert shell, which would be aimed at the planet. This outer shell was designed to ablate away as it entered the atmosphere, breaking up as a meteor might. The four duck eggs, along with decoy components, would separate to follow pre-designated paths to the target planet. The duck egg surfaces were designed to ablate away as well, slowing it down some before ejecting the Marines into the atmosphere some 10,000 meters above the planet’s surface.

The Marines would still be travelling quite fast, so a tight body position was a must. An arm could be ripped off before the flight suit baffles could take effect. At around 7,000 meters, the foil would deploy, allowing the Marines to navigate and descend to their actual insertion point.

All of this was done without any emissions. The entire evolution was mechanical. Oxygen for the trip was in chest tanks. No food would be taken, and while each Marine had a piss tube, there was no way to take a shit (which was the reason for the bowel evacuation). More importantly, there were no comms, either with higher headquarters or each other. It was possible for two Marines in the same duck egg to shout out to each other and be heard, but generally, it was silence for the entire insertion.

Ryck had made two training insertions, the longest one being eight hours. This one was calculated at 30 hours. No one was sure as to the capys' space surveillance capabilities, so no chances were being taken.

"You ready in there?" the yellow-shirted petty officer asked while looking in.

Ryck could feel Sams reach around him to give the thumbs up. The blood was going to his head, and he wanted the release of null gravity.

"OK, I'm closing up," the petty officer said. "God's speed."

The light was cut off as the side of the egg was put back and the seams sealed. Ryck could feel the duck egg shift as it was moved into position. With several minutes of jerking back and forth, Ryck's position was shifted until he was slightly on his side instead of straight upside down. It wasn't much of an improvement.

In the darkness, Ryck could only try to interpret the movements to try to understand what was happening. It wasn't until Ryck felt the pressure of the ejection from the ship and the shift to null grav that he knew they were finally on the way.

Thirty hours in complete darkness, without communicating, made it difficult to estimate the passing of time. The blood thinners they'd all been given to combat deep vein thrombosis had the side effect of keeping them more alert, so Ryck was lost in his thoughts. Many of those thoughts centered on Hannah. He'd cammed with her the day before, and she'd seemed almost normal, if you forgot the fact that they were husband and wife, not merely acquaintances. There were none of the little affections a married couple might use.

Ryck didn't know where they stood, but he still had hopes that they could get back together.

Despite the drugs, Ryck might have fallen asleep. When the duck egg started vibrating, it seemed shorter than 30 hours. But vibration meant atmosphere, and that meant they were getting close.

The vibration turned to shaking. Ryck strained his eyes, trying to pick up the glow of entry. If he saw it, though, before his duck egg was cast free, it would be a very bad sign.

Sams shifted beside him. He'd been very still during the transit, barely moving. Now, he was showing signs of life.

The shaking became violent, and Ryck had to brace himself to keep from being slammed about. There was a small, padded paper harness between the two Marines, but twice, Sams smashed into Ryck, once strong enough and in a location where Ryck would have doubled up if he had the space to do so.

When the duck egg broke free, Ryck was sure he felt the difference. The extreme violence abated a few degrees while vibration increased. Ryck became aware of a dull sound growing, penetrating his helmet. Not sure at first, Ryck began to see a glow as the egg's outer layers burned away. They would have between a five- and ten-second warning before they were ejected, but Ryck pulled his arms in and tightened up his legs. He'd done it too early, though, and he had just started to relax again when the longitudinal vents began to split, just as the flames started to die out.

Ryck quickly tensed up again, straining to get into position. Ryck's side of the egg split first, followed a fraction of a second by Sams'. This tiny difference kept them from slamming into each other. The shock of hitting the atmosphere was huge, despite the ablative slowing of the capsule. Ryck had been ready, but his position was almost flung apart. The helmet and the top of his flight suit kept his neck intact, but it could have been possible for him to suffer severe injury to his extremities. Ryck managed to keep his position, though, and within a few moments, he had stabilized. Slowly, and as taught, he extended into the age-old freefall position and started the next phase of the long insertion.

They had entered the atmosphere over daylight, but by the time they had ejected from the egg, Ryck and Sams had travelled into night. Ryck could see the light on the horizon, but beneath him, the planet was shrouded in darkness. Ryck glanced around, but he couldn't see Sams. He had to trust that their systems would not only get them down, but get them both down together at their objective.

The deployment of the foil was done mechanically. There was an emergency ripcord, but if he had to resort to that, he would be hopelessly off course and beyond any link-up with Sams. Ryck knew he had to rely on the equipment given to him, but free falling above a dark planet did nothing for depth perception, and he kept wondering if he had fallen too far. He was getting closer to using the ripcord when his foil deployed, and he was jerked to a steady descent.

The shock of the chute deployment pulled down a helmet overlay in front of his eyes. This was a clever designed developed by luxury watchmakers back on Utopia. All Ryck had to do was line up the horizon on the overlay with the real horizon, then keep the foil along the indicated glide path. How it kept adjusting to his descent, without any electronics, was beyond Ryck's comprehension. It had worked back during training on Tarawa and Johnston Landing, so Ryck simply accepted that it would work on HAC-440.

As he got closer to the ground, he could begin to make out features. First it was a hill to his left, then trees.

*TREES!*

Ryck swore under his breath as he tried to wheel his foil to the right. It was no use. He hit the trees, the branches grabbing at him, but not stopping his fall until he slammed into something big. He immediately grabbed onto the trunk, stopping his fall. He completed a quick self-check, but he was OK. Nothing seemed broken. Looking over his shoulder, he tried to see the ground, but in the darkness, it was out of sight.

Carefully, he unhooked his foil harness. It would disintegrate into its component molecules within an hour, so he could just leave it hanging there in the treetops. He was now unsupported. If he fell, nothing would stop him except the ground. Reaching into his cargo pocket, he pulled out a pair of gloves and put them on. Then, reaching around, he grasped the trunk and slowly began to ease his way down, hugging the tree for dear life. He inched his way down, once having to go back up a meter as he came down straddling a branch.

His senses were on full alert as he descended. Any capy out there would have him dead to rights. Finally, he could make out the ground. Another two meters, and he would be down.

"'Bout time you made it," Sams whispered from out of the darkness.

That was a relief. The system worked. They had made it down together.

Ryck slid down the last meter, placing his feet on the planet's surface.

The easy part was over. Now they had work to do.

## Chapter 18

Ryck pulled the sheet of plaspage out of his cargo pocket and looked at it for at least the dozenth time. His sense of direction was keeping him on track, but the map printed on the sheet was low res, taken from a visual image captured some 100,000 or more kilometers away and transposed over an old, but far more detailed planetary survey. The survey had been done close to 50 standard years ago by a Deep Space Agency scout team. The overlay had been done less than six months ago by a Navy picket-skiff. It showed what looked to be both herds of the capy minors as well as buildings where nothing had been before. The buildings Ryck could recognize. The capy minors? Ryck had to take the experts word on that. They could easily have been cows, sheep, or any number of other animals that gathered in herds.

Ryck and Sams had been moving carefully in the ancient forest for seven hours, all senses on alert. They hadn't spoken a word to each other, relying on hand-and-arm signals the few times it had been necessary.

Ryck could see the forest lightening up ahead. That had to be the start of the large, open basin that ran up to the mountains some 40 klicks ahead. This basin was one of the places where the picket-skiffs had spotted capys.

The basin was protected on three sides by steep mountains, and on the fourth side by the forest and a lower coastal range of hills. If the capy minors were livestock, as many of the experts surmised, then the basin made a nice, natural ranch. There was water, forage, and a means to keep them stationary.

Ryck held up his hand, and then spread three fingers. Sams nodded, understanding that it was 300 meters to the open grasslands. The trees were thinning out, changing from the huge giants to smaller, younger specimens of the planet's version of trees. About 15% of all known planets had something that looked and functioned as trees, so while the individual specimens were unique, the fact that there were trees on the planet was nothing extremely out of the ordinary. Xenobotanists would be interested, but to Ryck, they were just trees, scientific classification be damned.

Ryck was tempted to turn on his monocle. For such a small piece of electronics, it had a pretty powerful AI and sensing capabilities. He could use it to sweep the area ahead of him in any number of spectrums to try and pick up the capys. In his PICS, this would have been SOP[86]. In recon though, he was supposed to be a ghost, and without understanding the capy's capabilities, he was to turn on his monocle only as a last resort.

He motioned to Sams to get down, and the two of them low-crawled the last 300 meters, taking two hours to get to the edge of the treeline. Ryck's knees and elbows ached despite the crawl pads, but he forced the discomfort into a small corner in his mind. He stopped behind some sort of 3-meter fleshy plant that had no Terran equivalent that Ryck knew of, and pulled out the old binos he'd been issued. The normal recon visual glasses could be powered up for higher magnification, light amplification, and resolution enhancement. These were glass and light, nothing more.

He could see the capys with his bare eyes, and it took him only a moment to acquire them through the binos. These were the minors—the same kind as those the farmers had killed off, the same kind now in more than a few zoos. The meter-long animals were in a large herd, slowly cropping the local grass. From a quick guesstimate, Ryck figured there had to close to 2,000 of them, moving en masse. How the ones in the back got any grass to eat was hard to fathom.

The fact that they could eat the grass, and evidently receive sustenance, was pretty surprising. They were not on the planet during the initial survey 50-odd years ago, and it was pretty evident that this was not their home world. The existence of the capys on the planet was still classified, but scientists had been brought in, and one postulation was that the sentient capys had seeded this world as an investment in the future. Ryck, though, agreed with those that felt the little capys simply had robust digestive tracks. They had eaten Terran crops on GKN, and the specimens in the zoos seemed to do well on what their keepers fed them.

"What the fuck is that?" Sams whispered beside him.

---

[86] SOP: Standard Operating Procedure

"Where?"

"Past the herd, another 400 meters, at our two o'clock."

Ryck glassed over, picking up two buildings of some sort that looked like foam igloos. They'd seen the photos taken from the Navy ships, but those had been pretty low-resolution due to the distance from which they'd been taken. Seeing them up close was pretty interesting, but why was Sams so surprised?

Then he saw it. A huge, broad-shouldered creature walked on four legs in front of one of the buildings. It bent down, and then effortlessly stood upright on its hind legs with a large rock in its hands (paws?). As Ryck studied it, the obvious similarities spoke of a common evolution to the capy minors and majores. It had the same capybara-like appearance. It had the three eyes that the other two capys had. It was covered in a dense fur. But there, the similarities ended. This guy had to be twice the size of the soldier capys, and even at this distance, it moved in a way that spoke power. The rock it carried had to weigh 400 kg, but it hadn't phased the thing in the least.

"St Chuck's hell, look at the size of it," Ryck whispered.

"You see the belt?" Sams asked him.

Sams was right. The giant capy had a belt of some kind with things dangling from it. All of this bespoke intelligence.

*Are there two sentient species of them?* Ryck wondered.

Both Marines watched the big guy until it disappeared from sight down a depression.

"They never told us nothin' about no other capys," Sams said, sounding peeved.

"They haven't told us much of anything. I'm guessing this is as much a surprise to everyone as it is to us," Ryck responded.

All the briefs the Marines had were as much conjecture as anything else. Once, two scientist-types had actually grabbed each other on the stage and started to tussle over a difference of opinion.

What was known was that the *trinocular minor*, the little capys, were within earth-normal range of body temperature and respiration, and they had a circulatory system that almost mirrored that of earth-based life. Due to trace metals, the capys' blood was somewhat blue, but it acted in the same way to transport oxygen to the blood. The most amazing thing about them was that they were so close to earth biology. Many scientists took that as proof of some long-past mutual genesis—parallel evolution seemed too far-fetched and explanation to them.

There were differences though, the most notable being the three eyes. The lower two functioned in the same way as Terran eyes, and within much of the same wavelengths as a dog's. The third eye, higher on the forehead, was not as well-developed, and its similarity to the ampullae of Lorenzini that sharks used as electroreceptors meant that the capys could probably sense bioelectronics. Initial tests supported that theory, but those tests were not conclusive.

Two more of the giant capys ambled into sight. They sat back on their haunches and seemed to be communicating. The one on the right lifted on foreleg, and with a human-like gesture, pointed back in the direction that the first one had taken. Ryck could have sworn the second nodded, just as a person would have. It got up, trotted to the building, then picked up a rock bigger than the first one had lifted, and walking upright, carried it off. The one that had pointed simply sat still, an immense hunk of muscle and flesh. Ryck wished he could peer into the thing's mind.

"Well, Ansel Adams, about time you earned your paycheck. Start clicking away," Ryck told Sams.

Sams reached into his cargo pocket and pulled out the Leica replica he'd been given. With the requirement of no electronic signatures, no matter how small, the teams had been relegated to mid-20th Century, Old Reckoning, cameras. The real cameras were too rare to outfit everyone needing one, but replicas had been fabricated, complete with manual shutter speed and f-stop aperture adjustment. The Marines had gotten crash courses in their use, and while neither Ryck nor Sams had set the world on fire, Sams had been the better photographer of the two.

Sams put on the telephoto lens and began to take photos of the giant capy while Ryck pulled out his recon log to enter the sighting. The entry would be married to the photos later when the film could be developed.

This was big. In just a few short minutes, the little that mankind knew about the capys had been tossed asunder.

## Chapter 19

"Hey," Ryck said, kicking the sleeping Sams who was prone below him. "You're up."

The two Marines had been observing the capys for two days now. Other than that first bombshell, nothing surprising had occurred. The smaller capys had rotated their way around the basin. At the moment, they were a good 1,500 meters away, on the other side of the small group of buildings.

The more Ryck watched, the more certain he was that the giant capys were sentient. They had expanded one of the buildings and erected a stone wall. The wall didn't seem to lead anywhere, and Ryck couldn't come up with a reason for it, but the giant capys worked with individual purpose, not with the instinctive precision of earth ants or bees.

"Anything?" Sams asked, stretching his arms.

"Nothing of note. The giants still ignore the livestock. They've stopped building the wall, though."

"Doing anything with it?" Sams asked as he moved forward to where he could observe the basin.

"Nope, nada. It's just sitting there, a monument to nothing, and the giants are ignoring it now," Ryck said.

"What's with these things?" Sams asked. "In the scifi holos, aliens are reptiles, or dragons, or even big bugs, bent on eating all of us. But when we finally get contact, all we've got are teddy bears that just sit around doing nothing?"

"Don't complain. 'Nothing' is pretty good right now. You forget, I've seen them in combat."

Sams harrumphed, accepting Ryck's statement, then asked, "Well, do you think we should move yet?"

Ryck had been thinking the same thing. The assault was to take place in three days, unless something had changed since they'd been inserted. Ryck and Sams were almost opposite where the Marines would land, and they needed to be there to offer pathfinding for the incoming craft. It would take at least a day to move back, so they could leave early to get in position. On the other hand, the longer they stayed at the LZ, the more chance they had to give the position away.

"No, let's stay here another day. We've still got time."

"Roger, that," Sams acknowledged as he settled into position. "You leave me any bacon?"

"You son-of-a-bitch. Why'd you have to bring up bacon? I'd kill for some," Ryck said, grimacing at the thought of the base paste he and Sams had been sucking down.

The base was a homogenized version of the bases used in food fabricators, guaranteed to provide all the nutrients a hungry Marine needed. Not having gone through a fabricator, though, it tasted like shit, and it didn't come close to filling the belly.

"Well, those farmers said the capys tasted great. You saw that, right, on the vids? What say I sort of sidle on down there, grab one, and we can have a BBQ?" Sams asked, amused sarcasm dripping off each word.

"Sure thing, *Bobbi,*" Ryck said, using Sams' nickname, "you just run on out there and pick the fattest, juiciest one. Grab some BBQ sauce while you're at it."

"Think I might, at that. You like your sauce spicy or tangy?"

"Fuck you. Now I'm going to be dreaming about food, asshole," Ryck said, scooting back down the small rise to the hollow where they'd been sleeping.

He heard Sams softly chortle as he slid down past the flat spot where they slept and all the way to the bottom of the gully, another two meters in back of the crest. At about 2.5 meters below the highest point, he could stand up safely. Ryck stretched, and then wandered over to where some rocks protruded from the ground. Next to the big tree that marked the spot, he scraped away at the dirt between some rocks with a stick they had gathered, then undid his trou.

Ryck sighed with relief as he emptied his bladder. They had no idea as to the olfactory capabilities of the capys, but nothing the biologists had discovered indicated that it might be anything out of the ordinary. Anyway, the two Marines had to piss. The base paste might keep their other side blocked up, but not piss. He closed his eyes and let it flow.

Something interrupted the sound of the stream hitting the dirt. Ryck opened his eyes to see a giant capy walking towards him, dragging two huge logs. He glanced at the modified M72 HGL where he'd laid it against a rock.

*Stupid! Putting it down in enemy territory!*

He froze, alternating between diving for his weapon and standing still. The capy was 20 meters away, and it hadn't seemed to notice anything.

Ryck slowly slid his dick back inside, drips be damned. The recon skins had been adjusted through a calculated guesswork to be able to shield them. Ryck knew he was about to find out if they were effective.

The capy veered toward Ryck, and Ryck almost broke for his weapon, but the creature stepped into the gully, and then pulled the logs hand-over-hand to get them across. It climbed out on the other side, not even five meters from Ryck.

The thing was huge, and its muscles bulged under its fur. A musty, slightly pungent aroma filled the air. Just as it came abreast of Ryck, it turned its head and looked right at him. Ryck tried to will his heartbeat down, sure the beast could hear his pulse, skins or no.

The giant capy might have paused looking at him, or it might not have paused. Regardless, it didn't hesitate in its step and kept walking.

Ryck waited until the thing was out of sight before he dared to move. He picked up his M72, then made his way back to their hide.

"Did you see that?" Sams whispered excitedly. "One of them just came out of the woods, not 30 meters away!"

"Yeah, I saw it," Ryck simply said, sitting down to make the entry in his log.

With the giant capys, at least, the new skins seemed to have worked.

## Chapter 20

For the first time, the soldier capys, the same type that Ryck had fought, made an appearance. Four of them had marched out of the small stand of trees on the far side of the basin. The mountains rose up from those trees, so Ryck didn't know if they came down from the mountains, if they marched up from somewhere, or if they had been lifted by some sort of vehicle. They had just shown up.

The four seemed to examine the wall the giants had built. The giants (the two Marines had counted about 20 of them) ignored the soldiers just as the soldiers ignored them. That shattered the theories Ryck and Sams had come up with regarding the relationship between the three types of capy.

The soldier capys were much smaller than the giants, and they were far more slender, if still a bit pudgy by earth standards. They all carried the same energy guns that Ryck had seen before, the ones that looked like truncated jai alai *xistera* with a ball of light in the basket. One big difference, though, was that the soldiers had the faint blue glow of what had to be their shielding. That glow became more pronounced in the darkness, making them easily visible to the two Marines.

An incident before darkness closed in really caught Ryck's attention. A giant capy with a branch on its shoulder walked close to two of the soldiers. As he passed one of the soldiers, he turned at the same moment the soldier stepped to its left, putting it right where the back of the branch collided with the soldiers head. Ryck expected a shower of sparks as the shield deflected the branch, but that never happened. There was barely a pulse, and the branch struck the soldier in the head. The soldier went down hard while the giant continued walking.

The second soldier didn't seem upset, and it didn't chase down the giant. It merely walked to the downed solder and stood there. After a few moments, the downed capy struggled to its feet. Ryck and Sams both plainly saw the dark bluish-red blood on the side of the capy's head, even from their hide over 1,000 meters away.

The two soldiers moved off, even if the one seemed unsteady on its feet.

Ryck and Sams bounced the incident around for quite some time as the night wore on. If a shield could stop Marine energy weapons, if it could stop M99 darts, surely it could brush aside an accidental hit with a log. Sams figured that the soldiers kept their shields powered down to save energy until they were needed. Ryck had to admit that made sense, but something just didn't sit right with him with that explanation.

## Chapter 21

Ryck and Sams were still about 400 meters from the planned assault LZ when something big flew overhead, its shadow flashing over them.

*Was the assault already on?* Ryck wondered, taking a quick look at his watch.

No, it was not for another ten hours, right at dawn. Marines liked to fight in the dark, but the captive little capys seemed to be better suited than humans for darkness, so a daylight assault it was.

Ryck motioned to Sams that they needed to break off and get eyes on the basin. The two Marines moved forward at a slightly faster pace, knowing that the capys should be no closer than 1,000 meters from their position. Moving in a crouch, they went to their bellies for the last 20 meters, edging up to where they could see what was going on.

A blockish ship, perhaps 40 to 50 meters long, had landed close to Capytown. The back was a simple ramp that had already been lowered. This was Ryck's first glimpse of a capy ship, and it was surprisingly mundane to him. He had sort of expected something more exotic, like the alien ships in the flicks. This was nothing so much as a huge, flying cargo container.

"What do you think's up?" Sams asked as he snapped away with his Leica.

"Well, we've got more of the soldiers here now, what 30, do you think? And the giants seem to be—shit, is that another new kind of capy? Over there with the little ones?" Ryck asked.

Sams shifted his gaze, pondered a moment, and then said, "I don't know. It looks like a soldier without the gear. And check it out, it's herding the little guys."

Ryck studied the new capy. Sams was right about one thing: it was herding the little capys towards the ship. Whether it was an unarmed soldier? Well, Ryck wasn't so sure about that. True, it looked like one of the soldiers, but it was a little taller and a little more slender. "Gracile" was perhaps the right description. More than that, it moved differently, without the sense of purpose the soldier capys seemed to have. The appearance was close enough, though, so that Sams could be right.

As the herd of capys turned toward the ship's ramp, it immediately became clear what was happening. The little capys were being taken away. With the sudden appearance of more soldiers than the two Marines had seen before, the coincidence was too much to ignore. The capys knew something was up.

"They're leaving," Sams said, coming to the same conclusion. "Division's not going to like that."

The mission of the assault was not just to eliminate the capys from this one world. A simple planet buster could do that. The prime purpose was to engage the capys with an overwhelming force. Overwhelming to the point of ensuring victory, but not so much that combat was not engaged. Two capy-held planets were being attacked simultaneously, led by the Federation Navy and Marines, but with heavy reinforcement from the Brotherhood, the Confederation, several independent worlds, and three mercenary companies. Each unit, armed with every weapon imaginable, was to assault a specific objective independently. A heavy reserve force was to be kept to ensure no unit got into too much trouble, but the militaries of mankind wanted to analyze the effectiveness of various weapons and tactics in attacking the capy forces. Based on the analysis, the coalition could better plan to take the war to the capys in earnest. This was basically a rehearsal. But the capys had to cooperate. They had to stay and fight.

If Ryck and Sams' capys were leaving in such haste, then Ryck had to assume the rest on the planet were doing so as well. He wished he could contact any of the other seven teams (his three and Kylton Granger's four) to see if their groups were also leaving. But to do that would break emissions silence. It was possible that this was just a routine move, a pure coincidence.

That possibility was smashed, in Ryck's mind, at least, when the soldiers rolled out what was technically called a BFG.[87] It was manhandled (capyhandled?) to point to the planetary west, aiming in the only direction from which the basin was not protected by the

[87] BFG: Big Fucking Gun

steep mountains. This was the logical approach for aircraft. A second BFG was wheeled out of the ship, then a third.

By this time, the shepherd capy had about a third of the little ones rounded up and moving up the ramp. The giants were dismantling two of the buildings, carrying the components up the ramp and into the ship's hold.

Ryck was struck at how little the different capys seemed to interact. They moved aside for each other, but they didn't seem to communicate between themselves. The soldiers did not seem to communicate with the giants who did not communicate with the shepherd.

At this rate, Ryck figured the little capys would be loaded up within the hour. He didn't know how much dismantling the giants would do, and the soldiers were a big question mark. Were they there to cover the withdrawal of the rest, or would they stay to fight? If they stayed, given their proven ability to shield themselves from most Federations sensors, then those guns could prove deadly to 3/12, the Marine battalion assigned this basin as their mission.

"Well, boss? What's your plan?" Sams asked.

Without a fight, the mission would be a total failure. And the Marines were not scheduled to kick off for almost nine more hours. If the capys were egressing the planet, they would be long gone, leaving the forces of man an empty battlefield. He didn't know if the assault forces were in position to move up H-hour, but Ryck knew he had to try something. He had to get out the word.

"I'm going to notify Division," he told Sams, who merely grunted, neither agreeing nor taking issue with Ryck's decision.

By breaking emission discipline, Ryck was going against his orders. However, this was an emergency, in his opinion. If he didn't pass the intel, then the overriding mission would not be achieved and 3/12, by not having surprise as an advantage, could be in significant danger.

Breaking emission discipline could also put the two of them at risk. They'd remained undetected so far, but this could put them on the skyline.

Ryck pulled out his journal and encoded a quick message to the effect that the capys at this location could be gone in another hour. He also included the location of the three BFGs. He wanted to keep his transmitter powered for as short a time as possible, so everything was worked out before powering up.

"Ready?" he asked Sams.

"Go for it."

Ryck popped the powerpack, the two elements coming together and creating the electricity needed to run the MC884 deep space communicator. Within seconds, the pack was hot, generating juice. Immediately, he started keying in his message.

"Uh, the soldiers have stopped and are standing around, like they're looking for something," Sams said beside him.

*Shit!*

Ryck tried to rush, but that created mistakes.

*Calm down. Do it right.*

He finally got the message keyed in, and without hesitation, hit the transmit key. He then immediately pulled the powerpack and split it open with his Hwa Win combat knife, pouring the contents onto the dirt.

"Oh, shit! That did it," Sams said in a hushed tone as if the soldier capys could hear him at that distance. "I'd say they know exactly where we are now."

Ryck grabbed his binos and looked up. Sams was right. The capys were undoubtedly focused on where the two Marines lay in the low brush at the edge of the open basin. Within moments, about 20 of them unlimbered their weapons and started moving across the grass in their direction. There were a few flickers, then the round balls of light appeared at the muzzle of their weapons.

During the fight on GKN, Ryck had only briefly seen the capy's energy rifles. Even during the briefs back at Division, the actual construction of the weapons had been sketchy. Despite the oncoming capys, Ryck twisted his binos to their highest magnification and studied the weapons. Each gun looked the same. From the trigger on back, it could be human-made. Once again, the faintest flicker of the question of mutual evolution versus parallel evolution went through his thoughts, but he pushed those aside for another place and time.

From the trigger on forward, though, the guns were decidedly different. The "barrel" looked like the previously noted jai alai *xistera*, the muzzle flattening out into a spoon-like platform, slightly curved. In that platform, balls of blue light shimmered as they rotated in their cradle. When the capys fired, the balls of light shot off, barely visible as they left the gun and went downrange. Ryck had not seen the re-loading process before, so he didn't have a feel for how long it would take, or where the light charges were even stored.

"Uh, Ryck. They might be plodding along, but you think maybe we might want to get out of here?" Sams asked.

Ryck took his focus off the weapons. The capys had covered a good 150 meters and had another 600 to reach the two Marines. As on GKN, they didn't seem to be moving fast, but their progress was steady. Ryck didn't know the range of their weapons, either. On GKN, the capys had been firing from 500 meters or less.

"Yeah, 'bout time to diddiho. Let's, uh, how about Rally Point Bravo, the one with the grandfather tree?"

The grandfather tree was the name Sams had given a lone tree that emerged and towered a good 40 meters above the rest of the canopy. Its bare trunk reached up before spreading out into an umbrella-like crown.

"Sounds good," Sams said.

The two Marines scooted back, and then stood up. Ryck glanced once more in the direction of the capys, but he couldn't see them through the low shrubs and trees. He turned back and trotted behind Sams as they made their way to the grandfather tree, about 300 meters inside the treeline and another 300 meters back in the direction from which they had come. They moved cautiously, but having just covered the ground and confident that it was clear, they moved quickly as well. Within eight minutes, they had reached the base of the tree.

"I'm going up," he told Sams. "Cover me."

Ryck slipped on his van der Waals, what some Marines called their "geckos." The gloves contained hundreds of thousands of tiny hairs that created a strong enough molecular attraction—the van der Waals force that gave the gloves their name—that a full-grown man could climb up almost any surface. Granted, smooth surfaces were better, but the tree's trunk was not too rough. Coupled with the rough surface of his boots, Ryck didn't foresee any problems.

That did not take into consideration the sheer distance to the top of the tree, though. Ryck was huffing and puffing by the time he'd made it up, some 90 meters above the ground level. He was grateful for all those painful runs up Mount Motherfucker that had forced his body back into shape.

With the trunk between him and the open basin, he clipped into a safety strap, and then carefully peered around the trunk. The trees near the grasslands were low, more like shrubs, really, and they slowly changed, getting taller the further they were from the grass. Ryck scanned the low shrubs for sign of the soldiers but didn't see anything. Beyond them, the capy ship sat where it had landed. The shepherd capy had another bunch of the little ones almost to the ramp, and the giants were still bringing in parts of the buildings they were dismantling. The BFGs were in place, manned by a number of the soldiers. But not enough. The ones that had taken off towards Sams and him were not in sight. They had to be in the trees below him. And that meant he needed to get down so the two of them could get further away.

Just as he started to unhook his safety strap, he caught movement in the low shrubs down below him. He focused his binos and made out soldier capys moving through the shrubs, but away from him, back towards the grass.

Were they giving up?

The immediate sense of relief was quickly replaced with concern. If the capys went back, they could either lift out of there on the ship or stay to man the guns. Either option was bad. Ryck needed to split their forces, both to keep them there for the assault and to weaken any defenses they could mount.

He knew what he had to do. He looked down for a moment, trying to pick Sams out through the foliage, wishing he could give Sams a heads up. He couldn't see his teammate, so he unlimbered his M72 HGL from where he had slung it and aimed it in on the back of the closest capy soldier he could see. Normally, the HGL had a fairly sophisticated sighting system which took into account elevation, distance, air temperature, known wind values, and about every other factor that could affect accuracy. Ryck's M72 was on "iron sights," or a purely visual peepsight. With an M99, Ryck was fairly confident of his abilities with iron sights. The Marines had been issued the M72s, though, as they had proven to have had at least some efficacy against the capys on GKN.

Trying to figure in how the drop from tree-height-to ground-level would affect his round, he slowly squeezed the trigger. The 20mm grenade shot out slow enough for Ryck to follow it with his eyes as it arced towards his target. Ryck had overcompensated for his height, though, and the round landed high to explode 10 or 15 meters past his target. The grenade did a number on a local bush, blowing it to pieces as the capys all turned to see what was happening. Ryck adjusted his sight picture and fired off another round. This one ran true, hitting his target in the chest as it turned around. The grenade detonated, and the capy's shield flashed white and blue, making Ryck think it had deflected the grenade. But the capy fell to the ground, a bloody red-blue mess. Somehow, the grenade had penetrated the shield, but then exploded within the shield's confines.

Ryck popped off two more rounds before he felt the tingle that let him know he was being targeted. Luckily it was only a tingle. He must have been just out of range. Ryck slid back down the tree, somewhat recklessly taking huge chunks of length with each slide. He reached the bottom in less than a minute, slamming into the ground beside Sams, lucky not to have broken an ankle.

"I see you decided to get their attention," Sams said as if he hadn't a care in the world.

"Yeah, they had decided not to play, and I figured we had to convince them to hang around."

"Did you at least ghost one?" Sams asked as Ryck caught his breath.

"Oh, shit, ghosted it but good," he said, patting his M72. "The grubbing grenade exploded inside its shield, I think. Hamburger!"

"Really?" Sams said, excitement creeping into his voice. "This thing worked?"

"Sure did. I've got another 26 rounds, and you've got 30. That should hold us for awhile. But they fired back. Just got a tingle, not a full blast, so I think we're about at the edge of their range. We need to lead them further into the woods so they don't have time to haul ass out of here before our boys come, so we can't afford to have them lose contact. I want to find a gully or something close by so we can get close, but not too close, and see f we can take out another couple of them."

"Sounds like fun," Sams said with a tone of anticipation.

The two Marines ranged back and forth, ever listening for signs that the capys were near. Twicw, Ryck had Sams fire up through the trees and ranged so the grenades would land 200 to 300 meters away. Ryck hoped that would be enough to keep the capys' attention.

Finally, Ryck found what he was looking for: a rain-washed gully between the trees. It was only about three or four meters deep, but it was filled with bushes and vines that should impede movement. The two Marines set up on the far side of the gully, each protected by the trunk of a good-sized tree.

"You ready?" Ryck asked Sams.

When Sams nodded, Ryck pulled down his monocle and powered it up. He was hoping to see where the capys were, but as expected, if they were out there, their previously exhibited shielding capabilities would defeat Ryck's monocle. He kept it powered up, though, for 30 seconds, then powered back down.

Then they waited.

It actually took less time than they had figured. Within two minutes, they could make out forms moving through the trees toward them, easily highlighted by their softly glowing energy shields. The shields were beacons. How could they not realize that?

The capys still moved with that steady sense of determination. As before, Ryck was struck with the March of the Teddy Bears air about them. He knew though, that these were not Christmas teddies. These had a bite to them.

Shooting a HGL through trees was an iffy proposition at best. But when the capys made it to the other side of the gully, Sams and Ryck would have clear fields of fire for 25 meters. The arming range on the grenade was 15 meters, which kept the grenades from detonating if the gunner hit tree branches or the edge of a window on the way out.

The capys kept moving closer, and Ryck waited for them to begin to fire their energy balls. They kept swiveling their heads as they marched as if scanning the forest for them. They didn't scan as a person might, darting their eyes from one place to another. They twisted their heads in smooth arcs, covering their full frontage.

As the first capys cleared the trees on the other side of the gully, Ryck fired, followed a split second later by Sams. Both Marines hit their targets right in the chest, blinding flashes of light illuminating the small clearing. The two Marines shifted immediately to the next target, firing once more before Ryck realized that not only were the first capys they hit alive, but they were still advancing. One leveled its weapon in Ryck's general direction and fired. The shrubs in the gully between Ryck and the capy exploded into pieces, and Ryck felt the heavy tingle of another near miss.

"Sams!" Pull back!" he yelled as he jumped up and spun to run down his designated fall-back route.

He had selected this route specifically because it quickly offered cover from the other side of the gully. He ran a zigzag path to a huge fallen giant and dove over it, quickly turning and scrambling back to cover Sams.

"Sams, where are you!" he shouted, mindless of sound discipline.

There was a crashing sound on Ryck's right, and he spun around, M72 at the ready. It was Sams, who had retreated off line and had to come back to their rally point.

"I thought you said the '72 can take those fuckers," he said as he slid to the ground beside Ryck.

"It did! I mean, I saw the one I ghosted. He was dead," Ryck protested.

"Well, I hit that fucker right in the chest, and all it did was piss him off. My arm's about numb now from when he fired back at me."

"You too? I mean, only numb?" Ryck asked.

"Yeah, so what?"

"On GKN, they took us out at 400 and more meters. Here, they were, what, 25 meters?"

"Maybe they just missed our lucky asses?"

"I don't know. The one that shot at me, I think the bushes maybe absorbed some of the energy, like the bushes set them off instead of letting them continue to us," Ryck said.

"You mean, like arming them?"

"Maybe. I don't know. Maybe," Ryck said, unable to grasp an elusive something churning around in his mind, an answer, maybe.

"Look, I can hear them coming through the gully. I want you to move back to the rise over there. Cover me. I want to try something. When you see me coming, fire over me at anything you see, and if you don't see anything, I don't care. Fire. Got it?"

"Roger that. Don't get caught up on their direction of advance, though. They're soldiers, so they should know how to flank someone," Sams reminded him.

"So keep your eyes open. If anything comes up from the flank, fire away."

Sams moved down the fallen tree, then scrambled up the small rise until he had a position where he could observe Ryck and the area in front of him.

Ryck took out his Ruger. Most Marines carried the 2mm Ruger M31. Recon, though, had access to more weapons, and Ryck had chosen the Ruger M38, the chosen sidearm for the FCDC's SWAT operators. It fired a larger 3mm dart and packed a bigger punch. There was also a larger variety of dart heads, from armor piercing to small exploding mini-warheads.

Mindful of Sams' admonition to watch his flank, he tried to keep his eyes on both flanks as well as down toward the gully. Within 30 seconds, though, he first saw the glow of a capy shield from the shadow cast by a tree, followed by the capy itself. Ryck lowered the Ruger and popped off five shots. All five hit as indicated by the sparks which flew off the shield, but the capy never hesitated. Ryck ducked as the capy fired, and he sensed more than saw or felt the energy ball explode against the huge fallen tree. Keeping low, Ryck scrambled along the length of the trunk while Sams pumped shell after shell over his head and into the oncoming capys. Ryck reached the end of the trunk, then scrambled up and past Sams, who quit firing and followed Ryck. They ran up the rise, trying to keep as many trees as possible between the capys and themselves. A large rock jutted out of the humus-covered soil, and both Marines flopped down on the top side of it, looking back down toward the slope they had just climbed. Below them, the forest was silent.

"I think I got one of them," Sams told him between breaths. "Not the ones next to you, but one round went long and hit one of the ones in back, a seeing-eye shot through the trees. The fucker staggered, I'm sure as shit certain. I think it might have gotten back up, but I know it went down."

"That makes no grubbing sense," Ryck said, more to himself than to Sams. At close range, when they have the most punch, they're useless. At long range, they can be effective. That's bass-ackwards," he mumbled under his breath.

"You're sure about that? You saw it go down?"

"I'm sure it went down. I dunno. Maybe it just slipped in the blast. But the others, I've hit four of them already, and none of them even flinched."

Ryck mind was churning again. He knew there was an answer in there, one that could prove to be needed to keep them alive.

He turned to look behind him where the rise kept going. He could see the rock face of the mountains through the tree tops. They were running out of room.

It wasn't actually a click, but an idea slowly emerged as if crawling out of the mist. He hadn't even completely formulated his thoughts when he made a decision.

"Up and at 'em, Marine. We need to find the right terrain for this."

The two Marines continued to climb, and as they got closer to the base of the mountain, Ryck wondered if he would find what he was looking for. Finally, right at the base, he found it. The trees stopped about 200 meters from where the rock face of the mountain sprung out of the soil of the basin. Just to their left, above the rest of the treeline, a small copse of trees surrounded a huge rock, then petered out another 30 meters up the slope.

"Get up the slope and pick a vantage point where you can cover me over there," Ryck said, pointing at the rock and small trees. "How many rounds you got?"

"Eighteen," Sams said, not having to count them.

"OK, here take ten of mine," Ryck continued, handing them over.

"And what are you going to be doing?" Sams asked.

Ryck pulled out his small folding grappling hook. He sprang it open, the three blades falling back from the sharp point. It was designed to be fired by the auxiliary attachment that could be added to almost any weapon in the inventory. It could be fired over a lip, be that a rock or building, offering an anchor point for a climbing rope, or it could be fired directly into a wood door or wall, offering a set anchor point on a vertical surface. At the half-cocked position, Ryck snapped it into the firing attachment on his M72, then loaded the firing charge.

"You're going to climb the fucking mountain?" Sams asked, sounding bewildered.

"Nope. I'm going to seat this in a capy chest," Ryck said, turning his M72 HGL in a circle so he could admire the blades of the MA446, Grappling Hook, One Each.

"Uh, look Ryck, you're the lieutenant and all, and with all due respect, but are you fucking crazy?"

"Maybe I am. But I think the capy shields, well, they react to things that move fast. They stop energy weapons, they stop hypervelocity darts. They stop a 20mm grenade at close range. But when things slow down, they can pass through. Remember the soldier that got cold-cocked by the giant with the log on its shoulder? That was slow. When do our HGL rounds work? At long range, when they are slowed down."

"That's fucking ridiculous. Who ever heard of something like that?" Sams protested.

"Whoever ever heard of *trinocular majoris*, before, huh? Think of it. If their shields are so good, how does air get in for them to breath? They need oxygen, right? I think the shields aren't activated until something hits them hard and fast. If it is slow, the shields let whatever it is in. Like air. Like a grappling hook," he said, rotating his M72 again.

"But that's gotta be impossible. It doesn't make sense," Sams said, but with less force than he used before.

"Eliminate the impossible, and what remains, no matter how improbable, must be the truth,"[88] Ryck said.

"Who the hell said that gem?" Sams asked.

Ryck hesitated, then laughed. "I don't remember, actually. Some 20th Century philosopher, I think."

"You're basing this on a quote from ancient times?"

"Not really. But I feel confident about this. Look, we don't have much time. They'll be here soon, I would guess. So get up there and pick your spot. I need you to cover my ass."

"And if you're wrong?"

"Then, keep moving. If the capy's leave, so be it. You need to get the photos and notes to Division. Just wait until they get here," he said before taking his journal out of his cargo pocket. "Take this, too."

Sams looked at the journal for a moment, a frown on his face, before sliding it into his pocket. "Kick some capy ass, OK?" he said before turning to climb up the slope to the base of the mountain.

Ryck hurried over to the rock and trees. He had sounded sure to Sams, more confident than he really felt. He had to agree with his teammate that this was pretty farfetched. But it made sense, and if he was right, then the Federation had to get that knowledge.

---

[88] Eliminate the impossible, and what remains, no matter how improbable, must be the truth: a paraphrase of a several quotes by Arthur Conan Doyle in his Sherlock Holmes books.

He ran into the small trees around the big rock, looking for a good firing position. Nothing worked. He was too low, and he wouldn't be able to see a capy until it was too late. Finally, he gave up and climbed the rock. It was about seven or eight meters above the ground, and it offered excellent, if exposed, fields of fire. He settled down to wait.

As he expected, the wait was not a long one. The capys came out of the trees, but 150 meters to Ryck's left, where Ryck and Sams had come out of the trees as well. That was much too far to shoot a grappling hook. Ryck was tempted to stand up and shout, but this exposed, he knew the capys' energy ball guns would be quite effective. He lay prone on the rock, flipped down his monocle, and powered it up. Despite the stress of the situation, Ryck still marveled that while he could see the capys with his naked eyes, the monocle readout showed that nothing was there.

Ryck kept the monocle on for ten seconds, then turned it off. He risked a quick glance and was relieved to see that six capys had turned away to come toward him. Several of the other capys fired their weapons up the slope. Ryck hoped that they hadn't located Sams and were firing at him, or at least that Sams had taken cover.

Ryck waited, listening, trying to determine just where the six capys approaching him were. They just moved so silently that it was hard to tell. He finally risked another quick peek.

*Grubbing shit! They're right here!*

With a shout, Ryck jumped to his feet, HGL leveled. He triggered the auxiliary launcher, and with a bang, the grappling hook shot forward, trailing the climbing rope. The capy directly in front of Ryck tried to bring his gun to bear, but while the grappling hook was slow, the distance was too short. The hook slammed into the capy's belly, penetrating the shield to plunge deep into the flesh. The sensors of the hook released the half cock, and the blades flashed completely open.

For the briefest second, Ryck looked into the enemy's eyes, eyes that finally showed some sign of emotion. Or at least something. Was it the capy equivalent of despair?

Ryck stared in wonder. He'd been right! Then he realized how exposed he was. He turned and dove off the rock as several energy balls flashed through the space he'd just occupied.

His HGL was jerked out of his hands before he hit the dirt. The grappling hook was embedded in the capy on the other side. Ryck jumped back up to where the weapon dangled against the rock, and then hit the release, dropping the rope. He started his mad dash through the low trees and shrubs, finally aware of the sounds of Sams' 20mm grenades detonating.

Ryck reached the end of the little finger of trees and kept on going, willing his legs to get every ounce of push they could muster. Once, he felt the kiss of an energy gun sending his nerves twisting and turning, but he kept to his feet until he could get cover behind a rock not nearly as large as he would have hoped.

He turned back and tried to acquire a target. This wasn't as easy as he would have thought. The capys were not marching lemming-like to their fates. They were not hitting and rolling as Marines might do, but they somehow wove back and forth between each other as they advanced, and that had a very disquieting and distracting effect on the two Marines. Still, half a dozen of the capys were down when the firing from up the hill ceased. Ryck looked over, and Sams was looking down at him, holding his HGL upside down. He was out of ammo.

Using hand and arm signals, Ryck told him to take off. He had the camera. He had Ryck's journal. He had to get away. Sams had smartly picked a firing position that had a small egress from it, and Ryck was sure Sams could get far enough away that he could simply outrun the capys until the Marines landed.

Sams signed the negative. He was not going. Ryck once again signed for him to leave, this time using the final motion that made it an order. Recon or not, friend or not, Sams was still a Marine, and an order was an order. Even at this distance, Ryck could see Sams was angry. Ryck made the "this is an order" sign once more, and Sams glowered, but finally nodded. In a crouch, he saluted Ryck, then started running.

Ryck popped back up and fired three more grenades. He didn't hit anything, but he was sure that it was affecting the capys ability to fire. Ryck was giving Sams the cover he needed to make his escape.

Ryck fired his last two rounds, the first scoring a direct hit on a capy and sending him down. He did a quick inventory. He had his Ruger, which was ineffective. He had three grenades, but they would explode outside the capys' shields and be effectively worthless. He had two toads. Ryck laughed. It had come to this. He had first made his name with a toad, and it looked like he would go out with a toad.

He briefly considered making a run up the mountain, but to get to where Sams had made his escape, he would have to almost hand over hand it, and the capys were well within their energy gun range. No, this was about it.

He arranged the two toads in front of him. When the capys got close, he would simply throw them. They should penetrate the shield before flaring into small, white hot suns. He would burn the suckers.

After that, well, it had been a good run. He wished he'd been able to patch things back up with Hannah, but maybe it was better this way. She'd lost two of her manfolk to the Marines, so when she found out about this, it wouldn't hit her hard. Ryck hoped though, that she'd at least shed a tear for him.

*Grubbing shit, you pussy! Snap out of it. Get beserker and show these grubbing teddy bears how a Marine does it!*

He knew he was just psyching himself up, getting his nerve up to go out warrior fashion, but he didn't care. It was working. He risked a quick look and almost got fried, the hair on his head standing up in the side lobes of the energy blast.

He picked up the two toads, in one hand, the other hand ready to pop the fuze. Crouching in back of the rock, he drew a deep breath.

The explosions took him by surprise, the heavy blast waves squeezing the air out of his lungs. He struggled to his feet amid the chaos, pulling the fuze on the first toad, arm back ready to throw. A huge dragon was in the sky, spitting fire to the earth. Ryck stared in shock as the Navy Experion fighter peppered the hillside.

Ryck just stood there, toad in hand, only realizing at the last second that it was armed. He flung his hand backwards, sending both toads to the hill behind him. The armed toad detonated just a meter from his hand, falling to the ground in a blast of heat and light. It burnt a piece of the rock face loose and rolled back down at him, and Ryck had to leave his cover as it came up against the rock and started burning its way through.

Standing there, hyped up to fight only to find the battle was done, he tried to gather his wits. The Navy Experion was not a great atmosphere fighter, but its big kinetic guns simply overpowered the capy shields. The turf below Ryck looked like a plowed field, it was so chewed up. Capy bodies, or rather parts of them, were scattered about. Ryck had the field of battle to himself.

The Experion came low in front of Ryck and hovered, the two pilots saluting him before peeling off. It was only then that Ryck really looked to the basin below. The capy ship was gone, but the basin was full of activity as Storks and Navy shuttles landed. The three capy guns were more holes in the ground than anything else. Ryck couldn't see any sign of downed Federation craft.

Ryck took a seat on the rock to watch. There wasn't any sign of fighting, but the Marines buzzed about like a nest of disturbed fire ants. After about five minutes, a Stork took off, circled once, then flew up to the hill where Ryck was sitting. It landed in the chewed up dirt below him. Several teams in isolation suits got out and started to walk the battlefield. A fire team of Marines broke off from the scientists and marched up the hill to where Ryck was sitting.

"Are you Lieutenant Lysander?" the young corporal asked.

"Yeah, I guess I am."

"Um, is, uh, SSgt Samuelson, did he make it?" he asked, looking around.

"I imagine so. I think you'll find him up there along that path, but I'm sure he'll be down shortly."

"Well . . . uh . . . OK, sir. Uh . . . the colonel, that's Lieutenant Colonel Toritino, he said that Stork there is by his compliments, in case you want to come down and join him. He said you, and I quote," he said, pulling himself up straighter, "'saved the frigging day,' sir, only he didn't say 'frigging,' sir."

The corporal stood there waiting for Ryck to respond.

“Uh, so are you coming . . . sir?” he asked.

“Yeah, I think I am.  I think I am.”

# Pearson's Refuge

## Chapter 22

Ryck tried to adjust the Federation Nova that hung tight on his neck. Whoever designed the medal had to be a sadist. The sharp points of the exploding star dug into Ryck's chin anytime he lowered his head. He took a quick look in the mirror. He'd only had the medal for less than a day, and this was the first time he'd worn it with the neck clasp. The night before, at the medal ceremony, the Chairman of the Federation himself, Admiral Wulstan Yance, had put it around his neck, but with the ceremonial ribbon, so it had hung looser.

*Well, I've gotta admit, it sure looks good,* he thought to himself as he gazed in the full-length mirror.

Ryck still wasn't convinced he deserved the medal. If it wasn't for the photo Sams had taken, which caught him on top of the rock, grappling iron midflight between him and the capy, he was sure he wouldn't have been awarded it. But the photo—which Ryck had to admit caught the action just right, enough to make him *look* heroic, at least—looked pretty *taut*. The press had been using the word "iconic," but Kylee had used "taut" when she cammed him, excited that everyone at her school had seen the photo of her uncle. That had made her somewhat of a star. If Kylee said it, then taut it was.

He'd talked to the chaplain back on Zephyr-Hadreson about it when the word had first come out that he'd been put in for it. He'd even talked with Col Ukiah, the regimental commander, on the trip over to Pearson's Refuge for the conference.

This wasn't false modesty. Ryck knew he had stumbled across something pretty significant, one which would have eventually come to light, but still, this gave the forces of man a jump on developing tactics with which to fight the capys. And it had taken some balls to stand up on the rock and fire away. But no more than what other Marines had done. Like Joshua, who had been awarded the Navy Cross, posthumously. Or Felicity, Jones, and Hogger, who had gotten Silver Stars even though they had been doing the exact same thing as Joshua. Ryck wondered why he was getting the

Federation Nova when Joshua had insisted on giving up his life for the rest of the platoon and the civilians but only received the Navy Cross?

Col Ukiah, who had nothing higher than a BC2 on his chest, had seemed to understand. He acknowledged that there were politics involved, but the fact of the matter was that Ryck's actions would save far more lives than what Joshua and his three Marines had saved. This wasn't to denigrate Joshua, he quickly added when Ryck started to take issue with the statement, but merely to bring up cold, hard facts.

To say that there were politics involved was an understatement. The entire pageantry of the night before, where Ryck was paraded around like a prize stallion, was half politics and half marketing, although the differences between the two were almost indistinguishable. With Admiral Yance presenting the award in front of the First Brother of the Brotherhood, the president of the Confederation, and various heads of state of other planets and alliances as well as the top corporate chairmen and CEOs, this was a symbol of the Federation's claim of supremacy. They were taking the fight to the capys, or at least the brunt of it. It was a Federation Marine who was the big hero.

Ryck understood that he was a pawn in all of this, but he couldn't help last night but to be caught up in the atmosphere of it all. He'd been pretty keyed up while accepting the congratulations of the bigwigs. It hadn't been until he got back to his BOQ room several hours later that he lost some of his high. It would have been so much better if Hannah had come. The CG had almost insisted that Hannah make the trip, not caring when Ryck told the general's aide that he and Hannah were not together at the moment. The general had even called Ryck directly to try and pressure him, but Hannah didn't care what some Marine general thought.

The two had cammed several times, but Hannah had never even mentioned the upcoming award, something that had hit the newsfeeds, so she certainly knew about it.

He pulled down the Nova again, trying to seat it a bit lower. He would have been happy just wearing the ribbon for the conference, which was appropriate for the Alpha uniform, but the

PAO[89] had rather forcibly insisted that he wear the actual medal today. He gave his blouse one more tug and stepped out of his room just as Col Ukiah came down the passage.

"You ready there, devil dog?" the colonel asked.

"Yes, sir, locked and loaded."

"Yea, though I walk through the valley of the shadow of death," began the colonel, "that's still a far better fate than what we've got there, Ryck. We'll just sit in the back with the other peons and keep quiet. You get briefed again by the good LCDR Kangilla?"

"Yes, sir, in triplicate. I'm to shut up, and if asked by the press what I think, say we're going to win, and then defer to my seniors, in whom I have the utmost faith and confidence."

"Ha! At least you get to speak. All O'6's, and that includes yours truly, are to keep our mouths closed."

Ryck laughed. He'd never really met the CO. He wasn't sure he'd ever had much of a conversation with any senior officer before. But on the trip over, then all day yesterday, he'd gotten o know the colonel, and he rather liked him. He may have an eagle on his collar, but he was just a Marine like anyone else, one whose personality meshed with Ryck's.

They left the BOQ and headed over in the direction of the conference hall. The first talk didn't start until 0845, but as two in the mass of underlings, they wanted to get there early and at least get a seat. Standing up for several hours at a time didn't sound very appealing.

They had gotten only a few hundred meters when the bugle sounded. They stopped, came to attention, and saluted toward the flag pole where several sailors held the Federation colors. The Federation Anthem started up, and the sailors hoisted the flag. As the last strains died down, Ryck waited for the flourish that signaled that they could go about their business.

Instead of the flourish, though, the Brotherhood Hymn started up. It was only then that Ryck noticed the flagpoles in front of the 5th Fleet Headquarters building. A group of Brotherhood knights raised their flag while the Hymn played out.

---

[89] PAO Public Affairs Officer

The morning ceremonies didn't stop there. The Confederation, the Advocacy, Greater France, five independent worlds, even the autonomous Rottwilhelm Trust (the huge business conglomerate that operated by its own rules at the edge of explored space) had music played and flags raised. It took about 20 minutes before the flourish finally sounded and the two Marines could break their position of attention and drop their salutes.

"Well, now we know why the conference doesn't start until 0845," Col Ukiah said. "No one wants to be caught out in all of that."

"That's got to be some sort of record," Ryck said with a laugh. "But you know protocol. Everyone, no matter how small or if they've even sent troops into the fight, if they are here, they've got to get their acknowledgments in. If we'd left a minute earlier, we could have watched all of that from inside."

The two Marines made their way into the conference hall. It was one of the biggest in the entire Navy, and given that the planet was as close to the center of human space as a Federation World could get, Pearson's Refuge had been selected to host the conference.

Security was very tight. They had to show their badges and were scanned no less than three times. That did not include any number of discreet surveillance methods that Ryck could not even begin to list.

The two Marines finally made it to the cheap seats and found a place to sit. Within ten minutes, all the seats were taken, and the attendees just arriving had to stand in the back. One Confederation one-star didn't take it too kindly that he had to stand and raised a fuss, at one point ordering a Brotherhood guardian, their equivalent to a colonel, to stand and give up his seat. At that point, two ushers, who looked more like bodyguards, closed in to escort the recalcitrant general out of the hall.

At 0855, the conference still hadn't started. Most of the assigned seats in the first level had been taken, but the ones in the very front were mostly empty.

"I bet they're jockeying out there to see who comes in last," the colonel whispered into Ryck's ear.

"Are you Lieutenant Lysander?" a huge man in a tailored suit asked, leaning into their row.

"Yes, that would be me," Ryck said, wondering why he wanted to know.

The man spoke softly into some sort of hidden mic, but Ryck caught "GG-19."

GG-19, was Ryck's seat number.

"Thank you," the man said to him before turning away.

"What was that all about?" Ryck asked.

"I'd say you're going to get an honorable mention," the colonel told him.

Ryck was about to respond when the final worthies started down the aisles to their seats. Evidently, who could piss the highest had been determined, and everyone had their place in line. Within moments, all had found their seats.

The 5th Fleet Commander, resplendent in his whites, walked to the podium. "Heads of state, commanders, ladies and gentlemen, I welcome you to the United Federation Navy's 5th Fleet headquarters. I trust this be will an informative and productive session. If there are any issues of a personal nature, please contact any of my liaison officers. Without anything further, I am turning the opening ceremonies to the Chairman of the United Federation, Admiral Wustan Yance."

The Chairman made his way up to the podium. There was a smattering of applause, but it never seemed to really gain that groundswell. Admiral Yance gave the talk Ryck would have expected. It was full of exhortations for cooperation, yet it inferred a Federation primacy. When the chairman stated that the conference and the fight against the Trinoculars were beyond politics, the colonel whispered a quiet "Yeah, that will be the day." Ryck had to hold in the laugh that threatened to burst free at hearing that. For an O6, Col Ukiah was pretty grubbing cynical!

The colonel had been right about something else. Halfway through the chairman's speech, the admiral said "And one of those brave Marines is here today. First Lieutenant Ryck Lysander, the newest holder of the Federation Nova, awarded just last night."

A spotlight suddenly shone on him, and Ryck had to stand up and accept the applause. Col Ukiah noted that he got a much more robust round of applause than the chairman had received.

The chairman was surprisingly short and sweet, though, giving way to the First Brother. A few of the heads of state were a little long-winded, but most were fairly direct. Still, it took almost three hours to get through everyone. This without a break. When the last head of state, Princess Ryliar finished, there was a mad dash for the heads. Ryck had to wait in line until it was his turn up at the trough.

After lunch, the conference broke down into working groups. Ryck was not in any of the exalted groups, which was fine with him. Instead, he was able to choose, and both he and the colonel went to a brief made by a joint scientific team to listen to what had been discovered so far about the capys.

Of course, the big news was already known. Based on the DNA collected on the planet, the soldiers, the giants, and the little capys were one and the same. By inference, the shepherds, and several other types observed by other teams were probably one in the same, too. Evidently, the little capys were juveniles, and at some point, in a method still a mystery, they matured into different adult forms. There was extensive debate going on about how or why this occurred, but to Ryck, this was immaterial. As a Marine, he only needed to know which ones posed a threat.

The third eye on the soldiers was far more evolved than the simple biosensor on the juveniles. It was a pretty sophisticated organ, and it should be able to detect a wide range of electrical emissions. Some xenobiologists (and scores of biologists were now claiming that title) postulated that the soldiers did not vocalize at all, but communicated through their bioreceptors. When Ryck thought about it, he had never heard the soldiers make any noises, while the juveniles were constantly squealing and whistling.

Much of the biology was above Ryck's head, but the next working group on capy weapons was more up his alley. The capys' main weapon, the energy ball thrower was beyond human technology, but some secrets were being whittled out. At its base level, the weapon held balls of energy at the ready, and somehow shot those balls forward at its target. Details were sorely lacking, as were defenses against them. No human had been able to get one to fire. They seemed to have a limited range, and anything in the energy balls' paths dissipated their power.

The information gleaned seemed light for the expense in obtaining it. On HAC-440, most of the capys had gotten off the planet and evaded the Navy fleet. Combat had occurred in five locations, all with varying degrees of success. The humans had overwhelming numbers in each of the five assaults that culminated in combat, but while three of the assaults had minimal to no human casualties, two units—a Freison battalion and a Brotherhood host—had taken huge casualties. The Freison battalion had gone in with their meson guns, and the infantry had been almost powerless against a mere 40 or so capy soldiers. Without heavy Navy support, they Freisons might have lost the battle. It was a pyrrhic victory as it was. They had tested their tactics, and that was the intent, but the battalion had suffered 75% casualties.

One Navy frigate had been put out of action with 86 KIA. The cause of that still had not been determined.

The Marines had lost 18 KIA and three WIA, not including four Marines injured in a vehicle accident. Four of those KIA were recon Marines, and what happened to them would probably always be a mystery.

The Brotherhood-led assault on the second planet, K-65, had them landing on an empty planet. The Brotherhood cherubim, their equivalent of recon, had reported the capys leaving the planet, but the allied forces had not been able to react in time to prevent it.

Two huge operations with over 100,000 men and women involved, some heavy casualties, and the loss of one ship seemed like a lot of investment for a minimal payoff. Ryck just hoped that the payoff would be enough to tip things into mankind's favor when the next fight broke out.

# Zephyr-Hadreson

## Chapter 23

Staff Sergeant Gilroy leaned over and shot the "capy juice" at Sams face.

"Fuck, Buttercup, keep that shit away from me," Sams hollered, getting up from his seat.

He leveled a spray at Gilroy who had danced back out of range while laughing. Sams shook his head and sat back down, unwilling to chase Gilroy for payback. He'd get him later.

"Hey, you know what's better than capy juice?" Sgt Rogers asked Sams.

"No, what Jolly, in your infinite experience, is better than capy juice?" Sams asked sourly, his head down as he examined the trigger mechanism for the mister.

Sgt Rogers stepped up to the seated Sams, suddenly turned around, pulled down his trou, and let out a huge fart just centimeters from Sams face.

"This!" he shouted, before trying to pull up his trou and make his getaway.

"You vile mother fuck!" Sams shouted back, trying not to gag.

He dove forward as Sgt Rogers fell, tripped by his trou down around his thighs. The two Marines crashed to the deck as the other scrambled for safety, laughing uproariously.

"Get some, Bobbi!" several of the others shouted as Sams' arm snuck beneath Rogers' neck.

"What the hell crawled up your ass and died?" Sams asked. "I can feel it coating my throat you capy-lovin' freak!"

Sams pulled on Rogers' neck, bending the sergeant backwards and exposing his junk, as his trou were still at half mast. That brought more catcalls, most not fit for civilized company.

"Them's your boys," the newly promoted Capt Kylton Granger said to Ryck as the two team leaders checked their own misters.

"Yeah, and I'm so proud of them," Ryck said as a can of coke flew over to land on the two wrestling Marines, spray from being shaken drenching the two.

That broke the two apart, and Rogers finally got his trou pulled back up amidst comments on his physical inadequacies. He was gasping for breath, but still, he couldn't stop laughing.

Gunny Schmidt called out from where he'd been sitting, "If you two are done grab-assing, check your misters. You better not have fucked them up."

The misters were a new defense mechanism. With the scifi boys deciding that the capy energy guns could be attenuated, they had come up with them as a personal defense shield. The idea was that by spraying a fine mist of a glycerol mixture, the energy blasts would hit that first, and it could be enough to save the Marine being targeted. When the Marines had been briefed on it, they gave it about a rat turd's chance in hell of working, and they accepted the misters with about as much grace as could be expected. Derision would be an accurate description of their feelings.

Ryck had asked one of the R&D scientists how effective they would be, and that worthy had admitted that at best, the mist could absorb up to 10% of a capy energy blast, and that was using the most advantageous calculations. If that was at best, then Ryck thought the actual number would be from one to two percent, hardly enough reason to bother with the contraption.

"You really think this will do any good?" Ryck asked Kylton.

"Not really. But there's a lot of pressure on the R&D guys to come up with something to take the fight to the enemy. This is just one thing. I think the new blunderbusses are a better deal."

The "blunderbuss" was a short, flared-muzzle cross between a rifle and a handgun. It was retro-technology at its best. Using a compressed gas propellant, it fired an array of projectiles, all at fairly low speed, all designed to cause havoc on a soldier capy. The "harpoon" looked particularly nasty. It had four sharpened talons at the end of a staff. The staff was inserted into the blunderbuss while the talons protruded from the muzzle. Upon impact, the talons deployed. This was a weaponized version of the grappling hook that Ryck had used on HAC-440, and should be an order of magnitude more effective. The blunderbuss had an effective range of 50-60 meters, so each Marine also carried the same modified M72 HGL as well for distances further than that.

One good revelation was that the xenobiologists concurred that the capy bioreceptors were good, but they were not sensitive enough to pick out a person's heartbeat at anything over 15 or 20 meters.

"And of course, we're the guinea pigs once again," Ryck said sourly.

"Welcome to recon, Ryck. They play, we pay."

"At least these misters aren't very bulky. But I swear, if they get in the way, I'm shit-canning them," Ryck said.

"Combat losses are a bitch," Kylton said. "These things happen."

Kylton was one of the most laid back Marines Ryck had met. He looked non-descript, perhaps better suited as some Dickensian bookkeeper, but he was actually about the most physically gifted person Ryck had ever met. He was a superb five player, easily winning the division championship, and probably could win the armed forces championship as well. It wasn't just five; he excelled at handball, b-ball, billiards, and just about any other activity he undertook. But he was also a thoughtful, caring individual. His team adored him.

As if catching Ryck's thoughts, he looked up and asked, "So, how did your cam go?"

Kylton("Killer Angel" was his recon nickname) had never met Hannah, but he was a good shoulder, and Ryck had opened up about his personal problems to him.

"Not too bad, actually," he said, keeping his voice low as his team laughed and joked a few meters away. "Still, no sign of a reunion, but she sounded good. Looked good, too, not like before. I told her I wouldn't be able to cam for awhile, and she looked concerned, you know, like she understands what's up. She told me to be careful."

"OK, that's better, right? Give her time, and she'll come around," Kylton said. "When we get back, cam her again, see where her mind's at then. Who knows, after the duration, when all this is over, take a trip back and see how she feels when you two are actually together."

The thought of that scared Ryck. What if she officially cut their ties? Maybe seeing him face-to-face would make her decide she really needed to start her life afresh and in a new direction, one without him? He had almost accepted that, but still, as long as she had never voiced a request for a divorce, he had hope.

He was about to respond when the first sergeant came into the armory and bellowed out, "Your debark meal's about ready, and I tell you, it looks mighty fine. Someone sprang for real steaks, so unless you want me and the skipper to take all your chow, I'd suggest you get your asses in gear and to the messhall. You've got until 0330 until mount-out, and then a long day ahead getting to the spaceport and embarking. I'd suggest catching some z's after chow, but that's up to each team."

There were a number of "oo-rahs" at the mention of real steaks, and the Marines scrambled to stow their misters in the mount-out boxes. Everything else was ready—the misters were a last-minute addition.

"Real steaks? We must be important," Kylton said to Ryck as they stripped off their misters, tagging them so the correctly fitted mister would be re-issued before their drop.

"A condemned prisoner gets a last meal, too, right?" Ryck asked, hoping the similarity was not a foretelling of what was to come.

# GenAg 13

## Chapter 24

Ryck pulled on his toggles and flared in for a landing. He landed as light as a feather, as if stepping off the bottom stair onto a plush carpet. This was his second combat drop, and his mind was already past plummeting though the planet's atmosphere and onto his mission.

GenAg 13was in the last stages of terraforming, ready to be turned into a breadbasket. There had been approximately 400 staff on GenAg 13 when the combined science team studying the situation identified the planet as a probable target for the capys. Several teams of scientists had been deployed to the planet, along with some Legionnaires and GenAg jimmylegs for security, to be ready to observe if the capys did actually arrive. Ryck didn't know if the scientists were that accurate in their projections or if it was more in line with a blind squirrel finding a nut, but they had been right. Communications had been cut off with the teams on the planet, and with new Navy sensors that could detect the disturbance in space after something passes through it, they knew that ships had approached the planet. They couldn't detect the ships themselves, which was a pretty good indication that they were in fact capy vessels.

Without communications, the teams on the planet were cut off from most of the recently gleaned theories and facts about the capys. They had landed with some pretty sophisticated equipment, though, and the hope was that they had been able to gather more observations that would help the cause. This information could be invaluable.

The teams had been instructed what to do if the capys landed. The civilians were to gather at various rally points and hunker down, while the teams were to observe for 45 days, and then move to the rally points themselves.

All four recon teams from the division and two from Second Division were to be inserted and sent to the various rally points, gather the personnel, and move to designated LZs for extraction before the combined forces of man launched a full-out attack. Some of the planners didn't want to risk alerting the capys with more insertions. They wanted to leave the human groups on GenAg 13 to fend for themselves, to be picked up after the hostilities ended. But as the forces of man had no idea as to the number or disposition of the capys, it was vital to not only get any updates on capy capabilities, but to find out the number and positioning of the capy forces that would oppose the combined assault force.

Ryck knew that if the defense was too determined, the planet would be interdicted, just as GKN was. If the 450+ humans were still on the planet when that happened, they would be lost.

If the capys had landed in force, then GenAg-13 would be the site of the first major conflict in the war. This would be where the combined human forces would test their newly adjusted tactics against the Trinocular Army and Navy. Ryck and Kylton had discussed the potential for this to turn into a clusterfuck of epic proportions as every human organization with a military presence wanted to contribute, even going as far as those with quasi-illegal or outright criminal backgrounds. This made command a royal headache, but both Marines understood the importance of inclusion in symbolizing that this was man versus capy, not Federation versus capy, not Brotherhood versus capy, but all men.

Sams and Gutierrez came out of the low brush together as Ryck was gathering his chute. He rolled it up and shoved it under what looked, in the darkness, to be a bougainvillea, one of terraformers' favorite soil fixers. The chute would soon dissolve into nothingness, but there was no use taking any chances.

Ryck signaled the interrogative, then the number 4, asking if either of the other two had seen Caruthers. Each eight-man team had been broken down into four-man teams for the mission. Gunny Schmidt had the last three members and had dropped some 150 kilometers away.

Neither had seen Caruthers, so Ryck had them spread out to find their wayward corporal. It took about 20 minutes before he was spotted and the team was back together. With the other three providing security, Ryck got out his plaspage map and oriented himself. At least this time, they had been given some very accurate maps. Ryck plotted his position, then a heading to reach their objective, about ten klicks away. Ryck had wanted to drop closer, but if their target group had been overrun by capys, it wouldn't make much sense for the team to drop right in the middle of that.

GenAg 13 had a very odd magnetic north and south, both at the 60 degrees latitude in each hemisphere. This made for some extreme declinations when using a magnetic compass, but the calculations had already been made and the GM angle given to him. Within moments, the four recon Marines were moving through the low bushes. Their target was a small box canyon at the head of a stream. Box canyons offered no means of escape, and Ryck didn't like the idea of walking into one, but that was where it had been determined the best concealment from the capys would be best achieved.

The four Marines moved steadily, but cautiously through the low brush and into a new teak forest. The trees were only 20 meters high, indicating that they were only about 15-20 years old. Each tree was kept watered by a drip irrigation system. The fact that teak had been planted so soon meant the planet had been pretty close to earth-normal before terraforming began. Ryck came from a dry agricultural planet, but he wasn't ignorant about wet-climate crops. Normally, when a wet-world was first terraformed, the first large plants were species such as guadua bamboo, which grew faster and could handle a far greater range of soil conditions. Teak was only planted on mature worlds.

The fact that GenAg Corp owned a planet so close to earth-normal, not only in atmosphere and gravity, but in what could grow there, scratched an old scab of Ryck's. This was an agricultural paradise compared to his home world of Prophesy. His family had to scratch and fight to eke out a livelihood while in debt to United Ag, yet here, on a vast, rich planet, the corporate giant GenAg just sat there, having been granted a deed to the entire planet. The Federation granted deeds or limited licenses to compensate corporations for the cost of terraforming, but from what Ryck could see, this planet hadn't needed much to be ready for human colonization. It didn't seem fair to him.

The dawn began to lighten up the forest floor as they moved silently between the trunks. There were none of the low brush or vines that were so often planted while terraforming. This was already a working plantation. Without any undergrowth other than some nitrogen-fixing genmodded legumes above each root ball, Ryck and his team made quicker progress than planned. The sun hadn't made it over the horizon before they came up to the mouth of the box canyon.

*Pretty grubbing good, if I do say myself,* Ryck thought, considering he was using old, old land nav technology and had managed to come out right at their objective. Then again, he'd had the hypothalamus augmentation, so maybe he shouldn't feel so proud of the accomplishment.

The teak forest ended as the slope rose to be replaced by a mixed forest of native vegetation and earth-trees and plants. A creek came out of the canyon, babbling down the rocks until it was collected into the pipes that irrigated the teak.

With the dense undergrowth ahead, Ryck knew they would have to slow down. They couldn't move silently in all the vegetation. The very things that made the canyon a good rally point out of capy detection meant that the Marines would have difficulty moving forward.

Ryck motioned to the others to come on line with him. He contemplated using his voice, to let any local security know they were humans. He didn't know for sure, though, whether the area was free from capys or not, so he stuck with the hand and arm signals.

They slowed down, trying not to make too much noise, but the bushes and wait-a-minute vines tugged and grabbed at them. When the voice called out, Ryck wasn't sure he'd even heard it.

"Halt, who goes there?" a voice came out of the vegetation ahead of them.

Ryck looked at Sams, a few meters to his right, and rolled his eyes. If they were capys, well, capys couldn't understand Standard, so they wouldn't be answering, would they now?

"Federation Marines," he answered back.

"How do I know that?"

Ryck and Sams looked at each other in puzzlement. How was he supposed to answer that?

"Um, I can come forward and you can see me?" he finally offered.

"No! Don't come forward. I'm armed and I will shoot!" the voice said, panic evident in his tone.

"Look," Ryck said, exasperation beginning to show in his voice. "We're coming forward. We're not capys because we are speaking to you, right? You can shoot if you want, but I wouldn't suggest it. There are four of us here, and we are all quite well armed and trained to fight. If you fire at us, we will defend ourselves. We're here to get you out of here, so how about letting us come forward?"

There was a pause, then some whispering. There were at least two of them.

Finally, the voice called out, "OK, come ahead, but slowly. Remember, I'm armed."

"Sling your arms," he told his team. "Then let's move up, nice and slow.

"OK, here we come," he called out.

The four Marines pushed through the brush, taking it easy. After about ten meters, there was a small opening underneath some hoary old native tree, and under it were a man and a woman. Stark naked.

Well, the man had tried to hide his dick with some sort of Garden of Eden leaf underwear, which didn't hide much. The woman was completely naked, if filthy. The man held a large branch in his hand. That was his weapon? They were both nervous as the Marines came out of the brush, but that disappeared as soon as they recognized the humans facing them. The man had been holding himself tall, and Ryck could see him almost collapse in relief.

"Oh, thank God!" the woman said, rushing forward to hug a bemused Sams. Sams had hugged more than his fair share of naked women, but this was about as far from titillating as could be imagined.

"We're mighty happy to see you, but you've got to take off your clothes, now," the man said, moving forward to shake Ryck's hand.

That was not the greeting Ryck expected.

"Huh?" was all he could manage.

"Your clothes. The capys can sense them. You need to take them off."

"What gave you that idea?"

"The scientists and the GenAg security. They said the capys could sense them. We took them off and left them. but the security didn't. They kept their clothes and broke off, to lead the capys away, and sure enough, the capys followed them, not us. We made it here, but Lieutenant Galstone, he led the capys down that way," he said, pointing in the general direction of the DZ where the Marines had landed.

Ryck heard Sams start to laugh before choking it off with a feigned cough.

"The capys can sense a lot of things: PAs, AIs, communicators, biomonitors, energy weapons, just about anything that emits electric waves. But clothes? Not that. So we're going to keep our uniforms on, and I would suggest you get your clothes back on, too," Ryck told the man.

"But, but, Dr. Keasey, she said it. She said they had a . . . what did she call it, Tara?" he asked the woman.

"Ampullae of Lorenzini," the woman, Tara, said.

"So we ditched everything. And she—"

"Yeah, yeah, we know all about that," Ryck interrupted. "And they don't have exactly what a shark, has, those Ampullae of Lorenzini"—he stumbled over the term when the woman had just said it easily—"and they for sure can't sense simple clothing.

"What's your name?" Ryck asked.

"Oh, sorry. John Lancaster," he said, holding out his hand even though they had already shook once.

Ryck shook it and said, "First Lieutenant Ryck Lysander, Federation Marine Corps. Those are Staff Sergeant Sams, uh, Samuelson, Sergeant Clarence Gutierrez, and Corporal Francis Caruthers."

The woman, all 150 centimeters of her, stepped up and formally said, "Tara Jun, GenAg's Director of Information for GenAg 13."

"Director of Information" probably meant marketing or corporate misinformation, so she had to be fairly high on the food chain. She was filthy with bedraggled hair, a completely naked body, and bloody scratches and welts on her legs, but she looked Ryck right in the eyes with all the confidence in the world, her initial relief and Sams' hug forgotten.

Ryck turned to her, sensing she was more in control of the two despite John's initial actions. "Can you lead us to the rest? We've got limited time to get you out of here."

Tara led them back along a convoluted path, obviously trying to avoid the low bushes and branches. John stumbled twice, swore three times, and muttered to himself that he knew he should have kept his boots. The guy was suffering, but in front of him, where John couldn't see his face, Ryck couldn't help but smile. It wasn't funny, but then again, it was. The poor guy was suffering, and while Ryck felt sorry for him, he smiled nonetheless.

After moving back about 200 meters, they came to another opening beneath the trees where the undergrowth had either been cut back or hadn't grown. It was packed dirt on either side of the creek. A couple of dozen people were huddled around, some sleeping under make-shift lean-tos, but as the Marines came up, everyone got up and gathered around, excitedly.

Ryck quickly assessed the groups. He didn't show it, but his heart sank. Two were elderly with one man being helped by another just to stand. And one, St. Chuck's Hell, was grubbing pregnant, eight months if she was a day. The rest were scrawny, filthy, and very naked.

OK, they thought any man-made materials would bring the capys. But there was a grubbing creek right there, and they were filthy? This was a sure sign of people who have lost hope.

"Damn," Caruthers whispered next to him. "They look like they've given up."

"You got any food?" a tall man asked, looking eagerly at the Marines.

"Yes, we've brought extra emergency rats," Ryck said, pulling out a pack of base paste from his cargo pocket.

"Torque it, we've got that stuff. I was hoping for some real food," the man said, turning around and going back to a lean-to and sitting down.

Ryck was astounded. His team was there to get these people off the planet, and that was how the guy acted? The rest of the people seemed more excited, though, and he forced his thoughts back to his mission.

"Who's in charge here," he asked the group as a whole.

"That would be me," another woman answered, an older version of Tara. "Kata Jun."

"Lieutenant Ryck Lysander, Federation Marines. How many people do you have here?"

"We've got 25 GenAg staff and two of the commission researchers. This is Dr. Jarvis, from the commission," she said, pointing at the young, fit looking man who had stepped up to stand beside Kata.

"What about your security? Where are the legionnaires or company security?"

"We didn't have any legionnaires where we were. Just GenAg security. Lieutenant Galstone and six of the researchers took off to lead the capys away from us. If not, none of us would be here now," Kata told him.

"You were being pursued by the capys?"

"Yes, from the second day. We fled the best we could, but there was no way we were going to outrun them. Four of the security team went back to ambush them, you know, to give us more time, but I don't think it worked. They never slowed. So Dr. Keasey told us to take off our clothes. We ditched them into a well head, then ran into the bushes and hid while the researchers and the rest of the security team led them away. Then we came here to wait as they ordered us to do. We couldn't fight them, you see," she told him a little defensively.

"Who was the senior researcher here?"

"That would be Dr. Kopowski," Jarvis offered.

*Grubbing shit!* Ryck thought to himself. Dr. Georg Kopowski was on the list of "high value" researchers, one who had to be brought back.

"Where is Dr. Kopowski?" he asked.

"He went with the security team. He said he had to observe how the capys reacted," Jarvis told him.

"And where did they all go?" Ryck asked, wishing he didn't have to pull all this information out piece-by-piece.

"They said they would draw them away and either come back here or meet us at Station 448," Kata answered.

Ryck held back a sigh. "And where is Station 448?" he asked calmly, passing Kata the plaspage map.

Both she and Jarvis looked at it, and then Kata pointed to a spot on the map. "Here."

Ryck looked at it. His team had landed not 800 meters from the station. If he had known, he could have gathered them up and brought them here. Well, he had to go back.

"We need all of your group together, then we need to get to our extraction point here," he said, pointing to the primary LZ on the map. "Time is short, so I need you to get ready. I need everybody to clean up. There is a stream there, so use it. The capys probably have a good sense of smell, so we have to be odor-free."

Ryck didn't know if that was true or not, but he needed the group to have a purpose, to feel human again. Besides, he simply did not like their smell.

"I'm going to leave SSgt Samuelson and Cpl Caruthers here with you, and Sgt Gutierrez and I are going to go gather up the rest of you. We should be back in six hours if we make good time, so everybody, get ready."

He reached into his pack and pulled out his extra skivvies and his one extra blouse and trou, handing them to Sams. "Get more from the rest and get these passed out. We're going to be going through some thick shit, and they need all the protection they can. See if you can work up some Robinson Crusoe leggings, at least, for the rest while Crutch and I are gone. If we don't make it back in eight hours, take them to the LZ. We've got about 12 hours before pick-up."

"Roger that. Keep your head down. If you can't find them, don't waste too much time, OK, sir?"

"If I'm not back in eight, I'm either not coming back or we went directly to the LZ. So don't you do anything else. Don't try and find us. Get these people to the LZ. That's an order, Sams," Ryck said gently.

He turned to get some information about Station 448. It was an atmosphere monitoring installation. It sampled the air, conducting any number of tests that went beyond Ryck after "humidity" and then transmitted that data to a central relay. Ryck didn't like that it transmitted data. The capys would be able to detect that.

As he was about to leave, laughter rang through the camp. Three men and two women were splashing water on each other in the creek. One of the guys jumped on the other and pushed him under. They weren't clean yet, but they were getting there. It was amazing how a simple thing like getting clean could raise morale. Kata Jun should have realized that and kept discipline. Ryck might have been a little harsh on her, but she was the leader, so she should have led. It wasn't the Marines' job to come in and do that.

"You ready, Crutch?" he asked Cpl Caruthers.

"Born ready, Toad."

"Then let's diddiho."

Ryck gave Sams a wave as he turned to push back through the brush, following the creek until they broke into the teak forest. The team had just come through the same route, and while capys could have moved in during the interim, Ryck thought the chances were reasonable, and given the time crunch, he and Caruthers moved at a pretty good clip. Within two-and-a-half hours, they were back at their LZ. They slowed down then, becoming more tactical, as they covered the last 800 meters to Station 448.

A hundred meters out, Ryck knew something had happened, something bad. He couldn't see anything yet, but the feeling almost overwhelmed him. He motioned for Caruthers to move alongside him, and the two Marines, weapons at the ready, crept forward. The smell hit them first, and Ryck's heart dropped.

The first body was face-down in the grass. The bloated body, inflating the sky-blue uniform of GenAg security, left no doubt that the man was long dead. Ryck was tempted to turn the man over, but there was no real reason to do so. The two Marines moved forward as they came across more bodies, either separate or in small groups. Trees around them showed the scars of a recent battle, so the jimmylegs had put up a fight. The first civilian body was crouched by the base of a tree. Ryck didn't want to, but he pulled the corpse back so he could see the shirt. The nametag read "Mukado." He carefully lowered the body back to its original position.

It was Caruthers who found Dr. Kopowski. He softly called Ryck over. The doctor had one of the security guard's side arms, a huge .44 cal auto. It looked like he had gone out fighting. There were no capy bodies around the station, but Ryck hoped the doctor had taken a few with him.

Ryck pushed the body over. It wasn't bloated, but it was in a fairly advanced stage of decomposition. That was another sign of terraforming that had progressed quite far—Terran bacteria was present, Ryck noted dispassionately. He had to be dispassionate. Otherwise, he could lose focus.

He opened the doctor's side pocket and took out his PA. The doctor had a super, high speed PA, one with many more bells and whistles, the purpose of which Ryck didn't even begin to know. Ryck had been briefed on them, though, and he knew he was to retrieve it if the doctor himself could not be brought back. If it had been powered down during the fight, and the doctor would have been briefed to that effect, it should have survived a capy energy blast. If it had been powered up, it was toast. Ryck would turn it over when they got out of here and let the experts mine the PA for what was in it. Ryck hoped that whatever that was, it was worth the lives of the 18 people rotting around Station 448 on GenAg 13.

He and Caruthers checked the other bodies. They gathered up the lieutenant's PA, but even to the layman's eyes, it was obvious it had been fried. They took it anyway, not knowing if anything could be salvaged. One of the security team had a photo in his hand, the same hand that was clutched around the trigger of his beamer. A holo would have been fried, but the photo, embedded into an almost indestructible plaspage sheet, was undamaged. It depicted a young woman, her sari exposing her very pregnant belly. Ryck eased the photo out of the man's hand and promised to somehow get it back to the woman.

"OK, Crutch, take some shots of the area. Get each body. We won't be able to recover them now, and if the planet gets interdicted, we never will, so let's get a record and give it to GenAg so they can inform the families.

Marines generally had a low opinion of jimmylegs, even if many one-enlistment Marines signed on with the corporations after they got out. But these men had fought and died trying to save their charges. That deserved respect.

As soon as Caruthers finished with the photos, the two Marines left the station to make their way back to the camp in the box canyon. Three hours later, they emerged from the bushes and into the camp.

In the six intervening hours, there had been a sea change. The people were clean, but more than that, they were looking eager. Most were still naked, but the Marines' extra clothing had been partitioned out. Others had what looked like banana leaves, but probably weren't, tied to their legs. All of the men had their balls and dicks restrained with braided leaves of some sort, although Dr. Jarvis had claimed one of the sets of underwear. The other three pair were worn by women, as were the four pair of utility trousers. Those braided underwear were going to chafe, and they might not last long, but they could protect the men's junk for a little while, at least.

Sams and Gutierrez came up at their approach.

"All dead," Ryck said quietly. "Probably right after they led the capys away."

Kata and several others came up, and Ryck told them that the others were gone. One woman screamed out, almost collapsing, and was taken away by two other women.

"She was engaged to one of the security team," Kata said matter-of-factly.

Ryck noticed that she had taken one of the pairs of trouser. Her sister, though, Tara, was still naked. She had let others wear what the Marines had given up.

"We need to move out in 15 minutes," Ryck told those gathered around him. "Please, get everyone ready. For those who need help, let's assign two people each to them so one can take over when the first gets tired. We don't want to have to stop until we get to the LZ."

"LZ?" Kata asked.

"Landing Zone. Where the shuttles will pick us up. We need to be there on time. If we're late, we could get caught up in a full-fledged battle, and if that happens, no one will be worrying about what happens to us. OK? Let's get moving."

As everyone turned to get ready, Tara came up to Ryck and stood in front of him, hand on one hip in a pose of dominance. All cleaned up, Ryck couldn't help but notice that she was quite attractive. Short and compact, she looked both feminine and powerful at the same time.

"Yes?" he asked, wondering what was up.

"I told your Staff Sergeant there, Samuelson, to give his boots to Reiko. She's the pregnant woman there, and she can't be marching barefoot. We barely got her here, and that was when she was only six-and-a-half months along. He told me no."

"And?"

"And I want you to tell him to give her his boots. And you other three, we have some people who are going to have a hard time. They need the boots, too."

"No."

"No?" she said incredulously, stepping forward, thrusting her chest up and out in aggression with her fists clenched, not in any form of sexuality.

"That's right. No."

Ryck was about to explain when she went off, moving closer and putting her face centimeters from his chin. "You are here to support us. We pay our taxes for you, and it's your job. I'm telling you to give up your boots!"

Ryck put his hands on her shoulders and gently, but firmly, pushed her back. "No, our job is to save your lives. And if we have to fight, it will be up to the four of us. We need to be able to fight, and that means run, kick, whatever. And that, Ms. Jun, means we need to be wearing our boots. We are not giving up our weapons nor our boots."

With that, he turned and walked off before he could hear any reply she might have.

"She ask, I mean tell you about the boots?" Sams asked as Ryck walked over.

"Yep."

"Stupid little bitch. Kept harping on me while you were gone, threatening me with her 'powerful' friends who could kill my career."

"Yeah, stupid, but her heart's in the right place. Notice she's the only management type who didn't take any of our clothes?"

"What? You getting soft, Ryck? She threatened me!"

"No, not soft. And you know the threat's a non-player. She's just concerned about her own people. She doesn't understand what we do. So let it go and focus on the mission. Don't brood over it like you always do."

"I'm not brooding. I never brood!"

Gutierrez laughed out loud at that. "No, not you. You *never* brood, my friend."

"Oh fuck you both," Sams said, stalking off.

Ryck knew he would be fine. The bottom line was that he was a professional. He'd probably bring it up two weeks from now in the chow hall, brooding about it until then, but he'd do his job here and now.

Sams started getting the people in their order of march. If he was a little forceful about it, Ryck chose not to notice it. It took almost 20 minutes, but finally, they were ready. With Ryck on point, Sams in the rear, and the other two on each flank, they moved out.

Normally, Ryck wouldn't be on point. But as he was the one who had managed to master land nav with a magnetic compass, he had to lead the column. Initially, he didn't use an azimuth, though.

He made his way alongside the creek until he hit the teak forest. Then he went to his azimuth to take them to the LZ.

They slowly, very slowly made their way forward. Reiko, the pregnant woman, could barely waddle along, each step an effort. Ryck had a horrible thought of her going into labor. Mr. Saunders, one of the old men, was even slower, if that was possible. One of the younger men put Saunders on his back, but that lasted about 300 meters. Despite his intentions, Ryck had to call a stop before they'd gone a klick. They had to rest.

Ryck was staring at his watch, resenting each passing second, when Dr. Jarvis came up and said, "I assume you recovered Dr. Kopowski's PA?" And after Ryck nodded, "Can I ask you if I can take charge of it? I'm sure you know how important that might be, and well, if we have any problems, well, you're a Marine, and, well—"

"And I might get killed."

"I didn't mean it like that," Jarvis protested.

"Sure you did, and that's fine. You might have a point, there." Ryck considered it for a moment, then nodded and reached into his pocket, taking out the PA and handing it to Jarvis. "Better chance of it getting back with you."

Jarvis eagerly took it, turning it over looking for signs of damage. He looked into the dead screen, then flipped on the power.

Ryck stared at him in shock. "Are you fucking high!?" he yelled, grabbing back the PA and turning it off.

Jarvis paled as he realized what he'd done. "I wasn't thinking. I just wanted to see if it still worked. I'm sorry!"

Ryck ignored the trembling man, trying to figure out how long it was on.

*Two, three seconds? Was that enough to set off some sort of capy alarm? Probably not, right? Fuck! I can't take the chance.*

"Shart, get over here!" he shouted out for Sgt Gutierrez. "Sams, get them on their feet" he shouted, eliciting groans from half of the people.

As Sgt Gutierrez ran up, Ryck told him, "Look, we may have alerted the capys. I want you up ahead on point, but five hundred meters or more. You're our early warning if they're in front of us."

"But I can't use that fucking thing," he protested, pointing at the compass.

"You don't have to. Just follow the ridgeline. We've got four klicks or so to go. But remember, that's right at the edge of where it opens up to grassland, just like they told us the capys prefer. So if there are any capys here, that's where they probably are, so keep your eyes peeled. Got it?"

"Yeah, Toad. I've got it. Just . . . oh shit. I'll try not to get lost." He wheeled about, and Ryck heard, "*Dios te salve, María, llena eres de gracia . . .*" as he hurried off.

Sgt Gutierrez was a hell of a Marine, but Ryck knew he was petrified not of a fight, but of getting lost and not doing his job, not providing frontal security. He just had to suck it up and get it done. If he just kept the ridgeline to his left, he should be OK.

Ryck considered moving the column over a bit, closer to the ridgeline, but if they were moving this slowly through the teak plantation, then they would be crawling through the thicker mixed forest higher up.

Ryck told Caruthers to move out his left flank security. He told Sams to be conscious of capys to their rear, but he couldn't drop him back to give the column a buffer. He needed Sams to keep the stragglers moving. Ryck was naked to the left flank, but with the ridgeline there, that was his least likely problem area. Still, Ryck kept his eyes peeled towards the left as the column started up again.

Ryck pushed them. Or to be more accurate, Ryck led the way at a faster pace while Sams pushed them. Ryck could hear Sams, haranguing, pleading threatening, and using everything in his power to keep the slower ones moving. If the column separated, he knew Sams would send up word.

"Should some of us push forward?" Jarvis said, pulling up alongside of Ryck. "Some of them can't move very fast, and that's holding us back, so what about those of us who can move quicker, if we get going to make our pickup time?"

Ryck just glared at the scientist, evil intent in his eyes. Jarvis faltered.

"Just a suggestion," he said, before falling back behind Ryck. Somehow they made it one, two more klicks. He was beginning to hope that they would get to the LZ unmolested. He looked at his watch. Three more hours to go two klicks. Surely even this group could get that done. He slowed down the pace slightly.

When he saw Gutierrez running back, he initially started to point his arm in the correct direction of march. That was until he saw the sergeant's expression. His heart fell.

"Capys!" Gutierrez gasped out as he reached Ryck. "More than a hundred, all coming this way."

"Soldiers?" Ryck asked, already knowing the answer.

"Soldiers, yeah. No doubt."

"And do they know where we are?"

"They're coming right at us, Toad, and they're deployed for combat."

Ryck spun about and screamed, "Everybody, now, turn around! Sams, Crutch, to me!"

Some of the people stopped, looking confused. A few showed panic beginning to form on their faces. Still fewer, Jarvis being one of them, actually turned around and started heading back the way they had come.

"We've got trouble. Our LZ is out. The capys are heading our way from that direction. I don't think we can make the alternate LZ either, not with this group. Sams, I want you to take our charges and head back to our DZ. You can't make that, either, but keep moving. Try to get into someplace open, and exactly at 17:15, signal for a pickup."

He handed Sams three cylindrical tubes he'd bought at a hover shop back in Goattown outside base.

"You think this'll work?" Sams asked.

Ryck had shown the roadside flares to the others while enroute aboard ship. They were used by emergency crews responding to accidents, and were pretty old techno. They emitted a bright red flare that could be easily seen both in darkness or in daylight. A simple twist of the bottom cap set them off.

"If we can't use comms, we have to use visuals. This was the brightest man-packed, non-electrical light I could find searching the net. I'm guessing if they see our LZs are hot or we aren't there, they will see these. I hope.

"You two, we have to delay the capys. You're with me."

He pulled Sams in low to his face and whispered, "If it comes to it, don't wait for us. Get these people out of here."

Sams didn't protest. He just punched Ryck in the shoulder.

"Then make it back in time so we won't have to leave you."

With that, he turned around and started yelling at the column, getting it turned around and moving. Sams pulled out his Ruger just as Tara came up to find out what was going on. He handed his side arm to her and pointed to the front of the column, then used his hand to give a direction.

Ryck wouldn't have chosen the young woman as a point man, but he was already moving out with the other two Marines, and that was Sams call. Ryck put the column out of his mind as he led his two Marines into a fast jog to a spot where the trees were a little denser.

"Let's see if these things are as advertised," he said as he pulled out five tiny cylinders. "Crutch, run the trip lines. Give me, oh, seven meter lengths."

Ryck knelt in the dirt and emplaced the tiny mines. The mines didn't have regular fuzes. There were no sensors, no emissions. These were mechanically detonated. Very carefully, he wired the mines to nearby trees. Two were to larger trees, three to smaller ones. Then, he and Gutierrez attached the trip lines. For the smaller trunks, they attached two trip lines each, one to each side of the small trunk. For the larger two, only one was used, going away from the trunk on the same side as the mine.

He had watched the training holo on arming, and it was not that much different than with the more normal Marine Corps issue ordnance—with the slight problem that these could be prematurely set off if the hand was unsteady. He told the other two to back up while he armed all five, knowing he had to rush, but afraid of making a mistake.

"OK, that's it," he said, scanning the trees in front of him. "Now, over there to the base of the ridgeline."

The three Marines sprinted the 150 meters to where the rocks started up the ridge. They turned just in time to see movement in back of them.

The capys were moving slowly, but steadily. Ryck didn't know if the column was slower. Maybe so. But from experience, the capys never faltered. If the civilians had to stop, the capy's would crawl up their asses, one deliberate step at a time.

Something odd about them caught his eye, and for a moment, he couldn't make out just what it was.

"What the fuck are they wearing," Crutch asked in wonder. "Is that fucking armor?"

Then it hit Ryck. That was exactly what it was. Armor! This was a new twist. He pulled up his binos to get a better look. It was plate armor of some sort, covering their compact torsos.

"They ain't got no armor," Gutierrez said in bewilderment. "They fight naked!"

"They do now. It was stupid to think they wouldn't adjust. We adjusted, so why wouldn't they?" Ryck asked in disgust.

Of course they would adjust, but not in one brief, not in one brainstorming session, had anyone thought of that contingency. The assumption was that nothing would change, that the capys were a static entity.

They were approaching the trip wires. Ryck leveled his HGL and waited. Had they passed them? Did the stupid things even work? At least 40 capys were in sight, and nothing was stopping them.

The first mine went off with a sharp bang, felling four capys on either side of the small trunk. Two stayed down, but two struggled to get up. Ryck could see the red-blue blood staining one of the capys' leg hair as he made it back up before taking one step and falling down again.

"Hold your fire," he told the other two.

The capys reacted, moving into their synchronized dance formation. It shouldn't confuse him, but it did. He knew from the nature holos that fish schooling did the same thing, as did birds wheeling in flocks to confuse predators, but it didn't make sense.

Wheeling or not, the mines didn't care. Two went off almost simultaneously, downing another five capys. At this, the capys suddenly stopped as if on command. They started looking down, moving carefully. One capy bent over and reached down, hand out to pick up something. The blast of the mine is set off was satisfying.

"OK, gents, pick a target and engage."

All three Marines fired their HGLs. Ryck hit his target in the chest, and the grenade detonated, but the capy didn't go down. One of the other two Marines hit one in the unprotected leg, and the leg was blown off.

"Again!"

Three more rounds went off, but once again, two were hit in the armor. One seemed to be hurt, possibly from shrapnel blowing up to its muzzle.

"Up!" Ryck yelled.

The three stood up, and while the other two shouted and jumped up and down, Ryck turned on his monocle. Immediately, whether because of his monocle or the yelling, all of the capy heads swung towards them.

"Take off, and misters on!"

The three turned to run up the ridgeline.

"Shit!" Caruthers shouted. "That fucking burned me!"

Ryck wasn't sure if he felt any tingle, but he could have. Running up hill had its own sense of distress on the body. They made it over a slight leveling off of the rise and dropped down.

"You OK, Crutch?" he asked.

"I think I took a shot in the ass. It feels like my leg is asleep," he said, flexing his leg at the knee.

"Did you have your mister on?" Ryck asked.

"Sure as shit did. You think that thing actually saved me?"

"Who cares, Crutch. You're here now," Gutierrez said with the fatalism of a combat vet as they edged forward to look down the slope.

The bulk of the capys were heading their way. Ryck's heart sunk, though, when he saw a good 50 or so splitting off to follow the human column.

"Let's try and hit them," he told the others.

They were at least 500 meters off, and that was long range for an HGL. They each fired, but without hitting anything. Below them, 350 meters and closing, the bulk of the capys advanced toward the three Marines. They each fired two more times at them, hitting two and knocking one of them down and out of the fight. None of the others came to the wounded one's assistance. It just sat there in the grass as the others passed by it. It tried to lick the stump that used to be its arm, but evidently capy physiology wouldn't allow for that, so it quit trying and simply sat. Ryck had hoped that a wounded capy would take two more out of the fight as they helped the wounded one, but that wasn't happening.

"I want a string of mines here. Give me another five. No, give me two here, then two more over there," Ryck said, pointing to some trees another 50 meters in back of them.

Gutierrez and Caruthers hurried to comply as Ryck glassed the capys below them. As before, they didn't show an emotion recognizable to him. Ryck didn't want to anthropomorphize them, but he couldn't help but think they were soulless, mindless creatures based on their demeanor.

"Done," Gutierrez said as he slid back next to Ryck.

"OK, another shot, then we move back again."

Both Marines fired, this time getting two hits, both effective ones. Two more capys were down.

Ryck jumped up and started to run when Gutierrez shouted out "Stop!" and grabbed him by the arm.

"There's the trip wire!" he shouted, pointing to a spot just a meter in front of Ryck.

Ryck gulped. He lost concentration, and that almost cost him his life. He carefully stepped over it, then continued on.

"Crutch, where're your trip lines?" he shouted out as he came up to where he sent the corporal.

"Over here. You're OK," Caruthers yelled back, carefully coming back towards them before turning to face uphill. "This is clear."

"Let's head further up, then move over to the left a bit and see what they do."

They were masked from the capys below them, so they jogged upright. After only 20 meters, a tingle raised the hair on Ryck's head.

"Misters on!" he shouted, flipping the feed switch. He didn't know what would run out first: the compressed air or the liquid misting agent, but he had turned his off after they reached the level spot.

He turned to see the far group of capys, now more than 700 meters away. It looked like four of them were firing on the Marines. This was beyond their range, at least as far as Ryck had been briefed. Either they had developed a better energy ball thrower, or all the human conjecture was worthless.

They made it to the trees, out of sight of the far off capys. Ryck motioned the other two to slow down. They didn't want to outrun their pursuers. Two hundred meters from the second line of mines, they turned, using tree trunks as cover, and waited. The capys weren't showing. Surely they could have climbed the first slope by now.

"At the brief, they said the capys were from the plains, thc grasslands. You think they're having problems climbing, what with their short legs and all?" Caruthers asked.

"Of course!" Ryck agreed as he considered. "I think you've figured it out. Good thinking, Crutch."

"Yeah, but a broken clock is still right twice a day," Gutierrez said, unwilling to concede too much to the corporal.

"We should have thought of that. We could have sent the civvies up the slope. There's got to be someplace a shuttle can land up here," Ryck said, looking at his map, then scanning the area.

"I think I see it. Look, over there, by that second hilltop. According to this map, it's a flat spot, and from the photos, there're no trees there. We need to get our folks up there, and in two-and-a-half hours.

"No comms, and even if we turn them on, and if they work, Bobbi won't be listening," Gutierrez said.

Ryck thought about it for a few moments, then asked, "Crutch, how's your ass. Can you still run?"

"Not sure, Toad. I mean, I can move it, but it's numb. How long I can run, I don't know."

Caruthers was a long distance runner, so he should have been the logical choice. Ryck contemplated Gutierrez, but the sergeant was built for power, not speed. It had to be Ryck himself.

"OK, listen up. The capys should be hitting that first crest any minute. I want you to hightail it over to that side where you can cover the mines. When the capys arrive, light them up, then activate your monocles. I want you to lead this group as far in that direction as you can. But leave a way to double back. Give yourself a cushion, but get to that landing zone by 1700. I've got one more roadside flare," he said, giving it to the sergeant. "If you see the shuttle land somewhere else, light it for a pickup."

"What are you going to be doing?" Gutierrez asked.

"I'm going to chase down Sams and the civvies."

Ryck hefted his HGL. On impulse, he handed it over to Caruthers.

"You don't think you might need it?" the corporal asked.

"No. Maybe. It'll just slow me down. I've got my blunderbuss and Ruger, and that will have to be enough."

"You understand?" Ryck asked.

"Got it," they said in unison.

"Then take off. You need to cover the mines from that direction."

Both shook hands with Ryck, then started back. Ryck stood up, adjusted his equipment load, and then started off, running parallel along the ridgeline. The air pressure on GenAg 13 was a little higher than what he was used to, and that compensated for the slightly lower oxygen partial pressure, so Ryck felt comfortable as he ran. He picked up the pace. He tried to look through the trees on the slope to see either the column or the pursuing capys, but he couldn't catch a glimpse of either.

Behind him, a mine went off. The capys had finally made the ridge. The blast was immediately followed by the unmistakable reports of the HGLs. The boys were engaged.

Ryck couldn't do anything about that now, so he tried to focus, to calculate where the column would be. He didn't want to pass their position before heading downslope. Twice, he almost turned, but each time second guessed himself. Finally, he figured he had pulled abreast of the column and turned to start running down the hill. He had to be careful, though. Falling and twisting an ankle could spell disaster.

He reached the bottom quickly and was almost immediately into the more open teak plantation. He felt better about opening up his pace, and soon he was breathing harder and he pushed his limits.

He jumped an irrigation line and rounded a pump house when he saw them. Two capys were crouched on their haunches in front of him, focusing further into the forest. He slid to stop, his feet digging into the soft soil, not ten meters from them. They turned around in unison, emotionless as always. Both reached for their weapons as they stood up while Ryck fumbled for his blunderbuss. Ryck was quicker, and he flipped off the safety to fire. At the last second, he lowered his aim from the armored torso to the groin of the one nearest him. He fired the harpoon, which struck true, just above the leg juncture. It penetrated the shield and into the capy's body before flaring open. The capy collapsed in a heap.

Ryck had his Ruger, his grenades, and two toads, but the Ruger would be useless against the remaining capy's shield. Ryck hit the misters as he dove to the ground just as the capy fired. Ryck was going down, so the misters were probably ineffective, especially at close range, but by diving, the energy ball flashed over Ryck. Ryck felt the tingle, but nothing else. There was a whine that sounded like something charging. He knew he had to act fast.

His hand closed on his Hwa Win combat knife, the one he'd paid 350 units for at the Semper Fi shop back on Tarawa. He jumped up and charged, immediately closing the distance between the two of them. An energy ball appeared in the cradle just as he reached the capy. Using one hand to push the gun up past his shoulder, he tried to stick the creature with his knife. Immediately, as his hand penetrated the shield, his arm felt like it was going to sleep. The knife's tip skittered across the thing's armor, pushing up past its left shoulder. His legs whipped to the left, and that swung him around, almost past the capy. He held on with his right arm, though, and that acted as a pivot point. Somehow, Ryck ended up clinging to the back of the capy as it tried to turn and face him.

Ryck scrambled for a better position and managed to shift into a standing rear naked choke. He tried to pull back on the capy's head with his left arm to expose the neck, but the thing was unbelievably strong. The head wouldn't move. One of its hands reached down to grab Ryck's thigh, and Ryck thought he was going to yank his leg right off. In desperation, Ryck raised the knife and stabbed down, exactly as Sgt MacPruit had told them not to do back during MCMA training back on Alexander. Overhead stabbing was just not very effective, but while hanging from the back of the capy, it was his only option. The tempered durosteel blade slid into the capy's neck. The creature started wheeling about, trying to shake Ryck off. Ryck plunged the knife again and again, hoping to find something vulnerable among the heavy neck muscles. Ryck almost let go when the capy slammed him into a tree, but the creature was slowing, and the force was not quite enough to shake him. Finally, Ryck hit something vital, and with a huge exhalation, the capy went down. Still clinging to its back, Ryck stabbed it five or six more times for good measure.

The capy was still, but Ryck slowly pulled his left arm from under it and slid back. He stood and gave it a kick, but it was dead. He looked at the other one, and it was dead, too. Ryck tried to retrieve the harpoon, but the extraction function wasn't working. The blades were hung up in the capy's body. Without hesitation, Ryck cut the thing out with his combat knife, wiped it in the leaves, and loaded it back into his blunderbuss.

The fact that the capys had their own kind of recon team deployed shouldn't have surprised him. And if they could communicate through their bioreceptors, as the xenobiologists thought, they had to have sent what was happening to them, and if they had eyes on the column, that would have been passed, too. Ryck had to hurry.

He broke into a flat out run through the trees, trying to catch the column. Caution was gone: time was of the essence. He finally just caught sight of them 200 meters away as they passed between the trees. He called out, and in doing so, never saw the irrigation pipe. His left boot toe went under it as his body plunge forward. He shrieked as his tibia and fibula snapped.

"Mother grubbing fuck!" he screamed as the pain shot through him.

He looked back at his leg and almost threw up as shock set in. If he was in his PICS, drugs would already be flowing through his body. But he was in grubbing recon, where they were expected to grin and bear it.

He twisted to a sitting position, the pain of doing so almost making him pass out. But his tendons and muscles brought his bent leg a little more into line.

*Forget the pain. The pain is nothing. Get on with your mission!* He ran the mantra over and over in his mind.

He struggled to his feet and started walking. The first step was torture as he felt broken bone ends scrape against each other. The second was better. It hurt the same, but Ryck was beginning to compartmentalize it, to push it to a corner of his mind. He still knew the pain was there, but the rest of his brain began to be able to function again. Part of him wondered how much damage he was doing to himself, but his mission took priority.

Even with only one good leg, he started catching up to the column. At 100 meters to their flank, he tried to call out, but only a croak emerged from his throat. He swallowed, and then tried again.

"Stop!"

Miracle of miracle, someone heard him. A woman wearing his blue skivvies (he noted in a corner of his mind), saw him and pointed. The column stopped, and by the time Ryck had struggled forward, Sams had reached him.

Ryck collapsed on the dirt, his leg no longer supporting him.

"Ryck, what's going on? We've got to move it!"

"Change of plans. The capys' can't climb. We need to get to another LZ up there," he said, pointing in back of himself. "I've got Shart and Crutch leading the main body of capys away, then they're going to double back and meet us there. But I ran into two capys in the woods back there watching you, and the rest of them know exactly where you are. Even if you make it to the alternate LZ before them, unless the shuttle lands immediately, the capys will get there before you can load."

"But I don't know if some of these people can make it up a slope."

"They're going to have to. Turn now, and head up. Here's the map with the LZ. Get them there."

"But what about you? You can't walk."

"You heard him, Sams," Tara said as she came up, now with a blunderbuss in her hands. "We need to turn the column now and move it."

As she moved off to the front of the column, Ryck had to ask, despite the situation, a simple "Sams?"

"Ah, it was easier. She's been pretty helpful." He looked up and shouted "McManus!"

One of the men hurried over and knelt beside Ryck, looking at his leg.

"Can you do anything about that?" Sams asked.

"Oh, that's pretty bad. He needs surgery."

"Well there's no freaking surgeon here, is there now? You're the medic, show me what you can do."

The column began a ponderous turn to the right to move into the trees as McManus contemplated the situation.

"OK, this isn't enough, but get me one of those branches, one about yay long," he said, holding his hands about a meter apart. Then to Ryck, "Do you have any of those zip ties?"

"In my left cargo pocket."

McManus reached inside, pulling out everything and dropping it in the dirt before picking out some white zip ties. "Look, this won't be great, and these things are thin, so they'll cut your blood off if they are tight enough to give you support. When we get to the shuttle, we've got to cut this off, OK?"

"My leg?" Ryck asked, confused.

"No, this," he said as one might talk to a child, holding up the branch Sams had retrieved.

There was a blast, maybe 400 meters back along the columns trace.

"I heard your mines go off and thought I'd set a few of my own," Sams said. "They're getting closer. I think they've gained 300 meters in the last 30 minutes. Can you hurry it up, McManus?"

With sure hands, the medic placed the branch alongside of Ryck's leg, then with firm tugs, tightened the zip ties. Ryck had to bite back a scream.

"Can you get up?" the medic asked.

Ryck struggled to his feet. He gave a sort of hop-skip, putting almost no pressure on his leg, but it still hurt.

He kept his face calm as he said, "I can make it."

"Rancer! Come here!" Sams shouted over Ryck's shoulder.

A fit-looking man in his 40's came up. He was a little shorter than Ryck, his dark skin once again covered with the dirt and grime of the forced march.

"I want you to help the lieutenant, got it? Make sure he keeps up," Sams told the man.

"Shout out if you need more help," Sams told Ryck. "I've got to get these people moving."

Sams looked back to see if the capys were in sight yet, then started shouting out to speed up the movement towards the slopes.

"How do you want to do this?" Rancer asked, concern evident on his face.

"Um, well, how about if you give me a shoulder?" Ryck suggested.

Sams had been clever. With Rancer a little shorter, Ryck's left arm fit comfortably over his shoulders. Ryck took a hesitant step which drove jolts of pain from his leg all the way to his neck, but he thought it would be manageable.

Just as Ryck and Rancer moved off the path and into the trees, Sams raised his HGL and fired off two shots.

"Move it!" he screamed, physically pushing the last straggler into the trees.

The teak forest gave some degree of cover, and with no undergrowth, it didn't slow the column down in and of itself. However, with Ryck, Mr. Saunders, and Reiko, along with some other slowly moving people, the column was not making time, and if the capys got close enough, there was no undergrowth to dissipate their energy balls.

Ryck pulled out his blunderbuss and held it in his right hand, ready to use it if needed. With only one HGL in the group, every weapon was needed.

Tara came running back down the line, and Sams shouted out, "What are you doing? I need you up there!"

"No, you need me here," she responded, holding up her blunderbuss. "I've got Gracie leading the column. She's done sampling up there and knows exactly where to go. So how about you give me a couple more of the mines and you worry about keeping the tail end here moving."

Sams looked like he was going to argue, but then simply handed over three mines to the woman. Ryck felt like he should stop to make sure Tara knew what she was doing. The mines were sensitive, after all. But frankly, it was all he could do just to keep moving. Each step was agony, and he was having a harder and harder time compartmentalizing the pain.

Up ahead and off to the right, he heard the faint sounds of HGL fire. Gutierrez and Caruthers were still at it.

*They better be doubling back soon*, he thought.

If Ryck thought walking through the plantation was tough, once he hit the slope and the denser wild vegetation, it became torture. He couldn't swing his left foot as much and had to lift it higher to get it up and forward. After only a few steps, he stopped trying, using his right leg to step, then dragging his left to meet it, then the right again. The vegetation grabbed at is legs, trying to stop him.

An explosion sounded in back of him. He thought Tara had accidently set off a mine, and he looked back, but Tara was walking backwards only five meters behind him, blunderbuss at the ready.

That meant a capy had set off the mine, and that meant the capys were less than 200 meters behind them. They were closing the distance. If the column had still been within the plantation, the capys would have been within range of the rear of the column and they could have taken them under fire.

Ryck felt a rush of despair. This was the second time he'd been in full retreat, something Marines were not noted for. He'd lost most of his platoon on GKN with the capys chasing them. He'd joined recon so he wouldn't have to worry about being responsible for so many other lives, but here he was, running for his life, with 27 civilians in his charge. This was a wickedly devastating dose of déjà vu.

Ryck kept trying to turn around to spot the capys, and that twisted Rancer. The man didn't complain, though. Ryck knew the slope would slow down the capys as well, but if they got close enough right as the plantation ended, they could be well within visual and weapons range.

Ryck flipped the butterfly valve and started misting, but only in the back of him. He hoped the mist would cover Rancer as well. He didn't give it much credence, but maybe it had helped Caruthers, so it couldn't hurt.

There was another blast, just at the edge of visual range. Tara had made time to set at least one more mine with the capys on her ass. Ryck looked over at her as she made her way backwards up the slope. She had a big welt across her side, and one foot was bloody, but she didn't falter. Ryck had to admit that she was one tough hombre.

"There they are!" Sams said to no one in particular as he fired two rounds from his HGL.

"You got one!" Tara shouted in excitement. Both ducked low into the undergrowth, and in a crouch, pushed their way uphill. There wasn't any way Ryck could crouch, and Rancer wouldn't abandon him.

When Ryck felt the kiss of energy, Rancer cried out, "My arm! Bastards!"

Ryck wondered if the mister was actually helping. Maybe it only partially covered Rancer as well. That would explain why his left arm had received more of the effects of the energy ball.

Ryck had no time to contemplate that as Rancer physically dragged Ryck forward, each tug wrenching his leg. Ryck was lost in a sea of agony, only peripherally aware of anything else. He wasn't sure how long it took or how far they went. He was vaguely aware of Rancer cursing, of someone else, maybe Tara, coming over to take Ryck's blunderbuss and putting his right arm over her shoulder. He kept trying to walk, to move his legs, but he wasn't sure how effective he was.

And then, he was out of the trees, up on the grass and rock plateau. The fact that this was the new LZ registered deep within his mind, forcing him to shut out the pain and take stock of the situation.

Most of the civilians were standing in small groups, talking nervously among themselves. Several of them were down on their backs, the strain of the flight too much for them. A couple of hundred meters away, two Marines were running forward toward them.

Ryck felt a rush of relief. All of his team had made it. Whether there were capys on Gutierrez and Caruthers' tail, or whether the capys on the slope below them would make it up soon was immaterial for the moment. His Marines were back together.

"Sams! Is everybody up here?"

"Just did a head count, Ryck. Every swinging dick is here, ready to go. Where's your shuttle?"

Ryck's checked his watch. They still had five minutes. The timing had been close, which was good, but was five minutes too much time? How long before the capys made it up there?

"Shart! Crutch! Get over here and cover the slope. Where's my HGL?" Ryck asked.

"Here it is, Caruthers said, holding up the bunker buster." "Mine's out of ammo, so I'm using yours."

Ryck almost asked for it back, but it was better in Caruther's hands. Ryck had a brief flashback of giving a weapon to another Marine back on GKN, and what that had cost him. He forced the thought back down into the recesses of his mind.

"Give me the flares, then," Ryck said. "I want you two right there on those rocks. You see any movement below you, light them up!"

Tara and one of the men, both carrying blunderbusses, silently went to join the two Marines. Ryck didn't even bother to comment. If the capys made the plateau, it was over, anyway, so it didn't matter much if the two helped his Marines.

"Sams, get everyone ready to go. If the shuttle lands, I want everyone rushing it and onboard. If the capys get here, tell everyone to scatter. Maybe some will make it, and if there isn't an interdiction, they might get picked up later."

Ryck suddenly felt nauseous, and he bent over at the waist, afraid he was going to vomit. Bent over, he caught sight of his leg. That was the first time he'd seen his leg since he broke it. Shards of bone were sticking out of his skin and through his trou, and the foot was twisted 30 degrees to the right. Ryck almost passed out, but managed to fall to a sitting position. He refused to look at his leg as he took deep breaths, centering himself.

"Take it easy, Ryck. I've got it," Sams assured him.

Sams might be able to run things, but this was still Ryck's responsibility. He was the one who was tasked with extracting the civilians.

A shadow flitted across the grass, and it took a moment for Ryck to realize what it was. Two Navy Experions were making a run over the plateau. Of course! The shuttles would not come in without an escort!

At that moment, Gutierrez and Caruthers opened fire down the slope. Ryck heard the sharp report of one of the blunderbusses. The capys had to be almost to the plateau. Ryck scanned the sky, but no shuttle was in sight. Even with one on approach, it would be too late. They couldn't board it in time.

*I'm an idiot!* he berated himself. *We can't get into a Navy fighter, but they're pretty powerful birds, even within the atmosphere.*

Ryck turned on his monocle, hoping he had comms with the fighters. Nothing. Well, he had something else.

"Sams, the fighters are coming in for another pass, probably just to count us. I want everybody up and pointing to the slope where the capys are. Have them jump, have them scream, but point!

"Rancer, can you throw? You ever play ball?"

"Yeah, handball at my uni," Rancer said, looking puzzled at the question.

"Take these," Ryck said, lighting off two of the flares. "Wait until the fighters are almost over us, then toss these over the edge and down into the trees. Toss them high, so they arch. Don't wait too long, don't throw early. The fighter pilots have to see them. Think you can do it?"

"Hell, yeah I can!" he said, taking the flares.

"Do it, then!"

Ryck watched Rancer run almost to the edge of the plateau. He stopped and looked back, watching for the Experions.

The two fighters came back down to overfly them. The civilians all started jumping up and down. Not all were really pointing in the right direction, or pointing at all, to be honest. But Ryck hoped it was enough.

"Now!" he shouted at Rancer, but the man had already leaned back and thrown the first one.

It arched up, a bright red beacon, before falling out of sight into the trees below. He threw the second one, pushing it up higher. Ryck had envisioned both at once, but this made more sense. It gave the pilots a better chance to spot them.

The Experions pulled into an immediate climb. Had they seen the flares? Did they understand the message?

"Frack it!" Gutierrez shouted, jumping up and down, holding an arm. "Pull back five, then let them have it as soon as they poke their noses over the edge!"

The two Marines and two civilians stepped back from the edge and got down, ready to take on the first capys to make it up.

Caruthers reached into a pocket and pulled out a toad. He lit it off, then tossed it over the edge. Throwing blind didn't give him a good chance to hit one of them, but any action was better than inaction.

Ryck looked back up, trying to see the fighters. The sky was clear. Had they gone?

A low rumble filled his ears, and the tops of the trees not ten meters from the edge of the plateau began to come apart. The fighters had not left, and the pilots had understood the message. They had gotten altitude, and then swooped down on the trees below Ryck and his charges. They were chewing up the slope. The two Marines and two civilians pushed their faces into the dirt, hands covering the backs of their heads as pieces of trees flew through the air, pelting them. With one pass over, the second bird was starting its pass.

Cheers erupted from 31 throats. If Ryck wasn't the loudest, he had to be mighty close to it.

"Shuttles are inbound!" Sams shouted, barely heard over the roar of the Experions firing.

Ryck could see two shuttles gently coming in as if there wasn't a hellacious air-to-ground pounding occurring only meters off the LZ. All of Ryck's charges could fit on one shuttle, but the Navy had been prepared for the security and research teams as well.

Both set down and lowered their ramps. Several of the civilians rushed to the nearest one and climbed inside.

"Shart, get your team back and load them up," Ryck shouted.

"Shall we?" Rancer asked, coming back to Ryck and offering his shoulder.

"I'm going to take you up on that. Let's get the St. Chuck's Hell out of here."

Sams was standing by the ramp, counting each person as he or she got onboard. Mr. Saunders was carried by two others, and Reiko was helped up and into the shuttle. A younger woman was carried piggyback by another woman who had to be in her 50's.

Tara and the other man who carried the blunderbuss rushed by, the man shouting his inarticulate joy. Gutierrez and Caruthers came up and offered to help Ryck.

"No, Rancer and me, we're fine. Right Rancer?"

"Right, lieutenant!"

Ryck wasn't fine. His leg was no longer working at all, and he was lightheaded. The pain, thankfully, had faded a bit, probably because the nerves were just too mangled to transmit the signals. But he had only ten meters left, and nothing was going to stop him.

"We got everybody?" he asked Sams.

"Nine on the trail bird. Twenty-two on this one. We didn't lose anyone. You got all of us out."

"One more headcount, then we're out of here," Ryck said.

He looked back as the ramp slowly closed, cutting off his view of GenAg 13.

# *FS Frierson*

## Chapter 25

Ryck lay back in the rack, his leg in a portable stasis tube. The ship's doctor took one look at the mangled flesh and said he didn't even want to attempt working on it. The *Frierson* was a supply ship, and its sickbay was not fully capable. But it was an extra platform with plenty of room, so it made a decent emergency transport for the civilians while the warships did their thing.

He really wanted a drink, though, and he was abandoned. The stress of the avacuation had induced labor in Reiko, and all the medical staff was attending to her. Even for a supply ship, it was not often that someone gave birth on a Federation Navy vessel, and everyone wanted to be there for the event.

Mr. Saunders was resting comfortably in the next rack over, softly snoring. The old man had never complained, and Ryck had to give him credit for that, but age had been his enemy, and the man had been a liability to the entire group. Then again, he was part of a terraforming team, not expected to go into combat. Ryck listened to the snores, oddly pleased with the sound. They were proof the man had made it.

"Hey, Rycky Recon, you hanging in there?" Kylton said, sticking his head in the sickbay hatch.

"Kyle, when did you get in? How did things go for you?" Ryck asked, pulling himself into a sitting position.

With his leg in a semi-stasis, there was no pain, so Ryck was feeling much better. His nausea (simple shock, the doc had said) had completely faded away.

"Got a halfer. My pickup was nowhere to be seen. No sign, nothing. We pretty much sat on our butts until pickup. Cornball, though, he picked up 110 people and got them all out. No capys."

"You mean I'm the only one to run into capys?"

"No, the Second Recon guys were in it pretty deep. I got some of this during my debrief. It's not too clear yet for us here on the *Frierson*, but it looks like they lost a number of Marines and had heavy casualties with the civilians."

"That must have come in after my debrief. We were the first ones back. Still waiting for Klepto, though. This no comms BS is really grating on my nerves," Ryck said sourly.

"Did I hear my name being taken in vain?" Gunny Schmidt said, coming into the small sickbay.

Ryck's face broke out into a smile. "Thought you weren't going to join us for our leisurely voyage back."

"Wouldn't miss it for the world, sir," the gunny said, shaking hands first with Ryck, then the captain.

"So, how'd it go?" Ryck asked.

"Not so good," Gunny began as Ryck's heart fell.

*Who'd they lose?*

"The team's fine. A little banged up, but fine. You know those misters really worked? I never would've believed it. Ask Rabbit about it when you've got the time. His ass is numb, but he made it back.

"Our civilians, though, I didn't know how to handle them. They wanted to do things their way, not ours. The jimmyleg captain, he thought he knew more than us, snares and dead falls and such. Said they needed to ride it out. In the end, I took fifteen researchers and got out of there and to our pickup. I . . . I don't think those guys made it out," he said soberly.

"I've already briefed the failure to the skipper. He wants a full written report."

"Failure? You got 15 researchers out, and who knows what needed intel they have. You didn't fail," Ryck protested.

"It kinda feels that way, though," Gunny said. "But what's with this shit?" he continued, pointing at the stasis bubble around his leg. "Shart says you went hand to hand with two capys, ghosting both of them, breaking your leg doing it?"

"What?" Kylton asked in disbelief. "You did what?"

"Calm down. It wasn't quite like that. I did take out a capy with my blunderbuss, and I sort of did hand-to hand with one of them. My Hwa Min, the one you said was bullshit, Klepto, by-the-way, saved my ass, and I came out on top."

"You 'came out on top,' even with a broken leg?" Gunny pressed.

"Well, not exactly. After the fight, I sort of tripped on an irrigation pipe and broke it."

There was dead silence for a good ten seconds before both of the other Marines broke out in laughter.

"You what?" Gunny managed to get out.

"I tripped and broke my leg. What of it? It could happen to anybody."

"But not to the almighty Ryck Lysander, hero of the Federation," Kylton roared, tears coming from his eyes. "The mighty Lysander, master death dealer, trips on a water sprinkler! You couldn't write this stuff. This is brills, simply brills."

Ryck tried to glare at the two Marines, but he couldn't keep it up. He did see the humor in it. He chuckled, and that grew into a laugh. Then an uncontrollable laugh.

"At least . . . I tried . . ." he began before giving up.

He'd almost gained control when the gunny mimed walking along, weapon in hand, then tripping. That started the laughter going again.

The laughter was a release for Ryck. He'd been tight, both physically and mentally. Ever since Joshua's death, since Hannah left him. He'd been miserable. Recon was a refuge for him, where he could run away from it all. But he hadn't been happy, not like when he was a PFC, exploring his position in the Corps, finding out just what kind of man he was.

For the first time in a long time, he'd simply let go. He'd forgotten all the bad and just celebrated life. Maybe he was ready to move on.

The three Marines had finally gotten control of themselves when Sams and Tara walked in. Tara had on some sailor's overhauls, which were about four sizes too big. Both the leg and arm cuffs had been folded several times to shorten the sleeves and legs. Dressed, she looked like a much younger woman.

"It's a boy," Sams said.

"One of our civvies went into labor," Ryck said, cluing in the other two.

"Tell him the name," Tara prodded Sams. Literally prodded him, elbow to the ribs.

"Uh, well, she named him Bobbi."

"Bobbi, as in Bobbi Samuelson?" Gunny asked, eyes wide.

"Yeah, she named him for Sams. For what Sams did for us," Tara said defensively.

Ryck didn't know how to respond to that, and all five people stared awkwardly at one another.

"Well, I'll leave you here so you can visit with your friends. I'll see you at the first lunch seating," she told Sams, then "I hope you recover soon, Lieutenant."

Sams seemed interested in the end of Ryck's rack, rubbing his hand over the frame, looking down at it.

"'I'll see you at the first lunch seating, honey, and that's an order!'" Gunny said, his voice in falsetto.

"What the grubbing heck, Sams? I thought you said she was a bitch who threatened you? She was sure on your case about the boots," Ryck said.

""Yeah, but you didn't see her out there. She could be a freaking Marine. She was great, and without her, I don't think we would have made it. I just respect her, OK? Nothing wrong with that, right?"

"The great Sams, womanizer extraordinaire, with a girl in every port," Ryck began.

"*Girls* in every port," Gunny corrected.

"Yes, girls in every port. So do I hear the sounds of the ball and chain being dragged into position?"

Kylton started humming the wedding march, and the laughter grew the longer it went.

"Ah, screw it," Sams said. "So I like her. Big deal"

The Navy doc came in, drying off his hands. "OK, now that I've performed my first birth, we can get to you, lieutenant. As I told you, we don't have the facilities to do this kind of surgery on board. I've got your leg quieted down, so it shouldn't degrade while we're in transit. Francis here," he said, nodding at the corpsman who had followed him in, "will give you a shot, and that's going to make you drowsy. Then we're going to put you out for the duration. This isn't a true coma, like you've had for regen. I just don't want you moving about and putting any more stress on that leg. You'll wake up back at the Naval Hospital, primed and ready to go. Any questions for me?"

"This isn't a coma?"

"Nah, just a deep sleep. Nothing to it."

"OK, I guess you'd better have at it."

"Hey, buddy, I'll catch you on the boomerang, OK?" Kylton said as the corpsman tried to usher them out.

"Don't worry, Toad, I'll manage the crew while you're in dreamland," Gunny assured him as he left.

The corpsman pushed a button, and Ryck's entire rack lifted up and moved to a center examining table.

"You're going to feel drowsy, and you should fall asleep within 20 or 30 seconds. Then we'll take you deeper so you don't move around while under. You ready?"

"Go for it," Ryck said.

He immediately started feeling the effects. Snoring filled his senses, and he briefly wondered if that was Mr. Saunders or him before sleep overtook him.

# Zephyr-Hadreson

## Chapter 26

Ryck was surprised to see he was being wheeled through a corridor.

*Has something gone wrong? I thought I was supposed to be asleep?*

It took him a moment to realize that he wasn't on a ship. The white corridors were too wide, and there were too many people moving back and forth.

"Good morning, sunshine!" a totally too-cheery orderly told him. "Welcome home! Dr. Larkin is going to check you over, then we'll get you into surgery right way. You'll be good as new before you know it!"

*Lord save me,* he thought. It was too early for spunky overload.

He tuned out the orderly as his thought processes came back online. His leg felt fine, so it had to still be in stasis. But he knew they would want to get him to surgery as soon as possible after the bubble came off.

He was wheeled into a room, and the ever- chirpy orderly told him, "Dr. Larkin's our best, and he'll be here in just a spiff. If you need anything, press this button, and I'll be here in a jiff!"

*Oh, just go,* he pleaded in his mind, while saying "OK, if I need you, I will" out loud.

"'I'll be here in a jiff,'" a voice said from the corner of the room.

Ryck raised his head to see Bert Nidischii' sitting there.

"What are you doing here?" Ryck asked, happy to see his friend.

"Oh, you know, just in the neighborhood, so I decided to stop by and see how you were. You know how it is."

"Just in the neighborhood? And just when I get wheeled in to prep for surgery? Is this a command visit?"

"Could be."

"Maybe, to see where my head's at?" Ryck prompted.

"Well, I was asked if I could make the trip. You are a 'Federation asset,' as they told me, and they wanted to see what your plans are. You were ready to resign before, and now that the war is probably over—"

"What? Run that by me again?" Ryck asked incredulously.

"Ah, yeah, you've been out for a bit on your slow boat back. Well, it's not really over, but things are progressing. We took GenAg 13 pretty easily, with less than 1,000 killed and maybe that many or more of the capys. Did it in a day, too. But then over 2,000 capy ships appeared just outside the Blue Line[90], and they took an SOG ship captive, of all things."

"Two thousand ships, ships of the line?" Ryck asked.

"Yepper. Two thousand of the suckers, just appeared. They took this SOG ship, gave them a kind of book of pictures, is how it's being reported, and all 2,000 ships retreated some 130,000 kilometers and simply waited. The SOG ship hightails it back to one of the Navy's secret outposts and delivers the picture book."

"The SOG knows about secret Navy outposts?"

"Yeah, imagine that. Well, anyway, that gets copied and zapped back, and the xenobiologists and all their high-powered AIs are adamant that it's a request for peace. Sort of you stay on your side, we'll stay on ours."

"And we believe that?" Ryck said, trying to digest this.

"The Brotherhood is adamant about it, and they said they'll stop any more aggression until we figure it out. They threatened us with war if we pursued the capys before more was known.

"We're all still on full alert, but the capy ships are all still sitting there, unshielded. We've got a couple hundred facing them, well within our side of the Blue Line, though."

Ryck took a few moments to digest this. The capys were the enemy. They'd killed his friends, his family. Now they were at peace? It was hard to take in.

Bert just let him process the information.

It was almost five minutes before Ryck broke his silence. "So now that the war might be over, they don't have the legal grounds to

---

90 Blue Line: an imaginary line indicating the furthest reach of human space.

keep me in if I still want to resign. So they sent my good friend and mentor to see which way I was leaning."

"Yepper, that about sums it up. Of course, I can just wait until you are out of surgery and your regen coma. It's up to you."

"Yeah, we should make them wait. I'm not their pawn. They may think I am, but if anything, I'm using them. But no, you can tell them I'm all right. I got everyone out OK from GenAg 13. I broke my leg. But I'm fine. Ready to go back to a line company, too. I should be getting captain soon—"

"You're already on the list. Congrats on that."

"The list is out? Well, seeing as 95% of the eligible are on the list, that's no big achievement. Well, anyway, tell the wizards on high that I want a company. A PICS company. I'll take anything, really, but tell them I'll resign unless I get it, and I want Hecs as my company gunny. I might have a few other names, too."

Bert laughed. "It's good to see my bud is back. Turn the screw on them, Ryck. You deserve it. You scoffed at them calling you a Federation asset. You are, though. You may not be the asset they think, a political symbol, but to your Marines, you're about the best asset they could have."

Ryck felt tears start to well up, and he was saved by the great Dr. Larkin's entry, followed by his posse of white-cloaked followers. The doctor pushed Bert out of the way and signaled one of the others to deactivate the bubble around Ryck's leg.

*I guess he's too important to do that*, Ryck thought as Bert rolled his eyes over the doctor's head.

"Now let's see what we have," the doctor said as all his posse leaned in to observe.

"This is exactly what I told you before," he snapped in anger. "This man should have been immediately immobilized! If he had, it would have been a simple matter to set the leg for a quick ten-day regen. But he was forced to continue to use the leg, and consequently, there was severe damage to the . . . "

Ryck was lost on the more technical terms the doctor was throwing about. He caught the word "flensing," which Ryck knew from his days on the farm as taking muscle tissue off a carcass, and that grabbed his attention. But the doctor kept going on that Ryck was lucky (not "Ryck," but "this man") that he was present and could save much of the leg if he was gotten into surgery within the half hour.

Since the doctor was ignoring Ryck from above his knee, he motioned Bert over. "Can you do me a favor? Can you cam Hannah and tell her I'm OK? She would have gotten the casualty notice, but she won't know that it really isn't that bad," he said before lowering his voice to a whisper, "especially with Dr. Wonderful here to grace me with his skills."

Bert's face fell. "Already tried it, at least five times. No answer, no messaging. But I'll keep trying," he added hopefully.

*No answer? Why?* Ryck wondered. *Did she change her contact channels?*

Ryck felt his bed move again and four orderlies, this time, wheeled him out of the room. Ryck looked over his shoulder to see Bert, who rendered a casual salute.

The next five minutes were a blur as Ryck was prepped. The anesthesiologist, at least treated him like a person, not a lab experiment. His leg, out of mini-stasis, started to hurt, especially when they started to clean the mangled flesh.

"Hey," the anesthesiologist shouted at the prep team, "wait until he's under, for God's sake.

"Sorry about that, Lieutenant. Don't worry. Count down from 100 to one, please, and you'll be fine.

By 97, Ryck was out.

## Chapter 27

Ryck slowly fought his way through the cotton clouds. He was used to this now. He knew he was coming out of regen. If the doctor had been as good as he said, it should have been a short one or two week coma, and he faced a six month regen. If they had to amputate the leg, it would be more than a year.

That depressed him. He hated the regen process. He hated being a gen hen. Then there was the rehabilitation, or authorized torture at the hands of the physical therapy terrorists. Well, he'd be a captain by the time he was done, and if Bert had passed on his demands, he'd have a PICS company to command.

He kept his eyes closed. If he didn't open them, he could delay, if only for a few minutes, the official start of his rehabilitation. He deserved a few more moments to himself.

Finally, he opened his eyes to the darkened room. It didn't take him long to adjust, for things to make sense again. He looked over to see if he had a roommate in the next rack. It was empty, but someone was sitting in the chair in the corner, in the shadows.

"Bert," he croaked, his voice out of practice. "Did you get a hold of Hannah?"

The figure said nothing, but stood up and walked forward into a shaft of light coming in through the semi-closed blinds.

"Not until I got here," Hannah said as the shaft lit her features.

Ryck weakly raised his arm to her. "Hannah!"

She stood only a moment longer before running to him. "I'm so sorry," she started sobbing, putting her head on his chest. "I'm so sorry."

Ryck didn't know what to say, so he reached to stroke her hair as hot tears soaked through his hospital gown and onto his chest.

She sobbed heavily for 30 seconds before she began to gain control of herself. She wiped her forearm across her eyes and nose, and sat back up, with one hand holding Rycks'.

"I . . . I don't know where to start," she said.

"Ssh," he tried to calm her, reaching up to brush a remaining tear off her cheek.

"No, I need to say this. I knew I was wrong when I left. I knew it wasn't your fault. I was just so, so angry, and you were there for me to blame. When I got back, I tried to convince myself that I was right, that you were wrong. No, let me finish," she said when Ryck tried to stop her. "I just couldn't come to grips with what had happened, and I blamed you, even when I knew in my heart it wasn't your fault. And then Tand came to see me.

*Tand? Tand Ariana? What did he tell her? Did he turn her against me?*

"Tand came with his wife Cindi and his twin babies, Joshua and Greta. Yes, little Joshua. He told me what happened. He told me you refused to tell Joshua to stay and protect the rest. He told me Joshua insisted. It was Joshua's choice, Ryck, and I know it.

"Tand and his family stayed with us for a week. I insisted. I played with the babies, little ones who would not have ever been born if you hadn't changed your mind and let Joshua fulfill his destiny."

She was quiet for a moment, then slowly lowered her head to Ryck's chest.

"Hope doesn't blame you, you know. My mom doesn't. I spent time with Lysa and the kids. I spoke with the Deacon more times than I can count."

"Why didn't you tell me sooner? Why didn't you come?"

"You were at your new school, and I didn't want to get in the way.

"No, that's a lie. Deacon Inner Joy told me to be honest with myself. I felt guilty. If you were not at fault, then I was the one who was wrong. If I could cling to the chance that you really were to blame, then I would have been justified in walking out. But I knew that wasn't true. I've been unfair to you, the man I loved.

*Loved? Past tense?*

"The man I love," she corrected herself.

And when I got the message that you'd been hurt again, I panicked. A person doesn't do that about someone she doesn't love. I missed you, and I knew I loved you, but that was the dam breaking. Love broke through the wall I'd erected. Love. I love you. And if you'll have me back, I want to start again as husband and wife. I want you with me, until death do us part.

"So, and I can accept whatever your decision is, but I am asking you, will you take me back?"

Ryck reached over and lifted Hannah's chin until he could look into her eyes.

"Until death do us part."

Thank you for reading *Lieutenant*. If you liked it, please feel free to leave a review of the book on Amazon.

Other Books by Jonathan Brazee

## Fiction

**The Return of the Marines Trilogy**

The Few
The Proud
The Marines

**The United Federation Marine Corps**

Recruit
Sergeant
Lieutenant

Rebel (Coming Soon)
(This book follows Michiko MacCailín)

**The Al Anbar Chronicles: First Marine Expeditionary Force--Iraq**

Prisoner of Fallujah
Combat Corpsman
Sniper

To The Shores of Tripoli

Werewolf of Marines: Semper Lycanus
(Book 2: Coming January, 2015

Wererat

Darwin's Quest: The Search for the Ultimate Survivor

## Non-Fiction

Exercise for a Longer Life

## Author Website

http://www.returnofthemarines.com